The Quest

For exclusive insider info about the Quest Saga visit: www.jaflores.com

The Quest

Book I: The Roots of Evil

J.A. Flores

Copyright © 2006 by J.A. Flores.

Library of Congress Control Number: 2006908129
ISBN 10:   Softcover   1-4257-3359-X

ISBN 13:   Softcover   978-1-4257-3359-9

All rights reserved. No part of this book may be reproduced or transmitted in any form or by any means, electronic or mechanical, including photocopying, recording, or by any information storage and retrieval system, without permission in writing from the copyright owner.

This is a work of fiction. Names, characters, places and incidents either are the product of the author's imagination or are used fictitiously, and any resemblance to any actual persons, living or dead, events, or locales is entirely coincidental.

This book was printed in the United States of America.

To order additional copies of this book, contact:
Xlibris Corporation
1-888-795-4274
www.Xlibris.com
Orders@Xlibris.com
35616

For my parents
And for Yan, my own beloved Beauty

PROLOGUE

Sir Richard Viccon, Grand General of the Kingdom of Arcainia, was a tremendous warrior, the greatest in all of the Old World and perhaps even on Earth. He was a strong man with a virtuous heart, guiding his kingdom into an age of peace and prosperity. Sir Viccon was even looked upon for guidance by the other kingdoms of the Old World: Kuberica, Shazadia, Radinoz, and Holgrafia. A brilliant strategist with a mind for diplomacy, he united the five kingdoms of the Old World in a way that had not been seen for a very long time.

Sir Richard Viccon was the hero of the Arcainian people, coming out of obscurity as an orphan that joined the Arcainian Army at a young age only to rise in the ranks quickly and join the Arcainian Knighthood. Once secured there, he only further succeeded in impressing his superiors with his bravery and chivalry, turning the tides of many battles and bringing victories where there should have been defeats. Before long he found himself being appointed the rank of Grand General of Arcainia, the highest honor any knight could receive. Thus, the humble nobody had beaten all of the odds to win the hearts of the Arcainian people and became their Grand General, the highest-ranking military position who was both the king's top military advisor and the chief commander of all the military forces. Sir Viccon held this position with honor and pride, always fighting for his people and the good of the Old World. He was an inspiration to people everywhere, adored by the decent and feared by the wicked.

Richard's first wife had been Arcainian, such as he was, and they had had a son together in the first year of their marriage. However, she had unfortunately died from a complication during his birth leaving Richard alone to care for his infant son. He named his boy Kain and, after much grief, went on with his life. Knowing that he would not be able to raise the boy alone, he searched for a special woman to fill the void left by his departed wife. It was not until Richard was called to duty in the far away and exotic land of China that he managed to find such a woman. In a small park Richard and Hua Fang first laid eyes on one another and it was love at first sight for them both. By the time it came for Richard to return home to Arcainia, he and Fang were blissfully married.

Kain loved his stepmother deeply and never thought of her as anything short of his blood mother. She was very good to both her new husband and son and taught Kain much about her homeland, such as the Chinese language both spoken and written, the social customs, and even much of the colorful history. Kain soaked in everything she taught him and enjoyed the few short vacations he took with his mother and father to visit her family.

Later, Richard and Fang had a daughter together, and they named her Nancy. She was very beautiful and in time would grow to look just like her mother. Kain, whom was ten at the time of her birth, was very proud to be an older brother and enjoyed playing with his sister every chance he got. He was also equally proud of his father, whom was the Grand General of Arcainia, the most top ranking knight in the Queen's army and in fact her right hand military man. Kain vowed that he would practice and train as hard as it would take to become as great a warrior as his father and lead the greatest and mightiest army in the world.

* * *

With a low grunt, Richard Viccon finished his letter and looked up as his wife slowly walked quietly into the room, cradling their daughter in her arms. As she laid Nancy into her wooden crib, she asked where Kain was in a hushed voice so as not to awaken the snoozing child. Richard looked his young wife over as he told her "In his room, I think."

He then rose up and crossed the room to her. As he embraced her tightly in his arms, she nuzzled her forehead against his chest and whispered "Wo ai ni!"

"I love you, too." he smiled as he craned his head to plant his lips onto hers in a deep kiss. Suddenly, Fang felt her feet lift off the floor and gave a startled "Mph!" but calmed down instantly as she let Richard carry her to the bed.

He had just laid her down and was about to brush his lips against her soft neck when a loud and sudden burst of raps ripped through the romantic air. They both gasped and looked wildly at the bedroom door, expecting it to be their eleven year old son but quickly realized that it was a guest at the front door. Fang glanced at Richard with slightly concerned eyes while he simply shrugged his shoulders and planted one final kiss before rising up. As he crossed the room, he noted how dark it had suddenly grown outside.

'Hmph!' he thought absently. 'Guess it is a good thing I decided not to take Kain to the park today.'

As Richard turned the handle to the front door, a clap of thunder shook the sky. There stood a strange man whose very appearance made Richard flinch in surprise. The man was tall with a stocky build and broad, powerful shoulders. His skin was a pale greenish color while his eyes were ruby red and glew softly and his ears were pointed like those of an elf. When he grinned broadly, Richard could see his mouth was full of short, yet sharp fangs and his pointed tongue was a deep red.

His baldhead gleamed in the slowly fading afternoon sunlight. A red satin cloak, which could easily be wrapped around his entire body, was draped over his shoulders and he wore a simple black cotton suit under it. In his strong hand with pointed nails he held a long staff made of black ash with a sharp blade and diamond-shaped crystal attached to the tip. He was an impressive looking sort, and Richard was not quite sure what to make of him, or even what to say. He was quite sure he had never before seen the man, and yet something screamed in the back of his mind that he should know the fellow. However, the harder Richard thought, the faster the man's identity escaped him. He was a sorcerer or wizard of some sort, Richard could tell that from the start, but as to who he was or what he wanted, the Grand General had no idea and a deep uneasiness began to settle into his stomach.

"Ah, good day to you and a fine hello, Sir Viccon!" he said in a rather low but cheery voice that went with his wide, pleasant grin. Despite his odd looks, the man was very elegant and smooth and when he spoke there was a gentleman-like quality to his voice as if he were highly educated and cultured. This helped Richard to relax slightly as the stranger thrust his hand forward excitedly in a friendly gesture. "What an honor it is to finally meet you face to face!"

Richard gripped his hand firmly and shook it with a beaming smile of modesty. "And to whom may I give the honor of this meeting?"

"I am Noknor, warlock supreme!" he said smoothly as more thunder rumbled and the sky grew black as night with dark clouds.

Noknor. The name seemed even more familiar to him, and he began to search for the name in his memories. He didn't come up with anything right away, so he asked "Well, Noknor, how may I be of service to you?"

"How long it has been since I've had a worthy opponent!" he laughed and shifted his staff to his opposite hand.

"Begging your pardon?" Richard frowned, his hand instinctively reaching down for the imaginary sword on his empty hip.

"I wish to offer a challenge to you, Grand General." Noknor said simply. "A fight to the death, to be precise."

And suddenly Richard recalled where he had heard the name Noknor. He was a low level warlock that had been causing trouble around the Old World lately, small and low key stuff if Richard remembered correctly. He didn't think the warlock was very well known, and he wasn't even sure if he was actually wanted in Arcainia. Did he really want to challenge Sir Richard Viccon, the Grand General of the Arcainian Army, the greatest warrior in the Old World if not the entire world? Surely Noknor must be joking! Was he really that stupid?

As if reading Richard's thoughts, an amused grin formed on Noknor's lips and he uttered a dark chuckle. He swung his staff at Richard, the blade whizzing through air with the intent of cutting the knight in half. However, quick as a flash, Richard gripped the staff and gave it a hard yank. As Noknor tumbled forward, Richard kicked the warlock hard in the gut. He grunted and gasped for the air that had been forced out of his lungs as Richard dropped the staff and growled "Aren't very fair after all, are you? Sucker punching an unarmed man! How pathetic."

Noknor didn't have time to respond, for Fang had come up behind her husband and asked "Who is it, dearheart?"

"Ah, yes. I do remember hearing about you marrying a chink!" he replied smartly, coughing as he picked himself up and looked her lustfully up and down. Fang shrank behind her husband to hide from those dangerous eyes as Noknor licked his lips and commented "I do hope I win, for she is such a luscious prize!"

Richard exploded in fury at the statement and lashed out with a punch to Noknor's jaw that was so fast the warlock never saw it coming. The fist struck hard and there came a tremendous smack as Noknor yelped in surprised pain. His lip had been split wide open and blood gushed from the wound as he ran his tongue over his lips. The taste of blood, his own blood, enraged him and he hissed savagely as he tried to cut Richard with another swipe of his staff. Richard easily gripped it once more and flung him over his shoulder. The warlock sailed through the air and smashed into a large mirror. The glass shattering into a million tiny fragments sounds like a woman's shrill scream while Fang screamed herself in shocked hysterics. The commotion awakened the infant Nancy, who began to wail, and brought young Kain down from his room. He saw what was happening, so he ducked behind a large chest to watch his father as he rushed to deliver a violent kick to the strange man's side while his mother shrieked from against the wall.

Noknor was launched into the wall by the force of Richard's kick, again bouncing against the shattered mirror. He coughed roughly as he picked himself up, wincing as he pulled a large bloodied shard of glass from his shoulder. He savagely snapped, the words hissing past his lips with difficulty. "You are even better than they say! Unfortunately for you, Noknor doesn't die so easily!"

He rushed at Richard, but the Grand General easily defended against the onslaught of blows, ducking and dodging, batting away the bladed staff with his powerful forearms as it swung to and fro. In a sudden attack, Richard ducked under the staff and jabbed, his fist pounding into the warlock's belly. Noknor gasped and doubled over in pain, allowing Richard to bash in his face three times with his knee before lacing his fingers and pounding Noknor between his shoulders, his joined hands hitting like a blacksmith's hammer. Before Noknor could fall, Richard delivered a devastating kick to his face. Noknor flew backwards and landed hard on his chest, groaning as he painfully picked himself up onto hands and knees. Richard roared in fury as he ran forward, hopping the last few steps as he reared his leg back, and kicked him in the side. Noknor's kidney exploded in blinding pain as he sailed into the wall, the thud echoing as he rebounded onto the wooden floor. He moaned softly as he clutched his burning belly and painfully gasped "I . . . don't like . . . this game!"

"Finish him dad!" Kain whispered excitedly from his hiding place.

Richard stared down at Noknor, his frown expressing his contempt and disbelief at the audacity of the warlock whimpering like a scolded puppy. He just couldn't believe that Noknor had the kahonez to actually come to his house and think to challenge him to a fight. What in the hell would be worth proving by doing such a thing? And who would it be worth proving it to? In a sense, Richard almost felt pity for the man, if he could actually be called that. Was he really that desperate to make a name for himself, or was he just honestly that stupid.

"Pathetic." Richard snorted with disdain, shaking his head as if disappointed as a bemused laugh escaped his lips. "You come into my house where I live with my family, you insult my wife, and then you attack me while I'm unarmed. And still you didn't even make me break a sweat as I beat the bag out of you. Simply pathetic."

Richard lowered his head and took a deep breath before letting it out in a long, dissatisfied sigh. He lifted his head and spit upon his fallen opponent. "You wanted it to the death, Noknor. But you know what? You're not worth staining the floor of my home with."

Still holding his hard eyes upon Noknor, Richard slightly cocked his head and called out to his wife "Fang. Go next door and tell Entonio and Marie to alert the authorities. I'll wait here; this pathetic lump of filth won't be going anywhere."

Fang rushed to her husband's side to give her hero a congratulatory kiss on his cheek. When Richard turned his head to return the kiss with one onto the beautiful lips of his beloved, Noknor growled a bitter curse, blood spraying from his lips. With the Grand General's attention diverted for only the briefest moment, he scrambled for his staff laying a few feet from his hand. He leveled the jeweled tip towards Richard and Fang as his sudden commotion caught their eyes. Two reddish brown beams of energy shot at the pair as thunder ripped open the clouds outside and poured rain in heavy torrents. The first beam struck Richard in the dead center of his chest, throwing him backwards from the force of the impact as his heart was blown out of his back, painting the wall red. With a sharp gasp, the mighty warrior fell to the ground with his beloved, a victim of the same grisly affects.

"**MOMMY! DADDY!**" Kain shrieked in horror, revealing his hiding place. Noknor turned and fixed his evil eyes on the boy, paralyzing his mind with terror. Noknor turned his staff onto him and released another bolt of pure energy. At the last instant, Kain managed to regain control of his body and threw himself to the side. The beam exploded the chest, sending the contents flying. Kain took one look at the rubble and dashed to his parents' room.

"COME BACK HERE YOU LITTLE BASTARD!" Noknor roared, doing his best to pick his broken body up from the floor.

Kain slammed and locked the door before rushing to his shrieking sister's crib. With trembling arms, he reached down and picked her up, holding her close as tears poured from his eyes. The girl calmed down the second she felt her brother's protective arms around her. The door handle rattled violently before the door exploded off of its hinges. Noknor stepped in and cast his eyes around the room before grinning a vile grin as he raised his staff once more. Kain dodged to the side, just out of the way of the oncoming blast and dashed out of the gapping hole it had left in the wall, Nancy crying in his arms. He ran through the driving rain and howling wind. He ran as fast and as long as he could, thinking of nothing except for fleeing the terrible sight. When he finally couldn't run any longer, he saw a familiar house. Realizing that it belonged to John Accrue, his father's best friend and Second General under him, he hurried through the iron fence and dashed up the walkway to the front door, crying out all the while. John was quite surprised to see his best friend's son and daughter standing on his doorstep, crying their eyes out. However, he was horrified to hear Kain's traumatic story.

Three months later, John had finally found someone that could care for the two children. It had not been an easy task however, especially with the duties of Grand General suddenly thrust upon him as well as having to deal with the loss of his closest friend. Richard had no living relatives whatsoever, so Kain and Nancy were sent to Fang's brother in China. He was a merchant with a wife and two daughters of his own, and he was more than willing to take in his dear sister's children. He had loved her so very much and felt it was the least he could do. Also, he was very glad to have a male in the house that might take over his business for him when he retired while his wife was thrilled to have another infant under the roof.

His youngest daughter was named Li, which in the Chinese language means Beauty, and it wasn't hard to see why. She was a few months older than Kain and very friendly. As soon as her father escorted Kain and Nancy through the bright red gate, she went to them and bowed respectfully. She cooed over the baby for a few minutes before turning her attention onto Kain and looking him over for a moment, examining her new playmate.

"Hello, Cousin Kain!" she finally chirped happily. "I am very happy to see you again. I hope your stay in the Hua home is very happy for you!"

"Tuh-thank you . . . Cuh-Cuh-Cousin Luh-Li." he stammered nervously. He was very scared about being in a strange and new land without his parents. Of course, Fang had taught him so much about China and he had been there a few times before, but it was different actually being there without them. It was very uncomfortable. He was so different from everyone else. At least Nancy looked Chinese. Everyone would know that he was Arcainian. That he was . . . different.

Li noticed it, but didn't care anymore than she had in the past. She giggled and playfully mocked "Well, Kuh-Kuh-Kain, would you like to guh-guh-go play with me? Come on, now! Let's go play hide-and-seek in the garden!"

Kain loosened up a bit and mumbled softly "Okay, but I have to put my stuff away first."

"That's all right, my boy." his uncle smiled brightly, gently patting him on the shoulder. "You go play with Li. Have a good time with her. I will see to it that your belongings are put away."

"Thank you." he said quietly, almost as if he were ashamed of himself. Li grabbed his arm excitedly and dragged him off, chatting on and on about how much fun they would have together.

PART I

THE BEGINNING

CHAPTER I

"What a beautiful day!" the lovely Princess Elizabeth exclaimed as she walked with her father, King Edward the Bold of Kuberica, through the grand courtyard of their fine castle. The birds swung sweet songs of happiness and bliss as a fine, gentle breeze blew steadily across the grass, producing a rhythmic sway like the waves of the sea.

"I must agree with you, my dear." he remarked, stroking his long, gray beard. "It's days like this that make me glad that I rule such a grand kingdom as Kuberica!"

In the next instant, the calm, peaceful air was turned upside down as the earth shook underneath their feet as if a hundred thousand horses were driving past. The soft breeze turned into a powerful gust that whipped their hair and clothing about as a tremendous roar filled the air around them. The sky above quickly flooded with ominous black clouds, cutting off the rich sunlight and bathing everything into darkness.

"The hell?" Edward bellowed gruffly as he clutched his daughter's hand at his side.

The doors to the castle burst open and banged into the wall loudly as a young man in Kuberican armor rushed out. He was Sir Jonothan Fikit, the Grand General of the Kuberican Army. He gawked wildly around for a brief moment before spotting his king and rushing to his side, out of breath and gasping for air. "Luh-Lord . . . Edward! Are yuh-yuh . . . yuh-you all . . . . right?"

"Yes, my boy!" Edward replied. "Jonothan, what the hell is going on!"

"Interesting choice of words." the general wheezed before pausing for a brief second to catch his breath. "There is an . . . army approaching from the north! About five hundred yards from the walls! A devil army!"

"Devil army?" Edward raised shocked eyebrows. He pulled Elizabeth closer to his side, clutching her tightly. "Explain yourself!"

"It's a devil army!" Jonothan repeated. "Goblins, demons, and humans! There must be thousands of them! All dressed for battle! Oh, Goddess! It's terrible, simply terrible!"

"What does their flag look like?" the king asked anxiously, already fearful that he knew the answer. Jonothan didn't answer right away, and he just stared at Edward with a dumbfounded look, his terrified eyes staring through him. He was clearly still in shock at what he had seen. Edward was in no mood and barked "Answer me, boy! Don't they fly a flag?"

"Yuh-yes sir!"

"Well, what does it look like!"

"It . . . . it's half green and half black with a fiery demon skull in the center!" Jonothan explained in a wavy voice.

"Goddess help us!" Edward whispered weakly, his heart plunging into the pit of his stomach as all of the color in his face drained away. In a trembling voice, he uttered "It's him!"

"Who is it!" Elizabeth cried out with fear, her father scaring her out of her mind. She had always thought that her father was afraid of nothing and seeing him in such a distressed state crushed her and frightened her more than any devil army ever could.

"The Lord of the Dark himself! Quickly, my child! Into the castle!" He ordered, pushing her along. "Go up to the throne room! You'll be safe there."

The princess didn't question him, she was too frightened. She just tore to the castle doors, flung herself in, and ran to hide in the throne room as she was told. Edward watched her exit before turning to Jonothan and saying "I want you to gather all of our forces at the north wall. I have a feeling we'll need them!"

"I have already assembled them, sire. As soon as I caught wind of that hellish army, I told all of my troops to prepare for a battle."

"Good, good." Edward nodded, clapping his general on the shoulder. He glanced at the darkening sky once more before pulling him along by the arm. "I hope the Great Lady is watching over us today. I feel we will be doing battle with the Dark One, himself."

"You wound me with your words, Edward." an all too familiar voice behind him chuckled.

Both Edward and Jonothan stopped dead in their tracks and slowly turned to come face to face with the warlock. The evil fiend stood before them, his staff in hand, a large toothy grin spread over his face. The large crystal at the tip of his staff glittered in a sinister manner even though the sun was completely hidden behind a thick blanket of clouds.

Noknor had once been human, but even at that time his heart was black and diabolical. His power over the magickal arts had been mediocre at best and he had few, if any, real accomplishments under his belt. In a word, he was a nobody. That all changed the day he discovered the black power of the Dark One, an entity of pure evil, pure pain, pure suffering. Noknor called upon this power through dark, bloody rituals and when faced with the Dark One himself, he sealed a pact that instilled in him the power of the Dark forces, making him even more powerful and much more deadly. But, it was not a free gift and the price was high. He paid with his humanity and became a servant of evil, doing the bidding of the Dark One without thought or question. He had become the hand of evil, an extension of the

Dark One's will in his insane quest to destroy all that his Sister the Divine Mother had created and loved. And Noknor had yet to disappoint his bloody god of the Dark as he waged his own campaign to conquer all of the Old World and set himself up as ruler of all the land.

That was why Noknor had gone after Sir Richard Viccon, Grand General of Arcainia so many years before. He had figured that if he wanted to make a name for himself, why start at the bottom fighting pathetic scrubs. Might as well begin at the top, and at the time there had been no further top than Sir Viccon. He was the key to conquering the Old World, the glue that held not only Arcainia together but all five of the kingdoms of the Old World. With the assassination of the great Grand General Sir Richard Viccon, Noknor had anticipated the collapse of the Old World as Arcainia would blame the other kingdoms for the crime. After all, his plan had entailed no one knowing who had killed Viccon, thus blame would be thrown about freely. Each kingdom should have turned on each other and warred fiercely, thus allowing Noknor to swoop down and pick up the pieces as he set himself up with each crown until he ruled all of the kingdoms. What he hadn't counted on, however, was the survival of Viccon's brat son, and with his description of the assassin and the attack there was no doubt where the blame would be cast. And although there was chaos immediately following, Arcainia had held together tightly, remaining strong and stout in the face of such a terrible tragedy. Noknor was disappointed, but welcomed the reputation his murder had given him. He had spent the past few years gathering up forces, making small attacks here and there and building his power among the world of the Dark. He planned one day to take over a single kingdom, not Arcainia of course, but a weaker one, and continue to mold his strength until he could conquer each kingdom in turn. Unfortunately for the Kubericans, that day had finally come.

When Noknor grinned evilly and nodded his head in a mocking gesture of greeting, Jonothan was struck by a bolt of courage. He stepped in front of Edward, putting himself in between his king and the warlock, and drew his sword. He brandished it menacingly as he cursed Noknor's name viciously.

"My goodness! Such language!" Noknor scolded, a chuckle rumbling in his throat. He started to advance but stopped short when Jonothan thrust his sword threateningly forward. "It is really quite simple, even an uncultured moron such as yourself could understand it, Fikit. I'm going to take this failure you like to call a kingdom and turn it into a grand empire spanning the entire globe. One worthy of my rule." Noknor laughed quite heartily. "Of course, I must take you out of the picture first, good king."

"Go to the princess, your majesty!" Jonothan cried, brandishing his sword. "I'll rid you of this vile fiend!"

"How absurd!" Noknor muttered, tossing his blood red cloak back as he craned his neck from side to side so that an audible crackling was heard.

Edward looked at his general and frowned darkly. However, the brave knight gave him a reassuring smile and prepared to charge. The king, trusting his friend, made a mad dash to the castle doors, hurtling himself inside. Jonothan checked one last time to be sure the king had gotten away before shouting a fierce battle cry and rushing at his foe.

Just as he reached Noknor, the warlock spun his staff in his hands and thrust the blade forward, straight into the gut of the hero. With a painful gasp, Jonothan dropped his sword and clutched at the staff as he was hoisted high into the air and then slammed onto his back with such tremendous force that his spine cracked. When Noknor wrested the blade free, he looked down at the wretched human that laid on the ground groaning pitifully and writhing in agony. Uttering a demented chuckle, Noknor placed his foot to his throat and twisted his leg sharply. With a disgusting crackle, Jonothan Fikit was dead.

Noknor spat on the mangled knight before raising his staff up into the air and shouting in a devilish tongue. Instantly, a bolt of black lightning surged from the clouds and struck the crystal. There was a brilliant flash and the warlock was gone, teleported back to his minions. He stood upon a large wagon with his second in command, the Dark General Samhus Garrison, while his evil army cheered his name. The majority were humans, which Noknor had entitled Dark Knights. These men were evil, loathsome human beings that Noknor had handpicked for his evil forces. Greed had enticed them to join, for Noknor had offered a king's ransom to each man gained from his lifetime of misdeeds, while fear of a gruesome death and the loss of their souls kept them loyal. Garrison had been picked to lead the devil army because he had clearly stood out as the most vile, ruthless person Noknor had ever met. He was as greedy as the rest of the Dark Knights, but for him it was a sick pleasure to bring suffering to others, thus more so ensuring his loyalty to Noknor's cause. Plus, he was just spineless enough to be bullied by Noknor but vicious enough to bully anyone else.

Noknor immediately ordered for the battering ram to be prepared. It took twenty powerful orcs, ten on each side, to lift and carry the gargantuan three-ton log with a huge horned demon skull carved into the front end. When the warlock barked orders for his troops to fall into position for the siege, the entire army was ready for action in less than five minutes. With one final word on total destruction and the price for their failure, Noknor blew into a large spiraled horn, trumpeting the battle cry that led his massive army into battle.

Thousands of arrows rained down from the sky as Kuberican archers shot from the high castle ledge. The arrows that split the air with sharp stings rarely found an enemy soldier as most embedded into the large wooden shields on wheels that the demonic forces marched behind while other Dark soldiers advanced in the blind-spots of Kubrican Castle where no arrow could reach. The orcs bearing the battering ram quickly reached the massive castle doors, crossing the deep moat using large planks of thick wood that other soldiers had laid out. With several hard blows and a cracked headpiece for the battering ram, the wooden drawbridge was pounded into splinters. Kuberican arrows and blades mowed down the first of Noknor's forces, but as every one of the evil troops poured in, the Kubericans were overwhelmed and a terrible plague began to spread throughout a doomed body.

* * *

For seven hours the Kuberican Army clashed with the forces of evil and tried their best to fend them off, but to no avail. By the eighth hour of combat, most of the castle had been seized and more than three fourths of the Kuberican Army in the castle had been wiped out with only minimal losses on Noknor's side.

King Edward, Princess Elizabeth, and five of the best knights left sat in the throne room, one of the last safe havens in the castle, and awaited the inevitable. There came several hard assaults upon the heavy oak doors before they broke open. Dark Knights led by Garrison ran in and slaughtered the Kubericans protecting Edward as Noknor ever so slowly strode into the room, the look of the victor spread wide on his hideous face. Noknor looked to the throne and saw Edward clad in shining steel armor and a glittering steel helmet capped with a golden crown. He held tightly a powerful broadsword and a large oval shield, both quivering in fear and anticipation. Elizabeth begged her father not to fight the devil, for she knew that it was suicide. No one could face such a man and expect to survive. However, the king knew that if he could just manage to kill Noknor, the war would be over and he would win, since none of the Dark forces would continue to fight once their master was killed. All he had to do was kill Noknor. Just kill Noknor. It was much easier said than done. King Edward gave his daughter one final kiss on the cheek before leaving her on the throne and charging the warlock.

* * *

"There you go, my dear." Noknor chuckled and grinned evilly as he tightened the leather straps that bound her wrists together. "I trust you are comfortable."

Elizabeth stood as proud as she could next to Noknor's new throne, her hands tied and chained to the ghastly chair that had replaced her father's. She stared at the warlock with contempt burning red in her eyes, her very soul filled with hatred and abhorrence for the vile, heartless man that stood before her. She was devastated over the premature death of her father, a death she had witnessed with her own horrified eyes, but still she refused to crumble and shed even a single tear for Noknor. She wasn't about to let him have the sickening satisfaction of seeing her cry.

"Aren't you going to just murder me like you did my father!" she hissed through her teeth, her voice wavy and cracking. She noticed her eyes begin to water and sobs welling up in her throat and forced herself not to weep even though she wanted to. Even though she desperately needed to. She tugged hard on her restraints and roared "Aren't you!"

"Kill you?" Noknor smiled, a bit amused at the very thought. "Why, no my dear princess, I would not dream of killing you. At least, not yet. You see, you are just much too important to me. I need you." he told her in a low, sly voice, putting his fingers under her chin and lifting her head so that he could peer into her bloodshot eyes. Elizabeth jerked out of his grip and threw her eyes away from him as she mustered as much pride as she could to stand tall. Noknor frowned slightly. "I need you for insurance." He adjusted his gruesome new crown made from the skull and splintered bones of his deceased enemy, the once mighty and proud father of the princess, as he sat regally in the bone throne painted red with blood.

"I'm sure that news of my little victory here will travel far and wide." he sighed deeply, sounding exhausted from his evil workings. "And when the news hits some of the surrounding kingdoms, I'm positive I can expect retaliation. It's not that I don't have faith in my own warriors, I assure you. It's just better to be safe. Besides, how could I kill someone as lovely as you?"

The doors to the new throne room boomed open and Garrison strolled in with several of his underling Dark Knights. They approached the throne and knelt before their lord. Noknor looked the men over as he popped a small piece of dried fruit into his mouth and turned to the princess, telling her with a slight chuckle "Time for you to go, my dear."

As he began unbinding her from his throne, he told her "And just to show you that I'm not a total monster, I'm going to put you in the regal cell. Truly fit for a princess of your grace and beauty."

"You mean the room you had those wenches fix up?" Garrison inquired as he tossed his thumb towards the ceiling, gesturing to the room right above their heads.

"Indeed that's the one." Noknor smiled, nudging Elizabeth into Garrison's arms. "Take her away, Garrison. And please do be gentle with her!"

"You'll never get away with this, you monster!" she howled, her voice cracking and her eyes starting to moisten more and more as she fought Garrison with every step. "When Arcainia hears how you murdered my father, they're going to send Grand General Viccon after you!"

"Oh, I'm counting on it my dear." Noknor called matter-of-factly after them. "Oh, I am indeed counting on it!

* * *

The 113th Grand General of the Arcainian Army, Sir Kain Viccon and his Second General, Sir Raphael Boniva, were walking through the majestic halls of Arcainia Castle swapping stories on their break.

At a mere twenty-five years of age, Kain had assumed the position of Grand General a mere two years earlier and became the youngest man ever to hold the extremely high rank. Most of his rivals snorted that he had received it due to the connections he had, but while that had honestly been a small part of it, Kain was a very hard worker who had rigorously trained to be the best. He had truly earned the rank bestowed upon him and he carried it with great pride.

No one could deny that he was one of the best Grand Generals Arcainia had seen in a long time.

Like any pure blood Arcainian, Kain had black hair that he kept short as per military standards, dark eyes, and a tanned complexion. He was a large man, standing over six feet tall and very muscular, with a large chest and strong arms. However, like his father, his size was offset by his young and gentle, almost child-like face and soft features. Raphael, being originally from Kuberica, had light brown hair that was also kept short, small hazel eyes that occasionally hid behind round wire-frame glasses, and lighter toned skin than Kain's. He was slightly smaller than his friend, a few inches shorter and not as heavily built. He had achieved his high rank as Second General when Kain had picked him to be his second-in-command, as was the fashion.

"We were just fooling around, you know?" Kain said, relating an amusing incident involving his beautiful Chinese cousin Li and himself, which had occurred the night before. "I went to roundhouse her at the same time she front kicked at me. Well, I missed, but she didn't. She nailed me right in the basket! And hard, too! It still stings!"

"Good Goddess!" Raphael winced as he imagined being struck in that all too important and all too sensitive area. "What'd you do?"

"Well, I took it like a man." Kain smiled broadly.

"So, you grabbed yourself, tumbled to the ground, and curled into a ball while crying like a baby?" Raphael suggested with a grin.

"Exactly!" Kain laughed loudly.

Raphael imagined what a sight it must been to see his friend's reaction and began to chuckle. Then he thought about the look that must have been on Li's face when she realized what she had accidentally done and burst out laughing. Both men were laughing so much as they stumbled down the hallway like a couple of drunks that they failed to see a very nervous, low ranking messenger with a scroll in hand approaching them.

"Man, Li is something else." Raphael murmured, trying to catch his breath.

"You'd better believe it! You know, one time she—"

"Excuse me, Sir Viccon?" the soldier appealed uneasily, unsure what to make of his commander's odd actions. "This letter from Hurst has just arrived for you. It was marked extremely urgent on the cylinder."

"Eh? Oh, yes. It's from Hurst, you say?" Kain asked absently, taking the roll of parchment from him. He examined the scroll and found the unbroken seal of his old friend Deborah Hurst, mayor of the city bearing her family name.

"Yes, sir. It was marked urgent. Ah, extremely urgent, that is."

"Humph!" Kain grunted, wondering what Deborah had to say that was so important. "Well, thank you very much."

"You're welcome, Sir Viccon." the soldier smiled and saluted. He waited until Kain saluted him back before dropping his and heading off.

"Is it straight from the top?" Raphael inquired.

Kain nodded with a bit of a frown as he drew his dagger to cut the black ribbon that tightly held the parchment rolled up. "I haven't heard from her for a while yet."

"I wonder what's going on."

"I wonder why she marked it urgent."

"Extremely." Raphael corrected.

"Whatever. Ah, there we go." Kain murmured lowly as the ribbon finally snapped and the red wax seal broke. With intent and careful eyes, he slowly read what she had to say. He had only read a few lines when his eyes widened and his jaw dropped. His whole body began to quiver violently as the paper slipped through his hands and fluttered to the floor like a dead leaf.

"Kain? Kain, what's wrong?" Raphael asked in a very troubled tone of voice. He had never seen his friend in such an anxious state and it scared him to death. "Kain, what does it say!"

"Oh, sweet merciful Goddess, help me!" Kain whispered weakly, his wide eyes staring straight ahead yet seeing nothing. "He's back!"

CHAPTER II

Kain opened his front door and slinked inside. Once in the quiet comfort of his home, he slumped into a wooden chair, closed his eyes, and went into deep thought. He thought about the terrible letter he had received that morning and what he was going to have to do about it. He thought of all the good lives wasted in a gory fury. He thought about what he was going to have to tell his dear baby sister. But mostly, he thought about what he had witnessed so many years before, what had happened to his parents and who had caused his happy world to come crashing down around his very ears.

Suddenly, he became conscious of pressure on his shoulders as someone placed their hands on him. His eyes flung open and he leaped out of his chair, knocking back whoever had been behind him. He whirled around ready to fight and came face to face with his lovely cousin, Hua Li. Being Chinese, Li had jet black straight hair which she kept long, grown all the way to the small of her back. She often kept it up with hairpins in Chinese fashion, but this day it flowed freely like a cascading waterfall. Her eyes glittered like gems and her flesh was soft and fair as flower petals. She was always very graceful in her movements and her body, molded after many years of extensive training, was very trim and curvaceous while her long and shapely legs concealed powerful muscles. Her beauty combined with her dazzling personality made any room light up whenever she entered. After she had been left alone with the murder of her best friend, Kain had convinced her to stay at his home with him and Nancy for a brief period so she would not morn their friend alone. That brief period had turned into a little over a year.

"Goddess bless it, Li!" Kain bit out savagely. "I hate it when you do that!"

She recoiled slightly in surprise, but put her hands on her cousin's shoulders to sit him down as she scolded him sternly "Calm down! You know I didn't mean to scare you!"

"I-I'm sorry, Li." Kain murmured lowly. "I didn't mean to bite your head off, but it's . . . it's just that I'm a bit stressed out right now. I've had a . . . well, a bad day."

"I'm very sorry." Li said solemnly, gently massaging her cousin's broad shoulders. "My, you're so tense!" she murmured softly. Kain didn't say a word, he just surrendered to his cousin's soothing hands. Li looked at him with worried eyes and frowned. She had seen Kain on bad days, but he had never been so tense or so distraught. He acted as if someone had died.

Kain looked around and noticed that his sister was nowhere to be seen. That was odd, since she always rushed to greet him as soon as he came through the door. "Where's Nancy?"

"She went to the Square with her friends." she told him. They were silent together for several minutes before Li finally asked quietly "Do you want to talk about it?"

At first, Kain said nothing. He just sighed heavily, so Li figured he did not and decided not to press further. He startled her by suddenly muttering "I received a disturbing letter today. It said . . . it said that Kuberica had been attacked a few days ago." He paused and rubbed his face with a shaky hand. "Noknor led the attack."

"Noknor?" Li murmured, her mouth twisted. "Isn't he the one that . . . that . . ." She didn't want to say it.

Kain nodded gravely and sat back in his chair. "He murdered Edward and took over the castle. In the process he slaughtered a lot of innocent people. Good people, both knights and civilians alike."

"Oh, my!" Li gasped, putting a hand to her mouth. She was truly shocked by the news. Though she knew nothing of Kuberica, she felt for the people there. She knew how terrible and costly it could be to go though such a devastating ordeal. She also felt for her cousin. She knew how much of a friend King Edward had been to him, and for the aggressor to be the same man who had murdered his parents . . .

"From what the letter said, Edward and his men had put up a good fight and lasted long enough for Kuberican reinforcements to arrive, but it wasn't enough to stop him. They were just too overwhelmed and taken by surprise." Kain whispered, his voice faltering. "Edward himself fought him and almost beat him, but Noknor's men rushed into the fight just before the king could deliver the final blow. They . . . they . . . kuh-killed him in front of the princess."

'Just like he did you!' Li thought, fearing to say it out loud. The similarity hit her as sickenly ironic, but she didn't want to hurt him more by bringing it up.

"He did the same thing to my parents, that coward!" Kain roared, spewing curses from his curled lips as he leapt out of the chair and punched the wall so hard that it cracked and a nearby painting of his parents fell off its hook. Li jolted and uttered a startled squeak, but quickly caught herself, put her hands gently on his shoulders, and pushed him back down. As Kain sat, he winced and shook his bruised hand as the sting suddenly flooded his knuckles.

"I'm going to kill him, Li!" he growled. "I'm going to tear his heart out!"

"I know you will, sweetie." Li murmured, gently rubbing his even more tense muscles rhythmically. "I know you will."

"I swear this to you." he muttered, not talking to Li but instead looking at two invisible figures. "I will kill that demon and make him pay for what he did to you! For what he did to me! You took away my parents! You almost ruined my life! And now you're back! Well, I'm going do whatever it takes! If it's the last thing I do before I die, I will hunt you down to your dying breath!"

"It's all right now, Kain." Li whispered softly with rapidly growing concern, kissing his head. "Just—"

"DO YOU HEAR ME, NOKNOR!" Kain roared, jumping up so fast, he smacked into Li and knocked her back a few steps. She touched her throbbing lip and rubbed the droplet of blood between her two fingers as she looked back at her cousin. He had flown into an insane rage, grabbing the chair and slamming it down onto the floor, shattering it like fine china. Li screamed with fright and backed away from him as he bellowed madly "THINGS HAVE CHANGED, YOU FREAK! NOW I'M THE HUNTER AND YOU'RE THE HUNTED! AND WHEN I FIND YOU, I'M GONNA SHOVE THAT STAFF SO FAR UP YOUR—"

"KAIN!" Li shrieked as loud as she could, afraid for her cousin and for the very first time in her life frightened of her cousin. "Kain Viccon, stop it! You stop it right now, do you hear me! You've got to calm down! You won't be able to do anything until you calm yourself down! Why, if Nancy were to see you like, she'd be devastated!"

"Nancy . . ." Kain murmured in a small weak voice, remembering his little sister and how much she meant to him. He stood silently over the wreckage that used to be a chair and stared at Li.

Li, thrilled to have her cousin's full attention, sniffled and wiped her eyes. Her voice wavered slightly as she spoke "Yes, Kain. Think about Nancy. I know how hard this is for you, I honestly do. But, sweetie, you have got to calm yourself! Think about what seeing you like this will do to her. She's going to have a hard time with this herself. And she's going to need you to be strong, not some insane lunatic. If she sees you freak out like this, she'll be crushed! Please don't ever let her see you like this! Ever!"

"Yuh-You're . . . you're right, Li." Kain murmured lowly, lowered his head, and buried his face in his hands. Li rubbed his back soothingly as he bobbed slightly. It took her a moment to realize that he was weeping. She had never seen him cry, certainly not like that, and suddenly her heart crumbled into a million pieces.

"I'm so sorry, Li." he whimpered. Then, much to her surprise, he fled to his room. Li could only watch him go, she was powerless to follow. The door slammed behind Kain, leaving Li alone in the empty living room. She sighed deeply and stared at the door.

"Oh, Kain!" she murmured softly to herself as she lifted the painting of her uncle and aunt back onto its hook, a single tear sliding down her cheek. "I'm sorry. I'm so sorry."

She went to Kain's bedroom door and put her ear to the wood. Hearing nothing inside, she rapped her knuckles gently and opened the door enough to stick her head in. She saw her cousin sitting on his bed, his back to her, his eyes staring out the window, and his hand over his mouth.

"Kain?" she whispered. He didn't answer, he just sat on the bed motionless as a statue. It was even hard for her to tell if he was even breathing. "Kain, are you all right?"

Kain nodded slowly but made no other attempts at movement or communication. Li quietly stepped in and shut the door behind her. She was as silent as a cat when she advanced towards him and gently put her arms around him as she sat beside him. Li thought he would push her away, but he didn't. He simply sighed dully as he succumbed to her loving embrace and allowed her to put his head against her heart.

"Are you okay, sweetie?" she asked, gently rocking back and forth, his head in her arms, like a loving mother with her child.

"I . . . I'm all right now, I think." he whispered, his heart tearing apart inside his chest as he thought about what had happened those many years ago. Then, getting a firm grip on himself, he pulled out of her grasp, wiped his eyes, and quickly said "Yes. Yes, I'm all right now. I just had to release some steam, that's all. I've been holding it in all day long and it just kept building up. But I'm fine now. Thank you."

He stopped and thought about what had just happened to him a few minutes ago. He knew that he had upset his cousin greatly, and that hurt him even more. "Li, I'm sorry for losing it back there." he murmured, sounding ashamed. "I . . . I don't know what came over me."

"You don't need to apologize." she assured him. "It's good for you to get those feelings out. If you keep them bottled up, they'll just build up like you said. But you have to make sure you do it the right way, or it could just make things worse. It's good to lash out, it helps relieve the stress that builds up inside. But hit something soft, like a pillow. You don't want to break something." She looked at his red knuckles and put her hand over his as she gave him a warm smile. "Like your hand."

Kain snorted gentle laughter, and that made Li feel much better. It was music to her ears to actually hear him utter a happy sound after all that had just transpired. It was proof that he was feeling better and that his spirit was lifting. Li was all aflutter inside and it made her feel so much better to know that her cousin was starting to return to his normal self. They rested their heads on one another and sat together in silence.

Finally, Li broke it by inquiring "What are you going to tell the kid?"

"Well . . ." Kain murmured after a slight pause. "I-I'm not too sure, to be honest. I guess I haven't given it much thought." There was another pause, slightly longer than the first, as Kain tried to decide what he would eventually tell his little sister. "I guess . . . I guess I'll have to tell her that I'm going away on another quest."

"You are going to tell her who attacked Kuberica and why you're going on another quest?" Li inquired, looking Kain straight in the eye. Kain raised his eyebrows and quickly lowered his eyes from her gaze. Li sighed with a hint of displeasure on her breath. "You must realize that you not only should, but that you must tell her. Here, look at me Kain." She reached over and placed her fingers under his chin, lifting his head so that she could once again look into his eyes and know that she had his full attention. Li knew from experience that his eyes would give away anything he was thinking. "They, your parents I mean, mean as much to that little girl as they do to you. She loves them just as much as you do and she misses them just as much, even if she chooses not to talk about it. The point, I guess, is that Nancy was their child as well and she deserves the right to know the full truth."

"You're right, of course, Li." Kain murmured. "I didn't want to tell her, because, well frankly, I dread it. But I am her brother and she does have a right to know. I guess I'm just going to have to face the unpleasant situation head on and tell her the truth. We'll face it together."

"That's my boy!" Li beamed brightly, first rubbing than fondly patting his back. "It'll make it easier on both of you if you face it together."

Suddenly there came the distinct sound of the front door opening and then slamming closed right before they heard Nancy's voice call out Li's name, announcing that she was home. Li gave Kain's hand a loving squeeze before they went to the living room to greet Nancy and her two friends.

Nancy Viccon was a young girl, not yet fifteen, but she was a true beauty. She had long, shining black hair and black eyes just like her mother's. And with her long legs and slim figure, she got many glances from men as she strolled down the street. But they were always just glances. Kain's fierce protective nature was legendary and he was definitely not the type of man one would want after their head.

Nancy held a burlap bag in her hand that was filled with an array of different items Li had asked her to buy for her while she had been at the Square, the main market district of Arcainia City. She was so busy looking through it that she didn't see Kain standing beside Li. However, her two friends did and giggled sheepishly as they waved bashfully. Kain returned a simple wave and their hearts melted in their chests as their knees suddenly turned to jelly.

"He is sooooooooo fine!" Romi whispered into Dafne's ear. "Goddess, I wish he were my brother!"

"Not me!" Dafne whispered back. "If he were, what I'm thinking right now would be pretty twisted!"

Both girls broke into a fit of low giggles as Nancy, oblivious to what was going on behind her back, continued to check to make sure she had everything. Kain and Li were too far away to hear what was being said, but they pretty much knew what was going on. Li gave Kain a sly smile and nudged him with her elbow. Kain couldn't help but grin as he raised an eyebrow at her. He enjoyed being the subject of such girl talk; it helped to boost his ego way up. However, Li always told him that was the very last thing he needed boosted.

"Hello, Nancy." Li replied, still eyeing Kain with a crafty eye.

"Hi-hi, cuz." she mumbled, finishing her count. "I got everything on your list except for the burg weed. All three apothecaries were fresh out."

"They always seem to be." Li muttered in disappointment.

"Also, I—" she stopped suddenly when she looked up and saw her brother. "Kain? What are you doing home so early?"

Li took the bag out of her hand and said quickly "He took half the day off. Hello, Dafne. Hello, Romi. How are you two enjoying your week off from school?"

"It's been nice." Dafne smiled.

"Just fine." Romi murmured, still eyeing Kain.

As Li advanced towards them, she asked "Would you two like to stay for lunch?"

"Uh, no thank you, Miss Hua." Romi said, momentarily taking her attention off Nancy's brother to talk to Li. "I'd love to stay, but I have to get home. My mother wants me to help out around the house before Spring Festival ends."

"Same here." Dafne added.

"You sure?" Li asked. Then she leaned close to their ears and whispered "Kain's going to be free today. It could be your big chance!"

"Li! What are you telling them?" Kain inquired, his arms folded across his chest. The girls giggled loudly and Nancy rolled her eyes as she shook her head with a smirk.

"Oh, nothing! Just trying to entice them by telling them what they could be having for lunch." Li retorted nonchalantly as she strolled off to the kitchen and disappeared behind the corner.

"Hmph!" Kain grunted, following her out with his eyes. Then he turned his attention back onto Nancy and her friends and smiled as he politely asked "Are you two ladies sure you won't stay? You're more than welcome."

"I wish we could, but . . . you know." Dafne said with a dull shrug.

Romi leaned over and whispered into her ear "I wish we could . . . you know."

As both girls broke out into lascivious giggles, Nancy crossed her arms like her brother had and mumbled "You guys are so weird! What's so funny? What's the joke?" She knew exactly what it was, but wanted them to admit it.

"Oh, nothing really." both chimed melodiously.

Nancy rolled her eyes. "You two are so weird!"

"And you fit right in!" Dafne smiled and gave her arm a friendly nudge. The girls giggled as Romi looked at the large clock standing by the far wall.

"Uh-oh! We'd better get going or my mother's going to throw a snit-fit." she said, tugging on Dafne's arm. "See you later, Nancy."

"Okay. I'll see you guys for another round of shopping tomorrow." Nancy smiled brightly, waving her hand vigorously.

"Good-bye, Sir Viccon!" both girls called in harmony as they fluttered their hands and giggled airily. Nancy rolled her eyes once again and sighed loudly as her brother smiled and gestured a good-bye to them. When they didn't move from their spots, Nancy threw up her arms and proceeded to push them towards the door, muttering about how they'd catch more than snit-fits from their mothers if they didn't get going. As they stepped out, they called another farewell to Kain, who chuckled mildly with an amused shake of his blushed face.

Nancy shut the door behind them and put her hand to her forehead, shaking her head as she sighed "I swear those two! I don't know what to do with them sometimes!"

Kain chuckled emptily and watched her amble into the living room. As she tossed her purse onto the coffee table, she threw herself onto the couch, sighing deeply as she stretched her weary arms and legs. Then her body shivered violently as a sudden chill went through her body before she finally sprawled out comfortably. She gave another weary sigh and slowly closed her eyes.

"Are you feeling okay, pup?" Kain asked tensely.

"Yeah, just tired." She giggled. "Shopping with those two really takes a lot out of you."

She was about to relate an amusing anecdote of her and her friends' trip to the market when her eyes fluttered open and her gaze fell right onto the shattered chair. She stared at it with a raised brow, nearly asking what in the heavens had happened. However, she stopped herself before a sound could escape her parted lips when she remembered that her martial arts expert cousin was in the house. And Nancy knew that her warrior brother and fighter cousin often took it upon themselves to test their skills against one another just for fun. That was how they solved arguments, as well. Some people talked it out, some tossed a coin, and still others passed riddles. Her brother and cousin, on the other hand, fought for dominance and territory. This wasn't the first time Nancy had come home to broken knick-knacks or furniture. So, after the initial shock had passed, she didn't bother to ask. She figured she would get the same old story. Kain would blame it on Li who would deny it all and counter-blame him. Then they would start to argue and the whole process would start all over again. Nancy decided to save herself another headache and just not ask in the first place. She closed her mouth with an audible pop.

"So, what did you get?" Kain asked suddenly, drawing her attention away from her own little world of thought.

"Beg your pardon?" Nancy asked, sitting up and looking at him.

"What did you get? From the Square, I mean."

"Oh, nothing." she muttered, rising up and stretching her tired limbs once again. "For me, anywho. I just got a few things for Li. I did see a nice dress, though."

"Nancy, I need to tell you something." Kain blurted out in such a tone, a chill exploded down Nancy's spine.

"What?" she asked carefully, goose-bumps prickling her arms.

Kain pulled up a chair in front of her and hissed out a flat, apprehensive sigh. There was a short pause, but it felt like an eternity for them both. Kain wasn't sure how to put his words while Nancy was terribly worried about what he was going to say. Finally, Kain broke the uncomfortable silence by inquiring with a dull tone to his voice "How well do you remember mom and dad?"

Nancy flinched slightly. "I don't know. Okay, I guess."

"Well, you remember how they . . . uh, passed?"

For a split second, much too fast to really see, her eyes burned and she scowled. As she fidgeted uncomfortably in her seat, she mumbled "Yes, I do. I know what you've told me. Kain, what's this about?"

Kain stared at his sister with moistening eyes as he tried to come up with a way to break it to her. Suddenly, without thinking, he heard his mouth loudly exclaim "Noknor has come back."

"WHAT!" Nancy squeaked upstarting, jumping up to her feet.

Kain, realizing what he had just said, quickly reached out and grabbed her hands in his. He gently pulled his shocked sister back down into her seat. Then, still clutching her small, warm hands, he leaned over and kissed her pale cheek. After giving her hands a gentle, loving squeeze, he told her "Noknor has returned. He . . . he attacked Kuberica a few days ago."

"Wuh-what happened!"

"Well, he summoned up an army and stormed the castle. Kuberica didn't stand a chance against such a sudden and devastating onslaught. He took over the throne." Kain explained, unaware that his voice was beginning to crack in grief. "The king was . . . well, Edward was kuh-killed."

"Oh, Goddess, no!" Nancy mumbled in disbelief, snatching her quivering hands away from Kain's loving grip to cover her trembling lips. "What happened to Elizabeth? Is . . . is she—?"

"No. No, from what I understand, the monster has her held captive in the castle." Kain assured his young sister as he soothingly kissed her knuckles.

"Oh, my Goddess, Kain!" Nancy whispered, tears beginning to form in her eyes. "What are we going to do?"

"Well, to be perfectly honest, I'm not really sure." he told her, his gaze dropping slightly. "We really haven't had time to discuss the details. But, I do know that I'm going to be leaving on another quest. Michael's going to be joining me since the princess is involved. That's all I know right now. I have no idea when I'll be leaving, except that it will be very soon. Nancy, I love you!"

"I love you too, Kain!" she sniffled and rubbed her moist eyes before she threw her arms around him. She buried her face in his shoulder and began to sob, wetting Kain's shirt with her tears of sorrow and grief.

Kain enveloped her in a strong hug, rubbing her back and caressing her head. "Don't worry, my love." he told her as he kissed the top of her head and rocked slowing as if cradling a small child to sleep. "Everything's going to be all right. I'm going to make him pay for what he did to mom and dad. Even if it's the last thing I ever do!"

CHAPTER III

A soft, cool breeze dotted with tiny droplets of mist blew past the many headstones and monument markers of Arcainian Cemetery. Thunder rumbled distantly in the cold, gray sky as those people who had come to pay respect to their departed loved ones regarded the dark clouds. During the week there usually wasn't very much traffic within the large iron gates of the cemetery, but with the week's break for Spring Festival many families sought to take the time to visit the dearly departed. There were a few scattered individuals and groups around, lovers morning lovers, children looking after parents, friends visiting friends.

The cemetery was usually bright and beautiful with its many trees, lush grass, and magnificently carved markers. But on that particular day with the rain and gloom it was a dreary, desolate place, especially for one young girl who knelt in front of a large granite monument carved in the shape of a man and woman together in a loving embrace with the stone wings of a smiling Mother wrapped around them. They were locked in a symbol of love for all eternity, happy in each other's arms. While many of the grave markers showed the effects of time, this particular one showed none, it was as white and flawless as it had been when it had first been erected. Not even the slightest bit of green algae grew in the many pits and grooves of the highly detailed piece. It was truly a monument to an Arcainian hero and his beloved wife.

Nancy Viccon looked up at the carved names and dates at the foot of the statue and flicked off a bit of dirt. With a heavy heart and wavy sigh, she lowered her head and closed her eyes as she remembered her parents. Even though she had only been a year old when they had died, Nancy remembered them clearly. She always had. When she was younger, she thought it was because of how vividly Kain always described them, how colorful he made them seem. He was always telling her how great they were. How powerful and strong her father was, and yet so peaceful and gentle. How beautiful and caring her mother was, how wise and loving. They were two people very much in love who cared for their children deeply.

But as she grew older, she began to realize that she remembered them not as pictures painted in her head by her brother, but as actual people. She remembered things about them that Kain had never told her, things Kain could never tell her. Things like feelings and emotions. She remembered how she had felt when she was with them. What it felt like to be in her mother's arms in the middle of the night while her mother sang to her. She remembered how sweet and melodious her mother's voice was as she sang her lullabies to calm her or to help her fall asleep. She remembered the warmth and security she felt in those arms. She remembered her father holding her in his powerful arms and how safe he made her feel. How those arms, which could have crushed her in an instant, held her ever so softly and gently and made her feel special.

One of her fondest memories of her parents was when her father would take her out of her crib to play with her. He would toss her upwards playfully and catch her when she came back down, cooing to her as she giggled all the while. She always enjoyed it, the feeling of momentarily sailing through the air before landing safely back into his loving embrace only to be tossed right back up. She could still hear her father laugh joyfully and her mother shriek at him to be careful. He was always careful.

She had loved them both so much when they were alive and she loved them even more after she had lost them. And she hated Noknor with every bit of her being for what he had done. If it hadn't been for him, her parents would still be alive. That was why she could not bear to stand idly by and watch as her brother alone avenged the people who she also loved so dear. She had to do something to help. She had to be a part of Noknor's destruction. But she didn't know how she was going to do it.

She couldn't go to Kain. She knew exactly what he would say. 'No, it's too dangerous!' he would tell her. 'You'll get hurt!' Well, it might be dangerous, but she wouldn't get hurt!

"Hmph! I can take care of myself!" she mumbled to herself as she frowned bitterly. It just wasn't fair that Kain should stop her. She had every right to do it. Just as much as he did, at least.

"Look at me." she sighed. She felt ashamed of herself as she looked up to stare at the three beautiful faces. "I'm blaming Kain for things he hasn't even done yet. Or said, rather. And he does have every bit of reason to say those things, too. I'm not a warrior like him. Not yet."

The dark clouds rumbled deeply above her head. The other scattered people standing by the graves looked up with concern. The clouds would soon begin to drop their watery load upon their heads and they decided that it would be best to find some shelter rather than be caught in the rain. As they slowly began to disperse, they each mentally gave their loved ones heartfelt good-byes. The only one who knelt loyally by a grave was Nancy. She took no notice of the approaching storm as she sat silently still, her head lowered and her eyes closed as she continued her thoughts on her brother. About how much she loved and admired him.

Kain and Nancy had always been very close. When she was growing up in China, Kain and Li had always been her best friends. As she grew up, she began to respect him as a daughter respects her father. She looked to him for guidance and care, and he gave her plenty of both. Even though his career in the military and his aspirations to first become and then be the best Grand General of Arcainia had kept him a busy man much of the time, he made sure he was never too busy for her. He always told her that there was nothing so important that it couldn't wait for her. She really looked up to him and wanted to be just like him. That was why she felt so guilty for thinking so badly of him.

"Oh, mama and baba!" she whispered lowly, looking up at the statue. "I love you both so very much! I . . . I have to do something to be a part of Noknor's punishment for what he's done! But I know Kain won't let me. I can't . . . I can't really blame him, I guess. But . . ." she trailed off as she lowered her head once more, taking a deep, shaky breath. "Please help me. Please help Kain to understand how much this means to me. I miss you more and more each day, it just hurts so much! I know this won't stop the pain, but . . . I . . . I . . ."

A soft, gentle kiss touched her cheek as a low pitter-pat of raindrops striking the ground around her floated to her ears. She looked up at the figures. The rain had dropped onto them in such a way that it appeared that a small teardrop had drifted down their cheeks. Without knowing quite why, a smile touched the girl's lips as a powerful sense of comfort and well-being began to envelope her. She reached down the front of her white lace dress and withdrew a small heart-shaped pendant made of silver and inlaid with a sparkling sapphire. She opened it with a sharp click and gazed fondly at the two pictures painted with expert detail inside. As she stared at her mother and father with moist eyes, she heard her mother's gentle voice in the wind softly whisper 'What you dare to dream, dare to do.'

At that point, Nancy realized that she would join Kain on his quest, no matter what it took.

* * *

Later that afternoon, Li was in the living room working out, having been forced inside by the thunderstorm. After clearing all of the loose furniture out of her way and pushing the couch back, she stretched her muscles for a few minutes to get her blood warmed up again. Finally, she said to herself "Now it's time to get back down to business!"

She had just started to practice her kicks, punches, flips, and other fierce fighting combinations when the front door creaked open. From the depressing gray of the outside, Nancy walked in, her clothes damp and her hair in a wet disarray from the drizzle. She wiped the water from her face with the moist sleeve of her dress and regarded her cousin with a dull wave of her other hand.

"Nancy! Look at you!" Li scolded. "What have you been doing out in this rain? Without an umbrella, even!"

"I was at the cemetery." she replied softly.

"Oh, I see." Li murmured, slightly taken aback and feeling guilty for reprimanding her. She grabbed her towel from the couch and tossed it to her. "All by yourself?"

"Yes."

"Oh." she said, cocking her lip as watched her cousin rub the towel over her hair. "Are you all right, kiddo?"

"Yeah, I'm fine." Nancy told her, giving her a smile. Seeing how concerned Li was began to lift her down spirits once again. "I just have a lot on my mind is all."

"Well, I can understand that. A lot has happened since yesterday." Li said, returning the smile as she walked up to her. She took the towel and dabbed a few places around Nancy's face and neck before draping it over her damp shoulders. She looked into her eyes, offered a reassuring grin and inquired in a voice she hoped wasn't too pushy "Is there anything you want to talk about?"

"No." Nancy replied softly. "No, not right now."

"Okay, but if you ever do want to talk, you know—"

"That I can come to you, yes I know." she finished for her. She grinned broadly and wrapped her arms around her cousin in a tight embrace. "Thanks, Li."

Li smiled brightly and returned the squeeze. "You'd better go get changed out of those wet clothes. You'll catch your death! And, hey, if you weren't going to be doing anything else at the moment, I was wondering if you'd like to join me? I hate working out alone. I get so lonesome."

"Okay. Sounds like fun." Nancy giggled. "I'll be right back."

Within five minutes, Nancy was dried off and dressed in a tight black shirt and loose light green pants, practicing moves with Li. Li was very impressed by how Nancy handled herself. She knew Nancy could fight, after all she knew that Kain had taught her how to defend herself and she had shown the kid a few great moves herself. However, Nancy was now actually keeping up with her and not only matching her moves, but also pulling stuff Li had never seen before. Granted she was still a long way from even coming close to matching Li's skill and experience, but she was definitely improving tremendously.

"Hey kiddo, has your brother been teaching you some new moves lately?" Li asked when they took a break to get some water.

"Yeah, a few." Nancy told her, emptying her glass with large, thirsty gulps. "Why?"

"Because it shows!" Li told her with a proud smile, patting her on the back. "You are turning out to be a great warrior."

"You really think so?" Nancy asked hopefully. Li nodded her head as she sipped down the last few drops of her water before setting her cup next to Nancy's. "Wow! Thank you!"

Li grinned as she wiped her mouth with her towel and got into position. "I really liked that five hit roundhouse combo you did earlier. Let's see that one again."

* * *

The next evening, Second General Raphael Boniva and Prince Michael, son to Queen Vanetta the Beautiful of Arcainia and fiancé to Princess Elizabeth of Kuberica walked with Kain into the Viccon home, laughing rowdily as young men often do when left to their own devices.

"Hey, guys!" a surprised Li beamed brightly as she came from the kitchen to welcome Kain home. "What brings you two gentlemen out this way?"

"We just thought we'd tag along with the Grand General and get a chance to see the most beautiful woman gracing Arcainia." the prince grinned with a wink. Raphael held back a laugh and started to wish he could be as outspoken as his friend. He was always shy around beautiful women, even if they were just friends.

"Thanks." Li giggled sheepishly, blushing at the compliment.

A sudden and intentionally loud cough made them all snap their heads in Kain's direction to see him grinning slyly. As he slowly crossed arms, he jested "Hitting on my cousin, good prince? Are we forgetting that we are betrothed to another?"

"Not in the slightest! I was just complimenting the lovely Li on how she keeps herself." He winked an eye at the Chinese woman. "I was just being hospitable."

"Right, whatever you say, lover-boy." Li giggled and as she used silly flourishes to blow him a kiss.

After sharing warm laughter with the others, a delightful scent struck Raphael's nostrils and he sniffed the air lightly. "Mmmmm. Something smells good!"

"Dinner, I hope." Kain nodded as his mouth began to water at the scent. Suddenly, something in the air struck him as odd and out of place. He sniffed the air and caught a whiff of Li's wonderfully scented perfume mixed with boiling rice, braising beef, and a little something else. That little something was stronger the second time he sniffed, and yes, indeed, it did smell wrong. It almost smelled like . . .

"Do I smell smoke?"

Li shouted a Chinese curse in horror, spinning so quickly that she nearly threw herself to the floor and made a mad dash for the kitchen while the men had a good laugh at her expense.

"Man, that is some cousin you have there!" Michael smiled as he shook his head at the humor.

Kain snorted laughter and rolled his eyes. "You guys going to be joining us?"

"Love to, but I need to run these documents over to General Riet." Raphael responded, lifting his satchel as if to remind Kain of the order he had given him earlier in the day.

"Oh, yeah, that's right. Sorry. Your highness?"

"Naw, I can't stay either." Michael shrugged with slight disappointment. He was about to relay his own excuse when Li suddenly poked her head out from behind the corner and asked if they would like to stay for dinner. When they politely declined, Li pretended to be saddened.

"It was the fire, wasn't it? I'm a good cook, I swear! Tell them I'm a good cook, Kain." she ordered, grinning broadly and brandishing a huge cooking knife.

"She's the best cook in the land!" Kain laughed heartily as he held the door for his friends. "Honest."

"We'll just go ahead and take your word for it tonight." Michael grinned broadly before he and Raphael waved good-bye and started out into the night. "See you later, beautiful!"

"Take care!" Li called back as Kain shut the door.

Twenty minutes later, Li placed three plates onto the table. Nancy still hadn't returned home from being out all day and Kain was starting to get pretty worried. Li assured him that she was all right, that she probably just lost track of time, and suggested that they go ahead and start eating without her. So, they took their seats at the table and dug into the wonderful meal that Li had prepared.

As they ate, they engaged in lively conversation as they always did. However, this time Li noticed that Kain's mind seemed to be elsewhere. She saw him often glance at Nancy's empty place, fidget nervously, and toss his eyes over Li's shoulder at the doorway. Li was a bit concerned herself, but she knew the girl could take care of herself just fine. She had proven it to her the day before and she was about to tell Kain about it when he suddenly asked her where Nancy had said she was going.

"I'm not really sure." she shrugged. "She said something about visiting someone and headed out the door. I assume she's out gallivanting around the Square with Romi and Dafne."

"There's nothing open this late except for bars and taverns. Not their scene." Kain told her.

"There's a few dance clubs they like." she pointed out, gesturing at him with her chopsticks. Then, more to calm her own growing uneasiness than Kain's, she added "They might have stopped by one to check out one of those weird bands or something. Or perhaps they're at one of the others' houses sharing some girlish gossip and lost track of time." She paused and thought for a minute about what she had just said before she continued in a more confident tone "Yes, I'm sure that's it. She'll probably come running through that door any minute now apologizing for being so late and begging you not to kill her."

"I hope so." Kain mumbled, taking a bite out of one of Li's fabulous eggrolls. Once again, Li was about to try to set his mind at ease by telling him how much Nancy's fighting skill had improved, but before she could Kain replied "Oh, by the way. I talked to Queen Vanetta today."

"About?" Li asked, quite intrigued.

Kain looked at her for a moment as if she had just asked the silliest question in the world. "About having you join us."

"Terrific!" Li exclaimed. "What did she say?"

"She said that it was my call." he said, popping the last bit of eggroll into his mouth. "She said that I was leading this quest and that I could invite anyone I pleased. She has faith in my judgment that you have enough skill. I mean, no one has as much skill as you do." He paused thoughtfully as he considered. "Well, nobody except for me of course."

Li rolled her eyes and smirked as she shook her head. She knew the truth, and so did he even if he didn't like to admit it. She smiled, thrilled to be able to fight once again at Kain's side, as she whispered "Thank you."

"Don't mention it." he grinned, returning his attention back onto his plate. "You know how much I enjoy our adventures together."

"Wo ye." Li murmured, sipping her tea daintily.

After a few minutes and more chatting, he swallowed the last piece of food his stomach could hold and pushed his plate away. "That was delicious!"

He yawned and stretched before shuffling over to his cousin to give her a fond peck on the top of her head. "Xiexie ni, Li. You truly are the best cook in the land. But I thought you had burned something?"

"Oh, that was . . . heh-heh, that was nothing." she blushed, unable to hide the embarrassment in her eyes. It had actually been a sugar cake that she was going to surprise him with, but since he hadn't known about it, she felt there was no need in disappointing him. "Just a . . . a bit of grease, that's all."

"Oh, well in any case, that was a wonderful meal as always." he told her, yawning mightily as he grabbed his dishes from the table. "I guess I'll go ahead and start cleaning up now."

"No, you need your rest." Li told him assuredly, quickly rising and snatching the plate from his hands. "I'll take care of everything. Now go on and get yourself to bed."

"Well, I was going to wait up for Nancy, anyway."

"I'll wait for her to drag her little butt in." Li said in a very sure tone of voice that meant trouble for the girl as she set the dish back onto the table and crossed her arms. "I insist you go on to bed. You've had a big day today and you'll have another tomorrow. You need all the sleep you can get."

Kain started to protest but Li quickly put her fingers to his lips to quiet him as she hissed air through her lips and grinned. Kain sighed dully. He knew it would do no good to argue with her, especially since she was right anyway. He did have another big day ahead of him and he was exhausted. So he grabbed her wrist gently and pulled her hand away as he muttered "All right, you win."

"Was there ever any doubt?" Li giggled, making Kain roll his eyes and smirk.

"I guess I'll see you in the morning, then. Good night, Li." he told her, embracing her in a warm hug.

"Nighty-night, sweetie." she whispered, patting then rubbing his back. "Don't let the NightMare bite."

"Thanks. Now when Nancy comes home, be sure to give her a stern talking to." he told her in a lighthearted manner.

"Oh, you bet I will and more." Li replied, crossing her arms again and raising an eyebrow in displeasure. It was quite clear that Li was very upset and that she was going to give Nancy a big piece of her mind. "She had better have a darn good excuse, let me tell you!"

Kain chuckled lowly and gave his beloved cousin one final peck on the cheek as he whispered "It wouldn't be like her not to have an elaborate story all planned out. Good night."

With that, he sluggishly headed out of the dining room and to his room. Li followed him out with her eyes, her mouth forming a half smile. When he was gone, she turned back to her plate and listlessly prodded her food with her chopsticks. She was growing more and more worried about Nancy and she could only imagine what Kain was thinking. She hoped it wouldn't interfere with his sleep. It wasn't at all like her to stay out late, especially that late. She was always such a responsible girl. Li wondered what in the world was keeping her out so late. She was afraid the poor girl was out on the streets of Arcainia hurt or worse. Heaven only knew where she was.

Finally, Li decided that if Nancy hadn't gotten back by the time she had finished the dishes, she would go out looking for her. She thought about waking Kain when she did head out, but ultimately decided against it. She got up from the table and hurried to the kitchen to quickly finish the dishes.

* * *

After Kain had fallen asleep and while Li was in the middle of cleaning the kitchen, the front door opened with a soft creak and Nancy tiptoed in, trying to be as quiet as she could as she carried a small bag in one hand and a sword in the other. She looked all around to see if either Kain or Li had waited up for her. Seeing no one around, she breathed a great sigh of relief. She knew that she was going to be in trouble for being out so late, of that there was no doubt in her mind, but she would rather have them yell at her in the morning after having time to calm down than right as soon as she walked through the door. She figured them both asleep and walked silently to the couch where she tossed the bag onto the cushion and slid the sword out of it's sheath enough to read the inscription on the blade: "*To my little sweetheart, may the spirit of your father flow through your veins and give you the strength to be the great warrior that he was, Uncle John.*"

She smiled and sighed heavily, a tear forming in her eye as she slid the sword home. As she sat, she laid it beside her and took out a small scrap of paper from her pocket. She was carefully reading it with a heartfelt smile when Li came around the corner wiping her hands on a small towel and saw her young cousin. This immediately sparked an immense amount of relief as well as an equal amount of anger.

"Nancy!" she hissed in a low voice, tossing the towel to the ground in fury. "Just where in the world have you been! Your brother and I have been worried sick! Why, for all we knew you could have been dead in a ditch or some . . . thing." She finished her scolding blandly as she noticed Nancy's new toy and gave the girl a curious look.

The young girl gave a startled gasp and dropped the paper, which flittered to the carpet. Quickly, she snatched it back up and stuffed it into her pocket as Li examined the weapon beside her.

"Now where did you get that?" Li curiously inquired with raised eyebrows as she rubbed her chin thoughtfully, her newfound interest quickly pushing out all hostile thoughts of discipline. "And more importantly, why did you get it?"

Nancy put her hand protectively on her sword and pulled it onto her lap as she mumbled "I got it because I'm going with Kain to help him kill Noknor."

"I see." Li murmured thoughtfully, quickly realizing just what exactly this whole business was about. "And does your brother know about this yet?"

"No, not yet." Nancy whispered meekly. "But I don't care what he says. I'm going!"

"But why?" she asked with eyes growing misty, knowing full well what the answer was going to be.

"Because they were my parents too! I loved them just as much as him." she replied before thinking about what she had said. She lowered her head and quietly corrected herself "I love them just as much as he does. And it's not fair for him to keep me from helping set things right!"

"Nancy, how old are you?" Li asked softly, sitting next to her on the couch.

"I'm not too young!" the girl snapped defensively as she pulled out the piece of paper and pretended to read it.

Li snatched it away and whispered sternly "Did I say that you were? No, I was just going to say that it's not often that you find such a young girl so mature in her thinking. I know that your brother will welcome you in with open arms."

"REALLY?" Nancy squeaked hopefully and a bit too loudly.

Li put her finger to Nancy's lips as she giggled. Nancy blushed slightly and mouthed a 'sorry' as Li took her finger away. She smiled and handed the note back to the girl as she looked to Kain's door, expecting him to rush out. When it never opened, she figured that he must have been dead to the world and turned her attention back onto her young cousin.

"You certainly have enough skill, I'm sure." she told her in a whispered voice. "I mean, you proved it to me the other day when we sparred. I didn't know you were that good of a fighter, and I don't think that Kain does either. And I sure know that he doesn't know that you feel so strongly about your parents. I mean, you were so young then and I think he figures that you don't remember as much as you do."

"I think you're right."

"You remember a lot about your parents, don't you? More than you let on to your brother?" Li said softly, taking the girl's tender hand and giving it a squeeze. Nancy nodded slowly, her head slightly lowered and her eyes moist. "How much do you remember?"

"Enough." Nancy murmured softly. She turned her head away from her cousin for a moment as if she were ashamed. However, there was no shame when she picked her head up and looked dead into Li's eyes. Her eyes were different now, a lot harder with a flicker of burning hatred and scorn that Li had never ever seen. They were the same eyes Li had seen in Kain when he had smashed the chair to pieces in his rage. The day he had found out about Kuberica. They were the same except that Nancy's eyes were actually harder than Kain's had been, if that were possible, and it didn't look like Nancy at all. Staring into her cousin's eyes, Li felt as if she were looking at a totally different person, a person with a lot of anger in her heart. A very dangerous person. And when Nancy spoke, her low voice was more like a stinging bitter hiss than her normal high, sweet tone. "Enough to make me want to break Noknor's back!"

Li dropped her cousin's hand like a hot coal and shrank away. She suddenly wished she had never asked the question, that she had just kept quiet. She had never seen Nancy so vicious and hateful. This was not the sweet, innocent girl she thought she knew.

Then, as quickly as the hate had appeared, it vanished without a trace leaving Nancy her soft, tender eyes once more. The whole affair had lasted for only about half a second or so, but it was something Li would remember for a long time. It told her just how much hate for Noknor had built up in her cousin's heart over the years. At that moment, Li knew that Nancy had to go with Kain and she decided that she would do everything in her power to make sure it happened.

"I really miss them a lot, Li." Nancy suddenly replied, startling Li away from her heavy thoughts. "I know I didn't know them like Kain did, but it still hurts me to know that they're gone."

"I know it does, sweetie. I know that all too well." Li said soothingly as she put her arms around her shoulders and squeezed gently. The gesture was almost motherly. "But Kain's really the one you should tell."

"I am." Nancy replied, leaning on her cousin. "I will tomorrow."

"Good. That alone will probably soften his heart enough to have you along." she remarked happily before she added with a chuckle "You know what a daxiongmao your brother is."

Nancy nodded with a blushed smile as she pulled away from her cousin's grasp. "Thanks so much Li."

In reply, Li grinned affectionately and reached out to rub Nancy's head as she tenderly kissed her forehead. Then, in hopes of lifting the somber air that hung over them like a dense fog, she asked to see what all she had gotten. Nancy proudly showed off her new sword first. Li took it from her and removed it from its sheath. It was a small sword by any standards, but it fit Nancy just perfectly. It was about two and a half feet long, very lightweight, and looked to be as sharp as a fine razor. Li noted to herself that it was made of Rajima steel, some very powerful stuff indeed. It was the perfect steel for swords because it was nearly unbreakable yet extremely lightweight and it always seemed to hold its edge, never seeming to dull. Short of magick, it was the best steel out on the market, and as such was also very, very expensive. There was no way Nancy could have afforded it herself without Kain knowing, not even if she had saved her every penny for five years. Li was about to ask her where she had gotten such an outstanding weapon when the inscription caught her eye.

"John Accrue gave you this?" she asked. Nancy nodded vigorously, her knees pressed together and her hands cupped together in her lap. Li raised her eyebrows and muttered in a rather toneless voice "Oh. Well, that was sweet of him."

John Accrue had been Richard Viccon's best friend and his Second General, much like Raphael was to Kain. He was also one of the most powerful men in the Arcainian Court and one of Kain and Nancy's most cherished of friends. Ever since they had first arrived back in Arcainia a little over eight years before, John had helped them get their life back together and had watched over them like a blood uncle. And, since he had been closest to Richard and Fang, he told their children a lot about them and helped them to know their parents better as the great people they were. Even to that day, they often went to his house to sit down with him and chat over a cup of tea. They talked about many things when they were together, but mostly about their mother and father. John was forever telling them about their adventures and Nancy especially always listened to him with a great awe-filled fascination, taking in every detail and picturing her great father in action and the blissful love husband and wife shared.

Li slid the blade home and handed it back to Nancy as she asked if the girl had told John of her exact plans. The answer was of course yes. She had gone to him that afternoon and begged him for his help. She told Li that John had been very impressed with her but wasn't the least bit surprised.

"He told me that he knew it was only a matter of time before the warrior in my blood woke up and showed itself. That's why he wasn't surprised when I went to him." Nancy explained proudly as she stifled a small yawn. Li sighed tenderly and smiled. She couldn't help but smile because she had seen the decency in John Accrue that never showed itself to her and because he was absolutely right. It was only a matter of time before Nancy picked up a sword and followed Kain.

"Anywayz," the girl continued, "he told me that he wanted to help me as much as he could so he gave me a few things. He told me that he had gotten this sword a while ago and was waiting for the right time to give it to me. It was going to be a graduation present, I think."

"Well, I must say that I do like your new sword." Li told her. "It's a beautiful work and that inscription is just fitting. It'll be perfect for you."

"Thanks, Li."

"Ey, ah jest callz 'em lok ah seez 'em." she replied with a wink and a cocked mouth, imitating one of Nancy's favorite showmen. The girl put her hand to her mouth and giggled audibly. Li almost shushed her, but figured that if they hadn't already woken up her brother, a little laugh probably wouldn't hurt anything. Instead, she smiled and said "Here, show me what's in the bag."

Nancy perked up and eagerly untied the drawstring before pulling out a blowpipe, another smaller bag, and a spell book. Nancy loved magick and had many books on the subject, but for some reason the art seemed to elude her and try as she might she could not get them to work for her. Li grabbed the slender, hollow tube and asked if she knew how to use it. Nancy only smiled proudly and took it back. She loaded it with a sharp dart from the smaller bag and searched for a target. Finally, she directed Li's attention to a fat fly on the far wall. She aimed and fired, skewering the insect cleanly. Li was speechless as Nancy turned her head and grinned. She glared at her with wide, shocked eyes and asked "Where in the world did you learn to do that!"

"I've been practicing for a year or so."

"You taught yourself?" Li gasped, her eyes growing larger. When Nancy nodded with the simple honesty her innocent nature provided, her jaw dropped to the floor. She found it hard to believe that Nancy had taught herself that well, she knew people who had trained for years and weren't even half that skilled. But the proof was right there. "That is . . . amazing! Simply amazing! Truly a warrior spirit burns in your heart and flows through your veins!"

"I guess." Nancy blushed with a slightly lowered head and shrugged her shoulders, her modest nature getting the best of her.

Li sighed heavy-heartedly, silently wishing the girl wasn't so excessively humble. She seemed ashamed of her skills, and that wasn't right. The girl had some amazing abilities, abilities some people would kill for, and she should be proud of that fact. But what could Li do? It was Nancy's nature and only she could change herself.

'Well, it could be worse.' Li thought to herself with a subtle grin. 'At least she's not a narcissist.'

As she watched her gather her things, she patted her shoulder and replied "Well, anyway you have some great stuff. They're perfect for your first quest, especially that sword. And I do hope those moves I taught you will come in handy when you get into your first battle."

"I'm sure they will." Nancy smiled as she pulled the drawstring on her bag tight. "Thanks, Li."

Li smiled brightly and gave her a mighty hug. "Nancy, I am so very, very proud of you! You are growing up to be a beautiful and powerful person, just like your brother and I knew you would." Nancy mouthed another thanks and touched her lips to Li's cheek as her cousin opened her mouth wide and gave a tired yawn. She covered her mouth and murmured "Oh! Excuse me! Well, it's pretty late, sweetie. We had better be getting to bed."

"Okee-dokee. I love you, Li."

"Wo ye, kiddo." she replied before she wished Nancy a good night. Then she left her in the living room and headed straight to her bedroom where she undressed and climbed into bed. As soon as her head hit the soft feather pillow, she fell into a deep sleep. It had, after all, been a long and tiring day.

CHAPTER IV

A Dark Knight officer strode the length of the throne room to come to a halt in front of Noknor and Garrison. He bowed down to one knee and waited for his lord to give him the gesture to rise. He saluted both men, waited for Garrison's return salute, and replied "I do beg your pardon at your disturbance, my lord, but there is a messenger at your door requesting to see you. She says that she represents the Ladys of the Elements."

"Is that a fact?" Noknor murmured, raising a curious brow and stroking his chin thoughtfully. He said nothing for a long while and Garrison wondered if he was just going to have the captain kill her. Finally Noknor said "Show her in. I want to hear what those troublesome faeries have to say."

The Dark Knight bowed once more and executed a flawless about-face to march out. Not three seconds later, he returned followed by a human woman in a brown cotton dress and five more lower ranking Dark Knights flanking her. Noknor was a bit surprised as he had expected a faery girl for a messenger, particularly from such sprites that claimed to be as powerful as the Ladys did. He shrugged it off, as a messenger was a messenger be it a faery, a human, or a troll. Although he did have to admit that he would rather hear words from this woman than any troll any day. He threw a momentary glance at Garrison and could tell by the lustful grin and heavily concentrated look that he was already mentally undressing her and imagining her in various poses. Noknor gave a mental chuckle. He was such a vulgar creature, no sense of culture or class. But then, he was nothing more than guttertrash.

Of course, the girl was pleasantly lovely. She seemed to be in her twenties and Noknor could tell from her dark eyes, her dark hair hanging daintily about her shoulders, and her luscious honey skin that she was Arcainian. She wore the garb of a sorceress: a simple brown cotton dress with a rather large leather belt adorned with many colored gems wrapped around her slim waist. Her cloak was a darker brown than her dress and she walked with a large staff carved with pictures and symbols that Noknor recognized as faery in origin. As the girl approached, the warlock noticed that she was neither in fear nor in awe by his presence, but actually seemed to be annoyed. She sported a dark frown and bored eyes, a look that on this particular female served to make her even more desirable. However, it was a look that did not show the proper respect and a look that would have to change before she left. She would both fear and revere his newfound power.

When the group reached the throne, six of them bowed down to one knee. The woman regarded them with a raised brow and halfway rolled her eyes as she exhaled audibly. Garrison was quick to jump right down her throat, roaring "You little witch! You will bow before your Lord Noknor!"

The woman glared at him with such fire in her eyes that his barking fell brutally short. She wore a savage sneer which clearly showed her gleaming white teeth and . . . fangs? Noknor looked again for a very brief moment before she tightly pursed her lips together, but he did see them. Her four canine teeth were a bit longer and pointier than a normal human's. Not by much, but they were noticeable. Quite interesting, quite interesting indeed. Though, it probably didn't mean much, just an abnormality and nothing more. She was a human, perfectly normal. Her anger directed towards Garrison was not, however. The hellfire she threw at him with her eyes and sneer told that there was something more behind her fury than simply being barked at.

"He may be your lord, Mr. Garrison," she hissed his name savagely through her teeth. So, she did have issues with the cretin. "But he is NOT," she stressed the word harshly, venom dripping from her voice, "mine! I bow only to the Ladys."

"Be that as it may, Miss, but you are in the home of the Lord Noknor." Garrison replied, though not with near the same force as before. He made a gesture with his hand. "You will bow!"

The captain stepped towards the woman. She growled at him and placed a defensive hand onto his chest. Garrison thought she was going to try to push the man away and mentally laughed at the thought the moment before the Dark Knight burst into spectacular flames that engulfed him so fully that he was hidden completely from view. In the three seconds it took to reduce him to ashes, his constant wail of agony started at an ear piercing level and quickly drifted down to a low whisper. When the flames soaked back into the woman's hand, there stood before her a smoldering, charred skeleton in blacked armor. She followed it down with her eyes as the brittle bones collapsed in a dusty heap, leaving only the skull in its black steel helmet sitting with a morbid grin atop the rubble.

Another Dark Knight leapt at her, intent on running her through. However, a simple wave of her hand sent gray mist to cover him. Instantly, his legs grew too heavy to pick up and his arms too hard to move as his skin began to dry out and became rough and solid. He opened his mouth to scream but the air froze forever in his concrete throat as he was entirely petrified into solid stone. Another wave of her hand called forth a great gust that howled sharply and lifted the statue into the air, carrying it swiftly to shatter against the wall. The statue's head flew off the wall, hit the ground, and rolled to a stop at the feet of the remaining Dark Knights. Its wide stone eyes and stone mouth were eternally set in absolute terror as it stared back up at them as if to warn them against challenging the powerful woman. She held her sharp gaze for a moment to further discourage them before turning back to face the throne.

She snapped her wrist and sent a massive ball of fire screaming towards Garrison. He shrieked in horror and threw up his arms in a pathetic attempt to block himself from the onslaught. The fireball roared at him and exploded harmlessly as it crashed into an invisible barrier three feet from his face.

The woman turned swiftly to Noknor as he lowered his hand, every bit of rage showing in her burning face and clenched fists. "NOKNOR—"

"You came here on behalf of the Ladys for a reason, and I highly doubt it was to kill my men." he replied calmly. He glanced at Garrison, the man's eyes bulging out of their sockets and glazed over with a sort of blankness. His teeth were so tightly pressed together, Noknor thought that they would shattered like glass and his entire body was so stiff and rigid that it seemed he had been the one turned to stone. Clearly, he had the look of staring death in the eye. Noknor wondered momentarily if the man had soiled himself. "At least, not all of them." he continued, returning his gaze to the messenger. "State your business, if you will my dear."

The woman held her narrow eyes of contempt on him for a long moment before finally taking a deep breath and speaking, her words coming fast as she recited a prepared speech from memory. "Noknor, you are a most wicked man. By using the Swuenedras Amulet you have upset the balance that we four sisters have created and work to maintain. As such, you have deeply offended and insulted us. You are hereby requested to give up the Swuenedras Amulet to the custody of our Jestura and cease using faery artifacts to aid in your evil workings. We will not ask twice. Rest assured that if you do not come to agreement with this simple request, we will be a key element in your destruction."

She took a deep breath, held it in her lungs for a moment, and then sighed it out as she stood silently by for Noknor to give his reply. The throne room was as deathly quiet as a tomb as Noknor sat on his throne, clicking his talons against his armrest, the sharp sound echoing loudly. The only other sound came when the woman exhaled quite loudly in annoyance.

"Are you waiting for something, my dear?" he asked.

"Yes!" she answered briskly, thrusting her hip out to her left and snapping her hand onto it. "I'm waiting for your answer, you pompous ass!"

In a sudden instance of rage, Noknor hissed in fury and shot three purple blasts from his hand. The energy never reached the girl as an invisible shield stopped it inches from her nose. As the purple energy curved harmlessly around her body, illuminating her face, she closed her eyes and uttered an annoyed "Hmph!"

With the subsidence of the attack, her eyelids opened ever so slowly as her tongue ran delicately over her teeth. Behind her frown was a smug look as she replied "I am protected by those far more powerful than you could ever hope to be, *LORD* Noknor. Your little trinket has no affect on me."

"Be that as it may, messenger." he growled. "But can you turn all of my men into stone?"

"Perhaps you would be surprised." she spat out, her voice low and cocky.

"Perhaps I might, my dear." he returned, his voice just as low, his glowing red eyes held firmly against her dark brown eyes. For several eternally long seconds, they waged a silent war with their eyes before the woman was forced to admit defeat and look away in disgust.

Satisfied, Noknor cleared his throat and said "You may take this message back to your oh so powerful mistresses along with empty hands. Tell them that I will not part with my new toy, and if they want it so badly they are most welcome to come and take it. But they should be advised to be careful, because it'll take a war for them to get it from me. I am not afraid of a war, not even with them. Please also advise them against making empty threats. There will be a time when I will take care of old business, and I would hate to dirty my hands with them!"

The woman's scowl darkened in contempt. "The Ladys will be most dis—"

"My heart is breaking, truly!" Noknor cut her off, his voice gruff and booming. "Now, then if there is nothing more to be said, young lady, you may take your leave of my castle."

"Very well. Thank you for your time, Noknor. I'm sorry we could not come to agreement. Mr. Garrison," she cast ice-cold eyes onto the Dark General, "I shall look forward to meeting with you once again on more personal terms."

With that, a yellow mist began to cover the woman as she herself began to slowly fade away right before the eyes of the six men. In the next instant she was gone without a trace that she had ever been there, save for the shattered statue and the ashes that littered the floor.

Noknor turned to his wide-eyed, trembling general, raised an amused eyebrow, and chuckled heartily "My, but you sure have a way with the ladies, don't you?"

Garrison simply smacked his dry lips and gulped audibly.

*   *   *

Kain was the first one up the next morning, so he took it upon himself to cook breakfast. He made a fire in the stove and threw some fresh eggs into an iron skillet. As he flipped them, Li entered with a hand stifling back a very mighty yawn.

"Zaoshang hao." she mumbled as she walked over to him.

"I'm sorry. Did I wake you up?" he asked, handing her a plate of eggs and toasted bread as he directed her eyes to the steaming cup of tea on the counter.

"No, I woke myself up. Xiexie." she murmured as she shuffled into the dining room.

"No problem." he smiled, following her out with his eyes before he picked up his own plate and joined her at the table. As he sat and picked up his fork, he asked "So, what time did Nancy come in?"

"Hmmmm? Oh! Oh, ah . . . just a little bit after you had gone to bed."

"Did you get after her?"

"Yes, I did." she told him. It was a lie, but she knew that if he thought she had already scolded her, he wouldn't be so harsh on her.

"Where had she been?"

"John Accrue's house." she replied, sipping her tea. She thought Kain was going to question her further about why she had been there so late and she sure didn't want that because she felt Nancy should tell him her reasons herself. So, to take the heat off her, she quickly changed the subject by using her most pleasant voice to remark "This is very good, Kain. I do like the way you cook your eggs."

"Li, has Nancy ever talked to you about my parents?"

She sighed dully. "No, not really."

"What do you mean 'not really'?"

"No, she hasn't." Li replied, shoveling a fork full of eggs into her mouth. She really didn't like lying to Kain like that, but she knew that it was something he should discuss with Nancy. She hoped that if she played dumb, he would go to her himself. So, to push him along a little, she subtly added "Although at times I think she wants to talk."

"I know what you mean. I think she remembers more about them than she lets on. Sometimes I can see it in her eyes."

"Why don't you ask her yourself? She is your sister, after all." she pointed out, sitting back in her chair with her cup in hand.

"I know, but I really—" he stopped in midsentence when he saw Nancy stroll into the dining room with her nose held high, sniffing the air with a grin across her face.

"Good morning, all!" she squeaked brightly.

"Morning, kiddo." Li smiled, glad that she had woken up in time to catch her brother before he left.

"Hey." Kain murmured, wiping off his mouth.

"Something smells yummy! Is it eggs?"

"They're in the kitchen." Kain told her, throwing his thumb over his shoulder. Within two minutes, Nancy had herself situated at the table with a plate of eggs, three biscuits, and a glass of water. He watched her wolf down her food for a moment before asking "Nancy, where did you go last night?"

Nancy gulped and prepared for a hurricane as she stuttered nervously "I-I was at Juh-John's house." She paused to let him bark at her and was pleasantly surprised when nothing came. She breathed a mental sigh of relief. "I'm really sorry for coming in so late. He was telling me a story about daddy and I lost track of time. I'm very, very sorry."

"I know you are, darlin'. And I know Li has already gotten after you, so I'll save your ear. But just next time tell me or Li where you'll be going. I was really worried about you, Nancy." he told her gently as he patted her knee under the table. She looked into his eyes and smiled brightly. Kain returned it before asking "Which story did he tell you?"

"Ha? Oh! Oh, the one about daddy fighting the Dragon of Kitrad Doe." Nancy told him and it wasn't a lie. John had told her that story and it was one of the reasons she had lost track of time. "He's told it to me before, but it's such a good one. I just had to hear it all over again."

"I know what you mean. That's one of my personal favorites, too." he grinned as he finished the last of his eggs and looked at his watch. "Well, it's about that time, I guess. Pardon me, ladies."

When Kain had walked out of the dining room with his dishes, Li quickly turned to Nancy and excitedly said "Now's your big chance! Tell him you want to go with him when he comes back."

"No." Nancy whispered meekly and lowered her head in defeat. It was clear that she was getting cold feet.

"What! Why not?" Li's eyes widened. She couldn't believe her ears. Nancy just shook her head as Kain returned to say his good-byes for the day. Li regarded Nancy with discouraged eyes and sighed. She knew the girl just needed a little push to get her going, so she turned to Kain and said as innocently as she could "Uhm, Kain? Nancy has something she really wants to tell you."

"Really?" he smiled with raised eyebrows as he looked at his sister with heartfelt amusement. "What is it, pup?"

Nancy looked to Li with a trembling lip. Li simply gave her a warm smile and a reassuring wink as she nudged her under the table with her foot. Taking a deep breath, Nancy blurted out "I want to go with you on your quest to destroy Noknor!"

"Well, that's so swe-SAY WHAT!" Kain's jaw dropped to the ground and he fell forward against his chair. He was expecting a nice 'good luck on your quest' or something to that effect, but not that she wanted to go with him. His first thought was to say no way, out of the question! And he would have blurted it out if Nancy hadn't given her reasons first. He slowly sat back in his chair as he listened to her speak. Then, after hearing her out, he gazed at her with loving eyes as he told her "I never knew you felt this way! Why didn't you tell me before?"

"You were so upset about Noknor that I didn't want to make it worse on you." she replied in a quavering voice.

Kain quickly wrapped his arms around her in a mighty hug and kissed her cheek tenderly. "Goddess, I love you so much, Nancy! It wouldn't have made things worse, pup. It would have made me feel better! A lot better! I wish you had come to me earlier instead of holding it inside."

"I'm sorry." she whispered, lowering her head.

"Please don't be. I should have come to you myself. I've been meaning to, but . . . well, I guess I've been putting it off for the same reasons you had." he told her as he released her and sat back in his chair. He paused a moment and studied his sister with new eyes. "You know, I have always thought of you as a little girl, but now I know that you are maturing into a strong young woman." Nancy smiled brightly. However, it very quickly faded as her heart plunged into her stomach when Kain finished "That does not, I am very sorry to say, mean you can go with me on this one."

Both women began to protest furiously, but Kain simply held up his hand to stop them and continued "Let me finish, please. The reason is, sweetheart, that it's going to be too dangerous. And don't tell me that it's not, because you both know very well that it will be. I'm not trying to be mean or anything, pup. I really would like you to go, because I know how much it means to you. But you have no experience whatsoever and I just cannot and will not endanger your life like that. I am so very sorry, but I just can't. Please try to understand."

"I . . . I understand." Nancy sighed as she felt tears forming in her eyes. She fought with all her might to hold them back because she didn't want to upset Kain over it, so she turned away from him and was ready to give up.

Li, on the other had, was more persistent. She looked into Kain's eyes and pleaded "Come on, don't just knock her out. At least give her a chance. You don't know what she's really capable of. She surprised me the other day when we were working out together, and I know she'll surprise you. I'm sure she has more than enough skill to make up for her lack of experience."

Nancy perked up and fixed hopeful eyes on her brother. Kain stroked his chin as he glanced at Li before studying his sister and said nothing. He looked rather unmoved, so Li pressed further "Come on, Kain. There's nothing to lose. Just let her show you her stuff. It won't take but a minute."

Kain sighed and looked at his two relatives. Between Nancy's pitiful, hopeful look and Li's bright, beseeching eyes, they finally managed to cave him in. He sighed, throwing up his arms in defeat as Li and Nancy traded excited smiles. "All right, all right. I'll tell you what, Nancy. Go and get a sword and we'll see some of your moves. If I think you have enough skill to overlook the lack of experience, I'll let you go. If not, then you stay home with John and I hear nothing more on the subject. Deal?"

"Deal!" Nancy cried happily. Then she tore out of the dining room and to her bedroom to get ready. Li called after her not to forget her blowpipe, perking up Kain's ears.

"I'm going to be late, you know." he muttered dryly.

"Oh, come on! What are they going to do, fire you?" Li giggled, giving him a sweet look. She reached across the table and patted his arm. "Try not to go too hard on her. She really wants to go, it's very important to her."

"I'm going to be fair, Li." he told her, bringing his cup to his lips. When he found it empty, he grabbed Nancy's glass and took a drink. "I'm serious, too. I'm not going to let her go if I even have a hint of doubt that she wouldn't be able to hack it." Li grinned, but it was for the most part neutral and made it difficult to guess whether his words were upsetting her or not as he continued "I really want her to go too. I know how much it means to her. But I can't afford to be babysitting her, and I sure won't put her in anyone else's hands."

"I don't think she'll need a babysitter." Li muttered with a hint of offense.

"Well, I'm just letting you know right up front that I honestly don't see her going." he replied, looking at her out of the corner of his eyes. "Granted the kid's got skill. I mean, she is my sister and all. But I highly doubt it's near enough. And I don't want you to get all ticked off when I tell her she can't go."

Li raised an insulted eyebrow. "Kain, if you can honestly say that she doesn't live up to your standards after seeing all that she's got, then I won't get ticked off. But I think you are in for a surprise."

"We'll see." he grunted, taking another sip from Nancy's glass.

Nancy suddenly poked her head around the corner and told them "I was thinking. You know, it's kinda cramped in here. How about we move into the living room?" Kain agreed, so he and Li picked themselves up to join her. As Li stood and stretched, Nancy asked "Could you bring that basket of apples with you, please?"

Kain and Li sat on the couch watching Nancy, who was dressed in the outfit she had worn during her workout with Li, as she used her new sword to slice the air repeatedly in a variety of deadly patterns. An audible swooshing was heard by the pair as Nancy performed for a few minutes before stopping to rest and see how she was doing. Li was quite pleased with her and had a huge grin spread over her face as she swung her leg back and forth through the air. Kain was also smiling and seemed to be enjoying the show, and that was a very good sign for Nancy. Kain nodded his head for her to continue and Nancy turned her back to them. She asked Li to throw a few apples at her but not tell her how many. Kain was about to interject, but Li noticed and poked him with her elbow. He glanced at her before crossing his arms, sitting back, and plopping his mouth shut. Satisfied, Li took three apples and chucked them at her young cousin. Nancy twirled around when she heard the first one sail towards her and swung her sword. The first apple was cleaved cleanly in half while the second bounced off the blade when she raised her sword to defend against it before stabbing the third. All of the moves were fluid as if they were one. With a flick of her blade, Nancy sent the third apple straight up. As it fell back down, she gave one last mighty swing and sliced it into two perfect halves with a diagonal cut. Li threw two more apples, which Nancy easily dispatched. Li clapped excitedly and whistled loudly while Kain looked on with proud amusement.

"That was interesting." he grinned, quite overwhelmed with his little sister's performance. Li had been right, he was surprised. But he wasn't *THAT* surprised. "I must say, I am very impressed!"

"REALLY?" Nancy squeaked in delight.

"Yes, indeed. But there's only one small problem."

"And what would that be?" Li inquired with narrow eyes, crossing her arms and raising her brow.

"Apples don't fight back." he replied without taking his eyes off of Nancy. Li fidgeted in her seat and gave her male cousin a queer look, quite curious to know what sort of lamebrain idea was swimming around in his head. "If you want to go with me, you must know how to handle yourself as well as a sword in a fight. Pardon me a moment, my dears."

With that, he quickly headed off to his room. Nancy looked to Li with a worried frown and asked "Wuh . . . what is he doing?"

Li shrugged. She didn't have a clue. "I'm not sure. But hang in there kiddo. You've done terrific so far. I think you've got him hooked."

"You think?" Nancy smiled brightly, feeling quite proud of herself.

Li nodded vigorously as she jumped to her feet and headed for Kain's room. When she opened the door, she saw him riffling through his closet like a madman.

She coughed audibly and replied "Looking for something?"

"No, I'm fighting a dragon . . . ah-ha! Here they are!" he murmured triumphantly, producing a pair of wooden practice swords.

"And just what are you planning to do with those?"

"I'm going to give my sister a test." he told her.

"What sort of test?" she asked slowly, cautiously.

"She has to beat me or she stays here." he said simply.

"You can't be SERIOUS!"

"Oh, I'm very serious." he retorted, heading for the door.

"Kain!" Li cried out, jumping at him and grabbing his arm in a powerful death-grip. "You stop this right now! You can't be serious! She'll never beat you!"

"Then she can't go." Kain snapped harshly. "Look, Li! I am not going to let her go unless she can handle herself in a fight. I have to make sure she won't panic when she gets into her first sword fight. I want to know that she won't get intimidated and lose her cool. If she doesn't keep a hold of her wits she's dead out there, you know that better than anyone should!"

"Well, that's all well and fine, but she can prove that stuff to you without beating you!" she responded, trying not to raise her voice and start a fight she knew was boiling up. She mustered up the sweetest smile she could put on her face and drew him close to her. As she traced his arm with her finger, she told him "I know that you're just being protective of her. But Kain, she's not a little girl anymore. Like you said before, she's maturing into a strong and independent young woman and she doesn't need to be baby-sat. What she needs is to prove herself to you. And that won't happen if you set impossible standards for her. You promised me you'd be fair to her. Please don't break that promise to me or to her."

Kain was silent as he looked at her and pondered what he was told. Finally, with a dull sigh he told her "Okay, fine! She doesn't have to beat me. But she better come damn close to it."

"Fair enough." she smiled brightly, punching his shoulder gently. "Now let's go see Nancy wow you again."

When they walked back into the living room, they found Nancy practicing her swordplay. She stopped when she saw Li take her seat once again on the couch and Kain advancing towards her. He tossed a practice sword at her and she snapped her hand up to catch it on reflex so quickly that her arm didn't appear to move exactly, but instead teleport.

"What's this for?" Nancy inquired with a frown as she looked the mock weapon over.

"You're going to fight me with it." Her brother told her with a hint of a grin.

"Say what?" Nancy's frown darkened.

"You're going to—" he started to repeat.

"Fight you with it?" she finished for him. When he nodded, she looked to her cousin relaxed on the couch with wide, distraught eyes. "Li?"

"Don't worry, kiddo. You can do it!" Li assured her with a bright smile and an encouraging thumbs up.

"Okay." Nancy sighed, setting her real sword against the wall. Her little heart beat a mile a minute and her whole body began to shake intensely as anxiousness quickly set in. Feeling herself about to fall completely apart, she quickly shook her head to clear it and gently closed her eyes. She had to concentrate and keep a cool head no matter how impossible things might seem. She had to overcome and breakdown all the walls to shine through, just as her mother had told her. She had to do it, not only for her parents, but for herself as well. With moist eyes, she ever so lowly whispered "What you dare to dream, dare to do."

"What was that, pup?" Kain asked.

"Nothing." she told him as she opened her eyes and quickly wiped them. Then she looked dead into his eyes and grinned playfully as she told him "I was just thinking about how I'm going to kick your butt!"

"Alright, then let's play." Kain chuckled heartily and brandished his sword three times with audible swooshes before returning to his stance.

"Let's." Nancy remarked slyly as she copied him.

"Li, would you be so kind?" Kain asked, never taking his eyes off of Nancy.

"But of course!" she replied in a charming tone and smile. She stood and raised her hands into the air. She held them there for a few moments before throwing them down and loudly yelling a forceful "FIGHT!"

As the siblings rushed at each other, Li jumped back onto the couch and watched with great anticipation, her crossed legs moving up and down rapidly and her hand to her open mouth. Kain's first move was a powerful overhead chop that Nancy instinctively blocked. However, the force of the blow was so powerful that it knocked her off balance as Kain came around for a second blow. She dodged by ducking and rolling to the side as she chopped upwards, narrowly missing his chest. He was stunned by her speed but quickly recovered to throw furious blows at her. She managed to block each one as she was forced backwards quickly. She threw split-second glances around her to examine her options as she kept her concentration on Kain's blur of a sword. She planted her feet and then threw herself forward at him. Their wood clashed loudly as they found themselves inches from each other's faces. Kain chuckled at her spirit and shoved her away to squeak sharply as she was launched into the wall. The instant she hit, she planted her feet and kicked, throwing herself at her brother. Seeing her rebound so elegantly and with such fluid gracefulness shocked Kain and he barely had time to lift his sword to block her blade as she passed him in the air. She twisted as the swords collided and swung her sword once more. Kain didn't expect a second attack before she had hit the ground and she managed to hit his arm. As he cursed in surprise, Li hooted and whistled on the girl's behalf. Nancy landed on her feet and twirled the weapon in her hand before delivering three quick slashes at Kain's back. The only thing he could do to save himself from a bruising blow was to fall forward and roll away, his eyes wide and his jaw slack with disbelief.

Li sat upon the very edge of her seat, absolutely amazed by Nancy's performance. No matter how hard or how confusing Kain's combos had come, she had managed to either block or dodge them all. And while she was seriously outweighed by her brother, she compensated with her speed and agility, using skill that Li had never seen her use before. It was truly unbelievable. If Li hadn't known any better, she would have sworn that Nancy had been training for years.

'Truly the spirit of her father does flow through her veins!' Li thought, squeaking at Nancy's next move.

Nancy twisted the sword back in her hand and leapt forward, her sword held high. Being left on his back, Kain could only throw up his weapon to block and push her off once more. He jumped to his feet and tried to regain his senses. He had obviously underestimated her and now was paying for it. Instead of her losing her nerve and succumbing to panic, the tables were drastically turned. He rushed at her and threw three very uncalculated blows. Nancy blocked the first two as if she were simply idly swatting at a fly and ducked under the third one as she lashed out with her foot. She caught the back of his knees, unlocking them and sending him crashing hard onto his back. Like a hungry spider, Nancy was on her prey, sitting on his chest with her sword pressed menacingly to his throat. Li was so astounded that she leaped to her feet, both hands held tightly to her mouth. Kain shook his head and tried to figure out what in the hell was going on. It had all happened so quickly that he didn't even know what had happened. One second he was attacking, the next she was sitting on his chest with a victorious smile spread on her face.

"I win." she replied triumphantly, feeling quite proud of herself as she lowered her sword.

"Yeah, I guess you do." Kain muttered, trying to catch his breath.

He grabbed her thin waist and tossed her off. They both stood and dusted themselves off as Li rushed over to Nancy and threw her arms around her in an ecstatic embrace.

"Oh, Nancy!" she squealed in a high voice. "That was simply amazing! I am so proud of you! You certainly showed him! You kicked his butt!"

"Did I really do well?" she asked hopefully, looking into Li's eyes for approval.

"You did phenomenal!" Li told her and kissed her forehead as she rubbed her head. "Absolutely phenomenal! I mean, wow! It was like . . . like . . . WOW!"

"Yes, my dear! You did excellent!" Kain replied with a very proud grin and a cocked brow as he slung his wooden sword over his shoulder. "Where in the world did you pick up those moves?"

"I . . . I don't really know. They just came to me." She told them, a small frown gracing her lips. "I guess I just picked them up watching you and Li."

"I'm telling you, Kain." Li giggled, kissing the top of her head tenderly. "The kid's a natural."

"Of course she is. She's a Viccon. But still, that kind of skill is more than talent, and it sure as hell wasn't luck. Blind, beginners, or whatever you want to call it. You've had to have been putting in some serious hours behind my back." he said, his words hinting an explanation was in order.

Nancy only shrugged blandly and mumbled softly. Li took notice and was quick to cover. "Regardless! She had your butt on a stick and mopped the floor with it, Kain! Thrashed your tail from here to China!" she told him in a sure voice not even trying to hide her smile. Kain flashed her an amused grin.

"So, do I get to go with you?" Nancy pleaded with bright, hopeful eyes. "Do I?"

"Well, I don't know." Kain murmured lowly, putting his hand to his mouth as if in deep thought so as to hide his grin as he pretended to examine his sister. "I will admit that you did a heck of a lot better than I had expected you to. But I'm not quite sure if I'm quite convinced—"

"KAIN!" Li yelped in disbelief, savagely cutting him off as she spun on her heels and came face to face with her stubborn cousin. "How in the WORLD can you say that! She beat you fair and square! And if I remember the deal correctly, that is exactly what she had to do in the first place!"

"Li, darlin', I was just kid—" Kain started to explain but Li cut him off and wouldn't let him get in a word as she began to rant and rave.

"I mean, the girl's been blessed with a natural knack for combat! You stubborn man, what's it going to take to convince you that she's got an amazing talent!"

"I know what she's—" he tried again to no avail.

"What does she have to do for you? Slay a dragon? I mean, she showed you her skill with a sword, she proved that she can handle herself in a fight, and she just got through thrashing your tail from here to China! What in the world do you want from her?"

"Li, would you calm—"

"I know! I know just the thing! Nancy, I think it's time you played your yaodian!" Li grinned slyly as she nodded towards the table where Nancy had laid her things.

Nancy brightly smiled her understanding and strolled over to the small table where her blowpipe and bag of darts sat waiting for her. She leaned the practice sword against the wall and picked up the simple, slender wooden tube and two needle sharp darts.

"Nancy, that's really not necessary." Kain told her with a proud grin as he moved to stop her. "I was only kidding with you and your cousin blew it out of proportion. You know I'm a man of my word, and—"

However, Li quickly grabbed him by the arm and dragged him to the couch. She threw him down onto the cushion and pushed him right back down when he tried to get up. Then, holding his arms so he wouldn't budge, Li promptly took a seat herself and told her "Go on and show this pesky disbeliever what you've got."

"Okee-dokee!" Nancy cheerfully saluted before walking over towards the wall. With one of the darts, she etched a small circle in the paint.

"What are you doing, girl?" Kain asked with a confused frown.

"Shhhhh!" Li hissed with an excited smile. "Just watch!"

Finished with her scratching, she walked back away and loaded the second dart into the tube. As soon as she was ready, she looked to Li and asked her to throw another apple into the air.

"That one with the big leaf on the stem." Nancy instructed her as she placed the tube to her lips. Li did so and, after a very short moment, Nancy gave a powerful puff. There came a loud PUFT, followed by a sharp whistling then an immediate dull THUNK as the dart struck the wall. The apple fell to the floor and rolled to Kain's feet, seemingly untouched.

"Looks like you missed." Kain chuckled, not the least bit surprised as he bent low to snatch up the apple. "That's all right, though. I won't hold it against you. That was a pretty tough stunt, trying to hit an apple in mid air."

"She wasn't exactly aiming for the apple, Kain." Li giggled.

He was about to take a bite out of the fruit when something caught his eye. He turned the apple around in his hands and noticed that the big leaf was missing, clipped cleanly off the stem. His jaw dropped in shock.

"What do you think?" Nancy asked hopefully.

Kain didn't answer. He didn't even hear the question he was so stunned. He just stared at the leafless stem with wide eyes and a hanging jaw. Li giggled and grabbed the apple out of his hand. He slowly looked over at her as if to question her. She smiled as she shined the apple on her nightgown and took a loud bite out of the crunchy fruit. He tried to speak, but both his tongue and his mind were tied. He finally managed to croak out "That . . . that was very, ah . . . good. Very good, indeed."

Then it suddenly hit Kain like a brick why Nancy had been at the wall before. He jumped to his feet and rushed to the site. There was the dart, imbedded halfway in the wall in the dead center of the circle she had made. The shock of it made him blurt out an incomprehensible garble of words as he leapt away from the wall as if it had suddenly burst into flames.

Li laughed loudly as little gooey pieces of apple shrapnel flew from her lips. She wiped off her chin with her sleeve and snickered "Does this mean she's finally proved herself to you?"

"Yes, she has! Nancy, I don't know how you did that, but . . ." he grinned proudly, his eyes glittering as he approached his sister with an outstretched hand. "Congratulations."

Nancy totally ignored his hand and jumped straight into his arms, giving him a big kiss on his cheek as she did so. She was giddy with excitement as she cried out "Oh, Kain! Thank you so much! You've made me so happy! You won't regret this, I promise you!"

"Congrats, kiddo." Li smiled brightly. "I knew you could do it!"

Nancy released her brother and embraced her cousin tightly. She craned her lips close to Li's ear and whispered "Thanks, Li. I never could have done it without you."

"Yes, you could have." she whispered back. "I know it."

Kain cleared his throat and tried to assume a very professional attitude. However, he couldn't stop his lips from smiling. "Well, Nancy. Welcome aboard. It's going to be great having you along, I'm sure. Actually, since both of you are going to be coming with me, I think it would be a great benefit for you two to accompany me to the castle and join the meetings with the rest of us. Why don't you two go get ready? I'll wait for you here."

"Okay!" Nancy squeaked.

Li cleared her throat and grinned shyly as she murmured "I have something I need to tell you, Kain. You too, Nancy"

"What is it, darlin'?"

"I have decided that I'm not going to be coming with you on this quest." she told him. When both of her cousins began to protest, she let them get in a few words before she held up her hand and replied "Because last night, Nancy pointed out something very important to me." She paused and drew in a deep, wavy breath. "She has shown me that this is your battle, not mine."

"But we want you to come." Nancy told her, her voice drooping with disappointment.

"And I would love to go with you guys."

"So what's the problem?" Kain asked.

Li sighed and began to chew on her bottom lip before she tried to explain "This is your fight. You two must search out Noknor because he has wronged you. I don't even know who he is, just what you've told me. So even though I want to go very badly, at the same time I know I should stay. This is something very deep and very personal for the two of you and you both have to do this together. It's a Viccon thing, and I can't get in the way."

Kain smiled as he moved to wrap his arms tightly around her body. Her reason was honorable and he was very impressed with her sacrifice; he knew how much she had been looking forward to the adventure. He knew she had made up her mind and that it couldn't be changed. But he had to try anyway. He looked deep into her eyes and asked "Are you sure it has to be like this?"

"I'm sure. And I am sorry."

"I'm going to miss you, Li." Nancy murmured as she joined the hug circle.

"And I'm going to miss you, too." she told her, kissing the top of her head tenderly. "Both of you."

After a moment, Kain released his relatives and glanced at his watch. He noted the time with a grimace and said "Great, we're really late now. Come on Nancy, hurry and get dressed."

"Okay." Nancy smiled. "What should I wear?"

"Whatever makes you comfortable, I don't care. It's not like it's some type of formal gala or anything." Kain muttered, slipping his watch back into his pocket.

CHAPTER V

"It's about time you showed up, Viccon!" a tall and gaunt middle-aged man in purple senador robes growled as Kain and Nancy walked down the beautifully decorated main hall of Arcainia Castle. "You know, you may be the Grand General but doesn't mean you can skirt around your responsibilities around here!"

Senadors served as advisors to the queen and to the governors of Arcainia's territories, helping to keep a steady flow of communication between the queen and her subjects. The color of a senador's robes denoted his or her level of authority, and while this particular man was rather low on the ladder he liked to put on the air of someone of more importance. Given the way Kain heatedly rolled his eyes and swore under his breath Nancy could tell that her brother and this senador were not the best of friends.

"Get a grip, Ash." Kain sighed dully, hoping to be able to brush past him. "There were some things that I had to take care of at home before I headed out today, okay? Besides, I'm not that late."

"You are an hour and a half late!" Ash retorted with a sneer.

"Okay, okay. I'm sorry." he replied with a frown and a tone that was much more annoyed than apologetic. "I'm very sorry."

"You'd better be!" Ash snapped. He was about to continue scolding the knight when he noticed the strange girl beside him. He threw an opposing finger Nancy's way and snapped with great displeasure "Who is that?"

"THAT is my sister." Kain raised his eyebrows and crossed his arms in agitation.

"What's she doing here?"

"She just wanted to come along with me to see what I go through all day." Kain murmured and rolled his eyes as he silently wished the man would just go away.

"This isn't a very good time for that!"

"Are you kidding? It's the perfect time for it. She'll be able to see first hand how we prepare for quests."

Ash still wasn't sold, but there was nothing he could do about it. He eyed the girl with great displeasure for a moment before turning his attention back onto her brother. He raised a threatening finger into Kain's face and hissed savagely "You're so lucky you're not working for me, Viccon! I'm not weak like Miller is. I sure wouldn't let you or your friends get away with the sort of—"

"That's Grand General Viccon, *Senador* Ash." Kain replied abruptly as he pushed his finger away, cutting off the senador. "Now if you don't mind, Senador Ash, we're running late."

He grabbed his sister's arm and started to walk away as he sighed "Come on, Nancy. I'm sure the others are waiting."

"Of course they're waiting!" Ash rudely told him as they brushed past him. "They've been waiting for an hour and a half already!"

"You lousy son of a . . ." Kain hissed under his breath as he pulled Nancy along.

"WHAT?" Ash gawked in disbelief, his gleaming baldhead flustering bright red. "What did you say to me!"

Kain said nothing in response, he just kept right on walking with Nancy in tow. Ash stood in his place for a moment with his hands on his hips and his teeth grinding before starting after them. Kain heard his footsteps and hurried faster. It got to the point where he was almost dragging Nancy behind him. Ash finally gave up, snorted furiously, and huffed off in the opposite direction while Kain gave a sigh of great relief as he slowed back down.

"Sorry about that, pup." he told her, releasing her and stroking her head.

"That's okay." she said, rubbing her wrist and looking behind her to make sure that Ash was out of earshot. "Man, that guy is a total jerk! I mean, who in world does he think he is, the king or something!"

"He must." Kain grinned, biting his tongue.

"Can he really talk to you like that?" Nancy asked. "Why didn't you tell him something? I thought you were his boss."

"Well, technically, I'm not his boss." Kain told her with a sigh as he stuffed his hands into his pockets. "I'm military, he's civilian. We have no real bearing on each other, really. He just has a head bigger than a mountain. I could have told him something, but I figure what's the point in stirring up more trouble. I might as well take his—"

"It's about time you showed up, Viccon!" a voice behind them called. Nancy winced at the approaching battle as they turned to see a rather cheery, plump man in red senador robes hurrying towards them. "You were starting to worry me. I almost sent out some troops to make sure you were all right. For all I knew, that cousin of yours could have beaten the ever-lovin' crap out of you. Again!"

"Oh, stuff it up your—" Kain started, but remembered that his sister was standing right beside him. He glanced at her and saw that she had a very confused look spread over her face. He chuckled lowly and turned his attention back on to the senador. "I'm not that late, Miller."

"I know. You're just early for tomorrow." Miller laughed heartily as they shook hands. He noticed Nancy and smiled brightly as he extended his hand to the girl. "Well, hello there, Miss Viccon! It's a pleasure to see you again! How are you today?"

"Hello, Senador Miller." Nancy beamed radiantly as he kissed her knuckles.

"What brings you with your brother today? Did you tag along to see what he does all day?"

"Sort of." she giggled with a blush.

"She's going to be coming with us." Kain told him proudly.

"Come again?" Miller dropped the girl's hand in surprise and looked at Kain. "Did you say that she'd be going with you?" Kain nodded. "My friend, please don't take this the wrong way, but have you lost your friggin' mind?"

Nancy was hurt by his words, but Kain had been expecting such a reaction. He grinned broadly as he crossed his arms and asked quite simply "Why do you say that?"

"Kain, she's just a girl!"

"Correction. She's a girl with a lot of skill."

"But, Kain! She's not exper—"

"She's proven to me that she has more than enough skill to make up for her inexperience." Kain told him, proudly putting his arm around her shoulders. Nancy looked up at him and smiled, thrilled that he was defending her so. "Trust me on this one, Miller. I love this little lady with all of my heart. I would never have agreed to let her come if I doubted for one moment that she couldn't handle it. Now let's get a move on. I'm sure the others are wondering where in the world we are."

They continued down the hallway until they finally reached a small wooden door with beautiful brass trim all around. In the dead center of the door was a shiny brass marker with the words: *OFFICE OF THE GRAND GENERAL* prominently etched in Old Arcainian script. Kain tried the handle and found the door unlocked, so he knew that she was already in. He threw open the door and saw a rather tall and thin yet extremely lovely young woman with short raven-black hair and fair skin tidying up.

"Hello there, darlin'!" he boomed cheerfully, stepping into his office with his sister and Miller right behind him. "How are you doing this fine morning?"

"Pretty well, boss." she smiled brightly, setting a large pile of papers into a small basket on Kain's desk. She gave a brief wave at Miller and said "Hello, Senador Miller."

"Howdy." Miller waved.

"Sylia!" Nancy squeaked and rushed forward to shake hands with Kain's secretary.

Sylia, who pretty much towered over the girl, bent forward slightly and said in a cheery voice "Well, hello there, stranger! I haven't seen you around here lately. If it wasn't for the pictures on your brother's desk, I wouldn't have known who you are!" She gestured to the group of small paintings sitting around Kain's desk.

"I've been wanting to come up here to visit with you, but you know. School and all." Nancy said, finishing blandly.

"Oh, I know exactly how that is! It hasn't been that long for me either." Sylia laughed before she stood straight up once again and looked at Kain. "So what kept you?"

"I had some things to take care of at home." he told her, walking over to his desk and taking a seat.

"I was beginning to think that you weren't going to show and that I'd have it easy today." she teased.

"Not a chance, darlin'." Kain chuckled and opened the top drawer. He grabbed out some paper and a pen and began to scribble down some notes. "I really hate to do this to you, but I've got a few errands for you to run."

"Oh, well. That's what I get paid for, isn't it?" she smiled and leaned against his desk with her arms crossed over her chest so that she could see what he was writing.

"Good girl!" Miller laughed loudly as he plopped down in one of the two chairs in front of Kain's desk. Nancy took the other. "I sure wish my secretary had your attitude!"

"That bubblehead?" Sylia sneered. "Good luck! Why did you hire her in the first place?"

"Well, she has great handwriting, she's good with the books, and she makes a great cup of coffee." Miller responded, trying to hide his smirk but failing miserably.

"Oh, you just wanted to—" Kain started to mutter but stopped himself when he remembered Nancy was sitting right in front of him. He continued to write, Sylia snorted laughter, Nancy looked confused, and Miller just shrugged.

"So where are you going to have me running around to today?" Sylia asked as she stretched her long limbs.

"First, I need you to go to the schoolhouse and see if you can't get in contact with Nancy's teacher. I need to find out what we can do about her finals since she won't be here to take them."

"Why won't she be here to take them?" she asked, a bit concerned.

"Because I'm going with him!" Nancy blurted out excitedly, hopping about in her seat and clapping in ecstatic glee before Kain could even open his mouth to answer her.

"Well, okay. As long as you have a good-HUH?" Sylia gasped with wide, surprised eyes and a dropped jaw. "Excuse me? Did I just hear you say what I thought I heard you say?"

"Yes, you did." Kain smiled, pausing his pen. "She will be a part of my crew on this quest."

"May I be so, ah, inquisitive as to inquire why?"

"I felt that it would be a good experience for her." Kain muttered, returning to his note. He paused a moment, scratched out a few words, and continued. He finished up and fiercely marked his period before placing his pen gently back into the well. He then made a quick check to make sure he didn't miss any details. Finding everything in order, he waved the sheet up in front of Sylia's face, smiled at her, and said "Here you go, darlin'. All the info you need is right here."

Sylia gawked at Nancy for a few seconds before snatching the paper from Kain's hand and shaking her head. She never for a moment had ever dreamed that he would take her along with him on any of his missions, much less this one. She figured that it would be way too dangerous for such a young, sheltered girl like her. But over the time that she had known and worked for Kain, she noticed that his sister had quite a strong spirit and that she was well trained by her brother. Besides, she knew how much Kain loved his little sister and that he would never put her in harm's way. He always had her best interests in mind and wasn't prone to making dumb mistakes when it came to her well-being.

"How exciting for you!" she smiled brightly before lowering her head to look over the note. As she read, her head bopped slowly and she hummed tunelessly with every word. Kain's handwriting was sloppy and he wrote in shorthand, so it was almost impossible for anyone to read it. It was like trying to read some foreign language. However, Sylia had been reading his notes for quite some time, so she was quite used to it and had no problems whatsoever. "Okay, when do you need all of this stuff done?"

"I would like it as soon as possible, like by the end of the day if at all possible. If not, oh well." Kain told her, reclining back in his chair and putting his hands comfortably behind his head. "But I definitely need you to talk to her teacher first thing. Tell him that she won't be in for classes after Spring Festival and that-oh, hell, it's all written there for you. Just use your best judgment when it comes to the order you want to do the rest of that junk."

"I always do." she grinned. "Is there anything else I need to know besides this?"

"No. Are Michael and Raphael here yet?" Kain asked.

"They're in thirteen."

"Have they been waiting long?" he asked her.

"No, Raphael just got here about ten or twenty minutes ago. He had some delays this morning too. And Prince Michael lives here, so don't worry about it. Oh, and here's that study on Kuberica Castle you wanted." she told him as she pulled a thick leather folder tied with a green ribbon from the top of the pile of papers that she had just placed into the straw basket on Kain's desk.

"Thank you, my dear. You are too good to me." he said, accepting the folder and tucking it under his arm before telling her "Meet me back in here at the end of the day and I'll get all of the info from you."

"You got it, boss." she smiled and neatly folded the paper he had given her before slipping it into her pocket.

"Thanks a bunch, Sylia. You truly are a gem. I have no idea were I would be without you." he smiled as he gripped her hand and gave it a gentle squeeze. She grinned and returned the squeeze as she said "I'll see you later."

She gave the other two good-byes as well before heading out into the hallway. Kain grabbed a few more files and asked Nancy to carry his satchel before telling them "We'd better get going. I'm sure those two are waiting."

They then left his office and headed down the corridors until they came to a large door marked *CONFERNCE ROOM 13*. Kain grabbed the marker next to the door and slid it from *EMPTY* to *OCCUPIED* to signal that the room was being used and that they were not to be disturbed. As they walked in, Nancy saw Raphael and Prince Michael already seated at a large, round table. There were tons of papers, books, and maps scattered all over the table and more on the floor. To Nancy, as obsessively organized and tidy as she normally was, it looked as if a monstrous tornado had hit and she wondered how in the world they could keep track of anything in such a mess.

". . . And then I showed him." Michael chuckled, finishing up a joke as they walked in.

Raphael burst out laughing, hitting the table and rolling around on his chair. "Oh, man! That was a good one! Did you make it up yourself?"

"No, Delk told it to me."

"Man, that was funny. 'And then I showed him.'" Raphael smiled, regaining control of himself. He looked up and saw Kain and Miller standing before the table. "Hey, Kain! You've got to hear this joke Michael just told me! It's funny as—"

"No, tell me later." Kain replied quickly to cut of his friend, knowing full well that it was more than likely dirty.

Raphael was puzzled. Usually, Kain liked to start the day off with a good joke. He was about to ask why he wasn't interested when Kain stepped aside to let Nancy through. Both Michael and Raphael were very surprised to see her since they would have expected Li to join them before Nancy. They glanced at each other and shrugged, but said nothing. They both figured that she had just tagged along with him for the day and that Li was on her way in.

"Hello, guys!" Nancy beamed excitedly as she waved and smiled brightly.

"Hey, Nancy." Raphael smiled and waved back.

"What's going on, gorgeous?" Michael asked warmly.

"Nothing much." Nancy giggled with a blush.

Kain chuckled and said "Nancy's going to be joining us on this quest." Both men exchanged deeply concerned glances and looked at Kain with question. Before either one of them could open his mouth, however, Kain explained "Don't worry. She's proven to me that she can handle it and it means a lot to her. Like I told Miller, I wouldn't let her come if I didn't think she could handle it. In fact, that's where we've been all morning long. I was thoroughly testing her to be absolutely positive that it wouldn't be a mistake. Hell, she beat me in a fair sword fight this morning. If I had been her enemy, I would have been dead."

"Really? Wow, you really beat your brother!" Michael murmured, quite impressed as he stood up. She nodded and he, as he gripped and kissed her hand, told her "Well, congratulations, my dear. I'm sure you deserve it. And it will be great to have such a chipper young woman to keep us company."

Nancy blushed deeply and giggled "Thank you."

"That's terrific, Nancy." Raphael told her, also standing and shaking her hand, wishing he had the confidence to actually put his lips on her skin. "Even I can't beat your brother. Well, except on my birthday, I guess."

"Thanks, Ralph." she giggled bashfully, meeting eyes with him.

"Where's Li?" Michael asked Kain as he sat back down in his chair. "I thought she was going to be joining us too."

"She decided not to come on this one." Kain replied with a sigh. When Raphael asked why, Kain just shrugged and left his mouth closed. He didn't feel like going into a long explanation.

"Blast it all." Michael muttered. He was so looking forward to having her around. She was so witty and funny. Not to mention that after hearing all of Kain's stories, he was dying to see her in action.

"That's how I feel, but she's made up her mind. Anyway, it's late enough as it is and we really need to get down to business." Kain replied as he tossed the files onto the table and took a seat. Nancy looked at the table for a moment before sitting in between Kain and Raphael. Kain glanced at her and motioned for her to set the satchel down on the floor before remembering something important. "Oh, yeah. Uhm, since we've got company, I would like it if we kept this meeting nice and decent. Let's try to keep the swearing down to a minimum and keep the jokes clean, okay guys?"

While Nancy giggled, Raphael and Michael smiled and nodded their understanding. Miller gave an amused grunt as he crossed his arms and sat back in his chair, trying to get comfortable. Kain looked them over before slumping forward and replying "Alright, then. Let's begin."

"Okay." Michael replied, picking up a small scroll and looking it over. "This letter just came from Hurst this morning. We've got trouble, Kain. Big trouble."

"What great words to start the stupid day with." Kain muttered dully and sighed as he rubbed his face. "What is it now?"

"Well . . . you're not going to like this, but Noknor's found the Swuenedras Amulet."

Kain shrieked a curse loudly, jumping out of his chair. Nancy squealed in surprise and almost fell out of her own chair. However, she managed to catch herself and glanced at Kain with uneasy eyes as she sank back slightly.

"Is there a problem, Sir Viccon?" Miller mumbled, quite amused by Kain's outburst since he was the one that had imposed the language rule only moments before.

"You bet your sweet—" Kain started but stopped short. He glanced at Nancy and grinned uneasily. As he sat back down, he whispered with embarrassment "Sorry about that."

"That's all right." Nancy giggled and smiled as she patted his arm.

Kain immediately cast it off and turned his attention back to Miller. "Of course there's a problem! There's a big problem! Do you know what the Swuenedras Amulet is?"

"Yes, of course I do. Kain, I was just busting your—"

"So you know what it does?" Kain asked, slowly drumming his fingers on the table. Miller nodded slowly. "Then you know very well that we're completely and utterly-ah, well, as the prince said we're in a lot of trouble."

"Uh, Kain?" Raphael interjected, waving his fingers over his head for attention.

"What is it?" Kain asked his friend.

"Uh, what the devil's the Swu-Swu-Swuedrosad—"

"Swan-ed-rays Amulet." Nancy giggled, pronouncing it slowly for him.

"Whatever. What's that thing?"

"Well, it's a very powerful faery amulet. It looks like this." Nancy told him excitedly, eager to show off her knowledge of faery relics as she grabbed a pen and a piece of paper. She made a detailed drawing of a pair of serpents circling a diamond shaped gem and passed the paper to Raphael. As he examined it, she explained "It acts as an amplifier for magick, and can increase magick ability by a hundred fold. It's also supposed to bring out the ultimate warrior inside the heart of whoever wears it."

"And you can imagine what kind of ultimate warrior is inside Noknor's black heart." Kain growled heatedly. "I thought it was hidden!"

"Well, apparently he found it." Michael retorted cynically.

"Anywayz," Nancy replied, turning her attention back onto Raphael, hoping to impress the cute knight. "A long time ago, a hundred years ago, I think. Something like that. A hundred and some change, I guess. Anywho, a long time ago, a powerful sorcerer wearing the Swuenedras Amulet attacked Kuberica. I don't know the details, but the Kubericans defeated him and claimed the amulet as their own. They knew that it was much too powerful for them to use and that it could be very dangerous if it fell into the wrong hands. So the king decided to hide it. He only told two or three other people that he trusted where it was. Later on, when the king passed, the people he told decided that they were going to use it to honor their new king. They brought it out and presented it to the new king upon his coronation. That king then hid it away and told only three trusted friends. When he died, the same thing happened, and has happened ever since."

"I guess you can say that Noknor's crowned himself the new king of Kuberica." Raphael murmured, nodding his understanding. He gave Nancy a blushing smile and told her "You're really smart, Nancy!"

"Yes, she is." Kain mumbled, quite concerned over a new problem that had just presented itself. "So, if Noknor has this amulet and is so powerful, how are we supposed to beat him? That's a very good question." He glanced at Miller. "Do we have something in our arsenal that might at least help us? Something I haven't been told about?"

"Not unless I haven't been told about it either." the senator replied, his voice just as grave as Kain's. "Your highness?" Michael crossed his arms and gave him a defeated look but said nothing. "I'll look into it Kain, but it won't be very hopeful."

"I figure as much, but look as hard as you can." Kain told him, drumming his fingers anxiously on the table. "We'll need all the help we can get. I'll try to—"

A sudden light knock on the large wooden door sounded before it opened slowly with a slight creak, putting the meeting on pause as all turned to regard the intruder.

Kain frowned darkly and, already upset by the news he had just been given, opened his mouth to growl something along the lines of the intruder being blind and not being able to see the 'Do Not Disturb' marker. He stopped himself abruptly when he saw that it was his secretary.

"Excuse me." Sylia replied, her voice barely a whisper, her face slightly flushed. "I'm sorry to interrupt, but, uhm, Kain? You have a . . . well, you have someone waiting to see you in your office."

Kain was surprised Sylia had come in for that. "Tell them that—"

"I did, but, ah . . . she is rather insistent upon meeting with you as soon as possible."

Kain's dark frown darkened. "How insistent?"

"Very."

He debated the matter in his head for a moment before with a low grunt he finally turned to the others. "Let's take a five minute break. If this person absolutely needs to speak to me longer than that, she'll just have to schedule a formal appointment."

With that, he reached down for the handle of his satchel. Before he could reach it, however, Nancy snatched it and was on her feet wearing a bright smile. Expecting Kain to take it from her and leave her behind, she was delighted when he simply shrugged, turned, and headed for the door where Sylia stood waiting for them. Once out in the hallway, Kain asked "Did she say what this is about?"

"No, she wouldn't say. All she told me was that it was, and I quote, 'highly imperative that I speak with Sir Viccon immediately.' I tried—" She paused to return a wave to a friend they passed in the hallway. "I tried to tell her that you were very busy and set up an appointment for her, but she just repeated herself and promptly took a seat. I really am sorry for disturbing you, but there's something about her."

"What do you mean, like she's dangerous or something?"

"No, not dangerous." Sylia shook her head slightly. "More like she's a noble. You know how they are, expect you to jump when they speak. Actually, from her dress I'd say she were a sorceress of some sort."

"So I have a witch princess waiting to talk to me." he mumbled blandly.

"Sorceress." Nancy corrected at his side. "Don't call her a witch."

Kain looked at her out of the corner of his eye. "There's a difference?"

"Oh, yeah, there sure is!" Nancy uttered squeaky giggles. "You see, witch is a generic term for most Dark magick users. A sorceress is a woman who uses Light Magick; actually, their magick skills are based in the four elements. So, sorceresses, and any Light magick users for that matter, tend to be offended if you call them a witch, so I wouldn't—"

"Thanks for the warning." Kain held up his hand to cut her off as he reached for the doorknob to his office.

When the door creaked slightly as it opened, a woman who had been seated stood and turned to face them. Upon seeing Kain, she smiled radiantly and began to drift to him as he entered and the two ladies filed in behind him. Kain was immediately taken in by the woman. Part of it was that she was extremely lovely. With her dark hair that fell daintily about her shoulders, her sharp, sparkling eyes that seemed to trap one's mind, her soft, honey skin, and her slender, delicate body with a catlike agile look to it, he suddenly wasn't very annoyed with his meeting being interrupted. The other part was that he was quite surprised to see the woman in his office. He couldn't help but think that it wasn't just a friendly visit.

The woman extended her hand regally and offered a charming smile to Kain. He returned these with his own as he gripped her cool hand and brushed his lips softly against her knuckles. Nancy, who was frowning slightly at the sight of the woman, frowned darker when she noticed by the woman's smile that she was stranger still. Behind the woman's full lips lay four fangs and instantly Nancy was struck with a sickening sense of dread at the thought that the woman was sent by Noknor to ambush Kain. She quickly reached out to take her brother's hand to pull him away, but the woman spoke before her hand had gone three inches.

"Good morning, Sir Viccon." she said, her voice soft and pleasant.

"I am honored by your visit, my dear." he smiled.

"Why, what self-respecting Arcainian would not be honored herself to visit the great Kain Viccon, Arcainia's most eligible bachelor!" she snickered, giving him a wink.

"You're Arcainian?" Nancy asked, trying to push between the woman and her brother. She did not trust the woman one bit, and she wasn't about to let her get any closer to him lest she plunge a dagger into his chest or worse.

"But of course."

She had to warn Kain about the danger, but how? She decided to stall the woman. She quickly asked "Where abouts?"

The woman cast narrow eyes on the girl but kept her smile, slowly moving her eyes up and down as if sizing her up. Her words came slowly as she replied "Right here in Arcainia City. The Vaness district."

"Is that a fact? That's where we live. I've never seen you around." Nancy retorted, realizing that her tone sounded rather accusing but not caring in the least.

"I haven't lived there for years." she clicked her tongue against the roof of her mouth in mild humor. "Care to know my parents' street address?"

Nancy was about to snap that she would indeed like to know it but a hard shove on her shoulder from her brother cut her short.

"Really, Nancy! What is this, an inquisition?" he told her harshly. Then to the woman he said "Please don't be offended by her. She tends to be overprotective sometimes."

There was a brief pause before the woman looked to Kain and laughed airily. "Oh, think nothing of it. I can relate. I do have a brother, after all. A couple, in fact." She turned her eyes onto Nancy and smiled. "Despite what you may think, Miss Viccon, I am here to aid your brother against Noknor, not vice-versa." Nancy felt her face grow warm as her cheeks became rosy and she turned away slightly in embarrassment. Kain couldn't help but smile as the woman chuckled. She opened her mouth and ran her tongue over her sharp canine teeth. "And don't let these fool you. I was born with them." She looked at Kain and replied slyly "Do you remember 'Vamp'?"

Kain chuckled loudly. "That was your brother."

"No, that was you, Kain. His was 'Cottonmouth'. You two could be pretty cruel at times."

Kain laughed loudly, both by the sudden flood of memories and the woman's last comment. It was his turn to turn a slight rosy hue as he chuckled and replied "Come on, Mar. We were kids. The only reason we teased you so much was because we loved you. And besides, if my memory serves me right you did your fair share of teasing. Got in a few pretty good hits—"

Nancy snapped her head towards her brother with her face set in frown of disbelief. "You know her?"

Kain nodded. "Of course I do. This is James's twin sister, Mara Raptor."

"James . . . James Raptor?" Her frown darkened, her eyes widened. "Li's James?"

"That's right." he said. A thought popped into his head suddenly. "Speaking of, you still haven't met Li, have you?"

"No, I sure haven't. It's a pleasure to make your acquaintance, Miss Viccon." Mara giggled.

"Yeah, same here." Nancy told her shyly. "Sorry."

"Like I said, no big thing." She gave the girl a wink. "I get that a lot. You'd probably be surprised."

Kain raised his eyebrows and gestured towards the two seats. "Well, I don't mean to be rude, but I am a bit pressed for time so please have a seat and let me know how I can be of service to you, Mara."

"Would you care for a cup of coffee or tea, Miss Raptor?" Sylia asked her as Kain moved past her to sit behind his desk.

"Oh, no thank you." she told her pleasantly, taking one of the seats in front of Kain's desk. Nancy took the other while, with a final wave good-bye, Sylia headed out the door to run her errands. "And it's not what you can do for me Kain, but rather what I can do for you."

"And what would that be?"

"Help you conquer Noknor now that he possesses the Swuenedras Amulet." she replied simply, her tone quite nonchalant. Kain's jaw dropped in surprise. How in the world had she heard about it? He, himself, had only learned of it moments ago and this woman not only knew of it, but also was offering a solution for it. Mara couldn't help but giggle at his expression and said "I represent the Ladys of the Elements."

"Ah, yes . . ." Kain murmured, his mouth closing. "Well, Mara, this is quite an honor. But I'm not sure why such beings as powerful as them would help me."

Mara took in a deep breath, exhaled, and explained "They, being normally neutral in such issues, would not normally aid you. This would seem to be a mortal conflict, after all. However, Noknor has highly offended them by using the

Swuenedras Amulet. It belongs to the faeries and he is using it for Dark gains. And though he has not acted against us yet, the Ladys fear that once his power grows strong enough, he will most certainly attack the faery world. Obviously, this must not be allowed to happen."

"Obviously." Kain said. "But they are very powerful themselves. Not trying to be disrespectful or anything, mind you, but why help me? Why not go after him themselves?"

Mara opened her mouth to answer, but Nancy was quicker "Because they cannot use their powers to destroy a particular mortal unless he directly attacks them first. It would violate the Law of Moc Fae which says that they must remain completely neutral and impartial in regards to the mortal world. Just using the Swuenedras Amulet isn't enough of a reason unless he uses it against Light faeries."

"Well said." Mara replied, a bright grin on her face. "Do you study Elemental Magick?"

"Not really study." the girl blushed. "I just like to read about it. It's more of a hobby, I guess."

"It was once for me as well." Mara chuckled, giving the girl another quick wink. She then turned back to Kain and said "She is precisely right. They cannot attack Noknor directly. Not yet at any rate, and they do not want it to reach that far. However, there is nothing to be said of them helping a mortal should he, say, ask them personally." She paused to let her words sink in and continued "It has happened times in the past. In fact, the Viccon family is not unfamiliar to their aid either. They helped your father, after all."

Kain narrowed his eyes and thought hard for a moment. He jumped straight up from his chair, his knees striking his desk loudly but going unnoticed by the excited knight when what had been the perfect answer all along popped into his head. "The Elemental Sword, of course!"

The woman held a quiet, pleasured smile and nodded.

Nancy gasped in awe and murmured so lowly, the other two didn't notice "When daddy fought the Dragon of Kitrad Doe!"

"How can I reach them?" Kain asked Mara, his anticipation growing with each second.

Mara sighed dully and frowned slightly "I am afraid I can't tell you that myself. It . . . well, for lack of better words, it would make it too easy. We feel I'm already treading too close to the line set by the Law of Moc Fae just by coming to see you. You'll have to seek them out yourself, I'm afraid."

Even though the words were disheartening, Kain's brilliant smile never faltered. He rushed around his desk, limping slightly as the sharp bite of his busted knee began to set in, and grabbed Mara's hands. "Thank you so much for all your help! You don't know how much of a load this takes off my shoulders!"

"Oh, I can imagine, Kain." she giggled, rising to her feet with her hands still held tightly by her friend. "And I am quite glad to be of service to you."

"Well, I am in your debt, Mara." Kain replied softly.

A knock sounded from Kain's door just before a young page poked his head into the room. "Begging your pardon, Sir Viccon, but Senador Miller and the Prince Michael were curious as to when you were going to report back."

Kain glanced at the clock on his wall. He had been talking with Mara for almost twenty minutes! It sure hadn't seemed that long. He turned his attention to the page and replied "Inform them that I'm on my way back." Then to Mara he said "Well, I hate to run out on you, my dear, but I really must be getting back to my meeting, especially with the news you have given me."

"That's all right, Kain." Mara assured him with a warm smile. "I really must be getting along on my way, anyway. I have more duties I must attend to for the Ladys."

"Well, it was really nice to see you again. It's been a while since we last talked, hasn't it?"

"Not since after James' disappearance." Mara nodded. "Three years."

"We have three years worth of catching up to do. Too bad we don't have more time for each other at the moment. Would you like to make time later on? Say over dinner?"

"As in a date?" Nancy chimed in with a sly grin.

"No, just a friendly venture." he replied, regarding her out of the corner of his eye. "You could finally meet Li. She's staying at our place right now."

"It is quite tempting, Kain." Mara chuckled. She clicked her tongue. "But I am afraid to say, however, that as much as I would love to both be seen with you in a restaurant and meet my sister-in-law, like I said I have other duties I must attend to. But I shall look forward to it when this is all said and done."

She gave him a wink and then moved to kiss his cheek.

* * *

"It's about time, Kain." Miller replied as the Grand General and his sister stepped back into the conference room. "You said five minutes. What was that all about?"

"That, my good man, was the Goddess answering our prayers." Kain replied, a bright grin set on his lips.

"How so?" Miller asked with a raised brow as the Viccon siblings took their original seats at the table.

"She sent us word of a way to beat Noknor's Swuenedras Amulet."

"And that is . . . ?" Michael replied slowly.

"We just have to find something even more powerful."

"And what, pray tell, would that be?" Miller asked.

Kain slowly looked from face to face before he clicked his tongue and gently lowered his head. "Well, we have to find the Elemental Sword."

"Of course! Nothing is more powerful than that!" Raphael excitedly said, pounding the table with his palm.

"Not even the Swuenedras Amulet can stand up to that weapon!" Michael added, laughing in relief.

"Be that as it may." Miller broke in abruptly. "How exactly do you plan on finding it? It's not exactly sticking out of a stone in the middle of a lake."

"I'll take care of that." Kain told him, resting his chin on his fists. "During lunch and after we finish here for the day, I'm going to research it in the royal library, have Sylia help me. I'll talk to a few people later on as well. I think I know of someone in particular that could be a big help." The Grand General suddenly burst out "Well, hells bells! That changes everything. We're going to have to come up with a totally new plan of attack!"

"You can't do that, Kain!" Miller squealed, crushing the paper he had in his hand with an obvious joking flourish.

"And why not?" Kain raised his eyebrows.

"Because the original plans have already been set!" Miller explained, crossing his arms and pretending to be annoyed by the turn of events. "I've already written them down and sent them to the A.D. Department! Do you realize how much work it'll be to change—"

"Oh, come on, Miller." Michael grinned as he cut off the senator. "I'll do it for you, if you want."

"I think I can handle it myself, thank you!" Miller laughed and sat back in his chair. "You guys want me to start hitting the bottle after work, don't you?"

Everyone shared a good laugh as Miller shifted through some papers, trying to find a clean sheet. As he was doing this, Kain said "Don't worry, Miller. I'm not going to be making that many changes. Just for my unit, only. First, we won't be going straight through to Kuberica Castle. Instead, we're going to look for the Elemental Sword. Now I honestly can't tell you how long it will take or what route we will take if we do have to take a new one. I won't have that info until I do a little research." He paused so that Miller could write his notes. "Also, I want to nix the battalion and only take thirty soldiers total. It'll be easier to get around when looking for the Elemental Sword if I have fewer troops."

"Do you want thirty all together?" Miller murmured as he raised his head and his pen.

"No, thirty plus me and my crew." Kain replied, gesturing towards his three companions. "Master Scout Robert Grotz included."

"Do you still want horses?" Miller mumbled.

Nancy was expecting Kain to say something sarcastic but he didn't. He just slowly nodded his head. Apparently it was a standard question.

Miller was about to write something down when he looked up and gestured towards Nancy as he asked "Does she know how to ride a horse?"

"Yes, she's a very accomplished rider." Kain remarked proudly.

"I should have guessed as much." he grinned as he lowered his head once again. "She is a Viccon, after all. What type or types of soldiers do you want?"

"Let's see . . ." Kain sighed, rubbing his face. He had to think about that one. "Give me one scouting unit, one knight unit, and the rest infantry."

"Five scouts, ten knights, and fifteen foot soldiers." Miller murmured lowly to himself as he tallied down what he was told. "Okay, that comes to seventy total bodies."

"Seventy?" Nancy looked at Kain with a slight frown and inquisitive eyes. "Didn't you just say thirty-five?"

"Well, only thirty-five people." Kain told her. "They count horses along with the humans." She gave him a very confused look. He chuckled as he shrugged and replied "Beats me. They also count hunting dogs and hawks, and other animals if we take them. I guess because they're living creatures they like to keep tabs on them. Paper pusher formality." He paused and gave a sudden low chuckle. "No offense, Miller."

"How about if I just call you an arrow stopper and we'll call it even." Miller replied with a good-natured grin. This got everyone rolling around laughing so hard tears came to their eyes and it took a full ten minutes before enough order could be restored so that they could continue on.

Over the next three hours, they discussed more plans and more changes that were needed in a very light-hearted manner, which Nancy found quite strange. She had always pictured one of these little discussion groups as being very serious and down to earth, much like the classroom she was used to. However, many times over, someone broke in with a joke or a story that made everyone laugh. In fact, they probably spent more time playing than they did actually working, or so it seemed. And while the rowdy men found it difficult to be decent around the young lady, Nancy had no problem breaking them up many times with her silly jokes and cute antics.

Finally, a half hour after noon, Kain stretched and remarked "I think it's time we broke for lunch. Who's in agreement?" Everyone was, so he stood and grabbed Nancy by her arm. As he gently pulled her up, he said "Then the next thing I want to do is get you fitted for a battle uniform."

"Wait a second." Miller quickly said, holding up his hand to stop Kain. "Have you talked to the queen about her joining you yet?"

Kain released his sister's arm and slowly turned his head to look at the senador, quite surprised that Miller would bring up something like that. "No, not exactly."

"Then she can't get fitted yet." Miller told him in a rather authoritative tone of voice and crossed arms. "Anyone non-military can not be fitted for battle without first being approved by the queen herself."

Kain cocked his head and frowned slightly, not sure what to say or think. It was not at all like Miller, who always did his best to help Kain out. Everyone else carefully watched in silence what was about to transpire as Kain tried to explain "But—"

"No buts, Viccon." Miller grinned subtly. "You know the rules." Kain's frown darkened and Miller was not able to hold his playful grin in any longer. "But seeing as how she did kick your ass this morning, I'll overlook it this time."

Kain smiled and slowly shook his head while the others shared boisterous laughter. "She didn't kick my ass."

"Sure she didn't, Kain." Michael teased, looking to the girl for the truth. Her large grin said it all.

"Well, then I guess that about wraps everything up for now." Miller chuckled as he gathered up a few papers and neatly sorted them. "I'm going to go ahead and forward this stuff to the A.D. Department and then get some lunch with them. What time do you want to back here?"

"I'd say about thirteen thirty." Kain told him.

"Great! I'll see you guys then." Miller replied, standing with a handful of papers clutched in his right hand. He extended his free hand to Nancy and grinned "It was a very great pleasure to work with you, Nancy. Now that I have, I can understand why your brother speaks so highly of you."

"Thank you, Senador Miller." Nancy smiled brightly. "It was really fun working with you, too."

He grinned. "I can't want to do it again this afternoon. Ya'll enjoy your lunches!"

They all gestured a good-bye to him as he walked out into the crowded hallway. Kain pulled out his watch and regarded the time with a grunt before slipping it back into his pocket as his friends also stood and stretched. As they headed to the door, Michael inquired "Are you two going to be getting lunch first?"

"No, I want to go get Nancy fitted with a uniform first and get that over with." Kain told him, opening the door for his friends. Nancy and Raphael exited first and immediately began chatting intensely while the other two followed them out. "We'll grab something after that."

As they walked down the hall, Kain told Michael about his encounter with Ash earlier that morning while Raphael told Nancy how fun and exciting the quest was going to be. Kain angrily used some colorful words to describe the bigheaded senador, and when he realized what he had said he quickly glanced at Nancy to apologize for his language. She didn't hear a word he had said since she was so engrossed in conversation with Raphael. He returned his attention back to Michael and continued "I can't believe he had the nerve to attack me like that! Right in front of Nancy! The kahonez on that piece of—"

"You know he hates your guts." Michael told him, sticking his hand up to stop Kain from ranting off another string of violent curses.

"The feeling is more than mutual! Man, I would have told him off today if she hadn't been with me. Stabbed right through him!" Kain replied, subtly pointing his finger at Nancy as they turned a corner.

Raphael didn't notice the turn and Nancy was following him, so they just kept on walking. Without pausing in his conversation with Michael, Kain quickly snapped his hand out, grabbed Nancy's arm, and pulled her down the corridor. When Nancy squeaked in surprise, Raphael spun around and realized his mistake. He blushed deeply and felt embarrassed as he mumbled "Oops, sorry about that, Nancy."

"Don't worry about it." Michael laughed. "It's about time we left the two of them and go get something to eat, so we have to go down that way anyway. We'll see you two after lunch."

"Alright." Kain waved as Michael and Raphael headed down the hall, laughing and joking around. "Come on, Nancy."

"When do we get lunch?" Nancy asked, clutching her empty belly that rumbled and grumbled for something, anything to fill it. "I'm just about starving."

"We'll grab something after we get you fitted." Kain told her. He noticed her give a desperate sigh and grinned. As he ran his fingers through her hair, he told her "Don't worry, pup. They're just going to take a few measurements and we'll be done. Shouldn't be more than a few minutes."

"Okay." Nancy sighed hungrily as they came to a set of elegant double doors.

CHAPTER VI

Michael and Raphael were walking down a hall in Arcainia Castle when they spotted Kain and Nancy headed towards them. Both looked rather tired, but Nancy especially seemed to be beat. Michael could hardly blame her. It was the end of another long day and everyone at the castle was itching to get home.

The siblings were sharing a laugh together and didn't notice their friends. Kain strolled down the hall with his hands in his pockets while Nancy had a small sack loaded with goodies slung over her right shoulder and a rather large, tasty looking roasted turkey leg in her left hand. Kain said something that they couldn't hear, and Nancy nodded happily as she held up her turkey leg to her brother, who gladly took a bite. After he had swallowed, he thanked her and they resumed their casual chat.

"Ah, there you are my good man." Michael boomed cheerfully, attracting their attention. Both smiled and waved as they hurried down the hall to catch up with them. "I've been looking for you two. How did everything go?"

"Just fine." Kain smiled as he shook the prince's hand casually. Kain and Nancy had spent the past couple of hours getting the girl set up with her weapons and other important items she would need on the quest. "Teena didn't have her uniform ready but promised that she would have it finished by twenty tonight and we've already got her situated with the proper supplies."

"Terrific!" Michael grinned, kissing the back of her hand fondly. He regarded her turkey leg with a gesture as he said "That's one heck of a leg. And it looks delicious."

"Oh, it is." Nancy giggled. "Would you like a bite?"

"Would I!" Michael replied eagerly, grasping the leg that Nancy offered to him. He took a bite and chewed slowly, savoring the wonderful smoked taste. He handed it back as he swallowed and said "Man, that's one tasty bird! Where'd you get it?"

"Kain got it for me." Nancy smiled brightly, looking at her brother with appreciative eyes as she took another bite. "We stopped by the kitchen a few minutes ago. Would you like a bite, Ralph?"

"Sure." Raphael grinned and bit into it. "Thanks."

"So, what's the plan for tomorrow?" Michael asked Kain as Nancy shared her leg.

"I need to go to speak with John Accrue." Kain replied. "Hopefully he'll have some information I can use."

"Hopefully?" Raphael murmured, trying to look nonchalant about wiping his lips.

"Yeah." he mumbled, looking at Nancy and idly watching as she chowed down. In his mind's eye, he saw Li, who no doubt had dinner ready and waiting for them at home, chewing him out for allowing the girl to ruin her appetite. Then he thought about something. "Hey, Michael. Are you doing anything at the moment?"

"Not a thing. Why?"

"Well, I have to stay here until Teena finishes Nancy's uniform and I'm sure Nancy is dying to get home." Kain glanced at his sister once more and saw her nod her head vigorously with puffed out cheeks full of roasted turkey. Kain had to chuckle at the sight. "I was wondering if you wouldn't mind escorting my sister home."

"Well, sure! I'd be delighted!" Michael smiled brightly as he extended his arm out to the girl. "Come, my dear. Your carriage awaits."

"I get to ride in a royal carriage?" Nancy gasped excitedly.

"Well, uhm, actually it was just a figure of speech." Michael mumbled, blushing slightly. He thought for a moment and continued "But I'm sure I could pull a few strings to make it happen. I am the prince, after all."

"Cool beaners, mane!" Nancy squeaked, giving Michael her adorable smile as she hooked arms with him. Then they said their good-byes before trotting on down the hall, joyfully chattering away.

Kain grinned and watched them until he lost sight of them as they turned a corner. "Well, I guess I'll talk to you later, Raphael. I have to go see Martin."

"Martin? I thought you already went and picked out your weapons." Raphael grinned. Kain slowly shook his head as he stuffed his hands into his pockets and strolled off down the hall. Raphael gave a short chuckle and clapped his friend on the back. "Well, good because I haven't either. That means we can go together and I won't look like the only slow arrow."

As soon as they entered the castle's armory, a dwarf with a long, scraggly red beard and a shock of fiery red hair immediately walked up to greet them. Kain shook his hand vigorously and grinned as he beamed "Martin! Good to see you, man. I had come in earlier and your assistant had told me you had something to talk to me about?"

"Aye, that I do. Eric told me that yea were in 'ere with a fin young lass. New girlfriend, laddie?"

"Hardly." Kain chuckled. "That was my sister, Nancy."

"Yer sis, huh? Well, I ain't seen 'er in quite some time. Not since she was a wee one. I sure would enjoy seein' 'er, too. Yea gotta bring 'er in before yea leave."

"Oh, you can count on that." Kain replied. "Do you have all of my troops' weapons ready?"

"Aye. Weapons for fifteen foot-soldiers, ten knights, and five scouts all ready." Martin grinned broadly, quite proud of his swift handiwork. "Jest be needin' names for 'em."

"Oh, I'll have that list for you tomorrow." Raphael told him. "I'm going to work on it right when I get home tonight."

"Well alright, then. That's jest fin." Martin nodded approvingly. "Yea two be the only ones that still need to pick out weapons. The good prince came yesterday and I suspect that this extra order be for yer sis."

"That's right." Kain replied.

"In that case, why don't yea take a look around laddie?" he said, referring to Raphael. When he shrugged and headed for the many weapon racks, Martin beckoned to Kain "Follow me, if yea will, laddie. I be 'aving something that I been wanten to show yea."

They walked to the back of the room to a large Arcainian blue oak door. Martin took a silver key from his pocket and slid it into the lock. There was a sharp click as he turned the key and low squeak sounded as he pushed the door open. They entered and Kain found himself in a large square storeroom. All four walls were lined with racks loaded with weapons and the three circular tables in the middle had an array of different shields stacked high. The dwarf guided Kain to a large cedar chest at the rear of the room and opened it up. The powerful scent of freshly cut cedar wood drifted up to Kain's nostrils and he deeply inhaled the pleasant odor. From the chest, Martin took a queer looking instrument made of a hollow tube of iron held to a wooden stock with thick iron rings and with strange iron appendages.

"It came off the boat from the Chin." he told Kain as he showed off his prize. "I call it a glok. It be a well enough weapon, but I made a few improvements." He began to point out and explain the simple mechanics. "Yea see, yea put some Chin black powder into the barrel before yea add a lead ball and pack it down all nice and tight. This piece be the trigger, like on a crossbow. Yea pull this 'ammer back to lock it and when yea pull the trigger, it releases the 'ammer which causes the flint to scritch this and make a spark that ignites the black powder. That fires the lead ball like a blowpipe dart from 'El. Yea follow, laddy?"

"Yes, I think so." Kain mumbled with a frown, taking the weapon when Martin offered it and examining it closer. It was heavy for its size but the grip felt natural in his hands.

"Good, cause I be givin' it to yea." Martin told him. Kain was quite honored, but he couldn't just take his friend's interesting, albeit odd, weapon. He started to protest and hand it back, but Martin stood firm. "Take it, laddie." He grinned broadly. "Yea can field test it for me. Let me know if it be as good as them Chins say."

"Alright." Kain finally said. "Thank you, my friend."

Martin smiled and shook his free hand. Then he reached back into the chest and took out two small leather bags: one was thick and bulky and the other was slim with a cork stopper. As he showed them to Kain, he said "These be the lead balls and this 'as Chin black powder." He thought for a moment before taking the glok back. "Why don't I 'old onto these whiles yea choose yer other weapons."

"Okay, thanks."

Kain joined Raphael back in the shop. Being such high ranking officers, they were allowed to hand pick their own weapons as opposed to the lower knights and soldiers who had to take the generic weapons they were given. Kain picked out a large steel broadsword, a razor sharp dagger, a spear with a broad tip, a long leather whip, and a long bow with a quiver containing twenty arrows. Raphael had a steel sword, a dagger like Kain's, a spike-studded mace, a small morning star, and a small crossbow with thirty bolts.

After they decided that they were ready, they took the weapons to the counter and let Martin tally the items so that he could mark off his inventory. When he finally finished, he put the weapons, including the glok and pouches, into heavy leather sacks, tagged the sacks with their names, and set them on the ground behind the counter.

"Y'all 'ave a good night." the dwarf bayed them. "And be sure to bring yer sis by so I can take a gander at 'er."

"Will do." Kain grinned, waving as they walked out. He told Raphael "Now I have to go to the apothecary for Li. Want to keep me company?"

"Might as well." Raphael shrugged.

As they rounded a corner, a young woman hurried around and bumped right into Kain. The impact, as light as it was, didn't harm Kain in the least but sent the girl reeling back and she almost fell flat on her back. As Kain helped to steady her, he saw that it was Sylia.

"I'm terribly sorry about that, sir!" she quickly apologized as she dusted herself off. "I guess I was in a bit of a hurry. Could you tell me—Oh, it's you, Kain. Just the man I was looking for! You're terribly hard to track down, you know that?"

* * *

Later that evening, Kain and Raphael strolled through Kain's front door laughing loudly and carrying on like there was no tomorrow. Raphael had a black leather satchel in his hand full of scrolls and documents he was going to need to sort through while Kain had a dark blue outfit of some sort draped over one arm and his own satchel held in his other hand. Li was sitting on the couch sipping a cup of tea and reading a book. When she heard the commotion, she looked up and smiled brightly. Kain motioned Raphael to set his bag in a corner and threw the outfit onto a chair before he waved a greeting to her. Li saw that it was an Arcainian soldier's uniform. It was much too small for Kain, so she figured it must have been for the kid. Li always thought Arcainians to have such bland uniforms; she was going to have to make the girl her own fighting outfit one day, she thought mildly.

Kain, still talking business with Raphael, turned as he removed his dark blue cloak and hung it on a rack. When he turned back around, Li was gone. Both her cup of steaming tea and her book lay on the coffee table, but Li was nowhere in sight. Kain shrugged to himself as he invited Raphael to have a seat. Raphael thanked him and sat on the couch next to where Li had been sitting. Kain, himself, pulled up a chair as Li brought out two more cups of freshly brewed tea. The men thanked her as they were handed a cup and Kain asked her where Nancy was.

"She's in her room. Do you want me to go get her?" Li asked, regarding the uniform with her thumb.

"No, I was just curious." he said, sipping his tea and hissing as the hot water burned his lips and tongue. "I'll have her try that on in a little bit."

"Oh. Well, I must say that she seemed to have had a great time." Li replied pleasantly, taking her place next to Raphael. "It was all she could talk about when Michael brought her home. She is so excited about going with you on this quest."

"Good, I'm glad." Kain grinned, blowing on his tea before sipping this time. "It's going to be a great experience for her. I just hope she knows what she's gotten herself into." He raised a concerned brow as he mentally added 'and that I know what I'm getting her into'. "It won't be all fun and games out there."

"Did you get everything straightened out with her final exams today?" Li inquired.

"Yes. Her teacher said that it was no problem. She's his best student so he knows that she would pass the tests easily. And, I didn't know this but since she's first in her class she can be exempt from them anyway. The top five don't have to take the finals if they don't want to."

"Oh, really?" Li grinned. "Well, that's good. I'm glad there wasn't a problem with that. I suppose that's one less thing you have to worry about. So what about the quest details? Is everything taken care of with that?"

"Pretty much. There's only a few more details to flatten out, but on the whole everything's ready. If nothing else comes up, we should be leaving in a few days."

"That's wonderful!" Li exclaimed happily, clapping her hands. Then she thought about how she had sounded. "Well, it's not that wonderful. I mean, I'm going to miss you and everything. It's just that it's wonderful that everything's working out for you and all. I don't want you out of here or . . . anything." she finished blandly, her voice barely a whisper.

"I know, I know. You could still come with us, you know." he remarked, his tone a little more than hopeful. When she rolled her eyes, he grinned and took a small bag out of his pocket. Before tossing it to her, he told her "Here, I have a little something for you."

"Oh, Kain! Thank you so much!" she squeaked when she opened it up and saw what it was. "Burg weed! Now I can finally try that new recipe! How much do I owe you?"

"Don't worry about it."

Li leapt up and skipped happily to the kitchen while the two men discussed more things about the quest. When Li came back, she plopped back down on the couch and joined in on their conversation.

"Oh, by the way!" Kain said to Li. "You'll never guess who I ran into today!"

"James's sister, Mara." Li smiled. "Nancy told me. Seems like we always just miss each other."

"Seems that way." he shrugged. "I'm going to try to get in touch with her again. See if she won't stop by the house sometime, even if it's after Nancy and me leave so that you two can at least finally meet."

"That would be nice. I cannot believe that we haven't gotten together before. Of course, I guess we've both been pretty wrapped up in our own lives." Li grinned. She then asked about another detail of the quest and placed their discussion back onto the topic. However, with Li involved, it very quickly veered off as jokes and stories of past adventures worked their way into the conversation.

After a few minutes and one of Li's funny stories, Raphael was reminded of something that he been meaning to ask his friend. He turned to Kain and asked "When were you going to go see John Accrue about the Element—"

"John Accrue?" Li's eyelids fluttered with annoyance. "You don't need to go see him, Kain. He's a bad . . . no, a terrible influence on you!"

"He's not a bad influence." Kain sighed and rubbed his face. "And, yes I do need to go see him."

"What is it you don't like about him, Li?" Raphael asked with great amusement, noticing the disapproving look she was sporting on her face and the annoyed tone to her voice. He personally liked John. He was a funny guy, though he was a bit of a womanizer. And that was the understatement of the century.

Li promptly tried to blow away a bang that had drifted across her forehead. When she failed, she huffed, pulled back her hair, and crossed her arms and legs in a tiff. Then she growled "He's a perverted, sexist, little old rat—pig. He makes lude comments, offensive passes, and grabs my butt! How's that for starters?"

"Oh, he does that to everyone." Kain tried to defend his friend even though he knew that Li had a very strong point. Ever since Li had first arrived in Arcainia, John had made it his mission in life to bed her, a mission that had failed before it had even started.

"Everyone?" Li asked slowly and with a deviously cocked eyebrow.

"Yes, every—" Kain caught on. "NO! Just the ladies! I still have no idea why he would want to grab your ass!"

"Yeah, well at least I'm attractive!" she leapt up.

"By whose standards? A toad's, perhaps?" he blurted out.

"You would know!"

"Because you always tell me!"

"Why, you nasty little troll! You wouldn't know a pretty woman if she came up and kicked you in the—" Li started, but Raphael quickly grabbed her shoulders and promptly sat her down. Then he was swift to ask Kain to bring him a glass of water, saying that his throat was dry. Kain nodded and headed for the kitchen. As he left the room, Li rubbed her bottom and demanded "What was that for?"

"To stop you before you killed each other!"

Suddenly, Kain called out "Would you rather have some beer?"

Li opened her mouth so that she could tell her cousin where to shove his beer, but Raphael slapped his hand over her mouth and called back "No, water's fine."

As Raphael removed his hand from Li's lips, she turned and gave him a sly smile. He grinned nervously and blushed as Kain brought out a glass of water. Raphael drank it down in one long gulp and handed the glass back. Kain looked at it a moment before setting it on the table and following Raphael to the door.

"Are you sure you won't stay for dinner?" Kain asked, opening the front door. "I'm sure Li has prepared something very tasty."

"No, I think I should really be going now." he chuckled and looked at Li. He gave her a grin that said 'don't hurt him too badly' and waved to her. "Bye, Li."

Li returned the grin with a giggle and waved back. After Kain had shut the door, he heard his cousin say quietly, almost to herself, "If you want something to eat, you can fix it your damn self."

"What was that, dear cousin?"

"I didn't stutter!" she laughed and then retorted "What part of 'fix it your damn self' didn't you understand, Aizi?"

"Hey! Don't call me that." Kain grumbled. "I'm not short."

"Yes, you are Aizi."

"Stop it!"

"Aizi, Aizi, Aizi!"

"All right, Li! Fighting stance! Now!"

"Oh, please!" Li frowned and turned her head to examine her nails.

"Come on, Li. Unless you're scared of me, of course." he baited her.

Li snorted "**ME** scared of **YOU**? Don't make me laugh!"

"Well, you must be if you won't accept my challenge!"

She rolled her eyes as she slowly stood up and clenched her fists. She sighed "Fine, have it your way." Then she quietly added "Aizi!"

When they were younger, while Kain and Nancy were living in China with Li and her family, Li and Kain would occasionally have disagreements. However, instead of solving their disputes normally like the other children, since they both saw themselves as warriors they would fight each other. Of course, they were always careful and pulled their punches, they weren't out for blood after all. The loser would have to be the other's slave for the rest of the day. As things went, Li usually ended up freed from her daily chores.

Kain immediately tried to slap her cheek, but Li easily grabbed his hand. With his opposite hand, he cuffed her lightly across the head, surprising her into dropping his wrist. Hoping to catch her while she was momentarily stunned, Kain leapt at her with his arms ready to wrap around her body in a powerful bear-hug. Li foiled him by ducking at the last second and twirling around him. She kicked him between his shoulderblades, sending him sprawling face first onto the ground. He quickly rolled onto his back and leapt to his feet, kicking at her legs in an attempt to trip her. Failing that, he tried to punch her in the stomach. She countered with a slap to his face, which he countered with an elbow to her chin. He gave a headbutt to her forehead, using his hand as a cushion between their skulls. She backed up and shook it off as she rethought her strategy. Thinking fast, she charged at him and flipped over his head, twisting in the air as nimbly as a cat. As soon as she landed, she kicked him in the back of the knee, unlocking it and knocking him down. He was back up in a flash, but Li grabbed him and threw him into the wall. He struck with a tremendous THWACK, and when he rebounded off he tried one last feeble attack, but she slammed her arm across his chest and easily swept his feet out from under him, throwing him down at her feet.

Nancy was in her room laying on her bed and reading her new faery book. She heard the commotion, but didn't pay much attention to it until she heard the loud THWACK shake her wall, causing a small wooden faery statue on her dresser to topple to the floor. She rolled her eyes at it and shook her head before she returned back to her reading.

"Kain must be home." she mumbled to herself.

Li was pumped and ready for more. Kain, on the other hand, was not. He lay face down on the floor, their way of saying 'You win'. Li giggled and told him that he could get up.

"I don't think I can." he joked, his face red and warm as he slowly pulled himself up.

"You better, or I'll really get mad!" she mocked, stamping her foot menacingly. Kain leapt to his feet in a flash and Li giggled lowly. "That's better. Now then, let's see . . ." Li said thoughtfully. "I won, so that means you're my slave for the rest of the night. Since I never made supper and I'm hungry, you can make me something good to eat."

Kain didn't say anything right off, and it was clear he was not pleased with his present situation. "What would you like?"

"I bought some quails earlier today. How about you grill one of them up, slave? Oh, and one for Nancy, too." She snickered in good humor. "And if you have some time, I guess you can make something for yourself, slave."

Kain stomped off into the kitchen to do his chore while Li got her diary from her room and returned to the living room to take a seat. She opened up the book and looked at the drawing on the inside cover. It was a sketch she had long ago drawn of her lover, James Raptor. She sighed faintly as she traced a finger along the penciled cheek before kissing her fingertips and pressing them against the drawing's lips.

James had been a great warrior and was, in fact, a Knight of Auset, a powerful alliance of distinguished Old World heroes fighting in the name and glory of the

Divine Mother Auset to conquer all evil and to protect Her children wherever they went. They were trained in the ancient arts of their Goddess, using these old enchantments to aid them in their journeys and battles. They were believed to be able to turn invisible, move about in complete silence, breath underwater, heal themselves and others, and do many other extraordinary abilities. And they were so skilled in combat that it was said only a god could match the weaponmastery of the Knights of Auset. They were feared by the evil and wretched and admired by the good and innocent whom they protected with a furious vengeance.

James, himself, was the son of an Arcainian tailor. Before his untimely death, Richard Viccon and James's father had been very good friends, and as such Kain, James, and Mara, being the same ages, formed a strong friendship between themselves. It was during this time that James's strong curiosity of the Chinese culture began, mostly due to Kain's mother, Fang. He adored her and thoroughly enjoyed every opportunity he got to learn from her. He learned the language and the customs of China with her help and later with Kain's help. When Kain and Nancy traveled back to China to see their family, James had tagged along to visit the country he had grown to love so dearly. It was then that the two paths of destiny for the star-crossed lovers collided. It was love at first sight for both James and Li and for many years, they shared a wonderful and loving relationship. Then, on the eve of their wedding day, James was called to duty as a Knight of Auset to help the dwarfs in the infamous Dwarf and Goblin Wars. He had disappeared in battle and Li had not seen him since. But she had never given up hope that her beloved was alive and would return to her someday. She kept an eternal fire lit in her heart for him, turning down all other suitors who sought to take his place because she knew that no one else ever could. With a heavy, fond sigh of memories gone by, Li flipped through her diary, found the correct page, and began to write Chinese characters that read:

> *Kain and Nancy will soon leave on their quest against Noknor and I already feel my heart sinking. He has gone on many quests, and we've shared many adventures together. Nancy has proven herself very capable of handling herself. Still, I have a bad feeling about this one. Maybe it's just the fact that I'm going to miss them so much. I do want to go with them so much. I could really use some adventure in my life right now. No, I must remind myself that this is their fight, and I can't interfere no matter how much I want to. I can't let them see me shed a tear of longing for them. I have to be strong for them. It won't be very long, I'm sure I'll be hearing their stories in no time. I guess I'll delay my return home and stick around here until they get back. I'll house-sit, maybe have a party or two! Ha-ha! It's already been a year, what's a few months more.*
>
> *Still no word from James yet. I miss him so much. My true love, where are you?*

Suddenly, she felt someone tap her shoulder. She looked up and saw Kain staring at her. She had been thinking and writing for over forty-five minutes, but to her it seemed like seconds. He told her "Your supper's ready."

"'Your supper's ready' what?" she asked closing her book and straightening her dress. She crossed her legs, placed her hands on her knee, and looked up at Kain with amusement in her eyes and smile.

"Beg your pardon?" Kain frowned, his stomach suddenly unsettling.

"Come on, slave. I know you remember." she giggled, winking up at him.

"But that was years ago!" he protested.

"You got yourself into this. Now say it, slave."

"Fine! Your supper is ready . . . oh great . . . wise . . ." he grumbled lowly, his humiliated voice trailing off into garbled, unintelligible words.

She put her hand to her ear and mockingly replied "What was that, slave? I couldn't hear you."

"Your supper is ready oh great, wise, powerful, and beautiful Empress Li!" he said in a clear, stout voice dripping with sarcasm. "Happy?"

"Very." she covered her mouth to stifle a giggle. "Just be glad I didn't make you bow on your knees to me."

While she skipped to the kitchen and hummed triumphantly to herself, Kain snatched up the uniform from the chair and headed for Nancy's room. He knocked a few times and opened the door when he heard her call that it was open. She was laying stomach down on her bed, reading a book on faeries and faery magick. She looked up, smiled brightly and asked "So, who won?"

"Don't worry about it." Kain mumbled, blushing a slight crimson.

"I see Li did." Nancy snickered. "What's up, big bro?"

"Dinner's ready."

"Cool! I'm starved!" she squeaked joyfully as she marked her page and slammed her book shut. Her bare feet slapped against the wooden floorboards when she leapt off the bed and started to rush to join Li in the dining room. However, she never got past Kain. He grabbed her arm, stopping her with a jerk, and thrust the uniform into her arms.

"Here, I need you to try this on and tell me how it fits before you go eat." he told her and walked away.

Nancy looked at the clothing in her hands and sighed hungrily as she slowly closed her door. Then, with one final dull sigh and a sharp rumble in her belly, she tossed the uniform onto her bed and began to undress.

CHAPTER VII

"So, what's first on the agenda for today?" Nancy asked at breakfast. She was situated between her brother, who was looking over some documents he had been studying the night before, and her cousin, who was also curious since she had decided to tag along for the day.

"I have a bunch of errands I have to run." Kain mumbled to them, not looking up from his papers. Even when he shoved food into his mouth, he did so without looking to his plate. Li herself thought it was pretty silly looking while Nancy thought it was cool. Of course, she thought almost everything Kain did was cool.

Kain, still looking at his paper, went to skewer some eggs off of his plate but missed, the metal fork making a shrill squeal as it scratched the tin plate. The sudden noise startled Nancy, who snapped her head up with a wild look in her eyes and flung her own fork to the floor. She blushed slightly as she snatched it back up and silently resumed eating. Li had been watching him and thus expected it, so she just giggled at her cousin's foolishness. Kain lowered his map, grinned at Li, and watched what he was doing to second time around.

"What else do we have to do?" Nancy asked.

"That's pretty much it, I guess." Kain told her, shuffling papers. "Not a whole lot for you to worry about today."

"Cool. Maybe Li and I will get a chance to do some shopping whiles you're busy?" she smiled, trying to act nonchalant as she offered her suggestion.

Kain regarded Nancy and Li's playful grins with raised eyebrows.

* * *

Nancy wore a cute black dress with long sleeves and white lace around the neckline and wrists and dull black boots along with a dab of her favorite perfume. Her brother wore a pair of black slacks and a black shirt buttoned to the collar that was wrapped tightly around his neck. Both got their respective glances from men and women as they strolled through the majestic halls of the castle, but the real looker by far was Li. She wore a beautiful dark blue Arcainian-style dress. It had long, tight sleeves and a high collar that wrapped around her neck. The vest was a bit snug and hugged her shapely figure quite alluringly while the dress flowed like water around her legs with each step. Her long hair was put up in a tight ball behind her head while a few scattered locks hung down loosely. Both dress and hair made her even more voluptuous and attractive than usual. She was so enchanting that even Kain, who had bought the dress for her a few days before, did a double take when she had walked out of her room. 'It didn't look that good on the mannequin!' he had told her. She had only blushed and mumbled a thank you.

As they headed straight to Kain's office, Li gazed all around her at the immense beauty surrounding her. Li had been to Arcainia Castle many times before, Kain had even taken her once to actually meet Queen Vanetta the Beautiful herself, but she was still amazed at the grand scale of everything and how beautiful it all was. About halfway to his office, they ran into Raphael and Michael, who were on their way to report to him. They seemed to be in a rush and anxious to see him but weren't surprised that he wasn't already at his desk. They all stopped and exchanged greetings with one another.

"Nice dress, Li." Michael grinned as he looked her over carefully. "It really, ah, complements your figure. I can see that you certainly live up to your name."

"Thanks." Li blushed deeply and lowered her head slightly as she gave a sheepish giggle.

As they continued on their way, Raphael informed Kain as to why they had been in such a rush to see him. "You'll never guess what just happened in Kuberica."

"What, did Noknor give up peacefully?" Kain mumbled, hope vaguely invading his sarcastic tone.

"Not even close." Raphael snorted. "Shazadia gathered up their forces a few days ago and tried to attack, **TRIED** being the key word, I might add."

"Dare I ask?" Kain asked, knowing full well what had happened to them.

"They were massacred." Michael told him. "From the report we received this morning, it was quick and easy for Noknor, but far from painless for the Shazadians. The Shazadian Army was butchered, and I do mean butchered, Kain. It makes me sick to my stomach to think about it!"

"I can't believe he did that!" Kain growled, slamming his fist into the brick wall. All of the activity in the hall instantly stopped to see what the echoing boom was all about and for a short moment it seemed that time itself had stopped around Kain. Then as quickly as it stopped, all of the movement in the hall resumed faster than before and Kain and his friends continued along their way. "I can't believe he did that! How could he be so stupid? We told him that Noknor had that stupid amulet! He knew it would be impossible! And yet he knowingly sent his men in to be slaughtered! That pompous . . . ARROGANT, stubborn IDIOT!"

"Who's he talking about?" Li whispered into Raphael's ear, opting not to interrupt her cousin from his ranting.

"The king of Shazadia." Raphael told her, also whispering lowly. "He had wanted to send his troops in, but Queen Vanetta told him that Noknor was much too powerful. I guess he took offense and wanted to prove something."

"Sounds just like a man!" Li whispered to Nancy, who had been listening. Both women shared a giggle that was a bit too loud. Kain overheard and turned to glare at them. When they both gave him innocent grins, he simply snorted and shook his head slowly as he stopped in front of a large door and opened it. He ushered the others in before following.

Kain's office was tidier than he had left it the night before, but Sylia was nowhere to be seen. Kain shrugged and figured that she was around somewhere, so he took his seat behind his desk. The two men offered the chairs to the two ladies and stood beside them. Just as they all got comfortable, the door opened and the tall beauty walked in with a folder in her hand.

"Oh, hello everyone!" she chirped happily as she made her way to the desk. "Hi there, bossman."

"Morning, darlin'." he told her, rising. "Sylia, you remember my cousin, Li?"

"Oh, of course I do!" she said excitedly, instantly recognizing her. As they shook hands, Sylia chirped "How could I forget you! Kain talks about you nonstop!"

"All one sided, I'm sure." Li grinned.

"Yes, it is. But don't worry. I get the real story from Nancy." Sylia replied and they all shared a laugh, even Kain.

"Sylia, Michael told me that a report came in this morning. I was wondering if you could dig—" Kain started but stopped when Sylia waved the folder and smiled. As she handed it to him, Kain said "Does this girl know me or what?"

He opened the folder and examined the fifteen page report. Kain only skimmed through the pages, but it was more than enough to get the entire story. In it, it told of the Shazadian forces marching to Kuberica Castle waving their banners proudly. There was a brief skirmish on the grounds, but most Shazadian casualties had been from enemy arrows and catapult launched fire bombs. The Shazadians held their own against Noknor's initial ground force, although the Dark Knights were surprisingly savage and fierce. They made it to the drawbridge, which was left gaping open, and stormed the castle. Nearly one thousand Dark Knights were waiting, as was Noknor himself. The Shazadians fought valiantly, but their attacks did absolutely nothing to Noknor and their defenses were even worse. Every single weapon shattered like fine crystal when they struck Noknor as he casually walked among them and ripped once great warriors to shreds like paper dolls. The sick monster laughed gleefully all the while blood splashed the walls and screams of pain and torment filled the castle. The Shazadians' moral was demolished and panic swept through them like a plague, and nothing could have been worse for them. The Dark Knights easily overtook them ending the fight in less than half an hour. Those that had not been killed or managed to escape where taken alive and thrown into the dungeon to be tortured later with the Kubericans they had come to liberate. Noknor then ordered the outside walls of his castle to be painted with the blood of the Shazadian army while mangled bodies were staked into the earth and hung from the lifeless, naked trees on the grounds to serve as a warning to any others who might try and defy his awesome might.

When Kain finished the report, he lowered the papers and stared forward with empty, glazed eyes. He had never heard of anything so ghastly or disgusting. That was no way for a soldier to die and certainly not to live. To wait in a dismal cell knowing you will be killed in horrific ways. Not even Hell itself could have been like what Noknor had created. Kain didn't know if he should yell, cry, or throw up. He certainly wanted to do all at the same time.

"Let me see it." Nancy said suddenly, pulling him from his thoughts. She was quite curious as to what Kain could have read to make him react like he had.

"No." Kain replied simply. He knew it was much too gruesome for her. He gave a disgusted grunt as he tossed it onto his desk. Li made a reach for it, but Kain dolefully shook his head and she sat back without the report. Kain looked at Sylia and asked her if she had read it. She shook her head and he told her "Good. Let's not let curiosity kill the cat." He paused for a moment and sat back in his chair as he thought deeply. Finally, he sighed, leaned forward, and said "Well, there's nothing we can do about it. We warned him, he didn't listen, and his people suffered. If only one good thing can come out of this, it's that we know what to expect. We need that sword now more than anything. It's our only hope."

They were all silent, grieving for soldiers from another land who they didn't even know and wondered if that would be their fate as well. Kain began to have serious thoughts about dropping Nancy from the quest and forcing her to stay with Li. But he knew he couldn't. He knew it would devastate her, but he wasn't worried about that. He'd rather her hold a grudge against him than be dead, and especially like that. But there was something else, a sort of feeling more or less, that told him to take her. He wasn't sure why but he knew he had to. Perhaps it was destiny. So, he decided that he would give her one final test. He'd let her read the report when they were alone together and see how she reacted. After reading that horror story, she would probably volunteer to stay home with Li.

Kain rubbed his face and ran his hands through his hair before sighing. He noticed all eyes on him, so to brighten the dreary air, he said "That's not going to happen to us, blast it all! We're going to kick Noknor's tale clear across the world."

"Not to China, I hope." Li smirked, trying to help Kain out a bit. "We don't want his slimy hide over there. We've got enough to worry about. Send his sorry butt straight to Hell. I'm sure he'll fit right in."

The laughter was nervous at first, but soon they were all back in high spirits. They chatted amongst themselves for a bit before Nancy excused herself for a moment and Kain told everyone that he had to get some business taken care of.

"I need to go see John Accrue." he announced. "Now, I know Li doesn't want to see him." She snorted and crossed her arms and legs but said nothing. "Raphael, would you be so kind as to escort my lovely cousin to the Square for some shopping? Keep her entertained."

"You bet!" he chirped with a little too much excitement. He received a few sly looks and grinned nervously as he blushed and shrank back slightly.

"You don't want to go see John Accrue?" Sylia asked with a large grin as she looked at Li. The Chinese beauty snorted once more and rolled her eyes, making Sylia snicker "Gee, I can't imagine why. Not wanting your butt to feel like a pincushion?"

Suddenly, the door opened and Nancy strolled back in, taking her seat once again. She asked what she had missed, so Kain told her about Raphael taking Li shopping but left out the jokes about John. As much as Li and Sylia were right about his womanizing, John did treat Nancy very well and she did respect him.

"Do you want to go with me and Michael to see him or would you rather go with Li and Raphael?" Kain asked his sister after explaining the situation to her.

"Can I get anything?" she asked, her bright black eyes glittering hopefully.

"Whatever you want." he grinned.

"I'll go shopping, then." Nancy smiled brightly. Kain had figured so much and chuckled lowly to himself.

"What about me?" Sylia inquired as she lightly bumped her employer's shoulder with her hip. "Where are you going to have me running around to today?"

"Sylia, my dear, count your blessings. You are going to have it easy today."

"Yeah, I've heard that song and dance before." she grunted playfully, crossing her arms under her breasts. "What do I have to do?"

Kain opened the bottom drawer and took out a sack of Arcainian coins heavy enough to knock someone cold with. As he handed it over to his secretary, he told her "You're going shopping with Li and Raphael."

"What in the world do you want me to buy?" she asked, giving him an odd look after she saw the denominations of the coins. He had never given her such a large sum of money.

"Whatever the hell you, Li, and Nancy want." Kain replied. "You three ladies go nuts. Have yourselves a good time at the expense of good Queen Vanetta."

"Are you serious?" both Li and Sylia gasped in unison.

"Quite." he nodded.

"Do you need receipts?" Sylia asked. Kain scowled as he snorted and shook his head. Sylia's face brightened as she threw her arms around her employer in grateful glee. "Oh, Kain! Thank you so much! What have I done to deserve this?"

"What haven't you done? Consider this in place of those five gratitude lunches I've built up." Kain laughed, giving her waist a squeeze. Then he stood up, grabbed the file Sylia had given him and a few more papers, and stuffed all of this into his satchel. As he snapped the three brass locks closed, he said "Alright, let's all get a move on. Ladies and Raphael, meet us back here in about five hours."

* * *

Kain and Michael walked along the streets leading through the Vaness District, one of the many residential blocks in Arcainia City, until they got to a particularly large and elegant house. They walked through the waist high iron gate and up to the wooden door where Kain rapped thrice. A gruff voice suddenly called from within "Who's there?"

"Who do you think, you twisted old goat!" Kain answered with a grin while Michael glared at him with wide, shocked eyes and a dropped jaw. Even he wouldn't talk that way to John Accrue, and he was the prince!

"Only one good for nothing jackass would dare talk like that to me!" roared the voice as the door was thrown open. A well dressed, well built man of fifty-three with graying slick black hair and a graying black goatee stood before them, a large smile spread over his face.

"Kain! Your highness! This is a most pleasant surprise! Come in, come in the both of you!" he exclaimed, ushering them inside.

The living room was full of beautiful paintings, crafted furniture, and extravagant ornaments. Kain, as many times as he had visited his friend, was always impressed by the man's eye for art, both Arcainian and from foreign kingdoms. John headed to the kitchen to fetch three fabulously blown glass tankards of beer. He gave each man one and sat down in a beautifully crafted oak chair with his own. After a long sip, he replied in a nonchalant tone "Nancy came by yesterday. Told me that sexy cousin of yours opted to stay behind on this quest."

"Yep. Li decided that it would be best." Kain told him with a large grin as he chugged the beer from his mug. He knew what was coming.

"Your cousin's staying here all by herself? Why don't you send her on over here with me?" John asked, his lustful smile wide behind his mug. "I'll keep her company."

"She wouldn't come over here if I told her you were spewing gold out of your ass!" Kain chuckled as he shook his head. Michael burst out laughing while John grinned, shrugged, and sipped his drink. "She hates your guts, man."

"Why? Just because hand slipped once?"

"It didn't 'slip', it was a lot more times than 'once', and yes, because of that. You're lucky she didn't kick you across the room, or worse. She told me that if you ever even look at her funny again, she'll make it so that you won't have the kahonez to do it again. And she meant that in the most literal sense as possible."

"Ouch! She's a feisty one. I guess that's why I find her so hot." John smirked. As he threw his head back and swallowed some more of his beer, he thought 'That and the fact that she has some major T&A.' Then he grew more solemn and replied "Nance told me that Noknor actually managed to find the Swuenedras Amulet."

"That's right." Kain murmured, sitting back on the couch and slowly sipping his beer. All three men were now displaying a new seriousness about them and respecting the grave situation they were faced with.

"If he has that, he must be pretty powerful right now." John replied, wiping foam from his lips as he sniffled softly. "More powerful than conventional weapons at least, I'm sure."

"This will give you an idea." Kain told him as he took out the Shazadian report and tossed it to his old friend. John opened the folder and skimmed over the pages. As he read, his face went white and his mouth formed a disgusted sneer. He didn't read the entire fifteen pages, only enough to paint a vivid picture that would stick in his mind for quite a long time. He closed the folder with a slap and handed it back to Kain as if it burned his hand.

"Goddess help us!" he gasped lowly. "He's a devil! How in the world do you expect to beat him?"

"Well, that's what I need to talk to you about." Kain told him, placing his half empty glass on the black marble coffee table so he could put the report away.

John shrugged idly. "I'm not sure how I can help any. I'm not into that magick BS."

"No, but you were my father's Second General during his battle with Kitrad Doe." Kain grinned, noticing the sudden sparkle flash in John's eyes.

"Ahh, the Elemental Sword. Of course!" He sighed as memories of his dear friend Richard Viccon flooded into his mind. "If there is any weapon powerful enough to counter the Swuenedras Amulet, it's that sword."

"That's why I came to see you today. I was hoping you could tell me how he got it. I really don't remember the details myself. It was such a long time ago and I was so young then."

"He had to ask each of the four Ladys personally." John replied with a simple shrug, his tone implying that he had mentioned it plenty of times in his storytelling.

Kain chuckled, slightly embarrassed. "Yes, I know that. What I meant to ask is how did he find the four Ladys in the first place?"

"The Uraeus Sisters told him where their temples were." John grinned behind his mug as he slurped his beer. Again, such information had been contained in the stories he had told both Kain and Nancy countless times.

The Ladys of the Elements were very powerful faeries; some in fact called them goddesses although they weren't really worshiped as such. Collectively, they were called Mother Nature, though they were each a separate entity. Each Lady took control over the elements of Earth, Air, Fire, and Water. The Ladys were said to be the ones that ruled over the Faery World of the Light, but they also controlled the daily events of the natural world such as life giving rain and destructive storms, among other things. They went about their business with a neutral attitude to all mortals, doing what they did to maintain order in both the Faery Realm and the natural world and keeping the delicate balance of each in proper check. These four ladies in turn gave birth to three daughters, the Uraeus Sisters, spawning the sisters from a combination of the four elements. These faeries weren't nearly as powerful as the Ladys, but were still quite strong. They were observing faeries, watching everything that happened as mortals might watch a play. They occasionally played tricks on mortals, which they considered silly little creatures, to spice up dull moments and make things a little more exciting for them."

Before Kain could once again rephrase himself, John laughed "Yes, I know what you *meant* to ask is how did your father find them. The Lady's Jestura at the time had given him a map. Hey, isn't what's-her-name . . . ah, the Raptor twin . . ."

"Mara." Kain helped him, humored disappointment on his face. "Yes, she's Jestura now. I've already spoken with her. She's the one that actually gave me the idea to hunt down the Elemental Sword to begin with."

"She couldn't tell you more?" John frowned with disbelief dotting his tone.

Kain shook his head. "Something to do with faery laws. They can't get too directly involved unless Noknor hits them first, or something. I dunno. I guess faeries have to deal with bureaucratic BS too."

Both John and Michael snorted laughter, bringing a small grin to Kain's face too. The men were silent for a long moment, finishing their beers and thinking of many things. Finally, John sighed deeply and offered "The best I can suggest is maybe look for your father's old map. Try looking in Richard's memento chest. He showed it to me once or twice, but that was a loooong time ago. I want to say that it was printed on leather, but it could have been cloth. Faery leather or cloth, of course. He wouldn't have thrown something that important away and I never saw it when I was taking care of things. It's got to still be in there somewhere. And I'll bet you a beer that you'll know when you've found it."

* * *

Kain stepped up into his dark attic with a candle and tentatively surveyed the area before climbing all the way in. It had been quite late when Kain, Nancy, and Li had returned home from the day of fun and laughter at the castle and the Square. Michael and Raphael had followed them and the five friends had stayed up late into the night telling stories. By the time Kain had remembered to search the attic, it was too late and he told himself that he would do it first thing in the morning. However, come three in the morning, he found he couldn't sleep and decided he might as well have a look-see.

The low glowing fire didn't cast its light very far, just a few feet in all directions, but it was enough for Kain to make his way through the clutter. The flickering flame pranced about atop the candle and caused the shadows to dance wildly in a sort of frenetic phantom ball. More than once, Kain caught sight of a sudden movement out of the corner of his eye and quickly spun his gaze over his shoulder only to find nothing and chuckled at his foolishness.

He pushed his way through old and forgotten memories until he reached a large wooden chest almost free of dust and cobwebs sitting silently as if in wait for him. Kain gently set the candlestick down on the floor and knelt in front of the chest. He swept his hand over the top to remove a thin layer of dust that had collect since it had last been opened before rubbing the brass name plate over the brass latch. Kain gazed at it a moment and sighed lowly. It read: *SIR RICHARD G. VICCON, 109th GRAND GENERAL OF ARCAINIA.* It was in this chest that held assorted memorabilia from Richard and Fang's blissful life together. Nancy had found the small silver jewelry box that Fang had left for her in this chest. The jewelry box had held a silver ring with a small diamond set in it, a promise ring Richard had given to Fang when they had courted, and a silver heart-shaped locket with a large sapphire set in the center. Kain, himself, had found many of his father's old documents and papers that were in the chest to come in handy in his military life, and his father's quest journals especially where helpful.

When Kain and Nancy were sent off to China, John Accrue went to their house and shifted through all of the contents to see what was important and what was not. It hurt him to have to do it, but he trusted no one else with the fragile memories. Much of Richard's belongings went to the Arcainian Museum in honor of the fallen hero so that he would never be forgotten. The rest was packed away and put into the castle's vault until Kain returned to collect what was rightfully his and his sister's. The house was immediately destroyed so that Richard and Fang would be remembered as how they lived instead of how they died. When Kain and Nancy returned, they collected their inheritance and built a new house over their rightful land so that they could continue on as their parents wanted them to.

Kain flipped the twin latches and opened the chest with a dull creak that was loud in the still night air. With another sigh, he began to rummage through the love letters Richard had written to Fang, painted pictures and sketches of the happy couple and family, and other items that told the story of a cherished marriage and family. Everything was arranged differently than he remembered, with most of the military documentation buried under the love notes and tokens of affection. Kain's lips twitched with a heartfelt smile as he assumed Nancy had been the last one to browse through the chest.

As he searched for the map John had told him about, he couldn't help but closely examine just about everything inside. As such, he knew that his mission would take him ten times as long, but he didn't care. He took his sweet time to gaze longingly at the memoirs and grow misty-eyed as he fondly remembered the good times he had shared with his parents.

A sudden creak behind him startled him and made him jump, juggling and almost dropping a fragile clay ornament that had been one of his mother's favorites. He silently cursed himself as he caught it just in time and set it down gently beside him before turning to see who or what it was that was coming up the ladder. It was Li. In one hand she held a flickering candle high while she used her other hand to simultaneously hold the ladder and keep her robe closed. Her hair was slightly mussed and her eyes were tiredly held half closed as she peered as deep into the attic as she could.

"Kain?" she whispered sleepily. "Is that you up here?"

"Yeah, it's just me." he told her as he continued with his search in the chest. "Sorry about waking you, darlin'."

"That's all right, sweetie." she told him. She started to enter the attic completely but thought better of it and held her position. "It's four in the morning. What are you doing up here?"

Kain frowned and raised his eyebrows. It was already past four o'clock? He had been up there for over an hour and didn't even notice it. "I'm just looking for something."

"It couldn't wah—" she gave a mighty yawn. "—wait for morning?"

"I couldn't sleep, so I figured I might as well get it done now." he replied as he moved a large stack of papers and found a leather scroll that looked fairly new. He found it odd since anything in that chest had to be well over a decade old by now. Kain snatched it up, slipped off the red ribbon that bound it shut, and examined the contents. It was a map printed on white cloth that was neither yellowed nor ragged from age. It didn't look at all familiar, and Kain wondered how in the world he had missed it after going through the chest literally hundreds of times in the past several years. His suddenly very tired mind cast off any such suspicions as he looked the map over as closely as his heavy eyelids would allow. The ink hadn't faded one bit, but instead looked like it was written a few days before. The map itself led to a hut in a wooded area a few miles away from Arcainia. Kain gave himself a quick estimate that it would take a day or so to reach, depending on any complications that arose. Satisfied, he set it behind him and began to gather everything back up into the chest.

"Go on back to bed, Li." he told her after hearing the ladder creak dully behind him.

"What about you?" she asked, giving another powerful yawn.

"Don't worry, I'm finished." he assured her as he turned her way and gave her a warm smile. "Go on back to bed."

CHAPTER VIII

"Well, today's the big day, Nancy!" Li said with much enthusiasm in her voice. "I'll bet you're excited!"

All three sat at the dining room table enjoying a delicious breakfast that Li had prepared especially for the occasion. While Nancy had dug in voraciously and Li herself had not held back, Kain was reluctant to eat, complaining that he wasn't very hungry because he hadn't gotten much sleep the night before. Li knew that it was his nerves even if he didn't want to admit it. However, after some coaxing from his ladies, he had taken a few nibbles before finding his lost appetite.

"Oh, yes! Very!" Nancy joyfully chittered between mouthfuls. "I can't wait to get to the castle! I just know it's going to be so much fun!"

Kain regarded her with a raised eyebrow. "Fun isn't exactly the word I would use."

Nancy regarded him with a raised eyebrow of her own before returning her attention back onto her plate. Li took notice and grinned. The two siblings acted so much alike sometimes, it was uncanny.

"What time should we leave?" Li asked.

"Let's not worry about that." Kain told her, throwing a bright grin her way. "We'll leave when we leave. I want to spend these last few moments enjoying this wonderful food with the both of you in a nice, peaceful setting. Goddess knows when it'll happen again."

Nancy looked at him and smiled radiantly. Kain regarded her with a wavy grin. She didn't seem to be fazed in the least by the grotesque pictures the Shazadia report had created. He had let her read it the day before and he wanted to say that she took it better than he thought she would, but he really wasn't sure. He did have to admit, however, that she most certainly did have guts and determination, and plenty of both.

Sometimes that's all you need.' he remembered his father had told him many a time.

Kain had figured that the girl would have only gotten two paragraphs into it before she threw it down like a hot coal and begged Kain to drop her from the quest.

However, what had actually happened was far more different. She had read through it entirely, never turning away in disgust or gasping in horror. She hadn't cried, and although she had been clearly disgusted she hadn't seemed to be frightened by it. If anything, it had only served to enrage her further, her revulsion fueling her fury. As she read, she had been silent and had an eerie calmness to her. Kain had noticed a kind of fire in the young girl's eyes spark up that grew with each passing word. At first, she had simply murmured 'ICCK' and flinched slightly, but as she read on her eyes had grown harder and she had ceased to flinch even as her hate filled eyes had flittered over the most intense parts. Her face twisted not in terror, but in pure rage. Kain had seen the same look in the faces of his men on the battlefield as they lost close friends, but never so intense and most certainly never in his little sister. If Kain had still held any doubts about how she would handle herself in battle, they had been thrown out the window at that moment.

After she had finished, she didn't scream, cry out, or throw the papers to the floor like he had wanted to do when he had read it. Nancy had simply lowered the report from her gaze, neatly arranged the papers, placed them back into the folder, and handed it all back to Kain. She had done all of this with very calm and cool movements, slow and icy with her eyes hard and her once pretty face held in a vicious scowl. She had looked Kain in the eyes as she handed him the report and at first he had been afraid to accept it. He had never seen her like that before, and the seemingly cool and calm way she was moving despite the feelings her face gave away had gripped his heart in a block of pure ice. Kain didn't rightly understand the root of Nancy's hate for Noknor. After all, she had been so little, only a little baby when their parents were murdered. She hadn't witnessed their gruesome deaths as he had. She hadn't seen the look of tortured pain on their faces, or heard their screams as splashes of their blood drenched the spots where he used to play. Even more than that, she couldn't have remembered them as the wonderful, loving, kind people that they were. And yet, it seemed that she had even more anger boiling in her heart than he did. He could almost feel the hate emanate from her like a wave of intense heat wafting over him. He could literally see the anger boil in her ice-cold eyes. Her devilish sneer bared her teeth in such a way that she ceased to look like the sweet innocent girl he thought he knew and turned her into a powerful she-beast with vengeance in her heart.

And then, with nothing more, her face had softened and her mouth had loosened. The flicker of hate had still burned in her innocent eyes, but it hadn't been as prominent as it had moments before. She had seemed to be different. It was as if some very angry spirit had taken over her body and then had let her go. Kain hadn't been sure what to make of her and hadn't known what to do. Finally, he did the only thing that had felt right in his heart. He leaned forward and gave her a mighty hug to let her know that he would always be there with her.

"Well, we'd better get ready." Kain finally said, rubbing his mouth with his forearm. Li slapped at his wrist crossly and threw his napkin at him. He chuckled as he finished saying "I want to stop somewhere before we head to the castle."

They quickly set their plates in the kitchen sink and hurried off to their appointed rooms. Kain shut his door and went to his closet. He withdrew a neatly cleaned and pressed dark blue tunic and a pair of pants made from sturdy fabric of the same color and tossed them on his bed before taking out a pair of knee-high thick black leather boots, the top of the foot and shin armored with heavy steel plates painted dark blue. He quickly dressed, put on a dark blue leather-padded waistcoat with coat-of-arms of the Kingdom of Arcainia embroidered on the front. Then he clasped a heavy dark blue hooded cloak around his neck and wrapped his battlebelt around his waist. The cloak identified him as the Grand General of Arcainia while the battlebelt held the sheaths for his dagger and broadsword as well as pouches for his money, spare canteen, and any other special items he might need to have on his person. All of his other weapons, armor, and his loaded down backpack were waiting for him at the castle as were Nancy's.

Kain strolled over to his dresser where he took a small jade medallion that he placed into his pocket. Finally, with a sigh of satisfaction, he looked himself over in the mirror, grinned at the good-looking guy that stared back at him, and turned to leave. He made it halfway before remembering something special and moving back to his dresser. He opened the top drawer, grabbed another good luck medallion, this one of bronze, and stuffed it into his pocket as well.

Nancy and Li were both waiting for him in the living room. Nancy wore an outfit just like Kain's except for she didn't have an Arcainian Grand General's cloak and the markings on her padded waist coat were a bit different, denoting her as a soldier rather than general although there was no actual rank insignia anywhere on her uniform. Also, even though it was basically the same outfit, Nancy did seem to have a much more feminine look to her. Kain grinned as he thought 'Guess not even a soldier's uniform can hide that figure. Just like her cousin.'

He looked to Li and saw that she was wearing another Arcainian-style dress. Though it was not as luxurious as the one she wore previously and her long hair was hanging down carelessly, she still managed to look quite lovely.

"So, where are we headed to first?" Nancy asked after they all did a once over with each other.

"The Shrine." Kain murmured, gripping Li's hand fondly and wrapping his other arm around Nancy's waist as they walked to the door.

"Oh, goody! The Shrine!" Nancy cheered gleefully in excitement.

Nancy absolutely adored the Arcainia City Shrine of Auset. It was such an awe inspiring, heavenly place. The main part, the area open to the public, was a large and exotic courtyard complete with a long rectangular shallow pool filled with all kinds of attractive fish of all shapes, sizes, and colors. Many different species of plants, all with vividly colored flowers grew from the neatly trimmed lush green grass while tall sycamore trees were spaced evenly apart. Most of the trees had stone benches under the full branches so patrons could sit and just enjoy the beauty of the place. All of the bright plant life gave the Shrine a nice and warm lively sort of feel to it.

A cobblestone pathway made from brightly colored stones started at the stone entry archway, circled the pool, and wound its way to a small covered pavilion. Twelve massive stone pillars holding up the sky, six on each side of the courtyard, were carved with decorative pictures and inscribed with a different story written in elaborate Old Arcainian hieroglyphic script. There were even wooden poles with notches in them scattered around and when the wind blew, the poles each made a different whistling sound to create sweet music. The priests and priestesses that took care of the Shrine and conducted the ritual services were all very helpful and friendly, always ready with a smile to offer aid in any form. Everything about the Shrine was flawless, and it was a place of true serenity dedicated to the beloved Divine Mother.

The trio turned to go under the stone archway and Li gasped in awe. She had seen the place many times before, but it never ceased to amaze her, much like Arcainia Castle. They immediately caught sight of a young priestess not much older than Nancy sweeping the pathway ahead of them. She looked up and smiled brightly when she saw whom it was.

"Good morning, Sir Viccon and Miss Hua! Hello, Nancy!" she called, pausing in her work and resting against the broom.

"Hi-hi, Jennifer!" Nancy called back. As they walked towards her so that Kain could catch a few words with the priestess, a low mewl caught her ear. She turned to see a beautiful black cat sitting a few feet away from her.

The beautiful creature mewed lowly as it hopped off the pool's granite edge and minced over to where the young girl stood. Nancy grinned when the cat rubbed against her legs fondly and bent low to pet its furry little head and scratch behind its ears. It gave a low purr, arching its back and rubbing harder against her. When its tail swished back and forth, it brushed Nancy's nose and mouth, making her giggle.

"You're such a pretty kitty, yes you are!" Nancy cooed, her hand stroking the cat from the top of its head to the very tip of its tail and both loving it. "Yes, you are! Yes, you are! You're just the prettiest little thing! You're the sweetest little kitty—"

"Nancy! Come on, darlin'!" Kain called, catching her attention.

Kain and Li had already finished talking with Jennifer and were headed for the covered pavilion. The young priestess wore a smile on her lips as she watched Nancy kiss the kitty good-bye and hurry to catch up with her brother. The cat started to follow, but decided it wasn't worth the effort after a few steps. Jennifer continued her chore while the cat strode prissily back to its original spot to watch the fish with idle curiosity.

The pavilion housed a large rectangular altar made of polished sycamore wood. The front was decorated with bright colors and elegant hieroglyph pictures surrounding a painted picture of a gorgeous lady in a blue dress with long black hair and a willowy thin figure sitting on a golden throne. A small beautifully and vibrantly sculpted statue silently stood on the altar with a loving smile and outstretched arms. On Her arms were long wings with feathers painted in bright, brilliant colors and a pair of golden cow horns with a solar disc set between them stood atop Her head, a symbol sacred to Her children.

They were mildly surprised to find that no one else was there to pay homage and the long praying banister before the altar was empty. Nancy and Kain approached the altar and kneeled on the fluffy red cushion while Li hung back a moment before finally deciding to kneel beside Kain. Even though she wasn't of their religion, she figured that it wouldn't hurt any. Kain and Nancy bowed their heads, made a fist with their right hands and placed it against their left palm, and proceeded to pray. Li watched, but didn't follow in suite and chose to simply wait kneeling.

'Oh, my Divine Mother,' Kain prayed in his thoughts. 'I beseech you to please hear my prayers and watch over me and my sister in our greatest hour of need! Please guide us well on our journey and keep us well protected from all harm and evil. Please especially watch over my sister, she will need your loving wings of protection more than I. Please . . . please let me have made the right decision. Please watch over her and guard her closely. My Mother, I love you very much and I thank you for all of your blessings. Oh Beautiful Mother, Queen of Queens, Heavenly Enchantress, Goddess of Heaven Auset, please bless us always, and protect my Nancy always. Please helps us achieve victory over evil.'

* * *

When they finally arrived at the castle, all thirty Arcainian soldiers were already standing around the gym in clustered groups, talking excitedly about their upcoming battles. Raphael, Michael, and a third Arcainian Knight were standing behind a large podium on a small stage having a quiet conversation of their own. When Raphael saw them enter, he and the other two males instantly headed to greet them. Li immediately recognized the third man as Sir Robert Grotz, the Master Scout of the Arcainian Army. He was the general in charge of all of the scouting and reconnaissance units of the army, those specially trained knights charged with seeking out valuable information and detecting possible threats to better prepare advancing Arcainian forces. Sir Grotz had been strangely absent from the meetings, conducting some mission for Kain. Li had remembered her cousin voicing once or twice his fears that Sir Grotz possibly not making it back in time to join his team. She was very glad to see the scouting general as she knew that it was at least one load off of Kain's chest.

"Good morning, Grand General!" Robert boomed in a voice that wasn't too heavy but still quite strong. He and Kain gripped hands in the air as if arm-wrestling, flexing their arms slightly, their forearm muscles tensing in their macho handshake. "Together again, ne?"

"Glad you could make it." Kain said, finally releasing his grip. "I was afraid you wouldn't get back in time."

"Man, I wouldn't miss this party for the world!" Robert laughed boisterously.

"You have been briefed about everything, I assume."

"Hello, fair ladies." Michael delivered a fancy bow to Nancy and Li while Kain and Robert talked business. He reached for their hands, pecked their warm flesh, and clicked his tongue. "How are you today?"

"Fine." Nancy giggled, taking her hand back. "Hello, Ralph."

Raphael grinned brightly. Nancy was the only one who called him 'Ralph' and he didn't mind one bit. "What took you guys so long?"

"Oh, we stopped by the Shrine." she told him cheerfully.

"Cool. Guess I should have too. Oh, well too late for that now, I suppose. So, are you excited about going on your first quest?"

"Hey, Michael." Li murmured, pulling the prince back a little bit. "How old is Robert?"

"Grotz?" Michael said, glancing back at him. "Thirty-something, I think."

The prince started to call out to Robert, but was stopped when he heard Li ask "Is he single?"

"Why? Are you looking?" Michael laughed.

"Not for myself." Li grinned, throwing an implying look Nancy's way.

"LI!" Nancy yelped, her face flushing bright red.

"He's way too old for her!" Raphael scowled heatedly, crossing his arms faster than he should have.

Both Li and Michael gave him sly grins while Nancy smiled behind her blush, thrilled that he was sticking up for her. It was Raphael's turn to blush while the pair stared at him with cocked eyebrows. Raphael couldn't think of a thing to say that would throw the attention off of him, and he was dying under those grins. As luck would have it, Kain stepped forward and introduced Li to Robert.

"Greetings, Miss Hua." he told her. "It's always a pleasure to see you. I am a bit disappointed that Kain just told me that you won't be joining us."

"Thank you." Li smiled, bowing her head slightly. "It was a hard decision, but the right one I think." She gave him a wink. "I stand by it."

"Well, maybe something else will come up again where we can see you in action. Kain always brags how you make any fight more exciting." Robert returned the wink, making Li giggle and roll her eyes sheepishly.

"Is everyone here?" Kain asked his Second General.

"Yes, sir." Raphael saluted in professional manner. "Thirty men ready for your orders."

Kain stiffened as he turned to face Li. He looked her over fondly before he grasped her hands gently. They made eye contact and held it tightly, fighting back the tears welling up in their eyes.

"Xiaoxin!" Li yelped, fighting back a lump in her throat. She smiled with a sniffle as she murmured "I'm not going to be there to save your butt this time."

"Okay." Kain chuckled, giving her hands a squeeze. "Try not to get too bored. If you do you can always go see John."

She cocked her moist eyes and uttered a wavy snicker as her emotions began to choke her up. She threw his hands down and leaped into his awaiting arms for a strong hug.

"I'm going to miss you so much, girl!" he sighed, squeezing her tight.

She gave him a warm kiss on his cheek and squeezed him tightly once more before pulling out of his grasp. Li turned to Nancy and placed her hands on her shoulders as she told her young cousin "Looking good, kiddo! I'm sure you're going to become a huge thorn in Noknor's side!" She embraced her tightly and sighed "Ji xiang ruyi!"

"Xiexie." she whispered lowly, returning the hug with a kiss on the cheek. "I'm gonna miss you!"

In response, Li gazed into her dark eyes and ran her fingers through her silky hair before brushing her lips softly against the girl's forehead. She smiled as she wiped away the tear trickling down her cheek.

"Well, I'd better get going." Kain sighed, motioning towards the podium. "I'm sure the troops are waiting."

With that, he slowly started for the steps that lead up onto the stage. Li took a small step forward and felt something bump against her thigh. It quickly reminded her of something.

"Kain, wait!" she called, rushing to him. "I almost forgot! I have something for you." She reached into her pocket and pulled out a beautiful amulet. Three green jade Chinese dragons formed a triangle around a sparkling ruby heart that seemed to glow in her hands. The dragons were each inscribed with a word: *AMOR VINCIT OMNIA*. Li hung the brass chain around Kain's neck and pecked his cheek as a princess would award a medal to a brave knight.

He examined the strange piece of jewelry and gasped "Your Dragon Heart?"

The Dragon's Heart was a very special Hua family heirloom, passed down her father's bloodline for generations to the first born son along with a special fighting style and a strange weapon known as the Dragon Claw. As her father had not been given a son, Li had been passed these gifts to carry on the Hua family legacy. The inscription was a mystery to everyone and to Li's knowledge, Amor Vincit Omnia had never been translated. She just assumed, like every first born son before her, that it was the language of the dragons.

Li nodded sweetly. "Take it with you. It'll bring you luck and protect you in your hour of need. Wear it always and know that I will always be with you in your heart."

"Thank you, Li. I'll never take it off." Kain told her with a deep sigh as she put her arms around him once more. After a moment he grinned "I've got a speech to make."

Kain pulled himself out of her arms and headed up the stage. As he walked to the podium, he banged the wall with his fist for their attention. The hollow thud echoed over the men's voices and laughter, catching all of their eyes and instantly silencing the room to the point where one could actually hear the low breathing of every person in the room. All of the men obediently hurried to line up at attention for their general. As all of the soldiers hurriedly bustled around to their spots, Nancy followed Raphael to the front where Kain and Michael were standing.

When everything was at last quiet and calm, Kain looked to his troops and called out in a loud, clear voice "As you all know, I'm not one for speeches so I'll make this brief. You are all very brave knights and I wish to personally thank you for helping me on this quest. This one is very important to me and my sister, as I'm sure you all know. I trust you've all met her and will do your best to make her feel welcome in our little troop. It goes without saying that this mission will be very dangerous, the foe we are facing is powerful and deadly. So I want all of you to be careful so that every one of you to will come back safe and sound. After all, you must be able to relate the stories of your great Grand General in action to your families." This got a round of amused chuckles all over the gym. "That is really all I have to say, I guess. In closing, I'd just like to say **LET'S GO KICK NOKNOR AND HIS FELLOW FREAKS RIGHT IN THEIR TINY KAHONEZ!**"

There was a huge cheer that rocked the gym and startled Nancy so much that she jumped in shock and gave a surprised squeak. Then, as the cheering persisted, she glanced at Kain and, seeing him looking at her with an amused grin spread across his face, blushed deeply and giggled sheepishly. Everyone in the troop was hooting and hollering as they marched out of the gym, through the halls, and out of the castle to where their horses were ready and waiting. As they rode through the streets of Arcainia, Nancy saw that just about everyone in the city had turned out to see them off. All around her people crowded along the sidewalks cheering them and waving gayly. She saw teachers and students, friends and neighbors, and whole families gathered together, admiring the Arcainian soldiers. Admiring her, an Arcainian soldier. Why, even the schools had let out early and the merchants at the Square had closed their shops that morning to stand outside their businesses and catch a glimpse of the knights. The soldiers were congratulated with boisterous cheers as they proudly rode down the main street of Arcainia City. She saw the children looking at them with admiring eyes, dreaming of someday being the ones wearing shining armor and carrying powerful weapons to combat evil. She remembered that she used to be one of those children.

Then, suddenly, she somehow heard the sound of familiar voices calling her name over the roaring commotion. She looked to her left and saw Dafne and Romi on the sidewalk waving and shouting excitedly to her and jumping up and down in girlish glee. Nancy smiled and waved her hand vigorously back at them the whole time she passed her two best friends. Nancy was overwhelmed by all of the excitement that was exploding all around her and it wasn't long before the mood got to her and made her cheer loudly along side her brother as they rode out of the city and into adventure.

* * *

Noknor peered deep into the large crystal set in a massive hand of twisted black onyx and frowned slightly as he watched the small band of Arcainian soldiers exit the city.

"Excellent!" he chuckled lowly, running his hand over the glass ball. The image faded slightly and recast on another view of the marching army as Noknor's raven found a different perch in Arcainia City. "He's on his way."

"It's about time! I personally can't wait until you crush him like the bug he is. Just like you crushed those pathetic Shazadians." Garrison grinned at the thought, sitting back in his chair. Another thought entered his head and his grin widened. "Just like I'll crush that Chinese woman."

"Hmph. You underestimate your enemy, Garrison." Noknor replied, casting an eye the Dark General's way. He snapped his fingers and the image on the crystal suddenly vanished. "It will be your undoing, I'm afraid."

"I'll be damned if I let that chinky *woman* beat me!" Garrison snorted with disgust. Realizing the tone he had just spoken with, he sat straight up and quickly added "No offense, my lord."

"None taken." Noknor murmured lowly, pushing the air down with a flat palm. The twisted onyx hand shuddered slightly before being swallowed down into the ground. He sighed lowly as he sat back and put his chin in his hand, thinking about his next course of action.

"Speaking about her, my lord," Garrison murmured, a sinister smile setting onto his hard jaw. "When do you want—"

"We'll wait a day and let Viccon get far enough away." Noknor grinned a toothy grin as he reached a hand to his chest and gently rubbed. He could feel the amulet under his shirt warm slightly and he chuckled evilly.

CHAPTER IX

Li stood in the middle of Kain's cleared away living room, her brow moistened with sweat and her breathing slow and deep. She had been practicing and perfecting her already perfect fighting moves all morning long in the spacious Viccon backyard, moving with the soft breeze as easily as a leaf blowing gaily about. She twirled her arms about and spun on her toes, her legs kicking like a dancer's, flowing like water in a gentle stream. She executed each kick and punch combination flawlessly, looking very much at peace as she flew rapidly across the grass, her limbs making sharp swishing sounds as they cut the air as cleanly as a razor. Every movement of her Long Ching Shin fighting style came without thought or force, her limber body twisting and bending elegantly in a stunning display of deadly beauty and lethal grace.

After several hours, she had finally stopped and gone into the house for a short break. As she stood idly with a glass of refreshing water in hand, she tried to figure out what she would do for the rest of the day. She had spent the previous two days cleaning and straightening up the house and washing clothes because when Kain and Nancy finally came home, she wanted them to be able to relax in a fresh, sparkling house. After two days of work, she had run out of chores to keep herself occupied and so searched for other things to occupy her and help the days pass faster.

There was always shopping, or reading, or she could go out with some of the friends she had made while in Arcainia; they would be ready for lunch breaks soon. It was such a lovely day, maybe she could head to the park and do some sketching. But nothing really seemed to interest her. It just wasn't the same not having Kain and Nancy around. She hated being by herself and began to wonder if she should have gone with them after all. Eh, it was too late for that now. Might as well make the best of things. She'd find some way to entertain herself.

She took another long drink from the glass as her mind switched gears. Kain and Nancy. She missed them already. She just wished that there were some way that she could get in touch with them, but there would be no word until they accomplished their mission, of which Li had no doubt in her mind that they would most certainly do. Of course, that didn't stop the worrying one bit.

She reached the bottom of the glass and looked at the large clock.

'Break's over' she thought dully as she placed her glass onto a small table. She wiped off her brow and prepared to go back outside. A loud knock echoed through the quiet, empty house, the sudden noise startling her with a jump and a high squeal. She giggled at her foolishness as she went to answer the door. As she started to open it, the door was thrown open and a large man wearing a nondescript Arcainian style suit leaped upon her, pinning her to the floor.

"I don't reckon I've ever seen yellow breasts before!" he growled, his breath stinking of rotten filth as saliva seeped off of his green teeth.

"And I don't 'reckon' you ever will!" Li sneered in disgust as she put her feet on his chest and pushed him off. The man flew through the air and crashed into the wall with enough force to make him see stars. Li was on him even before his vision had time to refocus, and she gripped his head, throwing his face down as hard as she could. His skull smacked loudly against the floorboard, rebounded up, and was slammed right back down a second time as the thunderous *CRACK* echoed through the still living room. The man was either out cold or dead, Li didn't care which as she stood up, dusted herself off, and kicked the man hard in the side. She spat on his motionless body and muttered "Pig!"

Suddenly, five more men wearing similar Arcainian suits rushed through the door, surrounding her as they brandished their weapons of choice. Two had wide, flat swords and two had wooden clubs with the broad tips wrapped in what looked to be strands of rubber. The fifth man held a small crossbow that couldn't have been very powerful, but in such close quarters was still lethal. Li looked around at all of them, examining them. She had no idea who they were or why they were so angry with her; she didn't remember ticking anyone off lately. She quickly deduced that Noknor had sent them and that they were probably Dark Knights in disguise.

"Looks like my work-out just got interesting." she murmured to herself as a wide grin set on her lips. She smoothly shifted her body into her Long Ching Shin fighting stance and mockingly asked "Alright, you boys wanna play? Who's going to be first, hmmm?"

In response, the two Dark Knights with clubs approached her menacingly while the other three stood back and watched as Li examined her options. When the evil warriors rushed her on either side with their arms cocked back ready to send out a flurry of blows meant to pound her into submission, Li, quick as flash, ducked at the last moment in a spinning movement. Her leg lashed out, tripping one of the men. As he fell with a surprised grunt, Li continued to spin, pushing herself up just enough to kick the second man in the side. She leapt up in an instant, and before the man even had time to yelp at the pain in his ribs, Li smacked her foot across the man's face. The first, having picked himself back up, rushed at her, shrieking in fury. Li shifted her eyes and slid to the side, moving like a skater on ice as the man's club came down hard. The club was not meant to work as a lethal weapon, but instead to subdue an opponent as the rubber covered tip helped to cushion blows so that a person could be hit hard enough to knock the fight out of them but not do any serious damage. However, the force of the club coupled with the angle it struck the second man's head was enough to hammer his skull with a killing blow.

The first attacker was horrified at what he had accidentally done and Li took the chance to take him out. She used the split second of distraction to quickly wrap her arms around his neck and, with a sharp motion of her arms, snapped his neck like a dry twig. She dropped the listless body, which hit the ground with a dull thud, and turned to face the other three men with a smug smirk and innocent giggle.

This enraged the remaining attackers further, they were already angry about her so easily dispatching their two cohorts and the two swordsmen howled a horrid battle cry as they rushed to destroy the demure woman.

"No scratches!" the man with the crossbow barked at them. "Use the flats of your swords!"

Li pretty much guessed that he was the one in charge of such a loutish crew. Obviously she was to be taken alive, and that worked well with her. It just made it that much easier on her. With that in mind, she decided to have a little fun with them, make sure they regretted being assigned the job.

The swordsman to reach her first swung his weapon with enough force to lop off her head as the leader snarled at him to be careful, lest he pay the price with Lord Noknor.

'So they do belong to Noknor.' Li thought as she ducked clear and punched him hard in the gut, the breath instantly knocked out of him as he doubled over in pain. Li quickly jumped to her feet, broke his nose with a well placed punch, and leapt out of the way just as the other sword came crashing down, barely missing her ankle and sticking into the wooden floor. The Dark Knight swore violently as he tried to wrench his blade free. Before he could, however, Li's foot roundhoused his head, knocking him back. He hissed a curse as his eye began to swell into an ugly dark purple mass and rushed her again. Li sidestepped, placed her hands on his back, and brought up her knee up, catching him hard in the gut. Then she threw him down hard, right next to the sword still stuck in the floor. The Dark Knight quickly reached for it with both hands to try once more to yank it free. Li was instantly upon him. She placed both of her hands firmly onto his wrists, brought her knee up sharply into his elbows, and broke both of his arms with a resounding *CRACK*. He shrieked as excruciating pain flooded his limbs and howled madly as he watched his arms bend in horrid ways.

"Oh, shut up you big baby!" Li retorted with a snicker as she kicked his knee so that it bent at an odd angle. "Would you like some cheese with that whine? Tee-hee!"

The Dark Knight wailed in agony and crumpled to the ground, his body twitching in violent spasms. Li looked at him for a moment before she slammed her foot down hard onto his chest. His sternum splintered from his ribs, puncturing his lungs and crushing his heart without even breaking the skin. Li, pleased with her handiwork, smiled and lifted her foot off of the pitiful, dying wretch.

Suddenly, the remaining swordsman grabbed her from behind while his supervisor aimed his crossbow at her. She noticed that the tip of the dart glistened with a clear sticky fluid and she didn't know if it was poison or a drug, but she sure didn't want to find out the hard way.

Li struggled to pull free, but the slime held her tight and chuckled evilly at her futile attempts. She watched the Dark Knight's finger tighten on the trigger, waiting for the right moment and knowing that timing was critical if she wanted to live. When she saw him slowly pull it, she snapped her head back, the back of her skull crashing into her captor's already broken nose as a loud TWANG echoed through the now still house. His grip instantly loosened and she flew forward, just out of the way of the dart that struck his shoulder.

Li quickly grabbed him and threw him into his friend, both men tumbling hard onto the ground. The swordsman was either dead or out cold, Li couldn't tell and didn't really care as long as he was out of the picture. The other pushed him off his body with a struggle and stood up as he fumbled with his crossbow, trying desperately to reload it. Li punched him twice in the face, grabbed his ears, and introduced his face to her knee five times before using the heel of her hand to shove his nose fatally into his brain.

As she dusted off her hands triumphantly, Li cocked her eyebrow and retorted "Well, that was fun! I do hope there's more of them."

Suddenly, discreetly dressed Dark Knights poured into the house, all with murder in their eyes and clubs in their hands. As they rushed to capture her, she got into stance and sighed "Me and my big mouth."

* * *

Kain halted his troops in front of a large stone hut in the middle of a small wood. He pulled out the leather folder from his pack and untied the ribbon. As he looked over the piece of beautiful cloth, Nancy rode up beside him and looked curiously over his shoulder.

"Whatcha looking at?" she inquired.

"One of dad's old maps." he muttered, not looking up. After a few seconds, he finally closed the leather folder, tied the ribbon back up, and shoved it back into his pack. With a grunt and a shrug he murmured "This must be the place."

"Can I go in with you?" the girl asked. If Kain heard her, he didn't show it. Nancy sighed dully.

When Kain dismounted, the others followed in suite and gathered around their leader as he studied the simple hut of stone blocks trying to decide what to do. He had no idea what to expect going in there and had to be careful. It had been a very long time since his father had come here to see the Sisters and Kain wasn't sure if they would still be around. The place wasn't exactly a shrine to them, or at least didn't seem like one. It was very possible that they might have left and something else might have taken over the hut. Kain knew that forest trolls were known be in the area and that they could have decided to use the place in their absence. Kain walked over to the door and knelt down to examine the ground before it. He found no fresh tracks and deduced that nothing had gone into the hut for quite some time. Or come out, for that matter. By all points, it seemed that the hut had been abandoned and that little, if anything would be inside. Still, faeries like the Uraeus Sister probably didn't leave tracks.

"What do you think, Robert?" Kain asked his Master Scout. Robert voiced the same thoughts as Kain, so after careful consideration of these points, Kain finally looked over his crew and gestured to Michael and Raphael as he ordered "Okay, Nancy and I are going in. I want you two to stay out here and cover us. Robert, take your men and see what you find around the immediate area. Report anything that seems the least bit out of place."

They all nodded their understanding and saluted him as they hurried about their assignments. Kain saluted back before he turned to a brightly smiling Nancy. He wasn't sure exactly why he wanted her to go in with him, and nearly recanted his previous order. Howver, something gnawed at him to take her with him, so instead he told her "I'm not sure if the Sisters are still here or not so be on your guard. Come on."

With that, Kain gripped the handle of his sword and walked up to the large wooden door with Nancy right by his side. He knocked loudly but received no answer. He looked at his sister to make sure that she was ready before pushing the heavy door open and walking in first. Inside, the siblings saw three beautiful young ladies. They all looked exactly the same, a group of triplets, with long hair, fair skin, long limbs, and sharp facial features. There was only one difference and that was that they all had different colored hair. The first, Urd, had dark hair, Beldandi had brown hair, and Skuld had light, almost white, hair. Nancy had remembered that, among other things, the Sisters were elements of time: Urd the Past, Beldandi the Present, and Skuld the Future. She glanced at Kain, wondering if he also knew that or if she should tell him. Deciding it was unimportant and not wanting to draw attention to herself, she kept her mouth shut.

The pair watched as the beautiful ladies stood around a glowing ball of green light chanting in an odd tongue neither Kain nor Nancy had ever heard before much less understood. As the ladies chanted, the ball grew brighter and brighter and fierce howling like that of a powerful wind filled the air causing them to chant louder and louder until they were yelling to make themselves heard. The sisters' hair whipped about and their loose dresses flapped wildly even though nothing else in the room including the humans that stood less than twenty feet away were affected by the mysterious wind. The more the sisters chanted, the brighter the ball got and the fiercer the wind sounded until the light was so bright and the wind so loud that Kain and Nancy had to shield their eyes and cover their ears, impulsively bracing themselves from the wind that wasn't really there.

Then all of a sudden everything stopped. The throbbing ball of light was gone and the intense howling had been cut off by silence. It was like a candle's flame being snuffed out. The ladies, satisfied with their work, remained standing around a strange and colorful alter left behind by the ball of green light. Two of them immediately engaged in lively conversation while Urd looked straight into Kain's eyes and smiled brightly.

"*Why, sisters! It appears we have a guest!*" she squeaked joyfully. "*Look, it is Kain!*"

"*Kain?*" Beldandi and Skuld murmured with voices identical to Urd's.

"*Why yes! He has finally come.*" Urd told them.

"*And brought Nancy with him!*" Beldandi pointed and smiled at Nancy.

"*How goes you, Kain and Nancy Viccon, heirs to the Viccon bloodline?*" Skuld bowed. The other two took notice and bowed also as they asked "*Yes, how?*"

"How . . . how do you know who we are?" Kain asked slowly.

"*We are the Uraeus Sisters.*" said Urd.

"*We know all.*" said Beldandi.

"*We know why you have come to us.*" said Skuld.

"*You want the Elemental Sword to avenge the deaths of your beloved father and mother at the hands of the wicked, wicked Noknor.*"

"Yes!" Kain exclaimed excitedly. "Will you please give it to me! I beg you!"

At Kain's response, the sisters began to laugh gleefully as if Kain had just said the funniest thing in the world. And to them, he had.

"*You beg us to give it to you?*"

"What's so funny about that?" Nancy snapped savagely, not really remembering whom she was talking to as she tried to stick up for her brother.

"*Such a fiery tone of voice.*"

"*You must truly love your brother.*"

"*You risk your life barking at us to defend his honor.*"

"Please forgive her, Sisters! She didn't mean to attack you like that! She just—"

"*She did.*"

"*She'd do it again.*"

"*She did it for you because she loves you.*"

"*And that is the only reason we do not take offense.*"

Kain glanced at Nancy who had a worried look spread over her face. Kain smiled and gave her head a loving caress, gently running his fingers through her silky hair. Nancy grinned with relief and turned her attention back to the sisters as she constantly reminded herself to think before she spoke out in their presence.

"*The answer is quiet clear, human.*"

"*It is not ours to give.*"

"*It belongs to the Ladys of the Elements.*"

"Will you please tell me how to reach them?" Kain pleaded. "I need that weapon! I fear that I can not defeat Noknor without its power."

"*Yes, we could just tell you.*"

"*But how do we know that you, like you father, are worthy enough to wield the Sword of the Ladys?*"

"*Let alone stand before the mighty Ladys themselves.*"

"*We propose a test.*"

"*A test to prove your worth.*"

"*You must go into the Forest of Souls.*"

"Forest of Souls?" Kain raised his brow.

"*Are you frightened, Sir Kain Viccon?*"

"Of course not!" Nancy told them for her brother. "My brother's not afraid of anything. Isn't that right, Kain?" He blushed and started to mumble uneasily, but was interrupted by Beldandi.

"*You think highly of your brother.*"

"*And so you may.*"

"*He is your light.*"

"What do you mean?" Nancy asked with a confused frown, but the sisters appeared not to have heard her.

"*You must go into the Forest of Souls.*"

"*Siblings must work together.*"

"*If you hope to survive.*"

"Work together!" Kain exclaimed. "But I can't take Nancy in there with me! It's much too dangerous for her."

"*We didn't say you had to.*" Urd grinned.

"*We said you must work together.*" Beldandi replied.

"*Aid each other.*" Skuld told them.

"I understand." Kain nodded, even though he really did not at all. "What do I have—"

"*You must fetch us a gift.*"

"*A very special herb.*"

"*The mandrake.*"

"The mandrake!" Kain gasped in fearful awe.

* * *

When they finally got back outside, Kain told everyone what the Uraeus Sisters required of him. Michael was shocked to hear the impossible demand and voiced his opinions openly. Raphael had no idea what the mandrake was, but he kept his mouth shut for the time being.

"You are going to WHAT!" Michael cried out.

"I'm going into the Forest of Souls so that I can get the Uraeus Sisters some mandrake." Kain replied simply, as if he were simply going to the market to buy oranges.

"Have you gone insane?" Michael bellowed, faintly reminding Kain of the prince's mother. "The forest is bad enough without you messing with that damned plant!"

"Well, now I really don't have a choice, do I?" Kain returned without taking offense to the prince's tone as he tightened one of the saddlebags on his horse. He noticed Raphael's blank stare and asked what was wrong.

"What's so bad about mandrake?" he inquired.

Nancy was quick with an explanation. "The mandrake is a powerful herb . . . ah, a faery plant actually. The root resembles a person and is said to have a soul. When the plant is pulled up from the earth, the soul escapes and screams out. If you were to hear it, it would drive you insane. That's if you didn't die first, of course."

"Ugh! How awful!" he gasped, realizing why there was such a fuss.

"Yeah." Nancy agreed wholeheartedly as she wrinkled her nose in mutual distaste. She turned to her brother with an idea. "I think I might be able to help you, Kain."

"Unless you're a sorceress, I don't see how." Michael muttered blandly.

"I'm no sorceress, but I do have an idea. You see, I have some wax in here somewhere." she told him, probing through her pack. "When I get bored, I like to pass the time by playing with it and molding it into shapes. Anywayz, you can put a little in your ears. Then you won't be able to hear those dreadful screams and you won't go insane or die! Ahah! Here it is!" she smiled triumphantly as she produced a large wad of bee wax and handed it over to her brother.

Kain accepted it with great praise and thanks, frowning slightly behind his grateful smile. Nancy had just helped him with his task, and she didn't need to go into the forest. Was that . . . was that what the faery sisters were talking about?

After they had collected Robert and his scouts and had received their report, the group journeyed on towards the infamous Forest of Souls. Raphael rode up beside Nancy and mumbled in a weak, nervous tone "That-that . . . that was a great idea. You're . . . you're really clever, Nancy."

"Oh. Thank you, Ralph." Nancy whispered with a slightly blushed face as she flashed Raphael her dazzling smile.

* * *

Back at Kain's house, Li had taken out quite a number of Dark Knights before being overwhelmed and taken prisoner. Many armed guards ready to attack if she moved the wrong way, a menacing Dark General, and a very flustered Noknor escorted her down the hallway of the castle of blood in shackles. Even though she was seemingly at the mercy of Noknor and his minions, she was very rude to her "hosts" and delighted in causing trouble every chance she got.

"You'll never get away with this!" she snapped viciously in her most annoying matter-of-fact voice. "Kain's going to come and chop each and every one of you into itty-bitty pieces!"

Noknor spun around and thundered "If you don't shut that foolish mouth of yours right now, I'm going to gut you like a FISH!"

"I won't shut up! Do what you will! Kain's going to slaughter you!" she rebutted. Then she added for good measure "Fatso!"

Noknor snapped. With a tremendous roared, he shot a bolt of pure energy aimed for her forehead. It missed, coming inches from her scalp. Li looked at him with wide, heated eyes as if she couldn't believe what he had just done and shouted "Hey, watch the hair, you idiot!"

Noknor glared at her with stunned eyes and a dropped jaw, his hand impulsively releasing his staff, which clattered noisily to the floor and echoed through the hall. He shook his head to clear his mind and quickly snatched up his staff. Then, still watching Li with uncertainty, he spoke his orders, telling his minions to take her to the dungeon and get her out of his sight. Li grinned with satisfaction at the ever so slight tremble in his voice. The Dark General bowed and started to lead her away. Noknor thought for a second before holding up his hand and stating "No, I forgot. I want her in with our other special guest."

With that, he spun back around and made haste to the cool safety of his throne room. Meanwhile, Li, wondering what that was all about, was taken up a flight of stairs and to a strong oak door with a small window protected by iron bars. Inside was a young strawberry-blonde haired girl wearing round wire-frame glasses and a majestic dress. Li instantly guessed that she was someone of importance, probably the Princess Elizabeth herself.

The room itself was very nice and elegant. It had a huge red velvet couch, four red velvet chairs, a large cabinet and a few smaller matching cabinets. There were two canopy beds with heavy comforters and silk sheets. The room had a large window with a great view of the forest and was well lit by plenty of lamps. It was a nice room, indeed, but Li enjoyed making trouble for her 'hosts'. She lightly kicked the Dark General and said smartly "Hey, boot-lick. You really don't expect me to stay in there, do you?"

The other girl was shocked to hear this new woman talk to the Dark General in such a way. The general chuckled as he withdrew a razor-sharp dagger and placed it against her cheek. She felt the cold steel caress her soft cheek like a kiss from a corpse and pulled away. The general followed her head, keeping the blade pressed firmly against her cheek as he viciously spat out "You have such a beautiful face, Hua Li. It would be a shame if I were to rip it to shreds."

"That voice! I know that voice!" Li exclaimed in horror as the general removed his helmet, revealing a face with a long scar over the right eye. "GARRISON! You-you-you! I'll kill YOU! I'll rip out your heart and shove it down your slimy throat, you TWISTED BACKSTABBING—"

"Hello, Beauty. Long time no see, ne?" he chuckled as he kissed her lips roughly and gave her right breast a hard, painful squeeze. She squirmed to free herself so that she could destroy the man she hated so much, but the guards held her tight and the shackles bound her arms and legs, keeping her from lashing out. Garrison chuckled at her futile attempts and gave a silent order by simply nodding his head. He gave an evil chuckle as he called out to her "Have a great day, Beauty. I know mine's looking up! Hah-ha!"

As Li struggled violently, thrashing and tearing around trying to free herself so she could tear into Garrison while spewing violence and death from her lips, she felt a sharp prick in her arm. Suddenly, she felt very light-headed and began to swoon around. She tried her best to fight it, but it was no use. Everything around her began to slow down and blur to her eyes while the laughs of the Dark Knights were muffled, as if they were miles away from her. She tried to lunge at Garrison, only to slip forward limply. The last thing she saw was Garrison laughing maniacally as one of the guards opened the cell door before everything went dark and silent.

* * *

Li's eyes fluttered opened. Everything was still dark for a moment and the ground under her was hard and cold. Her head pounded, her whole body ached, and there was a terrible taste in her mouth. She didn't exactly remember what had happened until things gradually came into focus. She grabbed her wrists and found the shackles were gone. She noticed that the ankle shackles were gone as well. A definite plus added to the fact that she was still alive and in one piece. As she pushed herself up on wobbling arms and took in her surroundings, everything came back to her. Garrison! She couldn't believe she had finally caught up with him and now that she had, she was going to make him pay! She'd break out of her cell, find him, and make him suffer for what he had done to—

She noticed the young girl watching her with frightened eyes. Li blushed slightly as she waved her hand slowly and mumbled as sweet as she could "Hello."

"Are you all right?" the girl asked, her voice vibrating oddly in Li's ears.

"Yeah, I think so." Li sighed with a false grin as she fought the terrible hang over. Her own voice sounded out of place to her. "How long was I out?"

"A little over five hours, I think."

"Five hours, huh?" she murmured, rubbing her head and pushing herself against the wall. She closed her eyes and leaned her head back as she let out a low, exhausted sigh. "Feels like five days!"

She tried to stand, but her legs were jelly and she stumbled right back down. When the girl moved to help her, Li just waved her away, telling her in as strong a voice as she could muster "I'm all right. Just a bit dizzy."

"I was going to try and move you to the bed so you'd be more comfortable, but I-I was worried that it might do more harm than good to move you." the girl told her in an apologetic tone of voice, afraid that the new woman might be upset about being left on the granite floor for five hours. Li tried to talk to tell her not to worry about it, but she found her mouth too dry to speak, so she just waved her hand to brush off the issue. The girl understood and breathed a sigh of relief. Anyone that had to be drugged before the Dark General would remove the binders was probably powerful enough to knock her senseless if upset. She walked over to the woman and sat next to her as she explained "The general used solorga sap on you. It's a powerful poison, but can be used as a sedative in controlled amounts. I was really worried that he had used too much on you. I think Noknor was too. But you woke up, so you should be all right."

"Yeah, I'm starting to feel better already." Li coughed distantly. She opened her eyes a crack and frowned as she looked at the girl. "What do you mean 'Noknor was too'?"

"I heard him yelling at the general. He was pretty upset, too. He threatened to do the most gruesome things to him if he had killed you."

Li cracked a smile as she thought about how Garrison must have squirmed when Noknor ripped him a new one. It would have almost been satisfying to have died and know that Garrison would have had his spine ripped out at the very least. Almost.

"Garrison, you stupid . . ." Li murmured, her voice trailing off. The girl said something that Li didn't quite catch. Li turned to her as a sudden thought came to her and mumbled "Who are you anyway?"

"I'm Princess Elizabeth of Kuberica." Elizabeth said proudly, trying to hide the sorrow in her voice. "Or of what it used to be."

"Li." Li told her, still feeling quite drained and looking every bit of it. "Sorry to hear about your father."

"So am I." the other replied, her head hung and her eyes moistening. She wiped them away and looked back up. Li stared into her eyes with a mournful, sympathetic gaze as she reached out with a weary arm and put a hand on her shoulder. It was a look that said 'I feel your pain' and it was sincere. Elizabeth sniffled lowly as she pushed her glasses up on her face.

"Why are you here?" the princess asked, trying her best to sound strong and get the subject changed.

"Wha? Oh, I assume it's because I'm Kain Viccon's cousin." Li told her, her arm sliding from Elizabeth's shoulder. "I guess that's reason enough."

"Oh, Li! Yes, Kain and Nancy have mentioned you before!" the girl smiled, trying to sound excited despite the tightness in her heart. "It's such a pleasure to finally meet you."

Li gave a tired grin and murmured incoherently. She flexed her arms and legs the best she could and took a few deep breaths to clear her aching head. Elizabeth curiously watched her before sighing "I guess Noknor wanted double insurance protection."

"I know exactly how you feel, Princess." Li told her, hearing the despairing tone in her voice as she looked her dead in the eyes before lowering her gaze slightly. She sniffled and looked straight ahead as she dully replied "I lost my . . ."

She stopped and paused, as if debating whether or not to continue. Elizabeth thought she wasn't going to finish, but she finally said "I lost the only man I ever loved and then my best friend to Garrison." Elizabeth frowned darkly with deep concern, which Li mistook for confusion. "He's the Dark General that doped me up." Li hissed, tossing her thumb over her shoulder. When she continued, her voice was a soft, barely audible muffle "I can't believe I finally caught up with that maggot! He's got a lot to answer for and somehow I'm going to make sure he gets what he deserves, you can bet on that!"

"My goodness! I'm so sorry." Elizabeth murmured.

"It's a long story. Buuuuut, we'll probably be here for a while and we have nothing but time, time, time." Li sighed dully and used the wall to climb to her feet. As she tried to walk, she stumbled repeatedly. When Elizabeth rose to aid her, she waved her off and slowly made it to one of fancy chairs to have a seat and rest her weary body.

Then she began her tale.

PART II

LI'S TALE

CHAPTER X

Chen Wenchi had been my best friend since childhood. We were both born in the same town of Fuzhou which is on the southern coast of China, and we grew up like sisters. She was such a sweet girl, very kind and compassionate. Everyone loved her; I mean, how could you not? She always had a smile and it was always sincere. And she was so friendly to everyone she met. She always believed in the best in people. To some every person is a potential enemy until they can change your mind otherwise. For Wenchi, everyone was a potential friend even if you tried to change her mind otherwise. Some might call this naïve, but I prefer to think of her as eternally optimistic.

You know, even when times were toughest for her, and there had been some very tough times for her, she did her best to smile behind her tears. She always used to tell me that there was nothing so terrible that it couldn't get better and when it did she wanted to be ready with a smile. Sometimes . . . sometimes it's very hard for me to believe that, and I think that's the same for most people. Sometimes you wonder if it will ever be better. But Wenchi . . . Wenchi never stopped believing that.

She didn't deserve the fate handed down to her.

* * *

As I said, we were both from Fuzhou originally, but later we moved to another city called Wuhan for different reasons. Wuhan's a river town a little further inland from the shore. It's quite large and very busy. It sits on the Yangtze River, so it gets a lot of trade and stuff. I moved up there with my family when I was fifteen, and Wenchi moved up there when we turned eighteen. There had been a terrible fire in Fuzhou that year, and Wenchi had lost everything. Her entire family perished and so did all of her possessions, while she herself barely made it out alive. When she came to Wuhan, she did so with only the dress on her back. She moved in with my family, and later when my husband failed to return from battle she moved with me into my empty wedding house so that we could wait together for James to return.

I remember the day it all started. Sometimes the pain of it cuts as fresh as it did that day. I remember Wenchi and I were strolling down the wharf in Wuhan late one afternoon. I remember that the sun was already heading down and set the river on fire with red and orange hues. Heh, it's so funny the things you remember even a year later.

... One year. Has it ... has it really been that long?

I'm sorry, I'm getting sidetracked. No, no. I'm fine. Really. I could use a drink, though.

Anyway, that day we were watching the ships and junks load and unload cargo as we walked down the pier and fed the seagulls some rice we had just bought for our dinner when we would get home that night. We were heading for a small waterfront shop a friend of ours owned, because I needed to buy a gift for a friend of mine who was getting married the next day. Heheh, Wenchi had been ragging me all day long about being such a procrastinator.

We entered the shop and, after greeting our friend behind the counter, I immediately began to search for a wedding gift. Wenchi kept me company as I searched the many shelves, offering suggestions and giving her opinion of what she would prefer if it was her wedding. I was looking for something that was inexpensive but not cheap looking or stupid. After some searching I found a darling bronze wine vessel in the shape of a daxiongmao.

What's that? Never heard of a daxiongmao? Well, in my opinion it's just the cutest animal there is! It's kind of like a bear, with black hindquarters, black legs, a white body and head, and black ears and rings around its eyes. They're so fuzzy and adorable! I just adore them! Absolutely!

I saw the daxiongmao vessel and I knew I just had to get it, so I picked it up to examine the price. That's when it happened. That's when *he* came into my life a second time, only I didn't know it right at that moment. If I had, things would be very ... different today.

"What do you think about this wine vessel? Isn't it just adorable?" I asked Wenchi.

"Very! It is so you!" she giggled, turning her attention back onto the shelves to search.

"I know, right! I don't know whether to give it to Choa or keep it for my collection!" I sighed thoughtful indecision. "Here, help me look around for another one."

"Already on it." she smiled, pushing the other wine vessels around. She uttered a disappointed noise for me as she stood up and told me "Sorry, Li. There's a couple of frogs and dragons, but no daxiongmao."

"That's okay. I only have enough for one, anyway. I'll just give it to Choa. I already have enough—"

"Excuse me, ladies." a male voice called out close to us, startling Wenchi with a light squeak as she spun around and we both looked at the man approaching us.

He was a foreigner, probably with the trade circuit was my immediate guess. He wasn't very good looking, but he wasn't really a slob either. He had red hair cut short and he was clean shaven. His clothes were cheap but he wore them like they had been hand-tailored just for him. He walked with a cocky strut that went beyond confident and wandered more towards arrogant. As he stepped up to us, his eyes passed back and forth between me and Wenchi in a twitching sort of way, as if he wasn't sure which one of us he would choose to talk to.

Wenchi gave him a smile, I just raised an idle eyebrow. He muttered a chuckle that he tried to make sound slightly embarrassed but just came out sounding like the work of a bad liar and said "Excuse me, I'm sorry ladies. I don't mean to interrupt you, but I was wondering if you could give me a little help. You see, I'm not from around here . . . but, of course you could probably guess that."

He laughed at his joke as if to prompt us, and Wenchi gave him a giggle because it was the nice thing to do whiles I just roll my eyes at his obvious pickup line. The stranger picked his dove right then and there, turning straight to Wenchi and speaking directly to her.

"Could you give me directions to the Red Lantern teahouse?" he asked nicely enough. "I think it's on Lou Road, if you know of it?"

"Oh, yes! I know the Red Lantern!" Wenchi exclaimed brightly, glad to be helpful. That was just her nature.

"I'm going to go pay for this whiles you give him directions." I told her, being polite about it as I excused myself to take the wine vessel to the counter.

I greeted the cashier with a smile and handed over my purchase.

"I kind of figured this would catch your eye." he replied, making small talk as he looked at the price.

"Actually, it's for a friend of mine." I giggled as I handed him the money for it. "She's getting married tomorrow and I need a gift. But it's just so adorable. Do you happen to have anymore in stock? This is the only one Wenchi and I saw on the shelves."

"Not at the moment, but I should receive a few more like that in a few days. I'll hold on to one for you, if you like." he told me as he wrapped up my present in paper and silk.

"Yes, please! Thank you very much!" I chirped excitedly.

"No problem for one of my favorite customers." he chuckled. "So, who's getting married? Anyone I might happen to know of?"

"I doubt it. She doesn't come around here very often at all. She's way out in Shidiao."

"Oh, I see." he mumbled. He pushed the package across the counter to me and looked over my shoulder. "Hey, who's the waiguoren Wenchi is talking to?"

"Huh? Oh, beats me. He was asking her how to get to the Red Lantern." I told him with a shrug and turned to look at them also. They seemed to be talking intensely, at least more so than if they were just talking about street names. It looked like they were hitting it off quite well, all things considered. "Huh! Perhaps my little Wenchi has found a potential suitor!"

"If you ask me, she could do a lot better." he snorted his displeasure as he drummed his fingers on the counter. "I can't imagine what such a pretty girl would see in a . . . *foreigner!*" He dragged out the last word in a disgusted tone. I looked back at him and playfully raised an offended eyebrow. He noticed and was quite quick to add "Raptor was different. He knew our language and customs to the tee. Not like most of the other goatish dolts that ramble into this port. Raptor was like a Chinaman trapped in a Meigouren's body. And he was much better looking than that one, too."

"You got that right." I grinned, picturing my man. "You may be right, but it's not my place to say. If she happens to like him, she likes him. It would be wrong for me to warn her against him if I haven't met him. I'm sure he's no James, but he's probably a nice guy all the same."

"Maybe." he shrugged. "But you've got to wonder how a nice guy got a scar like that."

I frowned at him as I turned to have a closer look-see of the stranger's face. Taizong was right. I hadn't noticed it before, I hadn't paid much attention to his face, but the man had a long scar over his right eye. It ran from the top of his forehead to just below the middle of his cheek, but his eye was undamaged so the cut couldn't have been too harsh. It wasn't ugly and ragged, just a clean swipe, but now that it had come to my attention it stood out rather noticeably. But it didn't mean anything. James was, is rather, a very nice and sweet man and he has a few scars. Maybe not so prominently, but he does have them. He's a warrior, after all. And warriors tend to get cut in battle. But there was something wrong with the picture I saw. I couldn't place my finger on it, but it was there. A sort of feeling. But I cast it off as nothing.

Taizong and I talked for a few minutes more before I finally slapped the counter gently and said "Well, I guess they're going to be talking for a while longer. I'm going to wait outside so you can start closing up. I'll see you later, Taizong."

As I sat on the bench in front of the shop, I looked out over the water. The beautiful setting sun cast a gorgeous orange glow over the wharf. The ships had long since stopped loading and unloading their cargo and the bustle had dwindled to almost nothing creating a very calm and peaceful air over the wharf. Even though it was very pleasant, I wanted to hurry on home. My stomach was growling fiercely and I was tired from a long day of work. So, I waited for fifteen minutes until I was ready to go find her. I remember thinking that I was surprised that Taizong hadn't yet kicked them out.

Suddenly, I felt a hand on my shoulder. I stood and turned to face a dreamy eyed Wenchi. She looked as if she were lost in a fantasy world of her own as she replied simply "I think maybe I found a man, Li."

"That's gre—" I started to say but before I could finish my sentence she grabbed my hands and jumped up and down whiles she laughed "I FOUND A MAN! I FOUND A MAN!"

I giggled happily for her as I gathered my belongings and motioned her to follow, telling her to tell me all about her new suitor on the way home. We lived alone together in my wedding house, as I said before. We both worked very hard, her as a waitress at a local teahouse and me as a military trainer at the local fort. We were both alone, so we kept each other company, waiting for my James to return. My family was against me staying in the house, saying that it was bad luck, but it was the last place James had seen me and the first place I hoped he would look for me. So I stayed.

As we walked down the street towards home, she told me about her new man.

"Well, his name is Samhus Garrison." she told me. "He's a—"

"Samhus Garrison?" I gasped. She didn't seem to notice me shock, her being so wrapped up in the experience and all. "Did you say his name is Samhus," I choked a bit on his name, "Garrison?"

"That's what he told me." she laughed. "I assume it's his name. I mean, what type of man do you think he is?"

'A scoundrel!' I almost said aloud, but caught myself.

"Anyway, he's a free-lance warrior." Wen-chi continued to describe her new interest.

"Free-lanced?" I frowned. "You mean like a mercenary?"

"No! No, nothing like that! He's a Shazadian knight!"

"Shazadia, huh? That's not too far from Arcainia." I replied as I tried to remember what all Kain had told me about the Shazadian peoples. I came up empty minded, unfortunately, and returned my attention back onto my friend.

"Is it? Maybe Kain knows him then!" she chattered excitedly. "Samhus said that the Shazadian army lends him out to help out other kingdoms and cities in Meiguo with their problems. Hey, maybe he and Kain have worked together!"

'I doubt it.' I numbly thought as we walked up to our front porch. I grabbed the three letters out of the mailbox and fished the key out of my pocket. "What's he doing in China?"

"He's thinking of retiring from his work and moving out this way. He has a lot of friends here. Isn't that great!"

"Mmm-hmm." I grunted with a forced grin. "He . . . he sounds like a great guy. I can't wait to meet him."

"You will tomorrow night!" she squeaked out enthusiastically. "He invited me out to dinner and I thought you might like to chaperone us! Oh, I'm sooooooo happy!"

"Oh, I'm sorry, Wenchi. I won't be able to make it." I told her as I unlocked our front door and we entered. "I probably won't be back in time."

"Oh, yes! You've got that wedding tomorrow!"

"Maybe I could join you two lovebirds some other time?"

"Yeah! That would be great!" she smiled brightly, snatching the mail out of my hands. She shifted through it and gasped "Oh, look! You got a letter from Kain!"

I grabbed it out of her grasp and tore into it with growing anticipation for it had been three months at least from his last letter. Wenchi giggled and said that she was going to bathe whiles I read my letter and prepared dinner. It was my turn to cook that night. It's so funny how you remember the littlest things.

Anyway, as she strolled off to her room, I looked the letter over. It was basically just Kain and Nancy telling me hello, and Kain telling me about his new Grand General duties; he had just made Grand General the year before, but I'm sure you know all about that story. Kain bragged about Nancy doing so well in school, that sort of stuff. Reading it made me forget about Garrison for at least a few minutes.

When I finished I set the letter back down and set off towards the kitchen to make our dinner. As I cooked, Garrison once again weighed heavily on my mind. I couldn't stop thinking about him. Could he be the same guy who fought with James all those years ago? Who had betrayed my lover? The same Samhus Garrison who had shot James in the back with an arrow and left him to die on the battlefield? I kept telling myself that it wasn't, but I just couldn't convince myself. Maybe I just wanted it to be him because if it was, I could have found out what became of my lover and seen justice brought down on the man who had betrayed him. I began to picture just how I would pound my knuckles into his face, but quickly caught myself and tried my best not to think like that. I didn't even know if it was the same guy. For all I knew Samhus Garrison could have been a very popular Shazadian name.

I finally decided that it was pointless to dwell on the subject. It couldn't be the same guy, but if it were I'd find out soon enough. I did my best to push those thoughts back with cheerful thoughts of the wedding, but I could feel myself grow more and more anxious as I worried about Wenchi going to dinner with the stranger.

As I was setting the table, Wenchi came out of her room and asked what I had prepared. In response, I set a plate in front of her chair. She licked her lips as she sat and picked up her chopsticks. When I joined her in eating, I asked if she had gotten a chance to read Kain's letter whiles I was cooking.

"Li, you know that I can't read Arcainian." she giggled sheepishly.

"Oh, yes." I said, slapping my forehead. "I don't know where my head is today. You know, I'm going to teach you one of these days. Anyway, he says that they're doing just fine. And Nancy's number one in her class!"

"Well, good for her!" she beamed proudly.

"He and Nancy want us to visit soon. He said for me to tell you that he misses you."

"Oh, he's so sweet." she cooed. She had always had a thing for my cousin and him for her, but neither would ever really admit to it. I wish they had, especially now. "I can't wait to see them. I wonder if Nancy's found a suitor yet."

"I'll ask when I write back." I mumbled as I swallowed a mouthful of food. "Speaking of suitors, tell me more about your new man. Did he ever fight in the Dwarf and Goblin Wars?"

"No, he really didn't tell me about his missions. After all, we were only talking for ten minutes."

"Twenty." I corrected her.

"Pardon?"

"You two were talking for at least twenty minutes."

"Whatever." she mumbled, her eyes suddenly very suspicious. She must have picked up something in my tone or perhaps in my face. She was always good at that. "Why did you ask about the Dwarf and Goblin Wars?"

I wanted to avoid the question, so at first I pretended that I didn't hear her. I was hoping that she would drop the question. She didn't, however. When she repeated herself louder, I was forced to answer her. I tried to come up with a plausible excuse "Oh, I was just curious. It seems everyone in Meiguo fought during the Dwarf and Goblin Wars. Thought maybe he might have known James."

"Uh-huh." she murmured, slowly chewing her food as she eyed me cautiously. "Li, is something bothering you?"

"Not at all." I told her, trying to give as bright a smile as I possibly could. "Why do you—"

"You've been acting awfully funny since I met Samhus." she charged, cutting me off abruptly.

"What do you mean funny?" I replied, still doing my best to play it off as nothing.

"Nervous funny. Especially when I mention his name. What is it that's bothering you, Li?"

I sighed deeply. She had caught me. I guess I didn't do as well of a job hiding my feelings as I had thought. And I knew that there was no point in playing dumb anymore because Wenchi was much too smart for that. Taking a deep breath, I let it out. "I don't trust this Garrison guy."

"What?" she gasped, quite taken aback.

"Please don't take this the wrong way, Wenchi!" I tried to explain as best, and as quickly, as I could. "I'm sorry, but I just don't trust him for some reason."

I half expected her to jump up and turn the table over, yelling at me that I was just jealous because she was about to be in a happy relationship and I wasn't. To my secret delight, however, she gently set her chopsticks down, sat back, gave her full attention, and asked "Why don't you trust him? And don't tell me that it's just a feeling. I can tell that there's something more."

I really don't know why I thought that she would go ballistic on me. That wasn't the way Wenchi was. In my entire life, I'd never ever seen her angry, even when she was dumped on by her boss or the customers at the teahouse. She just took it and went on with her life. But, I sure didn't expect her to be so calm and cool about it. To tell you the truth, she sort of frightened me, kind of like the calm before the storm, you know?

"The man who betrayed James in battle was named Samhus Garrison. And I'm pretty sure he had been Shazadian."

Her eyes grew wide and her jaw dropped in absolute shock. If she had been holding her chopsticks, she probably would have dropped them onto the floor. She had never asked me details before and I never told her. I guess it came as a bit of a surprise to her. She looked me dead in the eyes and said "Li, I-I'm sorry. I-I . . ." She trailed off tonelessly, not knowing what to say. I couldn't blame her, I was pretty speechless myself. Finally, it's my guess that it was more to ease her mind than my own, she told me "But I doubt it's the same man. It's not the same man! I mean, what-what . . . what are the chances?"

"You're probably right, Wenchi. I'm sure you are!" I lied to her and myself. "But what if it is?"

"It can't be the same man! It just can't be! The man I met today was a perfect gentleman! He was so sweet and nice! It just can't be the same man!"

"All I'm saying is that I want you to be careful!" I told her. "If it is the same guy, then well . . . well, just be careful and don't rush into anything. Even if it's not the same guy, you need to be careful! A lot of guys wouldn't think twice about taking advantage of a pretty young girl like you. Especially foreigners."

There was a very long uncomfortable silence between us as she seemed to consider what all I had told her. As she sat brooding silently, I couldn't help but fidget around I was so nervous. I couldn't even bring myself to touch my food.

"You have a point, Li." she finally told me, looking at her half empty plate with flustered eyes. "And I know that you're only looking out for me. We've known each other for so long and you've never led me astray. I trust your judgment, even more so than my own. Maybe I should call off that dinner date tomorrow."

"I think that would be best. Just take it slow and easy and don't rush into anything too fast. At the very least wait until I get back home and can chaperone you guys."

"It's just that I thought I had finally met a man." She sighed dully. "Someone sweet and thoughtful that I could marry and be a good wife to. Honestly, now that I think about it, I really don't think too much of him. I mean, he seems sweet and kind, but he's really not the type of man I find attractive. But my parents aren't around to arrange a marriage for me and I guess I just wanted to rush into a relationship before it gets too late for me to find anyone. I guess I was just settling for someone who had shown interest in me."

"Don't worry, Wenchi." I assured her with confidence. "There are plenty of great men who would love to take you as their wife."

She snorted. "Like who?"

"What about Kain?" I offered without thinking. It just popped out.

"What about him?" she asked slowly, carefully.

"He's always been very sweet and thoughtful." I told her with a bit of a shrug. I don't think I really knew what I was saying at the time. "He's a great guy, he's great looking, and, last I heard, he's available. Why don't you get together with him?"

"Li!" she gasped, turning bright pink as she quickly turned her head away.

"What? You like him, don't you?" I asked, her blush growing deeper. "He likes you too. I think the two of you would make a great couple."

She sat silently. I began to fear that I had overstepped my bounds and had opened an unpleasant box. However, after a few moments, she raised her head slightly and whispered "Does Kain really like me in that way?" I smiled and nodded. "Does he ever talk about me?" Again I nodded. "What does he say?"

"Well, he thinks you're a sweet girl. And he's told me many times over that you're very pretty. Actually, his exact words were 'man, Wenchi sure is hot'!"

She giggled and blushed as she asked "Why didn't he ever tell me how he felt and court me?"

"I dunno." I shrugged, my mouth a bit full. With the heavy air starting to lift, I felt my appetite starting to return. After I swallowed, I replied "I think he was afraid that you might reject him." She gave me a curious look, so I thought I'd better explain. "We were all pretty close as kids and I think that he thought of you as family, sort of like a sister. I mean, you and I are like sisters, and Kain and I are like brother and sister, you know? I think he worried that you felt the same way and would tell him no, that you thought of him as a brother and that a relationship would be rather awkward."

"I wouldn't think of it as awkward." she murmured shyly.

I let a low giggle escape my lips as I offered to ask him, nonchalantly of course, if he might be interested in a relationship with my best friend when I wrote him back. Before I even finished speaking my thoughts, she cut me off with a squeak and a vigorous shake of her head. She'd rather I not in a letter and certainly not this one. She would rather wait until the next time we visited him or vise versa. She tried to play off that she was in no big hurry and that it really didn't matter when we saw him next or even if it would happen when we did, but the sparkle in her eyes gave her away and she constantly hinted that I sort of force ourselves into his house when I wrote him back.

"Now you realize that he's now the Grand General over there. You'll have to live in Arcainia if you two do get married." I told her.

"I wouldn't care!" she smiled.

"You'd have to learn to speak the language and the customs."

"For him, I'd do it with no problem!"

The both of us shared a giggle, especially me. I wondered how my cousin would have reacted if he knew what was going on that night. If he knew that we were talking about him in such a way. I rather doubt he would have minded. He probably would have been courting Wenchi long ago if he had known. I still think they would have made a great couple. They would be . . .

It had been a long time since I had seen Wenchi so excited about something. I was positively thrilled that she was so happy. With her life filled with so much recent tragedy, it was great to see things finally turn around for her. When I proposed to Kain that they marry, and I just knew he would jump at the chance, Wenchi's life would rise from the ashes and she would be happy again.

We talked about Kain for a few more minutes before I remembered to inquire "So, what are you going to tell this Garrison fellow?"

She shrugged and murmured something about forgetting all about him. I figured that was very good to know. "Where were you going to meet him? Not here, I hope. You didn't tell him where you live, did you?"

"Of course not! I'm not that hard up for a husband!" she grinned. We shared another laugh and I repeated the question once more. "We were going to meet at the Red Lantern."

"Just send him a message that you can't meet him tomorrow." I offered. "Tell him that you can't see him again for some reason."

"What should I say?"

"Be creative. Or just stand him up! I'm sure he'll get over it. You can come with me to the wedding tomorrow, if you want to."

She shook her head distastefully. "No, I wouldn't want to be a pebble in your shoe. Besides, I wouldn't know anyone there besides you. You know how I am about those situations."

"You won't be a pebble!" I told her. "You should come with me. It'll do you good to get out of the house!" She shook her head once again. "I think you'll have a good time. There'll be food!" She gave me a mock dirty look and I couldn't help but giggle. "Suit yourself. But if you change your mind—"

"I doubt I will, but thanks all the same." she grinned. I grinned back and stood to take my dishes to the kitchen.

"Li?" she stopped me, a somber look on her face as if she had been thinking of something for a while. "What if this Garrison is the same man?"

I guess the look on my face and the blaze in my eyes was rather harsh, because I noticed that she shrank back slightly. But there was neither no way nor no want to conceal the intense, burning hatred and crushing pain that I felt in my heart. It was there, and it would only get worse until I finally did what I had to do.

"I'll kill him!" I hissed darkly.

CHAPTER XI

The next morning, I awoke quite early. I knew I had a long distance to cover in just a few hours and needed all the time I could get. Shidiao Town was at least half a day's ride from the outer limits of Wuhan. Wenchi hadn't changed her mind, so I let her sleep as I washed and dressed in my finest silk gown before collecting my gift and heading out. I do remember peeking in on her before I left. I watched her sleep, trying to work up the nerve to wake her up and force her to join me. In the end, I decided she was too peaceful in her sleep, so I . . . I let her be.

The streets were still dark, save the street corners lit by lanterns. I saw an alley that led straight to the coach stables. It was quicker than walking all the way around by way of the sidewalk, so against my better judgment, I hugged my package tight and entered it. I didn't even make it halfway before I heard a gruff whistle. I turned and saw a drunk that looked as if he had spent the night in a pigsty.

"Hey, girlie!" he called in a gruff tone. "What's a sweet little thing like you doing out at this hour?"

I turned back around and started to walk away, but he grabbed my arm and whirled me around. He got into my face and snorted "Looks like I'm going to get a sweet piece tonight!"

"You couldn't get a piece from the corpse of a dog!" I retorted before spitting in his face.

The little scum glared at me with a startled look, then tightened his grip and growled "Looks like I'm going to have to teach you to respect a man!"

He let me go and tried to throw a punch, but I caught his hand easily and tossed it aside. Then I crushed his windpipe with a blow to the throat. He tried to scream as he sunk helplessly to the ground, but all that came out was a pitiful gurgling sound. Satisfied with my work, I kicked his wretched body in case any other hopeless romantics were watching and continued on my way. I reached the gates of the coach stables without any other complications and purchased a ticket. Since it was so early in the morning, I had the carriage all to myself. And that was just fine by me. I set my package down on the seat and reached into my pocket. I withdrew a few squares of silk that had painted pictures of my friends on them. I had one of Kain and Nancy of course, one of Wenchi and me together, and one with a very special person on it. He was my lover, James Raptor. Like I told you earlier, we were supposed to get married, but he disappeared in battle during the Dwarf and Goblin Wars.

Whiles looking at the picture, I got to thinking about my friend's own wedding and remembered when James proposed to me. I had been out shopping with Nancy and Wenchi and a few of my female cousins. When we got home, I found my mama and baba waiting for me with Kain and James. You know Kain, I'm sure; he's so easy to read! I could tell that something big was going on, because he had this really big, excited grin on his face. James was nervous about something, I mean really nervous. I'd never seen him like that before, he was fidgeting and hopping about, eating logan after logan . . . ah, a logan is a fruit, kind of like an orange but smaller and not as sweet. James loved them, but I mean he was popping them into his mouth like China was running out of them.

Anyway, Kain called me into the parlor where just about everyone had gathered to hear some big announcement. At first I had assumed that baba was going to say something, but then James got up, bowed with respect to my parents and asked for their permission to take me as his wife. Oh, I was so shocked! I could hardly believe what I had heard. I mean, James and I were very much in love, and I guess we both knew the day would come, but still! To actually hear it, it was very exciting for me.

Of course, my baba has always been such a jokester. He was trying to pick on his new son-in-law when he told James "I don't know if you're ready to handle my little Li. She can be such a handful. Maybe in another five years she'll be tamer."

Oh, I was so crushed! I was livid! I mean, how could my baba deny me a lifetime of happiness with the man I loved. I jumped right down my baba's throat, crying and yelling and carrying on. Of course everyone else, even James, knew that he was only joking, but the only answer I had wanted to hear from his lips was yes. It took three of my cousins, my auntie, and my mama to calm me down, and my father told me that he was just joking and that he completely consented our marriage, that he knew James would be a good husband to me. Oh, I was so embarrassed! I felt like such a fool! Of course, my baba wouldn't let it go, and all night he kept telling James "Are you sure that you want this one? You see how she treats her own father!"

That was such a fun evening, after the whole episode I mean. We all had a nice dinner to congratulate James and me, and drank toasts all night. I remember . . . I remember Wenchi telling me how happy she was for me and how we laughed together as we began to plan things out for the wedding. I remember that night thinking how good a couple Kain and Wenchi would be together, how they would give each other eyes and then quickly turn away as if ashamed of their feelings. I began to think, as I sat in that coach on my way to my friend's wedding, about how fun it would be the next time Wenchi and I visited Arcainia. I began to write the letter to Kain in my head and ended up falling asleep.

* * *

I was so excited when I finally got to Shidiao, I almost left my gift on the seat! I hurried to my friend's home filled with giddy, joyful anticipation. I could barely get a hold of the heavy brass knocker on the bright red gate, I was so excited. After I finally lifted the knocker and let it fall a servant opened the door.

"Miss Hua!" he exclaimed joyfully. "Miss Pan has been waiting for your arrival. She is in the Garden of Sweet Smells."

I thanked him and handed over the gift. Then I hustled to the garden as quickly as I could. I found Choa and her nurse, Lai, sitting on a bench. Lai was preparing Choa for her big day by brushing her hair. The nurse looked up and saw me. Her smile told me that she was about to say something, so I quickly motioned her not to. I walked silently behind my friend and took a handful of her hair from Lai.

"You know, Lai. I never thought I would ever find a husband." Choa murmured happily, thinking that I was her nurse. I bent my head low and replied "Nor did I, my friend."

It took her a few seconds to realize that it was me. When she did, she jumped up and laughed gleefully, twirling around to embrace me. "Li!" she cried "It really is you!"

"Sure is." I smiled, returning the hug. "Congratulations, my friend! I am so happy for you! Have you met your husband-to-be yet?"

"A few times. I really like him. He's very sweet and kind and thoughtful."

"Handsome?" I inquired as we sat down. Lai took back her brush and resumed brushing Choa's hair and prepared it with golden hairpins and red ribbons.

"Oh, yes, very!" she smiled, her heart so filled with joy. I guess she noticed I was alone because she then asked about Kain and Nancy.

"I'm afraid they couldn't make it. Kain's very busy with his new duties and Nancy is busy with her schooling. But they thank you for the invite and send their love and well wishes for you." I told her.

"Oh, they're so sweet." she cooed. "You must tell me next time they're in China. It's been so very long since I've seen them."

"How has Nancy been doing?" Lai inquired.

"Yes, tell us!" Choa insisted.

"She's doing just fine. She's turning into a beautiful young woman."

"I always knew she would. How old is she?"

"Twelve, I think." I replied. "Twelve or thirteen."

"Has she found a suitor?" Lai asked. I told them I had no idea.

"What about you, Li." Choa asked with a smile.

"What about me what?" I frowned, a little thrown off the by the sudden personal question.

"Have you found a suitor?" she asked. I looked at her for a moment before hanging my head. She sighed dully. "I'll take that as a 'no'. Who was your last suitor?" I didn't answer her. "It was James Raptor, wasn't it?"

"Yes, he was. So what of it?"

"Li, I know how much he meant to you, but he's gone now. You really should get on with your life. There are plenty of nice men who would love to marry you! If you want me to, I could arrange—"

"I don't want another man!" I barked, a bit too harshly, I suppose, for both girl and nurse jumped back. "I-I'm sorry about that, Choa. I didn't mean to snap like that. It's just that . . . you don't understand. I don't want another man! I want James back!"

"I know you do, my friend." she murmured, scooting closer to me on the granite bench. She reached over and placed a hand over mine, gripping it and giving it a gentle squeeze. "I know you want him back. But you must face reality! He's gone. Lost in battle. And you can't keep doing this to yourself, Li! It's just not healthy!"

I looked her in the eye before lowering my gaze. She didn't understand. I knew my beloved was out there somewhere. I don't know where he is or why he hasn't come back to me, but I can feel his heart crying out to me. But I couldn't really expect her to understand. Her marriage had been arranged. She didn't know what it was like to really be in love with someone else. That would come later.

So, to appease her and to help get the mood to the joyous level that it should have been, I conceded. "I guess you're right. I miss him so much, but I really need to get on with my life."

"So, you want me to arrange someone for you?" she asked.

That was the absolute last thing I wanted. "Maybe later. Let's not think about it any more. This is a happy event! I mean, it's your wedding after all!"

"I agree with Li." Lai replied, coming to my aid. "This should be a happy occasion. You two haven't seen each other in a long time and it's your wedding day. You two should be happy and chipper! I know you mean well, Choa but she doesn't seem to be too worried about her love life and you've got too much to worry about as it is without worrying about it for her."

"You're absolutely right, Lai!" I smiled, trading winks with her. "This is your day, Choa! It's something that you'll remember perfectly for the rest of your life. Let's not cloud it up with dreary discussions. Let's talk about blissful things!"

The three of us then talked about happier subjects, laughing and giggling like children once again until another servant came into the garden and said "It is time, Miss Choa."

"Thank you, Ling." Choa nodded. She looked at me and smiled "This is it!"

I smiled, gave her a hug, and congratulated her once again. Then I went to join the other guests. Firecrackers were exploded to signify the special event and the red sedan marriage chair was carried into the court. Red curtains hid the beautiful bride away from the rest of the world as the ceremonies began. They were quickly over and the newly weds bowed to the guests and each other. Wonderful music was played and many firecrackers were set off. They drank marriage wine from two cups tied together with a red string. They shared the wedding cake and professed their love.

At last, with the ceremony finished, the wonderful festivities began. Everyone laughed, danced, and had a great time. The food was delicious and the wine was grand. Even without Kain and Nancy, I managed to have a wonderful time. Oh, it was so much fun! I remember wishing that Wenchi had decided to come along. Now that I know how everything turned out, I wish it even more everyday. Or that I had forced her to come along, even if I had to twist her arm. If I had, she'd . . .

Wishing won't bring Wenchi back. No matter how many times I play each of the hundreds of scenarios in my head, no matter how many times I've wished I'd have done things differently, I have to admit to myself that it won't bring my friend back. And it just makes the pain that much . . . worse.

But I'm getting ahead of myself. Sorry. Now where was I? Oh, yes. I stayed a few hours and mingled with the many guests and had a wonderful time. When I found the hour growing late, I found Choa and her new husband and told them that I had to go. Choa and I gushed over each other as I congratulated the two lovebirds. They thanked me and I set off. I went to the coach stables and showed my ticket. Since it was pretty late in the day, I had the carriage all to myself again. Once again, that was just fine by me! As soon as we started to move, I found myself thinking of Wenchi again. I hoped she was all right and began to picture getting her and Kain together.

Soon, however, I felt my eyelids grow very heavy from food, wine and dancing. Before I knew it, I had fallen asleep. It had been another eventful day, though it seemed to be too short all the same.

CHAPTER XII

It was nearly morning when I arrived back in Wuhan. As I walked down the street towards my house, I felt an unsettling twinge in the back of my mind, so I hurried on a little faster. As I stepped onto my porch, I heard quite a commotion inside. There was a lot of yelling and screaming with loud crashes. I heard Wenchi scream loudly, but she was cut off. Having no idea what to expect, I threw open the door and was mortified at what I saw.

In the middle of the living room lay Wenchi in a pool of her own blood, her throat savagely slashed. Garrison stood over her with a bloody knife in his hand, panting and gasping for a breath. He looked up at me, fire burning in his eyes, that scar staring me right in the face.

"Well look who it is!" he growled dangerously. "Hello, Hua Li! Have you come to join the party? Well, you showed up just in time!"

In a horrified panic, I started to back out the door, not believing what I was seeing. However, I stepped on something that had been tossed around during the struggle and slipped. My head struck the door and slammed it shut whiles momentarily knocking me senseless. Whiles I was in a daze, Garrison took the chance to throw the knife at me. I awoke in time to see the blade screaming towards my face. I ducked at the last moment and watched as it was imbedded in the door all the way to its hilt. I jumped up and took a few steps away from the door as I stared at my sister's body and Garrison rushed forward to grab the knife. It took a few seconds, but he finally got it. He then turned around, laughing because he had the knife. I instinctively kicked it out of his hand and punched his nose. He howled in pain as he grabbed his face, blood oozing between his fingers. He roared and lunged at me, grabbing my collar and making as if to smack me.

The beast inside me snapped and I shrieked ferociously as I belted him hard in his stomach. He doubled over and wheezed pathetically, so I punched him three times in the face giving him two black eyes and a very busted lip. Blood and snot from his broken nose ran into his mouth and joined the blood from his lip in a grotesque combination. He wailed in agony and anger as he punched me in my jaw. As I was knocked back a few steps, he raised his hand and I saw the glint of something shiny and sharp. When he slashed at me with another small knife, I drew back on instinct, but it wasn't enough. The blade lacerated my belly just above my navel and I sank to my knees, clutching my wound as it burned furiously. Garrison stood over me, spread legged in triumph and chuckling evilly.

"You stupid girl!" he yelled, rubbing his face to clean off the blood. It was a useless gesture, for more blood just oozed out of his wounds. "I'm going to gut you and watch you bleed to death!"

I couldn't move, I couldn't speak. All I could do was cry, cry for my sweet sister as I saw her lying motionless on the floor in front of me, her eyes closed, her face pale. I couldn't even hear what Garrison was yelling at me, and my whole body felt numb. It was like all of my senses were dead, and I remember wondering if that was how it was going to end for me.

And then something inside me snapped. I wasn't going to die like that! I wasn't going to let that zazhong kill me! And I certainly wouldn't let **HIM** live after what he had done to Wenchi! She had to be avenged! So, I lifted my leg with great force and caught him in the groin whiles he was in the middle of his sentence. He dropped the knife, held his crushed crotch, and groaned dully as he sank to his knees. The pain of my torn stomach instantly forgotten, I jumped up and savagely kicked him in his jaw. I noticed a small white object shoot from mouth, probably a tooth. Garrison tried to get up, but I wasn't about to let him. I busted him in the face once again before grabbing his shirt and punching him repeatedly in the stomach, the force of my pounding fist lifting him back up to his feet. As he staggered, wheezing and gasping for breath, I grabbed him in an arm-lock. Holding his arm, I slapped him hard across his chest and cocked my arm sharply, breaking his. I still remember how he shrieked, and I still don't feel the slightest bit sorry for him. Not after what he had done to that poor, innocent girl. I was going to make him pay, and my only regret . . . my only regret concerning him directly, as I have many . . . regrets, is that I didn't kill him then and there.

I stepped back and kicked him in his face with all my might. He flew back, moaning and weeping from the pain. He started to get up, screaming because of his arm and his shattered nose and cheekbone, but I jumped up and planted my heel in his chest. He flew through the window and landed on the porch. I ran to the broken glass and watched as Garrison hobbled away, weeping like a child, his body crushed and broken. I could have caught him easily and made him suffer more before killing him, but heartache and grief took over. Instead, I ran to Wenchi's body, hoping against hope that I could still save her. But . . . buh-buh-buh-but she was already cold with death. I picked up her huh-head and placed it against my heart, her buh-buh-blood staining my clothes and my body. Staining my very soul. My bruises and cuts burned with fire, but the only pain I felt was right here . . . in my heart.

Her life had just been turned around! She was finally going to be happy! She had suffered so much tragedy in her life, but it was supposed to get better! She was a good person with a pure heart! She deserved to have a happy ending! It wasn't fair! **IT WASN'T FAIR!**

I held my sweet Wenchi close and wept.

PART III

THE MANDRAKE, THE SISTERS, AND THE DREAMS

CHAPTER XIII

"Wow! That's quite a story, Li!" Princess Elizabeth murmured from her position on the leather couch. Li lay resting on her soft bed with her hands behind her head as she stared blankly up at the underside of the canopy.

"Yep, and I'll always have the scars to remind me." she sighed as she sat up and lifted her silk blouse to her breasts. A long, white scar shone just over her naval. While she had been telling her story, she had found a whole wardrobe similar to her own at home in a large closet and had changed from the training outfit she had been captured in and into a pair of Chinese-style pink silk pants and a matching silk blouse.

"How awful!" the princess gasped, her hand over her mouth in horror.

"It happened long ago but it still hurts." she replied strongly as she tapped her heart with her fist. She lay back down and sighed "Now all I have are memories and scars."

"What . . . what do you think happened?"

"Well, the best I've been able to figure after talking to people at the Red Lantern and some others is that Wenchi elected to just stand him up." Li said dully, as if her mind were elsewhere. She paused to think a moment. After a few long seconds, she breathed a hard, wavy sigh and continued "I think that he had only one thing on his mind that day and was pretty upset that he couldn't get it. All that stuff he had told her, thinking of retiring in Wuhan and being with the Shazadian Army, it was all just trash meant to get her into bed. He must have asked around about her. Both of us were pretty well known at the Red Lantern, so he probably started there. He put together the bits of information he gathered, and found his way to our house. I think he was intending to rape her, but she must have put up too good of a fight, so he just sla—. . . killed her. I can't help but think 'if I had only been three minutes faster getting home' or at least forced her to come with me, maybe she'd be alive today."

"You can't blame yourself, Li." Elizabeth told her in a soothing voice. "It's not your fault. And you did beat Garrison pretty badly."

Li gave a half grin and chuckled emptily. "That sure felt good. It'll feel even better when I get my hands on his sorry carcass again! But it still won't bring her back. Oh, I miss—"

Suddenly, a small orc threw open the door and ambled into the room with a large tray of food in his massive paw. The creature, a demi-faery, was a grazing beast that lived on the grassy plains of the Old World, living in packs and was so named orc for the sound of its bark. Its head and shoulders were covered with curly dark brown fur, while the rest of its stout body sported short, tan fur. It had a massive head, resembling a cow with beady black eyes, a stubby snout, and a small mouth. It had two cow-like horns on its head, small and curved that jutted out from the sides of its skull just behind its tiny ears. Orcs were not the brightest of creatures, but being a demi-faery it was gifted with the power of limited speech and could be trained to handle simple, specific tasks. This orc had been ordered to deliver the dinner to the women, a delicious looking feast of roasted beef and corn with large, steaming rolls.

The orc set the tray down on a table near the door, regarded the two women with an audible snort as its ears twitched, and wandered back out. Elizabeth immediately leapt off the couch and rushed to gorge herself while Li just lay on her bed and wrestled with her thoughts.

Elizabeth took notice of her new friend's sullen state and asked "Are you not going to eat?"

"Nah, I'm not that hungry." she replied with a bit of a smirk, doing her best to remain strong. "The smell of that disgusting beast of burden made me lose what little appetite I had."

Elizabeth frowned deeply with concern but said nothing as Li lay back down on her back, her head resting on the soft pillow. She inhaled deeply, held her breath in her chest, and released it. Then she slowly rolled onto her side, away from Elizabeth, drew her knees up to her chest, and placed her hands under her head. A lone crystal tear grew pregnant on the corner of her eye and rolled down her fair cheek.

* * *

Kain and his troops finally halted at the edge of the Forest of Souls just after the sun climbed midway through the sky. He ordered a dismount and gathered his friends around for a briefing.

"Okay, here's the situation." he told them. "I'm going to take five of my knights in with me. From what I understand, the mandrake only grows deep in the forest, so I'm not sure how long this will take. It's not that big of a place, so it shouldn't take more than a couple of hours. To be honest, I'm really hoping to get out of there by sundown. If we're not out in two days time, you all have your orders."

Nancy raised a concerned eyebrow, the hairs on the back of her neck ruffling. She hadn't heard anything about such orders. But before she could press, Kain gestured to Nancy, Robert, Raphael, and Michael and continued "I want the four of you to stay here with the rest of the soldiers and set up camp."

"No, I want to go with—" Nancy started to blurt out but a glance at the forest cut her off. Every single tree she saw seemed to be dead and withered. They had knotholes in just the right places to give them ghoulish faces and their branches looked like the bony hands of a skeleton reaching out for her. There were ghastly shrieks and howls coming from deep inside the belly of the forest, and her active imagination began hearing the forest calling out for her. Nancy shuddered as she realized that the Forest of Souls had been named well.

"I th-th-think I'll stay behind and help watch the cuh-cuh-camp." she stuttered, not taking her eyes off of the trees as if she were fearful that the entire forest would reach out and gobble her up if she dared to.

"That's my girl." Kain chuckled, reaching out to pat her head. When he touched her, she gave a startled gasp and jumped nervously, her eyes wild with alarm. As she saw that it was only her brother, she gave a loud sigh of relief and blushed slightly as the men shared a laugh. "Okay, we're losing valuable daylight."

"Good luck, my man!" Raphael murmured, giving Kain a crisp salute. The others followed suit, even Nancy as she whispered her own well wishes to her brother.

"Thanks. I have a feeling we're going to need it." Kain smiled uneasily, looking into the forest before he returned the salute. Kain called all of his knights together and picked five out of the ten. After a few good-byes and good lucks from their cohorts, the small group drew their broadswords and held their shields in a defensive manner as they slowly entered the Forest of Souls. The warm, bright rays of the sun left them behind as the stale, dreary, dark air of the forest swallowed them like a beast. A soft, icy breeze encircled their bodies like the breath of a corpse, sticking to them and penetrating their armor to tickle beneath their very flesh, chilling their bones and running their blood cold. A faint moan echoed lowly sounding as if it came from all around them; it could have merely been the chilly breeze blowing through the knotted trees, but it certainly sounded more like the sharp whispers of the dead. Kain startled several times in only a few steps as queer dark shapes danced just at the edges of his sight and then disappeared when he spun his head with a gasp. As with the time he had been forced to enter before he had become Grand General, he noted that whether the forest was actually haunted or not it was most certainly aptly named.

The men hadn't gone one hundred feet into the gloom when a young woman appeared out of nowhere. Kain wanted to convince himself that she had jumped out from behind a tree, but the flaw in that was that the nearest tree large enough to conceal her was a good twenty feet away. She was a lovely young lady with deep blue eyes and short blond hair, giving away her Kuberican heritage. She wore a type of Kuberican dress that had been very popular thirty years earlier but had since gone out of style. She looked straight into Kain's eyes, her gaze piercing into his very soul. Her eyes were sad and her face dejected, as if she were prematurely morning their deaths. Kain felt his heart tighten. For several eternally long seconds, she held her gaze on the group in silence. Just as Kain was about to ask her if she needed help, the girl raised her arm ever so slowly and pointed at them with a long, thin finger that was as steady as stone.

"Leave this place. Now." she replied, her voice hollow and reverberating strangely.

The words surprised Kain into silence briefly before he tried to explain his situation. "I'm sorry, Miss, but we—"

"Leave! Now!" she repeated, her voice stronger, more forceful. "If you do not turn back now, you will never leave this forest! Please, go away."

"We—"

"Go AWAY!" she repeated once more, her voice frustrated and sad. She pleaded with them once more, her voice growing softer with each syllable. As Kain and his men watched, the girl began to simply fade from their view, becoming fainter and fainter until all that was left was a misty outline of a female, and then nothing. The last trace of her was a gentle crying whisper that floated on the breeze. "Go away . . ."

Kain stood for a moment staring at the empty spot where the girl had been, the icy breeze swirling around him and whipping his hair and cloak about. Finally, he turned to his men. Though they were all visibly shaken from the encounter, Kain could see the look of determination in their eyes. His loyal knights would not be scared away by a mere ghost. They would bravely face the dangers and the risks of the forest and follow Kain wherever he led them. It was their duty and it was their pride to do so.

"Be on your guard." Kain replied solemnly, turning back around and taking the first step deeper into the forest.

For thirty minutes, the small group stalked carefully through the forest. Though no more spirits presented themselves directly to them, there were the constant moans and wails from all around them, the intense feeling of being watched by dark eyes, and the shadows that jumped about out of the corners of their eyes. Besides the spirits that toyed with them, they had to contend with the local wildlife. There seemed to be no shortage of dog-sized lizards with sharp claws and terrible dispositions. Though they were fierce, they were easily dispatched with only minor scratches to show for them. And more than once, Kain had to cut the thick strands of spider silk to free one of his men who had inadvertently walked into the large webs that were common among the dead branches but very difficult to spot in the grey fog constantly swirling about them. Many times, they found themselves fending back the gruesome spiders that inhabited the webs, their swift movements and armored exoskeletons making them dangerous pests. However, even with these and a few other minor irritations Kain and his brave knights managed to make fairly decent time through the forest.

Suddenly, over the other unearthly noises among the trees, Kain distinctly heard a woman's distressed voice scream shrilly and call for help. He halted his men and listened carefully, trying to figure out from which direction it came from. Again the woman called for help, her voice closer to them. There came a heavy, abrupt sound of branches snapping underfoot and dead leaves rustling off to their right. Kain and his men turned their swords and shields in the direction of the noise, ready to defend against whatever unearthly creature threw itself at them. When a large shape tore from the brush, they brandished their weapons in a vicious manner, hoping to startle the beast. The woman screamed in a mixture of shock and terror as she fell backward, catching herself on a tree before she could topple onto her back. Kain, instantly realizing the situation, quickly lowered his arms in a gesture showing he meant no harm to her.

He noticed that she was an extremely lovely, if somewhat strange, young woman. She was a young girl, perhaps two or three years older than Nancy and she was about five inches shorter than Kain. She had long, jet-black hair with pale skin and gray eyes. Her face was very soft, giving her a bewitching quality. Her dress was odd, Kain thought, not something an average Arcainian would wear. She had on a bandana made of colorful glass beads and wore a long necklace made with similar, though larger beads. Her long dress was made of beautiful leather, Kain guessed it was deerskin, with brightly painted deerskin bracelets on both wrists.

Kain had the vague sense of having seen such dress before and wondered where she had come from. He wondered if she were, in fact, another ghost. Whoever, or whatever, she happened to be, he only hoped that she could understand them as he said in a soft and soothing voice "Please don't be afraid, my lady! We mean you no harm! We are Arcainian Knights and it is our duty to help you. Are you lost?"

The young woman looked at them with wild eyes, her face set in terror as she looked around for an escape. As soon as she heard Kain's words, her wild eyes stayed wide but took on a new sense of happy excitement while all of the fear melted away as joy brightened up her beautiful face. She laughed wildly as she threw herself at Kain, wrapping her slender arms around his neck and pulling close to him. Kain was quite startled at first, but found himself gently rubbing her back and telling her that everything was all right, that she was now safe. The woman pulled away and used her steel gray eyes to gaze into his dark eyes. Her voice was a bit low and heavily accented as she said "Yes, thank you so much! I am lost! I've been lost for hours and I thought I was going to die in this horrible place!"

"You're safe now, I assure you." Kain told her, giving her his warmest smile. He couldn't help but notice how much prettier she was up close. "Who are you?"

"My name is Demetra." she said. "I am Pocan."

That explained her dress and accent, Kain thought mildly. The Pocan were a nomadic tribe of people living in the areas around Arcainia and Kuberica. They were a pleasant, peaceful people who lived off the land, rambling into the various cities to make money selling their crafted goods and performing various shows for the citizens.

"My name is Kain." he said, gently pushing her out of his arms. "What are you doing in such an awful place, Demetra?"

"My family has set up camp near the edge of this forest. I came in to search for firewood and became lost! Oh, I was so scared! I didn't know what I was going to do! Why, my poor mama and papa! They must be so worried about me! Will you help me find my way back out? I beg you!"

Kain chuckled faintly. "Of course we will, my lady. We are Arcainian Knights, and it is our duty to help those in need." He paused and thought for a moment. "However, we are on a very important mission, ourselves. So I'll tell you what I'll do. I'm going to send you back to my camp at the edge of these woods. They will be able to help you find your family again, I promise you."

"Oh, thank you so much, Kain!" she squeaked in her deep accent. She smiled sweetly to him and slowly moved to give him a gentle kiss on his cheek. "Thank you very much! Will you be leading me back to your camp, Kain?"

"No, I'm afraid I can't." he chuckled pleasantly once more. "As I said, I'm on an important mission in this forest. But I will send you with two of my best knights. I trust them with my life, so I know yours shall be safe in their hands." He gestured to two of his knights. "Sir Azaca and Sir Yavic, would you mind escorting this lovely young lady to safety?"

"As you order, Grand General Viccon." Azaca stated gallantly as both he and Yavic saluted their general with great pride. To be hand picked by Sir Kain Viccon to accompany him on a dangerous venture into the Forest of Souls and then hand picked once again to lead a beautiful girl to safety in his stead was truly an honor. Both clearly knew that their careers were on the move. They also had the added bonus of escorting such a lovely young girl for company back to their friends who they would most surely boast to.

"It's not that far back; we've only been going for a little over half an hour. But don't let that lull you into a sense of false security. Be very careful and always stay on your guard." Kain told them, giving his brave knights an earnest look. "Her life is in your hands."

"Never fear, Grand General Viccon." Yavic replied. "We will take extra special care of young Demetra. Nothing in this forest will be allowed to harm her."

"Thank you very much, Kain. I will never forget your kindness to me." Demetra told him, giving his hand a strong squeeze and his cheek another kiss.

With one last longing look at him, she turned and followed Sir Azaca and Sir Yavic back towards the direction of the entrance to the forest. Kain watched them hurry away until the thick, yellow mist of the forest swallowed them up. He then drew his sword once more and ordered his men onward

* * *

Two hours later, Kain and his three knights were still trudging through the Forest of Souls. Since they had met the lovely Demetra they had been through a few minor scuffles, mostly the large lizards and spiders, although they had been attacked by an actual ghost as well as a group of skeletons. The ghost had materialized from a tree and scared them stiff. It was the most dreadful looking thing they had seen so far in the forest. It was somewhat transparent, but did have recognizable features. It looked human, or at least it would have before it died. Now it was nothing more than a rotting corpse in tattered rags floating about. Parts of his skull and his ribs were visible and one of his eyeballs hung from its socket by thick strands. It shrieked and howled insanely as it attacked them with a phantom axe that was quite real, as one young knight who had suffered a bloody, but superficial, wound could attest to. Their swords had simply gone through it at first until Kain, who had been relieved of his sword at one point, had cracked his whip with a mighty thunder, the frayed tip snapping through the phantom's eye. It screamed and disappeared, leaving the men tired and shaken, but in one piece.

The skeletons had been considerably easier to deal with in comparison. The four fleshless ghouls had surprised them by jumping from the branches, howling and cackling. They wielded wicked looking swords and shields studded with spikes, but they were much more frightening in appearance than in actual combat. The skeletons were slow and not very intelligent, and even though they had continued to fight when their arms or even their heads had been freed, persistent hacking eventually finished them for good.

Throughout the journey, Kain had kept a close eye on his watch. Even though he had told the others to give him two days before turning back to Arcainia City, he didn't relish the idea of having to set up a simple camp in the middle of such a vile place. Frankly, he didn't even want to be caught in the forest after dark. The things they had to fight during the daylight hours were bad enough, so he didn't even want to think about what came out when the sun went down. He took another look at his watch and grimaced. It was only about four hours to dusk. They had been walking for almost three hours already. If they didn't come across the mandrake soon, they would have to spend the night in the forest. But he and his men were tired enough from the long walk and many battles. He thought about just turning back if they didn't have results soon, but he knew that was not an option. The Sisters had given him this task. If he had failed, he would never get the Elemental Sword. Besides, what would Nancy think? She thought so much of him, what would it do for her spirits if her brother had turned tail to run away from the forest just because it got dark. No, he had to press on, no matter what.

"Grand General Viccon!" Sir Azul suddenly called out ahead of him. "I think I see some sort of light up ahead! It might be the clearing we're looking for!"

Kain looked ahead of him and saw it too. It was a soft golden light that could only be sunlight. With the cover of the trees and the yellow mist keeping most light out of the forest, sunlight could only mean the presence of a clearing. And since mandrake thrived only in the sunlight of the only clearing known to be in the middle of the Forest of Souls, it would be a perfect spot to find the herb he needed. Kain just hoped it wasn't another will-o-wisp. That was all they needed at the moment, to follow a ghost light around for hours and end up lost like poor Demetra.

Kain briefly wondered how the three of them had managed. More than likely they had already found her parents and were being showered with gratitude in the form of Pocan gifts.

"Most excellent." he replied. "Let's hope for the best and see what we've got."

Their pace through the maze of trees quickened until they could see a clearing that was devoid of trees, allowing the bright glow of the sun to rain down upon the lush grass that grew there. It was the only bit of green the men had seen since entering the dismal place and Kain was filled with a new sense of faith that he had finally come to the heart of his task. All of a sudden, Kain thought he heard voices, distinct voices coming from the clearing. He stopped and listened. They sounded like men, older men, and they didn't seem to be in peril. Unlike Demetra who had been crying and yelling for help, these men sounded as if they were just sitting around having a bit of a chat. There came the sound of their laughter and upbeat tones. Kain wondered who in the world could be having a picnic in the middle of the Forest of Souls and silently answered himself. Ghosts.

As they drew closer, he saw that the voices were, in fact, coming from a group of four men sitting in a circle just at the edge of the clearing, choosing to rest on the gray dead grass over the green living grass. As they burst through the trees, the men's conversation abruptly stopped as the four of them looked up at them and frowned, not out of fear or shock, but instead idle curiosity.

Kain had been right in his assumption. The four men were old timers, seemingly up in their years. They all had long silver-gray hair tied back in a single braid and each of them covered themselves with heavy dark blankets in such a way that only their heads showed. Though they were all roughly the same size, the one whom the others seemed to be gathered around had a long pipe in his lips that looked like it were made of white stone. It took Kain a moment to realize that it was most likely bone.

Kain shuddered at the thought of it possibly being human bone as the man puffed on his pipe and blew red smoke from his nostrils. Without moving to take the pipe from his lips, he smiled and said in a deep voice "Well, hello there, young adventurers!"

The other men all smiled in turn, the lips on their elderly faces showing genuine friendship without a hint of treachery. Kain was struck with the thought that they looked like a bunch of grandfathers sitting in a tavern and sharing stories of the good ole years. He gave a mental sigh of relief as he held his hand up and gave a friendly smile. "Hello there, good sir. We mean you no harm, we are Arcainian Knights."

"I was told that by your colors." the leader replied, taking a deep puff on his pipe. "You boys seem tired. Won't you take a load off and join us for a moment?"

Kain's knights looked at him with question, uneasiness in their eyes. Kain thought for a quick moment and decided that the men weren't going to try to attack them. And if they did, they were elderly. Kain and his men could easily take them on. He nodded with a warm smile and moved to sit next to the man with the pipe. "Thank you for your hospitality."

"You boys are a long way from home." he replied. He took another puff and exhaled the red smoke. Kain took a whiff and almost began to choke. It smelled terrible! It was a sickening sweet scent of fruit decaying. How in the world could the old man manage to breathe in the putrid stuff as if it were nothing but dry air? "What brings you out this way?"

"We are in search of mandrake." Kain told him, suppressing a gag. He gestured to the leafy green plants growing in the middle of the clearing and added "It seems that we have finally found it."

There was a pause as the man casually glanced back at the plants. "Yes, you have. That is our special crop, in fact, and we guard it with pride. It's some very powerful stuff, and we couldn't let just any fool take what they please."

"Oh, I see." Kain murmured softly. "Well, I would never like to offend you by raiding your garden like a bunch of thieving rabbits. Would you be so kind as to give me a few roots to aid my task?"

"No, we are not in the habit of giving it out." he retorted in a definite tone. "As I said, not just anyone can take it from the forest."

"I beg your pardon, good sir, but it is very important that I get these roots." Kain pleaded. "Please. I could pay you for them. What will you charge for just a few?"

For the first time since meeting him, the man's blanket stirred as he lifted his hand to take the pipe out of his mouth. Kain was shocked to see that it was a skeletal hand, the bones totally bleached white and devoid of any flesh. Red smoke poured out of the opening of the blanket, escaping from the old man's hollow rib cage. Kain guessed that his body had not a scrap of flesh on it, save his head. So, they were ghosts! Kain fought his surprised fear to control his feelings. Turning white would not help the bartering one bit. If he wanted to get the precious mandrake he had to keep a cool head. Giving in to fear would cost him the prize he so desperately needed at the very least. At the very most it would cost him not only his life, but the lives of his loyal knights as well.

"We have no use for money, young man." the phantom retorted, raising a silver eyebrow. He moved his eyes up and down, examining Kain. "However, my brothers and I are very fond of wrestling. I will make you a deal. My brothers and I will wrestle you and your brothers. If you throw us, we will give you anything you require, including our special crop."

He paused and stared Kain gravely in the eye. "But if we throw you, you will die."

Kain had no choice but to accept. As he and his men stood, the old men all threw back their blankets and excitedly jumped to their feet, their bones rattling and clanking together as they moved. They were all complete skeletons, the only flesh on their ghoulish bodies were their heads. Kain whispered a prayer to Auset for Her help in his battle as the skeleton men all picked an opponent. When everyone was paired up, the leader threw back his old head and let out a mighty bellow. Instantly, the other skeleton men seized the humans, who had been taken by surprise by the leader's shriek. One knight was instantly tossed to the ground like nothing more than a rag doll and his opponent immediately leapt atop his body, ripping and tearing the poor man's body to shreds with his sharp talons and teeth. The other humans were taken aback by the gruesome sounds that echoed in their ears, but managed to hold their ground.

Kain was surprised at the strength and speed of his phantom attacker. The skeleton man gripped him tightly by the shoulders, his sharp bone fingers digging into Kain's armor as he pawed the dead earth with his bone feet. He pushed Kain back, trying to knock the human knight off balance. Kain grit his teeth and fought back against the powerful force, but the harder he pushed, the more his attacker seemed to gain the upper hand. Through wincing eyes, Kain caught a glimpse of the old man's face. He wasn't even breaking a sweat but was in fact smiling enjoyably while Kain felt like he was pushing against a brickwall. The old man was toying with him!

Kain tried with all his might to at least come to a standstill, but was forced backward towards the sun-filled clearing. The closer they got to the sunlight, the less the man pushed. Kain managed to dig his heels into the soil and give a quick shove. The skeleton man was pushed backward away from the green grass and instantly pushed back with his original strength. Kain howled as his muscles buckled, but he refused to give in to the specter. He was shoved backward once more and again the man lost strength. Just as Kain was about to shove him back, he realized that it must be the sunlight that was weakening the man. He had to get the phantom closer to the sunlight if he wanted to have any hope at winning the struggle.

However, the skeleton man came to the same conclusion and quickly spun around on his heels, almost knocking Kain onto his back. Kain regained himself just in time but was now facing towards the mandrake clearing. Instead of being able to have the man push them towards the sunlight, he was now pushing them away. Kain groaned. The ghost shoved hard and managed to push Kain back a few feet, but the brave knight jumped forward, throwing all of his massive bulk into the skeleton's rib cage. He tried to catch his breath as the skeleton lost more strength, but it was short lived as the ghost refused to give up. The struggle continued for many minutes, but with no gain in advantage for either wrestler. Finally, in a final act of desperation, Kain grit his teeth and used a surge of adrenaline to give him the power to throw himself full force into the skeleton man. Both were knocked back to the edge of the clearing. The phantom squealed shrilly in fury and tried to muster enough of his waning power to get away from the sun, his bones hissing and smoking where the light touched him. In his weakened condition, the phantom paused for a split second to replant his feet. It was the opening Kain desperately needed and he grabbed the shoulder bones of the ghost tight as he jumped up and spun around. Using the skeleton's own weight and momentum, Kain flipped him over his shoulder to land right into the clearing. The man screamed loudly as he landed onto the green grass, bursting into flames as soon as he hit. He burned for several seconds before the ashes crumbled and floated away on the wind.

Exhausted, Kain bent forward and took deep breaths to fill his burning lungs. Gasping and panting, he slowly turned to see how his other men were faring, very afraid at what he would see. To his surprise and great relief, he saw that both men were alive, though just as tired and exhausted as he was if not very confused that their opponents had simply vanished in the middle of the bout. It seemed that when Kain had defeated their leader, the other three skeleton men had disappeared. His men had held out just long enough. Kain looked at the mangled body of his third knight and sighed lowly as grief began to fill his heart.

He walked over to the gore and looked it over. Kain always wanted to get his men who had died in combat back home for a proper funeral. But there was not enough left of the man to be sent back. With a shudder, Kain whispered a prayer in the memory of his deceased knight, begging Auset to be merciful and let his soul be free from the forest. It was truly agonizing, but there was nothing he could do now. With a heavy heart, he collected the fallen knight's metal ID tags from around what was left of his neck before he turned and started into the clearing to fetch his costly prize.

Kain stopped himself just in time as the myth surrounding the plant popped into his head. He silently cursed himself for being so careless as to forget something as important as his sister's protection from the screams of the mandrake. He reached into his pack and took out the ball of wax. He tore off two pieces for himself and firmly stuck one in each ear before tossing the ball to his two knights, who proceeded to do the same. When all were ready, Kain gripped three of the plants by their tough, waxy leaves and, with a mighty tug, yanked them out of the earth. Even with the wax, Kain thought he could hear the shrill, high-pitched squeals of the mystical plants, but whether they were real or not, they weren't enough to harm him or his knights thanks to his clever sister.

After a few seconds, Kain thought the maddening shrieking had ceased and he put the three humanoid-shaped roots into a small cloth bag. He grinned triumphantly as he tossed it into the air and caught it in celebration before stuffing it into his pocket and taking out his watch. Still three and a half hours until dusk. If they hurried they could be out before nightfall. But they had to move swiftly. He voiced his thoughts to his two knights and after they expressed their agreement, they gathered their wits and hurried away from the tiny clearing back the way they had come.

CHAPTER XIV

Nancy stood in a large meadow of grass humming sweetly to herself as she enjoyed picking the beautiful flowers. She plucked a large dandelion, drew in a deep breath, and blew with all her might. The many white fuzzy seeds billowed around her daintily and she couldn't help but giggle lowly as some tickled her nose. She looked at the almost bald head of the flower and grinned. Only one seed left. That meant that she would have only one child. She giggled in girlish glee and wondered who would be the father of this child. She began to fantasize over who she would like the mystery lover to be and failed to notice the sky grow dark over her head.

Suddenly, she felt the temperature around her grow cooler as a bone-chilling breeze blew over the meadow, motioning the grass like the waves of the sea. A shiver traveled up her spine and she whirled around. Nothing. The only thing she saw were the other troops at their makeshift camp. Robert, Michael, and Raphael were playing a card game with some of the other scouts and knights while the other men were doing something or other to keep themselves occupied. None of them seemed to notice the cold breeze or the shadow that had shrouded them. Nancy looked again and noticed that it was sunny where they were, the shadow stopping a few feet away from her. She shrugged blandly and tried to convince herself that it was just a cloud covering the sun.

Then came the smell. It was faint at first, making her wrinkle her nose in distaste. It was an odd smell, almost like food that had been left out in the sun and was spoiling in the heat. But as it got stronger, it grew worse and more disgusting. Nancy choked and her eyes began to water. She threw her head down as she tried her best to repress the gagging in her throat. It was the smell of rotting flesh. The smell of death. She looked all around and squeaked in shock as she came face to face with a horrid steed. It was a large horse with fiery yellow eyes and a coal black coat. When it neighed mightily, Nancy saw gleaming fangs in it's maw as gray dust and green saliva flew out. She gasped in horror and choked more as the putrid air gripped her throat like a vice. She looked onto the beast's back and began to tremble at the sight of the rider. He was a monster of a being, towering high over the girl in black armor adorn with ghastly skulls and bones. He was covered with a heavy black cape and a hood, which hid the features of his face in blackness except for his large eyes that glared a bright red like fire burning in his sockets.

With slow, even movements, he reached under his cloak and withdrew a large scroll that appeared to be made out of some sort of skin. As Nancy stood trying desperately to suck fresh air in past the rank filth, he threw it at her, smacking her in the face. She fell back and landed on the grass, gasping as she rubbed her sore nose.

Then the creature began to cackle with laughter that was so deep and hollow that it could not have been made by a human. A low growl reverberated from his throat as he clutched his large, clawed hands with a dull cracking. He reached his hand to the hood, gripped the black cloth, and whisked it away to reveal a hideous yellow skull with fire burning brightly in the sockets and blood covering the wickedly sharp teeth. He opened his jaw with a loud creak and hissed putrid air from his throat. Nancy tried to scream, but was unable to from the gasping and choking she suffered. She vomited onto the grass at her side and swooned as blackness crept in on her mind.

She felt a powerful hand grip her arm and haul her roughly upwards, lifting her as if she were merely a flower being plucked from the grass. She choked on her bile as her legs dangled in the air, her head rolling lazily on her shoulders as her mind spun dizzily. Running more on her survival instincts than anything else, she managed to find her dagger and limply lashed out, moving the weapon without any style or accuracy as she simply flung her arm outward. She felt the blade catch on something and heard a hellacious roar as the iron grip on her arm released and dropped her back onto the soft grass. Blinded by her dizzy dementia and slowed by her weak muscles, she drew her sword and hacked savagely out in front of her, swinging her sword about as if blindfolded. Again she felt her blade slow as it dug into something yielding and heard the distant bellows of a demon horse and the roars of the demon rider.

And then she felt nothing as she blacked out completely.

* * *

When Nancy came to, she saw that the monster and his steed were gone from the meadow along with the ice-cold breeze, the shadow, and the noxious air. Nancy inhaled the sweet, clean air deeply, filling her lungs greedily. She grabbed her aching head and sighed dully and she tried to pick her weary body from the grass. She felt several hands grab her by her shoulders, arms and back, but these hands were soft and gentle and she felt safe in their grasps. She heard frantic male voices call out her name, sounding very close to her ears. As the white cloud lifted from her vision, she turned to find Prince Michael and Raphael holding her up while Robert and several of the other knights and soldiers crowded around her with weapons drawn, all displaying concern and fear in their faces, but also looking at her with surprise and respect. As she stumbled, she kicked her sword and saw that the blade was greased with green slime.

* * *

Kain took his watch from his pocket to check the time on impulse. As he grunted with displeasure and dropped it back into his pocket, he carefully removed the Dragon Heart from under his shirt and looked it over, thinking of Li and wondering what she was doing at the moment. He hoped she was getting along well by herself. He raised a brow and pondered why he had been inclined to hold it. He hoped that it wasn't an omen and that his cousin was doing well. He shrugged it off. Of course Li was okay, there was no reason for her to be otherwise. She was at his house pretty much not doing anything, after all. Just sitting around waiting for their return.

After replacing the Dragon Heart under his shirt, he took out his watch again and glanced at the time. It had been a little under three hours since he had found the mandrake. As those three hours had passed closer to nightfall, it seemed that the supernatural forces of the forest were mustering themselves. They had come across less and less of the living creatures and more of the dead ones. They had fought more skeletons and had seen quite a number more phantoms on the way back to the forest entrance then when they had come. A few of the ghastly spirits had attacked, but most of them were there just to be seen, from adventurers who had tried to brave the forest and failed to people who had inadvertently gotten lost within the maze of trees. Kain realized that what the first ghost had said was true. It seemed that those who died in the forest became permanent residents. He hated to think that his brave but fallen knight was one of those lost souls.

Kain was so deep in his thoughts that he almost failed to hear a low grumble reverberate from the depths of the ghostly fog. A warrior's reflex took over his body and brought him to a sudden stop, freezing all movement. He held his position for several long seconds, only daring to move his eyes to and fro and nothing else. After an eternity, Kain exhaled the deep breath he had not realized he had been holding in and relaxed his tense muscles. Perhaps it had simply been a tree creaking in the wind, or branches rustling as some small animal skittered about. Or, maybe he didn't even hear it, perhaps it was just his imagination. As he slowly lowered his guard he reminded himself that the Forest of Souls was the type of place that loved to play tricks on one's frazzled mind.

A hideous snarl tore through the air followed by fierce growls like those of a dog or wolf, a very large dog or wolf. Kain gasped in surprise, ready to defend against any onslaught as he came face to face with only trees and fog mysteriously swirling around his body like the dead fingers of a long perished specter. The savage growling and snarling echoed all around the men, sounding as if they were surrounded by a pack of bloodthirsty wolves, but there was nothing to be seen. They looked all around wildly while trying to bring defense to all sides against an inevitable attack as they vainly scanned the trees for the phantom dogs. But only the sounds of drool-spitting yelps and harsh snaps greeted their frightened ears.

Then all was silent once again, cold and forbidding silence. The terrified men glared all around them, jumping at every wisp of fog. Kain suddenly realized that it had not only been the sounds of the dogs that had been silenced, but every other sound of the forest as well. The once moaning, groaning, laughing sounds of the forest were gone and only an eerie, intimidating silence was left, far more frightening than any other sound the forest had since produced. All three men, as very brave as they were, began to tremble. They were like the deer that could not see the hunter closing in but could sense it bringing their death.

When the shrill howl of a wolf broke the insane quiet, all three shrieked and nearly jumped out of their skins just before a large body jumped silently into view. Although the trees it had jumped from should have bent and snapped quite loudly from the bulk passing through, there was not a single sound, nor a single touched branch. The beast snapped its jaws fiercely and lowered its head as it clawed the ground with its massive front paws. The monster looked much like an over-grown wolf, standing at least six feet tall and about ten feet from its black snout to its bushy tail. It was covered in course gray fur that rippled as it snarled and its large mouth was full of razor sharp fangs dripping spittle. Five long talons grew from its huge paws, which were about the size of a man's head. However, its most frightening feature was its eye. It had only one large eye that sat in the middle of its face and burned a terrible yellow.

The phantom wolf pawed the ground, snapped its jaws and sprayed out slimy drool, and then threw back its head to wail its shrill howl before pouncing. Kain threw his shield up to defend himself against the powerful jaws and was thrown into the air by the impact. The other two knights rushed at the beast, swords raised high, voices roaring. It batted the first away as if Sir Azul were a fly, but took Sir Zanchaz's sword to the neck. There was a resounding thump, but the blade bounced harmlessly off its hide. It snarled and bit at the man, but he had leapt out of the way just in time. Kain had recovered and rushed forward to slash at the beast three times as Sir Azul lashed out twice. All five blows bounced off with no effect as the phantom hound barked gruffly and snapped savagely.

With a powerful bound, it leaped over the men's heads to land behind them. They twirled around just as it howled once more and opened its jaws wide. A powerful jet of intense flame started in the back of its throat and screamed towards them. Kain took the brunt of the fire with his shield, the flames licking around the edges of the steel. As Kain worked on holding back the flames, the other two knights each ran on either side of the beast and attacked the momentarily distracted phantom. They delivered mighty blows to its underside in a vain attempt to find a weak spot in the beast. Though nothing happened, it bellowed in fury and lashed out with its paws, catching Azul in the chest and launching him into a tree. Zanchaz took the blow to his legs and managed to roll away from the powerful jaws.

Without the fire to deal with anymore, Kain drew his bow and called out to his men "The eye! Try going for the eye!"

Azul picked himself off the ground and tried to regain the senses that were knocked away by the collision. The next thing he saw was the phantom hound bearing down on him. Kain fired his bow. The arrow flew swiftly towards the monster's eye and struck its shoulder. Kain cursed savagely as Azul took a blow to his shield that knocked him up over the beast and onto his back. Kain notched another arrow, but sent a wild shot into the air as he quickly raised his shield to stop another massive fire blast from cooking him alive. As Azul groaned groggily from the ground, Zanchaz rushed at the fire-spewing beast with a sword blow aimed for the large yellow eye.

The phantom hound snarled hideously and snapped at the man, the jaws clamping down on his arm. He howled in terror as the sword dropped from his hand and he was lifted off the ground. With a desperate plea to Auset, Kain targeted the single yellow eye and let the bowstring go. The arrow whizzed through the air and hit its mark, a perfect bull's eye. The phantom hound roared in pain, dropping the man to the ground as it clawed at its eye. It stood on its back legs and let loose a dismal howl as the gray fur covering its body burst into flames. Kain shouldered his bow on the run as he rushed to collect his injured knight while Azul hobbled to help. He grabbed his friend's sword and the three made their way away from the howling, burning beast.

As they quickly made their way through the trees, Kain looked at Zanchaz's arm. Though it was quite bloody and looked rather nasty, the bone didn't appear to be broken. That was a good sign for the man, but the wound was still serious enough to warrant medical attention. They would dress it with salve and wrap it in a sling as soon as possible and hope Zanchaz could make it to the City of Hurst for treatment. The young knight voiced that he would be able to make it without problem, stating that the wound looked more serious than it actually was.

They were so intent on the man's wound that they failed to notice the body laying face-down on the dead earth until they were right up to it. Kain jumped with shock and silently scolded himself for having let his attention be drawn away no matter how briefly as he looked down and examined the body. Noticing that the man wore the armor of an Arcainian Knight, his heart plunged into the pit of his stomach as a sour lump formed in his throat. Praying that it wouldn't be who he knew it was, he pulled the body's shoulders until it rolled onto its back. Sir Azaca's pale, cold face stared back up at him. Kain sighed dejectedly and stooped to examine the body. He concluded that the man had been dead for some time, noting that his body was as cold as clay and that the stiffness had already begun to set in. He had died from rapid blood loss due to a slit throat that was cleanly sliced. Cleanly sliced as opposed to savagely ripped, which implied that it had been done with an edged weapon and not an animal's claw. The area around showed no signs of struggle, so whoever . . . or whatever had done this to Azaca had crept up behind him without his knowledge, slit his throat, and left him to bleed to death.

Kain immediately tried his best to dismiss the first dreadful lingering thought to enter his head. He refused to believe that treachery had been involved in the death of such a fine soldier. He just could not imagine that one of his best knights had murdered one of his own in cold blood. He refused to believe it.

He breathed a huge sigh of relief and felt a dark weight lift from his shoulders when he saw strange prints in the blood stained grass around the body. They looked like the hoof-prints of a deer, except for they were much too large and were clearly made from a two-legged creature as opposed to something that walked on all fours. Kain deduced that Azaca had gotten separated from Yavic and Demetra for whatever reason and had met his fate at the blade of some monster or ghost, perhaps one that they themselves had fought along the way. Kain collected Sir Azaca's metal ID tags before he gathered his men around and led them in a prayer for their brave departed brother.

A hellish bellow shook the trees all around him. All three men jumped in fright as their flesh went white and their hair stood on end. They watched in stunned silence as two massive hands connected to two equally massive arms extended out from the cover of the mist coated trees. All they saw were the demon's arms, white and covered with wiry green fur, but from that alone the knights knew it must be monstrous in size. Vicious snorts and wet hisses spat out from the dense fog as the beast wrapped its long clawed fingers around Sir Azaca's legs and hauled him into the mysterious beyond of the forest as if he weighed as much as a feather. The horrid sounds of flesh ripping and bones snapping filled the air as a gruesome chomping was heard. The three men regained themselves and not wanting to wait for the devil to reveal the rest of itself to them, hurried away from the scene.

They had not run far when they came across another body laying in the grass, this time so mutilated that it was difficult to identify that it was even human much less who it might have been. The only way to tell that it was the second Arcainia Knight who had escorted the girl away were the tell-tale shreds of an Arcainian uniform and Arcainian armor pounded by a thousand hammers littered around the blood soaked ground around the man. Kain would later describe that the body was nothing but a pile of gory mush, looking like it had been trampled by a hundred horses and reduced to pulp. As Kain stared at the mess trying to make some sense out of it, he heard one of the two knights behind him heave.

All around the site there were the same tracks of the deer-like creature that had been around Azaca's body. It seemed that whatever had slashed Azaca's throat had gone even further with Yavic and trampled him to death, and then kept trampling him. It must have taken poor Demetra with it, because he did not see any sign of her. He slowly began to approach the body for a closer examination and stopped short when he heard the sounds of soft feminine sobs fill his ears. He looked all around trying to pinpoint the source but saw nothing save trees and the ghostly fog. Fearing that it was another phantom on the prowl, he listened closer. Finally, he decided that it came from behind a large tree to his left not far from where he stood. He tightened the grip on his sword and slowly tracked the sound, silent in his approach. He peered cautiously around the massive trunk and was surprised to see that it was Demetra alive but terrified out of her mind as she sat with her face in her hands crying her eyes out. At first, Kain said nothing, he just stared down at the pitiful girl in disbelief. Finally, he found his voice and softly murmured her name as he reached out to place his hand gently on her shoulder.

Demetra released a hideous shriek as she tore away from Kain's grip, her eyes wild with terror and her face stark white. As soon as she realized that it was Kain, her cries of horror subsided into sobs of relief and joy as she leapt into Kain's arms, holding him tight against her fragile frame. She flooded his cheeks with grateful kisses and wailed "Oh Kain! Oh, thank goodness it's you, Kain! Thank goodness! Thank goodness! It was awful! Terrible! Poor Sir Yavic! He's dead, Kain! Kain! He's dead! It came out of the trees and killed him! He's dead! Sir Yavic is dead!"

"I know he is, sweetheart. I saw him." Kain replied soothingly, rubbing her back and holding her close, turning slightly so that the frantic girl's eyes would be shielded from the gore. Poor Demetra had suffered enough.

"He's dead! That monster! It . . . it came out of the trees and pushed him down and stepped on him over and over and over and oh my Kain he's dead! I saw it! I saw him die! Kain, I saw that monster dance on his body! I saw him die!"

"It's okay, Demetra. It's over." he told her softly. "It is all over now. We're here and we're not going to let anything hurt you. It's all over now."

It took several minutes of comforting the hysterical girl, but she finally managed to calm down enough to be able to tell her terrible story. She spoke of the three of them having been walking for some time, she couldn't tell how long, when they had seen the ghost of an old man that begged them to help him. It had said that it was trapped in the Forest of Souls and the only way for him to be free of his supernatural prison was to have his bones dug up from the foot of a nearby tree and carried out of the forest. Of course the Arcainian Knights had agreed to help him but they also wanted to get Demetra out of the forest as soon as possible so they could get her back to her worried family. Azaca had bravely volunteered to find the old man's remains and catch up with Yavic and Demetra. That had been the last that they had seen of him. They had gotten to the spot where Kain found the remains of Yavic's body when a creature that Demetra could only describe as a horrific monstrosity, the largest thing she had ever seen with ghastly claws and hellish eyes, jumped out at them. Kain and his two remaining knights silently wondered if perhaps the creature that had snatched away Sir Azaca's body to devour had been the culprit. They suddenly felt guilty for turning tail.

Demetra began to try to explain what had happened next, but slipped into hysterics and had to be consoled once again. When she had somewhat regained control of herself, Kain pushed her away and into the arms of his other knights before moving to Yavic's body and kneeling beside it. He whispered another prayer to his brave knight and then withdrew his dagger to gently prod through the gore.

He winced as he picked through the ripped flesh, searching for the knight's tags. Finally, he found a small chain that was once wrapped around what used to be Sir Yavic's neck. Kain hissed a mournful sigh as he carefully pulled up the chain, taking the stained metal tags and putting them into a leather pouch to join those once belonging to Sir Azaca and Sir Tomaz.

As Kain weighed the pouch heavily in his hand, he began to lift himself back to his feet. As he stood, he happened to land his eyes onto Demetra's feet. He was so startled by what he saw that he gasped loudly and fell back onto his hip, his jaw dropping and his eyes widening as his dagger dropped from his numb hand. Below the hemline of her deerskin dress her legs were covered with course brown fur and her feet were large, black hooves as sharp as razors like those of a deer. He brought his shocked eyes to her beautiful face and met cold, gray eyes that blazed in fury, her mouth scowling darkly that her true self having finally been discovered.

Before Kain could react and shout a warning, the she-devil turned to Zanchaz, reared her deer leg back, and kicked him in the knee, the hoof easily slicing through his armor and leather pants. The knight shrieked in shocked agony and crumpled to the ground, clutching at his torn leg. Demetra then raised her leg and stomped down on his belly, her hoof easily piercing his steel armor. Then she stomped on his chest, her hooves coming down hard with furious anger again and again. She glared at the remaining two knights and hissed savagely as she clawed the air and pawed the stained grass.

By this time less than three seconds had elapsed and Kain and his final brave knight Azul had recovered their senses, standing ready for battle with their swords held high and their shields poised to defend. They rushed her simultaneously, Kain on her right and Azul on her left, the rage of their slaughtered friends powering their attack. Demetra roared and clawed at them as they approached. Just as they reached her and swung their blades, she stunned them with her swift agility as she leapt high into the air away from their deathblows. She flipped in air as she traveled, striking a tree with her hooves and instantly pushing off with extremely powerful legs so that she flew hard at Azul. Her hooves struck his shield with enough impact to dent the steel and knocked the man flat onto his back, stunning him as the wind was knocked out of him. The instant Demetra hit the dead soil she reared her leg back and kicked Azul in the temple, crushing his skull like a clay pot. Then she nimbly leapt away before Kain could lash out at her.

Kain was the last one left of those that had ventured into the forest of the dead, the deer woman claiming three deaths for her own and more than likely the fourth as well. His heavy heart filled with rage and the thirst for vengeance. He howled his battle cry, brandished his sword, and attacked. Demetra hissed and spat like a savage cat as she ducked and dodged away from his blows and kicked wildly at him. He managed to block with his shield but was surprised at the sheer power and ferocity behind her kicks, which gouged and dented the strong steel as if it were nothing but foil.

With her greater speed, agility, and strength giving her the definite advantage, Demetra soon took the upperhand, quickly lashing out to grab the Grand General by the collar and hoisting up the larger human before dropping him on his back. He released the grip on his sword as he grunted and wheezed dully, the breath knocked harshly from his lungs. Demetra kicked the sword far from his reach and was on her prey in a flash. She raised her black, blood drenched hoof over his face, and let loose a horrific wail of triumph. Kain gasped and shut his eyes tight to brace himself for the dark void of death. He heard Demetra's wail cut off harshly with a squeak and felt warm, sticky droplets touch his cheek. Kain opened his eyes to see her leg no longer hovering over him and that her hands were clutching at her throat, blood oozing from between her fingers as a low, painful gurgle issued from her trembling lips.

As Kain watched mesmerized, he heard the sharp sound of air being cut just before a second dart embedded in her eye. Her throat momentarily forgotten, she clawed at her new wound, unable to scream in pain because of the dart sticking in her throat. Mere seconds later, she took another blowpipe dart in the shoulder that sent her wild. Kain tried to roll away as her feet came stomping down in furious pain, but wasn't quick enough as her hoof clipped his arm and gave him a nasty laceration. He winced and picked himself up to one knee as he reached back and from his pack pulled the first thing his hand closed around: the glok weapon Martin had given him. With not even a moment to worry whether or not the queer weapon would even work, Kain leveled the iron tube and pulled the trigger. There came a tremendous explosion that thundered like a mountain collapsing as a thick cloud of sooty smoke blew out from the weapon, choking in Kain's throat. The lead ball zipped through the air, striking Demetra in the heart with the force of a mule's kick, knocking her back as she gave a short, sloppy grunt. She collapsed in a heap on the dead grass, her body limp and motionless. Not taking a chance, Kain immediately took up his sword and freed the deer woman's head.

Kain gave an exhausted sigh and clutched his bleeding arm as he looked in the direction the shots had come from. He saw his sister and Raphael running to his aid. Having heard the commotion coming out of the forest, Raphael rushed in to try and help his friend with the fierce deer woman but was a tad slow. Nancy had her weapon to her lips before he had even made it a few feet in, reloading it after each shot like a pro.

The pair rushed to Kain's side and upon seeing that he was exhausted but otherwise safe, they greeted each other excitedly. Raphael grimaced at the sight of his fallen brothers-in-arms, turning from the gruesome sight of their mangled bodies and sucking down his horror to ask Kain about the mandrake. Kain simply patted his pocket while giving a tired grunt but said nothing. While Nancy quickly dressed the gash on her brother's arm with ointment and a bandage from his pack, he reached over with his good hand and rubbed her head softly. "Thank you very much for your help."

Nancy simply smiled as she tightened the bandage. He winced sharply. "I would be dead now if it weren't for your skill with that blowpipe of yours."

"Well, I wasn't about to let that thing stomp you to death, big bro." she replied softly, putting her arm around him to support his weary frame. "Are you okay?"

"Yes, I'm fine." he said, pulling himself up out of her grasp. "How far is it to the edge of the forest?"

"Not far. Only about a few hundred feet or so."

Kain was quite surprised. He had not realized that they had been so close to the edge. But it explained why they had been able to hear the fighting. "Good. I want to get our fallen knights out of here. Think you two could help me drag—"

He was cut off by a ghastly shriek behind them. They all squealed in fright and jumped around to face the phantom forest around them. They saw the fog swirl and twist around the trees as if it were alive as small points of light began to pop up all over. Kain noticed that they were coming in pairs and it took him a moment to realize that they were glowing eyes. The glowing eyes of a dozen specters, each moaning and howling lowly as misty arms reached out for the adventurers. Not wasting another second, the three Arcainians quickly rushed from the scene as quickly as their legs could carry them as the forest shrieked in mad fury and the ghostly mist chased after them. They didn't even dare to stop once they reached the edge of the forest where the fading light of dusk greeted them as the angry voices were close on their heels. They ran all the way to the camp where a large group was already gathered to hear Kain's story.

As Kain attempted to catch the breath he had long ago lost, Robert walked up to him and took his hand in a strong grip. From the solemn expression on his face as well as on the faces of his other friends, Kain guessed that he was about to be told bad news and tried his best to prepare for it. However, his heart began to flutter nervously in his chest.

"Kain, I'm sorry to have to tell you this but . . ." Robert began in a low voice, but couldn't find the strength to continue.

Kain's heart did a harsh flop and plunged into the pit of his stomach. He wasn't quite sure exactly how or why he knew what he was about to be told, but suddenly the image of his cousin's face exploded in his throbbing head. "It's Li, isn't it?"

Robert nodded painfully. "Noknor captured her. He's holding her prisoner in his castle."

Kain felt his head go light and he began to topple backwards, but he caught himself. His lips trembled momentarily before he was able to ask in a feeble voice that was almost too low to be heard "Is . . . is she all right?"

"As far as we know, yes." Robert told him, releasing his hand and gently squeezing his shoulder.

"What . . . . happened?"

Raphael opened his mouth to tell Kain, but stopped short. He found his mouth was far too dry to speak even if he had not been taken speechless. Instead, he took the scroll from Nancy and handed it to his friend.

"Where did you get this?" he asked as he slowly began to unravel it with quivering hands.

"One of Noknor's demons gave it to me." Nancy told him before explaining her terrible experience with the vile creature.

"Did he hurt you!" Kain snapped as he reached out to grab her arm.

"Apart from making me barf, no sir."

Kain heard Michael inhaled a long, sharp breath, the unmistakable sound of someone about to say something he'd rather not share. Nancy flinched and tore her eyes away from Kain's piercing glare the moment before Michael told him "The . . . thing tried to kidnap her, also."

"WHAT!" Kain roared, his face white with a look of stark terror, making everyone jump. Kain shook Nancy roughly, yelping out "What happened! Are you okay? What did that thing do to you!"

Nancy screeched, trying to pull out of her brother's grip as his fingers dug painfully into her arm. Kain jerked her towards his body, grabbing both of her shoulders as he looked her over from head to toe, looking for the slightest scratch on his skin. The more she tried to pull from him, the tighter he gripped her.

"I'm fine!" she winced, squirming in a vain attempt to get away. "Kain! Please! I said I'm okay!"

"Grand General Viccon." Robert murmured softly, gripping his friend's shoulder and squeezing hard until he finally got the man's attention. "Kain, she's okay. She came out without a scratch, which is more than I can say for the demon. She killed it single-handedly."

"What?" Kain hissed, not sure if he had heard correctly as he loosened his grip on Nancy's arms but did not let her go just yet.

"Yeah, man." Michael replied, clapping Kain on his other shoulder. "You shoulda seen her! She is one tough little filly!"

Kain looked back at Nancy, finally released his hands from her as she stumbled back several steps, looking a little shaken and somewhat cross.

"That thing tried to grab her out of that meadow over there." Michael told him, gesturing to the spot he was referring to. "But she wasn't going anywhere without a fight. She cut that demon and his horse down, just pulled out her sword and started swinging until she pass . . . ah, until she stopped swinging, I mean." Despite the heavy air around them, Michael just had to laugh as he remembered the look of fear in the demon's eyes as Nancy's sword slashed into him over and over again as it fell helpless from his steed. "I don't think it was expecting THAT at all. I'll tell you this much, if Nancy hadn't killed it Noknor sure would have."

"You killed it?" Kain asked his sister. Nancy's response was a soft nod of her head, barely even noticeable.

"Yeah, she handed that thing its demon ass." Robert chuckled nervously. "We, ah . . . we burned the bodies of it and the horse it rode. We weren't sure if . . . ah, that is . . ."

"Had to make sure it was dead." Michael finished for him. "No better way than that."

Kain continued to stare at his sister with nervous uncertainty, his heart still racing in his chest and his mouth very dry. There was a long pause before Nancy replied in a strong, sure voice "I'm all right, Kain. Really."

Kain held his heavy eyes on her a moment longer, not looking very convinced. Then with a dull sigh, he pulled his gaze away from her to examine the scroll crushed in his hand. It was made out of skin, and knowing Noknor it was most likely human skin, and the writing was printed in a substance that looked and smelled like blood. Human blood.

My fine Grand General,

I have never before had the honor to meet you face to face since that time some years ago, but your reputation, as that of your father's, does do you justice, I'm sure. I realize that you have been sent after me by your queen to defend the honor of Kuberica, but I also know that you have your own reasons. I understand. However, you understand this. I am the most powerful being ever to grace this planet and I will never be defeated. And certainly not by a fool like you. I have your dear beautiful chink cousin as a guest in my castle. I dare say she put up quite a fight against my men, I'm sure you would be proud of her. But it was all for not as she is now mine. As for your dear sister, by now she must be well on her way to my castle, and I enjoy welcoming the lovely child to her new home. Though I assure you that both your cousin and your sister are quite safe currently, I tell you this in fair warning. Viccon, if you continue after me, not only will you never see their smiling faces ever again but the fate of your parents shall also befall you. I've killed two Viccons before and I will kill at least one Viccon more before this is all said and done.

You will do well to remember this.

Lord Noknor, Scourge of Evil

Kain's mind suddenly flashed red that Noknor would dare threaten his cousin and his sister and he didn't hide it one bit. In his fury he was about to crumble the skin sheet when suddenly and without warning a small flame began to glow in the center of the page. As Kain and his friends watched, the flames grew brighter and larger. When the flames licked Kain's fingers, he tossed the sheet down in reflex, swearing loudly. The paper then snapped into a blazing inferno before disappearing without leaving any trace of it behind.

Kain was now aflame with anger and scorn as horrid images flooded his skull. Nancy moved towards him to comfort him, but Raphael grabbed her arm and pulled her back, shaking his head silently as he did so. He knew it wouldn't do any good to try and talk to him. He knew Kain just needed to blow off some steam.

And blow off steam he did. He threw back his head and roared like a savage beast, turning bright red as his veins popped out of his forehead and neck. Nancy squeaked in fear and cowered away from him, terrified of her brother for the first time in her entire life. She had never seen him so enraged before and he scared her to death. And the worst part about it, she felt, was that there was nothing she could for him. She couldn't even get close to him.

CHAPTER XV

Lightning blazed forth brightly and thunder boomed menacingly overhead. Kain looked up at the black sky as a crack of lightning arched with a blinding flash, followed immediately by the grumble of angry thunder. He jumped at another bolt of lightning as he stared up the large hill standing mightily before him, his eyes trailing up the steep incline to gaze at the elegant house made of blue brick resting silently at the top. With the threat of a tremendous downpour lurking overhead, Kain started up the hill. When the sky bellowed with thunder, sounding like the pounding of a heavy drum in the sky, he ran faster to get to shelter, but the faster he ran the taller the hill seemed to become as the house always lay just out of reach. Just as he was beginning to think he would never reach the top in time, he was suddenly there standing in front of the house. He saw that the door was made from thick boards of the finest Arcainian blue oak bound tightly by powerful wrought iron. He seemed to remember seeing the door before, but he figured that it was just because everyone in Arcainia used that particular type of oak. However, there was something about the beautiful shapes of the iron that gave him a warm, homey sort of feeling. It was as if he should have known who lived there but couldn't remember their names or faces. He tried to peek through the narrow window beside the door but couldn't see much of anything except an inviting warm glow as he reached out with his fist to knock.

    A strong gust of wind blew and a few heavy raindrops began to splatter on the cobblestone path stretching beyond Kain as he went to rap upon the door. When his knuckles tapped against the wood, thunder ripped the sky apart and a tremendous rain pelted down from the black sky. Kain was soaked in seconds. He was about to try another knock when the massive oak door flew open on its own accord and unseen hands drew him in out of the rain.

    He stood in a very familiar house lit up by a light that seemed to come from nowhere but shined everywhere. Everything was familiar to him, the furniture and the way it was arranged, the knick-knacks cluttering all the available space on the shelves and mantle, and the artwork hanging on the wall. It all struck him so odd that it took him a few minutes to realize that he was completely dry. As Kain pondered over how such a curious thing could have happened, he looked over the fireplace and saw a large portrait of his parents, Richard and Fang Viccon.

Suddenly, the realization hit him that he was in his house! Well, not the house he now owned and shared with Nancy, but his parents' old house. That house had been torn down when Kain was just a boy living in China. When Kain and Nancy had returned back to Arcainia, he had recovered the land that was rightfully his and built his current house over the old foundation of his previous home. It couldn't possibly be the same house. But it was. He was looking at his old home, examining it closely, every aspect triggering so many wonderful memories that had been pushed far back into his mind and forgotten so long ago.

He stepped forward to bask in the glow of warm and cheery memories and instantly all went dark as the blackest night for a few seconds before all around him turned white as the purest snow. The whiteness soon faded and Kain saw a darkened room with two elegant satin chairs before a massive fireplace where a roaring inferno burned brightly.

A female voice speaking Chinese issued from one of the chairs, telling him in a sweet angel's voice "Come sit with me and warm yourself, Kain."

"Who . . . who are you?" he asked cautiously as he approached the fine chair.

"Someone who is very proud of you and your sister." was her reply. Her voice was so calm and soothing and rang familiar in Kain's mind. He finally reached the chairs and looked to see who it was. Much to his surprise, he saw Nancy sitting in the chair. Well, she looked exactly like his sister only a bit older, more Li's age or perhaps just a few years older.

"Mama?" he gasped, unable to believe his eyes.

"Yes, my darling son. It is I." Fang spoke Chinese as she smiled brightly, a tear already formed in her eye. She rose and stood face to face with her son, looking up at his face as her boy towered over her, just like his father. Both wanted to jump into each other's arms and hold on tight, tighter than they ever had before. However, for what seemed like an eternity, they both just stood and stared, not knowing what to say, not knowing what to do. The shock of seeing his mother again filled Kain with so many emotions that it was hard to think. Finally, when the passion reached its peak, he leaped into his mother's arms and pressed close to her body, feeling her loving arms wrap around him and her motherly warmth engulf him. He was no longer larger than his mother, and as she held him in her arms the boy fit perfectly in her grasp, resting his head on her warm shoulder. It was a feeling he had long ago forgotten and he wished it would last forever.

"Mama, I've missed you so much!" he gasped, his voice cracking as the words caught in his throat.

"Your baba and I have missed you both as well." she smiled behind a sigh, kissing his head while gently cradling her son. "We have been watching over you and Nancy since the day we . . . since that fateful day. And we are so very proud of what the two of you have become." She picked his head up, smiling into his eyes before giving him a kiss on his cheek while several wet tears slid down her face. "You and your sister . . . we're so proud of you! I want you to know how much we love you."

"We love you too, mama." Kain told her, tears coming to his eyes as well. "I love you so much!"

Fang reached over and wiped away the tear that had started to trickle down his face before grasping his hand and giving it a strong, motherly squeeze. She looked her son over and sighed happily. Her hand went to his cheek, the cool flesh feeling pleasant against his skin, and rubbed gently. Kain placed his hand over his mother's, his lips trembling.

"Where is dad?" he asked, suddenly aware that the man was not present in the strange room.

"Right here, my boy!" a male voice boomed from behind him. Kain spun around and saw Richard standing right in front of him. How could this be? Both of them, Richard and Fang, had died years ago! How could they be standing here talking to him? Kain didn't care, he was just so overjoyed to be with them. He rushed to his father and leaped into his arms more forcibly than he had his mother's, crashing into his father's chest but not budging the larger man.

"Dad . . ." was all Kain could utter as they embraced.

"I love you, boy!" Richard told him, hugging his son tight with powerful arms. "I'm very proud of how you've taken charge of your life! You took in your sister and made quite a life for the both of you. You've done well for yourself and for her. Very well indeed! And I'm proud that you're my son!"

"Dad, I . . . I've missed you so much!"

"Your mama and I have always been with you and we'll be with you always." Richard replied with a kind smile. Then he pushed his son away and raised a finger as he told him "Always remember that, boy. And always remember that I love you, Kain." He seemed about to say more, but paused as if he wanted to continue but couldn't. He looked his son in his eyes and sighed heavily. "I can't stay here with you tonight."

"What? Wuh-Why not?"

"I . . . I just can't. I have to go now. I'm being called away and I . . . I have to go now." he murmured, taking a step back. He reached out and gave Kain a strong squeeze on his arm. "Your mother has much to talk about with you. Listen to her words and she will help you."

With that, Richard kissed his son's forehead and walked towards the blackness at the far end of the room where the warm light of roaring fire didn't seem able to reach. Just before he stepped into the blackness, Richard stopped and turned back to face Kain. "Son, you are a fine Grand General. The finest Arcainia could ask for, especially now. Never forget that. And never, ever let anyone make you think otherwise. If you ever doubt yourself, and I know you will because it comes with the job, just remember that your old man knows that there could not be a better Grand General than you. I love you, son."

"I love you too, dad." Kain whispered back as his father disappeared into the empty void far from the fire's light.

Fang took her son by the hand and said "Come now, my darling. Let us sit and rest ourselves. As your father said, we have much to talk about."

"Like what, mama?" Kain asked taking one last look into the blackness as if hoping to see his father once again as he fell into the soft chair.

Fang looked her son over closely, taking in his every feature and aspect, before shifting in her seat and giving a low, tender sigh. "You are so very much like your father. You have all of his characteristics, right down to his fierce protectiveness over those he loves so dear."

Kain lowered his head slightly and his face reddened. He knew exactly what she was talking about. Fang smiled and leaned over to kiss his forehead tenderly. She placed her arm around his shoulder and pulled him close. Kain glanced around himself and saw that the two chairs had formed into a couch of the same style. Mother and son sat close to one another, their bodies pressed tightly together as Fang cradled Kain in her tender arms.

"I love them so much, mama." Kain murmured lowly, referring to his beloved Li and Nancy. "And to hear Noknor threaten their lives like that . . . it . . . it really hit me hard."

"I know, Kain." Fang told him, laying her head over his. "And it's good that you are so protective of the ones you love, but you must control your outbursts. I know how much it hurt you inside, but if you let your emotions cloud your mind and judgment, you'll make mistakes. Grave mistakes that could cost you your life, to say the least about your sister and your friends."

"I've always told my men that. But it's so much easier said than done, I guess." he sighed, sniffling a bit. He sat up and pulled away from his mother slightly to look into her face. "It really hurts me inside to know that he has Li held prisoner at that awful place. And to think that Nancy almost . . . almost . . . could have . . ."

"I know, sweetie." Fang smiled, rubbing his hand soothingly. "Noknor wants to take away those you love most because he wants to weaken your spirit. He knows that if he takes Li and Nancy from you, then you will be more likely to make mistakes and rush into certain situations unprepared and without a rational mind."

"Well, he's right about that." Kain chuckled uneasily, the words sounding very near to sobs. "I was almost ready to head straight to his castle without wasting time on the Elemental Sword."

Fang smile in pity and squeezed his shoulder. "He knows how to get at you, and he will do whatever it takes to beat you. But," she lifted her index finger into the air to strike her point, much has her husband had done moments before, "Noknor will never beat you. Only you," she lowered her finger and placed it gently against her son's heart, "will beat yourself if you are not careful."

Kain's face formed a perplexed frown as he thought about what she had said. Fang remained patiently silent, watching her son as his mind wandered with thoughts considering the answers she knew he needed to discover on his own. He found himself suddenly drifting away from his aching heart to visions of games of chess and cards. More often than he'd like to admit he had played foolishly, turning good plays into bad ones and practically giving the game up to his opponent. And a battle was no different from a game, although Kain was not as prone to foolish decisions on the battlefield considering the stakes were much higher than merely losing a bit of money. Still, Kain was only human and he had his regrets. But he never wanted to have a single regret when it came to the lives of Li and Nancy. And suddenly Kain knew his mother's point.

"Noknor has the advantage." he murmured softly, scratching his chin in a thoughtful manner that was so reminiscent of his father it made Fang giggle silently. "All he has to do is fight so that he doesn't lose. I have to fight to win. He has Li and he wants to capture Nancy, so I also have to fight to save Li and protect Nancy, as well as fight with the best interests of my men in mind. Noknor doesn't care about his men. He'd kill them all if it would help his fight even a fraction."

"That is correct." Fang nodded with a hint of a proud smile for her clever son.

"But just because he has the advantage now doesn't mean that I can't turn things around." Kain continued, not appearing as if he heard his mother. "I just have to be careful that I don't inadvertently give him more of an advantage by making foolish plays."

"Correct." Fang smiled brightly, giving his forehead an affectionate kiss as she stroked his cheek softly. Kain looked at his mother and smiled, but it was a sad smile. Fang could see in his dull eyes that although he realized what she was trying to tell him, that he must control his temper and let his emotions work for him instead of against him, it didn't ease the pain in his broken heart. It didn't allow him to swallow his dear cousin's abduction any easier. She took pity on him, feeling her son's sadness as if it were her own. She showed him a bright smile, making his just a little bit less dejected. "You have more advantages than you realize right now, Kain."

"What do you mean?" he asked.

"You think of it as a disadvantage that Noknor holds Li. After all, he could harm her if he felt it would help him beat you."

"Yes . . ."

"What you don't realize, and what Noknor doesn't realize, is that by capturing Li, Noknor turned what he thought was an advantage for him into a disadvantage."

"How is that an advant—" Kain began to object, but was cut off by a sudden warming on the skin of his chest. He looked down and saw a red glow pulsating under his shirt, beating like a heart.

Fang also took notice. "You wear your cousin's heart close to you own. Never take it off, because its jewel contains a great power that will help keep Li safe from Noknor's harm."

She paused as she turned to face the fireplace, her eyes glowing as they caught the flickering light of the flames. She sighed lowly as she stared thoughtfully off into the fire, considering many things in her mind. Finally, still with her eyes gazing into the fireplace, she spoke. "You and Li share a very special bond, and it is a very powerful bond. You always have, ever since you were children. Perhaps ever before either of you were even born. You share a common thread in your bloodlines."

Fang sighed once more, but this time it was upbeat and confident. She turned to her son and peered into his eyes. Kain couldn't help but smile as the tender, embracing eyes of his mother warmed his heart. Looking into those eyes he felt his mother's love and he knew that she would always protect him.

"Your cousin's Dragon Heart makes your bond even stronger." she told him, directing his attention to the red glow warming his chest. "It makes it even stronger than the amulet Noknor wears. And as long as that bond remains strong, he will never be able to hurt her. He will try, and as much as it terrifies you I will tell you that he has in fact already tried to harm her. But she is still strong and well. And she will remain so, always protected from Noknor's Dark magick.

"And that is why it is a disadvantage for him, because he does not understand and so he fears Li. He will try harder and harder to understand, but he never will and he will never be able to hurt Li. And this is why it is an advantage for you, because you know this."

She smiled and hugged her son tight. "So do not fear for Li, she is strong and she will survive. Keep your bond strong, and always wear her heart close to yours. When you need it most, the Dragon Heart will present its power to you. Just remember that in the darkest moment, hope shines the brightest."

She gazed into the flickering flames once again, her face growing serious with a look of deep, penetrating thought as if many ideas were flowing through her head and she was trying to grab a hold of the most important one. She finally murmured "Nancy knows that, yet is having a hard time believing it right now."

"Nancy . . ." Kain whispered her name as he sat back on the couch and stared blankly into the fireplace. With the way he had burst out, it was no wonder that she was having a hard time believing it. His anger probably didn't do anything but serve to lower her spirits, the one thing that needed to be the highest. She was probably already afraid for Li; well, there was no probably about it, she was terrified for Li's safety. And seeing her brother act as if it were the end of the world, surely she had lost all hope.

He turned to his mother and met her somber dark eyes, still shimmering like pearls in the fire. She told him "Your sister needs you right now. You're all she has and you must always be there for her. By letting your temper explode, you push her away because she feels that she can't get close to you."

"I didn't mean to scare her." he sighed remorsefully, remembering how she had cowered away from him when he lost his temper earlier in the evening. "That was the last thing I wanted to do."

"You must tell her that." she suggested with the hint of motherly order in her tone. "Yes, she knows it, but you must still tell her. Let her know that she can confide in you and you in her because you are both facing the same calamity. And if you don't face it together, you might as well not face it at all. Only with your combined hearts can you hope to overcome Noknor's evil."

Fang sighed deeply. "Your sister is more powerful than you realize, Kain. She has a strong spirit and a pure heart. And you will find that she will play a key element in your quest against Noknor."

"I know." he grinned, thinking back to when she gave him the wax and when she shot the deer woman off him in the Forest of Souls. "She's helped me out twice already. I have a feeling she'll do it again. But I can't understand it, momma! All of the skill she's shown, where does it come from? She's preformed moves I've never seen before! And that blowpipe of hers! She out shoots soldiers I know that have been training on it longer than she's been alive! The only way I could explain it would be to call it natural skill, but still all of that goes way beyond that! There has to be something more to it."

Fang smiled only a neutral smile and said "There is more to it. However, I cannot say anything of it. If you are to hear it, she will tell you. If not, she won't. So far, she hasn't, but she may change her mind later on. It's up to her."

"But why hasn't she told me? Every time I mention it, she blushes and turns away as if she's ashamed."

"She's not ashamed. Far from it, in fact." Fang shrugged "She just doesn't understand it, and in that is fear. As for confiding in you about it, it is all up to her."

"I love her with all of my heart."

"She loves you, too." she smiled. "She looks up to you. You're her hero and you must always guide her right."

"I will." he said. "I promise."

"I know you will." Fang kissed his cheek with warm, affectionate pride in her son. "You always have."

Fang looked over her shoulder towards the shadowed area Richard had left by and sighed. She turned back to Kain, looked him deep in the eyes, and murmured "It is time for me to go now, my love."

"Please don't!" Kain gasped, drawing his mother up in his arms. "Please . . ."

She giggled lowly, patting and rubbing his back in a soothingly circular motion. "I must, Kain. I have no choice. But I before I go, I must say one more thing about your sister."

She pulled him away and held his shoulders tightly with both hands as she looked deep into his eyes, her warm, soft gaze reaching all the way down into his heart. "She is your little sister, and you feel it is your duty to protect her from anything that would bring her harm. You have protected her well up to this point, and she is a much better lady for your caring and love.

"However, as I told you, she is stronger than you realize and there will be times when you must allow her to use that strength. Circumstances will come up when everything inside of you will be screaming at you to protect her, to shield her away from the world around her. And sometimes you must ignore those feelings."

"How will I know when to do that?" Kain asked, has hands already trembling with fear at such thoughts.

"Listen to your heart." she answered, placing her finger onto his chest. "And listen to her. Remember that this is something the two of you must face together, and the only way to get through it is by holding each other's hand all the way."

As she gave her darling son one last departing hug, tears dripping down both of their cheeks, she whispered into his ear in a quivering voice "Always know that your father and I love you very, very much."

* * *

Kain awoke with a start and sat straight up inside a small and cramped area, his eyes wide open and his breath coming in short, raspy gasps. When the initial shock finally passed him over, he looked around wildly, not really sure of where he was or even if he was still dreaming or not. As his eyes adjusted to the darkness, he began to see shadows creeping out of the blackness and realized that he was back in his tent in the middle of a large, grassy Arcainian plain on his way back to visit with the Uraeus Sisters.

The evening before when he had read Noknor's letter, Kain had become enraged with fury, ranting and cursing Noknor's name as he tore around the meadow. He held his fists so tightly as he shook them madly that his knuckles turned white, a terrible contrast to his red fists. His mouth was set in a horrid sneer as he bellowed and his eyes blazed with an icy intensity while his face burned a fiery red. Even the gentle breeze that whispered over the meadow only served to make him appear more as a madman by tousling his hair wildly about. He tried to calm the rage in his heart, but the horrid memories of his parents' demise and the thoughts of Noknor harming his beloved sister and cousin flashed brighter in his mind's eye and infuriated him even more.

Everyone, including his three closest friends and especially Nancy, were in fear of and for him. They all wanted to approach him, to tell him that everything would be all right, to talk to him and try to calm him down, but they dared not to even get close to him. For Nancy that had been the worst feeling she had ever felt. To not be able to help the person she cared so dearly for. Thinking back on how he was, he shuddered violently in his embarrassment. He wished that he hadn't acted so rashly and that he could go back and wipe away all he had said and done. However, the damage was already done, and all he could do now was to try his best to repair that damage, especially with his sister. He couldn't erase that horrible, stupid outburst from her mind, but he could at least try to explain it to her, to apologize for it. He knew what he had to do and knew that it couldn't wait until morning. He wouldn't get anymore sleep that night until he was able to lift the heaviness from off of his shoulders. He fumbled out from under the blankets and crawled out of his tent.

In the dim starlight, he made his way to Nancy's tent, silently peeled back the flaps, and stuck his head inside. Seeing his sister laying fast asleep under her blanket, he entered and watched her gently snooze for a bit. She was so beautiful and peaceful. She reminded him of an angel straight from heaven and instantly set his crushed heart at ease.

* * *

Nancy was busily setting the dining room table for four people while she hummed tunelessly to herself. As she did a double check of her handiwork, strong male hands came to rest on her shoulders. She looked up and smiled radiantly.

"Hello, daddy!" she chirped happily.

"Hello, my little darling." Richard Viccon grinned, bending low to give his daughter a peck on her forehead. Then, still holding her shoulders firmly, he twisted her around to face him so he could look her over. "You've grown so much. I am so very proud of you!"

"Thank you." she murmured lowly, smiling behind a deep blush. "I love you, daddy."

"I love you too, my sweet princess." he sighed deeply, his large chest heaving slightly. He looked her over once more and said "You're so beautiful. I always knew you would be. You're smart and beautiful, a great combination. Just like your mother. And, I must say you have become a powerful warrior. Powerful enough to stand up to even Noknor's evil."

"I owe you for that." she said, her voice and eyes waving a bit. "I could never have joined Kain without your help all these years."

Richard looked at her with a large, loving smile and chuckled audibly. He told her that she would have done it regardless if her old man had showed up, that the blood of a warrior flowed through her veins and fed a strong heart. Nancy blushed slightly before throwing herself at him, her arms barely reaching around his body in a strong embrace. She felt her father put his powerful arms around her and felt him, in an embrace that could easily have crushed her small frame, squeeze her as gently as a mother's kiss. She whispered how much she loved him in a trembling voice and he squeezed her closer to his body in response. Finally, he pushed her away and looked into her eyes, a cocked eyebrow and a playful grin on his face.

"What say we get in some last minute practice?"

"What about dinner?" Nancy frowned curiously, glancing at the table she had just set.

"Your mother's still cooking. We have a little time." he told her, tossing his head towards the kitchen door for emphasis. His grin broadened as he clicked his tongue. "Come on, pup. What do you say?"

"Okay!" she beamed excitedly.

With that, the dining room was suddenly filled with a bright white light, as if a million burning candles had burst into glorious flames. Nancy looked around her, not the least bit shocked or amazed. When the brightness faded, she found that she had changed out of her beautiful dinner dress and into a pair of loose green cotton pants and a tight, black sleeveless top. Her shoes and stockings were gone, leaving her barefoot. The dining room had changed as well, turning into a large practice ring in the center of a lush green forest. Off in the distance, Nancy saw rocky mountains jutting into the deep blue sky with a gushing waterfall spilling into a beautiful crystal-clear lake. A fine mist caused by the fall rose from the water and drifted out into the forest. Nancy giggled as it brushed against her face, tickling her nose.

"Are you ready, pup?" Richard asked from behind her.

Nancy turned and grinned. He father stood in the center of the ring, his casual attire changed into a pair of loose gray pants and a gray tunic. He stood at attention, his body ridged, his legs spread apart, and his hands behind his back. His serious military stance was shattered by his soft eyes and playful grin.

"You bet I am!" she cried out with great enthusiasm.

"Good. Come at me with a five point jump combo." he instructed her.

Nancy nodded her head and crouched into position. With a mighty push of her strong legs, she sprung at her father with her foot aimed for his face. When Richard blocked, she seemed to hesitate a split second before she backhanded at him with her right hand, punched with her left, struck with her right elbow, and punched with her left again. Richard easily batted her blows away before shoving her down.

"Too slow on the recovery." he told her, helping her back up. "Try again. Don't hesitate; you have to make it all one fluid movement. Flow like that waterfall over there."

"Yes, sir!" she bowed her head. She tried again, this time lashing out with her hands the instant before her feet hit the ground. She managed to score hits this time around.

She always thought it odd that no matter how hard she hit him, her father really didn't seem to be that affected by the blows. At first, she though it was because she was weak, but he always reassured her that her punches and kicks were quite hard hitting, proving it by having her break boards. Now she just figured that he was just really strong.

"Much better!" he congratulated her, slowly rubbing his sore jaw. "Much, much better! Try again."

She did, and scored one hit less. They continued on for what seemed like hours, practicing different moves and combinations, learning new moves, and exercising her weapon skills. The whole time they carried on, however, neither Nancy nor Richard showed any signs of fatigue. They just went on and on, pausing only when Richard had to explain something or correct her mistakes. There was not a single moment when Nancy thought it the slightest bit odd, to her all of this seemed as natural as breathing. It wasn't until she had a different, alternate reality to compare it to that it seemed strange, even frightening. She would ponder over what all had happened in that short and brief interlude and question her sense of sanity. But not now. Now was her special time with the people she adored and nothing else mattered.

After a while, Richard called for a halt and walked over to his little girl. He placed his hand on her shoulder and said "Nancy, I'm very proud of you! You are such a good student. You learn well and fast. Very fast. I wish I had more soldiers like you when I was Grand General."

"Thanks, daddy." she smiled brightly. "I really enjoy it. You're a great teacher!"

Richard started to respond, but something seemed to catch his attention. He looked up in to the blue sky and hummed lowly to himself. "It seems your mother's finished. We'd better be going back."

Whiteness once again engulfed the pair, this time taking them back to their dining room where Fang awaited, their clothes changing back into their dinner wear. Fang approached Nancy and gave her daughter a large hug.

"Did you have fun out there today?" she asked.

"Yes, ma'am!" the girl beamed. "Daddy and I had a lot of fun! And I learned a lot too!"

"That's good." she giggled, her eyes proud as she glanced at her grinning husband. "I'm glad."

"I love you guys!" Nancy chirped, grabbing both of her parents and pulling them in for a group hug. As they embraced, Nancy noticed a fourth body missing. "Where's Kain at?"

"Oh, he's coming right now." Fang grinned, looking towards the door.

* * *

Kain stood over his sister, not doing anything but instead just watching over her with a new sense of security filling his mind and heart. He had been watching her for a few minutes heavily debating whether he should wake her up or not. She looked so sweet and peaceful that he just couldn't bear to wake her. However, he knew that he himself would never get back to sleep until he got what he had to tell her off his chest. So, trembling from the anticipation, he reached out with a quivering hand to shake her awake. His hand stopped inches from her leg.

He just couldn't do it. He couldn't wake her up from such a peaceful slumber. He silently cursed himself for being so foolish as to think that a mere dream was so important that he had to wake his sister. But he knew that it wasn't a mere dream. It was a powerful message. Just thinking about it sent shivers throughout his body.

Nancy whimpered lowly in her sleep and kicked her blanket off her legs. Kain slowly reached over and carefully covered her back up before drawing back and sitting on his haunches. He watched her snooze for a few more minutes before sighing dejectedly and backing out of her tent. As he did so, his foot found a dry twig. The resulting snap shattered the still night air like a shout and carried for miles. Kain gasped lowly and froze in his place. Nancy stirred slightly and mumbled incoherently, but didn't seem to wake. Kain relaxed and breathed a low sigh of relief as he started back out once more.

"Who's there!" Nancy cried out as she shot straight up, the blanket clutched tightly to her chest as she snatched for the dagger that she kept close to her pillow. "What do you want! I'm armed! I swear I'll cut you!"

"It's just me, Nancy!" Kain hissed in a whisper, holding his hands up to block any oncoming blows. "Kain! It's Kain!"

"Wha? Kain?" she yawned, squinting in the dark. Her grip on the blanket loosened and her rigid body relaxed. "What are you doing? What time is it? What . . ."

"It's . . . it's late." he told her, slowing entering back into her tent. "I just came because I had to tell you something."

"What?" she mumbled, half asleep. "Kain, it couldn't wait until morning?"

"Well, it's kind of important, I suppose. I dunno, it's important to me, I guess." he told her, reaching out to grip and gently rub her small foot. "Darlin', I'm so sorry."

"For what?"

"For the way I . . . the way I reacted yesterday." he sighed dejectedly, looking downward like a shamed dog. "I shouldn't have burst out like that, especially in front of you. I'm sorry for scaring you like that. I didn't mean to."

"I know you didn't." she replied, a smile touching her tired lips.

Kain smiled himself. "It's just that it hit me really hard to hear Noknor talk about you like that. You mean so much to me, Nancy. I love you so much!"

"I love you too, big brother!" she gasped, crawling to him so she could wrap her arms around his neck in a weak, exhausted hug. She kissed his cheek fondly before collapsing back down onto her bed and covering herself back up. "Now go back to your own tent and get some sleep!"

* * *

Noknor hustled though the dank dungeon of his castle, his Dark Knights leaping out of his way and saluting their lord as he brushed past them without so much as a hello. By the look on his face it was plain to see that he walked with a lot on his mind, and most wondered silently what could trouble such a frightening man as their lord.

What Noknor would never allow them to know was that he was troubled by Viccon's cousin, that vexing Chinese woman. For all her sex appeal did for him, she was a most irritating woman and under normal situations he would have killed her long ago. However, he couldn't do anything to her just yet, and not just because he wanted to wait until Viccon arrived. For some reason unknown to him his magick couldn't harm the Chinese woman, as he had found out that first day when she was brought before him. Even with the Swuenedras Amulet some sort of shield or barrier was able to repel his magick. He considered himself lucky that she obviously didn't know the power she possessed. She talked big and showed no fear of him, but that was due to her tough nature and just general smart mouth.

He assumed that it had something to do with her amazingly strong will. He had heard that such a thing could form a defense around a person, basically casting a shielding spell without going to the trouble of casting one manually. He had never heard of someone's will being powerful enough to repel something like the Swuenedras Amulet, but he also thought that perhaps it had something to do with her being Chinese. There were probably a lot of factors that worked together to make her shield so strong.

Noknor wasn't terribly concerned about it at the moment, but he knew he was going to have to break her will like a mirror eventually. Preferably before she found out the power she possessed, of course. After all, letting her run around with that over his head was a weakness, and a god simply could not have a weakness.

He finally reached a door with the words *TORTURE CHAMBER* written in blood over it. He opened it and entered with a large smile on his face. He always enjoyed the entertainment this room brought to him. With the many and varied instruments of pain and death, Noknor relished the screams and delighted with the agony they brought with them. Not a day went by that he did not come down to the sublevels of his home at least once to both witness and take pleasure in the hell which was created for such unfortunate souls as the Shazadians who had survived the slaughter and the citizens of Kuberica who sought to stand up to him only to be pushed down hard. Death was never kind or easy when in Noknor's demonic hands.

"They are both ready for you, my lord." a monster of a man replied with a vile, toothy grin as he humbly bowed before Noknor. He was huge with a large barreling chest and arms as thick as tree trunks. He wore heavy boots with pointed steel toes and dull black pants, both stained with grim and blood. More blood was splattered over his chest and shoulders, dried and caked as it matted the thick black fur covering his enormous body. His thick head was shaved except for a long, black goatee. His gleaming scalp was strewn with queer tattoos, while his ears, brows, and lips were pierced many times over with huge golden hoops. "Two Shazadian pigs ready and waiting for your lordship."

Noknor looked over the man's shoulder. One man lay on a hulking wooden table with his wrists and ankles shackled with heavy chains. These chains were connected to massive wooden reels and gruesomely stretched the man's limbs. A second sobbing man knelt before a large steel vice. His wrists were cuffed to the vice's legs while a chain wrapped around his waist held him tightly down. His head lay on its side while the two steel plates held it snug enough without hurting him for the moment. Noknor immediately decided to do him first. He just loved the looks on their faces as their heads were crushed flat like grapes.

"Is everything all right, my lord?" the torturer asked, noticing the heavy look of concentration on his powerful master's face which he mistook for annoyance or far worse, anger. He absolutely dreaded the thought of being thrown into the machines he used so joyfully on others.

"Not for some." Noknor chuckled gleefully and started to advance to the vice. He brandished an evil grin that showed his gleaming fangs as the captured Shazadian Knight sobbed and begged for mercy, tears streaming down his dirtied, bruised face as he sprayed out snot and spittle. Noknor only snorted his amusement with his prey, his eyes sizing up the pathetic man stuck in the instrument of pain like a cat toying with a mouse. With a circular motion of his finger, the mighty screw atop the vice gave a shrill rusty squeak as it ever so slowly twisted down. Noknor laughed heartily as the Shazadian used his last breath to scream.

* * *

Li and Elizabeth lay in their beds in the dark room. Li was on her way into a deep sleep when Elizabeth thought she heard something echo through the castle. She sat straight up and whispered "Li! Are you asleep?" When she received no reply, she was afraid to be alone and called out again "Li! Are you asleep?"

"Not anymore. What is it?"

"Did you hear that?"

Li shifted to her side and mumbled "Yeah."

"That sounded like screaming!"

"I'm sure it was. Noknor must be having some more fun at the expense of some poor soul."

"Do you think we'll be—"

From the door came a loud bang and a gruff voice tiredly snapping "Shut up and get some sleep, you stupid—"

"Shut up yourself, maggot!" Li yelled back. She sat up and wrapped her arms around her knees, thinking about what Elizabeth had just said. Even though the princess hadn't been able to finish her sentence, Li knew what she was saying. "Don't worry about a thing. They won't hurt us. We're too important. Besides, do you think I'd be talking to them the way I do if I thought we were in any danger?"

"Yeah, I do." she chuckled nervously.

"Well, you're right." Li smiled and giggled softly. "But that's not the point, anyway, princess. Don't think things like that. Kain will come to rescue us and everything will be all right. Trust me. He's never ever let me down before and I know he won't this time either." Then she yawned and lay back down on her stomach. "Let's take maggot's advice and get some sleep."

As she sank beneath her covers, Elizabeth wished she had Li's strength and confidence. She knew her Arcainian friends were an accomplished fighting force, but wondered if Kain could really take on Noknor's entire horde when both her people and the Shazadians had failed so miserably.

Still quite frightened, she jumped at every sound and wondered if she would ever fall to sleep. After a while Li's gentle breathing finally lolled her to sleep.

CHAPTER XVI

The next morning, Kain awoke to find all of his troops were up and ready to start a new day. After a leisurely breakfast, they packed up their camp and loaded their horses leaving no trace that they had ever been there. All the while, Kain talked and carried on pleasantly with his band, seeming cheerily enough. No one, save Nancy, was exactly sure what to make of it after the day before and it was strange to see him in such high spirits. They finally all decided when Kain was out of earshot that it was amazing what a good night's sleep could do for a man.

Even though they had gotten a late start, they made it back to the hut in very good time. It stood just as they had left it, silent and looking completely empty. As before, he set Raphael and Michael on guard duty while he and Nancy went inside. However, Robert was curious to see the Sisters and he sent his scouts out before following Kain. Nancy entered first without incident, and then Robert tried to follow. However, he bumped face first into an invisible wall that barred the door. Kain reached out and his hand passed over the threshold without incident. Robert tried the same, but felt the barrier. Kain shrugged and followed his sister in, leaving Robert standing outside, curiously pawing the strange obstacle.

Once inside, Kain saw Nancy standing before the three sisters. They all wore large bright grins and glittering eyes. Kain bowed low before them and they acknowledge him with a slight bob of their own heads. They each in turn raised their hands in salute as they spoke.

"*How goes you, Kain Viccon?*" Urd asked.

"*You have passed our little test.*" Beldandi said.

"*You have earned our respect.*" Skuld grinned.

"Thank you very much, glorious sisters." Kain smiled, producing the small leather bag from his pocket. "Here are the herbs you have requested."

All three sprites waved their hands in the same declining fashion at the same moment.

"*Keep the mandrake.*"

"*We have no need.*"

"*It was simply a key in a grand test.*"

"*The test that grants both of you our respect.*"

The three sisters touched hands on their small altar and a bright flash brought forth a map printed on the finest cloth. Kain took it and looked it over, noting that it was much like his own map of the area but was marked showing where all of the Ladys dwelled. He smiled as his sister looked over his shoulder in curiosity.

"*Lady Earth waits for you in Mystic Cavern.*"

"*Lady Air awaits in the clouds atop Colossal Mountain.*"

"*Lady Fire lives in the Sulfur Pits.*"

"*Lady Water sits in the Aqua Palace.*"

"*All are tricky places to get to.*"

"*Tests in themselves.*"

Their long, beautiful faces lit up in glee.

"*We had faith in Richard Viccon.*"

"*Like father like son.*"

"*Daddy's little girl has grown up.*"

"*We liked him very much.*"

"*We like his children very much.*"

"*As we did for him, we shall give you something.*"

"*A gift.*"

"*To aid you on your way.*"

The Uraeus Sisters raised their hands in the air and threw back their heads as they began to chant "Earth, Air, Fire, Water, Earth, Air, Fire, Water, EARTH, AIR, FIRE, WATER, EARTH, AIR, FIRE, WATER, **EARTH, AIR, FIRE, WATER, EARTH, AIR, FIRE, WATER!**"

A shrill wind blew out of nowhere and shrieked around, whipping the Sister's hair and robes wildly about as they shouted louder and louder and the wind howled more fiercely with every word out of their mouths. Unlike before, however, the mysterious wind didn't just affect the faeries. Kain had to brace himself against the powerful force while Nancy held onto her brother as her long hair lashed around as if it had a life of its own. It was as if the sisters had called upon the mightiest hurricane and Kain was sure that the weak little building would be blasted to pieces with them inside.

Then it was suddenly over. Kain and Nancy slowly opened their eyes and saw a small round shield of silver and a quiver of beautifully crafted arrows floating just above the altar.

"*A shield for the girl.*"

"*It will watch over you.*"

"*It will protect you from harm.*"

Nancy took the beautiful round shield made of glimmering silver and gold and looked it over before slipping it over her arm as she gave the Sisters her grateful thanks. They smiled brightly at her and nodded slightly before turning their attention back to Kain.

"A quiver of special arrows for the boy."
"They will always fly swift and true."
"They will hunt down your prey."

Kain took the quiver made from the finest leather he had ever seen and looked at the arrows made of powerful wood that smelled of orange. He graciously thanked the Sisters as he slung it over his shoulder.

"Danger waits ahead for you." Urd warned.
"But we have done all we can for you." Beldandi added.
"The rest is up to the two of you." Skuld smiled.
"Fair thee well on your way." all three said in unison.

* * *

Later that evening, Kain examined his new map as he and his troops rode on. It was still quite a long way to Hurst and he noticed how much harder it was getting to read the paper with each passing minute, so he decided to set up camp. He picked out a spot near a small pond and a group of odd, almost human looking trees and ordered a hold. While his men erected their tents, he sat on a small stump and gnawed on a piece of dried meat as he thought about the City of Hurst and the woman who lived there.

The City of Hurst was well known for being as bright and exciting as it was big. It was the largest city in the world and wasn't in any particular kingdom, so it governed itself without hindrance of royal authority. It was situated on a major river that flowed through many of the different cities in the different kingdoms and was, without a doubt, the most important trading city in the Old World. Merchants and travelers from all over the world journeyed to Hurst just to see the city that never slept and sell their goods in the hundreds of markets and places of various entertainments.

The current mayor of the city was a woman named Deborah Hurst, the city having been founded deep in her bloodline, and she was a very beautiful woman. Her short blond hair reached the nape of her neck and her blue eyes shined like seductive jewels, so it was hinted that the Hurst's originally came from Kuberica. She was very sweet and gentle by nature but was hard and fierce where the laws governing her beloved city were concerned. Hurst had a police force equal to or greater than the armies of some kingdoms and they patrolled everywhere, some on foot and some on horseback, twenty-four hours a day. Punishments were dependent on the severity of the crime, with all heavy crimes such as murder or rape punishable by a harsh death. Executions were by beheading, burned or buried alive, or braking by the iron rod, and were made public so that other would-be lawbreakers would be able to see an example of what might await them if they sought wicked ways. Criminals so feared Deborah's swift and brutal justice that as a result there was very little crime in the fine crowded streets of the City of Hurst. It was truly a city one had to see at least once in their lives. Kain had seen it many times over and still enjoyed every visit, with or without specific relations with Deborah herself.

After they stopped in Hurst, they would travel through Dismal Swamp. It was the most dangerous place known in the Old World, even more dangerous than the Forest of Souls, but unfortunately Mystic Cavern sat dead in the middle of it. Kain rolled up the map and placed it in his pack, pulling out another piece of dry meat in its place. As he sat gnawing on it, something suddenly caught his eye. In the fading light, he noticed movement among the trees where many of his men sat telling stories around a campfire. He squinted past the glare and looked closer. Yes, there was indeed something moving among the trees, but it didn't look quite right. It was as if something was moving behind each tree. It was probably a trick played by the flickering campfires, he figured. He stood up and grabbed his sword just in case when he realized that he had been wrong. The movement wasn't among the trees, it was the trees themselves! And they were moving closer to the group where Nancy sat!

Ripping his sword from its sheath, he rushed as fast as he could to the spot, trying to yell out but not having the breath for it. Just as he reached his sister, a wooden hand covered with leaves gripped Nancy by the shoulder. She squealed and whirled about to face the creature. She heard it moan slightly just before Kain lashed out with his sword and freed the branch. There was a low moan as the tree used another branch to bat the knight away as if he weighed nothing. The other troops all jumped in shock but quickly recovered and drew their weapons. Kain picked himself up and shouted a battle cry as all men rushed at the attackers. The trees moaned and batted the soldiers away with their mighty leaf covered hands.

"WAIT!" Nancy squealed in a shrill female wail, quickly recognizing the bizarre creatures. "Hold off the attack! Wait! Stop! STOP!"

Her voice, being the only female voice for miles, instantly drew everyone's attention. The men, startled as they were, waited until their general ordered a halt and standby before they all backed away with their weapons still poised in attack position. They stood tensely ready but refrained from further attack. Nancy looked over the men before taking a deep breath and advancing forward, hoping she was right. She drew herself up to her full height but was still dwarfed by the massive tree and assumed her most diplomatic attitude.

"We do not wish for a fight, but your people startled us. What is it that you want from us?" Nancy asked the tree that had grabbed her shoulder.

At first, only a low moaning, like a breeze blowing through a knotted tree could be heard. Slowly, it turned into a low, wispy voice *"Weeeee meannnnnnnt noooo haaarm. Onlyyyy toooo knooooow whoooo youuuuu arrrrre."*

"My name is Nancy Viccon." she told him, slowly and easily reaching her empty palm out in front of her. "Hello."

The tree regarded her hand before ever so slowly extending its own. The leaves covered Nancy's entire arm, but she was able to find a small branch and grab it. Then in a most humorous way they shook hands.

"*Hellooooooo, Nancyyy Viccoooooooon.*"

"This is my brother, Kain, and this is his army, the Arcainian Army." she told the tree, pointing Kain and then making a wide gesture towards the other men as she introduced them. They all gave a motion of greeting, most of the men feeling more than foolish about giving out such pleasantries to trees.

"*Helloooo, fffffriends offfff Nancyyyy Viccooooon.*"

"What is your name?"

"*Weeee haaave nooo naaames.*" it sighed, slowing moving its branches up and down as it talked. "*Yoooou aaare goooood kniiiiights. Whaaaaat iiis yoooour queeeeest?*"

"We are on the way to fight Noknor and put an end to his evil deeds. Have you heard of him?"

"*Weeee haaave liiived fooor manyyyy ceeeeenturyyyys aaaand haaave seeeen aaand heeeard muuuuch. Weeee knoooow oooof Noooknooor's eeeeevil deeeeeeds. Ooooourrr mooooothersssss aaaaare mooost uuunhaaaappppppy withhhhhhhh Noooknooor.*"

"He killed my parents when I was a baby." she said in a low sigh, almost as low as the tree's moans. "He has killed a lot of innocent people since then and must be stopped! That is our mission."

"*Heeee iiiiis aaaaa moooost eeevil fleeeeesh. Weeee wiiish gooood luuuuck iiiiin yoooour queeeest.*" it told her with a smile, reaching out and caressing her with its leaves. Nancy couldn't help but smile as she grasped a handful and rubbed them against her cheek. It paused for a moment as if thinking and looked off into the distance before warning "*Thhhhere aaare manyyy daaaaangerouuuus fleeeesh thaaat cooome tooo thiiis poooond tooo driiink. Weeee willlll waatch ooover yoooou, Nancyyyy Viccooooon.*"

"Thank you very much, you are very kind." she smiled brightly, thrilled over making new, albeit unusual, friends. "But we can not let you risk yourselves for us."

"*Theyyyy feeeeear uuus, weee dooo nooot feeeear theeeem. Weeee feeeear nooooo fleeeesh.*" it replied with great pride. It bent to look straight at Kain as it said the latter.

Kain blushed a deep red as he crossed his arms and turned away. He muttered "Sorry about your hand." Or, at least he assumed it had been its hand.

"*IIIIt willll grooow baaack, broooother oooof Nancyyyy Viccooooon.*" it replied, its attention back on the girl.

"Well, thank you so much for your help, great faery tree." she told it, looking into the knotholes that obviously served as eyes. Then she kissed its leaves in respect and friendship and flashed it her dazzling grin. "You are very kind."

* * *

Later that night, the trees had surrounded their camp, warding off the night creatures as the soldiers rested for the evening for their trek into Hurst in the morning. Kain sat away from everyone else, going over his thoughts. Even though he thought about seeing Deborah and her city once again, most of his thoughts were on Li and the great adventures they had been on together. A sudden voice from behind startled him and made him jump slightly.

"Sorry." Nancy giggled, sitting next to her brother and patting his arm. "What are you doing?"

"Thinking." Kain replied softly, looking at her. "Nancy, how did you know that those trees weren't trying to hurt us?"

"They're called Ogam, they're Earth faeries. They're peaceful faeries, so I knew that they weren't attacking us." she explained. "They were just curious about us and when we started to attack them, they were just defending themselves."

"Well, I must say that I am very impressed about how you handled yourself and the whole situation." he told her, patting her on the back. "Diplomacy is very important. It plays a big role in any military situation, and is a great thing to have. Just like any important tool or weapon. It's good that you know how use it."

"Well, why fight when you can talk it out?" she lowly murmured, fingering a stone and tossing it away. "It's always better to make a friend than an enemy."

"Who told you that?" Kain asked, raising his eyebrows. He remembered his father telling him the exact same thing when he was just a boy.

"I dunno." she shrugged absently, grabbing another small stone. "Heard it somewhere. So what were you thinking about?"

"What? Oh, I was just thinking about your cousin."

"I miss her, too." she sighed, looking at her downhearted brother and taking pity on him. She smiled and gave him a peck on his cheek.

He chuckled and loosened up quite a bit as he put his arm around her shoulders and drew her close. Then he said thoughtfully "I was remembering our greatest adventure together. The one that made us both famous."

"Tell it to us." Robert said as he, Raphael, and Michael joined them.

"Yeah!" Nancy insisted. She loved to hear his stories.

"Well, it's a long story."

"I'm sure we're all in the mood for a long story, isn't that right?" Raphael remarked, sitting next to Nancy.

"I know I am." Michael said. "And it's not like we're going anywhere at the moment."

"Good point." Kain nodded his head. "Okay, I'll tell."

"Oh, goodie! Story time!" Nancy giggled, clapping her hands.

Kain looked at her with amused eyes for a moment before beginning his long story. "It started like this . . ."

PART IV

KAIN'S STORY

CHAPTER XVII

I was in the middle of teaching a class on basic survival techniques one summer about two years ago when a low knock sounded at the door. It creaked open and David Kantu poked his head in.

"Sorry to interrupt, people." he said before looking straight at me. He had a real serious look to him, so I knew something was up. But, then he always looks like that. "Pardon me, Sir Viccon. The queen wants to see you right away. I guess it's kind of important."

"Oh, okay. Sure. I'll be right there." I told him before turning back to my class and announcing "Well, I guess that about does it for today. Uhm, we'll pick up where we left off tomorrow. Good day to you all."

As the students gathered their belongings and bustled out into the hallway, Kantu slid in and joined me at the instructor's podium where I was collecting my own things.

"What does she want?" I asked as I put the last of my papers into my satchel and closed it up. I guess I sounded a bit nervous because he told me "I'm honestly not sure, but don't worry about it. Queen Vanetta seemed to be in a good enough mood. I'm sure it's nothing."

"I'm sure." I murmured, slinging my satchel over my shoulder and immediately heading for the throne room.

When I arrived I saw Queen Vanetta sitting in her marvelous chair speaking intensely with the then Grand General, Robert Zanchaz. They lifted their heads and smiled in a relieved sort of way. That set my heart a lot more at ease, let me tell you, but I was still pretty nervous. I saluted them both and stood silently at attention before them.

"Richard's boy!" Zanchaz exclaimed.

"Ah, just the young man I wanted to see!" the queen squeaked brightly in her sweet voice. "Pull up a chair and join us, my dear. We have much to talk about."

I obediently took a seat in the beautifully crafted wooden chair positioned in front of the throne as I looked between the two most important people in Arcainia and wondered what they wanted with me.

"How are you and your sister doing, Kain?" Vanetta asked me pleasantly.

"We're doing very well, ma'am. Thank you for asking."

"That's good, that's good." she nodded her head in approval. I got the sense that she had just been asking to be polite and that her response would have been the same had I told her we were struck with a plague.

"Sir Viccon, we brought you in here to discuss your future with the Arcainian army." Zanchaz told me.

"My . . . future?" I choked slightly.

"Yes, we think you have quite a future with us." he said, pulling out a file and flipping through it. "Your track record is quite impressive, Sir Viccon. You rose to Red General in record time with all of your past campaigns having been completed successfully with minimal loses and within the specified time frame. All of them! And you have received numerous medals for your courage and bravery in battle, more than anyone else! Now that's something! I've never seen a record like that from someone so young. Not even your father had a perfect record like that and he was the best! It must be that good old Viccon blood!"

"Do you aspire to be Grand General, Kain?" the queen asked with a bit of a smirk. The look on her face told me she knew what I would say.

"Yes ma'am, Your Highness! It's all I've ever dreamed of becoming since I was a boy!"

"Well, I, myself, want you to be my Grand General." she told me, giggling softly as she looked me over. "I like you, Kain. I always knew you'd turn out like your father."

"I must admit, I did have my doubts about you." Zanchaz replied matter-of-factly, scratching his chin. "But you have turned out to be my best knight."

"Thank you very much!" I blushed slightly as I bowed my head in acknowledgment.

"No need to thank the truth, my dear. But enough of that. We have business to discuss." Vanetta murmured, shaking her head and sitting back in her throne. "It seems Emperor Wu Di is having a bit of a problem with some sort of dragon over in China and has requested Arcainian aid. I know that you have a lot of experience with the land; you know the language, know people, that sort of thing. They're very busy with their northern boarders and we have a few matters over here ourselves, so it's going to have to be a solo mission. From what I understand it will be very dangerous, but I have full confidence in you. Would you like to accept it, my dear?"

"Yes I would, your highness." I told her. It's not like I could have said otherwise. "What are the details?"

"I'm not quite sure, it's very hush-hush. But I will tell you this much," she replied, leaning forward and lowering her voice as if she were afraid that someone were listening and might hear some sort of secret. "If you complete this mission successfully, I can promise you a shot at Grand General. Now, of course I can not guarantee the spot, but you will get your chance to apply."

"I'm sorry?" I looked at Zanchaz.

"I'm retiring, Sir Viccon." he smiled, amused by my reaction. I was indeed shocked by the news. He wasn't that old and he had been Grand General for only a few years so far. I just couldn't imagine why he would want to retire. He must have read my thoughts in my face for he chuckled and explained "I am getting too old for this sort of work. I have a wife, two daughters and a newborn son. I can't be trotting off on quests all the time, leaving them alone for months at a time. I would be able to work it out if I was the man your father was, but I'm not. And I've already missed seeing Jessica and Romi growing up, I don't want little Robert to grow up without his father around. It would be an honor to pass the torch to another Viccon."

"I understand." I responded, putting a bit of respectful sympathy in my tone.

"So, you are interested?" the queen asked with a hopeful pitch to her voice.

"Most certainly, Your Highness!"

"Excellent!" she smiled brightly, her eyes giving away her delight as she clapped her hands together. "Follow Robert to the A.D. Department. They will inform you of the few details we know of. And good luck, my shining knight!"

* * *

"Where will the ship take us?" Nancy asked for about the thirtieth time as she waited with me at the pier. The sun was setting and cast its warm glow upon the water. Mist cascaded from the waves as they crashed against the seawall and gulls called to each other as they swooped down and caught their dinner.

"To Nanjing." I told her. "I have to see the emperor."

"Then we are going to visit Li?"

"That's right." I murmured. I was actually scheduled for a vacation and was going to spend it taking Nancy to see Li. When this came up, I hesitated bringing her along for a few reasons, but she broke me with that pitiful look she uses to get what she wants. Even back then she wielded the look better than I can a sword.

The biggest reason I didn't want her to come was because the ship we would be taking was being considered on a war mission because it was taking me to China and I was on a quest. That meant that no one without proper military classification was allowed on board and that posed a big problem since Nancy was only a twelve year old girl. However, I'd say we took care of that problem pretty well, indeed.

"Straighten your hat, pup." I told her, reaching out and doing it for her. "You can't let anyone see your hair. It'll give you away for sure."

* * *

"Hold it a second!" Michael interrupted with a large grin spread over his face. He turned to Nancy, who was already starting to blush fiercely, and asked "He disguised you as a guy?"

"Yes, he did! And it was the most embarrassing thing I ever had to do in my entire life!" she chirped, her face turning bright red. "I still can't believe he made me do that! Can you believe at first he actually wanted to chop my hair off! See what kind of monster he is!"

All the men broke into wild laughter. Nancy stuck her tongue playfully out at Kain, who was chuckling himself. He threw his arm around her and drew her close, gently rubbing his knuckles against the top of her head. Soon, her flush was gone and she was roaring with laughter as well. This drew the attention from the other soldiers and they started to walk over to see what all the commotion was about. In no time, Kain had himself a nice sized audience with even some of the Ogam tree faeries eavesdropping.

"I told everyone that she was my mute page." Kain explained after the crowd had settled down. "Only Ben knew it was really her. He knew Nancy enough to have been able to figure it out, so I just told him when we booked the ship. He was a really good sport about it."

* * *

When we stepped on deck, my good friend and captain of the Lavinia, Ben O'Riley greeted me with a strong handshake and asked "How's it going, Kain?"

"Just fine. How have you and that wonderful wife of yours been doing?"

"Perfect bliss." he winked. "Are you going to be joining us on the return trip?"

"I doubt it." I replied. "Me and the mute here will probably stay a few extra weeks with Li and Wenchi."

Ben chuckled audibly and patted Nancy on the back as he pulled a dull bronze key from his pocket. As he handed it over, he said "Cabin's the same one as always. Since the kid here is supposed to be your page, I kept her . . . ahm, him in your cabin as well. I went ahead and split up that double bed just in case anyone poked their nose in."

"Thanks, man." I told him. Nancy was about to say something, but I nudged her to remind her she was mute. "Our bags already in there?"

"Sure are." he nodded. "I guess you two should get in there and into some privacy. From the look on he-his face, he has words to mime you."

We both had a good laugh before Nancy and I headed off to our cabin. It was quite large and roomy, yet didn't have much in the way of furniture. Just a large double bed which was split up with each half on either side of the room, two cabinets, and a desk with a chair. Our bags sat in the middle of the room in one big heap.

After I closed and locked the door, Nancy threw her hat on the bed and growled "I swear! The things you make me go through just for a stupid vacation!"

CHAPTER XVIII

The whole trip passed by pretty uneventfully. Nancy spent most of her time around me and Ben or in the cabin reading. She had gotten used to not talking unless we knew we were alone just as me and Ben got used to referring to her as a boy, so no one ever found out. It's not that it was a really big deal, but all the same Ben didn't want to start something that would come back to bite him. If he had let me and Nancy slide during that mission, then he'd have to let others slide, and next thing you know his battleship has more family on it than sailors. Besides, I didn't have quite the pull that I do now.

Nancy commented a few times how boring the trip was, and I really couldn't have agreed more. The days passed by uneventfully without hitch or stone, although that wasn't entirely bad, of course. However, on the last day, just before we reached China something big happened to change our attitudes completely.

"It's only eight hours to port, Kain." Ben told me as he joined me and Nancy on deck.

"That's terrific!" I exclaimed as I inhaled the salty sea mist that caressed my cheeks. The sun shone down brightly and bathed the ship with warmth. "We made excellent time!"

I thought it was a wonderful day to be alive, but that attitude soon changed. The lookout in the crow's nest shouted that a Valterian pirateship was off the starboard bow. Ben whipped out his telescope and scanned the sea. After only a few seconds, he quickly tore it from his eye and roared out "**BATTLE STATIONS!**"

Valterians are a nomadic race of berserkers that roam the sea bringing death like a terrible plague. These madmen attack like ferocious animals and have no mercy. Even if a ship has nothing, they'll still attack it just for the sake of killing. Sometimes, they go as far as to eat the meat and drink the blood of those the murder, so as you can see they are highly feared as rabid wolves of the sea. The Arcainian and Chinese Navies have sent out entire fleets specifically to wipe out these pirates and to date they have done pretty well, I must say. However, at that time there were still a good number of Valterians out there. We had the unfortunate opportunity to meet one of those ships.

I gave Nancy a short sword and ordered her to go below deck to the cabin and lock the door. I told her not to come out until I came for her. I watched her swiftly follow my orders before adjusting my shield and pulling my sword free. It was time to save the Lavinia!

Twenty archers lined the rails of the right side of the ship with notched arrows and drawn bowstrings. The pirate ship drew closer and closer at an alarming rate, never slowing their speed. It was obvious that the Valterians were intentionally aiming to ram us, hoping to use the massive steel prow of their ship to pierce the Lavinia's hull and cripple the ship. It was one of their more frightful techniques in subduing their prey and from what I had heard it was quite effective.

Ben ordered his archers to fire and instantly the air was filled with the swooshing of arrows sailing through the air, which was followed by the sounds of arrowheads hitting hard wood and soft flesh. Not two seconds later, the jagged steel prow of the Valterian ship splintered the wood of our hull and ripped a massive hole, the sickening sound of wood tearing reminded me of bones breaking. I was certain that the damage would sink us for sure, but I wasn't about to go down without taking a hell of a lot of them with me!

The Valterians gave a horrid battle cry as they boarded armed with a motley array of old weapons rusted by the salty air of the sea and mistreatment. They fought furiously, but the crew was able to hold its own against them. I saw that Ben had his hands full with two pirates when a third tried to stab him in the back. I drew my bow, notched an arrow and sent it screaming towards the pirate. It made a loud *THUNK* as it imbedded itself right between his eyes and the savage was dead before he hit the deck. Just as I lowered my bow, another savage lashed out at me with a sickle. I ducked just in time and kicked him hard in the gut. He dropped his weapon and doubled over. I swiped upwards with my bow and caught him in the chin. Then, with three hard punches to the face and a hellacious uppercut, I launched him over the side for the sharks.

A sudden scream sounded in my ears and I turned to see a sailor without his insides kneel before what could have only been the pirate captain. He was a monster of a man, standing damn near close to seven feet tall with huge muscles all over his body. His pants, boots, and cloak were made of tiger skin and he wore a tiger skull over his huge melon-head like some morbid helmet. He had a large curved sword and a gigantic shield that were both crimson with rust and blood. Three sailors ran up to attack him, but all three were decapitated with a single swing of that sword. He threw back his head and roared with laughter.

Then he saw me and his yellow eyes hardened. When he spoke, his voice was low and very gruff with a heavy accent to it. "You are Arcainian general!"

"You don't say, tiger lily." I spat out viciously, brandishing my sword in a threatening way.

"I hate Arcainian general!" he roared, cocking his arm back sharply and bashing a sailor in the face as he tried to sneak up behind him. "I kill Arcainian general!"

"Then let's play." I told him, making sure my mouth formed a mocking grin. "Or is that hot air just for the sails?"

He scowled hideously and yelled his war cry as he rushed towards me. I also charged, but at the last moment, rolled and swung my blade. It lacerated his side as he passed and he bellowed in pain and fury. He turned around and charged again, but I stood my ground and our weapons clashed mightily. We tore at each other, his blows denting my shield and my blows knocking off rust in huge flakes from his sword and shield. Finally, I saw an opening and jabbed forward, poking his gut. My blade didn't penetrate far into his powerful muscles, but it was enough to make him double over. Seeing my chance, I grabbed his massive frame and hurled him over my shoulder. He crashed headlong into the center mast of the ship and fell hard onto the deck. The resulting crack was so loud, I had thought the wood had splintered but it was actually the pirate's body. Blood poured from his wounds and a bone protruded from his broken neck whiles his eyes rolled back into his skull. He was dead, there was no mistaking that.

All fighting stopped at once and all of the pirates fled to their own ship when they saw their oh-so-mighty captain was defeated. As they ran away screaming bloody murder, our archers managed to pick off a good many berserkers, but some of the survivors escaped to the safety of their ship. They were able to pull their ship free from ours and turned tail to run, making a clear getaway because were we in no shape to give chase.

Ben thanked me for saving his ship and joined me as we rushed to my cabin. I unlocked the door and threw it open to find Nancy calmly reading a book. She looked up at me and brightly smiled "I take it we won."

* * *

Early the next day, we reached port. We had paused for a few hours on the sea to do what we could to fix the damage to the ship before limping our way to the Chinese port. Luckily, despite the horrible sound the collision had made, the hole in the side of the ship was of minimum size and we weren't in any immediate danger of sinking. It just took a little longer after making quick repairs because Ben didn't want to risk going too fast. Nancy and I were dropped off before Ben ordered the major repairs to begin.

We took the royal coach to the palace and were greeted by two servants that led us into the courtyard. Emperor Wu Di and his wife sat on a swinging chair suspended from a tree by vines. I bowed low before them both and said "Good day, honorable emperor and empress. I am Sir Kain Viccon, Arcainian Knight for Queen Vanetta the Beautiful of Arcainia."

"Ah, Sir Kain Viccon. It is a great pleasure to finally meet your acquaintance." he smiled brightly. "Your good queen speaks very highly of you."

"Good day to you, Sir Viccon." his wife bowed to me. Now, I don't know if it was just the royal glitz and glamour, but she was gorgeous. A true vision. She glanced at Nancy, who had changed into a beautiful Chinese-style dress along the way to the palace, and smiled brightly. "Hello, little girl. Who might you be?"

"This is my sister, Nancy Viccon, great emperor and beautiful empress." I told them, giving her a weak shove from behind to remind her to show respect before the royals. "I have brought her along to aid me through my journeys as I do your bidding. I do hope her presence is not an inconvenience to you or your court."

"Not at all, Sir Viccon." Wu Di assured me. "She is a child of the great Richard Viccon of whom I owe a great debt and thus very welcome in my house. Perhaps the young blossom would care to have a tour of my estate?"

"What do you say, pup?" I asked her. "Whiles the emperor and I discuss some business?"

"Okay." she whispered shyly.

"Most excellent." Wu Di grinned. He looked to his wife and gave a polite order "Would you be so kind as to guide the young lady through our home?"

"Of course, my lord." she said, bowing to him as she stood. She took Nancy's hand and gave me a large grin as she bowed low and murmured "A good day to you, Sir Viccon."

Then she trotted off with Nancy in tow, enthusiastically telling her all about the garden. Wu Di watched them leave before telling me "Perhaps we should retire into the library where there will be fewer ears to hear our conversation."

Once there, I sat in a beautiful chair carved from the wood of a cherry tree in front of his desk as he asked "Do you know of Gong Gong?"

"The Devil Dragon?" I wondered aloud.

"That's right. So, you have heard of him?"

"Sort of." I shrugged bluntly. "I remember my aunt telling me and my cousin that if we were bad, Gong Gong would come and get us. It was one of those tactics parents use to scare kids into being good. When we would ask who he was, all she said was that he was a devil dragon that gobbled up naughty children."

"I, too, was told that as a child." he chuckled. "Do you know his story?" I thought for a moment before shaking my head. "Well, I'll tell you now. Thousands of years ago, evil tried to rule this land. The ruler of the evil forces was a powerful demon by the name of Gong Gong. He was ruthless and slaughtered many humans and dragons alike as he tried to conquer China. And he almost accomplished his devilish mission but not for the grace of a hero. She was human, yet she was as powerful as a goddess. She and Gong Gong began a battle that lasted many days, with the tides turning constantly. Finally, the hero saw her chance and cast a spell that encased the evil dragon in a block of black ice. With the help of the other humans, she tossed the block into the sea and it sank to the ocean depths. With their general gone, the army of evil was then easily crushed and peace was restored to the land."

I asked about the black ice and he told me "It was enchanted, so it never melted while in the sea. Unfortunately, a few of his dark worshippers have found it and are in the process of freeing him. And when that happens, Sir Viccon, China and the rest of the world including your Arcainia shall be crushed under his might."

"Just a moment, my lord." I protested. "I thought all of this stuff was just a legend."

"Oh, I assure you, Sir Viccon, Gong Gong is quite real. And I need the very best to stop him. I see I have gotten just that." he smiled widely through his black beard. "I trust in good Queen Vanetta's choice and in the blood of Sir Richard Viccon. I know you are the one to stop this evil dragon devil."

He explained where he was and how to get there. I was about to tell him of my asking my cousin for help, but before I could, he told me that I was to take a barge to Wuhan. From there I was to travel to the Qinling Mountains where Gong Gong's cult had erected a temple to their dark god. Since Li lived in Wuhan, it was pointless to tell him about her, especially since he may not have been all too receptive of it. He spent a few more hours telling me a few more things before ringing a bell and saying in a pleasant but tired voice "I must take my leave of you now. I will have a servant show you to your room. Good day and good luck, Sir Viccon."

CHAPTER XIX

The trip to Wuhan was pretty uneventful, although the water was a bit more turbulent than it should have been. It took a bit longer to navigate, but we docked several evenings later. When we walked down the streets, I saw people come from the buildings and light the street lanterns. Since we were in Li's resident city, the first place we headed to was her house. I wanted to see her so badly and knew that she would insist that we stay with her, so I didn't bother trying to find a hotel. She knew I was coming for my vacation, she just didn't know when. Besides, I was planning to ask her to join me whiles Wenchi watched over Nancy.

Ah . . . Wenchi was my cousin's best friend at the time. She . . . ah, she . . . well, that's not very important to this story.

Anyway, I knew Wenchi wouldn't mind and that Li would be absolutely thrilled to have a little action in her life. I rushed to their house with Nancy in tow, thinking about how great it would be to finally see Li and Wenchi after all that time. Nancy griped about having to sprint to keep up with me, but I knew deep down she was just as excited as I was if not more. It took us a whiles to finally reach her place and I rushed to her door. As there came no answer to my impatient knocks, I began to pound harder. Wenchi finally opened the door, a damp robe wrapped tightly around her lovely wet figure.

"Yes, may I-KAIN!" she cried out in surprise, her hands going to her wide-open mouth. She immediately caught herself with a blush and pressed her robe close to her body as she squeaked "Nancy! It's so good to see you two! Come inside, come inside!"

"Where's Li at?" I excitedly asked her once we were situated inside. Wenchi had dried herself off and changed into a lovely, though simple silk gown and we were sitting on their couch having a lively chat.

"Oh, she has to close up at the Dragon's Flame." she told me as she carefully handed over two beautiful porcelain cups of tea. That was the name of the teahouse both of the ladies waited tables at.

We talked for at least an hour before I stood up and told the girls that I had to speak to Li immediately, so I was going to the teahouse to greet her. I asked Wenchi if she'd mind watching Nancy whiles I was gone and she said that she would love to. As I walked outside, their girlish chatters filled my ears and I smiled. It didn't take me all that long to get over to a teahouse known as The Dragon's Flame. I was about to walk up to it when I saw the door open and Li walk out. She lit the lamps and went back inside without seeing me, so I wrapped my cloak around my body and pulled my hood over my head, hiding my face and body. At that time your good Grand General didn't wear such a fashionable cloak as this, so I knew she wouldn't recognize me right away.

When I entered, a bell atop the door signaled my arrival. Instantly, Li greeted me and led me to a table, unaware of who I was. She handed me a menu and waited for me to decide what I wanted to order. From her deep, weary sigh as she tossed her hair back it was easy to tell that she was worn out from a long day.

"I would like the sweet and sour chicken, some beer, and to know what time you get off of work, beautiful." I told her in a very serious tone.

It took a moment for the line to register with her, but when it did she wasn't very appreciative of my compliments.

"What? Look, sir, it's late, I'm tired, and I don't feel like getting hit on. So, just lay off!" she replied with a dangerously annoyed tone in her voice.

That's when I pulled back my hood and said in my normal voice "Hello, Hua Li."

Her jaw dropped whiles she mumbled my name in a small voice. I stood and bowed. "Tis I, my lady."

She leapt into my arms and cried "It's you! It's really you! My goodness, it's been too long! Where's Nancy?"

"At your house with Wenchi. How ha—" I started to say, but a voice cut me off. I turned and saw the cook, Wang Anshi, approach us with a large grin spread across his face. He bowed and said in a booming voice "Hello, Kain! How have you been?

"Just fine." I remarked simply. What few customers were there had left, so Wang paused a moment to put the closed sign out. Li sat on the table and let her feet dangle as I asked how life had been treating her since we were last together just as Wang joined us.

"Decently." she replied. Then, she pointed a finger at Wang and giggled "This tyrant is working me to death."

"Work, nothing." he snorted. "You just sit on your pretty little butt all day long."

"I do not! I work hard for you!" she protested.

"And you can prove it by clearing that table." Wang chuckled, pointing his thumb to the table behind him.

"Hmph!" Li huffed as she crossed her arms. "I'll do it, but I want extra pay!"

Wang chuckled as she took the plates and mugs. We heard the dishes clang loudly as she put them in the basin. When she came back, she asked sarcastically "Happy, oh great emperor?"

"Somewhat. What are you in town for, Kain?"

"Business." I replied as Li jumped back onto the table.

She snickered and asked "What for? Trade?"

"Hardly. I'm on a secret assignment and I am not allowed to tell anyone what it is."

"Ohhhh, a secret assignment!" Li giggled. "You never were any good at keeping secrets. Why, I remember when—"

"Quiet, Li. Men are talking." Wang retorted, trying to hold back the laughter his joke had caused him. Li stuck out her tongue, leapt to the ground and flounced away into the kitchen. Wang burst out laughing and whispered "Oh, man! I'm in trouble now."

Li poked her head out from around the corner and asked sharply "What was that?"

"Nothing. I was just telling Kain good-bye. Don't forget to lock up!" he called. And with one final bow, he left.

Li came back with two mugs, one filled with beer for me and one with filled with wine for her. She handed me the beer and sipped her wine, asking "So, what's this secret business of yours?"

"I told you, I'm not supposed to tell anyone."

"Then I'll guess." she said. She closed her eyes and smacked her lips. "You're here toooo . . . stop Gong Gong's cult from raising him."

"How did you know that?" I asked, flabbergasted.

"I didn't. But I do now." she giggled and sipped more of her wine. "Like I said, you were never any good at keeping secrets."

"Well, I guess it doesn't matter since I was planning on telling you." I downed the last drops of my beer. "By the way, is it all right if we stay with you tonight?"

"Of course, Kain. You stay with us all the while you're here. You know you needn't ask. Now tell me more about your quest. Why are you the one going after the devil dragon?"

"I'm not really too sure, to be honest." I told her. "I was told that it's because China's having some trouble with the northern boarders and can't handle it at the moment."

"Oh, yes. I heard about that. Some invasions and whatnot."

"Anyway, I came here hoping that you would like to go with me. You're such a great warrior and I love having you by my side in a fight. It's been too long since our last."

"I'm greatly honored that you have asked for my help. However, Gong Gong is quite a tough character. Tell you what. You can walk me home and I'll think about it."

We went out into the night and Li locked the door to the teahouse with a dull iron key. As we walked down the empty road, I noticed that a full moon shone brightly in the star studded heavens and its light passed through the branches of the trees, causing a beautiful, yet somewhat eerie, effect upon the street. The wind picked up and chilled me. I glanced at my cousin and saw her shiver violently, so

I draped my heavy cloak on her shoulders. She pulled it tight, looked at me with appreciative eyes, and mouthed a thank you.

All of a sudden, a low scurrilous voice called "Look at the love birds. Ain't it sweet?"

I turned and saw a dirty slob of a man. I knew right off that he was going to be trouble, so I started to pull my sword. However, two large men grabbed me from behind and held my arms tight. The leader pulled out a long jagged dagger and advanced towards us. Li screamed out and cried "What do you want!"

"His money and to have your body, beautiful." the thief chuckled evilly.

Now, I knew we could take these pathetic gutter-trash punks no problem. Shoot, Li alone could have taken out all three in two moves with both hands tied. However, the fact remained that I was held out of the picture by two of the ruffians, thus leaving Li unarmed and facing an armed, potentially alcohol or worse influenced, opponent. They all certainly smelled the part. But be that is it may, there was still no a doubt in my mind that Li would be quite capable of handling herself. Thus, I allowed the two oxen to hold me back so I could watch the show. Of course, I played along with the whole concerned lover routine. No point in giving them a bit of foreshadowing.

"Run Li!" I shouted as I tried to break free. I really had to hold back myself to be honest as in their drunken state I was more holding them up than they were holding me back. "Run! Forget me, just save yourself!"

"I wouldn't. I might get careless with my knife around your boyfriend."

"FORGET ME! JUST RUN!" I yelled out and squirmed further. For my trouble, I received a sharp blow to my gut. For a drunkard, he sure did hit me hard. I lost all air in my lungs and we came very close to all collapsing into a heap on the street. Ironically, for that moment I really couldn't have been much help to Li even if I had wanted.

"If I stay and let you do what you want to me, will you let him go?" Li asked, her voice holding just the right amount of quiver to make it seem like she was really afraid.

"Yeah, sure." he snickered. I tried to yell, but there was no longer any breath in my lungs and all that came out was a pathetic wheezing sort of sound.

Li stood proud as the thief came closer and closer. He puckered up his lips for a kiss, but received quite a surprise when Li spat in his face. He reared back and wiped off his cherry-red face whiles his friends snickered. He turned to them and cursed loudly at them, threatening to slice them up. When they finally got quiet, he looked at Li and cursed her savagely before he roared "You and your gigolo are dead!"

He lunged forward, knife in hand. Li sidestepped and grabbed his arm. Then she bent it until we all heard the sickening sound of bone splintering. His screams filled the quiet night as a Li pulled his broken arm further back into an odd angle. She bent forward and hissed in his ear "Never underestimate a woman!"

Then she took hold of his broken arm with his grip still tight around the knife's handle, and used it to slide the blade easily into his throat. His loud screams were instantly replaced by muffled gurgling as he fell to the ground and slowly bled to death whiles convulsing violently. The other two punched me again in the stomach simultaneously and threw me to the ground helpless as I tried to get a breath. The first guy threw a punch, but Li swept him easily off his feet. As soon as he fell, she jumped at the other and kicked him in his chest, sending him reeling back. As the other rose, Li slammed her elbow into his face and his nose exploded in a bloody mess. Then she grabbed his ears and bashed her knee into his face a few times. He staggered and fell whiles his friend charged Li. She jumped straight up and stuck her foot out, catching him square in the face. He stumbled backwards, but didn't fall. Instead, he tried to kick her. She caught his leg with the greatest of ease and kicked him in the chest, then in the gut, then in the knee. I heard his ribs crack and saw as his knee bend at a queer angle and knew that there was no amount of alcohol that would numb that sort of punishment. She dropped him and silenced his screams of excruciating agony by slamming her foot upside his head with enough force to give him a serious crimp in his neck. Whether the blow killed him or not, I still don't know to this day.

The other thief had recovered enough to come to his somewhat good sense and turned to run, but I myself had recovered in time to beat the bag out of him, knocking him around with my fists until his face looked like an armless boxer's. With on final punch, I dumped him into some bushes, the impact disturbing several birds in the trees overhead and sending them flying into the night. Li rushed to me and looked me up and down as I did the same with her.

"Are you all right?" she inquired.

"Yeah. You?"

"Yes, I think so."

"The fun never stops when we're together." I replied with a cocked brow.

"I missed you too. Come on, let's get out of here." She urged with a hint of a giggle as she gripped my arm tight. Together, we ran off into the night.

* * *

Li fished out her key ring and inserted a brass key into the lock. As she turned it, the lock clicked loudly and made us jump with nervous giggles. As she closed the door and relocked it, I lit a few lamps. Wenchi quietly came out of her room and squeaked when she saw the mess we were in.

"Oh, my goodness!" she cried out in a whisper. "What happened to you two?"

"Don't ask." Li told her in a hushed voice. "Where's the kid?"

"In my room asleep. Are you two all right?" she pressed.

Li assured her that we were before she ordered me in an authoritative tone to get cleaned up. I mumbled a sarcastic 'yes mother' very softly. What can I say? Force of habit. Anyway, she must have heard me because she gave me a dirty look that sent me on my way. She's got great ears, let me tell you. Thirty minutes later, the three of us were sitting at their kitchen table sipping tea and talking about issues in our lives. We shared stories and jokes, laughing merrily into the night. I was afraid we would wake Nancy, but then again I almost woke her up to see Li anyway.

"You never gave me your answer." I finally pointed out.

"Answer for what?" Wenchi asked curiously.

"I never got your sweet and sour chicken and beer, either." she remarked with a grin, pouring more steaming tea into her white porcelain cup. "What you're asking me to do is very dangerous. Gong Gong is a very powerful demon. It is said that he can wipe out an entire army with just a snap of his fingers." She looked at me for a second and sighed before sipping from her cup and continuing "However, I realize that you'll need all the help you can get seeing as how both countries have jerked you on this mission and, as I said before, I am very honored that you came to me. My final answer is yes, I'll go. When do we leave?"

"When it's suitable for you."

"Then it's settled. We leave day after tomorrow. Say noon-ish?" she announced. "Wenchi, would you mind watching Nancy whiles we're away?"

"Why, I would love to!" Wenchi said happily, her squeaky voice sounding sexy to my tired ears. She was definitely quite a lady. Smart, clever . . . sweet . . . great cook. Just the perfect gal you'd want for a wife. She . . .

Anyway, Wenchi finished the last of her tea and bayed us both a tired goodnight before leaving for Li's room. Li and I talked a while longer before she yawned deeply a goodnight as well. I retired to Wenchi's room where Nancy was curled up on the bed peacefully.

CHAPTER XX

All of us woke up bright and early two days later. We had spent the whole previous day together sightseeing, shopping, and basically just sharing a relaxing day. Nancy was especially excited and spent the whole time as Li's shadow. You could have said that she was very thrilled to see her cousin again, and that would have been a major understatement. It was a nice time, a blessed relief to have even just a day's vacation before starting out on my mission.

During breakfast on the morning Li and I were to set out, the four of us talked and laughed over a delicious breakfast prepared by Wenchi and Nancy. Then we spent a good three hours if not more catching up before Li and I finally decided that it was time to get ready. I put on my armor and gathered all of my supplies together before going into the living room to wait with Wenchi and Nancy.

A few moments later, Li came out of her room, tugging at her leather-padded waistcoat. Her hair was tied back in a single braid and she wore a very loose dark blue Chinese-style tunic and dark blue pants that wrapped around her body, the folds flowing like water with her graceful movements. She wore no armor save for her waistcoat and her backpack was easily half the size of mine, holding only a heavy blanket, some food and water, some rope, a lantern, and a small flask of black liquid. Her weapon of choice was a queer looking glove covering her right hand. It had razor sharp steel blades on the fingertips like terrible claws and a circular gadget with a spout on the back of the glove. This spout spewed flames she told me, and the flask of black liquid was a special oil that gave fuel to her fire-breathing glove. This was her Dragon Claw, a weapon passed down through her father's family for many generations. She had received it upon her sixteenth birthday along with this talisman hanging around my neck. She had given it to me before we headed out for luck on our quest against Noknor.

After many good-byes and good lucks from Wenchi and Nancy, we headed out the door a little bit after noon. We were able to get our hands on a couple of horses fairly easily, which was a big plus considering Gong Gong's temple was a good ways away through rough hills. In fact, we spent the whole day riding through a forest only to come to a large rushing river. Back in Wuhan, it had taken us almost an hour more than normal to cross the Yellow River because the water had been so rough. I overhead a couple of the boatmen muttering about the river dragons being upset, and it seemed that they were probably right. If the Yellow River was bad, this one was even worse. There was no way we could have crossed it without drowning ourselves. No conventional way, anyway. But then, when have either I or Li been unconventional? Whiles I stood by the forest and leaned against a tree, Li advanced to the edge of the river and kneeled down on the bank before bowing forward a few times.

"Oh, great dragon of the river," she mumbled lowly in prayer. "Please look kindly on us in our journey. I do not wish to disturb you, but your roar is mighty and fierce and it is very important that we cross your great river. Would you please grant us permission to cross, oh River Lord?"

As she had prayed, the river actually started to calm slowly until it was as quiet as a lake at dawn. Li stood up, took three gold coins from her purse, and tossed them into the water. Then she turned to me with a large smile on her face and joyfully said "Okay, we can cross now."

Well, somebody was just a tad wrong, because all of a sudden there came a terrible roar as a gigantic whirlpool began to swirl right behind Li's back near the shore. It was the oddest thing, though, because whiles the whirlpool raced around madly, the rest of the river as far as the eye could see looked like glass, it was that still! In what seemed like a lot longer but in fact was only probably a few seconds or so, a colossal Chinese dragon swiftly rose from the depths of the whirlpool, dwarfing my cousin like you or I would an ant. It was huge! Its head alone was bigger then Li and it could have swallowed her whole if it wanted to. And from the look on her face, she was thinking the same thing! Our horses bolted away as fast their legs could carry them, taking most of our supplies in their saddlebags. I let them go, I mean like I could have actually stopped them anyway. To be honest, I was more concerned with dragon glaring at us than the loss of our rides.

The enormous beast looked us over with massive frowning eyes and gave a mighty bellow. Its roar echoed so loudly that the trees in the forest behind me shook and many scattered leaves fluttered from the branches. Now I will admit that I was shocked beyond belief. Of course I've seen my fair share of Old World dragons, but let me tell you there is something about the Chinese variety that makes them much . . . I don't know, grander perhaps? They certainly seem more frightening when they're pissed off, let me tell you. Anyway, point is I was shocked, but of course I was staring right at the thing. Poor Li was stilled turned towards me and away from the river, but she was absolutely terrified. She was stark white, her eyes were as big as I had ever seen them, and her body was as rigid as a post. She was quivering uncontrollably and her lips were drawn back, exposing her teeth that were clamped down tightly.

She slowly turned to face the monster and yelped loudly as she flinched in shock. The dragon lowered its head and looked her over closely before sniffing her lightly with its huge, round nostrils. Then it snorted loudly, the force of the breath knocking her back a few steps and almost off of her feet, before opening its mouth slightly and bearing the large gleaming teeth in its massive mouth.

"What do you want!" it growled in a booming voice.

Li took a deep, shaky breath, trying her best to collect herself and look presentable. She gulped and bowed low with respect to the dragon before blurting out "Please forgive us, Great Dragon of the River! I know you are mighty and powerful, and are greatly displeased at being disturbed in your beautiful home by mere humans! We only wish to beg you for your permission to cross your beautiful river!"

The dragon smiled at the flattery and when it spoke again, its voice was much more soft and gentle "Tell me, beautiful flower, why you wish to cross my river."

"We are in search of the temple of the wicked Gong Guh—" she started but didn't even get a chance to finish her sentence. The infuriated dragon pushed her down with its snout and pinned her to the ground as it hissed "Why do you **DARE** look for such a place!"

"Oh Powerful River Lord, please forgive me! I did not mean to offend you!" she yelped loudly. I seriously thought it was going gulp her down its throat right then and there, and I can only imagine what Li was thinking. "We do not wish to join such evil and wickedness, but instead quite the opposite! My cousin has been employed by my emperor to stop evil from being raised!"

It smiled brightly with relief that was infinitely smaller than the relief Li felt and backed off from her. It gripped her small hand his large paw and helped her back to her feet as he apologized "I am humbly sorry for my actions, dear lady. I should have known that a creature as beautiful as you would not be in league with such a devil. If the emperor Wu Di has sent you, you must be—" It stopped suddenly and frowned as it replied "Cousin?"

It brushed past Li and moved to me in order to eye me closely. "You don't look Chinese." Then, it sniffed me a few times as it had Li. "You don't smell Chinese." Finally, it flicked its long thin tongue against my cheek. "You don't taste Chinese!" It looked back at Li and demanded "Why do you call him cousin? You are Chinese and he is not! How can you two be cousins?"

Li quickly explained that we were actually half cousins and not related at all by blood, but that we had grown up together and considered each other blood. She told the dragon about how my father had met and married her aunt after I had already been born. It asked how we had grown up together, and she responded by relaying in short-form how Noknor had killed my parents and that Nancy and I were sent to live with her family. Upon the mention of my father's name, the dragon's jaw dropped and its eyes grew wide.

"You are the blood of the Slayer of the Doe?" it gasped loudly.

"I am the son of Sir Richard Viccon of Arcainia!" I told it proudly, stepping forward. "He is the Slayer of the Doe, and yes, I am his blood!"

"What is, or was, the Doe?" Li asked, a little confused by how the dragon had suddenly taken an interest in me.

Before I even had a chance to open my mouth, the dragon slumped down on the bank of the river, and explained "Kitrad Doe was a very powerful clan of dragons from the other side of the world, where your cousin is from. They were all very powerful and mighty, but also peaceful and honorable and they maintained peace with the world around them. However, one young and ambitious dragon began to make waves as he campaigned for the head of the clan. He felt that the elders were weak and cowardly, that the clan should use its power to gain instead of hiding behind ancient ideas and thoughts. He began to attract many dragon, human, and faery followers as he quickly schemed and connived his way up in the ranks of his clan.

"Then one dark day, after he had successfully placed his dragon followers in key positions in the clan structure like well situated chess pieces, he struck hard and swiftly. He assassinated the clan elders and placed himself as head of the clan. Those that opposed him were quickly and cruelly killed off. With no one left to challenge him, he grew thirsty for more power and treasure. He began a great effort to conquer the world, recruiting other evil followers into the clan and crushing all who got in his path. It wasn't long before the terrible new Kitrad Doe made their way over the sea. When we honorable Chinese dragons said we would neither bow before him nor join him, he kidnapped many of our children and used their lives to force us to his evil will.

"Then a great warrior, a human warrior, stepped forward and tackled him alone. After a great and bloody battle, the last Doe was slain and peace was restored to all lands whiles we got our beloved children back. The Council of Dragons owes the Slayer of the Doe a debt of gratitude. We were greatly saddened to hear of his passing, and the loss was felt by all of the council. If you are indeed the blood of the Slayer, we will do anything to aid you in your victory against our worst enemy Gong Gong."

"Thank you, great river dragon." I bowed low. "Please tell your council that any help will be greatly appreciated."

"I must take you before them." it mumbled, grabbing both Li and me and tossing us onto his back like a couple of rag-dolls. "Hold on tightly."

With that, it rose off of the ground and sped off high into the blue sky. It moved through the air gracefully, as if it were swimming rather than flying. As it swiftly flew, twisting and writhing like a great snake, I dared to peek over the side. I saw that we were very high up, that the forests below looked like tiny bushes and the mighty rivers appeared to be nothing more than slim worms. I looked over my shoulder and saw that Li clung on tightly, her face buried into the scales on the dragon's back. I chuckled lowly as the wind whipped through my hair.

CHAPTER XXI

After what seemed like only a few minutes, I began to notice that the dragon was spiraling downward. My first thought was that Li had fallen off and that he was swooping to catch her. However a glance over my shoulder proved that Li was safe and sound, still clinging as close as she could to the dragon's back with her face still pressed so tightly against its hide that the scales left indentions in her cheeks and forehead. Apparently my second guess that we had reached our destination was correct. The dragon alighted on a large, rocky plateau high above the land. From where we stood after climbing off its back, me and Li could see many miles of the beautiful Chinese landscape. It was truly a sight to behold.

The river dragon pulled us along and led us to an entrance into the mountain that was at least fifty feet high and almost just as wide. Inside it seemed as if the entire mountain had been hollowed out to make room for a grand hall of sorts. It was indeed a marvelous sight to see! It was the biggest room I had ever seen before in my life; think ten of the Grand Halls in Arcainia Castle. Golden torches lined the walls, lighting the room, and a large red carpet made of the finest silk ran down the center all the way to the back where a dragon sat on the most beautiful golden throne I had ever seen. The dragon was fairly large, but still smaller than the river dragon. It looked very ancient, at least a few thousand years old, and had a powerful air about him that was even stronger than any human king I had ever met. Suddenly, I felt very nervous.

Hundreds of Chinese dragons of all types stood or sat on either side of the red carpet as they chatted with one another. As the river dragon pushed us forward, they all stopped talking and looked at us, some curiously and some heatedly, before murmuring between themselves. I could tell that not many humans had ever set foot in the place. We were silently led to the throne and bowed before the dragon emperor. He looked us over with a frown, pawing the armrests of his chair with his five clawed fingers before glaring at the river dragon and snapping "What is the meaning of this!"

It recoiled slightly and laid its head on the ground before his master. "I did not mean to anger you, your greatness. But I felt that you needed to see this human. He has come from very far to combat Gong Gong."

"And who is this human that he is so important that he may be brought into the Great Hall of Dragons?" it roared, sitting straight up and looking every bit as menacing as he looked old. However, right about that time getting eaten was the least of my worries as being ripped limb from limb and then eaten ranked higher on the list. "And how can he even hope to combat such an evil devil as our enemy?"

"He is the blood of the Slayer of the Doe."

Instantly, the place went as quiet as a tomb and not a single sound was to be heard at all except for my cousin's agitated breathing. Even the emperor was struck speechless. After a few seconds, a low murmur was heard, followed by another, and then more. Soon the place was filled with the low buzz of excited voices. There was a slight rustling as the other dragons moved closer to get a better look at me; I swear I felt like an exhibit in the museum. The emperor opened his massive jaws and licked his lips as he eyed me with wide, impressed eyes.

"The blood of the Slayer of the Doe?" he finally uttered hoarsely, lowering his body slightly. "And this, your concubine?"

"No, most celebrated Emperor of the Dragons, she is his cousin." the river dragon replied before explaining the relationship between Li and myself.

"I see." the emperor murmured, after listening intently to all that was said. "And now you are here in your father's stead to combat a devil even more powerful than the Doe? This council has all of the faith in you that we had for your father. However, you will need aid."

He snapped his fingers, the sound echoing loudly as instantly a small female dragon, not much taller than me walked between me and Li bearing a golden sword upon a beautiful silk pillow. As she passed, she seemed to look me over and giggled bashfully before she handed the weapon to her emperor and retreated off to the side, watching me intently.

"Xiwang was one of the children the Slayer of the Doe rescued." the emperor looked to her and smiled. "A most beautiful child, she is my great-great-great grandchild and I owe your father much for her life. It deeply saddened me and this council to hear of his passing." There was a brief pause as he fingered the sword fondly before he continued "And now it seems that another hero from afar has come to aid us and rescue our children from our blight."

"I will try my best, great emperor." I replied strongly with all the pride I could muster.

"I have faith in you, for you are the new Slayer." he told me, presenting the sword to me. "But you will need help. This is the Dragon Blade, a very powerful weapon to combat a very powerful enemy. Please take this as a gift to use against Gong Gong, for though it will not guarantee victory, it will be of more help to you than your simple mortal sword."

"Thank you very much, gracious emperor." I said happily, taking the weapon from his grasp. The sword was very marvelous and was made of pure gold yet stronger then steel. The handle was crafted into the form of a Chinese dragon whiles the blade resembled flames shooting from its mouth. "With it, I will fight with all of my might for you and your people."

"Then, may happy luck be with you. Now off with you, for I feel it may already be too late."

* * *

On the back of the river dragon, we landed next to a small entrance into an underground cavern in the middle of Qinling, the Witch Mountains. An evil, stale air drifted out of the hole and covered us, chilling us to the bone. As the river dragon helped us off his back, he looked around nervously as if half expecting Gong Gong to jump from anywhere. Li and I checked ourselves over to make sure everything was in order and lit a lantern before lowering ourselves into the black abyss. As the darkness surrounded us, we heard the river dragon bay us good wishes for a grand victory.

We walked a long way, taking care to watch out for sharp stalactites and stalagmites and small bats that were certainly in abundance. We eventually came to a deep pit that was much too large to jump across and had at the bottom of it many sharp pieces of jagged rock. I tied my rope to my spear and tossed it at the outcropping rocks of the ceiling, snagging it tightly. I tugged hard on the rope to make sure it was secure before I grabbed Li tightly around the waist and together we swung across.

About fifty feet away from us was a large doorway from which light and chanting issued. As I put out my lantern, Li whispered something I didn't quite hear and I grabbed her arm as I pulled her to the doorway. Inside was a large room with the huge block of black ice in the center that had black candles arranged in an evil pattern whiles crude statues of Gong Gong horribly decorated the walls. Thirty people in gray robes and hoods knelt around the altar, chanting in a strange tongue that was a combination of Chinese and a sort of strange hissing. As we were about to rush in, the candles sent streams of green flame to the ceiling, leaving horrible burn marks. There was a heavy rumble and then a terrible hiss like that of a giant snake as the stone cube exploded, sending fragments everywhere. The thirty worshippers stood and cheered. We had come to stop the rise of Gong Gong and it seemed that we were too little too late.

A booming raspy voice came from an unseen body standing in the rubble, yelling something in that strange language that made the worshippers draw wicked daggers and turn to face us. It yelled again, and they attacked us like wolves. However, we fought like tigers. Li kicked the first in the gut and sent him crashing into one of the statues. A second struck at me with a downward blow of his sword, but I parried it with the Dragon Blade and kicked him in the gut. An upward swipe of the Dragon Blade cut him out of the picture. Filled with the frenzy of battle, we roared like dragons and leapt at the oncoming crowd. She slashed and stabbed madly with her claws like a woman possessed while I lashed out with the Dragon Blade, connecting my powerful blows to slice through them like a hot knife through warm butter. The worshippers were so shocked by our savage attack that they couldn't defend themselves properly and fell at our feet one by one. When we had finished that fight, we found that we were in for the battle of our lives.

In a flash of green fire, Gong Gong made himself known to us. He was a fearsome demon, standing thirteen feet tall, with massive shoulders that were five feet wide and four powerful arms with enormous hands armed with razor sharp black talons. His dark skin glittered like metal in the flickering torchlight and two horns as thick as trees grew from his thick head. He had the head of a China-man but his sneering mouth was filled with three rows of thin fangs sharp as needles and his two pairs of large eyes glowed bright red like coals straight from Hell. The temple shook when he threw back his head and uttered a devilish laugh as he clapped his four hands together.

"So, you are the new hero sent by that wretched council of lizards." he growled, stretching his mighty limbs, cracking his knuckles. "Haw-haw-haw-haw! Why, you little insect! You can't possibly think to defeat me! I could kill you with but a thought! However, since I am newly freed from that accursed block of ice and you will die soon enough, I will let you go so you can take your woman there home and give her one last good time. Haw-haw-haw! And what is she doing dressed like a warrior? Does she think she is a man?"

"You worm!" Li barked furiously, giving him a fireball blast in the face.

Gong Gong shook it off and hissed savagely "Foolish mortal female! How **DARE** you attack a god? For that insolence, for punishment I demand death!"

"Li, run!" I shouted, brandishing the Dragon Blade. She glanced at me for a second before bolting for the door. Gong Gong raised his hand and I, sensing great doom, flung myself shoulder first into the monster. I didn't do more than just bounced off his thick frame, but it was enough to knock him off balance a bit as he cast a stream of green fire from his hand and through the doorway. I heard Li scream and became overcome with fury. I lashed out with my magical weapon, giving him a nasty laceration on his side. Then I looked back at the door to see if Li was all right, a big mistake. I didn't even see Gong Gong's fist cruising towards me and he hit me so hard that I flew through the air watching the wall get closer and closer with just enough time to think 'this is going to hurt'.

Whiles I was in a daze, he tried to crush me under his huge foot, but I managed to roll just in time and slash his leg. He drew back, roared furiously, and used a powerful kick to my side to launch me across the room. I heard a horrible snap and was afraid it was a couple of ribs, but luckily it was just my bow. Sure felt like ribs though. Gong Gong lowered his head and charged at me like a bull. Just as he was about to mow me down, I leaped over his head and rolled down his back. He struck the wall hard, imbedding his horns deep within the rock. As he tried to free himself with frustrated snarls, I rolled under him and swung my sword a few times, deeply gashing his belly and his chest. I would have done more, but he swung his arms wildly and batted me away as he shrieked so loudly, the walls cracked, freeing him. I saw his wounds were bleeding black blood and that his body was covered in the stuff. He charged me again, swinging his fists madly. I tried to get in a hit, but he knocked me around like a rag doll. When I tried to get up, he grabbed me by my legs and intended to dash me against the walls.

However, I lashed out and cut off one of his arms. He squealed in pain as his limb twitched with spasms on the floor and gushed black blood. Gong Gong roared madly and began to shoot green flames as he bellowed curses at me. I danced around trying to avoid them and managed to block a few with the Dragon Blade. Then I pointed the sword at him and let a powerful blast of golden fire fly. It struck him square in that ugly face of his and almost took his head off as he flew backwards. He crashed into the wall and immediately grabbed three of his statues to throw at me. With three swipes of the Dragon Blade I smashed them to pieces before throwing another golden flame at him. It struck his stomach and tore through him with a disgusting splat. Black blood spewed from his mouth as he coughed violently and grabbed his torn belly.

He tried to rise once more, but I jabbed him in the shoulder with the tip of my sword and shoved him back down. Then, with a mighty roar, I leapt high into the air, brandishing the Dragon Blade as I flew. Just before I thrust the mystical sword straight into his heart, I saw his glowing red eyes pop open wide with fear, for he knew his end had finally come. He screamed in agony as the blade sliced into his chest up to the hilt. While writhing for a few minutes he tried feebly to knock me away, but I stood strong. Finally, the fire emptied from his eyes and the mighty Gong Gong was dead before he had a chance to live again. I laughed in triumph as I yanked my sword out of him and watched as his body burst into flames.

Suddenly, I remembered Li and ran for the door. I rushed out hoping to see her, but instead I was greeted by a shock. I saw Li, or so I thought. It looked exactly like her: same hair, same outfit, same face, even same Dragon Claw. But there was something about her that didn't seem quite right. Her skin seemed to be a bit pale and her eyes were a little red. Not bloodshot or teary, they just had a slight reddish hue to them. And when she grinned, her teeth looked more like sharp silvery fangs than her normal white teeth.

"Oh, my love! My darling!" she moaned joyfully as she rushed up to greet me. Her voice wasn't right either. Of course, that was not something she would ever say to me and certainly not in that sort of tone, and whiles it sounded like hers, it was hollow and empty, not up and perky as it usually was. "I am so happy you are safe!"

She threw her pale arms around me and planted her lips onto mine in a lover's kiss. I was shocked! I didn't know what to do and just stood there. When I finally tried to push her away, she just gripped me tighter the more I fought.

Finally, she pulled away from me and sighed in a hurt tone, her eyes filled with dismay. She gasped as if she were close to tears "My love! Why do you fight me so?"

I pushed her back a few feet and snapped "What are you talking about? What is wrong with you!"

She frowned and took a step back. She seemed to think for a moment before she scowled and hissed violently, raising her hand to slash at me. However, a rock whizzed from out of nowhere and struck her in the head. She uttered low a grunt and fell to the ground.

"So, can I kiss or what?" the real Li giggled, standing a few feet away. She was a mess, her body was scratched and bruised, her outfit was torn in several places, and she was covered in dust from head to toe. But at least she was alive and smiling. "I take it you did better than I did?"

"What in the world?" I gasped. "What happened to you?"

"I got into a fight with that . . . that . . . thing, whatever it is." she said, regarding the creature at my feet. "It was a pretty tough customer, let me tell you."

I looked at the fake Li at my feet and saw that she had changed into a weird looking creature. It was in the shape of a human, but its skin was as smooth as glass and it had no hair. Half of it was black and shiny like onyx and the other half was white as snow. Its eyes were blood red and filled with fury as it stared up at me.

"A doppelganger!" I replied, before realizing that its eyes were wide open.

It grabbed my leg and tripped me flat onto my back before leaping to its feet. It gave a horrible hiss as it quickly morphed into a Chinese man with a long, black whip. Li raised her hand to shoot a fireball, but the doppelganger cracked its whip and wrapped it around her arm. Quick as a flash, it gave a mighty tug and pulled her off her feet. When I got up, it wrapped its whip around my neck and proceeded to throttle me. However, three well-placed elbows in its stomach got it off me. It stepped back and morphed into an old Chinese man with a long white beard. Li jumped at it, but it shot lightning from its hand and knocked her out of the air. It tried to do the same to me, but I blocked it with the Dragon Blade and slashed at it. Before my sword reached its head, however, it morphed into me and blocked it with a mock Dragon Blade. We sword fought for a few seconds, our mighty blows doing nothing but clashing off one another. It seemed to know all of my moves and countered with ease. It was only a matter of time before it got the upper hand and took me out. However, Li rushed to my aid, slashing the fake me on the back and kicking its legs out from under it. It turned back into Li and slashed at her, but I knocked it on the shoulder with the butt of my sword whiles she blocked the doppelganger and kicked it in the stomach.

It staggered away from us and morphed into a Chinese archer, but not as quickly as it had before. It took an arrow and shot it at me before shooting at Li quick as a flash. I raised the Dragon Blade, splitting the arrow in two whiles Li simply ducked out of the way. Then, together we leapt at it. With both of us flying at it, it couldn't decide who to hit and panicked, allowing us to both kick it hard in the chest at the same time. It grunted and flew back against the wall, rebounding towards Li who gave it a mighty roundhouse kick to its head, the impact enough flip it head over heels. It turned back into its normal self as it spun the air and Li kicked it once again for good measure, sending it crashing into the wall. The doppelganger fell to the ground with a dusty thud, defeated.

As it laid whimpering and clutching its wounds and bruises, Li stood over it with a nasty scowl and growled "Your little tricks aren't so useful now, are they?"

We turned to leave, but it roared and leaped at Li, horrible black and white claws bared to tear out her throat. One swipe of the Dragon Blade detached its head, which rolled a ways before falling into the pit we had swung across earlier as Li thrust her claws straight into its chest. I set its body aflame with a shot of golden fire before Li and I proceeded to walk out of the cave. Once outside, I shot another golden flame into the air and we sat to rest whiles we waited for the river dragon to return. We shared some fruit and water as we recounted our earlier battles.

"When I ran from the room," Li told me after gulping down almost her entire skin of water. "I heard a loud boom so I hit the deck. As soon as I did, I felt the heat of the fire as it passed over me. The reason I screamed was because a hot piece of rock hit my shoulder when the fire hit the wall." She exposed her shoulder to me. She had a large, angry red burn and I offered to put something on it. She shook her head and told me that she already put some salve on it before continuing on with her story. "When I stood back up I saw that horrid monster in front of me."

"The doppelganger." I explained to her. "It's a monster that can change its shape and has a taste for human flesh. It always takes to shape of the person it's going to kill and if that person was in a group, it takes over his or her spot. Then it goes about knocking off the group one by one."

As you all know, a doppelganger is an Old World creature. Two of Gong Gong's cult members were Old Worlders, so Li and I assume that it either tagged along with them or maybe one of them trained it as a bodyguard of sorts. To be honest, we're still not pretty sure.

"Ugh!" Li continued with her story. "Well, anyway, that doppelganger leaped on me and pinned me to the ground. I was able to kick it off and get to my feet, but when I looked at it again, I saw that it was me! I was so stunned that it got the upper hand on me. I managed to defend myself, but for every attack I threw at it, it blocked each and every one. It was like it knew what I was going to do before I did. Anyway, it grabbed me and threw me into the wall. I, being the trooper I am, wasn't going to let it get the better of me and attacked it again. But the same thing happened. It was so embarrassing, getting my butt kicked by that thing. I think I managed to score a few hits, but that thing finally ended up grabbing me by the throat and tossed me into that pit we had swung across earlier. Remember, the one with the spikes at the bottom of it? Yeah? Well, I thought I was dead, but I landed on a small ledge and had the wind knocked out of me. I laid there trying to recuperate for a few minutes before I forced myself to scale that wall. When I finally made it, I saw that thing making kissy face with you. I thought you might be enjoying it too much, so I threw a rock at it. Pretty good shot, huh?"

"Indeed it was, my dear. Thank you." I told her, stretching out my sore muscles. "I guess it got the wrong idea about us. Must have figured us for husband and wife."

All of a sudden, we heard a familiar roar thunder across the sky and shake the ground.

* * *

The Council of Dragons had a great feast in our honor for defeating their sworn enemy. There was great and delicious foods of all kinds and wine that was the best I had ever tasted. The dragon emperor was thrilled to see us back and spoke at length of his pride in us. He was not only indebted to me, but to Li as well. She was positively rosy with excitement.

After his beautiful speech, I told the dragons tales of my father's conquests, to which they eagerly listened, especially the younger ones. They in turn told us tales of their ancestors, which I must say were very interesting themselves. I'll have to recant them for you all sometime. Li showed off her great moves in a spectacular dance and told funny stories to them. We had both earned the respect of the Council of Dragons, the greatest honor a Chinese could have. For my cousin, it was very special, indeed.

It was a wonderful few days that we spent as guests of the council, but it had to end much too soon. After about three days of feasting and celebrations, we found ourselves riding to the Imperial Palace on the back of the river dragon. Upon arrival, we went directly to the throne room to see the emperor. He greeted me with large smile but frowned upon Li. He gave her a look of distrust and asked "Who are you, woman? And why do you wear such clothes?"

"She is my cousin." I answered for her. "She helped me defeat Gong Gong."

"What do you mean 'helped'?" he asked.

"She is a very accomplished fighter." I told him. "And she has earned the respect of the Council of Dragons."

"The . . . the Council of Dragons you say?" he gasped, his mouth hanging open. "How did you earn their respect, young lady?"

I spent a whiles relaying the story of our journey and he listened intently whiles he nodded his approval and stroked his long, black beard. At the end of the recount, he turned to Li and asked "Would you be so kind as to show me some of the moves which gained you the respect of the Council of Dragons."

Li bowed nervously and began to do an array of punches, kicks, and flips. For almost five minutes, she entertained the emperor and his court. Finally, he told her to stop and offered her a seat. Li bowed again and sat as she said "Thank you, honorable emperor."

He whispered something to one of his many servants and the boy rushed out the door. Whiles he was out, I presented the Dragon Blade to Wu Di, telling him that as the Council of Dragons gave it to me as a gift, I was giving it as a gift to the great Chinese people in case another great evil ever rose up and plagued their land. Taking it from my hand, he smiled and said "Thank you, Sir Viccon. You are indeed a true hero. Much as your father before you."

That's when the empress came in and took a seat in the golden throne beside her husband. She gave me a beautiful smile, but frowned at Li, asking who she was without hiding her distaste. Wu Di explained her that she was my cousin and how she gained the respect of the Council of Dragons by helping me to defeat Gong Gong. The empress gave Li a very impressed look and smiled pleasantly at her, though her eyes still held a look of contempt. A minute later, twelve prisoners entered followed by twenty armed Chinese soldiers.

Wu Di turned to Li and replied "I wish to see you in action, my dear. These twelve men are sentenced to death for their crimes. I want you to fight them to the death. If you can beat them all, perhaps I might have a special position for you. After all, it is not often that a person, particularly a female, earns the respect of the Council of Dragons."

The empress looked at her husband with great distress as the criminals were given swords and spears. Li was given a choice of her weapon, but she waved them all away and pulled on her Dragon Claw.

One of the criminals approached the throne as close as the guards would allow and asked "So, all we have to do is kill this whore, and we can all go free?"

"I'm not a whore, you piece of garbage." Li growled.

"Shut your mouth, whore." he hissed.

"What are you going to die for?" she asked with a stingingly venomous voice as she clicked her metallic claws together and got into her fighting stance.

"I raped a stupid whore like you." he snickered vilely.

"What's the matter?" she laughed a mocking laugh. "The oxen kick you every time you tried to pet it?"

The criminal roared in fury as he charged at her with his sword swinging wildly. Li was able to grab his shirt and throw him to the ground without his blade even coming close to her. He jumped up and bellowed, but with a well-placed kick that broke his knee Li took him right back down. As he fell, he screamed wildly. Li leapt up high and slammed both of her feet onto his chest. There was a terrible, gut-wrenching crack as his ribs splintered and his heart was crushed. He began to spasm violently so just to be sure he was done for, she pushed down harder on his chest, a sickening wet crackle filling our ears as he gasped and winced painfully. She held her cold, venomous eyes on the other criminals as she pushed down harder still, twisting her feet around as she did so. Everyone tore their eyes away from her and the empress turned completely away from the gruesome sight.

For a minute or two, all was silent and all eyes were focused on Li and the dead criminal at her feet. Then the others attacked her violently, swearing and screaming as they all lunged forward. Now I won't go into detail because it's already getting late as it is and I want us to get an early start towards Hurst in the morning, but when the chaos finally ended, only Li stood strong and proud, and more importantly, alive. There was not even so much as a scratch on her other than those that were already there. As the guards rushed to pick up the mess, she turned to the royals and bowed.

Everyone was quite impressed as well as speechless, and even the guards gave her respectful, if not fearful looks. Finally, Wu Di began clapping slowly, the lone sound echoing loudly as he instructed her to have a seat before replying "Excellent. Most excellent. What did you think, my dear?"

"That was . . . most in . . . in-in-interest . . . ing." the empress remarked, looking as if she wanted to puke and cry at the same time. Her eyes no longer held contempt in them. Now there was only respect and fear.

"Tell me, what is that particular style? I must say I have never seen it used in any of our armies." Wu Di asked Li.

"It's called Long Jing Shin." Li answered, taking a deep, tired breath.

"Where ever did you learn it?"

Li took another deep breath and started her tale. "Well, it started many generations ago on my father's side. One of my ancestors taught his self and then taught it to his first son. That son taught his first son, and so on. My father was the first son of his family and thus was taught. Then he married my mother and had my eldest sister with her. He was disappointed that it wasn't a son, but was happy to be a father nonetheless.

"A few years passed and my mother got pregnant once again. My father hoped and prayed for a son to carry on the tradition. However, as things go, he received me. He was highly upset and wouldn't even look at me for my first month. He refused to hold me, but one day my mother forced him to, trying to force him to accept me. My mother was a smart and persistent woman and her plan did finally work. He realized that I was his blood, even if I was a girl. Pouting wouldn't change that fact and no matter what, I was his child. But he was getting older and he still had a tradition to carry on. So, rather than try his luck and hold out for a son that may never come, and incidentally never actually did, and instead of breaking tradition he ultimately decided to bend it slightly and decided to teach his daughter. By that time, my sister was too old for it to begin with her, so he began teaching me when I was about three, since that was tradition. He also gave me this Dragon Claw and this Dragon Heart talisman when I turned sixteen also as per tradition." she finished, bowing low before her emperor.

"Well, my dear girl, that is most impressive." Wu Di smiled brightly, twirling his long beard with his fingers. "I am sure the Chinese Empire would have great use for such a powerful person. Might I inquire when you reside?"

"In Wuhan, great emperor." she told him.

"Wuhan?" the empress remarked. "Did I not overhear that there is a fort in need of a trainer in Wuhan?"

"Yes, I do believe there is. Would you care for the position of military trainer in your village?" Wu Di asked.

"SURE!" Li squeaked with great enthusiasm at such an exciting prospect to have a job doing what she loved most. Blushing deeply, she regained her composure and hastily added "I would be greatly honored to serve my Emperor and my homeland."

PART V

JOURNEY TO HURST

CHAPTER XXII

"After Li and I arrived in Wuhan, Nancy and I stayed with her and Wenchi for a few more weeks." Kain finished his story with a mighty yawn. "In that time, I helped Li get started with her new position at the Wuhan fort. When we got back, I went out for Grand General and after busting my tail I got it."

"So that was the story of Kain Viccon's raise to Grand General, huh?" Robert murmured with a smile, clapping his friend of the back. "Well, it was a good one, I must say."

All of the troops agreed heartily as they started to rise and headed off to their tents for some sleep. Raphael yawned a good night to Kain and his friends as he also headed for his tent while Michael and Robert strode away chatting idly. Nancy stayed up with her brother awhile longer.

They sat silently together for several minutes before Nancy sighed dully and mumbled "I hope Li's all right."

"Oh, I'm sure she is. She's a very tough person." Kain told his sister as he put his arm around her shoulder.

"That's true." she replied with a grin, thinking just how tough her cousin could be. She thought of something else that had been on her mind. "Thank you, Kain."

"For?" he asked.

"Well, for letting me tag along. Thanks for letting me help . . . letting me help do what has to be done." she smiled.

Kain gave her an amused look before telling her "Thank you for being so mature in your thinking and mature enough to handle it. And, strictly speaking, you are not 'tagging along'. Anyone who has the skill you do is an important part of any battle unit. Besides, no one in Kain Viccon's army merely 'tags along'. And certainly no one who saves Kain Viccon's life merely 'tags along'."

Nancy blushed very deeply and said "Thank you, Kain. I love you."

"I love you too, Nancy." Kain yawned. "Now, go on to bed, pup. It's late. Early day tomorrow."

"Okee-dokee." she giggled. She gave him a peck on the cheek and skipped away.

Kain followed her away with his eyes before sighing softly and slowly picking himself up to make his way to his tent for some well deserved sleep of his own. He was surprised at just how much energy it took to tell a story.

* * *

Li was sleeping soundly in her bed while Elizabeth sat in the far corner of the room. She was examining a certain stone in the floor that appeared to be loose. She prodded it and nudged it, noting how it wiggled easily in its place. Suddenly, Li awoke with a start, yelping loudly and breaking the still air. Elizabeth was quick to rush by her side as soon as she heard her scream. Li was quivering terribly and sweating profusely with the sheet clutched tightly to her breast. Her eyes were wide open and she was shivering violently with fear.

"What is it! What's the matter?" Elizabeth cried out.

Li looked around in a wild panic, realizing that she was back in her bed in her semi-safe prison. She looked herself over and began to try to calm down, telling her friend "Nothing. Just a bad nightmare, that's all."

"Are you all right? What was it about?"

"I'm fine." she murmured, rubbing her face.

When Elizabeth pressed for details, Li told her that she didn't really remember any. The princess shrugged in acceptance and replied "Oh, well. As long as you're all right. Here, come see what I found!"

Elizabeth pulled Li by the arm and guided her to the stone. Li nudged it with her foot and found that it was indeed very loose. The princess explained that while it seemed to be fairly light as far as stone went, she couldn't get a very good grip on it to lift, so Li went to the closet and began removing the clothes that hung from a large iron bar. Elizabeth was just about to inquire what in the world she was doing when she pulled out the heavy bar. Then she walked over to the stone and wedged it in the large crack between the bricks. With a labored grunt and a sharp scrape of stone on stone, she pried the block up enough so that Elizabeth could grab and hold it steady. Li discarded the bar and helped Elizabeth hold the stone block. After making sure her friend had a good hold and was ready, Li counted to three and together they hauled it out of the floor with a bit of effort. The gaping hole was two feet by two feet, and both women could have easily fit through.

Elizabeth pointed out that they could escape, but Li just shook her head and replied "We could but I don't think we should."

"What? Why?" she inquired as she gave her friend a queer look. She couldn't believe Li didn't want to escape from such a horrible, dreadful place.

"Well, for one thing, we're pretty much safe here. Noknor won't hurt us, as I've said before. We're too important to him." Li told her. Elizabeth still wasn't sold, so she added, looking down the hole, "Besides, that's the throne room. We'd be leaping right into Noknor's lap. Now I'm sure he would love that, but I'm not too particularly thrilled at the thought myself."

Elizabeth looked down into the room below and saw that it really was the throne room. She also saw that it was empty. She mentioned it, but Li didn't appear to have heard her. She walked over to the small cabinet, opened the doors, and withdrew a flask of wine. She pulled out the cork with her teeth, put the bottle to her lips, and sucked down the wine in larger gulps than she normally used. She started to recork the flask before thinking twice and taking another gulp to help calm her nerves. The dream had been so horrid and it terrified her. All she could hope was that it wasn't a premonition of a dark future.

Suddenly, Elizabeth gestured for her to join her and to be quiet. Li knelt down beside her and peered into the throne room. Noknor was now sitting in his chair trying to get comfortable while Garrison had pulled up a chair and was sitting in it with his feet propped up on a small table. Noknor glanced at him and asked "So, you and that Chinese woman have quite a colorful history together, do you?"

"You might say that." Garrison smiled evilly as he grabbed an apple from the table. He drew his dagger and went about carving the fruit without much skill.

"What do you mean?"

"Well, I murdered her best friend." he laughed then thought for a moment. "Then I beat the bag out of her."

"You little . . ." Li hissed under her breath.

"Why didn't you kill her and be done with her?" Noknor asked idly, not really caring one way or the other. It was just conversation to him.

However, it caught Garrison off guard and Li enjoyed watching him squirm as he stuttered "I, uh . . . that is, she uhn . . . called some, uh . . . help . . . the authorities. And I had to ah . . . run or risk being caught by the authorities." Then, to quickly turn the heat off, he very hastily added "Oh, yeah. I also killed her lover in battle."

"So?" Noknor huffed blandly, not overly impressed in the least. "Every soldier has killed somebody's lover in battle."

"I was on his side and his best friend at the time."

"You betrayed him?" Noknor giggled with newfound glee while high above his head Li fumed in fury. "Why?"

"Money, of course." Garrison sighed happily. He snapped his head toward Noknor and said "And it's a great story, my lord! Would you care to hear it?"

"Oh, yes! It'll be excellent entertainment for dinner."

A small goblin brought a large tray piled with food and drink for the two evil men. As they dug in, Garrison began his devilish myth "Well, it happened five years ago. I, being a merc, had found my way onto the dwarfs' side of the Dwarf and Goblin war. To me it was just business, so I did the best job I could to earn as much money as I could. It was during this time that I met a Knight of Auset recruited to help out the dwarfs. His name was James Raptor.

"Raptor and I fought side by side all during the war and we became great friends, advancing together to higher positions within the dwarf army. Towards the end, we had become commanders for a large battle group with the dwarf king. Raptor often spoke of his woman and his life whiles I of course kept quiet about my past for obvious reasons, what with belonging to a criminal family. He was a decent guy, cool and fun to hang out with. A little too moral for my tastes, but at least he wasn't all about trying to convert me like some of those other pansy Auset Knights. A hell of a fighter too, let me tell you. I don't normally say this about anyone else, but I had to respect the guy. In a fair fight, he could have bested me easily.

"But there are some things even more important than respect and friendship: money. The dwarves paid me well enough, but I was a merc working for the highest bidder. And just when it looked as if Raptor and I had personally won the whole stupid war for the dwarfs, Grendal the goblin king personally approached me to ask something of me. Something wicked . . ."

* * *

"You want what?" I asked as I dropped my fishing pole and withdrew my sword. His two bodyguards immediately grabbed for their swords, but the king shook his head and they left their weapons in their sheaths whiles still holding the handles. Grendal offered his hand to me and told me that he meant no harm, unless of course if I answered his questions in the wrong way.

"I want you to help me. Join my cause and become a traitor for the goblins." he told me, showing no signs of trying to hide the direct order in his icy tone.

"What's in it for me?" I asked thoughtfully as I slowly put away my sword.

"Your damn pathetic life!" he roared, his red eyes blazing, his toothy mouth spurting goblin spittle.

"That's it?" I asked, not the least bit unnerved. "Certainly you have more to offer."

He gave me a shocked glare for a moment before bursting out in guttural laughter. He then remarked "I like you. You're my kind of human, willing to die for money. Tell me, friend, how much are those worthless moles paying you?"

"Five hundred thousand suns." I lied straight faced. The dwarfs weren't even paying anything close to that. Not that they couldn't afford it, but you know how greedy dwarves are.

"I'll double it. Hell, I'll even triple it." he chuckled and nodded to his bodyguards. They dropped their hands away from their swords and stepped back.

That pleased me. One million and a half suns would sure have helped me out during those harsh times. I extended my hand and said "Your lordship, you've got yourself a traitor."

He grabbed my hand and shook it vigorously. "Welcome aboard, human."

Grendal told me to get Raptor to lead our army through a certain mountain pass, one that the two of us had been debating about for a few days already. The goblins would seek refuge on the Argo Plains and wait for them to go through. Then they would ambush our army with arrows and quarrels as they passed. I, of course, was to stay back so I wouldn't get killed. The goblins would triumph, the dwarfs would lose their land to the goblins, and I would be one million and a half suns richer. I liked the sound of that, so I told Grendal that I would do as told. He smiled and left with his two bodyguards.

I guess I should have felt a little guilty at what I was about to do, but to me it was just business. I was a warrior for hire, working for the highest bidder and doing whatever they wanted me to do for a high profit. It just so happened that the goblins were willing to pay me more for my services than those cheap, money-grubbing dwarves. And a hell of a lot more at that. It was business, pure and simple.

That night there was a huge feast, for as you know, dwarves are quite fond of good food and drink. At the feast, Raptor, the dwarf king Dirnyn, and myself looked over a map of the area and discussed our plans for the final battle. Both sides were whittled down from all the fighting and the next battle would decide the victor of the war. As it looked to most, the dwarfs had the best chance of coming out on top. But of course, they didn't have the inside information that I had. Too bad I couldn't have placed bets on the outcome, I would have come out with yet even more money.

"We should go through this mountain pass and sneak up behind them." I offered, trying not to smirk.

Raptor thought for a minute before saying "No, too much of a possibility of an ambush."

"Those goblins are cretins!" I argued with him. "They wouldn't think of something like that."

"We can't risk it. I've decided to attack head on."

"But that's more dangerous! There is no cover on the plain." I insisted. "We'll be blowing a great chance that could mean the difference between a victory and a—"

"Yea sure are itchin' ta git me men in that pass." that pompous-ass Dirnyn butted in and shoved a fat, stubby finger under my nose.

"What the hell do you mean be that?" I shouted, knocking his chubby hand away. I always hated that little snot, and if it wasn't for Raptor, I would have punched him in that fat, red nose of his and tossed his dwarf ass across the camp.

However, Raptor got between us and growled "Calm down, both of you! Garrison, no one is insinuating anything. Dirnyn, he is just looking for the best way to win this blasted war! Perhaps he's right, but I just can't risk our men like that. If we did go through and they did ambush us, we wouldn't have a chance. And any risk like that is too much of a risk. We are doing a straightforward attack, and that's that! It may not be the best way, but it's the surest way."

I knew there was no getting to him, so I let it go. So what if I couldn't get Raptor to do it. If the goblins lost, Grendal wouldn't be able to do anything to me, so I was still in the clear. But I couldn't stop thinking of the money, so I decided to devise a new plan. A plan that would guarantee a goblin victory and get me that wonderful money.

The next day, we road up Argo Plain to the site of the battlefield. In only a few minutes, we had the goblins in our sights. They had not seen us, however, for all of their attention was focused on the pass. That little snot Dirnyn gave me the smuggest look I had ever seen and right then and there I knew Raptor wouldn't be the only one rotting on that field when all was said and done. Raptor sounded the attack and in an ironic twist we ambushed the goblins with few casualties on our side. Then the second wave hit. At least two thousand goblins mounted on timber wolves clashed with our army, the sounds of battle thundering the air. Dwarfs, humans, and mostly goblins fell left and right. I, myself, never got attacked. I hung back and got ready for my bold plan. Whiles Raptor fought with great skill, I crept up behind him, notched an arrow, aimed for the back of his head. I fired. I guess my aim was a little off that day, because I missed his skull. However, I did manage to hit him square in the back. For all of his stupid Auset tricks, he never saw it coming. If you ask me, most of that stuff about them is all rumors anyway. It really did pain me to have to do that to such a close friend, but the money I received cleared those queer sentiments right up.

After all, what good is friendship when you have to put food in your belly and women in your bed?

* * *

"You should have seen it, my lord." Garrison laughed evilly, as he excitedly mimed shooting a bow. "As soon as our army saw what I did, their morale was completely shot to hell."

"So, what happened?" Noknor cried with all the insane glee of a child presented with a new toy. "Come now, don't keep me in suspense!"

"Well, Dirnyn was standing next to me when I did the deed, so to speak. Before, he had been barking orders at me, that badgering little prick. But after he just stared at me. He was stunned at what he had seen, with his eyes wide and his mouth hanging open. He looked like some stupid bearded fish. I pulled out another arrow and put it right between his eyes. I didn't even notch it, I just jammed it into his thick skull. Thunk!" Garrison said as he jabbed the air with his hand and threw an apple core onto his messy plate. He chugged down the last of his beer and belched loudly. Noknor laughed, Elizabeth grimaced repulsively, and Li did nothing but fume full of hate for Garrison.

"Now, with two of their leaders dead at the hands of the third, the dwarves panicked." he continued on. "A few of the officers tried to calm the rest down, but it was no use. The goblins conquered easily and I, after explaining how Raptor refused to go through the pass, collected my money plus the gratitude of the goblin king, a very good thing to have at that time. I guess I should have felt a little guilty at what I had done, but like I said before, it was just business. All in all, I went home a very happy, very rich man. And, unlike some other so-called great warriors, alive. Thus ends my tale." he finished grandly, bowing his head lowly.

"And a might good one, too." Noknor laughed along with the traitor, daintily dabbing his mouth with his napkin.

Li was in a fiery rage. She saw herself jumping down the hole and ripping Garrison's stone heart out with her bare hands. She wanted to do it more than anything, but she instead jumped up and turned away. Elizabeth spun around in time to see her friend rush to the bed, leap onto the mattress, and bury her face into the pillow. Then, from across the room, the princess could hear the muffled sobs. She pushed the stone back into place before walking to the bed. She stood there for a few minutes, unable to think of what to say. She wasn't even sure if anything should be said at all.

Finally, she replied softly "Li? I . . . I'm sorry. I'm so very sorry."

Li had stopped crying, but didn't raise her head as she muttered "I had always wanted to believe that James's betrayal had been personal." She sniffled loudly and sat up, the pillow moist with her tears clutched tightly against her breast. "It would have been easier to swallow that way, I guess. To know that James had angered him in some way, that they had had . . . a disagreement of some kind, a misunderstanding maybe. But to know that it was just over money, that it was in fact just . . . *business!*" She hissed the word through her teeth in a frozen tone. "That just makes it even harder for me to believe."

"I know. I'm sorry." Elizabeth sighed, her head hung low and her hands clasped in front of her in a nervous sort of way.

Li sat up and rubbed her red eyes with the bedsheet to dry them. "But I know that James didn't die on that battlefield. He's alive and he's out there somewhere. It's a feeling I have in my heart. I can't explain it, but it tells me that he's still out there somewhere. And I'm going to find him. No matter what it takes, I'll find him. And I'll make Garrison pay for what he's done!"

CHAPTER XXIII

The first morning rays of light filtered into Kain's tent, forcing him awake. He shielded his eyes as he got up and closed the tent flaps. He was still very tired, so without thinking he climbed under his blanket and closed his eyes. Fifteen minutes passed, but to him it felt like fifteen seconds, and he heard Nancy call out cheerfully "Knockity-knock-knock. Are you awake, big brother?"

"No!" he grumbled loudly.

Nancy threw open the flaps and whipped off Kain's blanket as she told him "Wake up, Kain Viccon! Dawn's already broken and you did say you wanted to get an early start. Come on, Hurst is still a long ways off."

Nancy's cheerfulness annoyed Kain and he found himself mumbling "Shut it, Nancy. I'm awake. I'm awake."

She giggled as she threw the blanket into his face and replied "Fine, be that way Mr. Grouch!" before flouncing away.

Kain yawned and stretched as he rose up. He dressed and walked out, breathing in the fresh air. A wonderful scent filled his nostrils as he did so. His mouth cocked in a slight frown. It was a very familiar scent, and yet totally unfamiliar for the current situation. He looked to the fire pit and saw that Nancy had prepared a wonderful breakfast of eggs, roasted meat, and biscuits. When Kain asked where she had gotten all the food, Nancy explained "From the tree faeries. After I woke up, I got dressed and went to sit by the lake. The rising sun cast a beautiful glow over the lake and, oh Kain, it was so cool! Anyway, whiles I sat there, the tree faeries came up to me offering all this food. I have no idea where they got it, but they offered it to me so I took it with many thanks. Then I cooked it all and went to wake all of you guys up because I remembered that you wanted to get an early start."

"Yeah, I'm biting my tongue now." Kain chuckled.

"Huh?" she mumbled, a confused look to her face.

"Nothing. Skip it."

"Oh, all right." she shrugged. Then, she looked around and said to herself "Now, where is everyone?" She shook her head and then called loudly "Come on, you guys! Breakfast's on."

Michael, Raphael, and Robert joined Kain with a plate full of food. Robert yawned mightily and asked "Is that girl always like this in the morning?"

"No." Kain said with a broad smile. "Most of the time she's a lot more cheery."

"I only have one thing to say." Michael chuckled as he clapped his friend on the back. "That's one hell of a sister you have there, Kain."

"You have no idea." he snorted softly with a soft smile.

* * *

After they had all had their fill, they thanked Nancy for her great cooking and packed up their camp. They were ready to move out in under three minutes without a trace of their previous encampment, pleasing Kain to no end in his choice of warriors. He and Nancy rode in front, followed by Michael, Raphael, Robert, and the troops. Kain was joking around with Nancy and making her laugh while the three men were sharing stories of past conquests and cracking jokes, most being not for the ears of youngsters.

Michael put the jokes on hold by saying "Hey, Grotz. I heard you found yourself a new honey. And a new Shazadian honey, no less!"

"Who told you that?" Robert chuckled innocently as he glanced his way without exactly meeting eyes with the prince.

"Doesn't matter." Raphael prodded with a grin. "Is it the truth? Come on now, we'll find out soon enough."

Robert grinned tightly and looked them both in the eyes before turning forward and blushing slightly as he lowly murmured "Yeah, it's true." He was silent in thought for a brief moment before shaking his head and adding with a sly grin "And what's more, Robert Grotz will no longer be a swinging bachelor after we get finished with this quest."

"You mean to tell me that when we get through with Noknor, you're going to do the big 'M' word?" Michael gasped, quite surprised by the news. Robert nodded with a bright face as he ran his hand through his dark hair and looked forward. Michael and Raphael both gawked at him for a long while before the prince finally found his voice. "Man, Grotz! That is really something!"

"So, what's her name?" Raphael asked.

"Molly Duroe." Robert told them, her name rolling off his tongue in a dreamy sort of tone. "She's the daughter of a farmer from one of the Shazadian boarder villages."

"Wait a minute!" Michael gasped, a thought suddenly occurring to him. "Is this the same girl you rescued from that rogue dragon a few months ago?"

"Ten months, two weeks, and five days ago."

"I'll take that as a yes." Raphael laughed loudly, slapping his knee as he ducked to avoid a large buzzing insect. "So that was why you had missed all the meetings. You weren't stranded at all, were you?"

"Of course I wasn't! I was in Shazadia proposing to Molly." he replied. Then, as if reading his friends' minds, he added "And Kain knew about it. In fact, he's the one that had told me to take the extra time off."

"I figured he would somehow be in on it." Michael chuckled lowly, thinking of how Kain had helped out many others in the same sort of situation in the past. "So, she got the signature Shazadian red hair and fair skin?"

"Yep, with long legs and a thin figure to match."

"Shazadian, huh?" Raphael whistled lowly. "Now, those are some very beautiful women. Too bad they're stuck with those bullish brutes for husbands."

"Shoot, why do you think Grotz has himself a new honey?" Michael laughed. "They're all itching to get away from those trolls! That's why the Shazadians hate all the other kingdoms! It isn't because of trade or anything political like that. It's because we steal their women!"

Robert was about to throw a comment at him when ahead of them Nancy suddenly cried out "Look it! The city walls!"

The walls Nancy referred to were made of thick red brick and proudly stood thirty feet high. As usual, much traffic bustled through the large gates and it took a while for the Arcainian troops to finally make it through, even after being bumped ahead of the line with priority clearance. Once inside, they all chattered excitedly about what they were going to do first. As it turned out, the first thing they did was find a nice inn big enough to accommodate the large group for the night. Then, while Kain and his four companions started for the castle in which Deborah Hurst lived, the soldiers dispersed to various casinos and taverns to enjoy themselves with gambling and beer after such a long, eventful journey. They all knew to enjoy all that they could because it would be a long time before they had another chance. For some they knew that it could very well be their last chance.

It took Kain and his friends some time to find Deborah's castle, but they finally made it after purchasing a map of the city and many a wrong turn. Being so big and the roadways so complex, even native residents tended to get lost every now and then. They finally walked up to the large oak door and pulled a piece of rope that rang a bell, signaling their arrival. There was movement inside before a small window in the door opened and a pair of eyes peeked out, giving them an unsure look. A low, sharp voice snapped "What do you want?"

"I must speak to the Mayor of the city right away. Is she present?" Kain asked pleasantly as he bowed.

"Maybe, maybe not." the man said curtly. "What is your business?"

"It is private and none of your concern." Michael barked out harshly, furious that such a man would dare to talk to them like that.

"Hmph! No one sees Madam Mayor without an appointment!" the man growled.

Michael was about to snap at him again, but Kain only sighed and held up his hand to stop him. Then he turned towards the door, prominently flashed his Arcainian Grand General cloak so that the man got a clear view of it, and said "Fine. Just tell her Kain's here."

The little window closed with a loud bang and the four men and single lady waited.

* * *

Li sat in a chair beside the door as she quietly ate her lunch and watched Elizabeth pace back and forth. Finally, Li could take it no longer and she snapped "Must you do that?"

Elizabeth stopped and blushed. "Sorry." she said. "I have a tendency to pace when I get worried."

"So I noticed. What's eating you?" Li asked before shoveling a large piece of beef into her mouth. Her mouth was already full and all the meat puffed her cheeks out. That made Elizabeth smile and giggle.

"You look like a chipmunk." she laughed. "Anyway, I guess I'm worried about Michael."

"Prince Michael of Arcainia?" Li inquired with an unsure voice as she pushed her tray aside. She kept her glass of wine in her hand, however, and sipped. "What has that goober done now?"

"Nothing, except steal my heart away." Elizabeth smiled dreamily, making Li giggle loudly in tickled glee.

Suddenly, a bitterly gruff voice snapped sharply "Shut up, you dumb girl."

"Oh, leave us alone, you goon!" Li snapped as she threw the rest of her wine through the window.

They heard him curse and scream in fury "You little whore! I'm gonna kill you!"

"Bite me!" she hissed.

Suddenly, another voice joined the guard's. Li recognized it as belonging to Noknor as he asked "What's going on here?"

"That little whore threw wine in my eyes!"

"How dare she! Why, I'd bet you'd like to teach such an impudent woman respect, hmmmmmmm?"

When Li heard this, she backed away from the door slowly, frowning darkly. The guard happily growled "Oh, master! I would like nothing better! May I please?"

"Be my guest." Noknor told him as he threw open the door. He watched from the hall as the guard strutted in, giving Li a sly and dangerous grin.

"Oh, great!" Elizabeth gulped. "What did you get yourself into now?"

"Nothing I can't handle." Li smiled and got into fighting stance.

When the guard saw her, he burst out laughing. "Are you going to do that kung fu crap on me? Well, I know some of that crap, too! HE-AH!"

He tried to kick her, but it was slow and retarded as if he either was simply mocking her with a half-hearted try or trying his hardest and just wasn't any good. Li easily grabbed his leg and did an attack of her own, albeit not very graceful or traditional. She reared her foot back and kicked the guard as hard as she could in the groin. She kicked him so hard, in fact, that he was lifted two feet off the ground. She let him go and watched with a smile as he slowly put his hands to the crotch of his pants which already had a large, dark crimson circle growing. He uttered a high squeak before toppling over. For several minutes, he lay there, eyes glazed, mouth agape, and with no visible signs of breathing.

At last, Noknor called in some goblins and ordered them to take his body away. Then he approached Li, who still had her fists clenched tight and her legs ready to kick.

"Do not worry, my dear." he told her. "I won't hurt you. I just want to commend you. You have some most impressive moves."

"You really think so? Well, if you don't get out of here and leave us alone, I'll do those impressive moves on your ugly face." she snapped with such a sure and deadly tone that it startled Noknor.

This Chinese woman wasn't afraid of him, and he knew it. But why not? She must think that he could kill her with a wave of his hand. Did she indeed know the power she had, the power to somehow resist his magick? No, she couldn't have a clue, or she would have attacked him already. Killed him already. Either way, Noknor had to find a way to get around this strange defense. With a tremendous bang and a puff of smoke that made the girls' noses twitch, he was gone.

Li closed the door, wiped her brow and asked "Now, then. What where you saying about Michael?"

Elizabeth was still flabbergasted and her face showed it. Li giggled and repeated herself, only louder. Elizabeth jumped slightly before she replied "We're engaged to be married soon. I guess I'm just worried about him."

"Understandable." Li smiled sweetly, moving to the wine cabinet to refill her glass. "How long have you two been engaged?"

"Since we were born. It was arranged by our parents." she said. "Didn't you know? I assumed you had."

"Well, I knew you guys were engaged, I had heard it mentioned once or twice. But I didn't know Old Worlders arranged marriages too." Li said in a delighted voice, sitting in a chair and crossing her legs. "Do you want to marry him?"

"Yes, of course!" Elizabeth exclaimed. "He's a great guy. He's very sweet and kind. Not like some of those other creep princes that come looking for a princess bride. And he's very good looking, don't you think?"

"Yeah, he's a cutie. You'll be owning a pretty awesome guy when this is all over." Li snickered. She uncrossed her legs and crossed them back the other way. "A prince with a great butt. Quite a catch, princess!" Both ladies shared a girlish giggle before Li pulled back her hair and replied "Nancy used to have the hots for him."

"Nancy Viccon?"

"Yeah, when she was younger. Not anything big, just a little ten year old puppy love. She's forgotten about that already. Well, she still thinks he's cute, but you don't have anything to worry about. Speaking of which, what are you getting worried about again?"

"About Michael's safety!" she cried out. "I mean, I don't want him getting killed out there! What if—"

"Oh, he won't get killed. They'll be fine. They're all very experienced knights. You worry way too much" Li assured her. She raised her glass and suggested "Why don't you have a drink?"

* * *

Slowly, the large oak door creaked open and a small bearded man ushered them in. If it was the same man, he must have gotten quite a tongue lashing, because he was much more hospitable to the group. They were guided to a large, decorated door that led into the library. The man knocked for them and hurried away as Deborah called for them to enter. Kain threw open the door and immediately Deborah Hurst was in his arms, her lips planted on his cheek. When they parted, she gasped "Oh, Kain! How are you? It's been a long time."

"Indeed it has." he replied happily, pulling away from her grasp and looking her over. She looked great. In fact, she looked absolutely ravishing. Better than he had remembered. "I've been okay. How about you? Looking as beautiful as always!"

"Thank you." she blushed mildly. "Hello, Nancy. How have you been doing? Well, I trust."

"Hi-Hi!" Nancy waved, rushing to give her a hug. "It's great to see you again, Deb!"

"Same here. Hello, your highness."

"Hey, beautiful! My mother sends her regards." Michael told her as he gently gripped her hand and kissed it.

"How sweet. Hello, Robert. Raphael."

"Hey, Deborah." Robert replied, tossing a hand up.

"Hello again, Deborah." Raphael grinned brightly, clicking his tongue slightly as he looked her beauty over subtly. "It's always a pleasure. I must say, I am always impressed when I come to your city. It's such an awesome place!"

"Thanks. But the truth is, however, that I've been having some problems lately."

"Like?" Kain inquired, pulling up a chair. They others did the same while Deborah walked behind her desk and sat in the regal chair.

She sighed dully and said "Well, a gang of criminals have infested my city walls. There's ten of them now, not including their leader, Marcus Addison. A very nasty bunch, they've caused me a lot of grief over the past few months."

"What kind of crimes have they committed?"

"Some robberies and a few murders." she murmured. Then she explained "There were fourteen of them originally, but we managed to catch three. Through our . . . ah, special methods, we succeeded in learning everything about the gang."

Kain grimaced slightly. He knew all about Deborah's special methods. Though he had never actually participated in Hurst's interrogations, he did have the unpleasant opportunity to witness a few. They were not all that enjoyable for those withholding information from Deborah.

Nancy leaned over and whispered into her brother's ear for a few moments before looking at him with hopeful eyes. He thought something over before reaching into his pocket and taking out his coin bag. As he dropped a few golden coins into her cupped hands, he told her "All right, just don't get lost. Meet us back here in about two hours, okay?"

"Yes, sir." she smiled brightly as she stood up. "Bye, Deborah! It was really great seeing you again!"

"Same here, Nancy." Deborah waved to her. "Have fun!"

"Where's she going?" Robert asked after she was out the door.

"To get into trouble, undoubtedly." Kain chuckled, turning his attention back to his old friend. "What else do you know about this group? Maybe we can help you out some."

* * *

Nancy walked along the cobblestone road dressed in a simple black Arcainian dress and ruffled white blouse that she had changed into back at Deborah's castle while she admired the vastness and beauty of Hurst. Kain had told her before arriving that if she was going to go tromping about through the streets, to change into civilian clothes so as not to attract attention to herself. She still wore her cloak as it was, being simply an enlisted soldier's piece, fairly nondescript. It covered her body in such a way that it hid her dagger from normal view, insisting herself that she should at least have that on her. She felt safer feeling her blade bounce around on her hip with every step.

There were so many wonderful sights and sweet smells as she wandered in and out of the various busy shops. Hurst had everything one could possibly imagine or want, from gifts and trinkets, to potions and magick, to weapons and armor, to everything in-between. From the food vendors, the scents of different foods and drinks being prepared filtered into her nose and set her mouth watering. It wasn't long before the rumblings in her belly and the cravings overcame her. She examined the food stands around her and finally settled on some fried almond treats.

"Excuse me?" she called out, having to raise her voice over the bustling of the crowds around her. "Sir? Excuse me! Sir! How much for these almond treats?"

"One sack of ten for a moon." he told her quickly, returning his attention onto his other customers.

'A moon?' Nancy frowned dully. 'These better be pretty tasty for that much!'

However, the cravings won out and she looked at the coins Kain had given her. She showed one of the golden coins with a picture of a smiling sun inscribed on both sides to another one of the vendors and asked hopefully "Can you break a sun? I'd like to buy some almond treats."

"Yes, of course, little lady." he smiled brightly at her, grabbing a large tin box and opening it up. He took Nancy's coin and gave her a small paper sack of almond treats and nine silver coins with a picture of a smiling half moon in profile on both sides in return.

As Nancy reached out to take her change, she was shoved violently from behind. She caught herself on the table and started to turn around to snap at the jerk when she heard a man's gruff voice tell her "Oh! Please do excuse me, miss! I'm terribly sorry!"

"It's okay." she told him pleasantly without looking back, appreciating the apology. She took her money and stuffed it into her purse before walking away from the table.

She continued down the street stuffing her snacks into her hungry mouth as she looked at all the shops and boutiques had to offer. They were very tasty, indeed, though she rather doubted that they were worth a whole moon. At the Arcainian Square, she could have gotten the same thing and more of it than just ten for a lot less than that. But, then everything in Hurst was overpriced it seemed. It came with being such a large and prosperous city, she guessed.

Without warning, she found herself in a very crowded spot in the road and fought her way into a small alley to avoid all the pushing and shoving. It was as if all those people had just suddenly appeared out of nowhere. She decided to just take a pause in the alley and finish her treats as she waited for the crowd to pass by.

Suddenly, someone tapped her shoulder and she wheeled around, expecting it to be one of the other Arcainian soldiers that had recognized her and was coming over to say hello. Maybe it was even Raphael or Kain! However, she came face to face with two men, and they sure were not her brother or friends. One was dressed in fairly simple clothes and was totally nondescript next to the other, more elegant gentleman. He was a tall, well-built and well-dressed man. He had a handsome face and a lengthy black goatee, reminding her a little of John Accrue except for the fact that his head was shaved bald and he held a sharp dagger in his hand.

Startled, Nancy dropped her bag and slowly reached under her cloak for her dagger as she whispered "What do you want?"

"You dropped your dagger back there, Miss." the flashy man told her while the other seemed to look around nervously, his head twitching back and forth randomly.

Nancy looked beneath her cloak and saw an empty place in her sheath. She accepted the blade, feeling quite foolish for thinking badly about the man, and thanked him. With smooth movements, he put a cigaret to his lips and struck a match easily against the brick wall. "Think nothing of it. You can never be too careful with strangers. Especially with that gang of thieves running around." He lit his cigaret and shook the match out before tossing it behind him. "You're very pretty, but I'm sure you know that already."

That made her blush deeply, but she managed a smile as she told him "Thank you. And thank you for returning my dagger. You're very kind. A lot of people woulda just kept it."

He inhaled deeply, held for a moment, and slowly exhaled purplish smoke that smelled faintly of berries. "Like I said, think nothing of it. Are you a local?"

"No, just visiting with my brother." she smiled. She knew he was just making small talk, but she didn't think she should divulge the real reason she was there. She hadn't noticed it, but the other mousy man had been slowly creeping closer to her as she spoke, getting along side of her. "Right now he's visiting with Deborah Hurst."

"Is he now?" the man raised his eyebrows, nonchalantly moving the cigaret to the other side of his mouth.

Suddenly, the small man grabbed her by her shoulders and pulled her tightly against his body. She squealed in shock and tried to struggle to free herself, but the other held her tight from behind. The bald man advanced towards her with a grin on his lips and blew the smoke into her face. It made her eyes water and she coughed shortly before crying "What's going on! What do you want!"

"You know quite well what I want, Miss." the man said smoothly, the grin still on his face but his eyes hardened into an icy, lustful gaze. "I want that sweet little body of yours. And Marcus Addison always gets what he wants."

"Always!" the small man hissed in her ear, groping her neck and shoulder roughly with his thick lips.

"Let me go!" she yelped, her voice faltering as she struggled even harder and burst into a mad fit of tears. She looked around wildly for someone to help her, but the search was in vain. No one was around. "Go AWAY!"

"What's the matter?" Addison chuckled, gripping her blouse tightly around her neck.

"She must think you're not good enough for her!" the small man growled viciously. "Or maybe she just likes it from her brother!"

As Addison pulled her blouse, she howled in terror. The buttons popped off one by one and her chest threatened to fall out. In a swift and sudden turn of emotion, much too fast for one to comprehend, panic and fear were replaced by anger and vengeance. Nancy brought her knee up quickly in a wild rage, catching him square between the legs just before that final button that held her in could be ripped off. He instantly let her go and gurgled as he sank to his knees, clutching himself tightly and wincing in pain. He coughed violently and spit burning bile onto the cobblestone.

Before the small man could even react, she snapped her head back, smashing him hard in the nose. His grip loosened and she flipped her dagger in her hand. Then she grabbed his wrist and plunged the dagger backwards. She felt it sink into soft flesh as she twisted his arm around. He uttered a low grunt as she pulled the blade free and jabbed it into his shoulder, slicing clean through his joint. She kicked his leg and jabbed his back. He yelped in agony as he fell to the street, blood flowing freely from his burning wounds. She held his wrist tightly and sliced his arm deeply. She twisted it further as she roared in fury, her eyes aflame with rage. Her foot collided hard with his side, his kidney flashing with blinding pain. She kicked him again, and then again, and then again. She stomped his spine hard and swiped at him with her blade. A jagged, maroon line was left in its wake as it traveled swiftly all the way down his back. If the small man was still alive, he was undoubtedly wishing his boss had picked out someone else to harass that day.

With one final roar, she raised her smeared dagger high into the air, ready to send it flying down into his floundering skull. However, two booming voices shrieked for her to stop and put down the weapon. She looked up wildly, her eyes boiling, her mouth forming a horrid sneer as three Hurst police officers armed with crossbows rushed towards her and the mangled body under her as they sat alone in the alley. Marcus Addison was nowhere to be found.

CHAPTER XXIV

"I don't know what to do, Kain!" Deborah gasped hopelessly as she tossed herself back into her red satin chair. "I'm at my wits end with this entire mess! The only good thing about it is that it just a small gang. If it was an actual crime family, I'd be in trouble. And if I don't figure something out, it just may escalate into that!"

"Well, we'll do whatever we can to help you, Deb." he told her with a simple shrug, giving her a reassuringly sympathetic look. She gazed across the desk into his eyes and smiled brightly, a flicker of hope shining in her own blues. A gentle grin set on his face as he started to add "You know—"

A sudden thunderous boom cut him off as the massive doors were flung open, startling all in the library. They turned to see a tall and imposing figure stride in. He wore the full battle armor of a Hurst battle guard and was identified as a chief guard by a large badge on his arm. On his chest was a fiery sun, half black and half red with two bloody spears crossed behind it and a white rose in full bloom sitting dead center: the City of Hurst coat-of-arms. A large circular shield with spikes all around the edge on his left arm also bore the symbol, as did a black band around his right arm.

The warrior wore an eccentric steel helmet in the shape of a snarling wolf head complete with steel fangs and brightly colored phoenix plumage making a sort of mohawk back down the helmet. The wolf head covered the guard so completely that it was impossible to tell who, or what, was hidden beneath it. He was so menacing, that Raphael and Robert instinctively reached for their sword handles. Even Kain and Michael, knowing who it was, gasped lowly in surprise. Deborah was the only one to smile when she saw him.

"Anything yet?" the mayor asked, hoping against hope.

"Nothing!" the figure boomed in a slightly Shazadian accented voice that reverberated in a sort of deep metallic tone that was far less masculine than the figure was imposing. He reached up and undid a few clasps before pulling the monstrous helmet off. Long red hair fell about the shoulders just before a beautiful, fair feminine face showed. "Not a bloody thing! It's like they disappeared completely! Again!"

"They're thieves. That's what they do." Deborah sighed wearily, putting her hands to her face as if she were about to weep and wanted to hide her tears. She didn't however, nor would she ever have. Deborah Hurst was much too strong of a woman and had seen and experienced too much in her life to cry over something like that. Even if it seemed like an impossible, terrible situation, she had been in far worse ones. "Continue the street sweeps, I guess. Every ten minutes now. That's all we can do until something better surfaces."

"You're a woman!" Robert suddenly gasped out, being the first male to find his voice.

The lady glared at him as if he were a complete imbecile as she sneered coldly and retorted in a frosty tone "And you're a—"

"Can it, Landis." Deborah muttered, taking a deep breath and exhaling slowly. "Guys, this is my Captain of the Guard, Landis Dupree. This is Sir Robert Grotz and Sir Raphael Boniva."

Landis muttered a greeting to them both and waved absently before glancing at Michael and Kain. She replied a greeting without much tone even though she was absolutely thrilled to see them.

"Hey, Legs!" Michael grinned, waving his hand. She snorted and shook her head, trying but unable to hide her smirk. "Man, you look beat."

"I feel even worse." she sighed wearily, rubbing her forehead carefully so as not to cut herself with her spiked gauntlet. "You would not believe the trouble these jackasses are causing us. I bloody well swear!"

"I can only imagine." Kain muttered dryly. "Besides that, how have you been doing?"

"Surprisingly well, despite the fact that those blasted thieves are getting away with everything right under my nose." she hissed, her fair face flushing in frustration.

"Landis, don't be so hard on yourself. You have made considerable progress in the matter." Deborah told her in a confident tone. Landis shrugged blandly and grunted as she crossed her arms, her spiked shield covering her chest. Deborah frowned and told the others "In fact, she was the one that had caught those three thieves. Single handedly I might add. She was investigating a suspicious—"

"Sorry to disturb, Madam Mayor." an officer interrupted in an uneasy voice from the open doorway. It was, in fact, one of the three officers that had come to Nancy's aid. He slid in and drew himself up to his full height as he saluted.

"There is something rather important that requires the captain's immediate attention." He paused a moment. "As well as Sir Viccon's."

"Me?" Kain looked up at him, frowning as a dark tingling sensation crept into the back of his head. "Why me?"

"It's your sister. I'm afraid she was attacked."

"WHAT!?" Kain roared in shock, the others' hearts sinking as fast as he ran to the guard. "Wuh-what happened! Where is she? Is she . . ."

"She's all right now!" he quickly assured the frantic Arcainian while taking three rapid steps back without realizing it. "She's all right, just really shaken up. We have her in one of the private rooms downstairs. She needs you as soon as possible and needs to give a statement to you, Captain."

"Okay, we'll be right there!" Landis said, tucking her helmet under her arm. Instantly understanding the severity of the situation, while mentally hoping that it wasn't as serve as it very well could be, she decided that for the girl's own sake and sanity the less around her at the moment the better. "You three guys might want to go get a drink or something, we could be awhile."

Raphael started to protest that they should be with Nancy too, being her friends and all. However, Michael nudged him and shook his head. He knew the three of them would only be in the way down there. She didn't need them, she needed her brother. And the officer had said she was all right, so they really weren't needed at all. Raphael didn't like it one bit, but he kept his mouth shut.

After some very brief words about meeting again later, the three men headed off to a fetch some drinks in one of the castle's cafés while they waited. Meanwhile, Kain, Landis, and Deborah hurried with the officer as he led them to the private room. All the way down, Kain couldn't help but think the worst, and his paced picked up with every step.

On the way, the officer explained what he knew, that the girl had been attacked in an alley and Addison himself was suspected. While her clothes had been ripped, she had managed to defend herself before they could molest her in any way. She had managed to actually kill Addison's partner in the crime, but they had found no trace of Addison himself, except for Nancy's description and a freshly burning cigaret in the alley, Addison's known brand of choice. The officer choked on his words when he described the scene as he and his fellow policemen had found it, the girl blood stained and crazed with the mutilated body of the attacker at her feet. Upon hearing that, Kain broke into a full run down the halls with the others doing their best to catch up.

They found Nancy sitting in a plush chair, a heavy blanket wrapped around her shoulders. She did look quite fine, just tired if anything else. Her head was hung and she slumped forward slightly. Her face was a little pale and her hair was a mess, but she was alive and in one piece. Kain's heart did a quick somersault in his chest when he saw her. As soon as she saw Kain, she leaped up and jumped into his arms. She almost burst into tears, but fought them back when she saw Landis and Deborah enter. They went to her and consoled her with kind words, but she brushed them off gently, saying she was all right, that she had just been shaken by the whole experience. They sat her back down and took seats themselves. Kain sat right in front of her, his hands over hers and his eyes looking straight into hers.

"Now, Nancy," he murmured softly, squeezing her hands gently. "What happened?"

As she began to tell him everything that happened, Landis picked up a feathered fountain pen and a small piece of parchment from the table. She quickly wrote down everything that was said, almost as fast as Nancy was telling it. She described the two men, telling them of their clothing and the sweet smelling cigarette with a berry scent to it. She told what was said when they first approached her and after the small man had grabbed her. She told of dropping Addison to the ground and knocking back the other man. She seemed to consider something, but held back giving any more details, saying only that the rest had happened so fast that she wasn't really sure what had happened.

"He called himself Marcus Addison?" Landis asked, writing her notes down as the girl nodded vigorously. "Well, it certainly sounds like him. And where were you when he approached you?" She tallied what she was told. "He probably swiped your dagger from you in the crowd. Pretended to bump into you and whatnot. Okay, this is good. With this and the body of the guy you managed to take out, we may have a lead. I'm going to go check with the other officers and see what they have. Maybe, just maybe they found something on the body that will point out their hideout to us."

As she headed out, Kain embraced Nancy tightly and she sighed dully, sniffling lowly. He caressed her back and said softly "It's all right now, darling. It's over now. You're all right." He kissed her head and looked into her moist eyes before telling her softly, yet firmly "You're safe now."

"Yeah, I know." she murmured softly, feeling her body shaking uncontrollably. "It was just very . . ."

"Can I get you anything, Nancy?" Deborah said in a low, gentle voice, rising from her seat. "Some water or something?"

"No." she sniffled, wiping her eyes and trying her best to calm down. "No, I'm fine. Thank you, though."

"Goddess, I'm so relieved that you're okay." Kain sighed with a weary smile. He paused and then added "And proud at how well you protected yourself." She looked into his face and beamed brightly. Kain grinned as he reached out and playfully tussled her hair. "How hard did you hit that pervert?"

"He'll have to wear dresses from now on." she giggled as she playfully knocked away his hand, starting to return to the old Nancy. Kain chuckled in tremendous relief, the hundred pound weight finally falling off his chest.

A few minutes later, Landis entered. She had a disappointed look on her face; apparently she hadn't found much. She told them that the guy didn't have much on him: a dagger, some money, a nondescript brass key that could have come from any of the millions of doors in Hurst, and a flask of a greenish alcoholic drink available at any tavern or alcohol shop. Nothing about where they were hiding or anything pointing him to Addison's gang. It seemed that they were at a brickwall once again. Addison had lost some muscle, but had disappeared himself. And the police still had nothing to go on that would lead to him. Nothing had changed. All they could do was wait for something else to pop up and hope he'd make a mistake. Landis knew that was highly unlikely, Addison hadn't gotten as far as he did by sticking his neck out and making foolish mistakes.

"I think I know how we can flush Addison and his gang out of hiding." Kain murmured, almost to himself as he rubbed his chin thoughtfully and rose from his chair.

"What are you thinking, Kain?" Deborah asked in a suspicious tone, noting the look of hard thought on his face.

"Well, guys like that don't take getting ridiculed by a little girl very well." he explained, pacing while others watched him with curious intensity. "I think we should put Nancy up in an inn and spread a rumor throughout the taverns and streets that the girl who racked Marcus Addison is staying there. She told him that she was just visiting Hurst, and she has to stay somewhere. It's bound to reach his ears and he won't be able to resist going to get revenge.

"Let's see, he won't risk going through the front, he'll come through the window, so we'll need something first floor, second floor tops. We'll put a small group on guard outside her door, maybe in the room across from hers so it's not obvious. I'll stay in the room with her. Other than that, everything has to be low key. If he catches wind of a setup he won't show, or worse will find a way around it. But I'm very confident that we can pull it off. It might take a few nights, but when they do show up, we'll have them."

"Addison won't send all of his gang." Deborah bluntly pointed out. "We won't be able to catch them all."

"Doesn't matter." Landis replied, a large and bright smile on her face. "Kain's right! Addison will definitely show up. And if we can get him, I'm sure we can get a LOT of info outta him. You know, Kain, I think it just might my work!"

"It's going to be dangerous, though." Kain told his sister, looking deep into her eyes. "Are sure you up to it, pup?"

"You betcha!" she chirped excitedly. "I'm not going to let that jerk get away that easily!"

* * *

Just as Li and Elizabeth finished eating their supper, raindrops began to splatter against the window. Li slowly rose up from her chair and walked with her glass in hand to the window. Lightning flashed brightly, illuminating the forest for a brief moment while the sky rumbled lowly. Li sighed and sipped her wine.

"How long do you think we've been here?" she murmured softly.

"I've been here almost three months, at least. Probably longer than that." Elizabeth told her, pausing to think. "You've been here for about a month or so, I'd say. A little less maybe."

Li didn't answer, didn't even acknowledge that she had heard her friend. She just stared out the window as many thoughts spun wildly around inside her mind. A sudden flash of lightning illuminated her face while a booming crack of thunder made her recoil slightly, her jumping hand splashing drops of wine onto her slim fingers. She sipped her wine and gave another depressed sigh.

"Are you okay?" Elizabeth asked with some concern as she observed her friend.

"Yeah." Li mumbled turning to give her a weak smile. She breathed deeply and did her best to cast off the gloom. "I'm just so sick of this place, you know? It's so—"

The handle clicked loudly, stopping Li in midsentence just before the door flew open. Elizabeth gave a startled gasp as she recoiled in her seat, but Li simply stood her ground, giving the door a curious look as she sipped her wine. Noknor walked in quickly, a grim look set on his face. He nodded a momentary greeting to them both.

"I am afraid I'm the bearer of ill tidings." he told them in an obviously staged tone of grief. "Your heroes are dead. They were killed in a horrible—"

Li smiled, threw back her head, and chugged down the remaining wine in one gulp before cutting him off with her own mock-happy voice "Well, that's great news!"

"LI!" Elizabeth cried, not believing her ears. "You can't mean that!"

"Oh, of course I don't! What are you thinking?" she laughed, wiping her mouth with her fingers. She snapped her wrist and the glass shattered with a sharp ringing against the wall as she glared at Noknor and scowled. He jumped slightly, but did his best to remain calm in her presence. She walked right over to him, poked his chest hard with an opposing index finger, and growled "I don't know what you're up to, you ugly little troll, but you had best get your slimy carcass out of this room before I beat it into the ground, you cheap creep!"

The calm air he held shattered like the glass Li had thrown and he gazed at her with a shocked look on his face. Even though he stood more than a head taller than her, he seemed smaller before her as he slowly backed away from the fearsome woman. With a dark scowl, he turned on his heels and hurried out. Elizabeth gawked at her with wide eyes and asked how she had known he was lying. Li chuckled as she closed the door behind him and relocked it, stuffing a stocking into the keyhole so that it was impossible to insert a key from the outside.

"It's not hard to see through him." she said, strolling casually to the loose stone in the floor. As she gestured Elizabeth to come over and help her lift it out, she continued "He's not the best actor in the world and besides, he would have been thrilled about it, not upset. Second, if they had died, he wouldn't have said word one. He would have just come in here and killed us both. Well, probably have someone else do it, I doubt he'd have the guts to face me one on one. And last, but not least, it's going to take a lot more than a few bumbling Dark Knights and smelly goblins to do our friends in. Now let's see what his deal is."

Together they peered into the throne room just as the double doors were thrown open with such force that the walls were left cracked from the impacted. Noknor stormed in with an uneasy Garrison and two Dark Knight officers following close behind. He rushed to a table and threw it over as he roared with rage. Then he grabbed the closest officer and threw him hard into the wall. There was a sickening thud as his head struck the hard stone and he rebound back to pitch onto the floor, his limbs flapping about in violent death throes. Noknor roared for the other knight to take away the body before stomping to his throne and throwing himself on.

"It didn't work?" Garrison asked the air while the other knight tried to drag his friend away, his own body shaking uncontrollably at the thought that it could have been him.

Noknor screamed violent curses as he grasped a large bronze goblet and cast it at the Dark Knight, hitting him in the head and tearing away a large chunk of scalp. "Does it look like it worked, you idiot! Then she had the . . . the . . . the **AUDACITY** to insult and threaten me! **ME**! A god! Who does she think SHE **IS**!"

"I hate that little whore." Garrison mumbled, taking a shaky seat in front of his lord.

"The feeling's mutual, limp-wrist." Li muttered under her breath. Elizabeth heard and, despite what she had just witnessed, giggled a little too audibly.

Garrison raised his eyebrows and glanced around as he asked "What was that noise?"

"**I HEARD NOTHING!**" Noknor yelled so loudly that the room shook.

He threw himself back in a huff and crossed his arms tightly over his chest. Garrison sat before him, rigid as a pole. He was totally silent, fearing even to breath lest his master notice him and, in his intense rage, turn on him just as easily as he had two of his best fighters. His mind was flooded with things to say to cheer his lord up, but he found his throat refusing to work. He figured it was probably for the best anyway and kept his trap shut.

A sudden echoing knock boomed from the large doors. Noknor threw fiery eyes towards them as Garrison winced sharply. Whoever had chosen this particular moment to speak to Lord Noknor had just made the biggest mistake in their life, the last one they ever would. With some effort, one large door creaked open just enough for a tall, gaunt man with sunken eyes and a look of having the plague to slither through. He immediately dropped to one knee in a respectful bow.

"My lord, Korkic Tak-Naddo has arrived as you have summoned. He is awaiting your audience."

'The goblin prince?' Garrison frowned slightly, steeling himself for another onslaught from his master. 'Why would Noknor want to talk to him? Surely we're not going to league with the likes of that fool!'

To Garrison's amazement, Noknor's mood took a wild and drastic swing. A grin spreading from ear to ear quickly formed on his green face as he clapped his hands once in delight. It was impossible to believe that it had been the same man who had just brutally murdered two senior officers out of anger with a situation that did not even involve them. Whatever this goblin prince had to say, it must be pretty important, Garrison thought.

"Excellent! Most excellent, indeed!" Noknor smiled brightly as he rose up and stretched his limbs. He gestured to the two twisted bodies on the floor and ordered

Garrison in a cheerful sort of tone "Whiles I am meeting with Korkic, have something done about that mess."

With both Noknor and Garrison leaving the throne room once again, Li, thinking there was nothing more to see, pushed the stone back into place. She looked at Elizabeth and frowned in a curious way. "Do you know who that guy is Noknor's meeting with?" Elizabeth said she did not. Li's face set in a thoughtful pout. "Well, that was an interesting display, but still didn't tell us anything about why he paid us that visit in the first place."

"Maybe he was just trying to upset us." the princess offered with a dull shrug. "He's a sick monster. I'm sure he was just trying to get his kicks."

"Maybe. I wonder if it had anything to do with that Korkic person. What a bizarre name. I wonder . . ." Li muttered absently, rubbing her chin. She jumped and gave a startled screech of fright when the room filled with a shock of light and an echoing crack. Her face grew cherry red as Elizabeth snickered and reached out to pat her shoulder.

CHAPTER XXV

Nancy suddenly jumped in her bed with a shriek as a deafening crack of thunder split the still spring night. She hadn't noticed that she had been asleep, and she figured she had just dozed off for a moment, not realizing that she had slept for over two hours. She looked around the room, but found that she couldn't see a thing. It was pitch dark and eerily silent save for the rain that splattered against the windowpane with gentle taps and a continuous rumble over the roof. She was suddenly struck with lonely fear and began to whimper. Kain, who had not left her side since they had left the castle, quickly lunged to embrace her. She yelped in surprise but calmed down as Kain rubbed her back and soothingly murmured "It's all right, Nancy. I'm here for you. Everything's okay."

They had checked into the inn under assumed names the day before. All of the Arcainian soldiers had dispersed throughout Hurst to broadcast that the girl who had kicked Marcus Addison square in his kahonez was staying at the inn with her brother. Word had spread quickly, and almost immediately all the casinos, taverns, and shops were a buzz with the news as jokes concerning the incident instantly popped up. In no time at all the Arcainians were being told stories they had in fact started, how the girl had beaten Addison within an inch of his life and how her big mouth had the Hurst police force right on the gang's heels.

Kain was certain that at least one person in the gang, if not even Addison himself, had caught wind. It was a given that after being so openly mocked the gang leader would be fuming and thirsty for payback. All they had to do now was wait. At the moment, Michael and Raphael were sitting in the room across the hall just waiting to leap into action, while Robert and his scouts discretely patrolled outside. There were no police patrols around the inn other than the usual amount and the rest of the Arcainian knights and foot soldiers remained on temporary leave in the city, having been told the check back with Raphael every evening until it was time to move on. Kain knew that keeping cover was important, lest Addison and his gang catch wind of the trap. The thieves had to believe that it was only a girl and her brother on vacation in Hurst, nothing more.

Kain stood up and lit a small lamp. The illuminated room instantly chased away the frightening shadows, doing much to relieve Nancy's pounding heart. He went back to the bed and put his arm around her. Another thunderbolt made her jump and squeal lowly. Kain found that odd since Nancy usually loved a good thunderstorm. Of course, given the circumstances he wasn't really all that surprised. He kissed her forehead and asked "Are you all right, kiddo?"

"Yeah." Nancy managed a smile. She looked up into his face and replied "I'm just a bit nervous, is all. I know I'm being stupid and everything."

"No. No, you're not. I'm nervous about this, too. This is your first time ever to be used as bait, and I'm scared out of my wits. I don't think you ever get used to the feeling."

Nancy giggled and glanced out the window. A flash of lightning caught the silhouette of an angry man with murderous eyes peering through window. She screamed a split-second before the glass shattered inward, the explosion muffled by heavy blankets. Nine armed men jumped in and quickly surrounded the siblings as Addison himself slowly came through the widow, the broken glass crunching under his boots. Two of the intruders went to bar the door, but Raphael kicked it open just as they reached it. The door crashed into the pair of thieves, bashing their heads and knocking them out cold. The distraction gave Kain and Nancy the opening to draw their own weapons concealed under the pillows and deliver the first blows of the battle. Kain quickly lashed out and slid his shortsword blade between the ribs of one thief. With only six men left, Addison roared "Kill the others, but the girl is mine!"

Raphael and Michael stood back to back, Michael with his hand axe and Raphael with his mace. One of his two attackers tried to parry as Michael swung his mighty weapon downwards, but the axe shattered the cheap blade and continued on until it was imbedded in the thief's chest. The man fell still with the axe stuck in his chest, so with his main weapon lost Michael ripped his dagger from its sheath just as the other thief jabbed at him with a short spear. The prince caught the shaft with his free hand and gave a hard tug. As the thief flew forward, Michael jabbed his blade, but the man managed to block with only a small cut to his arm. He kicked at Michael, making the prince release the spear. He hit him in the side with the shaft three times, pounding the heavy wooden stick against Michael's ribs and arm, knocking him to one knee. The thief reared back to plunge his short spear forward, Michael grabbed it once more and leapt forward with an angry punch in the nose. As the thief was knocked back, releasing his hold on the weapon, Michael took the spear and began beating the man violently with the shaft until he submitted.

Raphael swung his mace around to bat away the blows from the thieves' shortswords before bringing it down with tremendous force. The spiked ball collided with the forehead of the first, killing him dead in an instant. The man slumped away as his friend stabbed at Raphael with his shortsword. The knight tried to bat the blade away, but he wasn't quick enough and it impaled his side. Raphael gritted his teeth as he fought back the blinding pain and arched his mace upwards. The mace bashed his assailant's chest, denting his cheap breastplate and sending him reeling across the room. Raphael tried to move forward, but his wound ripped sending horrible pain into the brave knight's stomach. Raphael clenched his teeth and bit back tears as his dizzy vision saw the thief rush at him, the brute howling in triumph. With no other ideas, Raphael reared back his arm and flung his mace as hard as he could. The heavy steel weapon smacked the thief square in the chest with enough force to knock him off his feet, the air driven from his bruised chest. The mace hit the ground and rolled within Raphael's grasp. Roaring in fury and using the pain of his wound to fuel his rage, Raphael leapt up and brought his mace down hard onto the gasping man's chest, the deathblow ending his life of crime. As Raphael slumped down clutching his torn side, Michael rushed to his aid fallen friend.

Both thieves attacking Kain did an overhead slice with their shortswords. Kain raised his own shortsword and blocked the oncoming blades. He gave a hard push to knock them away and furiously swung his weapon in skilled blows. With the odds two on one against him, his offense quickly reverted to defense and he found himself working double to defend his life from the two blades. As he began to tire, the two men once more tried a double overhead chop. Kain blocked these just as easily as he had the first time, but this time he drew his dagger as he kicked one away. Then in one continuous motion, he slit the throat of the thief whose blade he was still blocking and threw his dagger with deadly accuracy. It hit its mark, sinking deeply into the other's forehead. Both men fell as Kain turned to see how his sister was fairing alone against Marcus Addison.

While all the fighting was going on around them, Addison had managed to knock away Nancy's shortsword in less than two seconds and grabbed her by the neck. He hoisted her high into the air and held her in a tight grip for a moment before throwing her into the dresser. She crashed to the floor and the empty dresser toppled on top her. It was heavy, but she managed to crawl out right into Addison's waiting hands. He was immediately on her and tossed her into the wall. She struck with a loud smack hard enough to be dazed. Addison grabbed her around the throat one last time and started to crush it while he stuck his face right into her own and gloated "You little tart! This will teach you some manners!"

In reply, Nancy lashed out with her leg and caught his groin. He howled in pain and fury as he instantly dropped her, his testicles swelling almost immediately as his rapist erection snapped like an arm. She gasped for breath and coughed violently as she rubbed her bruised throat while Addison clutched himself and bellowed "AHHHHHH! You did it again! You busted me again, you tart! AHHHHHHHHHH! **I'M GONNA KILL YOU!**"

With rage and a sudden rush of adrenaline fueling his body, he leapt at her with his eyes on fire. Nancy grabbed his shirt, planted her foot on his chest, and used his momentum against him to flip him backwards. Addison flew out of the shattered window screaming, but was abruptly silenced when he struck a stack of heavy iron bars topped with pointed ends that were being used to repair the inn's fence. There was a tremendous clatter as the iron bars banged off of Addison and against each other, tangling in his flailing arms and legs. One of the large spiked tips struck his neck, silencing his howls of shock and fury. He gurgled, blood spewing forth from his lips as he shuddered violently and then went limp. The last thought to enter his dying, foul mind was to wonder who in the hell was that little girl that could have done such a thing to Marcus Addison.

Nancy coughed violently as Kain ran to her, but before her brother could lay his frightened hands on her she shrieked in horror and rushed over to Raphael. She quickly laid his head in her lap as she looked at his wound.

"My goodness, Ralph!" she cried out. "You're hurt!"

"It's nothing. Just a flesh wound." he assured her as he tried to lift himself up, wincing from the pain.

"You're bleeding!" she gasped loudly as she pushed him back down. He tried to tell her he was all right, but didn't stop her when she tore a piece of her shirt off, and put the cloth on his wound to cover the trickle of blood. As she held it there, she looked into his eyes and smiled with lips that melted Raphael's heart.

"You were very brave, Ralph." she sweetly whispered. "Thank you very much."

"Just . . . ngh . . . doing my job." he grimaced, shifting his bodyweight.

"How is he?" Kain asked, approaching them after making sure all were dead while Michael secured the unconscious three.

"He'll be all right." Nancy grinned, rubbing his cheek with a warm, gentle hand. "Are the police on their way?"

Almost ten minutes later, the city guard arrived with Deborah and Landis. They arrested the three thieves that had lived and started cleaning up the mess. Landis assigned five officers to stay and make a report, before going back to the castle with the others. Kain and his friends were shown to the main banquet hall where an impromptu congratulation party was prepared while Raphael's wound was treated in the infirmary. In only a handful of minutes he was enjoying the good food and drink with Kain, Nancy, and the others.

"Congratulation goes out to Sir Kain Viccon!" Landis announced as she pulled the cork out of a bottle of the finest Holgrafian champagne and began pouring for the small group that had gathered. She along with Michael, Raphael, Robert, Kain, Nancy, Deborah, and a few police officers and Robert's scouts were celebrating their new victory over the gang of thieves that had plagued the City of Hurst for some time. "Without him, we would still be worrying ourselves to an early grave over the matter!"

Kain blushed slightly and replied "Thanks much, Landis. But the real hero of the night is my wonderful sister, Nancy. She's the one that showed Addison what it meant to mess with a Viccon! Cheers to the lovely young lady I'm proud to call sister!"

"Cheers!" everyone burst out joyously before taking deep drinks of their champagne.

Nancy blushed a deep crimson, but gave her bright smile and curtsied for everyone before taking a sip of her own glass. Because of her great achievement, Kain had allowed her a share of drink to celebrate. A small band struck up a festive tune as everyone began buzzing lively chatters and danced up a storm. Landis took turns swinging around the room with Robert, Raphael, and Michael while Kain and Nancy flapped about merrily. Soon, Deborah found Kain and pulled him away into a dance of their own while Michael and Robert shared a good humored laugh after forcing a nervous Raphael to dance with a shy Nancy. The massive clock rang out with three bongs as the band played a slow, sweet tune for the dancing couples.

* * *

"Why are we in such a rush to get to the dungeon, my lord?" Garrison asked as he and Noknor rushed down the twisting stairwell.

"To see my surprise for the Chinese woman." Noknor panted, his heart and mind racing in anticipation.

"What is this surprise you keep talking about?"

"Just wait until we get there. You're going to love it! Just love it!" he grinned at the thought. "Now I can finally crush that Chinese woman's will!"

"Why is it so important that you—"

"Because she's much too powerful for my magick to affect her. I don't know why that is, but I'm sure that's connected to her strong will in some way." he told him, not really expecting Garrison to understand but explaining nonetheless. As they reach the bottom of the stairs, he grabbed the door and fiddled with the handle for a moment, his excitement getting the better of him. "Her will repels my magick, it forms a shield around her. Even with this blasted ornament," he fondled the Swuenedras Amulet roughly, "my magick has little affect on her."

"Well, if that's the problem, I could rough her up a bit for you, my lord." Garrison chuckled, a hint of pleasure in his voice as he rubbed his fist.

"That would be an impossibility." Noknor muttered dryly.

"No way, sire! I beat the bag out of her once, I sure as hell can do it again. No problem!"

Noknor gave him a sideways glare and rolled his eyes. He was much quicker to believe that the Chinese woman would . . . ah, beat the bag, as Garrison had so eloquently put it, out of his Dark General.

"Regardless." Noknor muttered without much tone. "I don't want her to even get a scratch on that luscious body of hers. Not until I have Viccon in my talons. I have big plans for them all. Big plans. Ah, here we are!" he boomed excitedly, looking into one of the dungeon cells. He gripped the rusted bars and leaned forward, a bright look of pride on his gleaming face. "What do you think, general?"

"Is that—" Garrison gasped, cutting himself off in his own shock. He opened his mouth and eyes wide in surprise, having to support himself on the bars to keep from toppling down as his knees turned to jelly. "I . . . I can't believe it! This is impossible! Impossible! How did you—"

"I acted on a hunch." Noknor grinned. "A strong hunch, but a hunch none the less. I'll tell you, it wasn't easy. Not easy at all. And it cost a fortune! But it'll all be worth it when my plan works and I crush that Chinese woman like the pathetic bug she is!"

He started to chuckle under his breath as he thought about how clever he was. The more he thought about it, the louder his chuckle grew until he began to laugh out loud. His booming cackling grew until it echoed through the halls and all over the castle like a twisted fog, stabbing an icy dagger into all those who heard it. Deep under their covers, both ladies shivered.

* * *

Early the next morning, someone tried to open the door to the ladies' chamber, but Elizabeth had propped a chair against the doorhandle before she had went to bed. After seeing Noknor's outburst the night before, she feared that someone would come in while they slept and hurt them. Li told her not the worry and that they weren't in any immediate danger, but Elizabeth felt there was no need to take chances; after all, Li had been the one to stuff the keyhole. When the person outside began to politely rap on the door, Elizabeth drew out of bed and looked through the barred window on the door. She saw two Dark Knights standing with a grinning Noknor. Elizabeth was never sure which she hated worse, Noknor's scowl or his smile.

"Good morning." he smiled nicely enough. "Could you go wake your friend? I need to speak to her and it is very important."

The princess decided to do as told, and hurried to Li's bedside where she shook her arm vigorously. "Li?"

"Wuh is it?" she mumbled and squinted as she looked at her friend.

"Noknor is at the door. He . . . he needs to speak with you."

"What!" Li growled as she laid her head back down and covered it with her pillow. Her muffled voice snapped "Tell him I said to go sit on an upside-down stool!"

"Li, please! He says it's important."

Li lifted the pillow and glanced at Elizabeth's worried frown. She finally huffed in annoyance and grumbled "This had better be good!"

She rose up and drifted to the door where she crossed her arms and hissed "WHAT!"

"Open the door, my dear." he said smoothly, not the least bit taken aback by her tone. At least, not the least bit physically taken aback. "I have a surprise waiting for you down in the dungeon."

"I don't like surprises from slime like you! Especially if they're found in the dungeon!"

"Oh, you'll like this one." He gave her a wink that made her skin crawl. "I guarantee it."

Li thought for a moment before responding "Oh, what the hey. If it'll shut you up."

She slammed the window's cover closed and pinned it locked before dressing for the day. She took her time, hoping that it was annoying the hideous man waiting for her. She even paused to pour a drink of water before deciding to toss the chair away and throw open the door. The two Dark Knights carefully approached her with shackles. Li guessed their intent and mocked "I won't hurt you on purpose, Noknor."

He gave her an icy glare as his knights bound her arms behind her. They led her down several corridors before arriving at the dank dungeon and shoved her down a corridor of cells. A few were empty, but most had Kubericans and Shazadians wasting away as they awaited death. Li felt such pity for them and her heart pained for their suffering. Her hateful eyes burned a hole into the back of Noknor's head as she prayed that her cousin would arrive soon to give the monster the punishment he so richly deserved. She was so intent on her dark wishes that she nearly bumped into his back when he stopped suddenly. The Dark Knights worked quickly to open the cell door and remove her bindings so that she would not be free for very long before they could shove her into the cell as fast as they could. She tumbled to the ground as the door of heavy iron bars clanged loudly behind her.

Noknor called out "Your visitor's here."

As she picked herself up and dusted off, she started to growl a retort until she saw who it was. The prisoner was none other than James Elaxander Raptor, her long lost lover. He was sitting on the dirty cot gawking at Li in disbelief. Her mind shut down as she just stood before him, her knees shaking and her hands quivering.

"Auset bless me!" James hissed a bewildered gasp, lifting himself up slowly on unsteady legs, his eyes refusing to close lest the vision of his beloved disappear on him. "Hua Li! Is that . . . is that really you?"

At that moment, Li took her body back as she rushed up to him and she threw herself into his awaiting arms, the lovers nearly tumbling down from the passionate impact.

"JAMES!" she cried out as she began to kiss his lips in crazed excitement. "Oh, it is you! Glorious heavens! James Raptor! It's really, really you! I can't believe it!"

James grabbed her around her waist and twirled her around while she giggled uncontrollably. She couldn't believe it! After three years, she had found her beloved James again. It was the moment she had been waiting for, she had been dreaming for, every day for three long years. She couldn't believe it was true, but there she was right in his arms just like so many times before. With so many emotions flooding her very soul, all she could think was that if it was, in fact, another dream, she never wanted to wake up ever again.

James drew her close, a tear forming in his eye as he kissed her neck and whispered into her ear "I was beginning to think I'd die without ever seeing you again, my darling!"

"I never lost hope, my love! I just never imagined that we would come together again in a dungeon!"

(kiss-kiss)

"Nor I!" James moved his lips over hers and down her neck. Li ran her hands through his long dark hair and along his back. James squeezed her arms and rubbed her shoulders. Both were trying to make sure that it was really true and not just another teasing dream.

"Wo ai ni!" Li whispered as she felt a tear slip down her cheek.

(kiss-kiss)

"I love you!" James returned, running his hand through her hair and caressing her cheek.

(kiss-kiss)

"My love, why didn't you return to me?" Li whimpered, feeling on the verge of tears.

(kiss-kiss)

Li repeated herself and this time James stopped and looked into her flustered eyes. He held her face and used his thumb to wipe away the lone tear that trickled down her fair and radiant cheek. He faltered as he struggled to find the words to answer "I-I tried, my China doll. I tried with all my heart and soul, but I couldn't. After that rat piece of filth shot me in the back, I passed out. I would have died had it not been for my Auset training. When I awoke, I saw that the battle was over and the goblins had massacred our army. The wild dogs and carrion birds had already begun to feast and were beginning to eye me. Goddess, the sight was so ghastly! I'll never forget it. I took off into the forest as fast as I could, but passed out again in my weakened state."

He stopped and looked at the cot, then to Li, then back to the cot. Li took notice and asked "What is it, my love?"

"Nothing." he replied in Chinese. "I was just thinking that it would be better if we sat down." He led her to the cot and closely sat hand-in-hand with her. He continued his story in Chinese as best he could, but Li had to correct him and help him out quite a few times. "The next time I awoke, I was in a small tipi, lying on a soft bed. It was the home of a Pocan family; apparently the husband had come across me as he was picking herbs out in the forest. He had brought me back to his tribe, removed the arrow from my back, and treated my other wounds. He saved my life, Li-Li. Anyway, I lived with the Pocan tribe for a while, I'm not too sure how long, a few months maybe, traveling with them whiles I recovered my strength. I had written you letters, but we were far from any villages where I could mail them and I was too weak to journey on my own.

"Then just about when I was ready leave them and come back to you, we accidentally wandered into what we assumed was still dwarf territory not knowing that it now belonged to the goblins. We were attacked. I tried my hardest to protect them, but those poor people never stood a chance. Those that weren't immediately slaughtered were taken prisoner, myself included. I was forced into slavery for all that time since. Until two weeks, anyway. I was told that I had been sold and well . . . here I am."

"You were a slave for goblins!" Li cried and held him tight as she gasped "How awful for you!"

"It was terrible. The work I had to do was very grueling and backbreaking. I tried to escape a number of times, but they always caught me and beat me, most times almost to death. But they never let me die. I was too good of a worker for them I suppose."

"Oh, James! However did you survive!"

"I always had my mind on you, Beauty. It was your memory and the thought that I would one day see you again that kept me going." he told her as he produced a small circle of metal that was hung around his neck. Painted on the metal was a very scratched and faded picture of Li's face and on the back was etched the Chinese symbol for her name. She looked at it and sighed happily as he put it back under his shirt and replied softly "Every day, every hour for three years I have prayed to my Mother to allow me to be with you again. To not die until I had held you one last time, told you how much I love you. And she has finally answered my prayers! Oh Goddess, I have never been this happy!" He kissed her lips fondly. Then he lowered his eyes and replied in a tone that held somewhat of a deep question to it "I was . . . I was afraid you had gone on with your life. That you had found somebody else to replace me."

"I have held my torch ever since the last day I saw you, James!" Li told him, assured him. "That torch has burned brighter and brighter for you, even against the so-called advise of friends in the hopes that it would burn bright enough to help you find your way back to me. If I had found out you had not made it, I still would have held that torch, awaiting the day that you and I would meet in the afterlife! No man could ever have replaced you in my heart. Our hearts are one, James. One and eternal!"

"I thought I couldn't become any happier, my love." James murmured softly, returning the squeeze she had given his hand as he rubbed his lips against her cheek. "But you've proved me wrong."

They sat together holding each other close and basking in each other's presence while Li spent over three hours telling him all about all about the events in her life that he had missed. She told of Kain's rise to Grand General of the Arcainian Army, their adventures together, Wenchi's premature death, her job as trainer for the Chinese Imperial Army, and the events that had led to that day. When she told of her battle with Garrison, James lifted her blue cotton blouse and growled "I can't believe he did this to you. I'll gut that son of a—"

"I get him first." Li cut him off with a sure voice as she placed two soft fingers to her lover's lips. "He took away my husband and murdered my best friend."

"Well . . ." he muttered as if thinking it over. "I guess you do deserve first crack at him. I'm so very sorry about Wenchi."

"Thank you." she murmured lowly, her head down. James put his fingers gently on her chin and lifted her head before looking in her eyes and giving her a kiss on her lips. They were silent for a long moment, just holding each other close.

Finally, James said "So, Kain's Grand General, huh? I always knew he'd make it someday. And you!" He grinned broadly and embraced his love as he sighed "I'm so proud of you, Beauty! Goddess, you earned the respect of the Council of Dragons! One in a handful of humans in ten thousand years! And the first female trainer in the entire history of the Imperial Army! My, you sure have been a productive woman!"

They talked and enjoyed each other's company for a few more hours before Noknor came down and boomed excitedly "Now it's time for the second half of my surprise!"

Li was led back up to her room, without shackles this time as she was so lost in the clouds of love that she couldn't have swatted a fly. Elizabeth immediately rushed up to her and examined her close, babbling about how worried she had been since Li was gone for so long. Li excitedly told the princess about James. If she had seen herself, she would have been reminded of her best friend when the prospect of marrying her cousin had popped up.

Suddenly, one of the walls changed into a set of steel bars that reached from floor to ceiling. The neighboring cell was much like the ladies', except it was made for a male prisoner. That prisoner was James. Li rushed over and passionately kissed him through the bars. The two lovers were so happy to be reunited that they didn't have a care in the world. Elizabeth, however, couldn't help but wonder why Noknor was being so nice to the woman he hated so much.

"He's scared of me." Li replied as she gazed dreamily into James's eyes. "So he's trying to get on my good side."

Elizabeth was still worried that there was a more sinister, darker motive for Noknor's actions. There always was with a devil like that. The only thing the princess could do was hope and pray that the Goddess have mercy on them and make her wrong.

CHAPTER XXVI

Due to the late night brought about by the celebrations for the liberation of Hurst from the Addison gang, Kain called for an extra day hold over in the City of Hurst. Having not lain in a bed before the break of dawn, Kain's crew welcomed the extra time to sleep in. As for the rest of the men, there was not one complaint about the extra time off.

On the morning of their fourth day in Hurst, the Arcainians left the city amidst great cheers and appreciation. They traveled on for several hours before reaching a large pond in the middle of a lush field of grass with a dense forest full of green not too far off. Kain called for a hold to let their horses rest and drink while they admired the peaceful beauty and tranquility around them. The sun shone down warmly upon their shoulders while a soft breeze billowed past in a lazy sort of manner. The chirps of a variety of songbirds filled their ears as the shrill calls of hawks echoed overhead. While Kain took a moment to fill his canteen with the sparkling waters of the pond, he couldn't help but think that under different circumstances it would be nice to enjoy the peaceful laziness for much longer than they could afford at the present moment. Longing thoughts of his cousin once again entered his mind as he thought how much she would enjoy sitting at the edge of the pond with her sketchpad in hand.

Suddenly, Nancy squeaked loudly and pointed excitedly off in the direction of the trees. Kain and his friends followed her finger and saw a lone unicorn stride regally out from the forest. It was a teenaged male from the looks of its decent sized spiraled horn and long white mane and tail. The sunlight glittered off its shiny pure white coat, seeming to make the creature glow. With its bright blue eyes that shimmered like sapphires, it looked across the pond at the humans and scanned over them with a mild sort of curiosity. Nancy was afraid it would run away at the sight of them, but Kain himself sensed no fear in the animal as if it was positive it alone could stand up to so many armed men. Kain was proven right when the unicorn finally disregarded them absently and meandered casually to the water's edge where it lowered its head and touched its horn to the water. The sparkling water seemed to become even cleaner and clearer as it reflected more light from the sun. Kain and Robert immediately dumped out the water they had just collected in their canteens and began to refill them once again, while most of the other men followed their lead. They knew that the unicorn's horn, among other things, had the magickal ability to purify water. And though the water had seemed clean enough for them, apparently it wasn't quite pure enough for the unicorn's taste.

"It's so beautiful!" Nancy cooed dreamily. She looked at it longingly and sighed "I wish I had one."

Robert looked at Kain and raised an eyebrow as he told his friend "You know, they say it's almost impossible to catch one."

"Well, I'm up for the challenge." Kain chuckled confidently. "Nancy, you will soon have a new pet!"

Kain started to sneak around the pond, taking care to not to make a sound as he clung to the trees that grew around it in large clumps. When he was only a few feet away from it, the unicorn lifted its head and peered curiously at him, almost looking like it was giving Kain a bothered frown. Nancy was afraid it would run away, but it didn't even move. Instead it snorted and she thought she saw it grin. She looked again and saw that, yes, it was indeed grinning at her brother, or at least as much as a unicorn could grin. It held a fierce look in its blue eyes that said 'go ahead, try it and see what happens.'

It lowered its head and resumed drinking. Kain, knowing that he had been spotted, decided to try the friendly approach. He walked forward slowly, his hands at his side to show he was unarmed and meant the creature no harm. In slow, even movements he extended his hand to pet it. The unicorn glanced at his hand for a brief moment before clamping its jaws down hard. Kain howled in pain and cursed the animal roundly as he examined his throbbing hand. It was bruised, but luckily the skin hadn't been broken. In his fury, he leaped at the beast and received a kick in the chest for his troubles. Kain flew against a tree and landed face first on the ground. He scrambled for its legs, but it sidestepped and kicked his side gently, just hard enough to humiliate the human. Kain roared and jumped to his feet. The instant he was up, the unicorn jabbed at him with its horn. Kain stepped back and threw up his hands to defend himself, wishing he hadn't left his shield with his horse as he was herded backwards. Suddenly, he tripped over a large stone and tumbled backwards into the pond where he made a huge splash. As he walked back to his friends with a very wet, very red face, the unicorn resumed drinking.

Nancy stood up and dusted herself off before she began to stroll over to the magical creature. As she passed Kain, he grabbed her arm and grumbled "Where do you think you're going?"

"I want to try." she told him, her voice carrying with it an all too familiar ring of Li's own devil-may-care tone. Raphael noticed that the unicorn perked up when she spoke. He blamed his imagination and cast it off.

"No." Kain shook his head slightly.

"Yes." Nancy nodded her head vigorously, mocking her brother.

"You're going to get hurt." he warned.

"I will not! I want to try." she insisted, trying to pull away from him.

"Fine. Do what you want." he muttered, releasing her arm and causing her to stumble with sudden surprise. He walked over to where the others sat and plopped down where Nancy had been sitting moments before. He nudged Michael and retorted "This should be good."

Nancy flashed him a dirty frown before flouncing on towards the unicorn. When she reached it, it lifted its head and peered curiously at her as it had done Kain. She extended her hand and everyone, sure that it would bite her as well, winced in apprehension. However, it licked the back of her hand, making. Nancy giggle and squeak "That tickles!"

It then nudged her with its snout and began to fondly lick her face as if they had known each other for years. Nancy giggled again and caressed its neck before straddling it. She rode it bareback to where the men were standing, gawking at her with wide, shocked eyes. She flashed a grin at them that to Kain seemed rather haughty and proudly called "I told you I could do it!"

"Only the purity of a virgin heart can tame the wild unicorn." Robert quoted with a grin. He gave Kain a jolly wink. "Guess I forgot to mention that part."

Now Kain was truly embarrassed as he strode over to Nancy's horse and began to unstrap the saddle without a word to anyone. Michael walked up behind him, clapped his back, and remarked "I've said it before and I'll say it again. That is one hell of a sister you have there, Kain!"

"You have no idea!" Kain laughed boisterously, shaking his humbled head.

* * *

Garrison knocked upon the throne room doors and opened them when he heard Noknor's booming voice call for him to enter. He did as told and shut the doors behind him. Then he quickly walked across the long red carpet and knelt before his master. "You called for me, my lord?"

"Indeed I did, my loyal Garrison." Noknor grinned a toothy grin. He motioned his general to rise and snapped his fingers. A pile of bleached bones next to the grand chair clattered loudly as they vibrated and began to rise up into the air. They quickly joined together in no particular order to form a simple chair. Garrison sat at his lord's gesture. "I called you in here to handle a special task for me. Now, I could have anyone do this, even one of those imbecilic goblins. But I'm going to give it to you, because you're most certainly the one who would most appreciate it."

"What's the assignment?" he inquired cautiously, moving his weight around to avoid the lumps in his morbid chair.

Noknor reached along side his throne and pulled up a long, gray whip studded with wickedly sharp thorns. As he handed it over, he explained "Take this magick whip and go up to Raptor's room."

"You want me to—" Garrison gasped, happily surprised.

"Precisely." Noknor nodded, licking his full, red lips. "You can make up anything you want as a reason for doing it, I don't care. Just make sure to do it in full view of the Chinese woman. And don't kill him. If you do, I'll definitely gut your sorry hide and feast on your entrails! Just beat him enough to provoke a rise from that woman, say five or six lashes. No more. Then have him thrown back into the dungeon. I'll deal with him myself as I see fit. Oh, and after you've done so, lash at her once with the whip. Not anything too harsh, mind you, just enough to see what happens to her. See if it hurts her. I'm quite certain after that it will."

"I understand." Garrison replied, bowing his head. An evil grin formed on his face as he fondled the handle and tested the sharpness of the thorns. He chuckled giddily at the thought of ripping his old friend's flesh to shreds. "Do you want me to do it right now?"

"No, wait a few days. Let the two lovers grow fat on their pathetic emotions for one another." Noknor told him, sitting back with his hands behind his head. He sighed heavily and closed his eyes to narrow slits. "Now leave my presence."

* * *

Three days after leaving the City of Hurst, the Arcainians stopped for a quick lunch on quiet grassy plains near a sparse wood. Kain figured that it would only take them another two days or so to reach the outskirts of Dismal Swamp and took some time to go over basics of swamp safety with his men as they relaxed under the slightly clouded sky and enjoyed a cool breeze with their meal. The knights and soldiers chowed down on dried beef and rice and beans quickly cooked over a several small fires as they listened to their Grand General, paying close attention to even the details they had heard many times before.

After finishing her lunch, Nancy managed to sneak away with her unicorn to find it some fresh wild barley to munch on, murmuring lowly to her steed in a sweet and pleasant voice as she rubbed its neck fondly. While she stood by idly and waited for her pet to eat his fill, she looked at the special faery shield the Uraeus Sisters had given her. It was very beautiful, looking more a work of art than any sort of weapon. It was made entirely of silver, with the round edge molded with flower stampings while the face was flawlessly polished, making a perfect mirror that reflected the sun's rays with brilliant flashes. A warm smile touched her lips as she noted that she hadn't even yet used it in any fights and she couldn't help but wonder when it would be broken in.

Her arm suddenly jerked up on its own accord, her silver shield flashing brightly in the afternoon sun. She felt something pelt it hard and heard a loud clang as a broken arrow fell to the ground, the tip dripping a sticky, clear liquid. She glanced at it curiously as her arm flew up once again on its own, ringing out with another impact. She gasped out as she realized the situation and twisted her head up to see five men dressed in black and dark green armor rushing at her while four similarly dressed Dark Knights sat in the tall trees of a nearby wood, arrows with drugged tips drawn back in their specially crafted sniping bows.

The Dark Knights were on her in a flash as she tried to mount her surprised unicorn, dragging her back down as she squealed with fright. Out of the corner of his eye Kain spotted some commotion where he had saw his sister head off to only moments before. As he turned, his terrified heart skipped several beats and plunged into his stomach, mixing very uncomfortably with his lunch. In his panic he couldn't even call for any orders and instead broke from the group without finishing his prior thoughts. He tore over the grass as quickly as he could fly, screaming out for his sister as three Dark Knights wrestled with her in an attempt to subdue her while the other two did their best to deal with her very irate unicorn.

The other Arcainians quickly picked up arms and rushed to the aid of the Grand General's darling sister, roaring ferocious battle cries. The four Dark Knight archers let a dozen arrows fly in only a few seconds, scattering the Arcainians as they ducked and dodged the arrows whizzing through their ranks. Kain felt the sharp breeze of at least three arrows as they grazed past him, not carrying if he was hit or not as he pumped his legs harder while another four arrows shot past him.

Nancy hissed a horrified squeak as she felt several hands snatch her legs and shoulders and pull her back to the ground. She heard her unicorn bellow enraged neighs as she slid down his slick coat. The creature reared back and kicked the air in front of it while blowing harsh snorts through its nostrils, its cloven hooves pawing at the Dark Knights' heads as they threw their hands up in defense and tried to drag Nancy away. She squirmed and wriggled in their grips, managing to free her right arm for just a brief second. She threw her elbow back as hard as she could, feeling it hit something hard as her arm was caught once again. She lifted her left foot and brought it down, slamming it atop someone's boot. One of the Dark Knights cursed heatedly and released her left arm, allowing her the bash him in the face with her shield. She struck him a second time, making the man see stars and then flung her shield over her right shoulder, the edge crushing the second Dark Knight's nose.

While only one Dark Knight held Nancy around her waist and two others writhed on the ground from their wounds, the other two tried to catch hold of the leaping unicorn's reigns with the hopes of dragging the animal to the ground to make it helpless. With shrill whinnies and neighs, the unicorn skittered forward, his front legs windmilling violently. A wild cloven hoof cuffed one of the Dark Knights across the head, the impact breaking his neck. The second Dark Knight drew his sword and sliced and jabbed at the creature in an attempt to drive it back, possibly even frighten it away. The unicorn wasn't frightened in the least, and jerked its head savagely about so that's long spiraled horn clashed with the steel. The Dark Knight was flustered by the vicious temper of an animal known for its peaceful nature and the unicorn had no trouble goring him in the stomach. As he double over clutching his wound, the unicorn spun around and delivered a devastating double kick with its hind legs.

Kain knew that the Dark Knights archers would pick him and his men off before they could reach Nancy, and with the crushing fear in his chest lifting as he watched Nancy and her unicorn hold their own against their attacks, he knew that his only chance of getting to his sister was to take out the archers. While still on the run, he threw himself down, skidding across the grass on his legs as he unshouldered his bow. When he came to a smooth stop, he drew up to one knee to steady his aim and notched a faery arrow in his bowstring. The branches of the tree shook as one of the Dark Knight snipers rolled from the tree and hit the ground on his feet, an arrow already notched and ready to fire. Kain's arrow arced in midair and shot straight for him. He dodged again despite his shock, but it followed and struck him square in his chest, his own arrow shooting wildly without danger to the Arcainians. Even before his first shot had found its target, Kain already had a second arrow flying and it also struck a second Dark Knight archer in the chest, knocking him from the tree. The other two archers knew they were no match for such an enchanted weapon or the overpowering force of the angry Arcainian soldiers running full sprint for the trees. They leapt from their perches and turned tail to run from the scene as fast as their legs could carry them. Knowing they would no longer be a bother, Kain was back on his feet rushing to help his sister.

Nancy pulled with all of her might, but the last remaining Dark Knight held her tight, lifting her feet off the ground as he struggled to haul her away with him. The unicorn snorted fiercely and pawed the earth with his cloven hooves, unable to advance because the Dark Knight held Nancy in the way. She met eyes with her steed and grit her teeth as she struggled further. She saw the unicorn twitch its horn and then jab forward with it. Nancy moved her head to the side, just out of the way of the unicorn's spiraled horn as it gashed the man in the shoulder. He swore more from the shock than the pain, releasing Nancy and dropping her back on her feet. She spun around, bringing her shield to hit him in the side. He grunted and then took the girl's tight fist hard across his jaw. She swung with her left, catching him across the face with her shield before punching him in the eye with her right. Suddenly, she felt her trusty steed charge up from behind her and jumped to the side well out of the way as the unicorn ran the dazed Dark Knight through.

Just as Kain reached her, she fell into her brother's arms and gasped "Thanks, bro!"

"I didn't do a damn thing!" he laughed loudly, overcome with relief that his sister was perfectly well without a scratch on her. She didn't even seem to be that upset by the sudden attack, a rush of adrenaline fueling her fighter's excitement. "That was all you!"

As the unicorn trotted up to them and nuzzled her fondly with its snout, Kain squeezed her tight, rubbing her head and back. As he let her go, he added "Your unicorn played a bigger part than me!"

Nancy wrapped her arms around her faithful stallion's neck and kissed him as she stroked his mane lovingly. She looked into his pearly blue eyes and whispered "Thank you."

The unicorn neighed lowly and caressed her face gently with his own. He extended his tongue for a kiss on her cheek, making her giggle as she uttered a suddenly exhausted sigh.

* * *

The Arcainians had stayed in the Kuberican field that day, pitching their camp a little under a mile from where the attack had taken place in case a stronger force came back for a second assault. Kain had known that they would not be bothered by more Dark Knights that day, but was still being careful. Although he had never muttered it aloud, he knew that it hadn't been so much of an attack on his force but rather another attempt to kidnap his sister. He was infinitely delighted and proud that once again she proved too much for Noknor's bumbling riffraff he had the kahonez to call knights. Kain had also been surprised by how well she and her unicorn had worked together and mentally noted that apparently Nancy had found a friend for life in the magickal creature.

Kain hadn't been too pleased about the delay setting up such an early camp would cause, but he had had no other choice in the matter as many of his men were not fit to travel. Although there had not been any serious injuries, several of the Dark Knight arrows had managed to strike their marks. And with the tips coated in what appeared to be a powerful sedative, they had all had to wait until the affects wore off from their brothers scratched by the drugged arrows. Still, the episode had been viewed as a small victory for Kain and his men, and they all agreed that it had been a small stepping stone in achieving their greater mission. As they rested and nursed their injured brothers back to strength, everyone remained in high spirits as they felt stronger than ever that they could overcome Noknor and his evil.

Two days later, they finally came upon the dreaded Dismal Swamp, immediately finding a large hole in the dense foliage that seemed to be an entrance of sorts to a path that lead deep into the dark, forbidding swamp. Kain examined his map and frowned, but said nothing as he turned to his men. He was very tempted to leave most of his men behind, Nancy included, such as he had at the Forest of Souls. But he ultimately decided against such a plan, as when it came to Dismal Swamp there was definite safety in numbers. Most of the creatures, even the larger predators, would be turned off by such a large number of human tromping through the swamp. The biggest danger would probably come from quicksand and sink holes, and again the more men watching your back, the more hands to pull you out of the bog.

"Alright, this is it." Kain announced boldly. "The infamous Dismal Swamp. It's not the most pleasant place in the world, so I want all of you to constantly be on guard and do not wander off this track. Remember what I told you: stay in tight clusters and do not get separated. If your horse starts getting antsy, listen to it because it's probably catching wind of something it doesn't like. Be careful and watch each others' backs. I've already lost enough men, and I don't wish to lose anymore. May the Goddess smile on us and protect us."

With that, they entered the swamp. Instantly, they were engulfed in shadows and the temperature rose a good ten degrees. A fine, sticky mist wetted their bodies as the horses carefully walked across the soggy ground, making a sloshing sound with each step. Wild creatures called to each other in an array of bizarre squeals and shrieks while the mighty hunters tracked their prey silently. The dark water on both sides of the wide track splashed as animals darted around and the muddy banks spluttered as mud bubbles formed and burst.

Nancy rode beside her brother, her nose wrinkling at the unpleasant odor that clung around them, and said "What's with this path? I thought you said no one had ever built a successful road through this place."

"I wouldn't knock it, girl." he murmured, his eyes shifting around carefully for any signs of trouble. "It's what'll get us to Mystic Cave in one piece. Hopefully."

"I wasn't knocking it." she replied, fiercely swatting at the buzzing insects that swarmed all around. She gave a frustrated snarl and slapped at her cheek. "I was just making an observation."

Kain, still keeping a careful watch around them, grunted in acknowledgment and explained "Both Arcainia and Kuberica tried to build a road to connect them through the swamp, but there had been too much, ah, trouble for it to ever be completed. They managed to build this path, but that's it. They didn't get very far in and there's not much left of it, either. It'll run out soon enough. Then we'll have to cut our own path through. Hopefully we'll be able to stay on solid ground."

"Oh." Nancy murmured nervously, jumping at a horrid screech that sounded too close for her ears.

Kain noticed and told her "Be sure to stay on guard, okay pup? This is not a place to let your mind wander."

"Thanks for the warning. Me and Uni will be sure to keep our eyes peeled for anything suspicious." she said as she lovingly rubbed and patted her unicorn's neck.

"Uni?" Kain raised an amused eyebrow.

"That's his name." she beamed brightly and stroked the long spiraled horn. Uni gave his approval with a cheerful whinny.

Twenty minutes later, they all heard a horse and man scream together and quickly turned to see that one of the soldiers had ridden slightly off the path and into a quicksand trap. The horse instantly disappeared as it struggled helplessly while the man fought to keep his head above the soupy goo. Kain and Robert instantly leaped to the ground and rushed over to help him as he paddled furiously, sinking quickly. Kain knelt at the edge of the pool while his Master Scout stood behind him and held him around the waist so he wouldn't tumble down to join the unfortunate soul. Just as the man was up to his mouth in quicksand, he gripped Kain's outstretched hand tightly. They had him pulled out up to his waist when a large purple snake suddenly sprang up from the sludge and coiled tightly around his arm, head, and torso. As the snake hissed and snapped at them, the soldier was yanked from their grasped and pulled down. His shrill screams were silenced when the watery sand flooded into his mouth and filled his lungs as he was dragged down. Both Kain and Robert were mystified, not really comprehending what had just happened, and stood at the edge of the pool as a few gummy bubbles plopped loudly, all that was left of the man. Suddenly, three more snakes slithered up and snatched at them, sending them leaping back onto their horses and quickly riding away with the others.

During the commotion of their getaway, a twenty-eight foot swamp alligator sprang out of the brush and attacked another soldier's horse. The attack was completely silent save for a gentle rustling of foliage and the startled grunt of the horse as the reptile grabbed the horse's legs and pulled it into the water, causing the rider to fly off. The man hit the moist ground hard enough to knock the wind out of him as a second alligator that was just as large as the first appeared. It snapped its powerful jaws down on his head, crushing his skull before easily tugging him away to be devoured in the dark abyss of the swamp. The attacks came so swiftly and silently, that all anyone else saw was a quick flash out of the corner of their eyes and then splashes in the black water. Kain drew his horse close to his sister's unicorn, watching over her carefully as he urged his men to press on. He personally could not wait until they were out of that horrid place and he seriously hoped they could find Mystic Cavern quickly. And the quicker, the better.

CHAPTER XXVII

"Enter!" the warlock's voice boomed, vibrating the oak door slightly. Garrison grimaced slightly and took a deep breath as he turned the human bone doorknob and entered as he was ordered.

It was pitch black inside the throne room, the only light came from the hallway through the partially opened door. Garrison gulped audibly and took a few tentative paces in. He looked around, but couldn't see anything at all it was so dark. All of the sudden, the heavy wooden doors creaked lowly and slammed shut loudly, cutting off all light into the room. Garrison squealed and spun around. No matter how many times he did this, it still frightened him to death. He mentally told himself that he should have had someone else do it, but he knew no one else would or could. Noknor would allow no one else into the throne room while he meditated and frowned very darkly even when Garrison did. The Dark General just hoped that he had made the right judgment and that his news was as important as he thought.

From the dark void of the room, Noknor's voice sighed dully "What is it, Garrison?"

"I-I'm terribly sorry to disturb you, my lord." Garrison called out into the shadows, sinking down to one knee and lowering his head. "The word just came in from Captain Whirter's squad." He paused slightly and drew in another deep breath. "I'm sorry to report that they—"

"Failed to capture Miss Viccon. Yes, I know." Noknor murmured, two thin slits of glowing red suddenly appearing far back in the darkness.

"Yuh-yuh-you know already, sire?" Garrison stammered, looking up but remaining kneeling. He cursed silently to himself that he had disturbed his lord with news he already knew. And terrible news at that! "How-how-how-how did you—"

"Find out?" Noknor finished for his Dark General once again. Much to Garrison's surprise and massive relief, Noknor chuckled lowly. "I see everything and I know everything, Garrison. I am a god. I am your god."

"Yuh-yes, my lord." he murmured softly. In a stronger voice, he asked "What do you want done over the matter?"

There was a silence as dark and forbidding as the room that lasted several seconds before Noknor replied "Were there survivors?"

"Yes, sir. Two of our archers—"

"Have them tortured. Other than that, nothing." He sensed his Dark General's confusion. "It would be pointless to waste more man power trying to go after her. They would probably fail as well. Anyway, she will come to this castle soon enough. I was just hopping to bring her here sooner than later."

"Please forgive, my lord. But why do you want the Viccon girl so much?" Garrison inquired, not sure if he should be asking but his curiosity getting the better of him. "I mean, you've already tried twice to—"

"I have big plans for her." Noknor told him with a hint of giddiness in his tone.

"I understand, sire." Garrison replied, even though he really didn't.

Noknor uttered a harsh sigh of annoyance and growled "You don't need to understand, Garrison. You only need to obey!"

"Of course, my lord." Garrison winced.

"Rise and come here, I want to show you something." Noknor ordered as a sharp snap filled the air, his fingers the Dark General guessed.

All of a sudden, torches along both walls burst into sudden life in a domino effect starting from the front doors and running to the back of the room. Garrison picked himself up and strode forward cautiously. Noknor sat hunched forward, peering deeply into a large dark crystal set in a massive bone hand that extended up from the floor in front of his throne. Garrison advanced to the large orb with as much courage as he could muster.

"Isn't she beautiful?" Noknor murmured, gently stroking the crystal fondly.

"Who, my lord?" Garrison asked, frowning and cocking his brow as he looked into the crystal. In it he saw an image of Dark Captain Mick Whirter's small squad attempting to kidnap Viccon's bratty sister. Garrison watched as the girl managed to fight her way out of the grips of three men, one of them Whirter himself, while another two Dark Knights went after what appeared to be a unicorn with a saddle on its back. Garrison frowned as the image blinked at regular intervals, much as a beast would blink its eyes. He assumed that the image came from one of those weird ravens Noknor had conjured up.

He watched the girl fend off two of the men before the unicorn, having finished off the other two, helped her by goring Whirter's shoulder. He snorted with disgust as he watched the girl punch him in the face as if he were a schoolyard bully.

'Hmph! Good riddance!' Garrison growled in his irritated mind, rolling his eyes. 'How did such a loser ever make captain? He can't even take a little girl child.'

"Isn't she beautiful?" Noknor repeated, also craning his neck for a better look. "Quite impressive fighting for a child her age, wouldn't you agree?"

"I guess." was all Garrison could think to say. He looked at his master and wondered what this was all about. Certainly his master wasn't falling for the punk kid! He didn't even think Noknor was even actually capable of such a thing. If anything, he just wanted to get his ashes hauled by her. Garrison gave a mental shrug. She was quite a lovely girl, cute with that sweet innocence to her that made her even more desirable. He'd jump her bones himself in an instant, by force if necessary. "But that's to be expected, my lord. I mean, look who her father and brother are. I'm sure he's taught her self-defense techniques and what not. Viccon wouldn't have let her go with him any other way, I'm sure."

"Oh, how I will delight in curdling that sweet, pure blood!" Noknor hissed through his teeth as he ran his thin, red tongue across his thick lips.

"Beg your pardon, my lord?"

"Nothing, skip it." he replied, softly stroking the orb with his hand. "I'm actually glad you came in here, as there's a matter I'd like for you to take of."

The image on the orb slowly faded and another quickly flooded to replace it. Garrison peered in and saw a vision of a small, cramped, poorly lit room in which sat five older men and one younger one looking over what appeared to be a map. As Noknor drummed his nails against the crystal, he said in a simple, almost conversation tone "There seems to be an uprising about to occur in Kuberica City." He paused slightly as if considering. "Crush it."

"I will take care of it, my lord." Garrison assured his dark lord, an evil grin touching his cruel lips as the Viccon girl was immediately forgotten in lue of duties.

Noknor glared at his general with brilliant, glittering red eyes. "Make them suffer."

"As you wish, my lord." Garrison smiled.

* * *

"This sewage tunnel leads straight to a vent just outside the throne room." Abe LeBloc murmured softly, as if he was suspicious that someone undesirable was listening. "We could kill Noknor where he sleeps tonight. Right now. Why should we wait for the Arcainians and let more of our people feed that demon's bloodlust?"

Five older men sat around the small circular table in the small, dark room silently, brooding over the idea that was being presented to them. Abe's eyes darted quickly to each of them, his arms quivering slightly as he waited for the last of Kuberica's royal court to answer.

"Can we be sure this map is accurate?" one man asked in a voice that was barely a whisper.

"My father helped rebuild the tunnels under Kuberica Castle for King Edward. This is his map." he told them. "It is accurate."

Another long, uncomfortable silence.

"Can we risk sending our young men there and leave the city unguarded?"

"Can we risk not? The longer we wait, the more our people will suffer and die. Besides, the city is already unguarded! Noknor comes in as he likes and takes away our family and who can stop him! This isn't even Kuberica City anymore! It's Noknor's city. And we must take it back! We must take Kuberica back!"

The older men glanced around at each other, their eyebrows raised, some of their faces showing hope, others showing doubt.

"I will only need a few men to accompany me." Abe continued. "I have already talked to those I wish to have with me and they all have pledged themselves to the cause for the good of Kuberica. We will see this through, that I promise you. Noknor will be stopped."

Several seconds passed before one former senator reached out with his fist slowly and tapped the table once. Another followed his lead before two more did the same. The last looked at his colleagues before hesitantly doing the same. Abe let out the breath he didn't realize he had been holding in and lowered his head in relief. He looked each of the Kuberican senators in their eyes and said softly "Thank you. We will not fail our kingdom."

"May the Goddess guide you through."

There came a thunderous crash and a sharp cutting of air as the first senator gasped and clutched the crossbow bolt that stuck in his throat. He wheezed heavily as blood sprayed out of his mouth and painted the map as his wide eyes raced madly. Abe stared at him in shock, not comprehending what was happening as the senator slumped forward onto the table, gurgling his last breaths. Abe spun around to run away and came face to face with the metal mask of a demon. He was grabbed by his collar and thrown into the arms of large men in black armor.

"What do we have here? Seems like a little rebellion in the works." the leader of the group growled viciously behind his steel helmet. "And after all Lord Noknor has done for you? You ungrateful slobs!"

"You can give this to your lord!" the third senator shrieked as he pulled a small but deadly crossbow from under his robes. He aimed, tightened his finger on the trigger, and then nothing. He looked at his bloody stump as the crossbow fell to the table, the finger hitting at just the right angle to finish pulling the trigger. The loud twang of the string was buried under the wails and screams of the senator as he grieved with agony for his lost hand. The Dark Knight swung his blood-splattered axe upwards and caught the senator in the chest, lifting him bodily and dumping him hard onto his back. Blood gargled from his mouth and dripped from his nose as the blackness of death shrouded his vision. The last thing he saw through his blood-covered eyes was Noknor's minions pouncing upon the others.

"Would anyone else care to retort?" the Dark Knight hissed savagely, ripping his axe free and waving it menacingly around. At the silence that answered him, he chuckled mildly and ordered "Take these lowly dogs away! The lord's hounds shall feast well on their bones!"

As he was dragged roughly through the door by three powerful men, Abe wondered how all of his carefully and painfully crafted plans could have died so brutally before they could even live.

* * *

By the next day, Kain's army was down two more good soldiers, victims of the horrid beasts that called the swamp home, while Raphael had become the victim of a noble gesture. He had seen a group of beautiful dark purple orchid-like flowers growing on an old and gnarled tree that hung close to the path. Thinking that they would make a lovely little token of friendship for Nancy, he quickly rode up to the branch to pluck a couple for the girl. As he gently gripped the smooth, red stem, he leaned his face close to inhale the pleasant aroma that he assumed they presented. However, he found that they had a somewhat bitter scent to them, but decided to pick them anyway. He gave a tug, but they were stuck fast and immediately spit out oily, green mucus from the beautiful bloom to cover his shocked face.

At first he was annoyed and cursed the plant mildly as he rubbed his face with his sleeve. Then his face began to itch, slightly at first but it rapidly grew worse with each passing second until it burned unbearably. He screeched and fell from his horse as he tore at his face, trying desperately to get the gunk off his skin, which quickly began to turn a vivid purple. His friends rushed to his aid and did everything they could to help him. They splashed clean water from their canteens on his face, they applied every kind of salve and ointment, and they even tried some of their much needed heal potions on him. And while the salves and potions took away the terrible itching, nothing seemed to help his face, which was such a dark purple and so bloated and boil covered that it was impossible to recognize him at all.

Robert and Michael immediately wanted to turn around and head back to Hurst to treat their wounded friend and Nancy was in full agreement with them. However, Raphael insisted that he was all right. The itching was gone and he could see just fine despite the puffiness around his eyes. If anything, it was just a nuisance and he was sure it would wear off eventually. They weren't very convinced, but Kain agreed with Raphael. As much as he pitied his friend, it wasn't the best idea to turn around after they had made it so deep into the swamp. They had lost enough men already and time was running out for them, so he insisted that they had nothing else to do but to push right on through with their mission and hope Raphael was right about the affects wearing off eventually. The others reluctantly agreed and they continued on deeper into Dismal Swamp. After that, Raphael wore his helmet with the facemask down.

* * *

The group had ridden all morning and well into the afternoon without the path even showing any signs of disappearing under their feet. Nancy made an observant note of it to Kain and he told her that if he were reading the map right, it should have vanished long before then. He was as surprised as she was.

By that evening, the path had led them straight into a large grove with a great hill in the center. Though the ground was still moist, it and the smell weren't near as bad as they had been in the darkness of the swamp. They looked up through the large hole in the tree line and saw a cloudless, star-studded twilight sky. At the top of the hill was a massive castle that seemed to be falling apart. Kain grunted as he examined his map in the fading light and found that his assumption was correct.

He scowled at the dilapidated castle and muttered dryly "This should NOT be here!"

"What shouldn't be here?" Robert asked as he rode up beside him.

"All of this! This grove, that hill, and especially that castle! And the path should have filtered out hours ago! According to this, we should be hacking through the undergrowth of the swamp right now!"

"The map must be wrong, then." Michael offered.

"Now who could miss a place like this?" Kain frowned.

"Oh, come on Kain." Nancy chided, joining the conversation. "You said yourself that this place was much too dangerous to build a road through, so it obviously hasn't been explored and mapped very well. I'm sure all map makers just figure its all swamp land, so that's how they map it."

"Very good assumption, Nancy. Very good, indeed." Kain grinned broadly, rolling up his map and slipping it back into his pack. She smiled brightly at the praise. "I hadn't thought of that, but it makes perfect sense. You're obviously right, although someone did explore far enough in to build a home at some point. Of course, why anyone would want to live in such a place is beyond me."

"Well, from the looks of that place, it doesn't appear that anyone's lived here for a long time." Raphael replied, is voice echoing under his facemask as he gestured at the castle. Then he muttered to Robert in a low, thoughtful voice "You know, I don't know what it is about that place, but it seems so familiar."

Robert shrugged blandly but didn't answer him.

"Are we going to investigate that castle?" Nancy asked nervously, glaring up at the rotting building.

"It doesn't look like there could be much of anything in that run down shanty." Kain considered, rubbing his chin thoughtfully. "No, we might as well just camp here at the foot of the hill. It's safe enough and I, myself would much rather look up at a beautiful sky than a roof that might cave in on me. We should be safe enough, but we're going to set up watches all night. Robert, start rounding up—"

Suddenly, a strong wind began to blow across the field and chilled them to the bone, the horses sidestepping uneasily by the unexpected gust. The sky above quickly flooded with black clouds that seemed to appear from out of nowhere as a booming crack of thunder filled the adventurers' ears. Soon, the whole sky over them was covered in black, ominous looking clouds that rumbled and grumbled angrily. It was hard to believe that the same sky that had been clear as could be mere seconds before now looked as if it would explode over their heads at any moment.

'That's odd.' Kain thought, feeling that this was no ordinary storm. Deep in the back of his head, he wondered if it was Noknor's doing. He questioned himself if Noknor even had that much power, but figured with the Swuenedras Amulet hanging around his neck, anything was possible. He glanced at each of his friends and noted that the two men had expressions on their faces that insisted something queer was awry. He was pretty sure Raphael had a similar look behind his facemask while Nancy had a look of pure terror splattered upon her face.

As the grove was thrown into the deep black shadow of the mysterious thunderstorm, Robert yelped in surprise and cried out "Look! There's lights in that castle!"

"Hey! He's right!" Michael agreed, having to raise his voice over the roar of the rising wind. "Someone's obviously up there, so it must be livable!"

"Or haunted." Nancy murmured dryly, her voice shaking.

"Regardless." Raphael said, looking over at her and wishing he had the guts to reach out to take her hand and console her. He cursed himself that if it hadn't been for his face he could have done just that. "I'd much rather take my chances with ghosts than with this storm."

"Well, it looks like we will be going up to that castle after all." Kain shrugged, yanking his reigns and spurring his horse up the hill. "Come on, we need to hurry."

"Wonderful." Nancy muttered under her breath as Uni neighed his agreement.

PART VI

THE ELEMENTAL RINGS

CHAPTER XXVIII

Kain and his company rode as swiftly as they could up the steep hill as the black sky bellowed with deafening cracks and blazes of lightning arced fiercely among the sinister clouds. Nancy and Uni were the first to reach the top just as the entire sky was briefly illuminated by a mighty explosion of lightning. The earshattering report that instantly followed nearly made both of them jump out of their skins as she clung tightly to her steed. She quickly shook it off and tried her best to conceal her fright as Kain and then her friends rode up to join her, though she couldn't control her shivering. They all dismounted and stepped away from their mounts as they crept to the door, save Nancy who hung back and clung tightly to Uni

The door to the mysterious castle was magnificent. It was made of thick boards of solid Kuberican oak that were firmly bound by iron strips that were as powerful as they were beautifully crafted. A large brass knocker was situated just below an impressive golden rose that glittered brightly despite the fact that the sky was masked behind thick clouds. Though the rest of the outside of the castle seemed to be falling apart, the door looked as if it could have come from the home of the wealthiest people in Kuberica. The knocker, itself, was quite heavy and required Kain to use both hands to lift it just halfway and drop it. As it struck the base with an echoing boom, a mighty clap of thunder ripped through the clouds and let loose a terrific tempest.

'This is too queer!' Kain frowned darkly as the rain pelted him and the others, soaking them in seconds. 'It's almost as if the knocker had somehow signaled it.'

"It's odd." Raphael told them, his voice echoing under his facemask as water dribbled in through the eye slits. He blinked rapidly as his vision clouded and continued "This place seems so familiar to me."

"Maybe you dreamed about it." Michael offered, spitting out the water that flooded his mouth as soon as it opened "A nightmare, I would presume."

"Maybe so." Kain muttered, reaching out to grasp the brass knocker once again. His hand hesitated. Deep in the back of his mind, he wondered if this was just one big trap for him and the others conceived by Noknor. There had been just too many coincidences leading to this castle since they had entered the swamp, and he wasn't sure exactly what to make of it. He couldn't stop thinking about the attempt to kidnap Nancy a few days before and feared perhaps all of this was little more than another shot at stealing her away.

He looked back at his troops and saw them all drenched and hopeful for a dry place to sleep. Nancy especially looked cold and miserable and it broke his heart. Looking at the lot, he decided that it was worth the risk of walking into a trap rather than catching their deaths out in the storm. As he reached for the knocker once again, he called out "Be on your guards at all times."

Before he could reach the brass ring, however, the door was thrown wide open, the iron hinges squealing shrilling. Everyone gasped in surprise, especially Nancy who half expected to see a ghost in the doorway. However, if it was indeed a spirit, it was the most beautiful one she could have ever seen. The maiden stood in front of Kain with bright, cheerful lights shining behind her and masking most of her features in shadows. From what they could see, she was fairly tall, standing an inch or two with Kain and she was slim and elegant as a willow tree. When she saw whom it was that had called, she took a step back and gripped the door as hesitation set onto her shadowed face. Kain was afraid that she would slam the door in his face and shut them out, but she held her ground with a stiff air about her.

"Good evening, my fair lady." Kain said in his most pleasant tone of voice despite the fact that the he was soaked to the bone and freezing. "My most humble apologies at disturbing the house, but we are Arcainian Knights. My weary crew and I are desperately in need of shelter until this unexpected storm blows over. I most certainly hate to intrude on you but—"

"You may leave your animals here." she cut him off in a hollowed voice that was somewhat frosted. Kain couldn't tell if it was from annoyance or just her normal voice, but she was inviting them in and that was a very good sign. "I will see that they are attended to."

While the others sighed in relief that they had found shelter, Nancy was reluctant to leave Uni. She had no idea who these people were or what they were like, and she was very well aware that alicorn, the spiraled horn of a unicorn, was highly prized by poachers. She shuddered to think that she would wake up the next morning with a dead Uni. However, he was able to take away her worries. His horn suddenly began to glow with a faint blue hue and there was a quick flash, which could have been nothing more than lightning. In that instant flash, Uni's alicorn was gone, having been turned invisible by the unicorn's magick. Now he was indistinguishable from the other horses, just another normal white steed in the bunch. With a bright smile, Nancy gave him a loving kiss and wrapped her arms tightly around his neck before rushing to Kain's side to be ushered in with the others.

A massive golden chandelier with one hundred burning candles illuminated the large main hall. Beautiful tapestries and magnificent paintings littered the splendid stonewalls. A huge swampbear-skin rug lay out in the middle of the marble floor right under the chandelier and there were three hunting trophy cases filled with impressive catches while other admirable trophies hung from the walls with the works of art. Whomever these people were they certainly had quite an eye for good taste, Kain thought mildly as his eyes grew wide upon recognizing some very rare works. The inside was so much more beautiful and cheerful than the gloom of the outside that it was very hard for Nancy to believe that it was the same castle she had been afraid of.

In the bright light, they were able to see the woman's great beauty more clearly. Her curly, sandy-blonde hair fell daintily about her shoulders and her large, bright blue eyes shined in the flickering firelight. When she walked and motioned, her long fingers and limbs, which seemed like they should have been rather awkward, moved with the fluid gracefulness of a swan. She was a true beauty and instantly caught Raphael's eye as well as most of the other men. Of course he dared not to even speak to her with his face looking the way it did. He hissed a low curse at himself for looking so ugly as he suddenly realized that she seemed even more familiar than the castle did. He began to wonder if the poison had begun to affect his mind as well as his looks.

After guiding them all into the main hallway, she closed the massive door and clapped her hands three times over her head. Instantly, three other young women entered from different doors, servants for the woman. She ordered them to tend to their horses and prepare rooms for them all.

"Then show them the way and alert the cooks to prepare meals for our guests." she said before returning her gaze upon the new guests. She slowly panned her blue eyes over the group with cool neutrality. "I'm sure they are as hungry as they are tired."

In total unison, the girls chimed "Yes, Miss Sarah." before they headed out to do their assigned tasks.

Then the woman turned to Kain and said "The mistress of the castle welcomes you to her home and wishes she could be here to greet you herself. However, urgent matters within have her tied up at the moment. Perhaps in a few moments she will be freed of her tasks."

"I understand." Kain murmured slowly with a bit of a frown. He was sure the tall blonde was the mistress given the fact that she had just given orders to the other servants, but he had obviously been wrong. She must be the head servant of the house; that would explain why she answered the door. No matter, he figured with a shrug. He gave her a bright, humble smile and replied "We would be very honored to meet her."

"And she you." the woman murmured lowly.

Out of the corner of his eye, Kain thought he saw a sudden movement in the shadows. He looked again, closer this time but couldn't see anything out of the ordinary. Just shadows leaping and dancing from the flickering torchlight. He figured it must have been a catch of his imagination brought on by the storm and castle itself. He cast it off as nothing but still glanced around casually as he said "One other thing, my dear lady." He grabbed Raphael by the arm and pulled him forward. Before the Second General could react, Kain pulled up his facemask and exposed his purple, blistered face. "I do hate to trouble you over this but my friend here had a run in with a poisonous sort of flower in the swamp. Would you perhaps have anything that might be able to help him?"

"Ah, yes." Miss Sarah murmured thoughtfully in her calm and cool voice, not the least bit taken aback by the sight. Kain began to wonder if anything ever bothered her. "We know of that flower quite well, the Virules Orchid. Yes, we have just the treatment for it." She clapped once again and another young girl, no more than twelve, entered the hall. "Take this gentleman to the infirmary and inform the nurse on hand that he needs treatment for Virules Orchid."

"Yes, ma'am." the girl bowed humbly before advancing towards Raphael. He quickly pulled the mask back down and once more grumbled a silent curse that he should look so repulsive in front of a woman as beautiful as Miss Sarah. The girl bowed her head to him and extended her hand as she said in a low, bashful voice "Follow me if you will, gentle sir. I'll guide you through the halls."

Raphael did his best to smile for her even though his face was hidden as he took her hand gently and swiftly followed the youngster out. Kain turned back to the woman and said "The lady of the house is busy, but where is the man?"

"There is no man of the house." another melodious female voice boomed through the massive hall.

Everyone gasped and turned their heads towards a large door set into the wall between two flaming torches. There stood a woman of immense beauty and elegance, seemingly appearing out of nowhere. Her long golden-blonde hung down to the middle of her back like the finest silk and her enchanting emerald green eyes seemed to capture one's mind while her skin was as fair as the finest porcelain. She stood shorter than the first blonde, but was still quite tall with somewhat broad shoulders and a very shapely figure and long legs. Her thin, white gown clung to her and helped even more to accent her elegant curves and features. She was the most cultivated and alluring woman Kain had ever seen, not even Queen Vanetta or her daughters possessed the grand and yet at the same time simple flourish that this woman held. And as Nancy looked at her, she silently noted that if the first ghost had been beautiful, this one was absolutely gorgeous. As for the others, they all instantly fell in love with the mystery woman as a thick mist clouded their minds in a sweeping rush of emotions. They saw nothing and heard nothing except for the goddess that stood before them and wanted nothing more than to be with her.

"Not any more, at least." she added with a hint of a smile as she glided daintily towards Kain.

"Our lady of the house, Miss Julie." the woman bowed her head slightly at the woman in acknowledgment. "Miss Julie, these are the guests we saw advancing into our grove."

"It is a great pleasure and honor to meet you, fair lady." Kain replied courteously as he slowly extended his hand to her, seemingly unaffected by her beauty to the extent as the other men were. She gracefully reached out to take his hand and he brushed his lips lightly against her sweet flesh. "I am Sir Kain Viccon, Grand General to Arcainia and this is my lovely sister, Nancy Viccon."

"Hi-Hi!" Nancy smiled brightly and waved bashfully.

"It is a pleasure, Miss Viccon." Julie returned the smile and cast her eyes back onto Nancy's brother, giving him a sweet and subtle grin as she nibbled on her bottom lip. Kain couldn't help but grin broadly.

"This is Sir Robert Grotz and Prince Michael of—" was about as far into his introduction of the others as he got out of his mouth. They all began to babble mindlessly in a feeble attempt to introduce themselves. After the sudden initial shock passed, Kain tried to call them to order but it was no use. All of the men were yapping wildly, especially Robert and Michael. In fact, they were worse than the others, bragging about their stations in life and trying to best one another but instead just coming out like a couple of jackasses. Kain had never in his life seen his troops or his friends behave in such a rude and obnoxious way and it both greatly shocked and insulted him. Even Nancy sported a very disapproving frown at what she was seeing.

However, before Kain could bark at them for silence, Julie called in a sweet, dulcet voice "That's all very nice."

They all went instantly silent with idiotic grins spread from ear to ear on their sleepy-eyed faces as if her voice were a siren's song and they longed to hear her speak again. Julie turned back to face Kain who was all ready with an apology. Before a single sound could escape his parted lips, she held her hand up to stop him and rolled her sparkling green eyes. Nancy snorted and began to giggle lowly as one of the servants reentered at the top of the stairs. The woman gave her mistress a motion of her hand and a head bob. Julie glanced up the stairwell and replied "Your rooms seem to be ready. If you would all care to follow my servant she will show you to your rooms where you can change out of those wet clothes and armor. I'm sure you are all very exhausted and would like to rest after your long journey."

"Indeed we are, thank you very much." Kain told her, bowing his head. "Your hospitality is very much appreciated."

The other Arcainian troops nodded dully like a bunch of brain-dead zombies at Julie's instructions and slowly drifted up the stairs like men lost in a dream. As they embarked up the richly decorated stairwell, they all threw wistful glances at their hostess, as if downhearted that they had to leave her presence even for a little while. Kain turned to follow as he mentally reminded himself to reprimand his men for their outrageously rude behavior. Rude and very peculiar behavior that was quite uncharacteristic of Arcainian Knights. He glanced at the mistress Julie out of the corner of his eye. Not wanting to upset such a beautiful woman, nor risk getting thrown out into the cold and rain, Kain held his tongue against making any immediate accusations. He simply turned his eye onto her lest she notice his sideways glare, bowed his head once more, and gave her a smile before turning to head up the steps with his men.

Julie stopped Kain with a sudden gentle tug. Nancy noticed the subtle gesture and was curious as to what it meant so she hung back with her brother while the others trudged dully, practically forced, up the stairs.

"I would be honored to have you join me for dinner!" she beamed, her eyes looking directly into his. She glanced at Nancy and hastily added "All of you, of course."

Kain looked at Nancy and chuckled at her vigorous, starving nods. He gave Julie a smile and answered "We would be quite honored to accept the invitation."

"Wonderful." Julie grinned, clapping her hands together and slowly licking her lips at the thought. "Very wonderful, indeed."

* * *

"What in the hell is wrong with the two of you!" Kain cried out when he was alone with Robert and Michael in the large room provided for them. "I can not believe the . . . the . . . the absolutely OBNOXIOUS way you—"

"I think she likes me!" Robert said in a dreamy tone.

"What! Who?"

"No way, loser!" Michael told him. "She loves me!"

"Who!"

"Oh, please! She didn't even notice you!"

"WHO!"

"JULIE!" his two friends shouted back before squabbling between themselves.

"Well, I don't see how that could have happened!" Kain growled, becoming more irritated every passing second with the whole ordeal. "You two, and the rest of the men for that matter, made total, complete asses out of yourselves and embarrass—"

"I know, isn't it great?" Michael sighed.

"I'm going to asked her to marry me!" Robert cooed like a schoolboy in love.

"What the hell!" Kain scowled, shocked at what he was suddenly hearing. Sure he thought the mysterious Julie was quite beautiful and tempting, but these men were acting totally ridiculous! "How can you two say that!" he roared furiously, doing everything he could to hold his fists back. "You both are engaged to other women! Great, beautiful women! Why throw them away like that to some stranger?"

But Robert and Michael either didn't hear him or were completely ignoring him as they fought back and forth over whom Julie loved more. Kain knew something was wrong, even a blind archer could see that much! But he couldn't place a finger on it. This castle that looked like it was falling apart on the outside but on the inside was grander than the finest home in Arcainia. The terrible storm, which had sprung forth from a cloudless sky only after Kain mentioned about passing the castle by. And perhaps strangest of all, besides the behavior of his own men, was the fact that Kain had yet to see any other men in the castle. All Julie had said was that there was no man of the house, or had said not anymore at least, thus implying that there had been at one point. What had happened to him? And what about male servants? He had seen several women, but no men. Why? Was there a connection between that and the way his troops had been acting?

Suddenly, paranoia flooded into his brain as he suddenly thought of the story of the Black Widow. An Arcainian scare myth, it told of a particular vengeful and murderous spirit who during life was betrayed by her lover as he shunned her for another. In a fit of furious passion, she murdered her ex-lover, planting an axe into his chest to cleave his heart in two just as he had broken her heart before turning the axe on herself. It was told that the Black Widow, her actual name lost over time, came back to walk the earth on the night without a moon, bloodied axe in hand. And should she cross paths with a lone man, her intense hatred and scorn towards the male gender as a whole overcame her and she would slam the blade of her phantom axe into his chest.

Kain shook his head vigorously to clear it out, the sounds of his arguing friends drifting into his ears once more. He turned to them, watched them carefully, but said nothing. Just what was happening to them? What did the mysterious Julie have on her agenda? All he could do was hope that whatever was going on, Noknor wasn't involved.

* * *

"Sarah! Could you come to my chambers? I need your help for a moment." Julie called into the air.

A few minutes later, the tall, blue-eyed, curly-haired blonde beauty rushed in and replied in her cool, neutral tone "You called, Miss Julie?"

"Yes. Could you fix my hair for me? I just can't seem to get it right." she sighed, handing over a golden brush to her head servant and best friend. She then sat in a chair and turned to face the large mirror on her dresser. She sat quietly while Sarah slowly stroked her long hair. Sarah found it quite odd as her mistress was usually very talkative when they were together.

"What troubles you, Miss Julie?" she inquired.

"Hmmmmmm? Oh, I was just thinking is all."

"If it is about that group you roomed, they are all under your spell."

"You mean . . . curse!" Julie murmured lowly, biting out the last word bitterly. "Are they all?"

"Well, all except for the girl and the one in the infirmary of course."

"Well, that's pretty much a given. What about Sir Kain Viccon? Has he started to show signs yet?" Julie asked hopefully. Sarah didn't respond at first, but finally shook her head dully. "I knew it! I just knew it! This could be it, Sarah! This could finally be the day that this damning curse is broken! I can have my powers back to normal! I can-OUCH!" Julie yelped as she jumped in sheer excitement. Sarah had been in midstroke when her mistress jumped for joy and caught her silken locks in the elegant brush.

"You must sit still, Miss Julie!" Sarah scolded as she sat her back down and resumed brushing. "At any rate, it is still uncertain if he is in fact the special one. Perhaps he is simply stronger than most but not quite as strong as you require. You won't know for sure until you put him to the tests."

"Yes, I know." she mumbled dejectedly, huffing air sharply out of her pursed lips.

Sarah sensed the discouraged tone in her voice, so she patronizingly remarked "At least we know it will not be Arcainia's finest babbling buffoons. What romantic stallions they all are!"

Julie was caught completely off guard and burst out laughing, barely missing getting her hair caught once again. It felt very good to her. "Yes, them." she giggled, pausing to wipe her eyes before continuing "Thank you, Sarah. I can always count on you to cheer me up when I'm down. You are a dear friend."

"As are you, Miss Julie. There, I am done." she said in her cool, neutral tone as she handed back the brush.

"Looks great! Thanks!" Julie smiled, posing for the mirror. She tossed the brush onto the dresser top before opening the top drawer and rummaging through the contents. As she did so, she mumbled in a distant voice "Did you ever catch the name of the knight in our infirmary?"

"No. Sir Viccon never divulged it and he is still under from the effects of the Virules treatment. Is his name important to you, Miss Julie?"

"Not at all, I was just curious. Ah, here it is!" she murmured triumphantly to herself as she produced a vial of glowing purple liquid. She carefully handed it over to her friend and ordered "Take this sleeping potion and put one drop and only one drop into glasses of water, enough for all of Sir Viccon's men. And for goodness sakes, please take care not to spill any onto your skin! Make sure to hint that it came from me, so that they'll be sure to drink it. And go ahead and offer a glass to Sir Viccon so he won't be suspicious, but do not put any into his glass. Don't worry about the girl, either. I have a spell that will fix her well enough." She paused and thought briefly. "I guess that's all. Do you have all of that?"

"Yes, Miss Julie." she nodded, closely eyeing the strange obelisk-shaped glass accented with golden flourishes.

Julie thanked her once more and Sarah hurried off to obediently carry out her task. Julie then closed and locked her chamber door with a silver key before she turned and held her fist high over her head. As she slowly opened her hand, the doors to her closet swung wide open silently. She floated gracefully over towards her bed and shed her gown as she eyed the many lovely garments. After much debate, she finally chose a dark red crushed-velvet dress that stretched to the floor and had so many ruffles that it rustled lowly with every step she took. The sleeves were long and ended in white lace at the cuffs while white lace also lined her low cut collar. The finishing touch to the ravishing attire was a brilliant silver brooch in the shape of a thorny rose that clung tightly to her breast. With hair, face, and dress finally prepared, she looked herself over in her mirror.

"This will have to do." she sighed dully as she tugged her sleeves and adjusted her brooch. She strolled to the center of the room and raised both hands over her head, palms facing each other. At once, a brilliant bolt of crimson energy arched between her palms. Then a flash of white light and a low humming like that of a swarm of wasps filled the room. The light quickly faded and left a large pink sphere like some huge, magnificent pearl floating between her hands. She brought the orb down chest level and gasped "Eye of Rosy Sight let me view Nancy Viccon!"

The Eye cleared as she spoke and an image faded into view until it was perfectly clear. Julie peered deep into it and saw the girl sitting on her bed reading a small book. Other than that, the room was empty and she was all by herself, as per Julie's orders. She needed to be alone with Sir Viccon at dinner in order to test him and that meant taking everyone else out of the picture one way or another. The men had been easy; they always were. The girl, unfortunately, posed a bigger challenge. Julie didn't want to risk using the sleeping potion she had given to Sarah because for some odd reason it had a particularly lethal effect on females, especially on one as young as Miss Viccon. So that left the other, more unpleasant, alternative. Julie began to concentrate on the girl until Nancy grabbed her head, receiving a massive headache. Then she clutched at her belly and lay down on her bed, groaning softly as she shivered.

Satisfied, though feeling a bit guilty, Julie then gasped "Eye of Rosy Sight, let me view Kain Viccon!"

Once again, Julie looked into the orb. The Arcainian general was sitting on his bed, throwing heated glances at his two friends as they snored loudly in their beds. A second closer look showed Julie that his glances were more troubled and apprehensive than angry. He knew something wasn't right and Julie only hoped that it wouldn't affect his coming to dinner with her. He looked down at a large scroll unraveled in his hands.

'Probably a map of some sort.' she thought to herself, hoping that it would give more insight into what he was thinking. She started to try and focus on what he was reading, but he suddenly rolled it up tightly and slipped it into his backpack before walking over to the door, still tossing glances over his shoulder at his cohorts. A servant greeted him and they exchanged a few words before he followed her out into the hallway. The Eye began to follow him out, but a sudden rap on Julie's own chamber door caused her to lose focus and thus caused the orb to disappear with a blip leaving nothing but the faint smell of rose petals hanging in the air.

"Yes? Who's there?" Julie called out cautiously.

"Tis Sarah, Miss Julie." a familiar voice responded. "The time has come for you and Sir Viccon to sup. Hurry, if you will. He is awaiting your presence."

Julie threw open the door and embraced her life-long friend. "Thank you, Sarah. Let's hope this is the one!"

"Good luck, Miss Julie." Sarah smiled.

* * *

Li sat against the bars in her room, holding James's hands tightly in hers while Elizabeth sat in a chair next to her. It had been almost a week since the two lovers had been reunited and they had not left each other's side since. They sat and held hands fondly while reminiscing about the past and preparing for their future.

"You know, James." the princess said with a smile. "Li has told me so much about you, but she has yet to tell me how the two of you exactly met."

"Well, I've known Kain since we were children." James told her, shifting his weight against the bars. "We grew up together. And hanging around him and his house, I was exposed to the Chinese culture because of his mother. Fang was . . . she was a great lady, really sweet and kind. Very friendly. She always made you feel welcome when you visited the Viccons, you know? I guess you could say she's the one that started my love affair for China, it seemed so strange and exotic to me back then. Of course I was just a little kid, but still.

"Kain's mother really taught me a lot. She taught me the language and started me in studying how to read the symbols, taught the history and the myths and legends. Even after her and Sir Viccon . . . after the tragedy Kain had to go through, I kept up my studies. And me and Kain still kept in touch with letters after he and Nancy were sent away. And when they got back to Arcainia City, we got together and hung out all the time . . . well, whenever we had time. He was off in the army and I was studying to be an Auset Knight, but we still managed to stay close.

"Well, after a while he got some vacation time and told me that he was going to China to see his family over there. I asked if I could tag along, you know, get a chance to actually visit the land I had learned so much about. So, we went over to stay with Kain's uncle and his family; they were all great people. Even though I was a stranger, they immediately accepted me as one of their own.

"Anyway, as I was introduced to the Hua family, I met the most stunning, gorgeous girl I had ever laid eyes on. I mean, she hit me like a million arrows!"

Li giggled bashfully and began to blush slightly as James gave her a wink and Elizabeth snickered.

"Well," James continued, "with Li and Kain being so close and Kain and I being best friends, Li and I saw a lot of each other during our stay. By the time Kain, Nancy, and I had to leave, I was courting the lovely maiden. We wrote letters all the time and visited each other when we could. And on one of my later visits to China, I proposed marriage to Li, her parents accepted me, and well . . . here we are."

"How romantic!" Elizabeth cooed sweetly, suddenly wishing she had her own husband to hold hands with.

Li opened her mouth to add something, but stopped abruptly when the door to James's cell was thrown open with great force. Garrison led five of his Dark Knights in and they quickly pounced on James before anyone knew what was happening. There was brief struggle, but James was finally shackled as Garrison pulled a thorn-studded whip from his belt. He chuckled evilly as his men chained James against the wall. The women were horrified and Li screamed out in terror "What are you doing! Leave him alone! What's going on!"

"Just business, ma'am." Garrison told her, flashing her a vicious grin as he slowly unraveled the whip in front of her quivering eyes. "Long over due business."

Elizabeth gasped sharply and Li shrieked at him to leave her lover alone, but the Dark General merely chuckled as he, with his crafty eyes still on Li, cracked the whip behind his back. James howled in agony as the razors tore through his shirt and shredded his back. Li screeched shrilly and sobbed madly as she clawed through the bars in a vein attempt to clutch Garrison. Elizabeth had to turn her eyes from the absolutely horrid sight, but the snapping of the whip and both of her friends' cries of torment rang in her ears, making her weep with fear. Garrison sarcastically blew Li a kiss before turning his full attention onto his old friend. He gave a sinister chuckle as he asked "So, how's the back after all these years, Jimbo?" James winced a savage curse at him and spat at his feet. "That good, huh? Well, trust me, we can change that. And remember, this will hurt you a hell of a lot more than it will me! Ha-ha!"

He laughed evilly as he cracked the whip again, and again, and again. Each snap ripped James' flesh, spraying his blood all over as he howled in agony. His shirt was quickly torn completely from his back and hung in loose, tattered rags soaked dark red. Li wailed like a banshee, tears streaming from her eyes as she sunk to her knees praying that she would wake up from the horrible nightmare.

"You were supposed to die, Jimbo!" Garrison muttered, pausing to rest his arm a moment. "I left you for dead in the middle of that blasted field. And you didn't die, Jimbo. Do you realize how that makes me look?" In the blink of an eye his demeanor turned from teasing to furious as he harshly cracked his magick whip. "DO YOU!" As James groaned and gritted his teeth against the blinding pain, a cruel smile touched the Dark General's lips once again. He licked his lips and reared back his arm. "You have to be taught a harsh lesson in life and death, Jimbo. So, listen well."

He struck, unleashing a fury of torturing blows with his whip. Garrison squealed in pleasure, swinging the whip with the glee of an artist, the whip was his brush and James's blood and back his paint and canvas. He thoroughly enjoyed the game and soon was lost in his own amusement as he tore away at James's back repeatedly. The cruel beating lasted several minutes, after which James was passed out, his back horribly scarred and completely stained a glistening dark red. His breathing was harsh and raspy, coming in short stuttering gasps as his unconscious body quivered violently.

Garrison stopped abruptly, suddenly aware of what he was doing. He realized that he might have gone too far in his excitement and had accidentally killed him. He quickly checked for a pulse and sighed in hidden relief when he felt one. As slow and laborious as it was, it was still there. As long as the idiot didn't die on him before he could get some sort of healing potion in or on him, he should be all right with Noknor.

"Take this infidel dog to the dungeon! I'll take care of him there!" he barked his orders, panting and flexing his tired arm as he wiped his sweaty brow. As his five soldiers unshackled James and carefully carried him away, Garrison suddenly remembered Li. In all the commotion, he had totally forgotten about her. He turned back to face her and flinched harshly at what he saw.

Li had stopped crying and screaming. Her cheeks were sprayed with droplets of red as she stood behind the bars like a statue, her eyes churning with fire and her hands clutched in fists at her side so tightly that they were stark white. Her lips were curled tightly over her grinding teeth and her face was set in the hardest look Garrison had ever seen on anyone. Her frozen, piercing stare burned straight into his very soul and chilled him to the bone. He shivered as he thought how lucky he was that those iron bars were between them and suddenly wished Noknor had instead given the assignment to a goblin.

He tried his best to conceal his fright, but wasn't very successful at all as he could only stutter "Wuh-wuh-what are you looking at, you little whore? I-I-I-I told you it was just business."

A low, audible growl sounded in the back of Li's throat and, out of reflex, Garrison lashed out with his whip and held up his other arm to shield himself as if he expected her to tear right through the bars. Li stood her ground, not even flinching as the tip of the whip whizzed swiftly for her face. The instant that first thorn stained with the blood of her lover touched her tear moistened cheek, the whole whip was reduced to dust in Garrison's hand. His jaw dropped to the floor as he gawked at the gray dirt that flittered about slowly through the air and took one more look at Li. There was absolutely no mark on her fair cheek and she had not moved in the slightest. However, her face had hardened and her growl grew sharper and more audible with each second. Seeing this, an ashen-faced Garrison fled the room as quickly as he could carry himself, clumsily stumbling over a chair in his haste.

Li stood as still as a statue, not moving, not speaking. It was even hard to tell if she were even breathing or blinking. She just stood and growled as the bars changed back into a brick wall and closed off the blood splattered room. Elizabeth was more afraid than ever before and she had no idea what to say or do, or even if she should do anything at all.

She finally managed to croak out a very feeble "Luh-Li? Are . . . are you all right?"

As if to answer in the negative, Li roared in fury and punched the wall so hard that it was left cracked and blood stained. The princess screeched loudly and jumped back several paces in fright. Li turned to face her, her boiling eyes and frozen sneer pinning Elizabeth in her spot while her bruised and slashed knuckles dripped splashes of blood onto the floor. There was so much venom in her voice that the princess cringed away when Li hissed in a low, almost whispered voice "When I get my hands on his throat, Noknor's wraith will be a tickle compared to mine! He's going to use his last thought to wish he had never crossssssssed me!"

Li then headed for her bed, threw herself down, and buried her face into her pillow. And then she wept as she hadn't wept in a year.

CHAPTER XXIX

As Julie entered her massive dining hall, Kain, whom was sitting at the opposite end of the extremely long and extravagant dining table, stood and bowed. She returned the gesture with a sweet smile and curtsy as she casually looked around at the empty spaces.

"Where are the other guests?" she asked nonchalantly, taking her seat and allowing Sarah to push her forward slightly. Julie thanked her and replied "That will be all, Sarah."

"Yes, Miss Julie." the servant bowed and quietly exited the room, leaving the two alone.

"Alas, my sister grew ill and my troops are in bed snoring their heads off." Kain answered her. "Quite odd, really. Very odd, indeed."

She sensed that he was trying to test her, so to try and throw him off she giggled airily then said "Well, come and sit closer to me, if you will. No one is around and I would wish to speak with my new guest without shouting."

Kain rose up quickly, carried his plate and goblet to the seat next to Julie, and blushed as he replied "I do apologize. And I want to apologize for the earlier rudeness of my troops. They are usually very well mannered gentlemen. Not at all like they were. I have no idea—"

"Think nothing of it." she said, throwing back her head and swallowing a bit of wine. She continued "Perhaps they were just exhausted from their long trek through the swamp. There are strange things in the air of the swamp that can make people act even stranger. A good sleep will do them well, I assure you. As it will your sister."

"I certainly hope so." he replied solemnly, taking a sip from his goblet. "May I be so bold as to inquire why such a lovely lady would care to live in such a place?"

"My family has lived here for many generations. Why, it's been said that we've been here longer than the swamp itself." she replied, giggling airily. Kain gave a hollow chuckle, hoping it didn't sound as such. Julie blushed slightly and continued "And it's not so bad when you've lived here all your life. It's very secure so I don't have to worry about raiders and the like. But on that same token, we also don't get many visitors here, so tell me what's a handsome man such as yourself doing this deep in Dismal Swamp?"

"I'm looking for Mystic Cavern." he said rather bluntly.

"Mystic Cavern?" she said, slightly taken aback. That was not really quite the response she had expected from an Arcainian Knight. "Why, whatever would you need to be in search of that place?"

"I'm looking for someone." Kain answered simply. He still wasn't sure what was going on and until he found out exactly, he wasn't about to trust anyone. If all of it was some grand scheme concocted by Noknor then he sure didn't want to divulge too much information to the woman. He was afraid he had said too much already.

"I see." she murmured slowly. "Is that your quest?"

"Part of it, yes."

Julie stared at him, her grin hiding her frown. She knew he was holding back on her, and that was both good and bad. It was good because it meant he wasn't coming under the effects of the curse as even the most shy of gentlemen would have babbled mindlessly about himself if that were the case. It also meant that if he wasn't affected, he might also be the one to break the curse and Julie was giddy with excitement about that. However, it was bad because if he was hiding anything it was most likely bad. But he was an Arcainian Knight, and the Grand General at that! Could he really be that bad? She finally decided that good or bad, whatever he was hiding wouldn't matter if he could free her from the curse.

"Well, I do hope that you find whoever you are looking for." she smiled brightly as she daintily began to cut her steak. "It would be such a shame to see such a handsome man as yourself fail in your quest."

"You flatter me with your words, fairest lady."

"As do you, gentle sir." she grinned seductively, slowly tracing her lush lips with her tongue. She slowly extended her hand and placed it onto his as she nudged his leg ever so lightly with her foot. "It has been such a long time since I have had male company. Far too long."

Julie drew herself up and closer to her guest, leaning toward him. Kain felt himself flush and tried to fight it away. The woman was being so forward and he was very attracted to her. With the combination, he found himself wanting nothing more than to touch his lips to hers, to be wrapped with her. But at the same time these feelings flooded his thinking she equally repelled him. He couldn't place it and it wasn't really tangible, but she repulsed him as she drew closer to locking lips with him. He wanted nothing more, but yet didn't want it at all.

Just as she was about to embrace him, he pulled back slightly and gasped "No, wait!" Julie hesitated and he continued as best he could. "We shouldn't . . . ah, what I mean to say, pardon me my lady, but this doesn't, uhm, seem appropriate. We shouldn't, really."

"We should! We must!" she moaned and wrapped her arms around the knight before he knew it had happened. He pulled back once more out of instinct and the momentum caused him to topple out of his chair and land flat onto his back. Julie leapt from her seat and straddled Kain before he could stop her, pinned him down, and drew her face close to his. With her lips mere inches from his, he could feel her sweet breath on his cheeks as she groaned "Take me! No one's around and I want you as my own so badly! Love me, Kain! Look into my eyes and love me! Kiss my hungry lips!"

Kain puckered his lips but just didn't have it in him. He wondered what in the hell was wrong with him, turning down such a voluptuous woman. He wanted to fight the force that held him back, but couldn't stop from blurting out "No!"

Julie stopped an inch from his lips and quivered slightly as she sat straight up. She glared at him with shocked eyes, as if he had just slapped her. Kain just lay there, trying to figure out what in the world was going on while Julie sat atop him with her lip twitching as if torn between laughing and crying in sheer joy. Finally, she jumped to her feet and cried out "You have refused me and resisted my enchantments! That means that it's true! It's really true!"

"So you are in league with Noknor!" Kain roared, leaping back to his feet as well.

"Who?" Julie asked, her tone confused. She quickly shook it off and leapt into Kain's arms before he could react and cried out joyfully "It doesn't matter, you're the one! The one to break the curse! Oh, thank the fates!"

Kain quickly shoved her away and snatched up a steak knife from the table so that he could defend himself when the witch tried to attack. It was pretty lame as far as weapons went, even he had to admit that much, but there wasn't much else around. So, he tried to look as menacing as he possibly could as he roared "So, that's why my men acted so strangely towards you! They were under your spell! And their passing out and my sister's illness! That was all from your workings too, wasn't it!"

"Guilty as charged." Julie replied, doing her best to fight back the giggles that were partly from overjoyment and partly from Kain looking so ridiculous and adorable. "If you'll just give me a chance to—"

"Save your blasted excuses!" he growled slashing the air in fury. "I know full well what all this is about! I don't know where Noknor managed to get you, but—"

"Who is this Noknor?" Julie charged, looking him dead in the eyes. It was a look that said she was telling the truth and really didn't know, but Kain wasn't about to take any chances. Julie huffed blandly and said "Look, I have no idea what you're talking about! All I know is that I need help, your help, in breaking a horrible curse that was placed on me." She started to glide to him slowly. "Please—"

"Stay back!" he poked the air viciously.

Julie stopped, put her hands up in a defensive manner, and continued "Please believe me. I know that you have no reason to, what with all I've done so far, but I had no other choice in the matter. I had to be certain that you were the one. Now that I know, I need your help. Please, Sir Viccon."

Kain held his ground, debating in his head what to do. He honestly sensed that her word was golden about everything she had told him and if it had all been a trap concocted by Noknor, Kain felt sure it would have been sprung the instant he had figured it out. He thought heavily but he finally snorted audibly and tossed the knife back onto the table. It clanged loudly on the plate and echoed in the still, silent air. He sighed lowly and replied "What were you saying about a curse?"

Julie giggled in glee, unable to believe it was all really happening and not just a dream, and gave a great sigh of relief as she replied in a shaky voice "Come with me to my study chambers and I'll explain everything to you in full."

Kain was still reluctant to follow the beauty until she grabbed his arm gently, looked deep into his dark eyes, and sweetly murmured "Please, you have my word that I won't try to trick or harm you." She paused then added "Anymore."

He followed her to the main hall where he and his friends had entered only hours before. The candles on the chandelier had all been extinguished and the only light came from a few scattered candles and torches. Kain scratched his head, wondering how they had managed the feat and if they did it every night. If so, it must be a sight to see.

The pair went towards a large door set between two large candelabras with candles that burned brilliantly and Julie ushered him into the pitch-black room. Kain started to walk forward when Julie tugged him slightly and snapped her fingers. Instantly, a row of torches lit in a domino effect up a winding staircase. If she hadn't stopped him, he would have tumbled headlong into the stone steps and bashed his face. He gulped at the embarrassing thought as he climbed upwards and entered a long hallway with many more doors. Candles in lanterns suspended from the ceiling illuminated their way while great paintings of different people hung majestically on the walls. Kain turned around to inquire what room to which Julie simply pointed down the hall to convey that it was far down. She brushed past him, her body rubbing against his in such a way as to cause the knight to blush and murmur an incoherent apology.

As they strolled down the hall together, a certain painting caught Kain's eye. It pictured a woman sitting in a beautiful golden chair and a tall, thin man standing behind her with his hands fondly on her shoulders. What got his attention was the fact that the woman was obviously Julie. The man also reminded him of someone, but the name escaped him. He had a long brown beard and somewhat long hair of the same color streaked with gray. His face, particularly his eyes, looked somewhat familiar, but he couldn't place it. He quickly cast it off and wondered aloud who he was, thinking he had been Julie's late husband or perhaps father.

Julie had stopped in front of the door directly across from the painting when she heard Kain and paused to explain to him "That is my grandmother and grandfather. Both were very skilled in the magickal arts. They were my teachers and taught me everything that I know."

"That's your grandmother!" he gasped, quite taken aback. "You look so much like her, I thought it was you! It's an amazing similarity!"

"Yes, it is." she replied softly. She unlocked the door and relocked it with a silver key after their entry. "My younger brother looks, or looked at the time, just like my grandfather. Grandfather was going to teach him about wizardry, but he left at thirteen, I believe, in search of adventure. I haven't heard from him since and don't know what's become of him."

Kain gave her a gentle smile and went over to sit on one of the two identical large plush chairs in front of Julie's desk. Julie plopped down in the twin next to him as she let out a dejected sigh. Kain looked her over and had a deep urge to put his arm around her shoulders, but fought it back. He didn't want his emotions to overcome him and cloud his thinking. He had to keep a clear head and a strong will if he hoped to help the beauty next to him. He wanted to say something to lift her up, but couldn't think of a single thing. All he could manage was a bland "So, how can I help you?"

Julie looked at him and frowned. "I suppose the best thing to do would be to tell you how the curse was placed on me. It's a bit of a long story, though."

"Take your time." He gave her hand a gentle squeeze and grinned reassuringly. "My ear is no rush."

Julie gave him a smile that melted his heart and murmured a thank you in a small voice. She looked away and sighed "It started about five years ago. No, that's not really true. It actually started long ago, when Grandfather was just a boy. Daniel Gregor was his best friend, and they were in school in Kuberica together. But as they grew older, they began to drift apart, as such is often the case. But I think in this case it was more from the rivalry that sparked between them when they became teens than just the normal drifting. Both were great wizards, each taught by their respective fathers. Grandfather, however, was obviously better. He was a very hard worker and studied diligently whiles Gregor was as lazy as could be.

"That did make them rivals, there is no doubt, but it was Grandmother that fueled the flames of rivalry into an inferno. Both were in love with her and fought to outdo each other as they wooed for her affections. But it was Grandfather she really loved and blatantly turned down Gregor's passion for her. Gregor was so overcome with a jealous rage that he challenged Grandfather to a Wizard's Duel. They fought, but it was Grandfather who came out on top and humiliated Gregor instead of killing him. Gregor swore revenge before disappearing."

Julie paused a moment with her face set in a deep frown and just sat silently beside Kain. He was about to say something to pull her away from her thoughts when she continued slowly. "Time passed and Grandfather and Grandmother married and bore my father. He grew up and married my mother, a Kuberican woman. They died shortly after my brother was born. I was three at the time. We, that is my brother and I, stayed in this castle under the care of my grandparents, helping them run the family business. I grew to look like Grandmother and she taught me the ways of the enchantress. My brother grew to look like Grandfather and had started receiving lessons on wizardry and on how to run the business when he left.

"Then one day, Gregor paid Grandfather a visit under the guise that he was sorry for all the things he had said and done all those years ago. He wanted to reconcile their friendship and tried to convince Grandfather to give him my hand in marriage, telling him that they would be family rather than just friends that way. It's my guess that he still wanted Grandmother and since I looked just like her, he thought he would be able to marry the woman he had lost so long before. I didn't want to marry him at all and expressed that to my grandparents. Grandfather finally told him that he was more than willing to reconcile but wouldn't give him my hand if I didn't want it. Gregor left the castle in a rage, ranting and raving that Grandfather would rue the day that he had crossed him. About a month later Grandfather came down with a serious, and fatal, illness. Grandmother followed a month later, dying of a broken heart."

She began to sniffle audibly as she fought to control her tears. Kain moved to wrap his arm around her and began to draw her close, but she gently pulled away and wiped her eyes solemnly. "I'm all right, I just needed a second. After I laid Grandmother next to Grandfather, Gregor came back for another visit. He expressed his condolences and then flat out asked me to marry him. Of course I refused.

"He just couldn't take no for an answer. He cursed me violently, calling me all other sorts of terrible names. He told me all wuh-wuh-wuh-witches should be buh-buh-buh-burned!" she stammered, tears falling freely down her rosy cheeks. Kain was quick to dab away the drops as he did his best to comfort her and help her regain control until she could continue.

"He shot a large fireball at me that was intended to kill me. I dodged and threw a bolt back at him in defense that caught him square in the stomach. I must have hit him pretty hard, because he was coughing up blood as he stumbled trying to get back up to his feet. When he finally did, his eyes were glowing with a blood-red light and his voice was eerie and hollow as he said 'I place a curse on you that your enchanting beauty will be your greatest enemy. All those men that gaze upon you or hear you voice will fall obsessively in love with you! They will all want to kiss you, but your kiss will bring only death to them. You shall never have any man!'

"The curse is real and my kiss is deadly. There have been a few that kissed me and were reduced to burning ash. And, as you can see by your troops, I speak the truth about all men falling obsessively in love with me."

"So, where do I fit into this?" Kain asked slowly.

"I'll get to that soon enough. Gregor died from his wounds and I burned his vile body and spread the ashes throughout the swamp. Then, after much studying I was able to find out exactly what the curse was and how to end it."

"Is this where I fit in?"

"It is set to end when 'the essence of a virtuous heart flows freely over the plagued heart to cleanse it of its troubles'." she sighed dully and frowned.

"So, I have to smear my blood on you?" Kain replied, raising an eyebrow. Then, in a low voice, he remarked "Why couldn't it just be solved with a simple kiss like usual?"

"Actually, I'm pretty sure it can be." she told him with a hint of a giggle. "Many of these curse cures are riddles and have double meanings. The unfortunate thing is that if I'm wrong about you, and you do kiss me . . . well, you will join the ranks of those others that have tried in the past."

"Hmmmmm. Just how virtuous is virtuous in this case?" he asked with a boyish grin, making her giggle. "Maybe the blood thing isn't a bad idea."

Julie put a hand to her mouth to cover her laugh as she gave his hand a gentle squeeze. Her mood lifting, she continued "Anyway, using the book, I was able to come up with three different tests that would tell me who this virtuous heart is."

Kain frowned and stared off with his hand gently rubbing his chin as he thought about all that he was told. Finally, he looked back at Julie and murmured "Well, I do hope that I can help you. What are these three tests?"

"I can't tell you. You must do them without knowing or you'd definitely fail them." she answered, rising from her spot and stretching her limbs. She directed his attention to a large painting of herself hanging over her bed. "Would you mind removing that picture for me? There's a paper I need hidden behind it and it's kind of heavy. It lists the tests for me."

Kain did as told and casually watched as she rummaged through a large hole in the stonework with many different papers. She found a small blue sheet with queer lettering all over it and asked him to replace the painting. Julie pretended to read the blue sheet while Kain studied the painting. Suddenly, she said "This is kind of hard to make out without my glasses. Could you read this line for me?"

"Huh? Oh, yes. Of course." he replied, looking over her shoulder. "It says 'if all three trials he overcomes, a virtuous heart he is'."

"Thank you." she smiled brightly, instantly overcome with rapture and joy as her heart melted in her chest. She absolutely couldn't believe it was all really happening, that it was all finally coming true! She slowly folded up the sheet and tossed it away as she prepared herself for the moment of truth.

As Kain examined the painting of the enchantress closer, the signature in the bottom right hand side happened to catch his eye. It read 'Julie Amora Boniva by Julie A. Boniva'. A sudden realization hit him and he whirled around to snap excitedly "Your family name is Boniva!"

"Yes . . . it is." she said slowly, confused at the question. Kain rushed to the door and tried to open it without success. Julie walked over and extended the silver key as she said "You need this. Why did you ask that?"

"Because, I believe . . ." Kain unlocked and threw open the door to take a closer look at the painting. He pointed to Julie's grandfather for emphasis as he finished "Raphael is your younger brother!"

"How . . . how do you . . . I mean, you know Raphael?" Julie stammered, eyes wide and mouth agape. "How do you—"

"Raphael Boniva is my Second General. He's—"

"The young man in the infirmary!" she finished for him as she too realized as well. Her long lost brother right there in her castle! She just couldn't believe it. Everything was rushing by her in a mad wave as she struggled to comprehend it all and she felt her entire body grow numb and weak. In a fit of passion and yearning that she couldn't hold back, she gazed into the knight's eyes and cried out "Kiss me! Please, kiss me!"

"What?" he gasped, startled by her words.

"Just do it!" she moaned desperately and threw her arms around his shoulders.

"But—" he tried to say something to her, but his mind went blank. He had no idea what was going on and wondered if it were the first of the three tests. He didn't know what to make of it or what he should do.

"DO IT!" she bellowed madly, pulling him to her. Without giving it a second thought, Kain grabbed her around her waist and planted his lips onto hers.

A great spark shot forth as their lips touched and a thunderous crack filled the quiet air. A great vibrating sound began to rumble through the castle as the splattering rain that had been falling since Kain and the others had entered the grove stopped and the black clouds parted to allow a beautiful star-studded sky to peer down. There was a flash of bright white light outside the building and a golden beam blasted down from the heavens to sweep over the grove. As it passed by, the entire castle seemed to change. What used to look dark and decrepit was brought back to its former splendor. The bricks faded from dirt-ridden gray to sparkling white, the roof tiles went from rotting black to lustrous blue, and the sinister statues cleaned and became the beautiful works of art they were. The whole castle looked as glorious and vibrant as if it had just been erected that day.

Back inside Julie's study chamber, the pair parted lips, though they still held each other tightly. Julie looked Kain over and gasped "You did it! You wonderful man, you did it! You broke the curse! Oh, thank you! I am in your debt forever, Kain Viccon!"

"I'd say the debt canceled itself out when you let me kiss such a lovely woman." Kain grinned broadly.

"Come on." Julie laughed, drawing Kain away with her. "I want to see my brother."

As they rushed together hand in hand through the elaborate hallways, Kain inquired "So what happened to those three tests?"

"Do you think I'd let you kiss me if you hadn't passed them all? You, Kain Viccon are truly a virtuous man."

"You're pretty wonderful, yourself." he chuckled. "But I don't remember any of them. What were—"

"The first," Julie explained, cutting him off excitedly as they rushed to the infirmary "was at dinner. I tried to seduce you and make you kiss me. Had you given in to me in the slightest all would have been lost. The second was the painting. While it looks normal enough, it carries a curse of sorts. To those affected by it, it is so heavy it would take at least three strong men to lift it off its wall peg. Also, the frame is extremely sharp and will cut a normal person's hands, making them bleed profusely. However, no lacerations will ever be found."

"How lovely." Kain grimaced mildly. "And the third?"

"That note that I took from the wall. It's written in a special language I made up especially for the test. No one can read it except for a virtuous heart. To him, it appears to be their native tongue. Of course, had I been wrong about you, your body would be nothing but a pile of ashes right now." she smiled and giggled airily.

"Oh, that's such a nice thought!" he laughed, trying to imagine himself reducing to a pile of dust. He didn't like the picture he saw and quickly shook it out of his head. "Well, at least it's all over for you. You don't have to worry about the curse anymore."

"All because of you." she sighed happily, throwing open a set of double doors.

Sarah stood right in front of them, her neutral face set in about as an excited look Kain figured she could muster. She instantly grabbed her mistress's arm and began to drag her through the darkened room past recuperation beds as she whispered "Miss Julie, you will never believe who is here!"

"My brother, Raphael!" Julie squeaked happily as they stopped beside a bed towards the back of the room. In it lay a peacefully sleeping Raphael Boniva, the blisters and purple completely gone from his face. Julie looked at him and gently reached out to rub his cheek as she thought how much he had changed, yet still looked like the little boy who used to chase her around the castle and play games with her in the garden. She noticed that besides the long beard and hair, he had grown to look just like Grandfather. "Kain told me that he was here. He's part of the Arcainian Army now!"

Sarah looked past Julie's shoulder at Kain and her smile grew wider still. She murmured happily into her friend's ear "So, Master Kain has finally brought an end to your plague?"

"Yes! It's over! It's all finally over!" Julie squeaked, moving to wipe a tear away from eye. Still gazing over her brother, taking in all of the features that changed over the years and all of the ones that had not, she murmured "Kain Viccon, you have done so much for me. You saved me from a terrible curse and have reunited me with my estranged brother after so long. I feel I owe you something in return." She paused and sighed deeply as she looked at her savior. "I want to help you with your quest. I know that it's important for you to get into Mystic Cavern and I can conjure up a portal leading directly into it. I could even do it right now, if you would like."

"Yes, I'd really appreciate that." Kain murmured, a warm smile touching his lips. "Thank you."

"We must be careful, though." Julie warned solemnly, also smiling. She reached out and grasped his hand gently, wondering how she could fall in love with a man she had only met a few hours before. "Many dangerous things live inside of it. But I know how to get around most of them, so we should be all right. If you go and get ready, I'll be ready and waiting for you in the main hallway."

Kain rushed out of the infirmary and to his room on the third level. Forgetting all about his sleeping friends, he threw open the door and although it banged loudly against the wall, neither of them even stirred. They just snored away in their beds while Kain slipped into his uniform and armor all the while thinking that Julie must have hit them with a pretty powerful spell.

He then checked on his sister. Nancy had kicked off her covers onto the floor and was shivering in her bed. She seemed to be over her sick stomach and that made Kain feel much better. He covered her up once more and kissed her cheek softly. Nancy sighed blissfully in her sleep.

"I'll be back soon, pup." Kain whispered into her ear as he slipped out as quietly as he had entered.

Julie was waiting for him in the grand hall just as she said she would. She wore a long-sleeve, light green satin gown that stretched elegantly to her feet with a dark green leather vest. Her golden hair was tied back and she wore a green headband with a large emerald surrounded by small diamonds on her forehead. Draped over her shoulders was a short cloak the same color as the vest and she held a long wooden staff. Kain suddenly felt his feelings starting to stir and wanted to comment how lovely she looked, but bit his tongue. Now was not the time for that sort of thing, not when he had a mission to accomplish.

"Are you ready?" Julie asked, her full lips set in a bright smile.

"As ready as I can be." Kain replied excitedly.

Julie put her index fingers together and her thumbs together so that a triangle of space was formed between her hands. As she concentrated, a pale blue light appeared in the triangle of space. The blue triangle suddenly shot forth and grew wider and taller as it traveled until it had grown large enough to fit two people on horseback comfortably.

"Hurry." Julie urged. "The portal won't last very long."

* * *

Garrison babbled mindlessly, clearly quite shaken up over the whole disastrous ordeal. It was hard to understand a word that spewed out of his mouth as it was all coming out so fast and jumbled. Noknor managed to pick out a few coherent phrases from his pleas of mercy to put the picture together himself, and it sure wasn't a work of art. From what Garrison squealed about, it was what Noknor had dreaded. The Chinese woman's will was much more powerful than he had anticipated. Even after witnessing the brutal attack, his power had no affect on her. She could kill him if she so wanted and he wouldn't be able to stop her. Thanks to Garrison's bumbling, that was probably all she wanted to do. And with the buffoonery that masqueraded as soldiers in his castle, it probably wouldn't be all that hard for her to get to him.

'No, that won't do. Won't do at all!' Noknor thought as he grimaced slightly and put his hand to his throat to rub gently. In his thoughts, he was completely oblivious to his Dark General still whimpering at his feet like a wretched dog. 'How can she be so powerful?'

Perhaps this power had no connection to her will at all, he offered to himself. No, but then where could it stem from? She wasn't schooled in magick. It had to be her will! And if it was, if it formed the shell around her, that shell must at least be straining after all she had been put through. She would crack soon enough. It might take seeing her lover's arms ripped off, but she would be crushed. The Chinese woman, no matter how powerful she was, was not as powerful as a god. She would cower before him. Noknor grinned behind his anger at the vision of that blasted woman crumbling at his feet just before he ripped her head clean off her body. He'd definitely make sure to have his way with her first, though. The vicious fantasies excited him and he had to clear his head quickly.

'Not yet, not yet.' he scolded himself silently.

The two lovers would die by his hand soon enough, but he had to have Viccon first. He wanted the boy to watch his oh-so beloved cousin's trip to hell as he tormented and tortured her uncontrollably. He wanted to feed on Viccon's pain and suffering, gorge himself on the young knight's screams of agony before sending him broken and mutilated to his pathetic parents. But, in order to accomplish that, he required certain things such as Raptor's living until Viccon and his sister reached the castle. Noknor cocked a brow at Garrison, who was still babbling madly for forgiveness and mercy, and thought for a brief moment before scowling hideously.

"Shut up, you stupid twit!" Noknor roared, backhanding Garrison across his face. The Dark General was flung back hard by the force of the blow, crashing into a table and falling roughly to the floor. As he slowly picked himself up, his cheek already red and starting to swell, he was cut off into dead silence. Noknor snatched out, grabbed him by his collar, and hoisted him to his feet. Then, with a fierce shove, he pushed Garrison into a bone chair. "Now listen closely, you little grunt! To what extent was Mr. Raptor injured?"

"Huh-huh-he's hurt pretty badly." Garrison quivered, gingerly rubbing his face. "He can't move or talk much, or at least he didn't say anything to me. And—"

"Gee, I wonder why that is, you dope!" Noknor snapped savagely. "I mean, all you did was beat the sorry bastard to the brink of death! I can't imagine why he wouldn't want to talk to you!" He threw himself back into his grisly throne and snorted air through his nostrils. "Did that salve work?"

"Yuh-yuh-yuh-yes sire." he gulped audibly. "He's unconscious again last I saw, but I'm pretty sure he'll live."

"No thanks to you, you simple-minded idiot!" the warlock snarled, raising his hand to slap the man again. Garrison cringed, but Noknor hesitated and dropped his arm slowly. The Dark General uttered a low sigh of relief as his master's red eyes narrowed to slits. "But, he'll live and that's what's important." He rubbed his hands roughly together and licked his lips.

In a flash, Noknor's powerful hand swiped out and clutched Garrison by the collar once again. He pulled him roughly to his face, meeting eye to red eye with his general as he hissed viciously "I ought to gut you for what you did! I specifically told you five lashes! And you haul off and just about kill him!"

"I'm sorry!" Garrison squealed, squirming in Noknor's icy steel grip. "Oh Goddess, I'm sorry!"

"Hmph! The Goddess can't help you now! You belong to ME!" he snorted in disgust and threw him back down hard. Garrison landed squarely in his chair and it teetered violently, threatening to collapse backward with him in it. He managed to steady it and gently set it back down on all four legs as he cowered before Noknor's wraith, looking as if he would heave all over his shoes at any moment. The warlock slowly reached into his pocket and drew out an all too familiar bronze key. Garrison yelped when he saw it and turned a ghastly pale as his chair toppled backwards. Noknor couldn't help but chuckle morbidly at his reaction.

"It's been too long since my torture chamber has had a guest." Noknor grinned, turning the key over in his hands. He didn't think a man's face could lose any more blood, but he was dead wrong. Garrison looked downright ill. Noknor tossed him the key, which fumbled about in his nervous hands. "I want you to prepare a few for me. One for the vice, one for the wheel, one for the needle king, and one for the acid pit."

"Yuh-yuh-yuh-yuh-yes, sire! Right away, sire!" Garrison yelped quickly, gripping the key tightly as he jumped off the floor. "I'll get right on it, sire!"

"See that you do. Oh, and Garrison?" Noknor murmured lowly, his voice frozen and menacing as his stare burned a hole straight into the general's soul. "You have one chance. Just one more. Any more screw-ups and I shall be promoting a new Dark General. And there won't be enough of the old one to fill a spoon!"

Garrison gulped, a large lump of bile clogging his throat as his knuckles went stark white from his death grip on the key. He finally nodded vigorously, more from pure dread than loyal obedience. Noknor raised his brows and snorted, a deadly signal for Garrison to hastily remove himself lest he use up his final chance. The Dark General fled the scene as quickly as possible, tripping over the chair in the process.

With Garrison gone, Noknor sat back in his gory throne and sighed dully. He closed his eyes and laced his fingers behind his head as he ran his tongue over his small fangs. He found his mind once again drawn to Viccon's sister, and he thought how wonderful it would be to have her in his clutches. Even when he tortured and slaughtered her brother and cousin, Noknor knew that he would surely spare the young Viccon girl. He couldn't throw away a fresh, young talent like hers without first trying to utilize it. She was as skillful as she was beautiful and she was so young and naive that her spirit could easily be twisted to his liking. It pleased him greatly to think that she would one day very soon make a nice additive to his forces. She would replace Garrison as his new Dark General after the things he would teach her, the power he would show her. Why, he could make her very powerful, indeed! And so much more. Together, they would be unstoppable. They'd rule the Old World together.

'How ironic!' Noknor thought to himself with a chuckle. The child of the great Richard Viccon and the sister of the rising Kain Viccon, an advocate of evil forces. The lover of the very man who had killed them both. It made him shiver violently to think about it.

It was definitely a great little thought, something he would most definitely fantasize on later. As for the moment, he had more pressing matters to deal with. He wanted to see for himself what Garrison's handiwork had done and if the Chinese woman's shell had finally broken. He wanted to crush her just enough to hear her beg for mercy. Her slow, painful end would come later, of course.

"Who knows?" Noknor sighed lowly to himself, his grin fading away as his eyes opened slowly. "I may just have that innocent girl kill them both. It would be a fine sight, and a good way to start her off as my wife."

"Prepare my dinner!" he called into the air. "And set two places for tonight."

* * *

"James?" Li whispered with a shaky voice as she dabbed his burning forehead with a damp cloth. "James, can you hear me?"

An unconscious James Raptor lay facedown on a cot deep in the dungeon. His bright red, raw back glittered in the flickering torchlight from the silvery slime Noknor had ordered to be put on him. His breathing was harsh and raspy, making him sound more like a slobbering troll than the man she loved. She put two fingers gently against his neck and sighed dejectedly at what she felt. His pulse was still irregular, drastically so. She touched his forehead and finding him burning with fever, took the cool washcloth from the earthenware bowl full of water and wiped his brow and head gingerly.

"Don't you dare die on me, James Elaxander Raptor!" she suddenly snapped in a wavy voice, feeling tears welling up in her eyes. "Do you hear me! Don't you dare die on me! I didn't live three long years without you just to become a widow all over again!" She fought the tears as best as she could but just didn't have the strength left. She had been driven to the breaking point, and her eyes exploded as waterfalls fell freely from them, etching clean lines down her dusty cheeks. She sobbed as she leaned close and whispered into his ear "Please don't die! Please!"

All of a sudden, she heard the familiar click of a key turning in the lock and she instantly stopped the flow of tears with great effort. She did not look at them when they entered nor acknowledged them when they spoke. She just squeezed James's limp hand tighter and wiped away her tears. She kissed his cheek tenderly and looked straight into his agonized face.

"I said come on!" the Dark Knight growled, advancing towards her. She snapped her head swiftly in his direction and snarled lowly. One look at her dangerous glare was enough to halt the man in his tracks and even take a step back. "Lord Noknor wishes your company for dinner."

Li scowled darkly and turned her attention back onto her fallen love. As she once again wiped his brow with the washcloth, she murmured "I'm not leaving his side."

"It's not like you have a choice in the matter." he replied, fumbling with something behind her back. "What Lord Noknor wishes is to be done."

Li turned back around to give a smart retort but instead saw a sharp needle speeding towards her. As it pricked her arm, she snarled savagely and leapt at the unfortunate man. He feebly threw his arms up in a vain attempt to defend himself, but was powerless against the onslaught. He took her knee square in the chest and was sent flying back. Without even slowing, she was instantly upon him, lashing out with her fists repeatedly, her blows connecting with solid explosions as the back of his head cracked against stone. She spun on her heels when the sound of chains hit her ears and saw three more Dark Knights enter the cell with shackles. She leapt off the man she had just beaten to death and roared in fury as she prepared to attack them all. She suddenly became very dizzy and began to swoon as everything became a blur. She swore violently as she stepped forward and fell into darkness.

* * *

"I trust you are comfortable, my dear." Noknor said as pleasantly as if he were about to enjoy a simple cup of tea with his dinner guest.

"Oh, I'm so very comfortable!" Li hissed dryly. "Would you quit doping me up! It's really starting to get on my nerves!"

"I do apologize." he chuckled briefly, shaking his wine glass in his hand before taking a long sip. "However, it's for your own safety. I just can't trust you to come peacefully with my soldiers. After all, you did just kill one of them."

"He deserved it just for associating with you!" Li snorted harshly in contempt.

The two of them sat at a large round table with a plate of scrumptious food and a glass of fine wine before them both. While Noknor had dug in heartily, shoveling forkfuls of food into his mouth, Li had yet to touch her own plate or even her wine. She sat in her chair, her ankles shackled together tightly with rusty chains and her wrists tied together with leather straps. Five Dark Knights stood directly behind her, ready to spring if necessary. Li looked back at them and frowned before examining her restraints, tugging her wrists apart to test the leather straps. They were pretty strong, that was for sure.

"No matter what you may think," she murmured, still testing the straps under the table. "I won't kill you. That's going to be my cousin's job."

Noknor grinned broadly at the thought as he snatched up his salad fork and gestured to the guards, ordering them to leave them alone.

"That doesn't mean, however," she finished coldly, "that I won't rip your arms out of socket the first chance I get."

His grin broadened as a low chuckle escaped the back of his throat. His guards paused slightly, hesitation settling in behind their masks. Noknor glanced at them and raised an eyebrow, a dangerous warning to them. They took notice and quickly hustled out of the room one by one, closing the door behind them with a shattering boom. Li followed them out with her eyes and turned back to face Noknor. One look at his queer grin sent shivers down her spine. It was a lecherous, evil gaze as if he were sizing her up and undressing her with his eyes. She felt like gagging at the disgusting thought.

"What are you looking at, you pig!" Li growled menacingly, all of her anger present in her fiery voice. Noknor gasped as if caught in a trap and turned away quickly as he took another sip of wine. "You look at me again and I'll knock your ugly head across the room!" And she was deadly serious.

Noknor flinched slightly as he gently stroked the warming amulet hanging around his neck as if for reassurance and muttered "You haven't touched your food, my dear."

"I'm not hungry!" she shot back harshly. "And I'd like to get back to my husband! What is all this about!"

"I just thought we should have a little chat, you and I." he replied, his eyes swinging back around to peer dead into hers as he clicked his long nails against the wooden table in a random, tuneless drone. "About the unpleasantness that has recently occurred."

"You mean about how you tried to have my husband killed!" she hissed, her teeth snapping.

"I did not try to have your husband killed, my dear." he replied smoothly, placing his hands under his chin. "But, yes. That incident. After all, what would I want to have to do with a dog like him? He is nothing to a god."

"A god!" Li shrieked out in shock, spittle spraying from her lips. "Is that what you think you are, Noknor? A god? You miserable worm! You're no god! And you will be stopped! Kain Viccon is coming and he's going to mop the floor with you, you arrogant—"

"Oh, he will try, my dear. He will try." he interrupted with a vile grin, licking his full, red lips with his sharply pointed tongue. "Just like the Shazadians tried."

Li stopped short in her rants and just stared at him with a loose jaw, her face showing signs of strain. She opened her mouth to speak, but no sound came out. Noknor's grin widened. Her shell was thinning, she would soon be at his mercy. And about time!

He sighed softly and sipped his wine casually before dabbing the corners of his mouth with a cloth. "But that is not the point of this company. I brought you here to share a fine dinner with a lovely young flower, as hard-nosed as you may be. I wanted you to know that I did not order my general to attack your lover."

"So, Garrison just picked up a whip and beat the living hell out of James on his own accord, huh?" she retorted. When Noknor simply nodded his head, she growled "I find that hard to believe, you lying troll! Then, why did you bring James here in the first place? What was your point to it other than to try to destroy him before my eyes!"

"I brought Mr. Raptor here so that the two of you could die together." he replied, his voice frosted with a hint of annoyance to it. "It is no mystery that once I have your cousin, you will no longer be of any use to me and that I will choose to kill you. I thought that perhaps it would be . . . sweet, I suppose is the word, for you two to die together."

"Oh, come on! Why—"

"Call it a momentary lapse in my good judgment." he stepped over her words roughly. "To be honest, I don't why I bothered to bring him here. I could have very well left him to rot away with the goblins. If you like, I could arrange for him to go back. He could die there for all I care!"

"You do and Kain won't have a chance at you!" she hissed violently, her voice low and frozen. "I will kill you myself!"

"I won't!" Noknor assured her with a slight gasp. "If no other reason, just because of the cost involved. Your lover can die here just as easily as he will there. And, from the looks of things, Death is standing right over him."

"James is a Knight of Auset!" Li snapped defensively, her voice cracking harshly and her moist eyes starting to drip. "Don't think that he's just going to roll over and die for you, or for Garrison, or for anybody!"

"Ha! A lot of good his little parlor tricks have done him so far!" he laughed, slamming his goblet down hard next to his plate, jostling everything on the table. "He'd be dead now if it weren't for me, you just remember that!" Li was thrown violently into silence by the statement. Noknor chuckled evilly, looking her dead in her misty eyes. "That's right, my dear. I saved his life. And if I have saved him, I can certainly whisk his life away just as easily."

Li was hit hard, much too hard for her to take in such a frail state of mind. She tried to fire back at him, but couldn't find any words, only broken phrases and harsh breaths. Her face melted from a harden scowl to that of a little girl desperately needing to sob her soul out. Her red eyes grew damp as her lips quivered violently. In a sudden instant, she jumped to her feet and slammed her hands onto the table, almost knocking it over as she shrieked "SHUT UP! JUST SHUT UP!"

Noknor yelped loudly and flinched away from her, but did his best to remain calm and remember that she was bound to the chair. She grabbed her wine glass and flung it away, shattering it onto the floor.

"Why don't you just shut up!" she slapped the table again as a low, muffled sob escaped her throat. With a heavy sniffling sigh, she threw herself back down into her chair and rubbed her face, trying to conceal the tears that had began to slip out. She finally glared at Noknor again and scowled bitterly at his smirk. She tried once again to say something to him, to put him in his place, but nothing came out. She stared into Noknor's face, her furious eyes wet and bloodshot, her fists clenched in rage, her heart ripping apart in her chest.

'I've done it! I've finally done it!' Noknor told himself, his eyes wide with excitement. He had finally broken her, beaten her down and shattered that diamond tough shell she had built around herself like nothing more than fine china. She was vulnerable now, exposed and powerless. And now it was time to test her.

Noknor subtly gritted his teeth and concentrated on Li's forehead. It pleased him when she flinched noticeably, however, he did not let it affect his blast as he focused with much more intensity, put more strength behind his slight attack. A bead of sweat formed on his forehead, a low wince escaped his throat. How his attack must be burning within her head, surely she was crying from all the power he threw at her. Soon, very soon, she would collapse from the searing torturous pain, and soon after her head would literally explode. But he wouldn't let it go that far. He didn't seek her death at the moment, just her pain. He would go only so far as to let her know who now held all of the cards. Just far enough to hear her beg him from down on her knees to stop, to release her from the torment. He laughed. He laughed at her pathetic pleas and concentrated further, hearing her cries echo in his ears. He laughed even more, pushed more, felt the surge out of his own mind and into the Chinese woman's. He tasted her pain, her agony, and he grew hungrier or more. He gorged himself on her torment, her—

"You have a problem there, Noknor?" Li asked hopefully, wishing a massive heart attack on him with a hint of a morbid grin on her face.

Noknor fell forward and almost crashed into the table but managed to hold himself with trembling arms. He had been so intent on his mind attack that he didn't realize just how much it had drained him. But surely his guest must be writhing on the floor, blood spewing from her eyes and ears after what he had done to her. With a guttural, exhausted chuckle, he looked at Li's chair and turned white.

Li sat in her chair, her flushed face set in a combination of curiosity and hopefulness, but still held the fragile look of a worn soul. Noknor read her demeanor and scowled darkly at her smugness. How dare she even think that he, the great god Noknor, would simply die at her feet! His fangs ground at the thought as he spewed icicles from his flaming red eyes. His powerful mind-blast had not a single affect on her! That protective force was still surrounding her, preventing him from doing anything to her! But how could that be? He had broken her spirits! He had torn her apart, made her weak and helpless! She should be on the floor now, flopping about like a fish out of water. But no! She sat in her chair, perfectly fine without a hint of injury. She sat in her chair smiling. She was smiling! After everything that had just happened, she was smiling because she thought that he had taken ill! He, a god! Obviously, he had broken nothing! Perhaps she had only a minute break of her will and had collected herself in time to repel his attacks. He had greatly underestimated her. She was much more powerful than he had thought, than he could have ever thought. And that enraged him. The thought that a woman, a simple, utterly weak woman could be such a threat to him attacked him as a god and for that she could not be allowed to live. But she was still ignorant of the power that had just saved her life. He could wait. He could wait for Viccon. After all, she would be sidetracked with her dying husband. She was of little concern to him.

"I am fine, my dear." he finally managed to say through his teeth. "Whatever made you think something was wrong?"

"Hummmmmm, I don't know! The fact that you looked like you were about to pass out, perhaps?"

"It's this appalling food!" he snapped, throwing down his napkin and fork in disgust as he swallowed more wine, partly for effect and partly to calm his still racing pulse. "I shall have the cook gutted for this!"

"Geez, calm down!" Li replied, not even trying to hold back her snickers. It felt good to actually squeak out pleasantly after what she had just gone through, losing her composure in such a way. "The food's not that bad. Certainly not worth someone dying over."

"You haven't touched your food." he told her with a heavy hint of matter-of-factness in his voice. He hastily added "And, by his death, I will be assured of a decent meal the next time. Fear of death is quite a powerful tool when controlling men. The more severe the death, the more of a hold you have on his comrades."

"You are a sick one!"

"I am a god, my dear. I demand respect. If it takes fear to gain that respect, what are a few lives more or less?"

"You are not a god, Noknor!" Li snapped back harshly. "What you are is a very sick, very disturbed—"

"I control the lives of my people." his voice boomed hard over her words. "I decide who lives and who dies. Their fates are in my hands. As is yours." He paused slightly and grinned broadly. "And your lover's." She frowned hideously at him, but she would not allow his words to affect her in the same way as they had earlier. "Is that not what a god is, my dear? One who sets the course of life and death?"

For a long while, there was a brutal silence that hovered in the room, spreading over them like a thick blanket. The only sound came from a lower, guttural grunt of satisfaction from Noknor and a dull sigh from Li.

"You are evil, Noknor." Li finally spoke, crumbling her napkin in her hand and tossing it onto her untouched plate of food. "There is no other word for it. You are an ugly, evil man. And you will get what you deserve."

"And what, pray tell, would that be?" he chuckled.

"My cousin's sword straight through that black, cold heart of yours." was her whispered answer.

"I am so afraid of your powerful cousin." he laughed, pouring every bit of sarcasm as he could behind his words. "I mean, after all, his father put up such a good fight!"

"From the way I heard it, his father kicked your ass!"

"But who's alive today?" he challenged.

Li gasped as she threw a hand to her mouth, her heart beginning to crumble away once again from the emotional blow. But she held on, she would not allow him to get the better of her. She drew in a deep, soothing breath, and exhaled in a wavy sigh. She wasn't going to lose it again. She knew that Noknor was intentionally provoking her, jabbing a stick of harsh words into her face. And she wouldn't give him the satisfaction of coming apart in front of him.

"Call your guards in, Noknor." she told him, her words soft and low but very strong and forceful. "I'm leaving this table and going back to my husband."

"As you wish, my dear." Noknor replied simply without even the hint of denying her. He had learned all he had needed from her. A large grin spread across his face as the snapping of his fingers echoed loudly within the room. "I certainly hope you enjoyed our little chat. I know I found it . . . quite informative."

As she was led down the hallway in restraints by many armed guards, Li trembled slightly and silently prayed with an anguished heart 'Oh, Kain! Please hurry! I . . . I don't know how much longer we can last here!'

CHAPTER XXX

Kain and Julie stepped out of the large triangle of blue light and into a completely dark pit. Julie pointed upwards with her right index finger and a small ball of yellow light burst into life at the tip like a match, casting just enough light for them to see their hands in front of their faces. Kain fumbled in his backpack for his lantern and a tinderbox. In only a few minutes Kain had his lantern lit and his supplies stowed, and while the lantern was small it illuminated their surroundings well enough. They found themselves in the middle of a large cavern that stretched far beyond their sphere of light in either direction.

"Who or what are we looking for exactly?" Julie whispered lowly, her hushed voice echoing dully from the terrific acoustics of the cave.

"The Lady of Earth." Kain grunted back, wincing slightly as his words were repeated several times over. Julie's eyes grew wide and her mouth formed a distorted smile of surprise, but she said nothing.

They walked on in silence before coming to a junction that split the cave into two different paths. Kain mouthed which way to which Julie's answer was a dull shrug as she took a silver moon coin from her pocket and flipped it in the air. It made a high whomping sound as it quickly spun upwards and fell back to her hand with a low thud. She looked at it, stuffed it back into her pocket, and gestured to the left. They crept along for a few hundred paces before they reached a large cavern chamber. Inside they found a very gruesome sight indeed.

In the dead center of the room sitting by a large, roaring fire was a large minotaur, a beast nearly ten feet tall with a body much like a human, except that its two legs were covered in dirty black fur and its feet were wide black cloven hooves. It had a huge barreling chest covered with wiry black fuzz and his muscular arms ended in broad hands with only three very thick fingers. Its head was that of a great bull with curved black horns and a long snout. Its maw was filled with razor sharp fangs while a mixture of blood and slobber seeped past its thick lips as it grotesquely sucked on the massive bone of what had been its dinner. Hundreds of bones from a variety of different swamp creatures as well as those of humans lay licked clean and scattered all around the floor, glowing eerily in the light cast by the fire burning in a pit carved in the stone floor. Above the fire pit there was a large hole dug into the wall that housed the monster's grim trophies: the skulls of its prey. The beast had a smell that was much like the rest of the room and made Kain and Julie gag. It was the smell of death.

The minotaur was a demi-faery beast, and much like the orc or the doppelganger it was not quite faery nor quite natural but somewhere in the middle. The minotaur was in fact the orc's utro, which meant that it was a close relative to the far more docile demi-faery orc such as the relationship shared by the dwarf and the goblin. While the orc was gifted with limited speech, the minotaur had no such gift, but it was blessed with a far greater degree of intelligence and was able to make and use crude weapons and build fires among other things. Its cleverness also made it a very cunning and savage hunter, and it feasted on only freshly killed meat. They were highly territorial with others of their kind, usually living only in pairs of a male and female and often brutally killed any creature it felt was trespassing. This, of course, was pretty much any creature with a pulse.

This particular minotaur appeared to have no mate unless she was still out on the hunt. Not wanting to bother with such a ferocious beast or worse yet be caught from behind by the returning mate, Kain and Julie slowly and easily began to creep away from the minotaur's home.

Suddenly, it raised its head slightly and snorted deeply, its huge nostrils flaring harshly to take in a new scent that had drifted over the familiar smells of its home as the humans gasped. It uttered a low growl and turned savagely to face the pair, its beady black eyes pinning them in their spot as its long red tongue lapped hungrily over its stained lips. The look it bore in its glassy eyes made the humans tremble, easily conveying the one thing on its hungry mind: fresh meat.

It gave a deafening roar and leapt to its hoofed feet as it snatched up its massive bone axe and swung it around wildly. Kain yanked his broadsword from its sheath as the monstrosity pawed the loose earth and charged, the cavern rumbling under its steps. The minotaur's size greatly betrayed its speed, for it was on top of them in an instant, bellowing madly and smashing its axe down hard in hopes of splitting Kain in two. Kain shoved Julie away and managed to jump back himself just as he slashed at the beast. Unfortunately, he missed. Julie did not, however, when she cast a large blast of magickal energy that charred all of the dirty hair off the beast's chest. It bellowed in shocked pain before snorting loudly in fury and making a charge at Julie with its head down and its sharp horns pointed right at her. Kain cracked his whip and wrapped the end skillfully around the creature's legs, tripping it up and sending it flying forward. As it fell, Julie pressed her hands tightly together and shut her eyes in concentration before shoving her palms outwards. A blast of bright yellow light burst out and struck the minotaur's large skull, striking like a blacksmith's heavy pounding hammer. The minotaur gave a short howl of surprised agony and collapsed to the ground, the momentum of its charge sending it sliding forward several more feet. Julie had to roll away before the horns could impale her. It shook its head groggily and snorted weakly as it slowly began to pick itself up.

Kain rushed to Julie's side and plunged his sword through the monster's heart, dropping it dead. He helped the enchantress to her feet before collecting his sword and together the pair ran quickly out of the room before more trouble arrived. At the intersection they took the path of the right tunnel.

It was almost an hour of trudging through the maze of tunnels, with Kain relying mostly on his instinct and luck with direction to guide them before they finally came to a large domed room. There was a carpet of lush green grass covering the dirt floor while many species of trees grew all around. Many faeries of the Earth, such as the lively gnomes, frolicked and played with each other in the fields of beautiful flowers. Kain and Julie saw a small group of humanoid faeries standing by a tree chatting idly. They appeared to be young women, but their skin was very pale green and their long straight hair was the color of the lushest grass. When the adventurers entered, all of the bustling play and friendly chatter stopped as all faery eyes stared at the humans with curiosity and interest but no fear or animosity. The twelve inch tall gnomes threw warm, rosy smiles at the humans while the green girls murmured softly amongst themselves and gestured towards the humans like gossiping hens. Kain saw large group of faery trees much like the ones he and his troop had met much earlier in their quest, Ogam if he remembered correctly what his sister had told him. They didn't appear to notice him and Julie, or they simply didn't care about them one way or the other. Kain vaguely wondered if they knew about his past crime of chopping off the hand of one of their kind.

At the far end of the massive room was a throne made of splendid granite more beautifully crafted than even the most skilled human hands could ever dream of carving. Sitting majestically in the seat was a woman more beautiful than any mortal female. She was tall and slender with long flowing brown hair and lovely rounded features while her skin was so soft and fair and her luscious eyes were so deep and invoking that she could only have been truly divine. Her flowing robes were green in color and conformed to her thin figure loosely. She was imposing in a friendly sort of way, like a mother to her toddler or a teacher to a fresh student. She was truly an impressive sight to behold, an undeniable faery queen.

Kain and Julie silently walked through the field to the throne, the faeries all following them with their inquisitive, curious eyes. A few of the more bold even walked closely with them to the throne where the pair humbly knelt before the woman. She looked down at them and smiled brightly as she said in a silvery voice "I have been waiting for you, Sir Kain Viccon. It is a great pleasure to finally greet you after all my Jestura has told me."

"Then you know why I have come?" he asked hopefully, keeping his head bowed in respect for the Lady just as he would to his own queen during an official greeting.

"Indeed." the faery queen nodded. "You have come in search of my ring. You, like your father before you, request our sword to aid in darkest times." She gave a soft sigh and, frowning slightly, told him in a low voice to raise his head to her. He looked up at her face while Julie kept her head bowed. "I feel your grief and understand your needs. However, you must prove yourself as worthy enough to wear my ring. And to do that, you must fight my elemental. Should you beat him, you will have earned my ring and my respect." She glanced at Julie and waved her hand as if shooing a fly out of her face. "You may have a seat and watch your friend, my lady. However, you may offer him no assistance."

"I understand. Thank you." Julie said, rising and moving to sit in a small granite chair covered with fluffy leaves that was far more comfortable than it looked.

As Kain drew his sword, the Lady Earth raised her hand and shot a green light from her palm that struck a large boulder. Instantly, the rock sprouted arms, legs, and a head with emerald eyes. The eight foot tall, four-foot wide elemental known as the golem bellowed gruffly and shook itself before rumbling a growl and pounding its heavy rock chest. The sound of grinding stone grated out from its neck as it swiveled its head slowly about, looking for his prey. Upon finding the sight of Kain, it snorted keenly and its emerald eyes flashed brightly as it clomped forward, its heavy stone feet pounding the ground with every step. It clenched its fists at its side, crackles and dust escaping from its palms.

Kain brandished his blade and rushed the elemental with a fierce battle howl, preparing an attack that he hoped would be enough to cripple it with only one blow. Just as he reached the monster, the golem reached out with blinding reflexes that were betrayed by its great size and the fact it was made of rock. It grabbed Kain and flung him against a tree as if he were nothing more than a rag doll. The tree did not break or give way to Kain's flying bulk, and his momentum caused him to flip around the trunk and crash onto his face, the plush grass somewhat cushioning his fall. The golem ripped a massive boulder out of the ground beside it and effortlessly threw it at the knight. Kain shook himself out of his daze just in time to roll out of its path and snatched back his sword from the grass. His dodge wasn't really necessary as the rock simply shattered against the tree with no damage whatsoever to the mighty oak. Kain rushed to the beast and skillfully swung his sword in an eccentric pattern, but each blow merely scrapped off its rocky hide. The golem grunted an annoyed growl as it swung its massive arm and batted Kain's head, knocking away his dented helmet. Kain thought his head was going to rip off along with the helmet, but it just rang like a church bell at a funeral as his vision went fuzzy and his hearing muted.

He gave a dazed, blind swing of his sword and struck the elemental in the side with all his might. The blade clanged loudly against the rock and wedged into a crack in the golems leg. With a foul curse, Kain tried to pull his weapon free, but had to leave it as he noticed a shadow descend over his head. The golem's arm swept down, shattering Kain's sword and sending metal slivers flying through the air. The handle of the broadsword and what was left of the blade bounced off Kain's chest and he caught it on impulse. Kain gawked at his broken weapon in shock and was pushed down hard by a heavy shove. The impact with the ground made him see stars, but he managed to roll out of the way as the golem's massive foot stomped down, making a large crater where he had just been laying. Kain tried to scramble away, but the golem snatched at him with amazing speed and grace, moving like a great ape. It easily grasped Kain and hoisting him high above its head. He lashed out blindly with his broken sword as the golem prepared to throw him and managed to clip its forehead with the jagged blade. There was a distinct metallic clang as a small area crumbled away, revealing a pulsating green gel. The elemental squealed and roared angrily as it dropped Kain nine feet down. He twisted in air and landed on his feet with catlike reflexes, instantly drawing his bow and a faery arrow as he did so. He leapt back a few paces as the golem pawed its head and grunted dully like a wounded animal. It looked up at the knight and bellowed furiously as it lunged forward. Kain let the arrow fly. It whizzed swiftly and hit its mark perfectly, making a low splurt as it imbedded deep in the forehead hole and sprayed a bit of the green jelly. The golem screeched shrilly as it tore at the arrow while a thick green liquid ran down its face and into its emerald eyes. Then, without any warning, it stopped and became silent as death. It twitched and shuddered slightly before crumbling into small stones and fine dust, the clatter echoing like a mountain collapsing. Kain gasped and panted tiredly as he stood and shouldered his bow, the high-pitched squeal of entertained faeries rocking the temple. He suddenly remembered why he had fought the elemental to begin with and immediately spun on his heels to face the Lady of Earth and bow.

The Lady, with a large grin spread on her face, cleared her throat and replied in a proud tone of voice "Very impressive, young Viccon. You have indeed proven yourself to me and the Element of Earth. It will be a pleasure to give you my ring."

She snapped her wrist and a handful of brown dirt flew out of her empty palm. As it hit Kain's hand, a glistening emerald ring appeared on his little finger. He gazed at it in awe and wonder as he thanked the Lady ecstatically. She smiled and nodded at him as she crossed her legs and folded her hands in her lap.

"You are a fine man, Kain Viccon. Like your father, it is my great pleasure to bestow my ring, the first ring, to you in your search for our Elemental Sword. I and my children," she waved her hand through the air, a sweeping gesture acknowledging the many faeries crowded around her, "wish you well in your quest against the vile Noknor. His evil has greatly upset our delicate balance and we would like nothing more than to see you restore it for us. However, your journey will continue to be hard and fraught with peril. I would like to extend to you a gift that will aid you on your way."

She snapped her wrist once more and flung a small, round stone at Kain. He caught it easily as it floated to him and looked at it, examining its features. He found that while it had the appearance and texture of wood, it was clearly a stone and made a crystalline sound when it lightly struck his metal gauntlets.

"This is will offer you protection in the swamp as you trek to Colossal Mountain, the home of my sister." Lady Earth explained. "While you hold this stone on your person, my children will keep the creatures that wish to bring you harm at bay. Take it along with my blessings and look well upon your way."

* * *

"So, how was dinner, my lord?" Garrison asked with a grin as he took a seat next to the throne. Noknor sat in his grim chair, examining something in that large orb of his as he stroked his hands gently over it. "I trust that our Chinese friend has finally crumbled at your mercy."

"Quite the contrary." Noknor murmured, his attention still drawn into whatever he was studying in the orb. "She has proven herself much more powerful than I had initially realized. I must say that has she impressed even me. Her will is very strong and my powers have as little affect on her now as before. But, I had an amusing time with her. She can be so defensive. You just have to know what scabs to pick at. It wasn't a total waste."

"But, you're not worried about her?" Garrison asked, quite confused. He was sure that the Chinese woman, being so furious that Noknor had instigated the attack, would have wanted the warlock's head on a platter.

"For once, your idiocy has paid off. She is too concerned with her lover to worry about anything but him. She is of no concern to me." Noknor muttered dryly. He tapped the orb and replied "I can't say the same for you, Garrison. I wouldn't catch myself in the same room with her if I were you. After all, I am not the one that beat her lover to Hell and back."

Garrison flinched and gulped audibly. "I . . . I'm not afraid of that little huh- whore! She . . . she doesn't scare me, not in the slightest!"

Noknor chuckled loudly and Garrison's face burned brightly. "I must say I am impressed with her lover, as well. He's doing considerably well, much better than he should be doing. I would have figured him for dead by now. A normal man would have breathed his last long ago. Perhaps there is something to be said of his pathetic religious order."

"I guess." the Dark General muttered under his breath. Wanting desperately to suddenly change the subject, he gestured towards the orb and asked "What are you looking into, my lord? Another potential uprising?"

"No, just a private matter. No concern to you, I assure you." he told him. He looked at his general and grinned brightly as he replied "And speaking of uprisings, you may not be such an idiot after all. Congratulations on the affair in Kuberica City. That was very well put together."

"Thank you very much, my lord!" he cried in excitement, quickly rising from his chair and dropping to one knee. He took the statement with great pride, as any compliment from Lord Noknor was very few and far between, especially after falling onto his bad side. "I live only to serve you, my lord Noknor!"

"Yes, I know." Noknor murmured, instructing him with hand gestures to rise and take his seat once more. "What have you done with that young man who was heading that pitiful revolt against me?"

"LeBloc? He's still rotting in the dungeon."

"Not literally, I do hope?"

"No sire. Unless he's hung himself with his shirt, he's still alive."

"Excellent!" Noknor beamed brightly. "I should like to have a little chat with him."

"I see, my lord." Garrison returned, his eyes noting the lustful glittering in Noknor's face. He grinned sadistically and asked "In the company of one of your persuasive friends?"

"But of course!" Noknor laughed heartily. "I should think the Needle King would be sufficient for his filth. Or do you think perhaps the Hot Bed?"

"I would go with the Needle King, my lord. The smell of burning flesh tends to cling in the hallways for some time."

"So be it!" Noknor replied as he tapped the orb and looked at the image that came into view. Garrison craned his head for a look, but Noknor quickly waved him off and ordered gruffly "Go and prepare my entertainment!"

With another respectful bow, Garrison turned away from the throne and strolled down the red carpet. Noknor watched him depart and then returned his eyes onto the orb. He grinned lustfully and licked his lips slowly as he gently rubbed the orb as if romancing a lady. The image of young Nancy Viccon faded from one of her in battle with his Dark Knights to one with her riding upon the back of her mystical creature.

"Soon, very soon, my dear." he whispered softly. "You will be mine!"

CHAPTER XXXI

Elizabeth stirred in her sleep, knocking her sheets around as she moaned softly. Then she was calm once more and lay still and silent, resting in peace. Her head flicked to the side and her eyes fluttered momentarily before ever so slowly opening. She stared at the ceiling still in a half asleep daze as she tried to wake up. Suddenly, her eyes popped open wide and she shot straight up in bed.

James! She had just remembered that late the night before Noknor had ordered him to be brought up into the ladies' room so that Li could better nurse him back to health. Elizabeth had found that the poor man was quite in a bad shape. He had been unconscious and burning red-hot with a fever, his back ripped and shredded. Li did her best to console his very troubled coma and keep him clean and cool. The princess seriously thought that he wouldn't make it through the night and she had fallen asleep only out of pure exhaustion. But now that the sunlight filtered through the barred window, she feared the worst as she looked around wildly in desperation.

She saw Li sitting in a chair next to her bed. James Raptor lay in the spot Elizabeth had last seen him and was still asleep, or so she hoped. She heard his wheezing gasps and saw his body slowly rise and fall with each troubled breath. He was alive! Thank the Goddess, he was alive! She let out a heavy breath of relief and watched the two lovers in silence.

Li held James's hand in her own as she looked at him with intent eyes, as if trying with all her might to will him better. Her mouth moved slightly as a soft, sweet melody sung in Chinese escaped her lips. She squeezed his hand every so often and gently rubbed it against her cheek as she pecked his flesh gently. Then she reached out to clutch the small blanket that covered his back and drew it back slightly, just enough for her to peer at his wounds. Elizabeth couldn't see for herself and Li's face didn't change in the slightest, so the princess didn't know what to think.

"How is he doing?" she suddenly heard her mouth say, and expected Li to startle.

However, Li did not jump at all. She did not even appear to have noticed her friend. The only hint of having heard her came when she murmured "Better. He's going to make it through, I think."

"Oh, thank the Goddess!" Elizabeth sighed, a smile touching her lips as her body began to quiver violently with waves of relief.

"He's been like this all night. I think he's having bad dreams." Li replied in a low voice as James shivered violently and moaned incoherent words. Li cooed softly in Chinese and brushed her lips on his head once again.

"You've been up with him all night?"

"For the most part. I've been dozing off here and there."

Elizabeth examined her friend and noticed that her whole body was sagging. Her eyes were red and had dark bags under them while her face was long and pale. For a woman who looked years younger than her actual age, she appeared to be older now, much older and withered. She was like a blooming flower that had begun to wilt without her sunshine.

The princess rolled out of her bed and said "You look pretty bad yourself. How much rest have you gotten in the past couple of days?"

"Enough." was Li's simple answer.

"I highly doubt that." she replied, moving to her friend. She looked at the fallen man and grimaced slightly. She really felt for Li. She must be going through so much right now. And for what? Just so Noknor could get his kicks? She scowled as hatred flooded her heart. However, it drained instantly as pity refilled it with one more look at Li. "Here, you need to go lie down and get some rest."

"I'm fine!" she snapped defensively, annoyance dabbing her cracking words.

Elizabeth didn't take offense and placed a caring hand on her shoulder. "Please lay down for a bit, Li." Before Li could bark at her again, she squeezed gently and quickly continued "You can't go on like this. You know it. Please, just for a little bit." Li drew in a deep breath but said nothing. "You need your strength. You have to be strong, Li. Don't let Noknor do this to you! He wants you to weaken. He wants to take advantage of you. You have to be strong enough to stand up to him, to put him in his place. Because no one can do that better than you! Trust me, James will be all right. I'll watch him for you. Get some rest, for his sake."

Li still remained silent, but with a strong squeeze of her husband's limp hand and one final kiss on his soft cheek, she let him go and walked to Elizabeth's bed, moving slowly and labored like an ill zombie. As she fell onto the soft bed, she closed her eyes and instantly fell into exhausted slumber. A lone tear trickled down her ghastly pale cheek.

* * *

"Miss Julie?" Sarah said, poking her head into the dining hall the next morning. "Sir Viccon is still sleeping."

"Oh, okay. Thank you, Sarah." Julie replied somewhat absently, preoccupied with an already full mind. She looked up at the servant pouring her coffee and waved her hand gently close to her cup. The girl stopped pouring and awaited further instructions. Julie looked at the others and asked "Is there anything else?" Negative gestures answered her. "That will be all, Nene."

"Yes, Miss Julie." the servant nodded obediently and turned to walk out of the room.

Julie took a long sip from her cup and looked over the other four people seated at the table with her. She cleared her throat and said "And that's about it, really. So, as you can see, I really had no choice in the matter. I know it's no excuse, really, and I want to once again tell you how sorry I am about it. Especially what I had to do to you."

Nancy gave her a pleasant smile and chirped "It's cool. No harm done."

"And it's not like you did much to us, anyway." Robert grinned. "If you ask me, you did the two of us a favor."

"If you ask me, we deserved the stomachache you gave Nancy. Worse, I think." Michael added, his grin playful. "But let's not tell our soon-to-be wives. I'd hate to be kicked out of my marriage bed before even having the wedding."

"Thank you all for being so understanding." Julie smiled with a bit of a relieved sigh, sharing the laughter that Michael's joke had raised. She took another sip, her hands still slightly shaking, and turned to look fondly at her brother. "How is your face feeling, Raphael?"

"Oh, I'm feeling one hundred percent better." he smiled, rubbing his chin and cheek.

"You look a hundred percent better." Nancy giggled. He glanced at her and blushed slightly, making her giggle more.

Raphael turned back to his sister and looked her over again with a heavy sigh. "Goddess, Julie! It's so wonderful to finally see you again."

"It's wonderful to be seen by you again." she replied, reaching out to softly touch his hand as if to make sure it was really him that she was talking to and not some specter. "I have really missed you, Raphael. And I know Grandmother and Grandfather did too."

The younger Boniva lowered his head slightly. Julie cocked her lips softly and squeezed his fingers. "What happened to you all those years ago, Raphael? We used to hear from you all the time, and then one day, poof! There was nothing. After a year or so, we never heard from you or anything again. It was like you had disappeared off the face of the earth, and I think Grandmother and Grandfather began to fear the worst. I know I sure did."

Raphael raised his brows and frowned. "I'm sorry, Julie. I really am. I . . . I don't know what exactly to say."

"Just tell me what happened to you." Julie said lowly, her gaze down as she released his hand. With a heavy sigh, she lifted her eyes and pleaded with her brother "Please, I must know."

Raphael looked over at the four pairs of eyes watching him, waiting for the truth. He knew he couldn't hide it anymore, it just wasn't fair to his sister. He thought about asking the others to leave, but he figured that there was no real point to it. They were already much too interested. They would pry and pry until he told them as well. So, with a heavy sigh and a dull groan as he thought of where to begin, he explained "Well, after I left home, I went to work in Kuberica and Radinoz, doing odd jobs and such just to make it through the days. Field hand, mostly. Most of the stuff I wrote in my letters was made up. I . . . I didn't want Grandmother and Grandfather to know that things hadn't exactly turned out like I had expected. I didn't want to let them down, you know?"

Julie frowned and lowered her eyes as she nodded her understanding. The others listened on intently, intrigued about what they were learning about their friend. Raphael used a shaky hand to grab his cup and took a sip before continuing "A couple of years after I had left here, I had found myself in a small rat-hole of a tavern in Radinoz as a kitchen hand. It was there that I had met a small group of fairly wealthy merchants.

"We somehow got to talking, I don't really recall how, and they mentioned that they were looking for someone like me, a young man to be their assistant of sorts and help them with their businesses. Of course I jumped at the opportunity. I mean, here was a golden chance to actually do something that I could tell the truth about to you guys. I was actually going to be doing something that was worth anything. I was young and stupid, I guess. I didn't even stop to think why a group of merchants with any money would be in a dump like that. I just jumped head long into it."

He paused slightly, long enough for him to take another drink and Nancy to let curiosity ask "What were their businesses?"

He cringed silently as he avoided the question and continued on "I worked pretty hard for them and they did take notice, I'll grant that much. They paid me quite well. I ate at some of the finest restaurants and wore some of the snappiest clothes and I still had money to spend. It was quite a ride, I must say." He looked his sister in her emerald eyes and seemed to plead for forgiveness with his own. "I wanted to write you and let you all know that I had finally made it. I guess I just got too wrapped up in the glamour of it all."

He turned away from her eyes and murmured in a low voice "I didn't find out for a while that the reason I was getting paid so well was because I was running odd jobs for a group of criminals. The merchant act was just a front to sell goods they stole and launder the large amounts of money they constantly received. They had lied to me and led me around by my nose the whole time! Of course I was furious when I had found out the truth and I instantly quit them." He paused and thought. "I should have just run off into the night, but, like I said, I was young and stupid. I had it out with them and threatened to report them. Well, they ended up beating the bag out of me and threw a bitter orange powder in my face and left me to rot in a ditch. They could have very easily just murdered me right then and there, but I think they really did like me. At least, that's what they used to tell me. I guess I do owe Grandfather for instilling such a strong work ethic in me.

"Anyway, after that, it had been hard to remember things. The only reason I was able to remember my name was because they so nicely left me with my identification and some money. I had forgotten everything else: this castle, my life here, my grandparents, you. I slowly began to remember some things, but they weren't much. Images, really. Like distant dreams. I still can't remember what those—" he glanced at the two women, and changed his words, "jerks looked like or their names or anything."

"But you remember everything, now." Julie said with a bright, hopeful smile, rubbing his arm with both of her warm hands vigorously. "About us, I mean."

"Yes, it's like waking up from a deep sleep, or like having your sight back after being blind for so long. It's quite a rush, let me tell you!" he said, grinning largely. A small chuckle rumbled through the group, shattering the melancholy and heavy air around the table.

"Datiwal seeds." a sudden cool voice said from directly behind him, causing all to jump in their seats slightly and gasp. Raphael spun his head around and saw Sarah standing behind him, having silently reentered the room with the unintentional stealth of a stalking cat. "Ground up, of course. It tends to cause amnesia, but rarely so extreme. They must have used quite a large amount on you."

"They used a lot, yes." he murmured, shifting in his seat slightly as the tall blond silently pulled out the chair next him and took a seat. "They may have used something else, too. I can't be for certain."

"I doubt it." she replied smoothly. "Datiwal seed powder is enough to erase one's memory by itself, but it would take quite a bit to do so completely. I'm sure that's why they used it, so you wouldn't remember them and be able to report them to the authorities."

"I guess that's why they let me live with a few bucks on me." Raphael shrugged. "They knew I couldn't remember enough to roll over on them, so I wasn't much of a danger to their organization. Let me tell you, I am lucky. People they didn't like . . . well, they had other ways of making sure no one would roll over on them."

"I'm sure." Robert said, crossing his arms and sitting back in his chair slightly. "No wonder you always kept to yourself, kid. I imagine it's hard to tell people about yourself when you, yourself, don't know anything."

Raphael gave him a sly grin and nodded. "Exactly."

"It must have been hard to get on with your life." Michael replied, fondling his cup gently in his two hands. "How'd you do it?"

"Well, they had left me close to Hurst." Raphael explained. "I picked myself up, licked my wounds, and used what little money they had left me to get to the city. While I was using what I had to live and try to find work, I met Kain. To make a long story short, we got to talking and he told me that he'd hook me up with the Arcainian Army. I didn't really have too many choices at that point. I couldn't even come home because I didn't remember my home, and so I took him up on the offer. We've been working together since then."

"I had always wondered why you never said much about yourself. I always thought you were just the really quiet type." Michael smiled with a cocked brow. "But I guess you have an excuse for not telling us that you had such a charmingly beautiful sister."

"You ol' smoothie." Nancy laughed as everyone, even Sarah, shared a chuckle while Julie blushed slightly. Nancy looked at her plate before turning to the servant girl close to her and asking "This stuff is really good! Could I have another plate, please?" The servant girl hid her tickled smirk behind her bowed her head as she took Nancy's empty plate and started for the kitchen. "Man, Kain's such a sleepy head! I can't believe he'd miss such a great breakfast!"

* * *

Kain arose from bed rather late in the morning, a hair away from noon. The night before seemed so distant to him even though he had only been asleep for a few hours, and he began to wonder if it might have all just been a whispery dream he had had. The plain emerald ring on his finger and the bumps and bruises that screamed murder at him as he rolled out of his bed were proof enough that he was, indeed, one forth of the way to his destiny of claiming the Ladys' sword. As he bathed and dressed for the day, he reflected back on all that had happened the night before.

After returning to the castle, the Grand General and the enchantress had stayed up well into the night and talked over a well-deserved dinner, since neither had gotten a chance to actually eat with all the confusion. Kain told her his story and how he had come to be sitting at her dinner table and Julie in turn told him more about herself and the Boniva family. Kain was quite surprised as well as impressed to hear that it was actually the Boniva family that owned and operated Djerrid Halberd Arms & Weaponry, the largest supplier of arms in the Old World. The weapons and armor that Kain's own troops used had come directly from the castle he was now in, and himself had been presented a new broadsword to replace the one lost in his battle with the Earth Elemental Golem.

Kain had found that Julie was as interesting as she was beautiful and it delighted him indefinitely. A guy could really settle down with a girl like her, that was for sure. But he wasn't sure that was exactly what he wanted, at least not at that particular moment. And especially with someone he hadn't even know for twenty-four hours.

He splashed his face with warm water from the basin and groped for a nearby towel. He had interests in other women, of course. He was, after all, Arcainia's most eligible bachelor. He had a few women on the line, however none of whom he had ever seen a relationship going past a few dates and into something deeper, more meaningful. Of all the women he had ever had in his life, there had only been two which he had seriously thought about, perhaps fantasized about was a better word he told himself, marrying. One was Mara Raptor. She had been his childhood sweetheart, at least until he had been eleven. She was, in fact, his very first kiss. He had cared very deeply for her at one point, and she for him. But they had both been kids, they didn't really know what love was.

However, when he had returned back to Arcainia, they had taken up a close, if somewhat rocky, relationship. Oh, they were very happy together, and when James, her brother and his best friend, had disappeared in battle they were guided even closer together, finding comfort in each other. But they both had their own lives, their own paths to follow. Mara had her aspirations to be Jestura to the Ladys of the Elements and Kain had his aspirations to be Grand General of Arcainia. They rarely saw each other, though they did very much enjoy the little time they shared. Nancy hadn't even gotten a chance to meet her, that was how little they saw of each other. And ultimately, it caused them to drift apart and halted their relationship. At least their lover relationship, at any rate. He knew they would always be close friends, no matter what.

The other woman he had loved, even more than he had Mara, was Li's best friend since childhood Chen Wenchi. Kain had loved her, and later Li had told him that she loved him in return. But they never had expressed those feelings as anything other than friendship. Even though he loved her with all his heart, he had never told her, never let her know. And why not? As Kain stared into the mirror, he sighed dejectedly as his heart crumbled all over again. He couldn't remember why not. He couldn't think why he let such a wonderful girl tragically slip through his fingers and away from his heart. Maybe there had never really been a reason, maybe it had been fate that things happened the way they did. But he didn't want to believe that. He didn't want to think that fate could be so cruel to him. It was much easier, less painful to think that it was his own stupidity that had caused him to lose the only girl he had truly ever loved. He knew that even if such a relationship hadn't spawned, no woman could ever take her spot in his heart. No matter whom he met, who he married, who he had children with, Wenchi would always hold a spot in his heart. Perhaps she was even the reason why he had found it so difficult to settle down and commit to a singular relationship.

With a heavy breath and a hung head, he closed his eyes and did his best to force these thoughts out of his head. He was about to go meet his friends, facing them with a very triumphant victory. Now was not the time to be heavy-hearted and melancholy, particularly over past regrets. He looked himself in the mirror once more before heading back to his room to get dressed for the day. As he walked down the large flight of stairs, Kain noticed Julie's D'Honneur, Sarah if he remembered correctly, coming up. She stopped him and said "Sir Viccon, Miss Julie wishes to see you in her study chambers. I trust you remember the way."

"Oh. Yes, I do. Thank you." he replied.

Sarah nodded and continued on her way while Kain quickly headed down into the main hall. It took him a few minutes and much backtracking, but he eventually found himself in front of her door, the painting of her grandparents staring at his back. He rapped gently on the wood and heard a faint voice call from within "It's open!"

He entered and saw Julie slumped down behind her desk with a feathered pen in hand as she wrote upon a large scroll of paper. She seemed intently focused on her work, so Kain simply took a military waiting stance in front of her desk, his hands behind his back, his legs spaced evenly apart. She wrote a few more numbers down before placing her pen back into the well and looking up. Upon seeing him, a warm smile graced her lips and her bright green eyes glittered even brighter.

"At ease, soldier." she giggled, gesturing to the chair in front of her. Kain chuckled softly and promptly took a seat. "Well, I suppose you're wondering why I called for you." She paused to grip his powerful hand in hers and continued "I just wanted to thank you again for helping me last night. I'm in your debt forever."

"Think nothing of it." he grinned, looking into her enchanting green eyes. "You did, after all, help me get the first Elemental Ring."

"You would have gotten it without my help."

"Maybe, maybe not." he murmured, his eyes shifting over her shoulder. "The point is you did make it a lot easier for me. Besides, you gave me a new broadsword free of charge! So, I'd actually call it even if anything." He gave her a wink and a witty grin. "Of course, it's not like I was keeping score or anything."

"No," she laughed, releasing his hand and backing away a step. "I guess you're not. But all the same." She gave him a wink. "Besides, all of my swords are guaranteed never to break."

Julie suggested that they retreat to the garden where they could get some fresh air. The sun was warm and bright and a sweet, cool breeze whipped gently around them. It was all so refreshing that Kain would have never guessed that they were right in the middle of a stale, stagnate swamp. The garden itself was a stunning sight. It was a huge display of bright, dazzling colors and bold, sweet smells. A narrow red cobblestone walkway twisted all around the massive garden, standing out prominently in the lush, cut grass. Many of Julie's servants were around in the garden, some working at pruning and planting while others were simply walking around and chatting mildly. Kain silently noted to himself once again that they were all female, and that all the others were female as well.

The enchantress seemed to read his mind, because she suddenly spoke up "There used to be male workers here, but I had to send all of them away. Well, those that survived long enough. A few did try to steal a kiss from me before I realized just how strong the curse was and ended up . . ." she trailed off tonelessly.

Kain grunted dully and simply shrugged. He felt sorry for the woman, having to go through that, but there was little he could say about it. He knew she was a strong one, and she had obviously pulled through, as did her servants. It didn't make much matter to him that the castle was all female, he just hoped his troops behaved themselves.

In the very center of the garden with the walkway wrapping around it like a serpent was a large and impressive willow tree. Even more impressive were the literally thousands of tiny golden bells hanging listlessly from the limp branches. However, even though there was a very weak breeze in the garden, the air was filled with the sound of each and every bell on the tree ringing as if a powerful gust was shaking the branches wildly.

"That is the Tree of the Whispering Bells." Julie said suddenly, pulling Kain's thoughts back down. "It was a token of love from Grandfather to Grandmother. He says that those bells call out to bring true love under its branches." She paused and glanced at him with a warm smile, her hand brushing his in what could have been an accident as she strolled under the tree and sat on the stone bench situated under the love bells. "Would you care to sit with me?"

Kain grinned broadly with a bit of a smirk and moved to sit down next to her in the shade cast by the whispering tree, just like her grandparents had so many times before Julie thought pleasantly. They were silent for a moment but slowly began to chat fondly with each other as she gave him warm glances. Kain returned them and wondered if perhaps Julie might be developing a passion for him. He gave a mental laugh as he thought about his cousin and what she had told him about his ego needing to be brought down a notch or four. Perhaps she was right. He doubted that Julie was falling in love with him. She was grateful, very grateful to him for helping her with a plague that had imprisoned her for so long. Nothing more. The more they chatted, the less he thought about it. They talked a lot about his quest, the details of which Julie listened to very closely.

Finally, she brought the conversation to a halt by clearing her throat and telling him in a nervous tone "Kain, I have something to ask you." As she lowered her head slightly, Kain wondered what in the world was going to come next. "Last night, you risked your life for me. If I had been wrong about you, you would be dead now. But you took a risk for me, someone you didn't even know, and you saved me." She raised her head and looked into his eyes. She opened her mouth to speak, but her mind went blank and all that issued forth was a short squeak. She blushed slightly as she tried to find a good way to put her words. "I . . . Kain, you have done so much for me. I would very much like to return the favor. Repay you for your courage. I know that you hardly know me and don't even know . . . know much about my magick. Heaven knows, you don't even need me, I'm sure. I guess, I just want to ask you . . . well, I know that there are rules and the like . . . I—"

"Julie Boniva, I would be delighted to have you join me and my friends on the remainder of this quest." Kain smiled with a heavy chuckle. "From what I have seen, your magick is quite powerful and I am very sure you would be very helpful in our upcoming battles." He paused and gave a playful grin. "After all, you're Raphael's sister. I'm sure he's not the only one in the family that inherited some battle sense."

"Thank you so much, Kain!" she gasped in ecstatic glee as she threw her arms around his shoulders in a tight embrace and pecked his cheek in thanks. "It's been so long since I've had any action to speak of! It's about time I got out of this boring castle and had some real adventure in my life!"

They continued to chat, mostly about the quest Julie was now a part of, until Kain just couldn't ignore the rumbling in his belly and had to ask "So, what's for breakfast?"

Julie gave him a queer look and said "Breakfast? My dear, it's already noon! Past noon, actually."

"Wow, really? I slept that late?"

Julie nodded and told him that she had already approached Nancy and the other three men and had explained everything to them. She said that they had all been very understanding and that Raphael in particular had been quite excited by the turn of events, for obvious reasons. As Kain thought about it, he began to wish he had been awake to see his friend's face when he came out of his recuperation sleep and saw his sister staring at him. He chuckled slightly.

Nancy was strolling around through the garden humming to herself when she noticed Kain and Julie sitting beneath the willow tree, so she skipped over to talk to them. She waved ecstatically and giggled happily "So, you're finally awake, huh big bro? You missed a great breakfast!"

"I imagine so. What are you up to?" he asked.

"Nutin' much. Just admiring the garden. It's so cool! It kinda reminds me of the one Li has at her house, only much, much bigger!" she said, spreading her arms out wide to help express her point as she spoke. She started to add something, but stopped short as something caught her attention. She glanced around with a bit of a frown and placed her fists on her hips thrust to one side as she asked "Julie, just what is that ringing sound?"

Kain grinned and jabbed his thumb upward. The young girl slowly gazed up and gasped in awe, almost falling down backwards in surprise. It took her a moment to find her voice and when she did, she whispered in awe "Wow! Did you do that, Julie?"

"My grandfather did it for my grandmother long ago. Do you like it?"

"That is so cooool! Oh, Kain! I want one of those!"

"Yeah, right! It'll fit perfectly next to your bed!" Kain snorted with sarcastic laughter, making Nancy and Julie giggle at the joke. "We already have to make room for your unicorn."

Nancy snickered and stuck her tongue out at her brother, making Julie chirp with squeaky laughter over the silly girl. Kain grinned joyfully as the two ladies then began to chat pleasantly with one another like old girlfriends. It was good to see them getting along so well, especially since it would sure make things more pleasant for Nancy to have another woman to hang out with now.

He blushed when his stomach roared loudly, catching the attention of the two ladies and causing their sweet giggles to join in the melody of the whispering bells.

* * *

"So, what's the master plan, boss man?" Robert asked at the long dining room table spread out with a dinner that was even more extravagant and delicious than either breakfast or lunch had been. He, Raphael, Michael, and Nancy shared a fine dish of swamp pheasant, assorted vegetables, dinner rolls, and rozenberry wine with Kain and Julie.

"Well, we have to go east to Colossal Mountain. I don't know how long that will take. A few days, probably longer depending on how difficult the route is." Kain explained as best he could as he chowed down heartily on the delicious meal. "According to the Sisters' map, the Air Temple is located there." He paused to chew and swallow. "Now getting there isn't really the problem. It's a hard enough trek, but the thing is it'll take time. And time is the one thing we can't spare right now."

"That's right!" Raphael exclaimed. "If the Arcainian Army hasn't headed out already, they will soon! And, if they get there before we do, they'll attack the castle!"

"And be slaughtered like spring lambs." Michael gasped, his voice barely a whisper at the horrible thought.

"Like the Shazadians." Robert added solemnly. Everyone shuddered as a dark chill went through their spines.

"Exactly." Kain said, pushing his plate away and propping his elbows on the table. "As you can see, it would appear that we're stonewalled here. If we head out to look for the rings and the other forces do get there first, they won't have a chance. If we by-pass the rings and go to warn them, we'll have even less of a chance. It's lose-lose."

"So, what are we going to do?" Nancy asked, her voice wavy in a sort of half-defeated, fully frustrated tone.

"Well, Julie and I discussed a few things in the library earlier." he muttered as everyone else slowly began to push their plates away one at a time, either from becoming too full or losing their appetites as the grim situation stared them dead in the faces. "What I've decided to do is both. We'll send a team, myself and a few others, to search out the other Elemental Rings while someone else takes the troops to the rendezvous point to meet up with the rest of the army before the big attack."

"A logical choice, of course." Robert murmured. "Except for both teams having to make it out of the swamp alive."

"Like I said, we've discussed it thoroughly, and Julie has offered to send three of her best hunters with the rendezvous team to guide them safely through. They are all very experienced with the dangers of the swamp and I am confident that they can lead that team without casualties. After all, they do it all the time with their weapons traffic."

"Will the same be done for your team?" Michael asked, his eyes slowly shifting over to the blonde beauty. "Or will Julie be your guide to Colossal Mountain?"

"Partly, but I also have something from the Lady of Earth that will keep the dangers away from us." Kain replied, reaching into his pocket and rubbing the strange wooden stone with his finger tips. "Now all that's left is deciding who I take and who leads the rendezvous party. It's obvious that Nancy and Julie will be going with me, but I need one of you guys to lead our troops."

"I'll lead them." Raphael volunteered, raising his hand slightly. "It's my responsibility to lead our troops in your absence."

"No offense there, Raphael," Robert interrupted his friend softly, "but you don't have the experience to lead our men through a place like Dismal Swamp." Robert glanced at Kain and noticed him grin subtly. Neither noticed Raphael utter a breath of massive relief. "Now granted Julie's hunters will be guiding us, but I'm sure they can't be expected to keep tabs on us. We need someone who at least knows what to look for in the swamp, someone who knows what they're saying with hand signals and such. Someone like a Master Scout. I'll take this one on, Raphael. You go with Kain and catch up more with your sister." He paused slightly as they reached across the table and shook hands. He smiled charmingly "Besides, think of how it'll look on my record. I can almost hear the pay raise."

Laughter erupted among the small group as Kain rose and extended his hand. Robert stood also and took his hand. With a wink, Kain said "Thank you, my friend. I know my men will be in good hands with you."

"Just doing my job, boss man." Robert grinned, giving Kain a salute and a playful shrug. "If I didn't want to earn my paycheck, I would have become a senador."

"Well, with that all settled I would like to propose a toast!" Kain exclaimed, pushing his chair back and slowly standing as he picked up his glass and raised it into the air. Everyone did the same, smiles spread over all. Nancy especially seemed quite enthused as she held her own glass of wine next to her brother's. Kain gave her a wink and announced "To our triumph and to the utter destruction of Noknor! May Auset watch us and steer us well in our quest! Blessed us be!"

"Blessed us be!" the group echoed in gleeful chorus as they swiftly raised their cups high and drank.

CHAPTER XXXII

The journey through the swamp had been long and quite tedious, but far from perilous for the small group of adventurers composed of the Grand General, his young sister, his Second General and his older sister, and the Arcainian prince. Though Julie had led them through a rough path of sorts, covering the terrain had been somewhat difficult for the horses as the ground was very soggy and mushy and the foliage had been very thick. Several times, they had had to dismount and lead their horses as they hacked their way through the thick vines and branches of the plant life that more than occasionally blocked their paths. However, true to her word, the wooden stone Lady Earth had given Kain had kept them free from the threat of the wildlife; they were never attacked, not even by the pesky insects that they could hear buzzing all around them. Kain was so confident in his magical token that without worry they set up camp when the hour grew late and the area around them permitted.

Finally, four days after leaving the sanctuary of Boniva Castle, they found light at the end of the tunnel of raw and dank life. The brilliant rays of the sun instantly blinded them all as the sweet smell of crisp, clean air rushed into their nostrils to displace the foul, rotting odors of the swamp that they had all gotten used to. When the white spots finally lifted away from their eyes, they saw before them a large field and then not far from where they stood, the foot of the fabled home of Lady Air, Colossal Mountain.

"So, this is where the second ring is, huh?" Michael asked, the amazement overpowering his voice. "I mean, on top of that huge thing, of course."

Kain nodded silently, his gaze still rising up the mountain as he had to crane his neck upwards. Even from as far back as they were from the actual mountain, there seemed to be no sign of the top as it lay buried behind clouds.

Nancy examined the plain emerald ring around his finger, looking at how it glittered brilliantly in the warm sunlight. She touched it lightly and asked "Does it do anything?"

"What?" Kain replied, shaking his head back into reality and looking at his sister. "Beg your pardon?"

"The ring. Does it do anything besides sit on your finger?"

"Not to my knowledge." he muttered, raising an amused eyebrow. "Just the fact that it is one more step to the Elemental Sword should be enough for it to do, don't you think?"

Nancy shrugged blandly and looked all around her at the lush green field blooming with vibrant life as they all dismounted from their steeds. It felt like forever since she had last seen such a splendid sight.

"We have to climb all the way to the top?" Raphael asked, his face set in a look that he hoped that the answer he was sure he would receive would be a joke.

"I assume so." Kain sighed dully.

"Will we be able to?" Michael asked. "I mean, forget about the fact that it could literally take us forever to do it. Will we be able to survive so high up?"

"Julie, do you remember when—" Kain started.

"I'm sorry." she cut him off, her tone just as dejected as his face was. "Teleportation only works if I know where I'm going. I've been into Mystic Cavern before, several times in fact, but never anywhere on Colossal Mountain. I am afraid I am at a loss with this, Kain."

"Wait a minute!" Nancy gasped lowly, reaching into her bag and taking out a small book. She unfastened the metal clasp that held it shut and began to flip through the pages. No one seemed to have noticed her.

"Hmmmmmm." Kain murmured, his eyes narrowing in thought as he slowly stroked his chin. "The Sisters said that Lady Air lived at the top. But how do we get up there. That's the challenge."

"Maybe there's a trick to it." Raphael offered. "Maybe there's something that you have to do here. Like an incantation, or whistle a tune, or something."

"If that's the case, what then?" Kain replied.

"It's a riddle for sure." Michael said.

"Here we go!" Nancy called excitedly, her raised voice startling everyone. She motioned them all to get closer to her and look into her book. "According to this, there should be a spot on the mountain that's reachable where we can get passage to the Air Temple. Look, see? Here's a map."

"What kind of book is that, child?" Julie inquired with a frown.

"It's about faery magick." she answered, reading intently what was written beside the crude map of a mountain with lines and arrows pointing out different features. Julie only nodded her head and blushed slightly, feeling quite out of her league. Her magick was based on her own energies and not so much the energies of the natural world around her. She knew nothing of faeries, that was sorceress business. •

Nancy pointed to a paragraph and told them "It says here that there's a small plateau where you can seek faery guidance to the Air Temple."

"To the top?" Michael asked.

"Just says to the Air Temple." Nancy shrugged.

"Sounds close enough to me." Kain said, a smile brightening his face. "How hard is it to get to? Is it far?"

"Uhm, from what this says it's a bit of a climb, but not that hard to get to. It should only take about a day or so, depending. Of course, not just anyone will be able to get the passage, just those the faery guide deems fit enough to bother her mistress."

"Well, I'm pretty sure that you at least fit that bill, Kain my man!" Raphael chuckled, clapping his friend on the back with a strong blow.

"How reliable is that book?" Julie asked her, a slightly distrusting look in her eyes.

"Very." Nancy told her with a proud smile. "It was written by Flora Hyzenthlay, a former Jestura to the Ladys."

"I have total faith in this Hyzenthlay lady and in my own dear sister. I say let's go for it." he grinned broadly. He placed his hand on Nancy's shoulder and gave a proud, loving squeeze. As she looked into his dark eyes with a sweet smile of her own, he told her "You never cease to amaze me, girl! If I haven't told you yet, Nancy I am very glad that you came along with me. I couldn't have gotten this far without you."

Nancy's heart melted away as her head rushed with a mixture of pride, joy, and surprise. She closed her book with a loud clap and threw her arms around his neck, pulling her elder brother close and planting her lips on his cheek in thrilled thanks. Everyone shared a warm chuckled at the sight as Kain patted her back, returning the kiss with a fond peck on her forehead. Then he turned back to the others and said "Well, if it'll take us at least a day, we better go ahead and start now. We won't get anywhere just standing around here."

"That's all very true, Kain." Michael said. "But how exactly would you like to go about that? That mountain climb's bound to be too steep for our horses."

Nancy stroked Uni's neck and proudly stated "Nothing's too steep for Uni." The unicorn neighed loudly and stomped his front feet as he nodded his head in agreement.

"That may be so, but our own horses won't make the climb." Julie replied as she stroked her own steed's neck. "I am afraid they will have to stay behind at the foot of the mountain. However, I fear for their safety, what with our being so close to the swamp's edge. They'll need to be cared for while we are gone. I mean, we can't just leave them all alone tied to a stake at the foot of the mountain."

"That is true." Kain agreed. He looked between his two male friends. "Someone will have to stay behind with them."

Uni began to neigh while Nancy listened intently. When he finished, Nancy nodded her reluctant agreement and kissed his neck softly. Then she turned to her brother and said "Uni says that he'll watch over the horses. He promises not to let anything happen to them. That way we all can go."

"Whoa, hang it a second, sweetheart!" Michael gasped, surprise showing in his startled face. "You can . . . you can understand what it says?"

"I can understand what **HE** says, yes." Nancy answered, a frosty hint of annoyance in her voice as she corrected the prince.

"Amazing!" Raphael replied with a chuckle. "Must be a type of bond you two share."

"Well, thank you very much, Uni." Kain said, reaching out to pat his neck. Uni neighed a return to which only Nancy could understand.

Nancy placed her hands on his long face, looked deep into his bright, blue eyes, and murmured softly "Now you be careful and don't be getting into trouble, you hear boy?" Uni licked her cheek fondly, making her giggle. She kissed his forehead just below his horn and whispered "We'll be back soon."

With all of the supplies they could carry hanging on their persons and a simple camp set up at the very base of the mountain for the horses, they started their long trek up the side of Colossal Mountain. They hiked all afternoon, stopping only to rest when they were tired and breaking for light snacks that consisted of dried meat and fruits and water from their packs. The mountain was aglow with life, from the tall and lush mountain grass and brilliantly painted wildflowers, to the sharp buzzing and chirping of insects, to the many rabbits and birds that meandered around lazily in the afternoon sun. Nancy, herself, counted no less than twenty-five different colors of butterflies that fluttered all around them constantly. The sun shone down brightly from the reddening sky, bathing them in warmth as a cool, crisp breeze blew around them, causing the willowy mountain grasses to sway like the waves of the ocean. It was a wonderful day to experience and all five knew their Mother was looking down upon them and smiling.

As dusk began to break, they reached a high mountain mesa that Kain felt had to be at least halfway to their destination. He called for a halt and they set up a very simple camp. While Michael stayed behind with Julie and Nancy to build a fire pit and pick berries from the many bushes that surrounded the area, Kain and Raphael headed off to hunt for dinner. The sounds of feminine laughter caused by the prince's jokes echoed reassuringly in Kain's ear as he and his friend set off down the rocky slope with longbow and crossbow in their respective hands.

* * *

Robert glanced at the raven-haired beauty that rode silently a few feet away from him. Carrie was her name. She was the head scout for Julie's hunting and exploring parties, and it seemed she had definitely earned the title of D'Elite. She was the best tracker that he had ever seen, and it didn't threaten him in the least to include himself. And he was the best Arcainia had to offer. She never made any unnecessary sounds at all, not even a single slight cough or sigh. She was constantly on alert, seeing things around them that Robert wouldn't have even thought to look for, and she seemed to know anything and everything about the swamp, from the wildlife to the plantlife. She and her two fellow trackers were experts, and Robert had to admit that he and his scouts had much to learn from these highly skilled women. Of course, he thought, they had trained in the middle of Dismal Swamp, the same place where experienced scouts such as himself and his men feared to tread, much less train in. It was no wonder that they were the best. And as a result, even after a few days worth of travel, they had zero casualties to report.

They traveled down the same path that had led the Arcainians to Julie's castle. It was the only such path that actually went completely through the swamp. Carrie had explained that it had been built by the Boniva clan long ago when they had first settled in the swamp and that very, very few people even knew about it. It was used to connect Boniva Castle to Hurst, so that the products made by Djerrid Halberd Arms & Weaponry could be transported to the city and then be distributed to the various buyers around the Old World. Later the Bonivas had continued the path straight through to Kuberica so that their weapons could be easily transported to the north as well. The path was kept hidden so as to avoid a large amount of traffic that it would surely bring as conquering the swamp had been an Old World desire for centuries. As such, it was not used quite often enough to keep it safe and manageable. It had seemed that the Arcainians had stumbled upon the secret road purely be accident. Or perhaps, Robert thought mildly as he considered higher forces watching over them in their fight against evil, it was not as accidental as it had seemed.

Suddenly, the redheaded Rebecca, who rode further ahead of them, spurred her horse to a quick stop and thrust her fist into the air. Robert silently called his men to a halt and watched as Rebecca's head swayed ever so slowly back and forth, scanning the low canopy of dense leaves. Though he could neither see nor hear anything, he sensed something was amiss and prepared himself for a battle. Her head stopped as her eyes focused onto something sitting in the trees most likely waiting for potential prey to pass under it. She jabbed her fist three times into the air and gripped her eight-foot long pike with both hands. Robert recognized the gesture and motioned his men to draw their weapons, most of who were already prepared to defend themselves. Rebecca thrust her spear suddenly into the leaves.

A shrill roar filled the air. The pike jerked around in circles, but Rebecca held her ground on the back of her horse. As the unseen creature fought with the spear, it hissed and spat much like a large cat. Finally, the human triumphed and yanked the beast hard off the branch by rolling off her steed and onto her feet. As soon as the heavy two hundred pound body slammed onto the moist grass, Rebecca drew her short sword and thrust it into its side, piercing its heart before it could regain its senses.

It looked like a swamp cat of some sort, with soft tan fur and long, thin ears with tuffs of fur at the tips. Robert estimated that it was roughly five feet long not including its odd tail, which was about nine feet long and very muscular with a sort of club of reinforced bone at the end. One side of this club was smooth while the other was studded with long, hook-like spikes.

"A sliver cat." Carrie said softly.

Robert's eyes widened slightly in interest. He had heard of these beasts in his scout training, but he had never had a chance to see one in the flesh. He remembered from his classes that the sliver cat sits hidden in the leaves of a low hanging branch, waiting with much patience. When prey walks right under it, it swings the heavy club on its tail and knocks the prey literally senseless. Then it quickly twists the tail in air and uses the spikes to hook the prey and drag it up into the branches where the cat will feast at its leisure.

Rebecca mounted her horse once again and studied the canopy ahead of her. She held up three fingers, made a swirling motion with her index finger, and held up four fingers. Then she held her palm up.

"She has counted twelve more sliver cats up ahead and wants to know the next course of action." Carrie whispered.

Robert frowned. "Is it possible to kill them like she just did before they attack us?" Carrie jabbed her pike into the air a few times. Rebecca answered by twisting her hand so her palm faced down and then lowered it slightly. Then she made a fist and punched the air in front of her. Carrie solemnly shook her head. "I'm sorry, Sir Grotz, but they are too clustered. It would be too dangerous."

Robert's frown darkened, as he thought for a moment. Not a single idea popped into his head, so he replied "To be honest, I would like to hear your thoughts on this. I've never even seen one of those things much less have the know-how to best deal with them."

"Well, we could crawl under them." she told him with a hint of a smile. "Their tails aren't long enough to reach that far. Your men have crossbows?" Robert nodded. "A few of your men can crawl under them and fire shots into the trees. What they didn't hit would most likely move away long enough for us to pass. These cats are for the most part lazy and don't like to be attacked."

A sudden sharp whistle startled them as the scout following the rear called "Alligator attack middle left!"

The soldiers situated at the middle of the group drew their bows and aimed towards the black water on their left side. The attack was very quick and sudden, making the men jump with screeches and gasps, but they managed to fire accurately enough to drive away the massive swamp alligator before it could claim a horse and rider for its meal.

"Excellent eye, Kassandra." Carrie praised with a proud smile. Kassandra had been given the assignment to further her experience and it seemed she was quite well equipped for the task. She would surely rise in rank with this under her belt.

"Thank you, D'elite Himiniz." she answered, still trailing her eyes over both sides of the paths, looking for another hint of an attack.

"That sounds like a good idea to me." Robert shrugged. "Let me rustle up a few guys for the job." He then motioned Rebecca to ride back to them so they could get the exact positions of the remaining sliver cats.

* * *

"How about something to eat?" Li asked her husband as she held a piece of bread in front of his face.

James grimaced and did his best to shake his head, wincing as he did so. He coughed and said in a low voice "No, thanks. I don't think I could stomach anything."

"You need to eat, sweetie." she told him softly, reluctantly placing the bread back onto the tin platter. "You have to get your strength back up."

"I don't need food for that." he grinned. "Your caring touch and beautiful face give me all the strength I need."

A rosy smile brightened her face. "You need to eat."

James didn't acknowledge his lover's words, but instead grit his teeth as pain exploded through his body when he drew in a deep breath. He did his best to concentrate past the pain before wincing slightly and replying "You've kept in contact with my family?" Li nodded silently, not bothering to remind him that they had had a similar conversation a few times already. She had noticed that her husband had become somewhat scatterbrained since his cruel beating and prayed he hadn't suffered permanent damage to his mind. "How are they?"

"They're all doing very well." she told him, stroking his cheek fondly. "Your father's tailoring business is still doing very well, pretty much the same as always, and your older brother is still helping him out, learning the trade and such." A slight look of distaste crossed her tired face. "He married that girlfriend of his about two years ago."

James chuckled slightly, as much as his body would allow him to. "You never have liked her much, have you? What about my younger brother?"

"He's doing all right, I think. Doing his best to get into Arcainia's gladiator circuit. And your eldest sister has finally found that teaching job she wanted in the castle. That was about the same time as your brother's wedding."

"Seems I missed a lot in my absence. You haven't mentioned anything about my twin."

"Mara?" Li's eyes widened slightly. "From what Kain has told me, she's doing very well for herself. I think studying elemental magick. I'm not too sure what she's really doing. We . . . we still have yet to meet face-to-face."

James frowned in disbelief "After all this time?"

"We always seem to miss each other. Bad timing, I suppose." she replied as she shrugged blandly. "We've kept in contact through letters, but . . . you know. We both keep pretty busy."

"I see. Well, you two will definitely meet now that I'm back." he chuckled. "Any new nephews or nieces to speak of?"

"No, still just Debra's little boy. He's such a cutie! He reminds us all of you." Li giggled softly. "You're still his favorite uncle, you know. And he really misses you." She paused slightly, a low sigh escaping her lips. She looked away and glanced out the window, as if she were thinking of what to say next. "They all miss you, James. They took it pretty hard, your disappearance I mean. Especially your parents. I know it crushed them to pieces. I don't think they've ever really gotten over it." When she looked back at her husband, a bright smile was on her radiant face. She leaned close to him, touched her lips to his ear and whispered "Just think of what seeing you alive and well will do! I can only imagine how excited they will be!"

"If we ever get out of here." James muttered.

"We will." Li assured him, gently placing her lips against his earlobe. Into his ear she whispered "Trust me, we'll get out of here very soon."

"Well, I do hope you're right about the soon part." he replied, raising an eyebrow. "After all, I have a new life to start over again. We do, I mean. And I'm rather anxious to do so. But you know I don't . . ." he trailed off and hacked roughly. "I don't understand it. Why is he helping me? Why doesn't he just let me die?"

"Because he knows that if you do, I'll kill him. Or die trying." she replied with a bit of a smirk to her face. "And he can't have either of those things happen."

"Why is it so important to him that you live? Not that I'm knocking it in anyway, of course."

"Of course." she giggled. "I'm not sure, to be honest. But whatever the reason is, you know it can't be good for any of us." She paused and offered a goblet of water to his lips. As he sucked down the cool liquid, she replied "I think it's because he wants to kill us all together. Or at least Kain and me. Sort of a grand coup of sorts."

"Probably." James muttered blandly. "But it still doesn't make sense! Why would Noknor have me almost beaten to death only to save me?"

"Actually, from what Elizabeth has told me from spying on the throne room, Noknor honestly didn't want you beaten as badly as you were." she told him. "Garrison was just supposed to hit you a couple of time, enough to upset me." James frowned darkly. Li read his confused eyes and shrugged with a fierce scowl. "There's no telling with him. And, frankly, I don't want to know. So long as he leaves you alone from here on out."

James smiled and sighed dully as he gave her hand a weak squeeze. "Beauty, I love you so much. With all of my heart."

"I love you too, airen." she smiled, her heart warming in her chest.

The sudden click of the door caught her attention and she twisted her head, expecting it to be her princess friend back from her trip outside. Her bright smile instantly melted into a hideous sneer when she saw Noknor enter with a smug looking Garrison right behind him. After them came eight armed Dark Knights, each with that same drug dripping from the tips of their weapons, and then four more Dark Knights carrying a cot.

Li's eyes widened and she hissed "What do you want now!"

"My dear, we are moving your lover back into the dungeon." Noknor told her, his voice slightly strained as if he were tired from a long, hard day.

"WHAT!" she roared jumping to her feet. She advanced towards him and the guards prepared to jump on her. Noknor waved them down with a slight hand gesture. "What do you mean you're moving him back down there! Why!"

"He is doing quite well since the . . ." he regarded his Dark General out of the corner of his eye, "unpleasant incident. So much so, that I feel he no longer needs a nursemaid. It's quite apparent that—"

"So what!" Li snapped harshly, clenching her fists.

"It's quite apparent that he's not going to die." Noknor continued, sighing heavily, his tone taking on an annoyed air to it. "He can recuperate just as well down there as he can in here. The simple fact of the matter is that this is a ladies' room. It is not very proper for a male to share this room if he is no longer unconscious."

"What the hell's your problem?" Garrison replied through a sneer. "It's not like you won't get to see the gimp any—"

Li's fist flashed through the air so quickly that no one even knew she had moved until her knuckles connected with Garrison's face with a painful crack. His head was whipped sharply backwards by the force of the blow, straining his neck muscles as he howled and grabbed his nose already spewing a mess of blood between his fingers. He roared a furious curse and bellowed "You little chink slut! I'm going to—"

"You are going to shut up, Garrison." Noknor replied, his voice booming just loud enough to get his attention. "I told you to keep your stupid fool mouth shut." Garrison's eyes widened in surprise and he began to turn his anger onto his master without realizing it. When Noknor cast his red eyes on him, the look melting into Garrison's brain, the general lost all of his steam and closed his bloodied mouth quickly. Noknor raised an eyebrow and growled "Go make sure everything is ready downstairs before I do more than make your nose bleed. And do not **EVER** forget whom you serve!"

As Garrison gave a shaky nod and turned to walk out quickly, Li called out "You need to thank him, he just saved your ass! Next time, it'll just be you and me!"

Noknor held his gaze on Garrison to keep him from retorting before turning his attention back onto Li. "Now, then my dear." he told her. "He is going down there. Let's not make this any harder on either of us than it has to be."

"I'll make it as hard as I—" was as far into her venomous threat as she got before her husband coughed loudly and called her name as sharply as he could in his weakened state to get her attention quickly.

When he spoke, his words were Chinese. "My love, don't argue with him. You know you won't win, at least not right now. It'll just make things worse than they already are. Just let him do as he wants, I highly doubt he's going to do anything to me. As long as I still get to see your beautiful face and hear your voice, I don't care where he puts me. Please, for me."

Li scowled savagely, but listened to what her husband had said. She didn't like it one bit, but James was right. If Noknor was planning to hurt him, he would have done it already and wouldn't go to the trouble of faking anything for her benefit. She hated it, but there was little she could do about it.

"Fine!" she hissed through her teeth. She shoved one of the Dark Knights preparing to lift James onto the cot and gripped her husband's hand. "But I'm going down there with him right now!"

"Whatever you wish." Noknor replied, giving a sarcastic bow before turning and leaving the room before any more of their lovey-dovey cooing could make him sick.

CHAPTER XXXIII

Late into the afternoon of the next day, the adventurers finally reached their destination with the help of Nancy's book. They found the plateau to be as flat as a table and totally barren. It overlooked the land around for miles, giving them all a spectacular view with the clouds seemingly just beyond their reach. A sharp, crisp wind blew around them, howling lowly like the voice of some unseen faery as it fluttered their loose clothing and tussled their hair. They all felt a sense of calmness and serenity, and, just like the book had said they would, instantly knew that they had found a spot that marked a gateway between their world and the Faery Realm. But as to where the door laid, they were at a loss as they could find nothing on the empty platform.

"What now?" Michael asked with a skeptical eyebrow raised.

Kain shrugged blandly just before Nancy grabbed his arm and gave a sharp tug as she pointed and gasped "Look over there!"

They followed her finger, which fell onto a spectacular golden gong glimmering brightly near the center of the plateau. It was the most beautiful instrument they had ever seen, inscribed with marvelous designs of air faeries.

"Where did that come from?" Raphael asked, frowning slightly as he rubbed his chin thoughtfully. "That wasn't there a minute ago! Or did I just overlook it?"

"I don't see how you could." his blonde sister muttered softly. "It's not like there's anything else to hide it. It just appeared."

"Guess this means you're good enough to bother Lady Air." Michael replied, nudging his friend with his elbow.

"I guess." Kain murmured in a low voice that was barely audible over the wind.

He strolled over to the small gong and grabbed the brass mallet that hung listlessly from the instrument by a silver thread. He struck the small dish, which gave off an immense clang that startled Kain so much that he dropped the mallet as the sound echoed into the sky. Instantly, the wind began to pick up as the clouds just over their heads began to part slightly. They saw a small round cloud seem to detach from the rest and drift slowly down to them. As it grew closer, they could see a figure standing upon it. As it drew closer still, they saw that it was a young maiden, clothed all in white with a long staff in her hands. When the cloud raft alighted upon the plateau, they saw that she was quite a lovely faery indeed. Her white hair fluttered softly around her shoulders like the strands of the finest spider silk and her eyes where the purest white, glittering like perfect pearls. Her flesh was as fair and soft as new fallen snow and so pale that she almost seemed translucent while her flowing gown whispered in the wind, clinging to her and accenting her far too slim figure. She was like a breath from the Lady Air.

The faery looked among the group but said nothing at all. Kain wondered if she would allow them all to go, or just himself as she held an outstretched hand to him. Kain was unsure what the meaning behind the gesture was, and turned to his sister for a clue. Nancy looked from the faery's hand, to her brother, then back to the faery. Finally, she told him that he was to give the faery a silver coin, one for each of those that would be riding.

Kain shrugged and reached into his pocket to extract five moon coins. He gingerly placed them into her hand and watched as she very slowly closed her long fingers around them. Still remaining perfectly silent, she lowered her staff and gestured for them to advance onto the raft. After all were onboard and situated, she pushed off the plateau with her staff and they floated quickly up into the clouds.

In what seemed like seconds, they felt the raft come to an abrupt stop. The faery gestured for them to depart with her staff, and one by one they stepped off into a large area of white stone. They looked around with puzzled faces and found themselves in a massive arena of sorts with large pillars all made from the white stone and masterly carved with detailed inscriptions, holding up the clear blue sky over their heads. A soft breeze caressed them all as they looked around to take in the curious place. All around them they could see air faeries of many kinds. Nancy, with her proud knowledge of the fae pointed out sylphs, which seemed to be everywhere they looked. They were very small, seemingly transparent and very light in color, making it impossible to see only one by its self, but plain to spot since they were all mostly in groups, hovering in midair while their small wings remained perfectly still, seeming to be only for show. They also saw many pixies fluttering all about, chittering rapidly with one another in their high-pitched voices. Julie smiled brightly as she thought that they were the most beautiful creatures she had ever seen, with curving bodies, soft features, and dazzling wings which resembled those of the most radiant butterflies. When any of these air faeries caught sight of the group, they chittered even more and buzzed around them momentarily before flying away and conversing among themselves over the strange guests. They appeared to be just as curious and interested in the humans as the humans were of them.

Suddenly, Nancy gasped loudly and tugged on her brother again with ecstatic glee and she pointed wildly "Lookit! Ohmigosh! I don't believe it! The Seelie Court!"

Everyone turned to look at a large group of the most beautiful faeries they had seen thus far tromping along in a sort of parade not far from where the humans stood. They chittered in much the same way the pixies, but there was more of an actual language in their words. The humans could even pick out a few understandable words from their chats as they marched across the stone floor. They made their way past the humans, not paying them any mind and acting as though they weren't even there until they finally came to a stop in front of a large staircase. The human group watched as they went silent and then bowed all in unison before detaching their gaze from the faeries and following the stairs up to a marvelous throne in which sat a gorgeous woman with long, flowing blonde hair, thin and sharp features, and wearing a pure white gown that fell over her very curvaceous and delicate body. They gasped in awe as they realized that it was the Lady Air herself.

The great faery did not seem to notice them as a young human female, whom Kain and Nancy immediately recognized, spoke rather intently to her. When this woman saw the guests, a bright smile touched her lips as she gestured towards them and spoke excitedly to her mistress. Lady Air glanced at them and smiled radiantly as she traded a few more words with the human. Finally, with an obedient nod of her head, the woman bowed at her side and then rushed down the stairs at an excited pace to greet them. Upon reaching Kain, she threw her arms around his neck and pulled him in for a tight squeeze. After a momentary pause of surprise, Kain returned the hug and chuckled as he received a light peck on his cheek.

"I am so happy to see you here!" she cried out, releasing him and stepping back slightly to give him room. "I must say, I am thrilled that you have made it."

"I'm pretty thrilled myself." Kain grinned, reaching out to take her hands and squeeze them gently. "I'm kind of surprised to see you here though."

"I told you I represented the Ladys of the Elements. I have been informing them to expect your arrival." she giggled, offering him a pleasant wink. "I'm sorry to have missed you at the Earth Temple. But I see—"

"AHEM!" Julie coughed loudly, cutting Mara off in midsentence. All turned to look at her, her eyes cross and her mouth forming a greatly displeased frown with her fists clutched at her side. Mara glanced at her, her smile not fading in the slightest although her eyes sparked with catty humor. Julie immediately tried to soften her attitude as she asked "Are you . . . a friend of Sir Viccon's?"

Mara didn't answer right away. "Yes, an old, dear friend of Kain's. I am Mara Elaxandra Raptor. And you are?"

"I am Julie Amora Bonival!" Julie snapped, almost over Mara's words. "I am a CLOSE personal friend of Sir Viccon's."

"Hmph! Charmed." Mara replied, her grin wry and sarcastic. "A witch?"

"I am an enchantress, thank you!"

"Of course you are. One can always tell." Mara replied, nodding her head slightly as she clicked her tongue against the roof of her mouth. Before Julie could say anything more, Mara turned her attention back onto her childhood friend. "I see that you're already a fourth of the way there! I do wish I could have seen you challenge Lady Earth's elemental. I bet you put on a grand show!"

"It was very grand indeed." Julie told her with a teasing grin as she crossed her arms.

Mara threw her a quick scowl before covering it up with a warm grin and telling Kain "Well, Lady Air is ready for your audience. However, I am afraid that your friends will have to stay behind." She threw a snide smirk at Julie. "No matter how close of a personal friend they are."

Julie glowered darkly, throwing burning icicles at Mara from her eyes as the sorceress gestured for the knight to follow her up the steps, the others sharing an amused chuckle at Julie's apparent jealousy behind the enchantress's back. Apparently, her feelings for Kain ran deeper than they had thought.

Kain followed Mara up the grand staircase to stop in front of the massive chair of white stone. It towered over the pair from their position and they had to crane their necks slightly. While it looked as if it should have been quite hard and uncomfortable, Lady Air appeared to be quite as relaxed as if she sat upon the softest cloud. The pair bowed down to one knee and they held their heads down in respect until Lady Air told them to rise, her voice soft and gentle like a sweetly caressing breeze.

"It has been a long time since a Viccon has kneeled before me to request my aid." she replied. "I was very pleased as well as honored to receive your father. And now, I am just as pleased and honored to receive you. You are a good man, one any father and mother would be proud of. Your quest to reach me has been full of difficulties and there are many more awaiting you after you leave my home. It is against my will that I add to these difficulties by giving you a test I know you shall pass."

"I understand, beautiful Lady of the Air." Kain told her as he bowed his head. "And I am very grateful for the opportunity to come before you today and make this request."

With a warm smile and a wave of her hand, Kain was lifted into the air as if he were nothing more than a feather picked up by a breeze. He was slowly carried down the steps into the middle of a large circle of air faeries which had eagerly gathered around to watch the show. Even the Seelie Court had taken away from their spot at the foot of the stairs to join the crowd. There came a shrill roar of faery chirps and squeals as Kain looked around at all of them, wondering just what this elemental would be like. He glanced up at Lady Air and noticed that Mara had taken a seat next to her. The Arcainian woman noticed his eyes and gave him a sweet grin and a reassuring wink for good luck. He turned to his friends and saw that they all had found seats as well. With a small sigh, he hoped he didn't have too much trouble with this test. Or at least, that he didn't look too foolish if he did.

Another wave of Lady Air's hand sent a gray mist flying to land in front of the knight. He watched as it formed a vaguely humanoid shape but held no features such as a nose, mouth, or eyes. It seemed to just be a man shaped mist. Kain frowned as he noted that it didn't appear to have any weapons and he wondered how it would attack him as he quickly reached for the handle of his sword. His hand didn't even get a few inches. The mistie was on him and delivered three blows to his body that launched him backwards before he could even comprehend that it had moved. He flew through the air and hit the ground with a hard thud. As he tried his best to pick himself up onto his hands and knees, coughing violently, Nancy shouted "You can do better than that!"

Kain looked up at her and gave her a sarcastic grin with annoyed eyes. He started to turn around again and saw a blur as he took three more blows that came so fast it felt like one all over his body. He quickly retreated back many steps to try and examine the situation, the shouts and cries of his friends and the faery folk cheering him on ringing in his ears. He watched as the mistie went to the right, moving so quickly that it appeared to have teleported rather than move. It stopped for a brief moment, then went to the left, stopped, then went back to its original position. It suddenly shot forward and Kain barely had time to dodge the rapid blows that came in the blink of an eye before the mistie retreated back to its original spot.

Kain tried to draw his sword, but his hand closed around air. He looked at his belt and was shocked to find his sword gone as was his dagger. He looked back at the mistie and saw his weapons strewn on the ground just behind it. It had been so quick that it had not only hit him, but also disarmed him without him realizing it. Kain could only stand by in stunned silence at its speed as it once again flew to the right, then to the left, then back, and finally rushed to attack. Kain had absolutely no time to react and was knocked around like a training dummy. When the mistie retreated back, he stumbled forward and tried his best to regain his senses. There was no way he was going to beat it if he couldn't do something about that fierce speed.

He watched it, trying to examine its moves as it went right, left, back, and forward. He jumped back just out of reach as it shot backwards. It attacked once again, moving in the same fashion. That was the pattern! Now all he had to do was time it all right. Much easier said than done with that blur. He wasn't even sure he could count that fast. The mistie attacked once more, and Kain lashed out with a fierce punch, only to be struck by a fury of savage blows. With the retreat of the mistie, he rubbed his very sore jaw and chest and prepared to try again. He missed a second time, but had managed to avoid the blows. Finally, he took a deep breath, did his best to calm his nerves, and cleared his mind. He had to be exact, even a split second off one way or the other would mean a miss and more than likely he would be pummeled. He couldn't let this thing beat him. He had gotten much too far for that to happen. Besides, he wasn't going to let a stupid piece of mist get the better of him in front of the ladies, or at least any more than it already had. And he had a reputation to hold up to with his friends. So, with a silent prayer to Auset that his fist be true, he grit his teeth. The mistie went right. He clenched his fingers tightly in a hard fist. The mistie went left. He cocked his arm back. The mistie went back. And let his blow fly as hard as he could.

Kain's hand melted into the elemental's head, a cold, damp feeling engulfing his arm. His heart melted into his stomach as he realized that his blow probably had to hit a specific part, like with the golem, and with his luck it was in the chest and not in the head. He closed his eyes and prepared for another onslaught of blows to his ribcage.

The only thing that greeted him was an eruption of cheers from all around him. He slowly opened his eyes and saw his hand holding rigid in the air. The mistie was gone. He looked around and saw the air faeries flying all about, dancing and shouting in wild glee at the wonderful show they had just witnessed. His friends were just as thrilled, whistling and hooting on his behalf. When he turned to face Lady Air, he saw the great faery sitting silently by, a very happy, very impressed smile on her beautiful face. Mara held a very pleased look herself, and gave him a wink, but made no other move at her mistress's side.

"It appears our young Jestura was right to speak so highly of you." Lady Air called down to him, gesturing towards Mara. "And so she should."

Nancy gasped loudly, her friends taking notice. Michael looked at her and said "She's talking about Kain's . . . ah, friend, right?"

Nancy nodded with a dropped jaw. Raphael chuckled slightly and asked "What's a Jestura?"

"That's a very, very high spot." Nancy explained, seemingly thrilled at what she had just heard. "The Jestura is like the main assistant to the Ladys of the Elements!"

"It means she's a go-fer." Julie muttered dryly, crossing her arms.

Raphael chuckled and replied "I think your eyes just got a shade greener, sis." The other two shared a small giggle as Julie's face blushed brightly, her mouth closing tightly.

"You have done quite well, young Kain. You are, indeed, worthy of my ring. As I had been told you would prove yourself to be." Lady Air said, her beautiful voice echoing in the grand temple.

She raised her hand once more and a soft wind shot forth from her palm, covering Kain's hand in a cool, refreshing mist. When it disappeared, Kain saw that a ring made of crystal was around his right ring finger. As he examined the simple, yet beautiful ring, he gasped loudly in awe and in glee, knowing that he was halfway to claiming the Elemental Sword as his prize.

"The roads to the homes of my two remaining sisters are quite long, much longer than you would like them to be. Time is of the essence for you, young Viccon. The longer the vile Noknor holds power, the more our realms suffer. Please take this gift from me and let time be on your side."

The Seelie Court marched up to him, their heads held high with pride as they carried something to him. As they drew closer to him, he saw that it was a flute, simple and made from some kind of feathery wood. Upon reaching him, Kain stooped down to take the instrument they offered with his many thanks and praises. They all squeaked a return and watched as he stood back up to examine his prize.

"When you play a tune upon this special flute, you will summon my faery guide and her raft." Lady Air told him. "She will take you where ever your need dictates. Now go, and take my wishes for a strong victory, Kain Viccon, for the fate of both of our worlds rests tightly in your hands."

CHAPTER XXXIV

The raft maiden landed her cloud at the edge of the Sulfur Pits, a large barren area of black and red granite, active volcanoes, and lakes of magma with thick, black clouds of soot blocking out the sun. Not that the sun was needed, the red and yellow light cast from the burning rocks greatly illuminated the area with an eerie glow like that of a thousand thousand torches. Kain vaguely wondered if there was much difference between night and day in such a place. The harsh fumes all around flooded their nostrils, burning them with the vile stench of burning sulfur and bitter ash. There was not an abundance of life around, with only a few species of plants that could survive in such an inhospitable environment scattered around. The only animals they actually saw were the many beautiful phoenixes flying gracefully overheard dragging their long, colorful tails behind them, but they heard many different calls, including those of dreaded hellhounds on the hunt.

Kain turned to thank the raft maiden and ask her if she might point out the path to the Fire Temple but was surprised to see that she was already gone. Apparently she didn't care to stick around long after depositing her fare. He sighed dully and asked his sister if she had her faery book handy.

"Already ahead of you." she murmured softly, wiping the sweat from her forehead. Though the heat was uncomfortable, it was not unbearable or dangerous for the group.

"It says that the Fire Temple is located in a sleeping volcano." Nancy murmured. She paused to look up and scan the mountains ahead of them before looking back into her book. "Uhm, let's see . . . according to this, if we're right here, then . . . the Fire Temple should be about right . . ." She glanced up and pointed to a large mountain. "There."

True to the book's word, it did seem to be a volcano without violent life to it, free of large puffs of smoke billowing out of the top or molten rock bleeding out of many holes and crevices.

"Well, that doesn't look very far at all!" Michael replied in an upbeat tone. "It shouldn't take us very long to reach it."

"Thank the Goddess!" Raphael muttered. "This is not the kind of place I would like to stay long in. I certainly wouldn't like to set up camp here."

Kain frowned slightly and spurred his horse into the direction of the volcano. "Come on. Let's go."

They hadn't ridden very far when a group of small, red feathered birds much like quail darted frantically in front of the horses from a large outcropping of rock, startling them and making all the steeds save for Uni rear back slightly. Kain idly wondered what had been their hurry and realized with horror a split second before a vicious snarl filled their ears. With a mighty roar, a large hellhound leapt from behind the boulder and snapped at the air with powerful jaws. Kain's horse startled, throwing its rider to land onto the ground with a dull thud and a sharp curse.

The beast was as large as a horse, with reddish-brown fur covering thick, solid muscle, large black eyes, and a huge muzzle filled with long fangs that were stained red from a freshly caught kill. When it pawed the ground, its strong claws carved grooves into the granite. Just as Kain drew his broadsword and the others prepared their own weapons, two other hellhounds that were just as big and vicious appeared to join the first.

Kain swung his sword, but the first hellhound simply batted it away and pounced at him. Julie caught it in midair with a powerful bolt of lightning. It howled and yipped but hit the ground on its feet and prepared to attack once more. Uni kept the second at bay with his horn while Nancy put her blowpipe to her lips and gave a hard puff. The dart struck the beast in the nose and it snarled in fury as it pawed its snout. As Michael did his best to keep the third one from pouncing with harsh lashes of his whip, Raphael trained his crossbow on the beast and fired. The bolt embedded in its shoulder, but the muscle was so tough that the hellhound didn't even seem to notice. It snapped at them and clawed as Raphael quickly reloaded and Michael drew his own bow. As it got ready to pounce, they fired. It retreated slightly when the arrows hit the soft flesh of its underarm, but was only momentarily deterred.

Uni thrust his head forward, goring the second hellhound while Nancy lashed out with her sword, clipping its ear. It yipped loudly and bit at Uni's neck, but the unicorn dodged and kicked at it, moving swiftly and gracefully despite the rider he carried while Nancy rode her steed as if she were glued to his back. With a fierce neigh, Uni attempted to gore it once more while Nancy tried to jab it in the eye, but it moved suddenly and lashed out with its huge paw. It caught Nancy, knocking her hard from her saddle and giving her a nasty laceration on her arm. The hellhound instantly made to pounce on her, but Uni spun around and delivered a powerful kick with both of his hind legs while Nancy ignored her burning wound and rushed forward to hack at it before flipping away from another swipe of its paw.

Julie shot a purple beam from her hand that exploded a nearby rock as it missed the hellhound. It roared and snapped at Kain, but the knight swung his shield to strike the beast in the face as he chopped with his sword, cutting into the hellhound's front leg. It charged and butted him with its massive head, knocking him backwards and sending his sword flying. Julie threw another beam at it, blasting fur off its short tail. It howled in fury and lashed out savagely, frightening her horse into bucking her off. Julie barely had time to cast a small shield of light over her that took the brunt of the fall, but the sudden impact of the hard ground knocked her senseless as the hellhound reared back to pounce, its teeth bared and its claws ready to slash her to ribbons. There came a tremendous explosion and a great puff of black smoke as the hellhound gave a short yip and it collapsed to the ground, missing an eye and the back of its head. Kain stood with his glok still aimed towards it, a whiff of smoke drifting from the hot barrel like the many volcanoes around them.

The sudden thunderous noise startled all, but the other two hellhounds more so. Uni rushed forward and impaled the second hellhound's throat with his horn as Nancy jumped onto it, wrapping her legs around its thick neck to steady herself as she held her sword high with both hands. It gave a muffled gurgle as Nancy brought her sword down with all her might, running it into the massive skull all the way to the hilt. The third hellhound, with ten arrows and bolts embedded all over its body, took Raphael's mace and Michael axe to its own head in one expertly timed deathblow.

And then there was an eerie calmness. The warriors paused to take deep, tired breaths and rest their racing hearts. When Kain saw his sister's blood soaked arm, he gasped in horror and rushed to her. Nancy yanked her sword out of the skull of the beast, the blade covered in thick hound blood. She moved to clean it as she gave a weary sigh just before Kain whisked her into his arms, startling her.

"Kain!" she yelped, trying to pull away. "I'm okay!"

"The hell you are!" he cried as he grabbed her arm, his fingers smearing with her blood. "Look at this! Oh my Goddess! Your arm!"

As Uni and the other three humans rushed to her side, Julie gently pushed Kain aside and touched her hand to the three deep gashes in Nancy's arm. Her fingers glew with a warm, pink light, soothing the girl's wound and slowing the free flow of blood. After a few seconds, the bleeding had stopped, leaving only glistening red marks.

"There, she's all right now Kain." Julie told him with a reassuring smile. "But I'm afraid that it will leave a scar."

"Oh, thank you so much Julie!" Kain replied, throwing his arms around the enchantress in relieved joy. Julie's smile grew brighter as she returned the gesture. Kain turned to his young sister, expecting her to be upset over the incident. However, to his shock she was actually grinning and giggling as she proudly showed off her arm to her friends as if it were a trophy.

"Awesome!" she replied with glee. "My first battle scar! Just wait tell I tell my friends about this!"

Michael glanced at Kain with a broad grin. "That is one tough little filly I must say!"

Kain couldn't help but chuckle, the act releasing a large load of tension from off his shoulders. After Nancy had proved herself to him, he had no doubt that she would be able to handle herself. But he had in no way expected that much from her. She kept amazing him more and more and all he could do was wonder what would be next. He suddenly wasn't very surprised when the thought that she might actually be the one to deliver the fatal blow to Noknor entered his head.

They dressed Nancy's arm to keep the wound from reopening and continued on their way with much haste before the slaughtered bodies of the hellhounds could attract more of their kind, or something much worse. They reached the dormant volcano quickly and without any further incidents or attacks. The large opening leading deep inside was like a mouth ready to swallow them all whole as they entered. At first, all that surrounded them was black porous rock, but that quickly gave way to bright red granite speckled with glittering gems that sparkled in the red light of the glowing walls. They crept through the maze of hot rock for a few minutes until they came to a smaller opening.

Just as they were about to enter, a faery woman leapt out to block their path, startling them with loud gasps as they fumbled clumsily for their own weapons. The faery woman barked out unintelligible words and gave threatening gestures with her long spear until they left their weapons alone. When they showed her empty palms, she lowered her guard and examined them as they took the moment to do the same with her. She was a lovely creature, with pale orange skin and soft features. Her eyes were creamy orange without a trace of pupils to them and she had long tongues of flame instead of hair sprouting from her head. She was completely nude with fire licking around her breasts and waist to cover her as other small flames danced around various other parts of her body. When Kain tried to advance towards her with his hands well away from his belt, she scowled darkly and swung her long spear around to aim at him. He held up his hands in a defensive manner and was about to explain himself when a familiar voice stopped him with his jaw held slightly open.

"It's all right." Mara replied as she stepped out of the entrance. "Lady Fire is expecting them. They are her guests."

"Very well, Jestura." the faery said obediently, pulling her spear back and stepping out of their way. She smiled at them as they filed past her and bowed her head slightly with a newfound friendliness, although there was not a hint of apology in her eyes or smile.

"Don't mind her. She's all show." Mara told them as she led them through the tunnel. As she glanced at the group she happened to notice the stained bandages wrapped tightly around Nancy's arm and remarked "Miss Viccon was injured?"

"Yeah, we had a bit of a run in with some hellhounds on the way here." Kain told her. "A scuffle, but nothing major."

"How unfortunate." she replied softly. "But very fortunate that there were no serious injuries. Lady Fire is eagerly awaiting you, Kain." She looked into his eyes and offered a radiant smile and a wink to him. "Lady Air was very, very impressed with you. As were the other faeries. You were all they could talk about. I'm sure you'll be equally impressive here."

"Well, I'll do my best." Kain grinned.

They entered a large room with the mouth of the volcano far above their heads and a very massive bridge of rock that stretched all the way to the other side over a pool of magma several hundred feet below. Dancing and flying all about where many small licks of flames that held a vague humanoid shape while black lizards with red spots and intelligent eyes scuttled over the rocks playfully. Nancy told them these were fire faeries, and that the dancing flames were drakes and the lizards were called salamanders. Mara grinned broadly and nodded her head approvingly as she stopped them. She asked them to wait for a moment while she took Kain to speak with Lady Fire. The sorceress guided Kain along the bridge of granite to a massive chair of black onyx in which sat Lady Fire, her fiery red hair falling daintily about her beautiful face while her red gown clung to her wispy thin figure. Both knelt down on one knee before rising back up upon her command.

Mara stepped forward and gestured at the knight as she announced "May I present Sir Kain Viccon."

"It is a pleasure to finally see you in the flesh, my young sir." she told him with a cocked grin and bright eyes. "Clearly, nothing my young Jestura has told me can do you credit."

"Thank you very much, beautiful Lady Fire." Kain smiled with a slight blush.

"I would like to say that it pains me to have to put you to a test for that which you seek from me. But, after all I have been told of your triumphs before my two sisters, I am very eager to see you tackle my elemental. If you would, young Kain, stand under the mouth of my home."

Kain bowed in obedience, and quickly walked back to the center of the bridge directly under the mouth of the volcano. The many drakes squeaked and chirped wildly as they flew to gather in a circle around him while dozens of salamanders scuttled around the platform and the sloping walls of the volcano for better views. Lady Fire snapped her fingers and the floor rumbled as the parts connecting the bridge at both ends crumbled, leaving Kain standing upon a floating platform above the sea of boiling rock. She snapped her fingers once more and a large black dragon flew from the pool onto the platform. Upon its back was a large figure made entirely of flames. The fire elemental jumped to its feet and the dragon growled loudly, its mighty bellow shaking the entire temple, before flying back to where it had came from.

Kain drew his broadsword and brandished it as he adjusted the shield on his arm. Suddenly, the fire knight rushed at him. He threw up his shield to block and was shoved back hard by the force of the impact. He winced as flames wrapped around his shield, giving his arm a warm lick. The fire knight rebounded and landed on its feet where it raised its arm and fired three large balls of pure fire. Kain managed to knock the first one away with his sword and blocked the second two with his shield before rushing at the elemental. The fire knight leapt into the air to dodge the hard blow of Kain's sword as it skidded upon the rock and hovered in midair for a quick moment before turning into a large ball of flames and diving down. Kain threw up his shield just in time to repel the attack as he stumbled backwards, the blow shaking his entire body. He was just about to lower his protection once again when a brilliant flash caught his eye the instant before another blow rocked his body, making him silently compare it to that of a rampaging orc.

Sensing a third attack was about to come, Kain gripped the handle of his sword tight and swung it with all of his might. The blade ripped through the fire knight, splitting it cleanly in half. Kain began to breathe a sigh of relief, but it died in his throat as he saw the two halves turn into balls and then reform into twin humanoid shapes equally half the size of the original fire knight.

"That was smart!" he hissed through his teeth, quickly backpeddling to get a better position so as to try and figure out just what he was going to do about the situation.

Both twins raised their arms and each fired three blasts of fireballs that roared at Kain. As the shield took all six blows full force, Kain began to feel his arm warm as the shield was heated like a frying pan. There was no way he could last very much longer against this foe. He had to figure out a way to beat it, and quickly or he'd be burned to a crisp. The twins jumped into the air and dove at him. Kain dodged the first, who hit the ground and rolled for a few feet. Using the momentum from his dodge, Kain swung at the second attacker. His sword sliced through it as if it was nothing, but the fire knight was once again split in two. Kain winced as the thought hit that he had gone and made the same mistake twice. However, his breath of relief finally came out as he saw both fireballs hang in the air for a moment before zipping towards the first fire knight. They were absorbed and the fire knight grew back to its original size.

Kain's shield took three more vicious blasts of fire, and he gasped as his arm warmed drastically. One more attack, and he'd have to discard the only protection he had or risk receiving serious burns on his arm. It was time for a drastic action. Thinking quickly, Kain rushed to the edge of the platform and waved his shield at the elemental, trying to tease it. Like a bull with a red cape, the fire knight was provoked into charging. The elemental came fast and furious, but Kain's timing was flawless. Just as the fire knight was right on him, Kain spun on his heels just out of the way and lashed out with his sword, catching it with the flat side and sending the fire knight tumbling down into the lava pool below. Exhausted, Kain gasped and threw his shield down as quickly as he could as he rubbed his warm arm and watched the elemental splash into the lake of melted rock and disappear. A sharp snap caught his attention as the bridge reformed to connect the platform on both sides. Over the sound of rumbling rock, he heard the delighted squeals of the drakes and excited hisses of the salamanders as his friends cheered for his triumph.

He looked to the throne and saw Mara standing over her seat, her hands clasped together at her breast and her face holding a look of joy and admiration. Kain couldn't help but smile as he saw her wink at him and mouth a sweet congratulations. He picked up his shield, now cool but blackened from the harsh attacks of the battle, and quickly made his way to bow in front of Lady Fire.

The faery queen smiled brightly down at him, her face radiant and her eyes filled with joy. She motioned him to rise to his feet and said "You have done very well, young Kain. A true testimonial to the first Viccon to visit me. You have, indeed, earned the right to wear my ring. It has been quite a long time since I have given it out. Wear it with pride and honor." She shot a fireball from her palm that exploded upon impact with Kain's hand. When the painless flames had disappeared, there was a ruby ring shining brilliantly upon his middle finger. "You are an extraordinary man, Kain Viccon. The path to my sister's temple, the last temple you seek, is a long and difficult journey. I'm afraid not even my previous sister's child can take you close enough for it to be any aid to your waning time. I wish to offer you a key for a swifter way. Please accept this small token from me." A group of drakes bearing a small, glowing orb flew before Kain, chittering excitedly. Kain took the orb with many thanks and looked it over. It was about the size of a grapefruit and was as smooth as glass, though it had no weight to it as it glew with a warm, yellow hue. "You hold in your hand the power of the sun. Take it along with my respect. Now go and right that which has been made wrong."

* * *

Garrison sat in a rather uncomfortable bone chair eating a mild lunch with Noknor. He had to shift his weight around constantly to relieve the terrible pressure the lumps brought, but it was all in vain as every time he fidgeted the pressure moved to a different spot on his back and legs. He silently wondered if Noknor made the chair that way intentionally to watch people squirm before him, perhaps for the effect sitting on such a ghoulish piece of furniture had on those who sought an audience with him, or if it was just a coincidence. In any case, it made for a very unpleasant meal. However, eating with the Lord of the Darkness made it quite interesting enough to be withstandable. As if he had a choice in the matter. Garrison gave a mental chuckle. Of all the people both human and non in Noknor's army, nay the world, he was probably the only person who could actually feel that way. The truth of the matter was he rather enjoyed being around Noknor.

Well, except when he ventured onto his bad side of course. Then to be anywhere near the warlock was just plain suicide. But at a time such as the meal they were sharing, it was exciting. Garrison was the only person Noknor really had any actual contact with on a one-on-one basis, and it made the others revere and respect the Dark General. Garrison could kill anyone in the castle on a whim, same as Noknor, without incurring the wraith of their lord. Well, almost anyone. He was the Dark General, but he wasn't Lord Noknor. He may have been spared on several instances where Noknor would not only have killed anyone else but revived them only to kill them again in a more gruesome way, but there were limits. Garrison counted himself very lucky that he had not crossed those limits after coming dangerously close to tiptoeing over them. When all was said and done, thanks to Noknor, Garrison was a man with power, and lots of it. How long he had dreamed for such a position. And he had no intention of ever giving it up to anyone. Certainly not to some punk girl. That little slut-child could kiss his—

A knock echoed on the double doors, spoiling Garrison's thoughts, and they opened to reveal a high grade officer. He was clearly agitated over something, and it appeared to be on something other than disturbing Lord Noknor during his lunch. He threw himself down onto one knee and shot back up to his feet where he gave a quick salute. Garrison thought Noknor was going to turn on the man for impudence, but the warlock gave him one look, snorted lowly, and carried on with his eating.

"My lord, begging your pardon for this intrusion," he said, his words coming in-between gasps for air as if he were winded from running through the castle. "But there is an army approaching from the east wall!"

Noknor sipped his wine and then ever so slowly dabbed his napkin at the corners of his mouth as if he hadn't even noticed the man. Garrison raised an eyebrow, but kept his mouth shut. Noknor folded his hands on the table in front of him, clicked his tongue, and replied in an almost idle tone of voice "Is that a fact?"

"Yes . . . yuh-yes, my lord." the man said in a very slow and cautious way, clearly confused that his master was taking such a calm and reserved manner to the situation. There was a long, cruel silence before the man finally parted his lips to speak "They . . . they appear to be Arcainian."

"Yes, of course they would be." he remarked casually, not even looking at the man, but instead seeming to be speaking to Garrison. "Who else would they be?"

"Uhm, yes sire. We haven't yet established if Sir Viccon is heading the unit. We have yet to see him."

"Of course he's not there. He's still off tramping about looking for aid from those pathetic faeries. A fat lot of good it will do him. I'll crush them soon enough." He chuckled evilly. "I do wonder what a faery would be like."

A vile grin cracked on Garrison's lips. "Much better than a blasted village wench, I'm sure." He licked his lips and laughed heartily at the thought. "At least much more interesting!"

The two men chortled loudly as they continued to eat and drink. The officer looked between the two men, expecting an order for the situation. When several seconds passed without one, he started "My lord, what should—"

"Thank you for the update. You are dismissed." Noknor replied, waving the man off. The officer nodded his head and made a hasty bow before quickly making his way out of the room. Noknor sipped the last of his wine, gave a small burp, and sat back in his chair. "Send out a couple of squads, Garrison. Nothing too much, just enough to meet them and keep them occupied. I want Viccon here to see me rip his men to pieces before any serious damage is done."

"As you wish, my lord." Garrison murmured with a grin, bowing his head slightly as he tossed down his napkin and stood.

* * *

"Well, there's the castle." Robert murmured softly, as if afraid that even from so far away Noknor himself would hear him.

All looked and gasped in horror at the grisly site. The grounds all around were brown and gray, the grass long dead and rotting as many gnarled, leafless trees jutted out of the earth in mutated forms. Where the ground wasn't brown or gray, it was red, painted with the spilled blood of thousands of knights and Kuberican citizens. The Arcainians took in the horrible sight and many began to lose their stomachs as they caught sight of Noknor's "Stake Forest". Dozens of tall, sharp wooden stakes were planted in the ground around the front of the castle, each one with the body of a person impaled. Most of these tormented souls were long dead, rotting while carrion birds feasted grandly upon them. However, even from the distance, Robert and the others clearly saw the tortured writhing of newly planted people kicking the air and grabbing the stake with weak, dying hands as their wails of agony echoed lowly across the field like a wind moaning through a crypt. There were men and women, soldiers and civilians. It didn't seem that Noknor had any preference of who he made suffer.

The sky directly above the castle was filled with coal black clouds that twisted and turned like some living blob eating away at the crisp, blue sky around it. The castle, itself, seemed to be decomposing like a corpse. Every bit of it was covered with dirt and dust while dark green moss grew all around the bricks and the dark maroon paint flaked away. It took them a moment to realize that, much like the grass, the morbid color of the castle bricks came from blood. A sharp, cool wind blew across the area like a dead breath, striking them and chilling them to the bone as shivers traveled over each of their spines. Carried upon this filthy breeze was the smell of an open grave. Many of the Arcainian soldiers that had managed to keep themselves together up to this point now found that they no longer had the strength to do so and more than a few began to weep openly.

"Oh, Goddess!" was all that Robert could say as he began to quiver uncontrollably. "We have walked into the blood fields of Hell!"

Many of the men began to panic, but with both Robert and Carrie's quick, forceful leadership, the group remained calm and would not be deterred from their duties. Robert was quite surprised by how the woman had taken charge, barking at the men with orders and motivational words as if she had fought beside them for years. And should anyone feel the need to ignore this outsider woman, the fiery Rebecca was quick to bite their heads off more savagely than any Arcainain Army boot camp instructor.

It was clear that the sight had greatly frightened and disgusted the Boniva hunters, at least as much as it had him and his men, but it was even clearer that these women were not going to let it cripple them. They were stronger than that, tough enough to overcome their fears and raw emotions. They were just the kind of people Robert wanted next to him in battle. Deciding quickly, they ushered back into the cover of the forest and set a crude camp far enough in to where they would neither be seen by Noknor's sentries or be able to experience the grotesque scene, lest it whittle down at the very core of their moral.

They decided to set up perimeters around their simple camp to avoid detection and there was a watch posted at the forest's edge to look for the approaching Arcainian forces. Only the strongest men with steel stomachs were given this task. As it turned out, it was less than two days before the watch came back to report that he had detected the Arcainian troops marching towards the castle. Robert left the camp in the charge of a trusted scout before he, the three women, and a few chosen others rushed out to intercept the army before an attack could be mounted.

Robert went to the first high-ranking officer he could find and presented himself with a salute. "Sir Robert Grotz, Master Scout Green General Three Star. Who is heading this battle unit?"

"That would be myself, Sir Grotz." a large general a few years older than Robert answered with a salute as he approached the Master Scout. "Sir Henry Riet, Blue General Four Star. Would you care to explain what in the hell that is!" He gestured towards Noknor's home.

"That, my good general, is Hell. I have no other explanation for it."

"What's going on here? Where is Sir Viccon?"

"He . . . he'll be along shortly, I hope." Robert answered before quickly filling him in on everything that had transpired since they had left Arcainian Castle.

"D'Elite Himiniz, what are we to do now?" Kassandra asked her superior while the Arcainians discussed their business.

"We go home." Rebecca told her simply. "We have completed our orders, so now we go home. This is the Arcainians' fight."

Carrie looked at her, her depressed face sagging. With a lowered head and a soft voice, she said "No, I'm afraid it's not that simple. We are going to stay and help them."

"What was that?" Rebecca scowled, turning to glare at her with disbelief. "I'm not sure I heard you quite right! Did you just say you want to stay here?"

Carrie looked up and frowned. "Yes. Yes, that is exactly what I said."

"Are you insane!" Rebecca gasped, her face quickly flushing almost as red as her hair. "Why? I told you, we did our part! We got those Arcainians here safe and sound. Miss Julie would be pleased! Now we get to go home and tell her so she can be pleased!"

"We are staying." Carrie growled, her frown darkening.

"You're crazy! Why the hell should we!"

"Because I am ordering it so! And I do not care for your tone, Rebecca! Do **NOT** forget who is in charge here!"

"Oh, I am so sorry, D'Elite!" she bite out harshly. "I didn't realize you would be so quick to order us to commit suicide!"

"That is enough!" Carrie roared, her face turning as red as her soldier's. "Do you hear me!"

"That's what it is, you know! Suicide!" Rebecca snapped, not heeding her words and not caring about the repercussions that would surely follow. "Carrie, just look at that place! We stay here and it'll be us impaled so that birds may peck at our corpses! That's not how I want to die!"

"That's not how I want to die, either." Kassandra replied in a voice so low it was barely heard. Both women ceased their arguing and turned onto the girl. She winced sharply at their eyes. "I'm afraid to stay here." Rebecca smiled smugly in triumph as Carrie's frown melted into despair. She had been counting on Kassandra to back her up, but now with both of her hunters turning against her Carrie might as well give up the fight.

The youngest looked between the two women before taking a deep breath. "I am very scared to stay. But I am more afraid to go. We have to stay." Both women were stunned by her words, not even sure that they were hearing correctly. "Rebecca, you are wrong. This isn't just the Arcainians' fight. It's ours too. If Noknor wins, he won't stop with this place. He'll go on becoming more and more powerful. And sooner or later he'll happen upon us deep in the swamp, and by that time he'll be so powerful, not even Miss Julie will have a chance against him. At least if we stay here, we have the help of the Arcainians. And I . . . I just can't go back knowing that we could have helped them. How could I wake up tomorrow with that in my heart? I mean . . . I know that we will most likely not even make a difference in this battle and we'll more than not be killed here. But how could I look to the others . . . how could I look to Miss Julie when deep in the back of my head I would forever wonder if maybe, just maybe we could have been the turning tide in this war."

Both women were silent. A tear slipped down Carrie's cheek as her mouth smiled with great pride. She rushed to throw her arms around the youngest, knowing that one day Kassandra would become D'Elite, such as was her dream. And what a fine D'Elite she would be! Rebecca crossed her arms with a frown as she watched them. With a dull sigh, she threw up her hands and moaned "Okay, you're right. We stay and help them." She then advanced to them and they opened their arms to her, a smile cracked on her face. "It's still suicide, you know."

"Maybe it is, but it would be an honor to die with the two of you." Kassandra replied.

Before either Carrie or Rebecca could offer a reply in return, the shouts of the Arcainian soldiers interrupted them. They turned to look in the direction of the pointed fingers and shocked faces and saw the massive wooden drawbridge begin to creak with rumbling thunder as it opened ever so slowly.

"Oh, Goddess, no!" Robert whispered, his face losing all color as his heart plunged into his belly. As he and the rest of the Arcainians took up arms to face whatever onslaught would be bearing down upon them in the next few seconds, many men prayed "Please be with us, Auset!"

CHAPTER XXXV

"So, you kinda like Kain?" Nancy asked Julie as they rode together far enough behind the men who were engaged in intense conversation over the battle they would soon face to have their own private female conversations.

After a very long ride, the Raft Faery had dropped them off on the sandy shore of an extremely beautiful lake glittering in the fading light of the setting sun. Gentle waves washed onto the shore, lapping softly against the beach and then retreating as the cries of white gulls echoed with the birds flying overhead. Looking out at the lake it was so large one would have thought that it was in actuality the ocean itself. It stretched either way for miles and the opposite shore couldn't even be seen it was so wide. It held many strange and wondrous mysteries, being more than three miles deep in some places. One of these mysteries was the Water Temple, hidden deep beneath the cold, blue depths. They had only Nancy's faery book as a simple guide to help them find it, and even it raised more questions than answers.

"What do you mean, Child?" Julie inquired with a slightly raised brow as her cheeks began to grow warm and rosy.

"You know what I mean." Nancy giggled. As Uni strode through the soft sand, she looked out onto the water. Gazing out upon the sparkling lake colored orange by the fading sunlight, she felt a sense of calmness and serenity about her. A crisp breeze blew past, ruffling Uni's mane and her long hair, carrying with it sweet smells of the lake. She sighed dully, a smile touching her lips as memories of happier times filled her head, memories of her and her brother and cousin enjoying a day at a similar shore with their Chinese family and their friends. She looked back at the enchantress and gave her a sly grin as she giggled softly.

"Why . . ." Julie started, but trailed off as she turned her head away from the girl in a brisk motion. She found her gaze fall onto Kain and smiled sweetly. There was a slight pause as she regained her composure and turned back to the insightful young girl. "Why do you ask, Child?"

"Well, I've gather it from the way you are around Kain. Little things. We girls pick up on that stuff quicker than the boys do, you know." she replied, running her hand fondly through her unicorn's mane. She raised a brow and added "Plus, you were pretty touchy with Mara Raptor."

"Oh that! That was nothing more than magick rivalry. I'm not . . . I'm certainly not jealous of her in the least. Not in the least! After all, she is a sorceress. They can be so—" Julie stopped herself abruptly, looking at Nancy with a bit of a frown spread on her face. "You aspire to learn faery magick, do you not?"

"Well, it is the one I read about the most. I guess you could call it my specialty. But I'm not so sure I'd want to be like Mara and become a Jestura. That's rather taxing and you have to be very dedicated. Or so I've heard. Eh, I'm not really interested to learn magick, so to speak. I just kinda like faeries is all."

"I see." was all Julie could think to say in return.

"I don't blame you for liking him." Nancy continued, not fazed away from her original question despite Julie's attempts. "Most of my friends have crushes on him. And I know a lot of other women have the hots for him." She giggled loudly. "He's Arcainia's most eligible bachelor."

"Well, he is quite a guy." Julie grinned, returning her eyes onto the general's back. "He's not like any of the other men I've met. Of course, to be honest, being in a castle in the middle of a swamp and then being burdened with a curse for years, one doesn't come in contact with too many potential husbands. But, all the same, he is a rather special man. Even I can tell that much in the short time I've known him."

"Yes, he is." Nancy murmured, looking back out over the water now covered with a twilight sky. They paused in their ride across the sand to pull out their small lanterns and light them to provide illumination. They fixed the burning lanterns onto long poles that they attached to the saddles of their steeds before continuing their trek. Nancy gave the enchantress a wink and asked "Would you like for me to put in a good word for you?"

"Oh, goodness no!" Julie squeaked loudly enough for it to echo across the cool, night air. The men turned to regard the women with curious looks and raised brows, but said nothing as they returned back onto their own conversations. With a deep blush still burning her face, Julie smiled and tried to retain some sort of dignity as she replied in a softer tone "No, my dear. Don't be silly!" She paused briefly. "But thank you very much for the offer."

"No problem!" Nancy laughed. "No problem at all! But if you ever change—wait a minute. Hey, Kain! I think this is the spot!"

She pointed to a small rectangular boulder jutting out from the sands of the beach a few feet away from the water. The group crowded around it and examined it closely under the light of Kain's flickering lamp. It seemed to be an oversized tablet of sorts, old and cracked with many chips, most of the beautiful carvings of water faeries and strange etchings worn away with time. The one part that seemed fresh and untouched by the harshness of the elements was a short inscription written in a weird form of calligraphy that none of the men had ever even seen before. They turned to Julie hoping for an answer, but were met by eyes as bewildered as theirs and an apologetic shrug. She was at just as much of a loss as they were.

Nancy pushed past them to examine it closer, touching her finger under what must have been letters and murmuring incoherently to herself. She paused for a moment to open her book before continuing on. Finally, she stood up and told them "It says two things. This first part here says 'across the waves center of the shores my home awaits beneath the swirling depths.' Guess it means that we're supposed to get to the middle of the lake."

"Gee, let me pull my yacht out of my pocket!" Michael growled in frustration, throwing his arms across his chest in an agitated manner. "Of course, that won't help us when we have to dive to the bottom anyway!"

"What does the second part say?" Kain asked, not paying attention to the snide comment. He was fairly used to it, what with dealing with both the prince and his mother on many bad day occasions.

"Uhm . . . it says 'give light to my child to illuminate his way home.' Oh, that must be this little guy here." She pointed to a carving of a small fish within a circle just below the words.

"So, what does that mean?" Raphael asked.

"Well, I guessing that you have to shine a light on this spot where the fish is. It must summon a faery that takes us to the Water Temple."

"Very well done, Nancy!" Kain told her with a proud clap on the back. Nancy blushed and mouthed her thanks as her brother took his lantern and placed it close to the tablet.

Flickering light brightened the stone even more with the fish in the center. They looked around and waited, not sure what to expect. Only the still night air answered them.

"Maybe it has to be a special light. Sunlight or moonlight, or something." Raphael offered.

"Well, there if that were the case, we'll have to wait a few days for the next full moon." Michael said dully. "The sun won't be up for another ten hours at least. And since it'll rise behind it, we'll need a mirror to direct the light onto that particular spot. There's no telling how long it'll take to align it all up perfectly enough."

"That may not even be the answer." Julie added.

Kain grunted and reached into his pack to pull out the shining orange orb Lady Fire had given him. As his friends began to argue over what to do, he looked it over momentarily before holding it close to the tablet. A soft, warm glow was cast onto the stone, and the fish sparkled like a gem under its light. A low rumble filled the night air as the sand bounced under their feet. They looked around wildly, not sure what was going on when a large ripple formed in the lake close to the shore. The water formed a hump, as if some sort of large, ferocious beast were rising from the depths. All humans gasped and the horses neighed wildly as they backstepped away from the water, their riders holding the reigns tightly to keep them from bolting.

As the water began to break away, a rock pierced the surface. It continued upwards, climbing higher and higher out of the water until they saw the mouth of a cavern begin to form. Suddenly, all became still and silent once more, only the sounds of the waves crashing against the rocks and the dripping of water echoing from the dark, forbidding cavern accompanying the startled gasps and quick breaths.

Kain quickly made his way to his horse and consoled it as he climbed back into the saddle. He looked at the other's bewildered faces and called in a booming voice that betrayed his excitement "Come on, let's get going. We're almost there!"

The others joined him at the mouth of the cavern, blocked out by a wall of water. They looked at the eerie barrier with slack jaws and wide eyes, the water looking as if it were held back by glass, though there was nothing to stop the water as it should have come spewing out. However, it simply rippled softly, as if it were a gentle pond, the gentle murmur of the swirling water singing to their ears. The horses neighed loudly and stomped fiercely, but would go no closer to the cavern, afraid of the faery magick they sensed. The humans, stricken with curiosity, dismounted and approached with caution, expecting with every footstep for the water to come crashing down on them like a powerful wave. However, it held back calmly as they examined it without daring to touch it or even breath hard, as if afraid that it would burst some sort of bubble.

"Is . . . is it supposed to be like that?" Michael asked in an awe-filled whisper.

Kain could only shake his head slowly. "Nancy?"

"I have no idea!" Nancy replied, gulping audibly. She tore open her book and flipped through the pages in a vain attempt to track down any sort of answer. "It doesn't say anything in here about-**AHHHHH!**"

Without so much as a warning, a face appeared in the wall, a face made of crystal clear water. It looked to be a feminine face, with large eyes, high cheekbones, and a small, round nose. It moved slowly around with the ripples, peering at them with curiosity in her clear eyes. She smiled and cocked her head with as much curiosity for the humans as they had for her as her face extended out slightly. She looked them over and made a soft clicking sound that they figured must have been a giggle of some sort.

"I . . . I'm looking for Lady Water." Kain told her, stepping forward slightly. "Are . . . are you our guide to her."

The face made the sound again and then opened her mouth to let out a string of clicks and whistles, apparently talking to Kain. He frowned and, still keeping his eyes on the face, murmured "Nancy, what is it saying?"

"She said 'you're cute'." a voice answered from behind them. They spun around to see a familiar sorceress walking towards them. She offered a warm smile and a sly wink "I think she's taken a fancy to you, my friend." She tossed a wry smile at Julie. "You have that way with girls, it would seem."

Julie blushed brightly as she glared at her. She sneered heatedly as she hissed "Just what are you doing here, sorceress?"

Mara glanced at her with amusement in her eyes as she clicked her tongue. "Why, my job, of course. It is my duty to aid Sir Vic—to aid Kain." She gave a soft, baiting giggle as she raised an eyebrow. "I'm sure the concept is beyond you, enchantress."

"Why, you little—" Julie started, her fists clenched tightly at her side as she took a threatening step forward.

"AHEM! Ah . . . excuse me, but, ah . . . Mara?" Kain interrupted, quickly moving to step between the two women with a flushed face as Nancy and the two men shared low jests and chuckles under their breath. "Uhm, let's not forget why we're out here to begin with. We need to get to the Water Temple. I assume you can help us with that?"

The sorceress gave him a sweet grin and walked straight up to the face, which was clicking and whistling at her in gleeful excitement. Mara began to make sounds similar to the face and they traded words for a few moments, all the while the group wondering what would be the outcome. Mara turned to gaze at Kain with a large smile as the face chittered and giggled gleefully. Mara nodded her head and answered her before the face glanced at Julie. With a reply, both faery and sorceress broke into giggles as Mara nodded her head once more and made a reply of her own. Julie fumed in fury, her teeth grinding and her eyes boiling. Finally, after a few more words, Mara returned her attention onto them, Kain in particular. "Are you ready to see Lady Water?"

"Yes, very ready!" he told her, excitement in his voice. "Will she take us to her now?"

Mara threw her eyes over her shoulder and made a short whistle-click. All of a sudden, the face disappeared and the wall of water exploded out to wrap around them like long, delicate fingers. They barely had time to gasp in shock and surprise as they were pulled into the sparkling water filling the cavern, leaving Uni gawking in stunned silence at what he had just seen. He snorted and shook his head as he looked back at the other steeds. Obviously, it was up to him to watch over them again. How lucky for him, he thought dryly.

* * *

Li sat with James in his cell in the dungeon of Noknor's Castle of Blood. Only a little more than a week had passed since the brutal beating James had suffered, but he was doing remarkably well. He was doing much better than one would have expected, considering a normal man would never have lasted a few minutes, though he was still plagued by terrible pain, breathing problems, and an inability to move much that left him stuck on his cot. While his back slowly mended, he found his mouth quite willing to work, and conversed freely with his lover though she did her best to try to get him to rest and conserve his strength. She found it a difficult task as her heart wasn't very much into sealing his lips unless it was done by the use of her own. After such a long time without hearing his voice, she found herself wanting to hear it at all times, as if to convince herself that he was real, that he was actually beside her this time.

"Li, you look great!" James replied, his voice strained and raspy.

"Shush! You must rest." Li told him, wiping his brow with a cool, damp cloth.

"Seriously! You are so beautiful! Have I told you that?"

"Only five times in the past three minutes." she giggled with a soft blush.

"Oh." James muttered, frowning slightly. "Well, you are."

"Thank you. You look great yourself."

"Yeah, right! Look at me! I'm a mess!"

"You're a handsome mess." Li giggled once more.

"I've missed you so much, Li-Li!" James told her in as strong of a voice as he could muster as he winced sharply. "I can't even begin to describe the hell it was to be without you all that time."

"You don't need to. I have a pretty good idea."

"Yeah, I guess you would." he sighed dully, laying his head back down on his pillow and resting a gentle hand upon Li's leg. He gave a simple rub and a squeeze of her knee. His breathing rumbled in his lungs before he hacked roughly, his lips dampening with blood. With a startled squeak, Li snatched up a cloth and dabbed his chin. "I'm okay. Really . . . I am. Anyway, as I was about to say, I love you."

"Wo ai ni." she forced a smile, still distressing over his coughing up blood.

"You know, we obviously have something special." he grinned, meeting eyes with her. "I mean, the way we waited for each other. Well, me, it's not like I had much of a choice in the matter. But you! I still can't believe you waited for me all that time!"

A true smile brightened her face. "James, I would have waited an eternity for you! You are the only man I've ever loved! You are my destiny."

"Yeah, but to wait for someone like that, doing your best to fight all the grief and the temptation to—"

"There was never any temptation." Li assured him in a confident tone, offering him another sip of water. "There might have been opportunities presented by my friends; you'd be surprised just how many people can get so interested in your love life when there's a lack thereof. But there was never any temptation. There were only the constant hopes, prayers, and fantasies that I would find you once again. Our bond is eternal."

"Now that's love!" he cried out in glee, reaching to grasp her arm and tug gently to bring her lips closer to his. "It reminds me of the love my divine Mother and Father share. I guess there's a little Auset in you and a little Ausar in me."

"There's a lot of both." she whispered, closing her eyes gently.

As they kissed, a Dark Knight opened the cell door and entered with a great deal of caution behind his steps. He tried his best to sound forceful as he told her that her visiting time was up, but instead came out sounding even more uneasy and fearful. Li opened her mouth to blurt out a rude comment, but James grabbed her wrist and shook his head, knowing full well what sort of words were about to come out. As much as he enjoyed the way she made him laugh, he knew they didn't need the trouble. It was better to keep a low profile, especially since something had taken Noknor's attention as of late.

Li grinned and pecked his cheek. As she headed out peacefully and without a fight, James called "Now, you stay out of trouble, you hear?"

"Who, me?" Li asked innocently. James chuckled and drank down the last of his water. Li was guided back to her room and Elizabeth instantly approached her to ask how James was doing.

"He's still in bad shape, but he's getting better. Any news from the throne room?" she asked, seeing that the brick was still pulled out since the last time they had eavesdropped.

"Nothing much." the princess answered. "Just Noknor eating dinner, I think. I wonder when ours will be up! I'm starved!"

Li strolled over to the hole and peered down in a fairly casual sort of way, not really expecting to see much of anything. She saw Noknor glaring at her from his throne, his green face stark white and his red eyes bulging as his jaw dropped down to his plate. She jumped back as if she had been burnt by a hot plate.

Elizabeth rushed to her side and asked in a low, worried voice "What happened! What was it? What did you see?"

"He saw me!" Li said. "Noknor saw me."

"Oh, no!" Elizabeth gasped.

Suddenly, the door was thrown open and ten Dark Knights rushed in, overpowering Li before she knew what was happening to them. As their hands were tied behind their backs, Elizabeth cried out "What are you going to do with us!"

"We're moving you two ladies to more suitable quarters." the officer in charge answered her. "Lord Noknor doesn't seem to think you two are exactly trustworthy for this fine suite."

They were taken to the dungeon and thrown into the cell that was right next to James's. He was quite surprised to see his beloved back so soon and with almost two dozens guard flanking her. With a sarcastic grin, he asked in a semi-mocking tone "What have you done now, woman!"

* * *

Before the group even had time to gasp in surprise from being whisked off the beach, they found themselves deposited in the middle of a vast lake. A sea of perfectly still water stretched out before them as far as the eye could see with a dense mist swirling about all around them. There was not a sound to be heard, save for their own startled breathing. No birds, no ripples in the water, no fish splashing about, nothing. Just a gentle, if not eerie, calmness all about them as they stood underneath a dull yellow sky that seemed to be made up of the mist that completely surrounded them.

"Wasn't . . . wasn't it night when we left?" Raphael asked with a dark frown as he peered up through the mist.

"That's the least of my worries!" Nancy gasped, being the first one to glance at the ground, or rather the lack of it.

They squeaked and startled in alarm, flabbergasted when they saw that there was no sandy beach under them, nor any wave beaten rock to stand on. There was only water, reflecting up at them like mirrored glass. With what should have been several hundred feet of watery depth below them, they were actually walking on the water! They immediately turned to look at Mara, and even Julie's cattiness had been replaced by a look of overwhelmed astonishment.

The sorceress couldn't help but giggle softly as she grinned and replied "You are in the realm of Lady Water. This is a magickal place, one where things aren't exactly the way you would expect them." She tossed an amused smiled towards Nancy and asked "This was omitted from your book, I take it?" The girl answered her with a silent, though vigorous, nod of her head. Mara giggled and gave her a wink. "Overlooked, I'm sure. I'll have to be sure to mention it when I write mine. Well, if you will all hold for just one moment, I shall summon my mistress."

With that, she slowly began to sink under the water until she was gone, not even a slight ripple or a single bubble to mark her disappearance. Before they could even start to converse between themselves, the water around their feet suddenly began to ripple and in several spots the water churned and gurgled violently as if something rather large was rising up. Suddenly, pillars made of brilliantly colored pearl and coral began to break the surface and jut high into the air. These were followed by smaller reefs decorated with bright colors upon which sat different water faeries relaxing and chatting idly. Upon coming above the water, their talks stopped abruptly and their attention was cast onto the humans who stood by admiring the beauty around them.

Nancy quickly pointed out the plentiful undines, small water faeries that appeared to be tiny humanoid figures with features of fish, such as fins and webbed digits. Lounging by a particularly large reef was a group of six beautiful young maidens with pale white skin and long green hair. Nancy labeled them as Rusalkis, faeries who were not deliberately hostile, but whose games sometimes tended to become rough and dangerous to humans. Also splashing about in the water around them were the merrows, beautiful creatures of both male and female genders with the upper body of a young adult human and the lower body of a brightly colored fish. They giggled playfully as they moved about freely both under the water and on the surface, sliding around in a game of sorts. They pointed and happily observed the humans, the females giggling bashfully as they regarded the males in a flirtatious manner.

"Welcome to the Realm of Water." Mara greeted, advancing towards them quickly. For someone who had just slipped beneath the surface of the water, she was completely dry, not even a single lock of her hair seemed to have been touched by moisture. "Lady Water is most pleased to see you, Kain."

She gestured to a large throne made of pearl and painted shells. In this marvelous seat sat a true vision, as beautiful and alluring as her three sisters. Her long hair was black and hung down daintily about her shoulders bringing out her soft skin as pale as the foam cresting the wave with the help of her dark eyes. She wore a simple blue dress that clung to her slim figure tightly, bringing out her lovely curves. When she saw the group, a large smile formed on her face and she gestured towards Mara. The sorceress nodded her head and gently laced her arm with Kain's.

"The time has come for your fourth and final test." she told him, her high voice exposing her excitement. She threw her head over her shoulder and giggled to the others "You all know the drill by now."

She led Kain before the throne where they both bowed down and rose only after Lady Water had motioned them to do so. When she spoke, her sweet voice sounded like a babbling brook "It is a pleasure to finally have the audience of the great son of Richard Viccon. We have long been watching you, young Kain, knowing that the day would come that you would stand before us to follow in those mighty footsteps. I have heard many wonderful things of you, from my Jestura and from our three beloved daughters who have been keeping an eye on you. As you know, you will have to earn my ring through combat. But I know you shall not disappoint me and my court." She offered a wink. "Good luck, Kain Viccon."

Kain bowed his head in respect as he marched with his head held proudly high to the center of a large circle created by his friends and the water faeries, all of who were excited to see some action. Kain looked around as he adjusted his shield on his arm and gave a mental grin as he was vaguely reminded of the scuffles he used to get into when he was a young teen in China. He remembered how the friends of both boys fighting for whatever reason circled them like vultures and cheered on the one in their corner, yelling and screaming until one came out on top or the scene was disrupted by an authority of some sort. He used the term boys lightly, as there had been quite a few times he remembered that Li had found herself in the center of that juvenile gladiator encirclement, and not just with another young lady. And while he had had his rather small number of losses to account for, she had always, always come out on top no matter who her opponent had been or how many they were. At least, until she had gotten home to her parents. They just didn't deem it very lady-like at all for a maiden to be fighting, particularly with boys twice her size, and they let her know it each and every time. However, Kain had always noticed that his uncle was never too harsh with his cousin as he hid a gleam of pride behind his eyes. There had even been times when he had turned his head ever so conveniently upon word that his daughter and nephew had thrashed another bully. Kain and Li had always made a terrific team, even at a young age. Together, no one could push them around and they rose to be known as bully busters for the other children. Kain idly noted to himself that it was interesting how those bullies got more and more dangerous the older they got, even though it was pretty much the same scene. He just hoped that they all made it out of this alive to be able to enjoy future battles together—

Kain was pulled out of his thoughts by a powerful blow that sent him splashing down onto his back. A loud, unanimous gasp echoed around him as he shook his head to displace the ringing in his ears. As he tried to recollect himself, he mentally cursed himself for being so foolish as to let his mind wander and let his guard down before the battle even started.

'Well, that's a sure way to impress Lady Water and get her ring!' he thought with angered sarcasm.

He realized he was doing it again in time to see a large blob of water falling swiftly to smother him. Acting on reflex, he rolled to the side and felt a spray of mist as the blob crashed right next to him. He leapt to his feet and backed away a few steps to get a look at his opponent and examine his options. The blob of water swirled around like a mass of jelly before quickly forming a humanoid shape. Kain frowned. While the other three elementals had not shown any signs of gender, this one did. And it appeared to be feminine in a nature. His frown turned into a look of surprise as the body formed into a curvaceous, although clear, figure and the face formed into one that was rather familiar. He instantly recognized it as the face that had been in the wall of water he had seen on the lake's shore.

As Kain stared at her, the water girl smiled and a sharp whistle-chirp of giggles echoed in what should have been her throat. She leapt into the air and dove straight into the water, disappearing under the surface. Kain groaned and drew his shield close to his body as he peered down into the depths of the lake beneath his feet. The water churned under him the split second before a column of water burst upwards, catching him and sending him flying by the force of the blast. He managed to land on his feet, his sword gripped tight after coming very close to losing it, and he looked at where he had just stood to find the water girl standing there, giggling bashfully. As he tried to quickly guess how he was going to beat this one, she rushed at him, flowing forward as if surfing rather than moving her legs to run. She was quick and he barely had time to throw his shield up before she struck with a large splash. His thoughts that he had defended himself rather nicely were very brief as he saw tentacles of water reached around from the front of his shield, slithering around like hungry snakes. He shrieked in panic and swung his sword at them, but his blade merely passed through them as they wrapped around his arms and body. They constricted tight and raised him high into the air, holding a two hundred and fifty pound man with the added weight of weapons and armor up as if he were nothing but a child. He gasped as the air was forced out of his chest by a harsh squeeze from the water wrapped around his body before he was thrown onto the surface, landing with a resounding smack that caused both human and faery spectators to wince.

His warrior instinct took over and rolled him out of the way of another expected attack as he gritted his teeth against the pain that burned his body and took to his hands and knees. He coughed violently and threw himself up to his feet. Thinking that the water girl would follow up her attacks, he dodged backwards and searched for her. She had not moved from the spot where she had grabbed him, his sword and shield laying at her feet. He cursed as in one swift motion he snatched his dagger from its sheath and threw it with deadly accuracy, even through slightly blurred vision. He had expect her to at least make some sort of movement, but she only stood by and let the dagger strike her in the forehead. She giggled as the dagger melted into her head and the others watched in fascination as it traveled within her body past her neck, through her arm, and to her hand to exit out into her palm where she wrapped her fingers around the handle. She released it and let it drop to join with his other weapons.

She gave Kain a flirtatious wink and once more dove under the water. Kain gave a silent prayer and rushed forward, leaping into the air and rolling as he hit the ground to come to a momentary stop next to his weapons. He snatched up his sword just as the water began to churn beneath him and rolled just out of the way of the large column of water that shot up. He gave a weak back swing of his weapon, the blade slicing through the column with no effect. He sprung up and twirled around the come face to face with the water girl, arching his sword upwards as he did so. The sword struck her arm, cutting it off and sending it falling to the ground. Before it had fallen halfway, it soaked back into her body and her arm regrew itself instantly. Not deterred in the least, Kain lashed out once more, bringing his blade down to cut right through her neck. A low whistle exited her parted lips as her neck rejoined when the blade passed through and she raised her arm into its path. As the sword struck, her arm twisted and wrapped around the blade like a serpent, catching it and holding it firmly. Kain tried to wretch it free, but she held it tight and it would not budge. He kicked at her, his foot doing nothing but becoming entangled in her leg. Her body began to flow around Kain, moving swiftly to bind him in watery tendrils. Expecting to be crushed like a rat trapped in the coils of a snake, Kain held his breath and shut his eyes. After a few moments, he flung his eyelids open and lost the air held in his lungs as he was startled by the water girl's face inches from his own. She offered him a smile and whispered lowly to him, her voice nothing but whistles and chirps that he couldn't even begin to piece together. And suddenly he was released, landing onto the surface of the strange lake on his posterior. He looked up and saw the water girl gazing down at him as if to tell him to strike. He frowned as he tried to examine her as closely as time would allow, trying to find the weak spot he had clearly missed. And then he saw it, a small pink ball floating listlessly in her chest. That had to be it!

He gripped his sword tight, roared, and lunged forward, the blade piercing her chest but missing the ball as the ripples pushed it away from the metal. He cursed himself roundly as the water girl began to flow around him, her water tentacles slithering around his body and limbs as she chirped and squeaked words of sympathy he couldn't understand. His sword was sucked from his grip and spat out of the water girl's back. Strands of water wrapped around his wrists and forearms as he struggled violently to free himself. Clenching his teeth, he pulled his left arm back with all his might and tore it loose with a sloppy slurp. Before the water girl could react, he plunged his left hand into the cool clear water of the elemental's body. His fingers wrapped around the ball, a perfect pearl, and yanked it free with a roar of triumph. The water girl gave an airy giggle as if the act had tickled her and quickly began to melt off of his body, very gently lowering him back onto his feet as her clutching tentacles soaked back into her feminine form. As Kain watched with curious eyes, the elemental gave him a wink before leaping up and splashing back under the surface of the water.

All of a sudden, the water began to churn under his feet and he winced harshly at the thought that it wasn't quite over. He took a defensive posture, looking wildly around for his weapons. They were no where close and he clenched his fists tightly as the water girl rose up from the depths, not as an explosive column but instead as her humanoid form. Kain was stunned, finding himself unable to throw a punch at a woman smiling so sweetly to him, even if she was a faery and she had just been knocking him around moments before. Her squeaky clicks were obviously laughter as she reached up and tapped Kain's fist. Surprised, his fingers uncurled impulsively exposing the pink pearl he had taken. Before he could react, she plucked it from his palm, swallowed it down her clear throat, and giggled loudly as she sunk back below Kain's feet.

The echoing cheers all around him startled Kain so much that he almost fell backwards. It wasn't until the voice of Lady Water called out in congratulations to him that he realized he had achieved victory. He spun around to face Lady Water and dropped down to his knees, glancing around as he did so and catching notice that the water girl was now standing with Mara, whispering so lowly only their moving lips gave away their chat. They looked like a couple of teen girls admiring him from afar and he felt himself flushing brightly.

"Rise and face me, Kain Viccon." the great faery queen announced, her voice ringing with joy and pride. "You, just like your father, are a remarkable person and are truly deserving of my ring as well as our sword. Take it along with my fondest wishes for a swift victory over evil."

She raised her palm and sent a large ball of crystal clear water to splash over Kain's hand. He looked and saw that upon his index finger was the fourth ring of sapphire glittering brilliantly. A warm smile of unbridled joy touched his lips. He had done it! Finally, he had done it! Now it was time for payback!

Lady Water grinned softly and told him "I would like nothing more than to offer you a gift to aid you further in your quest. However, there is nothing more that can be done for you. All of the tools you will need are in your hands, use them all and use them wisely. I offer you my blessings and open arms to you. You are always welcome into my home and the homes of my sisters." She paused and turned half her attention onto Mara. "Time is slipping away very quickly now. My dear Jestura shall offer guidance to the Elemental Temple where your gift is eagerly awaiting you."

Mara bowed her head in acknowledgment and smiled brightly as she replied "It would be my honor and pleasure to do so, my mistress." She quickly advanced to him to offer a fond embrace and a heartwarming smile. "Congrats, Kain! I knew you could do it! I always had faith in you!"

"Thanks." he replied, looking past her at the water girl now standing looking at him and talking with a few merrow females, giggling like school girls. "What's that all about? I thought she'd be at least a little upset losing to me."

"I told you that she thought you were cute." Mara laughed loudly and gave him a sly wink. "Even faeries know when they see a good man."

CHAPTER XXXVI

The cloud raft landed softly onto the lush green grass next to a sparkling blue pond in front of a small temple surrounded by perfect trees. The building wasn't very large, but its craftsmanship more than made up for the small size. It looked to be carved from a single massive block of marble with four large columns guarding the large opening. Etched into these four columns were beautiful pictures and words written in the strange calligraphy of faeries. Although Mara and to a lesser extend Nancy recognized them, to the others it was all completely alien to them.

All dismounted their steeds as the raft faery pushed off the grass-covered ground with her staff and quickly faded into the clouds above. Nancy in particular seemed very excited as she immediately started for the temple and beckoned the others to follow.

"I am sorry, Miss Viccon." Mara told her, holding her hand up slightly to stop the girl in her tracks. "I must take your brother in alone."

"What? Why!" Nancy retorted with a hurt frown.

"Only the one who possesses the four elements may enter the Elemental Temple." she replied, sighing slightly as she offered a smile begging forgiveness. Nancy began to interject, but the sorceress continued "I am sorry, Miss Viccon. I really am. Unless you have all four Elemental Rings, or work for the Ladys of course, you can't even cross the threshold."

"There's nothing much going to happen in there, anyway pup." Kain told his disappointed sister, patting her gently on her back. "I'm just going to go in, grab the sword, and come out. That's it, nothing exciting."

"You'll have more fun with us out here, anyway." Michael said as he reached into one of his saddlebags. He pulled out a stack of small, rectangular pieces of thin sheets of wood bound together with a green thread. As he untied the thread and began to shuffle the many cards in his hands, he offered with a grin "Me and Raphael will teach you to play Arcainian Hold'em."

"Wonderful!" Kain chuckled loudly, giving Nancy a gentle shove in the direction of the prince. "Corrupt my poor, innocent little sister even more!"

"How else is she going to shark the tables in Hurst?" he laughed with a wink. "Come on, Julie. We'll show you too. It's really fun and easy to learn."

The four situated themselves in a circle near the pond, and Michael began flipping through the deck explaining what each card was and explaining the basic rules of the game while Raphael snatched a few handfuls of loose pebbles to act as checks and passed them around. Still chuckling lowly, Kain and Mara started for the temple. Kain's pace was quickened by excitement, but Mara kept them at a slower, more patient stride as they walked through the ankle deep carpet of verdant grass.

She looked over her shoulder and, when she figured they were far enough away not to be overheard by the group, casually remarked "How'd you pick up the witch?"

"Julie?" Kain murmured idly, throwing his eyes over his shoulder to look at the group who were laughing and carrying on gleefully. "She's Raphael's . . . ah, my Second General's, sister. It's a long story. Why?"

"Hummmmmmm? Oh, I was just curious." she muttered with a slight pout.

"Jealous?" Kain prodded, throwing his eyes onto her and suddenly wondering if he sounded too hopeful.

"Should I be?" Mara retorted with a laugh as she raised her eyebrows. Kain chuckled modestly and looked forward once more, shaking his head slightly. "Yes, maybe I am a little. I mean, my ex beau, my first kiss even, is dating a wit—ah, an enchantress, after all. Who wouldn't be jealous?"

A laugh rumbled in Kain's throat as they climbed the magnificently carved steps of the temple. "Julie and I not dating. We're just friends, that's all."

"Not to hear her tell it." Mara giggled, giving him a sly wink. "But I can hardly blame her. I know from experience what a catch you are."

Kain blushed deep and mouthed a low thank you as they stepped over the threshold and into the temple. He gasped audibly as he marveled at the fantastic sight. It was a grand room, much larger than it should have been from looking at the outside. The white marble walls were lined with finely crafted statues of faeries of all types and sizes while the marble floor was so highly polished that one could actually see their reflection gazing back up at them. Stretched out before them was a luxurious red carpet made from the finest silk that had not even the slightest hint of dirt or wear. Two hundred feet from the entrance to the temple the red carpet came to a stop in front of a large stone altar. A good-sized marble orb sat perfectly still in the center, so flawlessly round and polished that it looked as if it would roll off at the slightest disturbance. Placed in front of the orb were four small earthenware bowls spaced evenly apart, each bearing an elemental marking. Behind the altar and situated in line with the respective bowls were four golden statues, crafted with such lifelike perfection that no human could have sculpted them. Lady Earth sat upon a sleepy tortoise. Lady Air perched upon a large butterfly. Lady Fire rode on the great wings of a phoenix. And Lady Water straddled a grinning dolphin. All four ladies had large smiles and glittering eyes, as if the faery sculptor had predicted that they would be proud to see any human before them.

Kain and Mara started for the altar, their pace across the red carpet quickening with every step from sheer excitement and unbridled joy that after so many hardships and trials he had at last come to the end of his search. This feeling was surmounted by the awareness that his quest was far from over, the anxiety of knowing that his toughest battle, his lifelong pursuit for vengeance, was at last very near. It didn't seem real to him. It felt more like a dream, a dream plaguing him for many years.

When they reached the altar, Kain took a moment to examine the area before glancing at his friend. Mara grinned brightly and cocked her head towards the bowls. Taking the hint, Kain removed the Ring of Earth from his finger and dropped it into the Earth Bowl. It clinked as it bounced about, the sound echoing in the tomb silence as the elemental symbol etched into the bowl began to glow with a soft, white light that throbbed like a heartbeat. The same happened as he dropped the other rings into their respective bowls. As soon as the Ring of Water found itself inside its bowl, a loud boom shook the temple as bright light shot from each bowl, illuminating the temple with such intensity that the humans had to shield their eyes. When the strange and sudden show had subsided and they were able to open their eyes once more, they found themselves looking at the Ladys themselves, their statues becoming the beautiful faery queens in the flesh. Their steeds called out gleefully as the Ladys laughed with great joy and spoke in complete unison, their voices expressing every bit of pride as their bright eyes showed.

"Kain Viccon, for such a long time our sword has slept quietly as peace reigned throughout the land. Now that evil has once again come to plague and threaten our children, it stirs waiting for a hero to take its handle and wield it in battle. It pleases us that you are that hero, for there is not a more deserving person. It is an honor to bestow upon you our greatest gift, the Elemental Sword."

They each held up their right hands which began to glow brightly in their respective colors: green, yellow, red, and blue. Chatting so softly only a gentle murmur was audible, they touched their fingers and brought them down onto the orb on the altar. There was a flash of bright white light that blinded Kain for a moment. When his eyesight returned to him, he saw a sword imbedded in the marble orb that looked more like a work of art rather than a weapon.

"Use it wisely and you will conquer the bane of evil." they told him, returning to their original positions as they slowly began to fade back into beautiful golden statues. "Your heart commands our power."

He murmured a soft, heartfelt appreciation as he reached up to grip the golden handle. There was a sharp sound of metal on stone met with a shower of sparks as he withdrew the Elemental Sword and marveled at its splendor. The diamond blade was long and as transparent as glass, it's edges sharper than the finest razor blade. Its hilt was made of silver and glittered brightly as did the handle made of pure gold. It felt as if it had no weight at all and sliced through the air with the greatest of ease, feeling as if it had been made especially for his hand.

The sorceress sighed dully as a tear trickled down her radiant cheek, her mouth forming a large smile. Before Kain could react, she threw herself into his arms.

"Congratulations, my dearest friend!" she squeaked, gripping him tighter as he returned the gesture. "I knew you would do it! I always had my faith in you."

"I couldn't have done it without your help, Mara." he told her gently, his lips close to her ear. "Thank you so much! I owe all this to you."

"I was just doing my job as Jestura." she grinned, pulling away from him slightly. She leaned close to bestow a fond peck on his cheek before drawing away completely and lowering her head. When she looked back into his eyes, her face was different, more somber as if she was about to plead for his help. "Actually, there is something I need you to do for me when you get to Noknor's castle."

"Anything for you, Mara." he smiled sincerely.

"I . . . there's a man there. Noknor's second in command, I think his title is the Dark General. His name is Garrison. Anyway, he's . . . he's the one that . . . murdered James."

"I see." he murmured, his eyes flashing heatedly as he immediately knew exactly who she was talking about. He was well familiar with the name Samhus Garrison.

"I . . . I'm not asking for you to save him for me or anything. I mean, I would like nothing more than to deal with him myself, but that's just not feasible. I want you get him for me, Kain. Avenge my brother's betrayal with his blood. Please, for me."

"You know I would do it not only for you, but for myself as well. James was my closest friend. I . . . I miss him." he replied, reaching out to take her hands in his. As he gave a reassuring squeeze, he told her "However, Noknor has my cousin Li, your brother's lover. If what you say is true and Garrison is there, she will see him dead by her own hand, if she hasn't gotten to him already. He's done more to her than to anyone else."

"As long as justice is delivered to his head." she said, closing her eyes as she leaned slowly forward, pulling him close and wrapping her arms delicately around his neck as she put her lips onto his, a kiss as sweet as their first for her hero.

* * *

"I win again!" Nancy laughed excitedly as she triumphantly threw down her cards in front of her and reached for the small pile of pebbles to add to her collection. "You guys must be letting me win!"

Michael chuckled as he took back everyone's cards and began to shuffle them. "Maybe it's beginner's luck."

"Or maybe you're just a natural player." Raphael added with a playful grin as he looked his new cards over. Keeping his physical smile, he grimaced mentally at what he saw.

"Yeah, right!" she laughed. "Then let's start playing for real money!"

"Please, girl!" Michael snorted, tossing three pebbles out in front of him. "Your brother would kick my ass . . . beg your pardon, my rump. Speaking of . . . hey, Kain!"

The small group turned to look as Mara and Kain strolled out of the temple, something new in his sword sheath shining in the bright sunlight. As they jumped up and rushed to greet him, he pulled out the faery flute from his backpack and called out to them "Hurry and collect your stuff. We're going to Noknor's castle! It's time to finally settle an old score!"

* * *

"So you see, Garrison, that is why—" Noknor was explaining to his Dark General, but cut himself abruptly off with a dark, concentrated frown.

"What is it, my lord!" Garrison cried, jumping to his feet and grabbing the handle of his sword as he looked around wildly, fully expecting the Chinese woman to be rushing at them.

Noknor said nothing as he closed his eyes and took a deep breath, which he held for a long moment. Finally, he released it as a long, slow sigh and opened his glowing red eyes to narrow slits. "Viccon is on his way."

"What? How do you know?"

"Is everything ready?" he murmured softly, paying no heed to the question. Garrison nodded vigorously, not sure what to make of his lord. Noknor put a thoughtful hand to his chin as he ordered "Good. Then prepare our little greeting."

* * *

Li twitched violently as if waking up from a nightmare, dropping her lover's hand to fall against the iron bars harshly and startling the princess Elizabeth. The girl rushed to her side, gripping the bars that separated their cell from James's with one nervous hand while putting the other on her shoulder.

"What is it? What's the matter?" she asked in a very concerned tone of voice.

"Are you okay, Li-Li?" James replied with a heavy frown and a dull cough as he quickly reached back through the bars to grip her hand.

Li didn't say anything right away, she just sat silently by staring off into space. James gave her soft hand a loving squeeze and her jaw slackened slightly as she shook her head to clear it. She glanced at Elizabeth before returning James's squeeze and replying "Kain . . . Kain and Nancy are on their way here."

"Right now?" Elizabeth asked.

Li nodded slowly. "Yeah. They're coming."

"What makes you say that, my China doll?" James murmured softly, reaching out with his free hand to take her hand in both of his. He hissed and grit his teeth as pain flashed through his body from the stretching the movement caused.

"I . . . I don't really know." she answered him, looking deep into his eyes as if to plead with him not to think her crazy. "I just have this sudden feeling in my heart that's telling me salvation is on its way to this castle."

PART VII

THE FINAL BATTLE

CHAPTER XXXVII

At the edge of the coal black clouds rumbling over Noknor's castle, the pure white clouds parted just enough to allow a smaller cloud to quickly drift through and glide swiftly into the trees of the forest. As the cloud raft landed silently upon a cushion of crisp leaves and soft grass, Kain looked around for any signs of friend or foe, nearly expecting to be immediately attacked by some of Noknor's minions. The small group rode off the cloud one by one, followed lastly by the Grand General still keeping his eyes watchful and his ears open for the slightest snapped branch. When Kain tipped his head and thanked the faery girl for all her help, she smiled under her hood and held up her hand, slowly moving her fingers to wave farewell. Though her lips never moved, he distinctly heard a soft, female voice whisper a reassuring good luck to him. Even with the churning in his stomach, the grip over his heart loosened and his managed to muster a bright smile as he quickly spurred his horse onto the ground.

"What do you think, man?" Raphael asked him in a voice so low most of the words were buried under the silence of the forest. Kain had told them to keep as low of a profile as possible, since there was no telling how far Noknor's scout patrols reached away from the castle.

Kain frowned and his eyes narrowed as he shook his head silently. He thought for a moment before replying in a voice as muffled as Raphael's had been "I'm not sure. But the first thing we need to do is find Robert and the rest of the troops." He paused and looked above at the canopy of leaves over their heads before scanning the trees ahead of him. "On the way down I noticed that there seemed to have been a recent battle, but it looked to be a pretty small skirmish. I'm pretty sure our forces have already arrived and that Robert intercepted them. We're pretty deep in the forest, so we shouldn't have to worry about any enemy patrols, but let's just be on the safe side and keep ourselves covered."

"How are we going to find the camp?" Nancy whispered, gently caressing Uni's trembling neck.

Seeing the sight of Noknor's gory hell had upset them all, but Uni especially seemed disturbed and Nancy was doing her best to console him. She had surprised everyone on the raft by being the one least taken aback by the sight. While everyone had thought that she would have turned away before the rest, she had actually never taken her eyes off the sight, taking it all in and letting anger and disgust fill her heart. Filling it with a furious rage that she would let loose first upon Noknor's army and then onto the dark lord himself. At that point not just Kain, but everyone with her realized the power the girl held within her spirit.

"I'm not quite sure yet, kiddo." Kain replied with a dull, dejected shrug of his broad shoulders. "Unfortunately, the cover the trees provide not only prevents Noknor from seeing it, but also prevented us too as we came down. I'd hate to have to split up, but maybe we should. Pair off and I'll go by myself. With any luck one of us will be spotted by an Arcainian patrol or maybe—"

The echoing sound of dry leaves being crushed under foot silenced him instantly as he drew the Elemental Sword. It gleamed brightly, even with the sun partially blocked out by the heavy trees. It seemed that its luster came from within itself, glowing as if it were alive. The others followed his lead and drew their own weapons as they induced their horses into a tight circle to guard against all sides. There came utter silence, with no insects buzzing, no birds chirping, and no animals skittering about in the underbrush. Not even a wind blew to shake the branches or rustle the leaves. All was perfectly still, and very unsettling. It was a predator's silence.

Kain listened closer, but nothing except for his own heart beating rapidly in his chest filled his ears. His knuckles wrapped tightly around the handle of the Elemental Sword. His eyes narrowed to slits.

'We've been spotted!' he thought savagely, adrenaline gushing through his veins. He dared not move his body at all except for his free hand, which he used to caress his steed's neck to comfort it and keep it under control. He glanced at his friends. 'They know it too. Good. They're ready for it. But why haven't we been attacked? Hopefully we out number them. Or maybe—'

Three sharp, quick whistles sounded from the brush, which could have been nothing more than a forest bird. However, Nancy and the three men knew better and exhaled the breaths they had been holding in their lungs audibly and sighed in relief, small chuckles unconsciously coming from each as they lowered their guards. Julie was the only one that kept herself poised to attack anything that dared to show itself from behind the thick wall of trees, her fists glowing with a throbbing yellow light. Kain took notice and quickly waved her down, giving her a trusting smile when she conveyed her reluctance. After she had finally lowered her guard, though keeping her mind set to act at a moment's notice, Kain cupped his hand at his mouth and gave two long whistles of his own followed by two short whistles.

There was a short pause before a loud commotion stirred within the brush and three Arcainian scouts, their light leather armor covered in leaves and moss, stepped into full view. Kain didn't recognize any of them as being a part of the original band of scouts headed by Robert, so he immediately knew that his previous assumption had been correct. It was definitely a good thing that he had sent Robert and the soldiers ahead of them.

"Sir Viccon?" the highest ranking scout gasped as all three men's faces fixed into a mixture of shock and overjoy. He quickly regained his composure and went rigid with a stiff at-attention stance, the two enlisted scouts taking his lead. He delivered a snappy salute and held it proudly as Kain returned it.

"At ease, captain." Kain replied in a pleasant, hushed voice. "We sure are glad to see you."

"Not as glad as the rest of us are to see you, sir!" he said in a very excited, quite boisterous voice. "Morale's been shot to hell, but as soon as you step into the camp, it'll go sky high! Thank the Goddess!"

"You're being awfully loud, don't you think?" Nancy snapped, her frosty tone merely a raised whisper. She would have thought more from a scout captain than to carry on as if it were a homecoming party. "It's a wonder Noknor's patrols haven't pounced all over us already."

"Oh, you don't have to worry about that, uhm . . ." the captain told her, stumbling at the end of his sentence as he looked for her rank insignia. He should have been more than a little annoyed at being barked at by a youngster that couldn't have outranked him by a long shot, but the excitement over seeing his Grand General made the manner of her words pass right over his head.

"Soldier will do just fine." Kain told him.

"Yes, sir." he nodded his understanding. "As I was saying, ah, soldier, Noknor doesn't seem to have any scouts, other than a few winged demons we've seen flying around the castle grounds. And even then, they don't come very close to the forest, much less this far. It would seem that either they can't cross the edge of those black clouds or are just not interested in anything beyond them. Either way, we're perfectly safe from their patrols as long as we stay in the forest."

"That's good to know." Michael replied. One of the enlisted glanced at him and fumbled for a salute. The other two looked at him and then to Michael before also saluting the prince uneasily. The prince gave a quick return and waved them off with a humble grin.

"Perhaps bad to know. With his power right now, he may not have any need for scouts." Kain muttered dully, his eyes narrow as he scanned all around them for any sign of a potential spy. There was a short pause before he seemed to cast off his search. "Why don't you take us to our camp, Captain."

He engaged in small talk with the captain while the others conversed with the two enlisted as the group moved swiftly through the forest. Kain had figured if Noknor just didn't want patrols or could spy on them with sorcery, it didn't much matter if they crept along to conceal themselves or if they moved quickly without regards. Personally, he rather they get to the Arcainian encampment as quickly as possible.

When one of the enlisted scouts, quite taken in by the young girl, asked Nancy why she wore no rank insignia anywhere on her uniform, she told him that she was the Grand General's civilian sister along at his request. It took a moment for it to sink in, but when it did both enlisted men became even more nervous and uneasy and any sort of eyes they had on her instantly went blind. They repeatedly stumbled on their words as if they tried to make sure of each word as they came out of their mouths lest they inadvertently make a comment that would get them harshly barked at, or worse, for insolence. Nancy giggled lowly. Apparently they weren't used to contact with people as high up on the pole as Kain and his crew, so she decided to be extra pleasant to them.

After a few inquires as to what they had learned from serving watches as scouts, Kain asked the captain "How long have you been here? I mean the army as a whole."

"Just a few days." he answered. "General Grotz came in contact with us just as we came up Tosica Hill. He told our commander about your being along at a later time and the actual plans to wait until you arrived before mounting a full-scale attack. I'm sure you already know this, sir, but there is rumor of Noknor having something of a secret weapon with enough power to mow us down."

"He does at that, Captain. I did notice that there seemed to be a recent battle on the fields not far from the castle. Explain?"

"Yes, sir. Uhm, there was a small battle, but only a handful of casualties. I think three deaths and ten injuries. Only two of those where serve enough to warrant concern."

"That's it?" Kain asked, quite taken aback.

"Yes, sir. It's thought that Noknor just wanted us to know that he knew we were there. He didn't throw a very large force at us, and most of the injuries actually came from castle archers. Because of General Grotz's report we had already begun pulling back before the attack came. Noknor himself didn't show, so it's thought that he's waiting for something."

"For me." he muttered blandly. "Who's in command?"

"Four Star Blue General Riet, sir."

Kain nodded his head dully with no change in his outward expression. His only response was a simple "Excellent."

* * *

Inside the largest tent of the crudely and hastily fashioned Arcainian camp, Kain stood in front of a large tree stump being used as a makeshift table. Raphael, Michael, Robert, Carrie, and Riet were quietly crowded around him, while nearly two dozen other high ranking officers stood in the tent. Everyone wore long, grave faces as they waited for their Grand General to speak. Laid out on the stump was a simple map of the area the Arcainian scouts had put together in the course of their patrols. It showed the castle and the grounds around it as nothing more than squares, circles, and labels. It was quite simple to see that many different hands had gone into making it up, but Kain wasn't looking at it in order to critique its style and form. It provided the information needed to plan an attack and a backup plan if a hasty escape was needed. That was its only job and it did it quite well, indeed.

"What do you think, Grand General?" Robert inquired. Kain didn't answer for several moments as he stood and glared at the map, brooding with narrow, intent eyes and a sharp frown. Finally, he replied "Do we have any rolling shields?"

"Yes, sir. I believe we have four squads." Riet told him, his own voice carrying a disappointed tone to it. "Not many, I'm afraid. But I'm sure we could rig something up with logs from the forest to make more. Rather crude, I know, but—"

"No, that's unnecessary and it would only serve to tire the men out before the battle." Kain said bluntly.

"But four squads won't be enough." Raphael hastily replied. "Especially if they bombard us with catapults."

"If they use catapults, it wouldn't matter if we had a hundred squads." Kain told him in a simple point-of-fact tone. "However, the lay out of the castle itself should provide a majority of our forces quite a bit of cover protection."

"I was noticing that too." Carrie voiced strongly. Despite being the only female, she held herself with great pride, not intimidated in the least by the men. And none of them, especially after hearing her expertise in tracking and warfare as well as watch her take charge of the soldiers during the previous scuffle, thought of her as anything other than their equal or their superior. Kain, himself, had bestowed upon her the honorary rank of One Star Green General in charge of several scout squads under Robert Grotz so as to aid such a costly battle. "It seems that not very much thought went into its construction. Either that, or way too much."

Upon the curious looks of the others gathered in the tent, Kain explained, touching the paper as he spoke to give a visual. "Archers will line up along the front edges of the castle and will be able to rain down arrows roughly from here to here." His finger traced a rectangle on the field in front of the castle. "However, these towers on either end, actually all four towers at each corner and these two as well, are not archer-friendly at all. What few windows there are are way too narrow and odd shaped and they're staggered in an almost random order. It's impossible to fire a decent shot out from any place in any of these towers. And there's no way to get a catapult up there, the roofs are much too slanted."

"Why would they have been made it like that?" Raphael asked, his face distorted in a look of disbelief but holding a flickering gleam of relief.

"It's just what Himiniz said. Too much thought went into it. Something thought up by a bureaucratic bookworm." Kain told them. "One of those things that looks good on paper, I guess. It's supposed to help cool the castle in the summer and warm it up in the winter. The thing is too, that the towers also cut off the line of sight from the front and sides. If you notice, the square shape of them creates a cone shaped blind spot as far as archers on either side of the towers are concerned. You can't see anything from the positions on the outer walls. And what you can't see, you can't hit." He paused and rubbed his chin thoughtfully as he took in a deep breath. "For years I've been trying to get Edward to correct it. To flatten the roofs at the very least. I think that was a big reason Noknor took the castle with such ease. But then, fate has played the same card against him. Lucky us." Kain paused once more and examined the map. He glanced back at Riet and murmured "Four squads, huh?"

"Yes, sir." the blue general answered. Even though he was several years older than the Grand General, he had the utmost respect for the man. He took his orders without question and listened intently whenever he had anything to say. He knew, after seeing Sir Viccon in battle and directly working with him in the past, that age didn't necessarily determine skill or natural leadership as far as the Viccon heir was concerned. Kain was the best damned general he had ever seen in his long history with the Arcainian armed forces, and he was not ashamed to admit it to others and to himself. "With two per squad, that's only eight shielders."

"I think that should be enough." He gestured to the area in front of the castle that would surely be bombarded with archer fire and said "Here is what I want to do. We're going into three teams. Team A, of which I will personally lead, will be smaller than the others and advance directly forward. The shielders will provide the protection from ground forces and ground archers to a lesser extent. We'll just have to deal with any catapult fire and castle archers the best we can."

He pointed to each of the cone shaped blind spots each tower would provide as he spoke. "Team B will follow the cover given by the tower on the right. Team C will take the left. Grotz, I want you to lead B and take my sister and Julie with you. I'll be damned if I'll take them into the inferno with me. Boniva, Your Highness, I want you two to go with Grotz and keep an eye on the two of them. A **CLOSE** eye!" He stressed the word harshly. "I'm entrusting their lives in your hands."

"Don't worry, Grand General." Raphael assured him with a deadly serious tone. "We'll die before we let them fall into harms way."

"You can trust us, my friend." Michael added. "After all, we've grown pretty fond of them ourselves."

A grin touched Kain's face as he nodded his head softly and then it just as quickly disappeared when he continued "Riet, I want you to lead C. All three teams will meet right here at the doors to the castle. Drawbridge up or down, we'll figure out how to advance in." He stopped and looked up, his eyes falling on the only female among the leaders. "I will leave it up to you as to what team you want your unit to go with. Whichever you feel you will be able to give the most to."

"My team would very much like to go with you into the inferno, Grand General." Carrie replied firmly.

"Are you sure?"

"Yes, sir. Very sure." she nodded with bold confidence.

He looked around at his friends and battlefield brothers. "Ten battalions will hold back and be our reinforcements." He named off the ten commanders to head these battalions, each man saluting his pride and obedience as his name was mentioned. "Each is only to enter the first moments of battle as needed and only one at a time. We have too many men for a siege and if we bring everyone in at once it's just going to be a giant fuster. However, once we are able to break into the castle each battalion is to march in, one at a time." He pointed at three of his commanders. "Your battalions are to monitor Kuberica City. It's a sure bet Noknor has at least a few garrisons stationed there and it would be rather easy for them to flank us. Should that happen, you three are to intercept them. The city's far enough away that any action should be noticed well in time. If any of his Dark Knights try to run, you will intercept them as well. None of them will escape justice!"

He took in a very deep breath and let it out slowly, looking over his loyal and brave knights. "So that's it, people. Are we all clear as to what's going on?"

All of them silently nodded their understanding. Robert looked him in the eyes and asked quietly, almost in a whispered voice "When does it happen?"

"Tomorrow. At dawn." was Kain's answer, his fingers drumming on the tree's flat surface. "I know there isn't much time, but it's a safe bet that Noknor knows I'm here and will launch an attack. Frankly, we've run out of time, so let's spread the word. We only have a few gut wrenching hours, and they'll be over before you know it."

CHAPTER XXXVIII

The dark sky was lit at the distant horizon by the tip of a rising sun, dashes of brightness showing among the white clouds as dawn began chasing away the night. The morning birds sung softly as they spread their wings for the dawn of a new day while a few large gray owls gave their last few hoots before silently flapping their wings to take air and return to their daily resting places. Insects buzzed and chirped as a cool, gentle breeze drifted through the forest to carry the many traces of life along its breath. Droplets of mist from the night's fog clung thickly in the air, a cold, dense moisture caressing the Arcainain Army, ten thousand strong standing ready and waiting for orders from their great Grand General.

The horse took Grand General Kain Viccon to the head of the army to deliver his final parting speech. As he rode, he looked around at all of the tired, haggard faces all filled with fear, every eye overflowing with uncertainty and terror for the rapidly approaching battle. He heard several men retch onto the ground, heard the muffled, sobbing whispers of prayers being said. They knew they were about to walk into the fires of Hell and that they all stood a very good chance of never making it out alive, of never seeing their loved ones again. They had no doubt in their minds that they would very likely rot on those very fields and be pecked at by the carrion birds and ravaged by the wild dogs. It was a most gruesome fate for anyone to befall, but even more they knew that it was a terrible tragedy to suffer for their families that were already so frightened for their brave soldiers. Kain knew these fears quite well as he had those very thoughts himself, for himself and for his sister. And as brave of a man as he was he was scared to death. However, though deep inside he could not stop trembling at the bloody visions that raced through his mind, he would never show any outward signs that would threaten to cause morale to sink even lower. Years of fighting brutal wars had taught him to develop an iron shield of savage coldness that would not only hide his inner workings, but also both strike terror into his enemies and give strength to his own men. And now, with his mind racing and his heart pumping faster than a roaring river, he knew that this battle was something that must be done and could only be done by him and his group.

He would run into battle and fight as bravely as he could no matter what. And if he or his sister did die, he took heart in knowing that their souls would live on with Auset and with their parents. It was not a pleasant thought, but it was much more reassuring than the alternative thinking.

Kain spurred his horse to a stop and yanked on the reigns to turn it snorting to face his men. The horse's right front leg slipped on a patch of grass made moist by the morning dew, causing it to stumble slightly and neigh angrily as it regained its footing. Kain looked down and frowned. His men were already exhausted, and he wondered if any of them had managed a decent night's sleep. He himself hadn't slept a wink as he stayed up all night praying. But even as ragged as they looked, he had much faith in his soldiers. He knew they would fight with honor and never give up, no matter what. They were Arcainian Knights. They were the best. And he knew they would not be beaten, certainly not by Noknor. He just had to make sure they knew it better than anyone else did.

"We are soon to head out into battle." Kain bellowed out, his booming voice loud and carrying to every ear. "I will not lie to you, it will be very dangerous." He paused slightly and his poignant frown darkened. "Noknor and his army will give us the fight of our lives. But it is a fight we can and most certainly will win! We will triumph over this great evil! Because we are better than anything Noknor can throw at us. We are the best! I know many of you are afraid, for I know these emotions well. But do not let your fear consume you. Do not let fear cripple you when there is so much at stake.

"And indeed the very world is at stake today! Remember, you are not fighting for me. You are not fighting for the glory of Arcainia and our great Queen. Today you are fighting for the good of the world! Because Noknor is evil and such evil cannot and will not be allowed to infect this world. Because the world is counting on you today to pull in victory over the great evil that is Noknor! Your family, your friends, and everything you cherish and hold dear are at stake here to today. For if Noknor wins, then all is lost. I have already lost enough to him, and I will not lose anything else to Noknor and his evil. I may die today, I may lose my life! But I would rather die with a sword in my chest and a hundred arrows piercing my flesh than to live as a coward in a world ruled by evil.

"We are Arcainians! The toughest of the tough! The best of the best! The whole world is watching us, praying for us in our swift victory. And we shall not disappoint today as we ride into glory and the immortality! We shall fight bravely and if we fall, we will fall with honor so that when we walk the golden halls of the Heavenly Palace and come upon the throne of Auset, She will welcome our souls as heroes and usher us into the paradise of Heaven!

"If your brother should fall by your side, know that he will be watching you, so honor him and fight for him! Make him proud! Make your family proud! Make Auset proud! Fight bravely, fight with honor, and you will never be destroyed!" With quick, sharp movements, he snatched the handle of his sword, tore it from its sheath, and thrust it high over his head. Though the morning sun still had not been able to penetrate the canopy of the trees, the crystal blade glittered brilliantly and reflected light over his face and body. "Now, let us ride out onto that hellish battlefield and fight! Let us fight until we are called home, to Arcainia or to Auset! Let us fight to **WIN**!"

The massive army rose as one, their tremendous roars and shouts filling the still dawn, their weapons and shields clanging loudly with the intense pounding as thousands of men roared and bellowed to make the very earth tremble at their intensity. A thunderous rumbling vibrated the ground as each of the large, thick wooden shields slowly started to roll, pushed by four men each. They stretched high above at a sloping angle to catch arrows that rained down like hail and each wielded wicked steel spikes to mow down any enemy forces that dared get in their ways.

Kain watched his sister ride upon her unicorn, her mood even more angry and vengeful than any of the most seasoned troops. He urged his steed a few steps towards her, wanting to follow her as she fell in line with her advancing team, refusing to take his eye off of her. This was it, the end of their adventures that had brought them where they now stood, the beginning of perhaps the greatest, most important fight for them both. He did not want to let her leave his side, fearing that this would be the last he saw of her. But he knew he had to leave her, he had to let her go. It tore his heart apart in his chest, but there was no choice in the matter. Fate had long ago stepped in. He only prayed that Fate was feeling kind this day.

With a heavy sigh, he touched his fingers to his lips and blew his baby sister a farewell kiss that she did not notice. "I love you, Nancy. Please be careful."

With that, he replaced the Elemental Sword into the sheath and spurred his steed to gallop behind the rolling shields. As he rode swiftly past his men, each saluted and raised their weapons proudly to him, honoring him with cheers and hardy shouts. He weaved his way to his spot finding Carrie, Rebecca and Kassandra there waiting. Their faces were filled with the same odd mixture of pride, excitement, and tension as he knew his was. However, the youngest seemed especially excited and determined. She reminded Kain so much of his sister, and he again bowed his head slightly to whisper a prayer on her behalf. He hoped that her strange determination for Noknor's blood would not cloud her thoughts and make her do something that would forever scar his soul. Especially if he weren't there to save—

"Good luck, Grand General." Carrie replied softly to stir him from his thoughts, a wavy, false grin on her trembling lips. "We'll need it."

Kain frowned as he glanced up to gaze at the top ledges of the castle and saw archers, much too many to count, already lined up with arrows notched and bowstrings drawn. Several grotesque winged demons circled overhead just high enough to avoid the rush of Dark Knight arrows but low enough to swiftly and easily swoop down to claim an Arcainian soldier and rip them to shreds. It was the first wave of Noknor's horde, and probably the easiest to deal with.

His horse bucked, nearly throwing him off as it was startled by the hellish squeal of one of those demons. As he did his best to regain control, he was slapped in the face by a leathery wing. He turned to see one of the demon creatures attacking a rider in an orgasmic frenzy right next to him, shrill hog-like squeals and bellowing horse neighs issuing loudly from the mass. He drew his blade and forced his steed to close in, but dared not to lash out for fear that he would inadvertently hit the person being attacked. As he drew closer, shouting and trying to frighten the demon away, he recognized the enraged swears of a female voice belonging to Rebecca. The monster rose slightly, just enough for him to catch a glimpse of her stabbing at it furiously with her dagger while screaming and cursing in rage, the extremely close quarters allowing the use of nothing else. He noticed that she had blood streaming down her face from a nasty gash above her eye from the sharp talons. Deciding that it was better to chance hitting her than watching her surely be torn to shreds, he reared back his arm and calculated his blow. He nearly dropped his weapon as he startled when the demon squealed in a very high-pitched howl and a spray of thick green syrup followed the tip of a Boniva lance that exploded out of the side of its gruesome head. It lashed out in death throes, its talons slashing air and its wings giving weak beats. Kain barely had time to throw up his shield as the clawed tail as sharp as metal thorns whipped around, sent a shower of sparks as it carved a groove in the steel. Rebecca's horse collapsed from exhaustion, its own dark coat matted with blood from its wounds, and sent Rebecca crashing hard onto the ground. Screaming and spewing savage curses, she rapidly crawled to the demon and began to hack at it with her dagger to spray the green slime that was its blood onto her, totally oblivious to her burning wounds in her berserk rage. The green ooze enraged her further, and she jabbed harder and faster, her clenched jaw grinding in fury.

As Kassandra tugged on her lance still skewering the demon, Carrie fell off her horse to rush to her crazed friend. When she first tried to pull her off the mutilated corpse, she almost took a dagger to her stomach as Rebecca's wild swings came dangerously close. She bellowed at the insane woman, jolting her out of her bloodthirsty trace to gaze at her superior with a stupefied look in her dull eyes and slack jaw. She shook her head slightly and took a deep breath as she looked at the creature at her side and gave it one more savage thrust. With a heavy, drained sigh, Rebecca pushed herself up and slowly stood on very shaky legs. Her entire face was a crimson mask, blood gushing from the large slash on her head. She had scratches all over her body, most small and superficial but some very deep and nasty, and a large puncture wound where the tail had impaled her side literally spewed like a fountain. With such a massive loss of blood, she was even paler than normal and those soldiers around her wondered how she was still even able to stand. She was in terrible shape and needed medical attention quickly, but before either Carrie or Kain could even open their mouths, two Arcainian medics were at her side, helping to steady her as they attempted to dress her most serious wounds first.

"I don't need a medic!" Rebecca spat out fiercely, pushing the Arcainians away and almost falling in the process. Rather than listening to her, the medics gripped her arms and held her weak frame up, holding her tight against her stubborn tugging.

"The hell you don't!" Carrie told her, her voice powerful and forceful and her eyes hard and striking. "You are to go with these soldiers and receive the medical attention that you need, Rebecca! That is an order!" She looked into her friend's disappointed face and her own softened slightly. "I'm sorry."

Rebecca's eyebrows arched slightly and she stood as tall and proud as she could in her state. She knew there was nothing more she could do, no matter how much she wanted to fight. She would die if she didn't heed the order, and that was enough to immediately kill her pride. She raised her arm in a Boniva salute and said in a weak voice "Aye, D'Elite."

Suddenly, she felt too drained to even walk on her own, and so she allowed the medics to guide, practically carry, her to a horse-drawn cart large enough to hold four injured and wounded as they tried to stop her bleeding. She turned her head and called out in the strongest voice she could muster "Thanks, Kassandra."

The young girl smiled proudly and gave her a departing salute. As Carrie mounted her horse, Kain idly thought that if the red hair and pale complexion didn't give away her Shazadian heritage, her fiery temper sure did. He glanced into the sky and noticed that the demons were breaking formation, if it could actually be called that, to fly towards the other two groups. His heart flopped in his chest. Clearly, Noknor had realized the design flaw and was sending them to cover for the lack of archer fire. If enough of those demons were to attack, which it seemed there would be more than enough as the rate at which they flew out of the castle didn't seem to slow in the least, Nancy would be in just as much danger as if she were riding right beside him. He truly had faith in his two friends, but even that began to falter when he saw several of the demons dive onto his men. Many failed as the men lashed out with their weapons to kill them or at least drive them away. However, lives were still claimed by their claws and Kain shruddered to think that the fate could befall anyone, particularly someone who the demons would target as easy prey to begin with. As much as Kain had seen from his sister over the course of their journeys, she was still his beloved little sister and he couldn't help but think of her as anything but the meek little girl he had always known. These thoughts slowly gave way to sullen realization that the battle had yet to start and they were already down one very good Boniva scout and several men. They were running deathly short on time and good luck.

"By the Goddess!" Carrie whispered at Kain's side, just the mere tone of her voice enough to make his spirit weaken.

He looked back up to find that the sky was pitch black, covered by a thick shadow. It swarmed around wildly like a provoked hive of insects as it flew, seeming to drop down at an alarming rate. Kain's own heart shattered as he recognized that they were not insects at all, but something with a much more deadly sting.

"INCOMING!" he roared at the top of his lungs, throwing his long, curved shield over his head to make an umbrella against the deadly rain. The sound like that of an immense wave from the ocean filled his ears, followed by many more all at once. There came the metallic clangs as he felt a dozen arrows strike his shield and shatter, the dull chunk as they embedded into the massive shielders, and the screams of fallen soldiers and horses that could not protect themselves in time.

When he felt the danger had passed, he lowered his guard and urged his steed onward. He had only made it a few feet when he had to stop and yell the warning once more. As arrows rained over them in a hellish torrent, a tremendous explosion rocked the battlefield. He dared to raise his head enough to see a large orange glow in front of his unit. He lowered his guard and saw a large bonfire crackling in the dead grass where nothing else was. He contemplated what in the world could have caused it and figured it out the split second before two enormous black balls trailing thick clouds of smoke and long tails of flame shot from the castle and sailed through the air with a strange whistling. As they reached their peak height and began to fall swiftly, Kain could only stand by staring with dread-filled shock, unable to call out the warning. Both balls struck the front line, erupting into searing infernos upon impact. The resulting explosion blasted two shielders to burning embers and vaporized the crews of each as well as several soldiers and their riders that had happened to be too close. Two other shielders were disabled to the point at which they could no longer move, their crews burned and crushed. This left only four working shielders to defend against the barrage of arrows and the ground troops Noknor was sure to now send out. Those that did not perish instantly as bodies where torn to charred pieces from the blasts screamed and writhed as they ran around wildly and rolled around in vain, their bodies so consumed by fire that the only way to distinguish them from the many other fires scattered around by the blasts was by the squeals of their agony as they very slowly suffocated to death.

Kain gasped as bile filled his mouth. They were losing the battle more and more quickly with each passing moment. With damp eyes, he removed the Elemental Sword and gazed into the blade as if looking for some secret answer within the mystical weapon. The only thing he saw was his own sorrowful face reflected back. All of a sudden, to his surprise his own face disappeared and was replaced by the four beautiful visages of the Ladys of the Elements.

"Your heart commands our power." they told him in unison, their collective tone tender and warm in a motherly sense.

Kain was stunned, stammering "Wuh-what . . . what . . . what do you-you mean? My heart?"

But it was too late. His own face had replaced theirs. *Your heart commands our power.* What had they meant? He clutched at his chest, feeling Li's talisman press against his heart. The Dragon's Heart! Could that be it? He pulled it out as another explosion shook the earth. It was as cold and inanimate as any other piece of jewelry. He placed the Elemental sword close to it. Nothing. As he brought his shield up once more to protect against the barrage of arrows, he touched the blade to the ruby heart. Nothing. He swore violently as he dropped the talisman back under his armor.

"Your heart controls our power." the Ladys' voice drifted softly from the blade.

Kain glanced at the weapon and frowned. Without knowing exactly why, he held it outstretched in front of him and pointed at the fires killing his men. He thought of water quenching the flames and a hard stream of cold-water shot from the blade like a roaring river. The water splashed everywhere, instantly putting out any fire it came in contact with. As it struck those men that still lived, it soothed their burns and wounds faster and better than any ointment the medics could put on them.

Kain looked up and saw three more fire bombs and another sea of arrows bearing down upon them. With a simple wave of the sword over his head, a bellowing wind swept overhead. It blew with such power that it grabbed each firebomb and threw them away to crash back where they had come from. The black sky was lit up with a red glow from the resulting explosion, the castle ripping apart to spew rubble as the Dark Knight forces responsible for the arrows were totally decimated. The arrows in flight were picked up into the wind and carried over the battlefield. A large whirlwind began to churn and collected the arrows into a large collection. As quickly as it came in, the whirlwind disappeared and deposited the arrows harmlessly onto the field. The missiles were not the only things affected. The demons were whisked away, squealing and squirming as they were taken out of sight and out the hair of the Arcainian Army, writhing in a vain attempt to escape the winds that tore them apart.

Kain's eyes narrowed and a large grin of renewed hope brightened his face. The tides, he knew, had now changed. His men knew it as well, as cheers and applause took the place of arrows and firebombs in the air. Without needing further urging, the Arcainian forces pressed harder and faster towards the castle knowing that their Grand General was a match for any superweapon Noknor could wield.

* * *

"What is it now, Garrison?" Noknor muttered with frosty annoyance as his Dark General burst into the throne room excited and out of breath.

"Vuh . . . Viccon . . . has . . . has . . ." Garrison gasped, doubling over as he huffed and wheezed.

"Would you PLEASE collect yourself!" Noknor snapped fiercely, turning his head to bark before returning his attention back onto a glowing orb. He watched as Viccon rode his horse swiftly cross the battlefield, leading the Arcainian forces onward. In the span of seconds, literally mere seconds, the entire disposition of the Arcainians had turned around. First cowering behind their shields, very slowly advancing forward as they were picked off one at a time, they trembled as his Dark Knights rained a plague of fire and death upon them. But now they had taken to hooting and wailing like savages as they tore across the field, energized with a newfound sense of hope and determination. They followed their Grand General with an intent hell-bent loyalty that Noknor would never see in his own troops. Whatever Viccon had done to eliminate his archers had not only served to prevent further attack from the sky but had also boosted the morale level of his men to insane levels. Of course it would be all for not. No amount of help those foolish little faeries could give Viccon would make the slightest difference when the deciding moment finally came. Let them have their precious moment of inane glory. Archers and catapults would be but child's play compared to what awaited them after Viccon's defeat at his personal hands.

He grunted and sniffled slightly. "You can not know just how vexing that is!"

"I . . . buh-beg your . . . pardon . . . sire." Garrison gasped, pausing slightly to draw deep breaths of air into his lungs. When his heart-rate had slowed and he regained control of his breathing, he replied "I'm sorry, my lord. I ran all the way from—"

"What is it!" Noknor barked roughly.

Garrison squealed and flinched. "Ah, Viccon has conjured up some type of force to drive away our arrows and fire bombs. Ten squads of archers were completely obliterated and we lost all of our catapults! There is severe structural damage to the castle as well. We have no way of delivering an aerial—"

"And?" Noknor raised a brow.

Garrison was thrown into momentary silence from the much unexpected, simple comment he was interrupted by. "Ah, and what would you like done, sire?"

"Send out the ground forces, of course!" Noknor frowned darkly, his hissing tone low as if Garrison had asked him what color the sky was. Even that cretin should have made that obvious decision himself. Apparently Viccon's recent actions, while strengthening his own men's spirits, had shaken Noknor's troops rather harshly. He'd have to show them that whatever power was on Viccon's side was no match for the black powers of the Dark.

"Go get the women and the cripple and bring them to my chambers." he ordered, tapping the orb. It grew dark as the picture of the battlefield faded and began to shrudder as it was swallowed into the ground. He raised his right hand and snapped his fingers, his staff whisked away from the side of his throne to land squarely in his awaiting hand. He twisted his head first to the left, then to the right as a sharp crackling echoed in the quiet room. He straightened his head, licked his lips, and said "Now, if you don't mind, it's time I met the great Grand General face to face and let him know just who he's come up against."

* * *

A shruddering boom rumbled through the air that could have been nothing more than thunder calling from the black clouds or another firebomb exploding onto the battlefield. However, the clouds as black and ominous as they were would not yield rain or thunder and there would be no more fire bombs launched from Noknor's powerful catapults, Kain and the Elemental Sword had made quite certain of that as was evident by the shattered castle ledges where several fires still burned. Kain frowned and his eyes narrowed darkly. He pushed his horse hard and fast over the dead land, the Elemental Sword held high over his head as he gave sharp, intent thrusts with his arm to urge his loyal knights onward into the battle. Close behind his steed rode One Star Red General Carrie Himiniz and Captain Kassandra Erte, their long Boniva lances held in front of them, their Boniva banners waving proudly in the wind. While the general's lance was still virgin, the captain's was stained with the green blood from the demon she had saved her friend from, drying gobs flinging off. Behind them rode Kain's small company, small in comparison to the other two companies advancing well ahead of them under the protection of the castle towers but still one thousand strong, less the mournful casualties they had regrettably suffered. They used the pain and sorrow of their fallen comrades in arms to fuel their anguished hearts as they roared and bellowed, their hellish battle-cries carrying loud and far as they rushed past the Forest of Woe where hundreds of decomposing bodies rotted on stakes thrust through their bodies. As disgusted as they were with the putrid sights and smells they experienced, the brave Arcainians would not allow such a grisly detour make their hearts go numb and turn them away as before. Now they allowed it to further add to the fires in their souls and push them on with more determination and bravery. They took compassion on those that still writhed in agony, delivering them a quick end to their suffering as they rode past the horror, rage building for the blood of the ruthless Noknor and his horrible men.

As he recognized the groaning of timber and the clanking of chain links, Kain slowed his horse, his army following his lead as they all came to a stop to watch as the massive drawbridge slowly lowered one chain link at a time. A heavy thud shook the ground under them as a large cloud of dust and grime kicked up when the drawbridge slammed onto the soft dirt just past the moat. And then there was silence. Not a sound was uttered from the Arcainians, not from Kain's company or from those two companies under the commands of other Arcainian generals, which had also come to a complete stop in nervous anticipation. Only the occasional whinnies and snorts from scattered horses as nervous as their masters could be heard as all stared into the black void, waiting for what would come at them. Many expected a hellish army, so large and overwhelming that it would make them look like nothing more than a troupe of parading school children. Others were sure that a horde of terrible demons would spew out, ready to devour them all alive while others thought that only one or two demons so monstrous as to put even the fiercest dragons to shame would be necessary. Kain, himself, steeled himself while he prepared to finally meet Noknor, sure that the warlock would step out to test his enormous magickal powers on him and his men. He gripped the handle of the Element Sword tight with one hand and drew up his shield, soundless words from his broken heart on his lips. His parents, his sister, and his very self would be avenged this day. This vow came forth strongly and proudly.

A low murmur extended from the mouth of the castle, and it slowly rose to higher levels. Within the shadows came movement. Nothing more than simple twitches in the dark, they quickly spawned into wild spasms as the murmurs rose to shouts. Across the wooden plank came Noknor's army, a vast collection of Dark Knights on midnight black steeds. Their cries came fiercely, just as strong and powerful as the Arcainians' had come mere moments before. The heart of every Arcainian tightened within their chests and anxious tremors shot through their bodies. This would be a heavy battle, one which all knew they may not live to see the end of. But each warrior of the Light swore that if their time upon this world had come to its end, they would take a hundred of Noknor's men with them.

Kain scowled hideously and a coarse growl grated his throat. With stone cold eyes and a rock hard jaw set in an almost humorous mixture of rage and annoyance, he snapped his arm upwards. The blade burst into bright orange flames, crackling and spitting. There came no change to his face or demeanor as he slowly brought his arm down to point the tip of the burning blade towards his rapidly advancing enemy. Without even the hint of what was about to happen, the evil horde took to the field, the commanding officers riding before the others urging them onward for the glory of their Lord Noknor. The blast came so hard and so fast that their cries of battle did not even have a chance to turn to squeals of terror. A massive pillar of fire blasted through their ranks, instantly incinerating several of the Dark warriors and horribly burning others with the heat so scorching it warmed the faces of the Arcainians and spooked their horses. Those Dark Knights not killed outright or permanently disabled scattered in wild panic, fearing to run back into the castle to face Noknor's wrath for their failure. They continued onward towards the Arcainian forces, but with their the bulk of their leadership wiped out and dread flustering the very core of their morale each Dark Knight fought only for himself, racing across the battlefield like crazed rats abandoning a sinking ship.

Kain lowered his arm, every Arcainian gawking with utter disbelief at the insanely impossible feat their Grand General had just accomplished. With a simple stroke of his sword, he had destroyed Noknor's ground force, had obliterated the onslaught of bloodthirsty warriors with but a thought and sent them running like frightened hens. They had all heard stories of Noknor dealing a thousand deaths with nothing more than a wave of his hand, and these had long plagued the hearts of the Arcainians like horrible nightmares. But it was at that moment that they realized that despite all they had heard, regardless of what they had believed, their Grand General had evened the odds. Whatever weapon of power Noknor had in his evil grips, Kain Viccon held the equal in his virtuous hands. And as such, they were not simply riding into the slaughter like so many lambs. They were fighting a battle that they could win. That they would win. That they must win.

The heavy clank of rusted chains and the dull groan of wood cut through the silence like a razor. Kain watched the drawbridge slowly make that feverish, labored climb back up to prevent entry and watched as a ragged wave of blundering, frightened Dark Knights advanced towards them as if they would continue running without stopping to fight. A triumphant smirk graced his hard lips.

Kain pulled hard and sudden upon his reins to bring his steed onto two legs, neighing with a tremendous bellow as he thrust the Elemental Sword into the air, the blade once again burning brightly with living flames. A tremendous roar lifted from the Arcainians, and the entire army as a whole spurred onward, following Kain as he rode with determined intent, brandishing his blazing sword high over his head as he urged his horse faster.

What was left of Noknor's ground forces were cut down by the hard assault of the Arcainian Army, and Kain never once slowed his pace as he swatted Dark Knights away like so many pathetic flies. He rode over the grounds, his breath coming quickly and his pulse racing just as fast as if it was he that ran across the field, kicking up dead grass stained with blood of past battles and large clumps of rotted dirt. The constant, rhythmic pounding of each powerful hoof was all Kain heard as he body jerked roughly about in the saddle. He watched the castle grow larger and larger, the strong scent of scorched flesh drifting up to his nostrils as his horse trampled over the charred remains of what had only moments before been a strong Dark Knight battle force. A small, satisfied grin touched his lips as he heard the crunch of charred bones under his horse's hooves. He would soon deal with Noknor in the same fashion. With the power of the Elemental Sword he would let loose years of aggression and pain, would make that cowering bully feel the pain he felt and then some. Kain's heart began to beat even faster.

Both teams were already waiting for him, gathered proudly together. As the rest of his troop fell in with the other soldiers, Kain, Carrie, and Kassandra rode through the narrow gap of Arcainians to come to a stop at the edge of the moat where some familiar faces had gathered. He was very pleased and extremely relieved to find Nancy perfectly well. As the vice on his heart loosened, he was surprised at just how much of his tension had to do with her well-being. They all dismounted their steeds to trade greetings and warm congratulations. Kain was very surprised to find that Nancy had indeed been attacked several times by Noknor's demons, but had for the most part defended herself with only the help of her unicorn until Raphael had rode closer to her to try and deter further attacks. Kain held this interesting news inside and only gave his sister a slight bob of his head before carrying onto the pressing matter of gaining access to the castle.

The moat was at least two dozen feet across and there was no edge on the other side, just the sidewall of the castle, thus immediately killing the idea of jumping across. Kain peered over the edge of the embankment to look down into the deep ditch. He had expected water, or at the very least nothing at all, just an empty pit perhaps filled with more stakes. He saw a river of a dark maroon substance, swirling about in a rushing frenzy. It moved much slower than water would, looking as if it had a thicker consistency. When the distinct sharp coppery smell hit his nostrils, he held no doubts as to what the grotesque liquid was. He snorted in contempt, wondering just who had supplied such a massive amount of blood. He closed his eyes and gave a silent prayer for their departed souls. When he opened his eyes once more, they instantly focused on something that appeared to be floating just below the surface. It moved about in the current and formed a lump on the surface as if it wanted to break through but just couldn't quite make it. Kain hissed a breath of surprise as a skull suddenly broke the surface, stained red as the thick liquid dripped from it. It continued upward, revealing a hollow ribcage as the current pulled it along slowly. It stared up at them as if in warning. It seemed to say 'Don't press any further or you'll be just as dead as I am!'

"I don't think we'll be swimming across." Robert muttered, wriggling his nose with disgust as the skeleton twirled when it got caught in a rift and sunk back below the surface.

"So how are we going to get in?" Nancy asked. Her tone was hard and there was no disappointment or frustration in her voice. She would not be defeated so simply. Not this time.

Kain raised the Elemental Sword high above his head, arcs of electricity coursing along the shimmering blade. He twirled it with a high-pitched swish and then thrust it down into the ground with a powerful stab. As it sunk halfway down into the dead earth, the power surged into the dirt and directed itself toward the drawbridge. The earth rumbled intensely, shaking and cracking from the magickal earthquake that shuddered the drawbridge. Wood creaked and splintered as the heavy chains shattered to let the massive wooden plank fall just in front of the Elemental Sword with another earth shaking boom.

"That's how." Kain responded, tearing the faery weapon from the dirt, the blade sparkling clean.

"Bravo, young Viccon! Bravo indeed!" a boisterous voice called from the archway across the bridge accompanied by the slow slapping of palms together. "I do congratulate you for making it this far."

Kain looked up and scowled darkly, his eyes flaring with hellfire as his knuckles tightened around the golden handle. He had thought about, perhaps obsessed about was the better term for it, what he was going to say and do the second time he was to lay eyes upon the man that had forever scarred his soul. From shrieking swears and cold threats to an instant bloodthirsty attack, he had conceived of nearly every possible way to react. But when it was all said and done, now that he stood before the man he had sworn to kill, he found his tongue unable to move and his feet firmly planted.

Noknor chuckled once more, the sound as filthy as the moat beneath him. He licked his lips with his pointed tongue and replied "It has been quite some time, hasn't it. You have changed much from that sniveling brat I last saw running away from me with his tail between his legs." His red eyes shifted from brother to sister, narrowing as a lustful glow filled them. "And I do see that young Miss Viccon has changed much herself. She has . . . developed very finely indeed."

Kain roared, swinging the Elemental Sword in a high arch to release a large ball of fire towards the warlock.

With a simple laugh, Noknor shifted his clawed hand around to catch the attack as if it were simply a ball tossed to him by a youngster. With his arm outstretched in front of him, Noknor's hand burned brightly as the flames licked around his fingers. "Young Viccon, such a quick and fiery temper you have." A chuckle rumbled in his throat. "So just like your father. Your **DEAD** father."

In a swift motion, he cocked his arm back and pitched the ball of fire into the air. It sailed whistling through the sky, threatening to land onto the battlefield and burst into a searing inferno, its destruction ten-fold that of two firebombs. As several unfortunate Arcainian troops cowered underneath their approaching death, screaming out in terror and hellish wails, Kain's scowl hardened while Noknor's eyes beamed morbidly. In a sudden flash of movement, Kain spun on his heels and lashed out, shooting out a forceful stream of blue water from the blade of the Elemental Sword. It struck the fireball just as it was about to incinerate his men and quenched the angry flames. Kain continued to spin, stopping to point the quivering tip of his blade towards Noknor once again.

"Not bad." Noknor admitted, a vile, twisted grin touching his lips.

With a low chuckle that rumbled deep in his throat he held his hand out in front of him. As they watched, a small purple ball of light began to glow brightly in the center of his palm. As Kain steeled himself to prepare to block the oncoming blast, Noknor's grin widened.

"Just to let you know I could have, Viccon." the warlock winked.

Noknor shifted his hand slightly and with a tremendous roar like that of a large waterfall the ball of light turned into fifteen arrows that screamed towards their target. Kain gasped and flinched reflexively as his eyes followed each arrow. As the first shaft of blackened wood pierced his shoulder, Robert Grotz screamed in pain and surprise. The second, third, and fourth struck his torso, the echoing squish of each filling the air as his lungs and stomach were impaled. He began to spasm in a gruesome dance of death as his entire body became riddled with arrows, one after another as his shrieks filled the air. His cries were cut off into a gurgle of frothing blood as the ninth arrow tore into his throat, sending a spray of crimson that peppered against Nancy's cheek. She flinched in surprise and reached her hand up to rub her face, looking at her fingers as she rubbed his blood between them, the coppery scent filtering up to her nostrils. In an uncomprehending daze, she looked back to her friend and watched as three more arrows embedded into his body, making him look like a large, gory pincushion. In a matter of seconds, Robert Grotz was pierced by fourteen arrows, each one tearing his armor as easily as they tore his flesh. The fifteenth and final arrow struck him square in the forehead, slamming into him like a runaway horse that knocked his head sharply back as it slid halfway up the shaft. He uttered a low, soft gurgle that almost sounded orgasmic as he twitched and collapsed to the ground. He splashed into the pool of his own blood already collected into a large puddle and jerked about reflexively. Though his eyes remained large and wide, horror forever filling them, his vision slowly blurred and faded into darkness as death took away his final thoughts of his sweet, beloved Molly Duroe.

His friends were thrown into unbelieving silence as they watched his body lurch violently for one last time. They were too shocked to speak, too bewildered to act, too struck to even think, to comprehend what had just happened. It didn't seem real. Their friend couldn't be dead. He just couldn't. Not like that. It was impossible. It had to be a dream. A nightmare!

Nancy roared violent curses the likes of which had never before passed her lips, spittle flying from her horridly sneered mouth, tears of rage splashing down her dirtied cheek stained with Robert Grotz's blood. She brandished her sword and leapt at Noknor with her friend's death throwing her and fueling her attack. Her blade gleamed as she swung with all her might, her piercing wail of anguish splitting the air. With a simple wave of his hand, Noknor caught her in an unseen force and held her in the air as she swung her bladed fruitlessly

"Don't even try, my dear." Noknor replied with a sinister chuckle, twitching his fingers as if beckoning the girl to go to him. Still floating, she began to drift towards him, kicking and screaming not in terror but unbridled fury.

With the roar of a hellhound, Kain leapt forward to grab his sister's arm and at the same time flung his sword with enough intensity to pop his shoulder. A burst of flame as powerful as any dragon could muster spat from the tip, aimed at erasing Noknor from the world. The warlock uttered a short yelp covered up by the howling flames and with a bright arc of light and a harsh crackle he was gone. Nancy immediately fell, gently landing onto her backside. She was back on her feet in a flash and ready to make a mad dash into the castle.

"Get back here **you COWARD**!" Nancy screamed, throwing herself forward. Kain kept a firm grip on her willowy thin wrist as he sank down to his fallen friend's side. Nancy tried to wretch free so she could go after Noknor, but her throes were futile. Kain wasn't about to let go as he dragged her down with him. She pulled with more violence. "Let me go, Kain! We have to catch him! Let me go!"

"**ENOUGH**!" Kain roared savagely, tossing her hard onto the ground. She uttered a sharp grunt as she struck and glowered at Kain with fire in her eyes. A glare from Kain's cold steel eyes kept her mouth shut and her body unmoved. Content that he had gotten his sister's attention, he looked at his good friend and loyal knight lying in a pool of his own blood, his body ravaged and torn. Kain's lips trembled slightly as his eyes slowly began to moisten. It was hard to believe that after so many adventures together, it had to end like that. It was such a cold-hearted manner that Robert's young bride-to-be had been deprived of a loving, caring husband. It was a crime that Kain would not forgive Noknor of, added to the many crimes of which he would answer for. A single tear trickled down Kain's face as he sniffled softly a final good-bye to Robert Grotz, his brother.

"Medic! Fallen general! We need a medic now!" he roared, knowing full well that there was nothing they could do for him. He rose to his feet, his rage boiling. Taking a deep breath, he tried his best to calm his surging nerves and slow his pounding heart. His eyes opened slowly, burning with a fire none had ever seen before. When he spoke, his voice was loud and forceful, devoid of sorrow but rich in ravenous fury. "We're going in, and we're going in hard." He turned to face Generals Riet and Himiniz. "Riet, you and Himiniz lead in the attack. I want the castle scoured top to bottom, every dark corner. Every one of Noknor's men are to be found and dealt with. Every one, including whatever monstrosities he has on his roll. Use lethal force as necessary."

"Yes sir!" both voiced boldly in a rigid stance as they gave crisp salutes, Riet the traditional Arcainian and Carrie that of the Boniva Guard.

"Go!" he barked.

"Yes sir!" they responded.

At Riet's lead, the Arcainian forces began to pour into the castle to do hand combat with Noknor's skilled forces. The air was shattered with the sounds of their tramping across the drawbridge and their ferocious war cries. They poured into the castle, the force of the Arcainians' attack so brutal that the second wave of Noknor's forces, already devastated by Kain's annihilating attack on the first wave, were slaughtered without much effort with many actually running away down the maze of corridors. The Arcainian forces quickly spread out, taking every path and every hall of the castle.

"Raphael, I want you and Michael to take a small squad in there and go after Li and Princess Elizabeth. I would assume that they are being kept in the dungeon, but it's possible that Noknor could have put them anywhere. Find them and get them out of here. Take them back to camp, double time!"

"Yes sir." Raphael acknowledged his Grand General, his and Michael's Arcainian salutes sharp and quick. "What about you?"

"I'm going straight for Noknor's throat."

"Alone?" Raphael gasped. Michael continued "Kain, don't you think—"

"I think that those are my orders and they are to be followed!" Kain snapped with the harshness of an officer pulling rank. Both men flinched and refrained from further opening their mouths. A small grin touched the Grand General's lips as he replied "Besides, I won't be alone. I'll have the Ladys of the Elements behind me." The grin instantly faded as he continued solemnly "I can't have anyone else in there with me. They would be in way too much danger and only get in my way. Noknor's much too powerful. It has to be me against him."

"Just make sure that it's not the personal aspect of this battle that draws you to fight alone." Julie told him, sure to incur a fierce wraith, but not caring. It needed to be said, and she didn't have any rank to lose. She prepared to flinch from his venom.

He turned on her with flaming eyes, but the storm never came. Instead, much to all of their surprise, his face softened and his dark scowl loosened into a dreary frown. His eyes showed pain, harsh pain and deep sadness.

"Yes." he said, his voice low with a hint of a wave to it. He paused to take in a deep, shaking breath. "Yes, it is personal." For a brief moment, they thought he would change his orders as he paused once more. However, he allowed emotion to flood his mind to regain the fierce hardness. "Julie, Nancy, go with them."

"No! I'm going with you." his sister told him firmly. When he turned his full attention onto her, his eyes hard and forceful, she held his gaze and refused to back down. When she spoke up, her voice was low but her tone was powerful and there was no trace of meekness. This was not the little girl he thought he knew. "This is my fight too and it's personal. I'm going with you."

Kain studied her for a brief moment, his cool eyes not giving away what he was feeling or what he was going to tell her. She refused to back down from her words, even though she said nothing more her body conveyed that she would never take no for an answer. Not this time, not with something this important. But Kain couldn't possibly risk her life in such a way, it would be the same as if he killed her with his own hands. And then his mother's words echoed in his mind, 'Listen to your heart. And listen to her.'

"Michael, you guys get out of here." Kain ordered, not removing his glare from his sister's. She furrowed her brow and narrowed her eyes. He turned to the prince "Find my cousin and your wife and find them now! Get them out of here and take them into the forest. And . . . tell Li that I love her." He sniffled slightly, not being able to believe what he was about to say next.

"Nancy, let's go hand Noknor his ass the Viccon way!"

CHAPTER XXXIX

Four Dark Knights roared in fury as they threw themselves at the siblings, their swords drawn back for a deathblow as their commander barked orders at them. Nancy shouted a warning to her brother, her shield rising on its on accord to block the attack that was launched upon her. Kain, startled from his careful examination of the hallway around the corner, threw up his own shield just in time to have it ring with two blows as the Elemental Sword blocked the third. Nancy squeaked and then growled fiercely as her shield sang once more.

"You idiot!" the commander snapped. "Lord Noknor wants her alive! Use the flat of your sword! The flat!"

Kain's heart sank as he recalled the three previous attempts Noknor had made to capture his sister alive, dodging the three blades that were intended to kill. He swung his own sword twice before having to revert back to defense. He would never allow that fiend to violate her! If he had to fight Death off long enough, he would do so. If he had to sell his very soul, he would do so. But he would NEVER allow Noknor to take his sister. Never! Emotion flooded his heart and powered a swing that was strong enough to behead one of his three assailants.

Kain took a very risky glance at the instant he batted away the blades of his two attackers and grinned at what he saw. Nancy was holding her own against the Dark Knight, whether from her own skill or from his lack of trying as hard as he could. Kain could tell, however, just from the split instant he saw before he had to return to the defensive, that it seemed to be a combination of both, although it was quickly reverting to weigh on her skill as the Dark Knight's temper began to flare violently at Nancy's intensity. He had expected it to be quite simple to overtake such a young girl, and became increasingly irritated as she proved that it would be far from simple. His superior's barking voice did not serve to help his disposition any.

"Idiot! I said the flat!" the commander roared, tearing his own sword free from its sheath. He began to make his way towards the pair. "What is wrong with you! How can you be having so much trouble with a girl!"

The comment infuriated the soldier and he momentarily took his attention off the girl to confront the commander's badgering. It proved a fatal mistake as a moment was all Nancy needed. She launched her sword forward to sink deeply into the man's stomach, pushing the blade so far that the needle tip exited out of his back. His eyes bulged in shock and his mouth formed a painful sneer as a weak gurgle escaped his lips. His sword clattered noisily onto the ground as he gripped the handle of Nancy's sword and fell back several steps. His lips moved slowly, but no sound came out of his mouth other than a few muffled words of fear. Then with nothing more he collapsed, leaving Nancy without a sword.

The commander roared in fury, bearing down on her fast with his weapon poised to kill. In his rage at seeing one of his best men slain by nothing more than a lucky shot by a weak little girl, he suddenly forgot the very orders he had only moments before been barking. He didn't care if he did kill the girl, he would just put the blame on someone else. Either that or run away. And knowing Lord Noknor's temper and history of taking his anger out on anyone and everyone, running would more than likely be the better choice. He cocked his arm back and flung his sword in an arc powerful enough to lop the girl's head clean off.

Nancy ducked under the whistling blade and threw herself forward, hitting him squarely in the chest with her shield. He gave a startled grunt and stumbled backwards as Nancy rolled on her shoulder to stop at the dead man's side. She gripped the handle of her sword still impaling the Dark Knight, but instantly let go when she saw the commander coming at her. The instant her shield flew up to guard, her entire arm shook violently from the impact. She whipped her dagger free and slashed at him, catching him in the thigh. He gasped at the unexpected assault, giving Nancy time to pull her blood-covered blade free and leap over the body to come to a defensive stance. The commander lashed out at her with an overhead chop and followed it up with a left slash. Nancy easily countered these blows and delivered her own chop. The commander was caught totally off guard, not expecting her to attack from her defensive pose. Her blade caught his wrist and sent his hand still clutching the handle of his sword falling to the ground. He stared at his stump, not comprehending the events that had transpired so quickly. When the pain suddenly hit him, he opened his mouth to scream, but her sword passed through his throat.

Nancy drew a deep breath and turned her attention onto her brother. Two Dark Knights lay dead at his feet as he fended off the third. Just as Nancy started on her heels to aid him, the Elemental Sword began to glow with a gray light. Kain swung his sword weakly, cutting the man on the arm. The wound was very small and didn't even appear to bleed very much. However, it wasn't the size of the wound but the nature of it that doomed the man. He stopped in his tracks as all of his muscles locked up instantly, refusing to move. With a low crackling sound like pebbles being crushed underfoot, the man froze in his stance, quickly turning to stone. Kain snapped his head in the direction of a low gasp and saw a lone goblin glaring at him with terror clouding its eyes. In its hands was a small spear that quivered violently.

The impotent goblin dropped its weapon and spun on its heels to run straight into Nancy, who pushed it back towards her brother. Kain caught it by the throat and tightened his grip so that the metal fingers of his gauntlet dug into its flesh, drawing blood. As it gurgled and gasped, clawing at the knight's wrist and arm, Kain lifted it bodily off the ground and demanded the way to the throne room. The best the goblin could do was point wildly and whisper weakly, trying to pull out of Kain's steel grip. Kain growled lowly and tightened his fingers. The goblin's eyes bulged out and it gave a high pitch wheeze. Kain threw the beast down hard enough to bounce twice and turned to his sister. Finding her good and well, he urged her down the hallway the goblin had pointed to.

The pair traveled swiftly through the hallways, not coming into any more contact with Noknor's troops. It seemed that their path had been totally cleared and Kain could not help but wonder if it had been intentional. He was almost certain that Noknor wanted him all to himself. And that suited him just fine. He was prepared to give Noknor the fight of his life.

At last, they spotted a large set of elegant double doors at the end of a long passageway, red in color with eccentric, though grotesquely morbid, designs engraved into them. Kain held no doubts that they had come to the throne room and that Noknor awaited them inside. He wondered with a grimace at just how the doors had gotten their red color, noting that if the rest of the castle was an example he should utter more prayers. Two Dark Knights stood ready on either side of the doors, decked out in full armor with a more devilish look to their helmets and larger swords and shields than the average Dark Knight. Kain figured these to be Noknor's personal guards. They would be very well trained and prove to be quite formidable enemies. Kain, losing patience fast for Noknor's blood, decided to just be done with them in one swoop. As they turned their heads to regard the pair, Kain raised his sword at them. Before they could even utter a word of warning, a large blast of fire hurled towards them. They raised their shields on skillful instinct, but they might as well been holding their bare arms up as the flames engulfed them, swallowing them like a snake gulping down its prey. They screamed for a very short moment before their ash bodies blew away, scattering among the hall like so much confetti.

Nancy started forward, but Kain gripped her to halt her in her tracks. She jerked to a stop and whipped her angry face around to growl lowly at her brother. The harsh glare he fed her stopped her words and softened her anger as he murmured "I don't want you going in there, Nancy."

She gasped in utter shock as fury rushed back into her face, her sneered mouth quickly opening to deliver a harsh string of words. However, Kain's upraised hand directly in front of her face ceased her actions and prevented further speaking as he continued with what he had to say.

"I don't want you to go with me. But, I know that I can't keep you from it. And I understand why. You have to, I guess, for the same reasons I have to face him. And, what can I say, you've got the Viccon stubborn streak. You'll go in no matter what. Plus, mom said . . . I, I mean . . . Look, what I'm just trying to say is be careful in there."

"I will."

"I mean it, girl. Watch your back, do not allow your emotions to get the better of you, and absolutely do **NOT** under any circumstances take any unnecessary risks! If it gets too hot, you high tail it out of there and get to a safe spot. Don't worry about me. If anything were to happen to you . . ."

Her grin was playful, but her eyes held serious as she replied "I'm not going anywhere anytime soon, big bro."

Kain nodded his head as his own pursed lips smiled slightly. He tightened his grip on his weapon and replied in an almost playful tone "Let's play, shall we?"

The double doors were thrown open with a resounding boom that echoed through the throne room as the siblings threw themselves in, their weapons and shields held ready for the immediate attack they felt would be launched at them. To their surprise, nothing came at them, no men, no arrows, no fireballs or blasts. They took the time to examine their surroundings and simultaneously their eyes fell onto the massive throne of black stone set at the end of a long and lavish red carpet. Noknor sat calmly upon his seat, his hand held thoughtfully at his mouth as he looked over the interesting pair. He smiled, but it was a hideous, twisted smile perverted by evil intentions.

"Welcome, young Viccons, to my humble abode." he called out to them, removing his hand from his chin and shifting slightly to sit up in a tight and rigid posture. His voice had all the pleasantness of a tea party greeting, but it could not completely cover the vile tone underneath.

Once again, Kain was thrown into a silence caused by a hundred words trying to exit his mouth at once. His teeth ground behind his tightly pulled back lips as his eyes burned with such an intense, savage fire that he could have melted ice with only a glance. His silence was like that of a statue.

It was Nancy who hissed savagely "You are a dead man!"

"Oh, is that a fact, my dear?" he chuckled, the sound vibrating from the back of his throat to echo eerily throughout the entire room.

"Yeah. It is." she returned in a lethal voice that was so low and so full of venomous malice that it even made Noknor's smile falter slightly in disbelief that it could have come from such a lovely young girl.

Noknor's smile disappeared completely and was replaced with a dark frown as he slowly rose to his feet. With a hideous growl, he leaped high into the air, his cloak spreading widely out like the wings of a bat as he flew forward. His feet struck the stone floor with an echoing thud as he whipped his arm to the side to call his bladed staff to his hand. He twirled it over his head with the pitch of air being cut before stopping it abruptly at his side, cocked slightly and quivering like a serpent ready to strike in a split instant. He twisted his mouth in a wry grin and raised an eyebrow.

"Two on one, hmmmmm?" he chuckled. "Those aren't very fair odds, now are they, great Grand General?"

"Since when have you ever used fair odds!" Nancy spat out viciously, rearing her arm back to deliver the first blow.

"Ah, point taken, my dear." Noknor snapped his staff away from his body, blocking Nancy's sword before sending the blade hurtling towards Kain.

Kain threw up his shield to receive the tremendous blow that sent out a rough shower of sparks as Nancy jumped forward and lashed out at Noknor. With blinding speed, Noknor spun his staff around to parry her blow with a clatter of steel-on-steel. Without even a moment of hesitation, she launched another shot as Kain delivered a powerful blow of his own. Noknor uttered a very labored grunt as his staff cut air with a loud swish followed by the clanging of steel as he blocked their blows. He was suffering heavily, having to work harder than he ever had to before so as to fend them both off as they relentlessly pounded on him. He had no doubt whatsoever that he could take the girl without problem, even while holding back to preserve her for his intentions. And he told himself that he could take Viccon himself one on one. But even he knew full well that he was no match for them both at the same time. He hissed savagely and floated backwards at an incredible speed, just barely missing their blades as he did so. He landed his feet on the ground several feet away and smiled as he slowly ran his tongue over his ruddy lips, hiding his strained breaths.

"I had thought that I would test my battle skills against yours, boy!" he growled, his eyes burning. "But since you, yourself, possess faery magick, as weak and pathetic as it may be, it would be only fair, ne!"

Noknor puckered his lips and snapped his head as if spitting at Kain. However, instead of saliva, a small ball of fire streaked towards him as fast as a bolt of lightning. Kain raised his shield and steeled himself for the impact. Despite its small size, the fireball proved to be much more powerful than it looked. It hit the center of his shield and exploded in a blast that rocked the shield and pushed Kain backwards, almost catching him off balance. Flames engulfed the steel, forcing him to discard it with a surprised curse.

'Good!' he thought fiercely, brandishing his sword at his side before reverting to a two handed stance. 'Just one less thing to weigh me down.'

As he saw Noknor prepare to spit once more, he steeled himself to dodge. The fireball, bigger than the first, screamed towards him and he bent his knees as he readied to leap away. All of a sudden, from out of nowhere, Nancy sailed through the air right into the path of the fireball. It struck her silver shield and, as she held it at a slight angle, was deflected towards the wall where it exploded harmlessly. Kain, as surprised as he was, leapt into action to take full advantage of Noknor's own stunned shock. As Nancy's feet hit stone, he swung the Elemental Sword, unleashing a massive ball of fire of his own. The warlock stirred with barely enough time to cast a small shield of light that took the force of the fire. However, he did not have time to block or dodge Nancy's shield heated by the fireball, which she had flung at him as soon as she landed. It slammed into his mouth, knocking his head backward as he shrieked. He swore violently as he grabbed his bloodied face, back peddling many steps as he swooned about in furious blinding pain.

He turned back to glare at them with furious rage, cursing them both violently, but especially Nancy, before pausing to spit a mouthful of blood and tooth chips onto the floor and growled "You two work well together. But even you can not compare to a god!"

A bright blue fire engulfed Noknor, covering his body completely. Kain, feeling a sharp twinge in the back of his neck, quickly ordered Nancy behind him and used the Elemental Sword to produce a protective barrier of wind around them. Just as the whirlwind began to circle the pair, the blue fire exploded out away from Noknor's body, sending out a powerful shockwave that ripped the heavy throne out of the floor and sent it flying against the wall as the room shook violently, cracks spiderwebbing the walls. Kain and Nancy were relatively protected from the blast, though Nancy felt her ears pop as the wave passed over them.

When they looked at Noknor now, they saw that he had changed drastically. He was much larger than before, almost twice his original size, and he had four powerful arms. He had discarded his staff in place of two swords and two single bladed axes. He twirled his weapons about with excellent skill, producing a whirlwind of sharp steel. He smiled hideously, showing needle-like fangs that were both longer and sharper than before.

Noknor rushed forward with speed inhumanly fast and was on top of them in the blink of an eye. His attacks came incredibly quick with two hands for each sibling, his swords and axes blazing down on them with relentless fury. Without shields to defend them, both siblings found it increasingly difficult to not only match his speed but both defend and attack with their swords as fatigue and desperation wormed away at them. Nancy, feeling herself slipping under the onslaught, waited for her chance before she found the opening she was looking for. Ducking under his sword, she curled herself up and tried to roll away to a safe distance. Her winded muscles howled and slowed her at the most crucial moment. As she twisted herself, she caught Noknor's second axe across the back of her shoulder, opening a deep gash. She squealed and plunged forward, striking the stone floor hard. Fighting back the stars, she flipped herself around and jerked her blowpipe to her lips. Kain, hearing his sister call out in pain, startled and left himself wide open for a blow that sped towards him. Noknor yelped, his voice much deeper and guttural than normal, as the dart impaled his forearm, throwing his arm wild as the sword spun from his grip. Kain recovered quickly, replanting his feet for a stronger blow as Nancy's well-thrown dagger struck Noknor's side. The warlock recoiled from the attack, and launched his two axes at Kain. As feeble as his uncalculated blows were, they were enough to save his skin. As one parried away the Elemental Sword, breaking from the impact with the faery weapon, the other struck Kain in the arm with the flat of the blade, bruising the knight but not seriously injuring him.

Noknor roared, his glowing red eyes blazing as the whole room shook. Once again, he leaped away from the pair and landed several feet away from them, tossing away his remaining weapons and wrenching Nancy's bloodied dagger from his side. Upon hitting the ground, he raised all four of his arms as his hands glew with bright purple lights. With an intense bellow, four large purple blasts tore at them while filling the air with a deafening explosion that was like the roaring of the largest waterfall. Nancy dodged the one blast sent her way and quickly set upon reloading her blowpipe. Kain did his best to slip past the first two, but the third struck him dead in the chest. With an agonizing grunt that took away all the air from his lungs, he was lifted bodily off the ground and thrown hard onto his back, the Elemental Sword flying out of his grasp as his chest armor sizzled.

Nancy managed to divert Noknor's attention with another dart to his body while Kain reached out to thin air. A roaring wind gripped his sword and carried it swiftly to his waiting hand just as four more blasts bore down upon him. Acting quickly, he struck the ground at his feet with the tip of his sword, producing a large pillar of rock that jutted up from the floor and took all four blasts, exploding in the process. Nancy quickly loaded her blowpipe once more, but before she could get the tube to her lips a bright white light struck her, pushing her backwards and throwing the weapon from her hand. She instantly recovered from the weak, though distracting, attack and began to scour her body for some other missile weapon. Finding none, she gripped her sword with both hands and scowled darkly as she fixed deadly eyes upon Noknor.

Kain spun his sword in his hand and cocked his arm back ready to deliver a blow even though Noknor was much too far away. The blade of the Elemental Sword sparked into a bright orange flame the split instant Kain began to swing. Like water flinging off the blade, the flames screamed towards Noknor. The warlock caught this first attack easily, but was struck by the following blasts of flame as Kain swung twice more. He grunted in pain as his clothing burned and his flesh scorched, sending him stumbling back. Seeing her chance, Nancy yelled a fierce battle cry to fuel her body as she raced across the room with her sword held poised over her head. Kain scowled and swore loudly as he watched his sister rush into harm's way, sending a blast of frozen water to slam into Noknor's furious face. He was blinded just as Nancy reached him. She sprang upwards, slicing down with her sword as hard as she could. As Noknor twisted from Kain's attack, Nancy's blade, while barely scratching the warlock, ripped through his shirt and revealed the Swuenedras Amulet as it glew with a bright red luster and seemed to pulsate swiftly like a heartbeat.

Furious and fully recovered from the blinding water, Noknor snapped two of his four arms at the girl, snatching both of her arms and hauling her into the air. With a savage, reptilian hiss, he completely forgot that he had wanted to take the girl alive at all costs as he bared his long, razor-sharp fangs with the intent of ripping her throat wide open. Kain's heart floundered in his chest as he looked for a clear shot at his foe. However, Noknor held Nancy as she kicked and tried to worm free of his steel grip in such a way that he was shielded by her body. Thinking quickly, Kain notched a faery arrow in his bow and sent it flying. It twisted in the air, moving around Nancy body and was caught by one of Noknor's free hands. Clenching his fist tightly, Noknor snapped the faery arrow in two. Swearing violently as Noknor brought his jaws down on her, Kain flipped the Elemental Sword in his hands and brought the blade down hard into the ground.

A tremendous rumbling filled the room as the floor began to move roughly under their feet. Above the shaking came the morbid snap as cracks opened up all over the floor and the walls, sending dust and small debris cascading down. Noknor cursed Kain darkly as he began to stumble around, trying in vain to keep his footing during the quake. He released one of Nancy's wrists, leaving her dangling in the air by one arm. As she twisted around trying to free out of his remaining grip, her eyes fell onto a large crimson spot on his body. Realizing that it was the spot where her dagger had struck him, she mustered all of the power and strength she could to straighten her body so as to give her the best position possible. Then she kicked her legs backward and immediately snapped them back in front of her, causing her to sway back and forth. Using the slight momentum she had given herself, she reared back her leg and let her foot fly as hard as she could. Though the impact wasn't as harsh as she had hoped, it was more than enough. Noknor howled furiously as his side suddenly exploded in pain, sending electricity throughout his body. He released Nancy to grab his wound instinctively, dropping her safely at his feet. Kain roared for Nancy to remove herself, but she couldn't just leave such an opening. She leapt up into the air, spinning like a ballerina to land her foot dead in Noknor's chest. The impact was strong, but it only seemed to enrage Noknor further. He began to swipe at her with his four clawed hands, but she displayed amazing agility as she danced perfectly around his blows until she was enough out of the way for Kain to launch another fireball. Noknor, so engrossed with Nancy, did not even see it coming and was completely engulfed by fire. Nancy rolled away from the heat, grabbed her sword from where it had dropped, and rushed back to her brother's side. Kain was much too impressed by her moves and relieved that she had gotten away from Noknor without so much as a scratch that he didn't even think to bark at her as they watched the fire burn intensely.

All was quiet in the battle scarred throne room, with only the sound of the crackling fire and their own content breathing pounding in their ears. Suddenly, a hideous roar filled the air, startling the siblings. They watched the fire grow larger and slowly turn a bright green as Noknor's roars boomed with more intensity. Kain, realizing that their battle was not yet finished, put up another wind shield with barely enough time as a tremendous shockwave, even more powerful than the first, rocked the room. When they looked at Noknor again, their hearts froze in their chests and plunged into their stomachs.

Noknor was had grown even larger than before, filling the entire room with his nearly twenty foot high frame. His lower body had turned into that of some enormous black spider, his eight legs covered in course hair and ending in wicked claws like scythes that could slice through steel as easily as flesh. Noknor's four arms were now bigger than tree trunks and his talons were little more than daggers while huge bat-like wings attached at his shoulders. When he flexed these wings, they brushed past the walls on either side and gouged large slashes as if the stone were nothing more than pig fat. His head was like a keg with large ears, huge red eyes that glowed like coals straight from Hell, and a fang filled mouth that could have bitten a man in two. Sitting on his chest, dwarfed by the rest of his body, was the Swuenedras Amulet, pulsating rapidly in bright red flashes. He bellowed loudly, his hellish voice ripping through the air like thunder and causing the pair to wince away in pain as rocks broke loose from the ceiling.

Without taking his stunned eyes off of the monster that now stood before him, Kain drew in a deep breath, held it for a long moment, and then released to murmur "Nancy, get out of here." She didn't respond to him, didn't even appear to have heard him. In a stronger voice, though still shaky, he told her "Nancy, get out of here!"

"No." she replied strongly.

"Get out of here now!"

"No, Kain!"

"**NOW**!" he roared.

Nancy threw her arm towards him, making him flinch instinctively. However, she was not aiming for his face, she wasn't even throwing a punch. Before Kain knew what she was doing, let alone have a chance to react to stop her, she pulled his glok from his pack. Quick as a flash, she cocked back the hammer, aimed with both hands supporting the weapon, and pulled the trigger. With an earshattering explosion and a puff of black smoke, Nancy found herself sitting on the ground, groaning in bruised surprise while coughing up the soot that covered her face. As Kain rushed to the aid of his sister, the heated lead ball tore through the air.

Noknor flinched reflexively at the explosive retort of the strange new weapon, though due to his immense size he could not move very well as again his wings ripped through the walls. Though the blast had kicked her down, Nancy's aim was true and the lead ball struck the Swuenedras Amulet dead center. With a sharp click and a squealing zip, the lead ball ricocheted off the magickal talisman without so much as scratch on the gem. The lead ball continued on its new path for a very short distance when it struck Noknor's arm. Once again, it was repelled and dropped harmlessly to the ground.

As Kain picked Nancy back up to her feet, he noticed a strange light in Noknor's huge mouth. Thinking quickly, he gave Nancy a hard shove that threw her bodily into the air and jumped the other way just as a large blast of purple energy smashed into the ground, ripping open a jagged rift all the way to the room beneath them. Kain winced sharply as a red-hot stone struck his arm. While he nursed the new wound with a rigorous rub, the vice grip crushing his chest grew tighter as he realized Noknor was definitely playing for keeps. He wasn't toying with them anymore, and if Kain hadn't been so quick on his feet they would have been annihilated. And if anything Noknor threw at them hit on target, be it another blast or those deadly claws, it would without a shadow of a doubt be the end. He swore in dejection. He had been counting on Noknor wanting to savor the battle, especially with Nancy. He grew sick at the knowledge of why Noknor wanted Nancy alive at all costs, but at the same time that had further helped to keep her just that much farther out of harms way. However, it seemed that he longer cared to have Nancy alive. He wanted them both dead and he wanted them both dead now.

    He turned to yell to Nancy once again to leave, to order her as her commander and as her older brother to find safety, but was shocked to see her grip her sword offensively as she steeled her legs. She was about to charge that monster! Kain swore violently. Didn't she have any fear? She was going to get herself killed! In the split instant before her legs snapped into action, Kain decided that she wouldn't listen to him and he didn't have time to intercept her himself, so he began to swing his weapon to throw massive balls of fire at Noknor in hopes of distracting him enough to let Nancy find out her weapon would have no effect. Maybe then she would decide to leave it to him.

    The distraction worked even better than he had hoped. Noknor had to use all four arms to bat at the fireballs as if he were swatting flies and even then several got past to explode against his body. Though he didn't appear to be taking any actual damage, he bellowed loudly in annoyed pain and fury. That put a very slight grin on Kain face as he pumped his arms harder to throw a fury of fireballs, sweat beginning to bead on his brow. He lost track of Nancy as she disappeared under Noknor's body, his eight legs crashing down furiously as he swooned around from the pummeling. Kain prayed Nancy wouldn't find herself under one of those legs at the wrong time.

    After several long minutes, Kain's arms began to slow and grow sore from overwork, though he refused to quit until he saw Nancy return to his view. The lagging of Kain's attack was all Noknor needed. With a maddening howl, he flapped those gigantic wings on his shoulders to create a sudden powerful gust that caught Kain's fireballs and sent them right back at him. With a horrified shriek, he jumped and ducked around his own attack, explosions blasting all around him. As he danced around in a spasm of fright, he failed to notice his position and after a quick turning dodge found himself teetering over the gapping hole in the floor. Just as he began to lose the battle with gravity, he was suddenly hit in the side hard enough to knock his breath out and drive him safely away from the murderous fall.

    As he tried his best to suck in a new breath, he saw a small hand extended out to him. He trailed the arm to Nancy's concerned eyes and worried frown. With a gasp of thanks to her, he reached out to take her hand in hers so that she could help him to his shaky feet. His hand closed around air as Nancy was suddenly whisked away from him. He followed the direction she had flown and found her pinned to the wall, stuck with some sort of spider webbing. She pulled and strained as best she could, kicking and writhing like a trapped animal, but she was stuck fast without a chance of freeing herself.

Kain considered leaving her where she was, thinking her out of the way and safe. However, he had no doubt that Noknor would launch some sort of an attack at her at any moment. And if such a thing did happen, she had no way of dodging or protecting herself. Leaving her stuck was just as bad as if he slit her throat himself. He stabbed towards Nancy, sending several strings of flame whispering off the tip of the sword. The thick strands of webbing melted like wax as the flames gently licked around Nancy's body. Kain breathed a deep sigh of relief when Nancy's feet finally touched the ground once again. She took two steps and stopped dead in her tracks, her eyes wide and her lips parted in a silent scream. Her face was a terribly strange mix of stark terror and anxious hopefulness, like a student awaiting the results of a crucial exam to be called out only on a much grander scale. Kain drew in a deep breath and was afraid to turn around, however did so with a startled jump when Noknor's echoing boom of laughter erupted.

Noknor pawed the ground beneath him with his spider legs, the claws scratching deeply into the stone floor. Kain's heart dropped as he realized Noknor's intent. The monster was going to rush at them with the grim intent of trampling them and slashing them to literal ribbons. Without even thinking about it, Kain stepped in front of Nancy as if thinking that he could shield her with his body. Kain gripped the Elemental Sword with both hands, positioned himself in a warrior pose, and closed his eyes as he tried his best to relax his racing heart and shot nerves. He wasn't so much trying to find peace right before death so much as looking to take the full advantage of the Elemental Sword and heave anything and everything it would throw. Earth, Air, Fire, Water. Something had to be able to keep Noknor from charging, or he had won. His own life aside, he couldn't let Noknor win, for his sister's life and for the honor of his parents. His eyes slowly opened.

Noknor chuckled, the sound rumbling like thunder off in the distance. A large smile showing his many sharp teeth spread on his lips, his eyes narrowing. The look that crossed his face was the same when he had murdered Richard and Fang Viccon. It was the look of the victor. With a ferocious battle cry, Noknor's eight spider legs began to move swiftly. The front legs snagged and Noknor was thrown into shocked silence as confusion shadowed his massive face. He glanced down as he stumbled and found Nancy's rope and Kain whip, which Nancy had stolen from her brother when he had shoved her away from the tremendous purple blast, tangled around four of his eight legs. Kain gawked in utter disbelief as he saw it too. Nancy hadn't run at him to hack away with her sword, she had used her rope and his whip to tangle up Noknor's legs. It was an ingenious trap and it worked perfectly.

Noknor struggled to keep himself up, but he had thrown himself forward with such force and his frame was so massive that the momentum was much too great. He pitched forward, his four arms flailing franticly and his legs kicking wildly. Noknor struck the ground so hard the floor cracked and groaned, threatening to crumble out from under him. Dust flew up into the air in a great cloud, scratching his eyes and burning his throat as he coughed and wheezed. He did his best to hoist his body up with his arms and try to figure out what had happened. In the process, he exposed the Swuenedras Amulet on his chest.

Kain saw his greatest opportunity and leapt on it without a second thought. He twirled the Elemental Sword in his hands to point blade down, raised it high above his head, and roared his fierce battle cry as he bolted towards Noknor. The mutated warlock shook his head as his blurred vision slowly came into focus. It took him a moment to realize just what was charging at him, but when he did his red eyes popped open and his jaw dropped. His green face no longer held the smugness of a winner, but instead had gone a sickenly pale white as for the first time in a long time Noknor felt terror. That terror paralyzed him for only an instant, but an instant was all it took to end the battle.

With a powerful thrust, the tip of the Elemental Sword struck the very middle of the Swuenedras Amulet. The talisman that once held an unstoppable power shattered like fine crystal and Noknor's screams filled the air. There was a powerful blast that drove Kain backward and a powerful arch of blue lightning as Noknor began to shrink and loose his monstrous features. His wings melted into his shoulders, his extra pair of arms disappeared, and his legs reformed out of the spider body. His cloak, now torn and ripped, hung loosely from his body in tattered rags. He moaned painfully as the lightning scoured his body, feeling like a hundred bees pricking him at once. He had never before felt such pain as he toppled to the ground and squirmed and twisted about, trying to suck in air that was continuously forced out of his lungs.

Then it was over. Noknor lay out on the floor, gasping and coughing for a breath while wisps of gray smoke drifted up from his twitching body. It took several seconds for his body to regain feeling. With a pounding head and aching limbs, he slowly picked himself back up to his feet. He raised his head and startled violently at what he saw. Both Viccon children stood before him, their weapons held tightly and their faces set in deadly looks of contempt. Noknor's cold heart froze in his chest and skipped a beat, terror pinning him in his place. Somehow, in the span of seconds he had gone from almighty god to just another pitiful mortal. He had been beaten, and to add an insult to such an injury, by a second-rate knight and his snot-nosed brat sister. His knees wobbled under him as he realized he was now at their mercy, or the lack thereof as told by their burning eyes.

"For the blood you have spilled, the blood of a thousand innocents and the blood of my own parents, you will pay with the spilling of your own. May you burn within the belly of the Gobbler for ten thousand years." Kain murmured in a tone of murderous intent as he started forward with the stride of an executioner, the Elemental Sword held ready to bring down justice.

"We beat you!" Nancy growled through sneering lips

"Hardly, you little tart!" Noknor hissed savagely as he shoved his hand behind his back and whipped out a small but deadly crossbow. Taking only a split instant to point and aim, he pulled the trigger tight and sent the bolt whizzing towards his enemy.

Kain reacted quickly to Noknor's sudden movements and prepared for a surprise. By the time Noknor had it pointed at him he already knew what he was going to do and dodged to the side to let the bolt speed past him. He raised the Elemental Sword high into the air, the blade exploding into life with bright orange flames. With a triumphant roar, he brought his weapon down. It struck Noknor's still outstretched arm, slicing through his wrist as if cutting air, the flames instantly cauterizing the flesh so that not a single drop of blood was spilled as the hand still gripping the crossbow fell to the ground. Noknor shrieked in horror as he grabbed his burning stump and fell backward to writhe in agony over the loss of his hand, spewing weeping curses from his thrashing lips.

Kain turned back to Nancy so as to pass on the deathblow to her, feeling she had earned it. He was mortified to see the crossbow bolt sticking in her chest, blood covering her breast. She clutched the shaft as she looked at her brother, her soft voice nothing but a sad whimper as she collapsed roughly to the ground.

"No . . ." Kain gasped in a voice so small it was barely more than a whisper. His grip loosened and the Elemental Sword clattered to the ground with a resounding echo. His jaw dropped and he almost crumbled to the ground as his entire body grew limp, all of his life energy sapped from his being. At first he couldn't believe what he was seeing, couldn't comprehend the severity of the situation. His mind was like a ceramic vase, strong to a harsh breaking point and, like that vase being throw to the floor with the powerful force of a bear, his mind, his very soul, shattered. He refused to accept what he was seeing, refused to believe that such a thing was possible. After everything they had been through, after how they had braved so many obstacles how could such a thing happen? They had stood up to Noknor, together they had beaten him, together they had pounded him into submission. They had won, avenged the honor of their parents. So, it was impossible that Nancy had fallen, impossible that he had lost her. Impossible that his Mother would allow such a thing to happen. After all of his prayers, after constantly asking, begging, throwing himself at Her feet that She watch over her, Auset had turned Her back on him. And that was the most impossible thing of all.

Kain closed his eyes tight, his tears pressed between the lids and dripping down his cheek, and held them tighter still while a string of prayers rattled through his head at an insane pace. Though he had greatly mourned the loss of his parents, he had accepted it with a proud stature and a determination not to allow their deaths to be in vain. But he could never, would never, accept the loss of his sister. That was a loss that he would never recover from and as such he might as well have taken the arrow in his own chest. As it was, his heart was pierce by a thousand arrows at that moment, each burning with a fierce flame, the fiercest he had ever known or could ever know. And the agony ripped his mind apart, destroyed his spirit. But he would not accept what was, would not allow it to be truth.

He slowly opened his eyes to allow a river of tears to stream down his face, expecting his passionate prayers to have been answered and to find his beloved sister standing in front of him, a smile on her beautiful face and no arrow in her chest. When he saw that nothing had changed, that his baby Nancy still lay in a puddle of her own blood that grew larger with each passing moment, he was at first lost and frustrated, like a little boy who couldn't find his way out of a forest. Then, as suddenly as a gentle breeze explodes into a rampageous tempest, rage washed over Kain like a waterfall of emotions. It hit him so hard that he was physically affected. He lurched violently as if struck by a blow and shuddered from a sudden cold bleakness that penetrated to his very bones. His body spasmed as his heart and every other muscle tightened into a steel grip on his body and he spun around his heels so fast, he threw himself off balance so that he had to take several steps to keep from pitching forward onto his face. At any other moment with any other reason behind it, it would have been humorous, even laughable. But not then. Not to Noknor. For him it was utterly frightening, like staring into the black void of Death's cowl. In that very instant, the warlock knew he truly was a dead man.

"Not her!" he hissed savagely through his teeth, his face twisted into that of a demon. His eyes were clouded, glazed over like that of the dead and they burned like searing hot pokers that pieced Noknor's skull and bore through his mind. **"NOT HER!"**

With an eruption of mad howls and savage curses, he threw himself forward with enough force to break through a brick wall and tore across the room with his hands stretched out for Noknor's throat, his fingers curled like the talons of an eagle. With a horrified shriek, the doomed warlock threw up his arms, instantly forgetting about the agonizing pain of his stump wrist. He couldn't move, he couldn't think, he couldn't even defend himself in the feeblest manner. Not that it would have mattered, there was nothing he could do that would have stopped Kain from tearing out his heart. The knight was upon him, leaping like a jungle cat as he howled like a madman. In that most critical split instant, the simplest instinct man had retained, that of his own survival, struck Noknor. Biting past his pain and quelling his fear for just a brief moment, he did his best to concentrate on one last magickal spell. It was just enough and a large circle of glowing purple light opened in the floor under him. Even though he had created the portal, Noknor yelped in surprise as he plunged downward. The portal closed up instantly and the anguished knight struck the solid ground hard enough to bounce as he went skidding.

The impact left Kain dazed as he tried his best to pick himself up off the stone, holding his head and wondering what had just happened. Rage began to boil within him as he put things together and realized that Noknor had escaped. However, it did not have time to come to a head for the plight of his sister struck him harder than the floor had. His dizzy head sent him tumbling forward as he spun on his heels, but in a mad frenzy he crawled like a spider to his fallen angel. Her eyes were closed softly and she seemed to have a gentle glow of peace about her, as if she were sleeping. However, it was not slumber that had caused her skin to go ghostly pale while making her flesh bitterly cold to the touch. Kain lifted her small, limp form into his arms, tears streaming down his face.

"I love you, my sweet Nancy." he whispered softly to her, touching his quivering lips to her forehead. He knew, deep down in his dying heart he knew, it would be the last kiss he ever gave her as he wept over her.

CHAPTER XXXX

Michael, Raphael, and Julie rushed through the twisted narrow hallways, desperately looking for any clue as to the whereabouts of the dungeon. Michael had ordered the soldiers that were to accompany them off with the notion that it would be far easier for the three of them to slip past most guards than it would have been for the large lot of them. Neither he nor Raphael should have had any trouble locating the dungeon, as they had been given tours of the entire castle several times in the past, the last one having only been a few months before for Michael. However, Noknor had perverted the grand Kuberican castle so greatly, that neither of them could tell which way they were going and had no idea where they would end up next.

All three were so worried that they had become lost and would never find the ladies, that when they spun around a corner they almost ran into a small group of Dark Knights being barked at by a Dark General. The three of them gasped lowly and darted back around the corner, listening with rapidly beating hearts for the order for their heads to be given. When the air surrounding the evil soldiers had not changed for several seconds, they exhaled great sighs of relief before craning their ears to listen to what was being said. Only Michael dared to allow one eye to peer around the corner.

He saw several Dark Knights that appeared to be of various ranks standing rigidly before an opposing figure that could only be the Dark General, a rather prominent scar over his eye marring his face.

"You three!" he thrust his index finger at each of them with harsh strokes. "Go down and get those two women and the gimp. I don't care if he's too weak to come. And if the chink gives you any trouble, drug her. But they better not be harmed, or I swear I'll rip your hearts out! Understood!"

"Yes sir!" they shouted in a strong, unanimous shout, giving crisp, sharp salutes.

The Dark General sneered harshly and didn't bother to return the salute as he gestured to the rest to follow him down the hallway. When the two groups went their separate ways, Michael turned to the others and used hand motions to get them to follow him. They waited for several seconds before feeling that they would be far enough behind not to be noticed before rounding the corner and slinking down the halls after the three Dark Knights.

After many twists and heart-stopping moments where they felt they had been spotted for sure, the Arcainians found themselves in a dank, rotting area lit only by a few burning torches. There was the disgusting smell of sweat and filth issuing all around them that penetrated their nostrils and made them gag in repulsion. A collection of sounds from soft sobs, to mumbled prayers, to whimpers of agony echoed throughout the chamber, sounding like ghosts rather than prisoners held in such a ghastly place. All three couldn't help but wonder if some were in fact spirits cursed to spend eternity in the dungeon hell.

With three different ways to head down, they weren't too sure where to begin until they saw the movement of a torch. They hurried down the cellblock and came upon the three Dark Knights they had been following collected around a cell at the far end. One shook rather violently as he tried his best to calm himself enough to insert the rusted iron key into the lock and all three Dark Knights were extremely edgy and fluttered, as if they were terribly afraid of who, or what, was waiting for them behind the bars. They looked and saw both Li and Elizabeth sitting on their cots, one sneering and one trembling as they glared at the cell door. Julie wondered what had made the Dark Knights so upset. Perhaps they were in fear that they would anger that Dark General and be severely reprimanded with death or worse. Surely those two women couldn't pose that much of a threat to three devilish Dark Knights.

With a sharp metal-against-leather sound, Michael tore his sword from the sheath and called in a booming voice "We will be more than happy to handle the transportation of those two beautiful ladies!"

All three Dark Knights startled, dropping the keys into the dust. Time seemed to stop in that cellblock. The three Dark Knights stood staring with shock filled eyes and dropped jaws, not even comprehending exactly what was going on. Both women gasped in surprise and were stunned into silence with the disbelief that their friends were actually there clearly showing on their faces. Raphael gripped the handle of his mace in one hand and his sword in the other and grit his teeth as he mentally prepared himself to attack. Julie stood just behind the two males, her fists beginning to glow with a soft, pale yellow light that slowly intensified with each passing second.

Suddenly, the still calmness was broken. The Dark Knights fumbled clumsily for their own swords and Michael and Raphael roared battle cries as they leapt into action, their weapons held cocked back. Just as the Dark Knights managed to free their swords, there came the flash of torchlight on steel and the sound of air being cut. A Dark Knight howled as a bright beam of yellow light struck him like a runaway orc, and that was the end of the Dark Knights.

Raphael rushed to the cell door and snatched up the keys. Upon trying the fourth key, there was a loud click and the bars parted with a shrill, rusty squeaking. The Kuberican queen rushed out to throw herself into the arms of her king, holding him tight and kissing his lips in ecstatic glee. Li walked out slowly, regarded Julie with raised eyebrows, and then wrapped her arms around Raphael. She gave him a warm smile and giggled softly as he blushed slightly. She took the keys and then unlocked the cell next to her old one before tossing them back to Raphael and walking in. After a few minutes, she slowly walked out, a beaten and battered man hanging from her shoulder.

"Now, let's free everyone else and get our happy-pappy butts out of here!" Li replied, her smile brightening her dirty face as she trembled slightly, partly under James's weight but mostly from the excitement of finally being free. Actually leaving such a grim and gruesome place with only distant memories never again to set a foot within the dank was more than enough to put a smile on anyone's face. She turned and her smile instantly melted into a dark scowl, her eyes blazing with hellfire.

Garrison chuckled, the sound as vile as it could get as it rumbled in the back of his throat. He stood in a proud, victorious stance, his arms crossed and his legs spread apart. The Dark Knights who had been with him earlier stood behind him, along with several others. All held weapons tightly in their grips and bloodlust in their eyes.

"Well, well. Now what do we have here, hmmmm?" he remarked in a sinister manner, his eyes glowing with pure evil. He clicked his tongue "I'm sorry, are we interrupting your little orgy, Beauty?"

"You are a . . . dead man!" she hissed with such venom in her voice that it made everyone cringe.

Even Garrison's grin faltered slightly, but he reassured himself with a caress of the sword nestled snugly at his hip. He snorted "Why don't you put your money where your mouth is, harlot." He chuckled once more and raised a brow. "Or better yet, why don't you save us all a lot of trouble and just put your mouth on my—"

A savage curse spewing from James's lips cut him off as he tried to make for the general. However, he simply stumbled forward, held tightly in his lover's arms. Garrison scowled darkly and jabbed a threatening finger towards him as he snapped "Shut your damn mouth, gimp! I'll finish what I started with you as soon as I take care of old business!"

In reply, Li slowly and calmly handed her beloved into Elizabeth's arms, never taking her boiling eyes off of the man she loathed so. The cold and deadly way she moved sent a shiver down Garrison's spine. Merely touching his sword wasn't enough to comfort, he drew it from the sheath, the blade of red metal gleaming in the flickering torchlight.

"The chink and her gimp are mine!" he barked at his men, brandishing his sword. "Kill the rest . . . now."

Li strolled forward, her fists clenched so tightly her knuckles crackled loudly. She did not acknowledge the Dark Knights screaming past her, did not even seem to know that they were there. Michael, Raphael, and Julie held themselves ready as the attackers rushed forward. With a mighty battle cry of their own they struck out at the onslaught, the prince and the knight throwing fierce and skilled swings of their weapons to bash armor and bodies while Julie cast yellow and orange beams of energy and formed a large purple ball around herself to protect from the attacks of her enemies. Elizabeth cringed against the wall, her body trembling as she turned her face away from the sight, much too afraid to watch her king fight. She knew she wouldn't be able to see him being struck down. She prayed for them as she tried her best to keep James up. James could only stand by, supported by the princess, not wanting to watch his beloved and yet not being able to turn away.

"You know, I can't seem to hurt you with any weapons Noknor has provided." he muttered, fingering the handle of his sword and running his finger over the blade. "Then again, he didn't provide this one." He cocked his brow and gave her a devilish wink. "I'm pretty sure you can tell who did."

Li's eyes widened as she did in fact recognize the blood red blade inscribed with Chinese symbols and designs of a dark and sinister origin. Her fiery sneer darkened fiercely as she growled "Heide Xueye!"

"That's right, Beauty. The Clan of the Black Blood." Garrison nodded. "What, did you think I was just in Wuhan to rape young girls? I spent quite a bit of time with those savage animals and learned a few things . . . like this!"

Garrison thrust his sword forward, intent on running her through. Li slapped her palms over the blade, stopping it inches before it could pierce her chest. With a savage curse, he put more force behind his sword and tried to shove it into her heart. Li kept a firm hold as she stepped to the side and then released the blade, causing Garrison to gasp in surprise as he tumbled forward. Li bashed her elbow into his mouth as he passed, splitting his lip wide open. He roared in fury, spitting a mouthful of blood onto the wall. His eyes blazed with fire and he leapt at her, his sword swinging fast and furious. Li jumped back and ducked away from the deadly steel, but the sudden swiftness of his attack startled her and upon his fourth swing she took the blade across her leg. She winced sharply as she saw a deep red line trace her thigh, blood instantly glistening on the wound. She crumbled and fell down in the dust away from Garrison.

He stood over her, laughing in triumph with his sword held high over his head. His eyes glittered as he prepared to bring it down hard. The split instant before he chopped Li threw herself forward, her wound burning like a flaming coal as it tore open further and dust settled within it. She flew so swiftly, Garrison didn't have time to alter the course of his sword before he took a solid fist in his gut. He was knocked back several feet as he doubled over, his lungs violently launching every bit of air they held. As he gasped and wheezed painfully, Li leapt to her feet and slammed both of her palms into his chest, cracking one of his ribs and severely bruising several others. He smacked against the wall, bashing the back of his head hard enough to see bright stars. Using the rebound and the furious pain, he lurched forward and swung wildly. Worn down by weeks of harsh captivity, Li's reaction was slow and she could only put up a feeble block to receive a nasty slice on her arm from the weak and uncalculated blow. She chirped in alarm and spun to the side to avoid the follow-up swipe, which tore her dirty silk shirt but luckily not her flesh that time around. With an enraged scream, she launched her foot upwards as his arm came back around for a third slice. The kick connected soundly with his wrist, cracking bone and killing nerves while causing his whole arm go numb and send the weapon clattering onto the floor. Even more momentum was added to his body, twisting his waist halfway around. He squealed in agony and clutched his throbbing wrist as it instantly began to swell into an ugly, purple mass. His screams were cut short as Li delivered three quick punches to his body and an open thrust to his jaw, slamming it shut. His entire face flashed with fire as three of his teeth shattered.

Li threw another body shot, but Garrison managed to get his hand up to block and spun around to deliver a devastating kick to her gut. As she grunted dully and doubled over, he jabbed her in the mouth with his good hand and slammed his forehead into hers. She was thrown back but stayed on her feet to shake off the blows as best she could. Her brow began to dampen and she threw her arm across it to wipe away the sweat. She shocked herself when she saw her forearm smeared crimson. Still in a daze, she gazed up in time to see Garrison dashing towards her, sword in hand. Acting more on instinct than anything else, she threw her leg up, her foot catching him square in the sternum with an impact loud enough to be heard and felt by all. He crashed down onto his back, his eyes watering and his fractured teeth grinding as he clutched at his crushed chest and desperately fought back the blackness that quickly began to creep around the edges of his vision.

He squirmed and then managed to roll onto his hands and knees to push himself up. For all of his trouble, he received a hard kick to the kidney that made him hack up a mixture of blood and bile onto the dust as he tried to crawl a few feet. As Li reared back for another hard kick, Garrison snatched up a nearby rock, howling in agony and crumbling down onto his side as his weight was put onto his swollen wrist. He sucked back the pain and heaved the rock at her head. Though the throw was very weak and feeble, the stone clipped her shoulder, stopping her in her tracks as she swore and gripped her bruised shoulder. He took the brief moment he had bought to recollect himself before throwing his body at her with a hellish shriek. She took his shoulder hard in the chest and flew backwards as he tackled her to the ground. She crashed onto her back and her head exploded in pain as Garrison drew back his blood smeared fist for another blow to her injured forehead. Li lashed out with her left arm and batted away the fist bearing down hard on her head, striking his already injured wrist in such a way that electricity traveled up his arm as he went numb once more. His sudden yelp was cut short by a fast, though weak, punch to his nose followed by a short pause while she repositioned herself. Then she unleashed a fury of angry blows that pounded his face until he rolled off of her, weeping and moaning over his broken face as rage took over.

Both fighters leapt to their feet, adrenaline gushing through their veins and killing away the tearing agony that their wounds and injuries brought, a bottomless pit of hatred and fury causing both to refuse to give up until the other lay dead at their feet. They rushed each other, dust kicked up by their heels, blood and sweat flying from their bodies. Garrison began to throw swift and furious blows, his broken wrist screaming but the rage of his humiliation ordering him to ignore it. Though hurting and weary, her own thirst for vengeance gave her the strength and speed she needed to easily block each blow as she slowly stepped backwards, tossing her hands to and fro with such skill and ease that it seemed she wasn't even in control of her body, that her mind was a million miles away. Garrison tried his hardest to score at least one hit on her, but was surprised to find that he was now being pushed backwards. Li had turned her actions from defensive to offensive so subtly he hadn't even noticed. It took all of his waning strength to just keep up with her speed and accuracy, but even that was not enough. He took several slaps to his body and head before falling backwards.

Li stood back, her whole body held loose and relaxed, her head rolling around her shoulders with a limp neck, as she waited for him to try again. Garrison was slow to get back onto his feet and he staggered about momentarily as he struggled to get his senses back. He advanced on her once more, his fists coming much slower than before. Li blocked every punch, an air of annoyance that she had to fight such an easy opponent gracing her bloodied face. With a dull sigh, she turned the fight around. Garrison took her hands as if he were nothing more than a bag of rice. Each time she connected, her fists came faster and faster, her scowl darkening as she grew more and more furious until she was roaring madly as she pounded relentlessly upon him. He danced around like a ragdoll, his blocks nothing more than feeble gestures recoiling each time he was struck.

As his arm flew up limply, Li snatched it and twisted around to come side by side with him. Before Garrison could even comprehend what had happened, she snapped his arm at the elbow as if she were simply breaking a dry noodle. He screamed as a well placed elbow into his side shattered the remaining ribs that had not yet been broken during the battle as she, in the same movement, lifted her leg and brought it down hard on top of his, bending his knee into an impossible angle. Garrison squealed like a butchered hog and began to collapse. As he fell, Li reared back her leg and slammed her knee soundly in the small of his back, snapping his spine loudly. His crumbled body fell to the dust, sobbing and crying in hellish torment. He was beaten. He was dead.

Li glared down at him and side stepped as she began to collapse from exhaustion. Taking a deep, refreshing breath, she held herself up proudly and refused to fall as she turned to her friends. She found all the other Dark Knights had been beaten and the Arcainians standing in utter silence, gawking at Li with disbelief at what they had just bore witness to. Only her husband's look was one of pride and relief for his beloved. She had taken a beating, but she had come out on top and more importantly she had answered her blood-vow.

All of the others' wide, staring eyes and tense faces showed fear and uncertainty. As she slowly limped towards them, they all couldn't help but shrink away slightly.

Though she was clearly in need of attention, they unconsciously held back, more afraid of her than for her. They had seen Li unleash the true power within her soul that few ever lived to see again, and while they would never admit it afterward, at that very moment each and every one of them were terrified of the beautiful woman they called a friend.

Without the slightest word, she stepped towards Raphael and reached for his belt. He gasped and flinched at the sharp sound of his dagger sliding swiftly from its sheath. Li looked at the razor sharp blade and raised a tired brow before turning and walking back towards the weeping mess on the ground. With a low, sore grunt, she bent over slowly and gripped Garrison by his collar. When she slammed him against the iron bars of a cell and pulled him upward, he shrieked out as his many broken bones ground together and ripped his flesh to pieces. She held her grip on him tightly as she gripped the handle of the Arcainian dagger tight enough to turn her knuckles white. She leaned close to Garrison's face and spat into his tear spewing eyes, stinging him like the poison of a cobra.

"Burn in Hell." she hissed through clenched teeth.

Garrison quivered violently, sweat and blood glistening on his face as he whimpered incoherently. His eyes were glazed with a pathetic mixture of fear and begging for mercy. In a split instance his eyes bulged wide, his mouth opened to scream, but all that was heard was a poor wheeze and gurgle. His body became rigid in Li's grasp, his head twisting in violent snaps as she slowly pushed the dagger deeper into his heart. She pushed the dagger all the way to its hilt, twisting it and grinding it to increase the pain even though Garrison's eyes were already glazed over and his breathing had stopped. She poured out all of the anger, all of the hate, frustration, and agony that had been collecting within her heart, growing in her very soul. And when those exasperated emotions could no longer give strength to her jaded muscles, Li dropped Garrison in the lake of his blood and spat onto his dead body once more.

Everyone gasped as she gave a withered sigh and took several weak steps backwards. As she began to collapse, Raphael broke the spell of paralysis and rushed towards her to catch her falling body safely in his arms. He began to pick her up to her feet when she inhaled deeply and pushed away from him to stand on her own wobbly legs. She looked down over Garrison's body once more and a small smile touched her weary lips.

"Wenchi, my beloved sister." she whispered softly, speaking her native Chinese tongue so that her deceased friend could hear her. "Your death has finally been avenged. May your soul rest in eternal peace."

CHAPTER XXXXI

Kain drew his beautiful sister close, her body limp and drawing cold and blue as her life slowly slipped out of his hands. Blood seeped from her chest, staining Kain's arms and hands as a small pool began to collect on the ground beneath them. Her breathing came slow, but even with the arrow piercing her chest it was calm and easy, though marked with remorse. She looked into Kain's eyes, her own filled with sorrow not from pain or her own impending death, but instead out of failure. Failure to her parents, to her brother, and to herself. Noknor had still lived after she had vowed to kill him, to make him pay his own life for those that he had taken. And, as she lay dying in her brother's trembling arms, she had failed. That hurt her heart more than the arrow piercing her ever could. Her eyes began to water as a sorrowful tear trickled down her fair cheek.

Kain sniffled and hugged her close, kissing her forehead tenderly before placing his head gently against hers. He felt the warm, wet blood that moistened his clothing against his skin as the bitter scent of Death flooded his nostrils. He pulled her tight once more before pulling away slightly to look down at her with moist eyes and a trembling lip. He couldn't believe it. He just couldn't believe that his sister, the person he held most dear, the person who he thought would always be with him was now drifting away right in his arms. It wasn't possible that he was losing her after everything they had been through. He couldn't even comprehend what it would be like without her. Nothing else in his life held any meaning when compared to her. She was his life. Without her he couldn't go on. That would be impossible. He didn't know what he would do now. But it didn't matter, he couldn't even think along those painful lines even if he wanted to. His heart was filled to overflowing with an agony he had not experienced even when he saw his own parents murdered before his eyes. He couldn't even pray for his fallen sister as his mind fell apart, his world crumbling down around him as he sat losing his whole reason for being. She was more than his sister, Nancy was his daughter and his best friend. And now she was gone.

He looked into her eyes. She winced sharply and moved her lips very slowly as if asking one last thing of him, her last wish, but no sound came out of her throat.

Kain's eyes burst and a flood of tears began pouring down his cheeks, dripping upon her. She closed her eyes slowly, the last amount of strength she had going into a gentle squeeze of his hand with her own. Her arms fell away weakly and her head rolled on her shoulders before pitching back. Her lips stopped and her chest ceased to rise and fall. Kain wept openly over her as he drew her close, her skin growing colder against his cheek. He whispered incoherently into her ear, begging her not to leave him, pleading with her to stay with him for just a moment longer. Then Kain Viccon, the Grand General of the Arcainian Army, threw his head back and howled mournfully.

Past the desolate sorrow, the vice-grip on his heart, and the million other emotions ripping his soul to pieces, he felt a strange warmth upon his chest. As soon as he noticed it, it began to grow warmer and warmer until his skin began to burn. Cursing loudly, he reached under his shirt and wrapped his fingers around Li's now very hot talisman and yanked it out of his shirt, snapping the chain around his neck as he did so. On reflex, he threw it away as he examined his hand, expecting it to be scorched. His hand appeared perfectly normal and there was no longer any stinging pain of a burn. Without a second thought, he turned his attention back onto Nancy, failing to realize that the clattering of the talisman as it struck the ground never sounded. As he clutched his sister in his arms, a sudden radiant light fell upon them. The bright pink light burned intensely, as if the sun itself was within arms reach. Kain was forced to place his sister's body on the ground and draw out of the light or risk blindness and terrible burns or worse. He looked around wildly trying to find the apparent cause of the mysterious light and his jaw dropped when he saw Li's talisman hovering motionless several feet above Nancy, the pink light emanating from the heart shaped ruby. Kain watched in shocked silence as Nancy was lifted bodily off the ground by unseen forces, her limbs falling away limply. The arrow buried in her chest suddenly burst into bright blue flames as cold as ice that lasted several seconds. When these queer flames subsided, the arrow was gone, leaving no trace save for a gaping hole in her flesh. Then the pool of blood slowly rose off the ground, collecting into a massive ball to form a perfect sphere that floated above her body. Kain watched as a dark maroon tentacle stretched out from this ball, slithering its way into the hole in Nancy's heart. It took Kain a moment to realize that the ball was growing smaller as all of her blood flowed back into her body, taking away the cold blue hue of death as her flesh began to regain it's beautiful flush.

When there was no more blood to be placed back home, the laceration closed as it by a ghostly zipper and left not even the faintest trace of a scar. Nancy floated back down to the ground and the light cut off, Li's talisman falling to the stone floor with several sharp clicks immediately thereafter. Nancy began breathing softly once more as her eyes fluttered momentarily before opening with a worn out look to them. Kain, still thrown into a paralyzing shock, could only watch as she slowly pulled herself up to a sitting position with her hand on her head as she looked around to survey her surroundings. Her eyes fell onto her brother and she stared at him for a long, awkward moment.

"What . . . what just happened?" she asked, her voice strained and tired. "I remember . . . I guess I blacked out for a second."

Her voice stuck Kain like a hard blow and ushered him back to life, filling him with a warmth and happiness that he had never felt in his life. It was a sense of relief so powerful he was not likely to feel it again, ever. He rushed to her side, helping her to her feet so he could throw his powerful arms around her and hoist her into the air, crying tears of utter joy and laughing uncontrollably the entire time. He planted his lips upon her cheeks and forehead repeatedly, squeezing her tight as if afraid that letting her go would result in losing her once more.

"Thank the Goddess!" he gasped, choking on his breath with emotion. "Oh, Nancy!" He kissed her cheek. "Thank You, Auset! Thank You my sweet merciful Mother!"

"I love you, Kain." Nancy whispered softly, a tear slipping away from her eye.

Kain looked into her eyes with a bright, glorious smile radiating his face and mouthed a return as he placed his forehead gently against hers. "I thought I lost you, girl! I thought I lost you forever!"

"I . . . I'm not going anywhere anytime soon, big brother." she replied, starting out with a shaky voice and ending with a low giggle. She opened her mouth to say more, wanting to reassure him as well as herself that everything was okay, that everything was all right. Well, almost everything. She shifted her head and looked away to the spot where Noknor had slipped out of her brother's grasp. She closed her mouth and tried her best to hold back her very dejected sigh as she closed her eyes, a tear trickling from either eye, and succumbed to her brother's embrace.

After all of the fighting, the travels and adventures. After all of their blood, their sweat, their tears. Their hard work and their sacrifices. Her own near death. After everything, Noknor had escaped the hand of justice. Their justice. He was still alive and to Nancy, that was the harshest blow that could have been dealt to her. Her vow to her parents and to herself had been broken, smashed to pieces the instant Noknor jumped through that portal. It was as if everything she had worked so hard for had been for nothing. True, they had stopped him. But he was alive with still so much to answer for with his blood. She had failed.

She suddenly became conscious of eyes upon her, as if she were being watched. Expecting to meet eyes with her brother as she glanced up, she was surprised to see his eyes closed while the feeling intensified.

"Congratulations." a female voice called out to them.

They slowly released each other and turned to face Mara Raptor who stood fondling her staff with a proud grin set in her full, red lips. Her own eyes were moist and held a glint of joyful affection in them. "Congratulations on a grand victory to you both. I knew you could do it."

"But we failed." Nancy muttered weakly.

Mara chuckled slightly and gave her a reassuring grin and wink. "My dear, you most certainly did not fail."

"But, Noknor's still alive."

"Yes. Yes, he is. However, you stopped him and that was all the Ladys required of you. And, in the process, you saved many innocent lives that surely would have been lost had he not been stopped. I would hardly call that a failure."

"Besides, sweetheart." Kain replied, looking down at her with a smile. "He'll turn up again. Either on his own or by us hunting him down, we'll face off again."

"Indeed." Mara agreed with a simple nod of her head as she fingered her staff. "He's like a bad copper star, and we know how those always have a habit of turning up time and again." She turned her attention onto Kain, looking his weary frame up and down. "You have done very well. Both of you. You have impressed many, particularly my mistresses. They are very proud of you. Very proud."

"Well, we couldn't have done it without their help, that's for sure." Kain chuckled lowly, a grin crossing his beaten face. "Or yours, Mara. Thank you."

Mara's smile brightened as she simply bobbed her head once in regard. Kain glanced to his side and saw the Elemental Sword lying on the ground where he had discarded it upon seeing his sister fall only mere moments before. He nudged the girl and gestured her to retrieve it for him. Excitement guided her to cover the short distance in long, quick strides. She had never actually held the sword since Kain had gotten it, she hadn't even touched it for that matter. For her, bringing the fabled Elemental Sword to her brother, though it would actually only be in her grasp for a few short seconds, was a monumental treat for her. She bent her knees and reached down to wrap her fingers around the cold golden handle. Expecting it to weigh quite a bit, she gave a hard tug and knocked herself off balance, almost tumbling backwards in surprise that it was much lighter than she had anticipated. She glanced at the others and blushed slightly when she saw amusement on their faces.

"Thank you, sweetheart." Kain murmured as he accepted it from her.

Nancy gave him a bright smile and flicked her head to one side in silent response. He turned to Mara, brandished the blade once at his side, and held out the handle to her. She reached out and gripped it, deliberately letting her fingers fall over his fondly. When his grin widened slightly, she offered him a gentle wink of an eye. She looked the blade over, admiring its splendor.

She opened her mouth to speak, but was abruptly cut off as a tremendous boom echoed in the room and shook the walls, knocking several bricks out of place. The three startled wildly as several resounding echoes shook the ground under their feet.

"What was that!" Nancy cried out, ducking reflexively as several large rocks tumbled down around them.

"It would seem that with all the fighting the structural integrity of this castle has been compromised." Mara explained, looking around with raised eyebrows. She closed her eyes and lowered her head slightly as her brow furrowed with concentration. As her body began to slowly grow hazy and fade right before their eyes, she continued "It is crumbling, rotting like a dead body so to speak. I would make haste out of here, if I were you. I would hate to think you two buried along with the rubble. After all, you still owe me a dinner, Sir Viccon."

And she was gone, making her way across the astral plane to the Ladys of the Elements. Kain urged Nancy to follow him in taking the sorceress's advice. They took several long strides across the throne room, taking care to dodge the large chunks of rubble, which were now falling all around them like hailstones. Suddenly, Kain hissed a sharp breath as he remembered something, stopping so abruptly that Nancy crashed into his back and bounced off to land on her backside. As she picked herself back up, he turned on his heels and rushed back to the spot where Li's lifesaving talisman lay on the cracked and pitted floor. A large rift opened up next to it as the floor began to give way, the talisman teetering on the edge and threatening to plunge into the dark void below. Kain quickened his pace and dove to snatch it up before it could be lost. With a heavy, labored sigh of relief, he jumped back up to his feet and rushed back. Just as he reached his sister, she copied his actions, dashing back to the center of the throne room.

"What are you doing!" Kain cried out, having to shout at the top of his lungs to overcome the earshattering roar of the castle falling. Nancy made no reply in return as she flew swiftly to the spot which Noknor had last occupied before disappearing. "Come on! We have to get out of here!"

He started to advance towards her as she stooped low to snatch up something on the fly before pumping her long legs hard and fast while jumping over cracks and dodging debris. Kain saw something large in her hand, but couldn't figure out just what it was. As they drew closer to each other, Kain's jaw dropped in shock when he was finally able to see that she had a tight grip on Noknor's severed hand, the fingers still clutching the small crossbow tightly.

"What . . . ?" he gasped, pausing and watching Nancy rush to him.

"Souvenir! Come on! Let's go!" Nancy replied shortly, reaching his side and grabbing his arm with her free hand to urge him onward.

Together, the pair rushed from the throne room just as the roof completely caved in to expose a bright moon and star studded sky.

* * *

"Do you see them yet?" Raphael asked his sister, quickly clutching and relaxing his hands repeatedly with uneasiness.

The enchantress Julie Boniva straddled the large branch of the tree she had chosen to roost in, her green eyes glowing with a strange pale orange light. She had used a spell to make her sight that of a hawk's eyes and was intently scanning the area around the castle for any sign of dawdlers that might not have yet made it out of the collapsing building, particularly the Viccon siblings. No one had seen or heard from them since Kain had given the order to separate, and all were worried.

It was obvious to everyone that something had happened to Noknor, death more than likely as not a person there, especially Kain's friends, held any doubt that the Grand General would kill the warlock rather than take him alive. However, just because Noknor had been defeated didn't mean that the Viccon siblings had come out of it unscratched. Or that the pair would make it out of the crumbling castle before it crushed them in the rubble.

Upon the onset of the collapse of the castle, total panic had engulfed what remained of Noknor's army. All of them, human and non alike, knew that the impossible had occurred, that their lord and master had fallen. In the span of a second they had all went from fighting together out of fear of their master's wraith to every man for himself. Escape was the only thing important to each of the dark warriors, escape from the Arcainian forces. Not even money was important to them as they rushed past the many fine and priceless articles scattered about without so much as a second thought. After all, what good was a golden candelabra or a jewel encrusted silver mirror when one was sitting in an Arcainian dungeon awaiting execution. Provided that they even made it that far. The Arcainians were taking prisoners faster than they could round them up. Noknor's once mighty army was now reduced to tumbling over one another like frighten rabbits trying to escape a weasel invading their burrow. There were no more friends or allies anymore, not with defeat bearing down on them like a ravenous animal. As such, the Arcainians quickly and easily seized control of the situation, snatching up Noknor's forces like lost children and ushering out of the crumbling castle that seemed to fall apart more quickly as the seconds ticked by.

They fled to a safe distance so as to treat their wounded, to deal with their many prisoners, and to boast about their battles. A large group had gathered at the very edge of the forest to establish a sort of rendezvous point that was far enough away from the castle to avoid any hazards yet close enough to be easily spotted by Arcainian troops which still fled the collapsing building. Among the first to set up such a post had been Kain's party.

Julie had immediately ascended into the tree to pose as a watch while her brother uneasily paced back and forth repeatedly under her asking every few minutes if she had seen Kain and Nancy yet. At first, she gave him full answers, put as Raphael asked more and more, each time her answers shortened until they were reduced to dull grunts. Finally, Julie failed to answer at all. However, it didn't stop him from asking. The prince and princess had not let each other out of their arms since reuniting and had taken under a large tree to discuss their future now that they were the new king and queen of Kuberica. Medics had instantly taken James under their care, giving him different elixirs and ointments to relax him and ease his pain. Li had at first resisted medical attention, fearing that to do so would mean she would be separated from her beloved. However, insistent coaxing from her friends and her husband and assurance that she would be treated with James by her side finally persuaded her to get her many serious wounds looked at. Carrie and Kassandra were also in need of the medics; Carrie herself had almost lost an arm in the midst of battle. However, through the quick thinking and expert actions of her young companion she had survived to make it out to better care. As her arm was placed in a sling and a large scrape on Kassandra's head was bandaged, the D'Elite continuously gave praise to the young girl, spouting out about how she had more than proven herself in the Boniva Guard. Kassandra merely smiled and acknowledged her superior modestly, knowing that while the elixirs had freed Carrie's tongue, the words were heartfelt and sincere.

Uni seemed particularly agitated as he paced back and forth and snorted anxious neighs of concern for his teenage mistress. The Arcainian soldiers, many of who had never before seen a real unicorn in the flesh, were quite surprised to see any animal show so much emotion over their owner. Even Raphael and Michael commented back and forth that they had never seen such loyalty in a beast before.

"What's she doing up there?" James Raptor replied, wincing sharply from the breath as the Arcainian medics treated him the best they could with what supplies they had. Li tried to shush him sternly but it was covered by her wincing hiss as they smeared a sticky gel on her thigh and began to wrap bandages around her leg.

Suddenly thinking of his sister, James added "Is she a sorceress?"

"I, good sir, am an enchantress." Julie corrected him in a somewhat annoyed manner, casting off the distraction immediately to concentrate on her search.

Li threw narrow eyes and a dark frown up at her, not particularly appreciating the tone that she had used. Her own voice was frosted over when she called "So? Do you see them or don't you!"

Julie was slow in answering, during which time Li seriously contemplated jumping up and kicking the woman out of the tree regardless of whose sister she was. "I see several more people, they look like Arcainians. Yes, they are, but . . . I don't see Kain or Nancy among them. They appear to have a few prisoners with them. No, I don't see . . ." Her voice trailed off into silence. Suddenly, she gasped out "Oh!"

"What!" several different voices called up hopefully to her.

"Here they come!" Julie cried out joyfully. There was a brilliant flash of bright orange light from her hand before she carefully climbed back down to the ground. "They saw me, they're heading this way!"

There was only a few minutes of waiting to be had before the Viccon siblings burst into view, rushing at them in full stride. Upon hitting the homestretch to their companions, the pair slowed to a jog, huffing and breathing heavily. By the time they reached the cheering group, they trudged along as if their legs were stone. They were mobbed by roaring congratulations and excited questions, but both were much too tired and winded to answer. Kain simply held up his tired hand as he and Nancy moved through the crowd. Raphael, Michael, and several other officers managed to muster enough control to get the soldiers to make way for them, following closely behind themselves.

Nancy and Uni quickly found each other as his ecstatic whinnies and neighs echoed loudly. She kissed her unicorn, rubbed her face against his neck, and slowly began to slide down to the ground. Uni sat down himself, allowing the girl to use his body as a cushion. Nancy was so drained that she couldn't even muster up the energy to giggle when he began to nuzzle her fondly.

Kain was guided to his cousin, whom he embraced in the weakest hug he had ever given her. They spoke no words, only exchanged pecks on their cheeks before parting. A bright smile, brighter than it should have been, graced Li's face as she gestured behind her. Kain's excitement at seeing his lost old friend was conveyed with wide eyes and a low mumble of incoherent words. He threw himself down onto the lush grass and closed his eyes for a moment as he drew in deep breaths. When asked for the details of his fight by those around him that were all quite thrilled at his return, he simply raised an exhausted arm and slowly pointed his finger at the castle.

All turned to look and witness the final remains of Noknor's unsuccessful conquest shatter. A tremendous rumble, like rolling thunder right over one's head, shook the forest as what was left of the castle collapsed into itself, filling the air for miles around with an earth shattering explosion of cracks and deafening booms. A cloud of dust as large as the castle kicked up, billowing like smoke as it rose in thick gusts around the rubble that had become the ruins of Kuberica Castle.

* * *

Even with limited supplies, the Arcainians had managed to have quite a wonderful celebration feast in the streets of Kuberica City with the overjoyed citizens. The wounded were treated in the soft comfort of many inns and though there was still enough beds for every Arcainian to have a much needed comfortable rest after such a brutal fight, the indebted people of Kuberica City freely opened their doors to welcome in their heroes as honored guests. It wasn't very late into the night before even the most excited people began to feel the exhausting affects of the day's battles and headed away for much needed rest. They knew that the next day would bring the true festivities, and everyone wanted to be well rested for what was sure to be a spectacular event.

In the waning hours of the night, only Kain and a select few remained in a small banquet hall at one of the more luxurious inns discussing the aftermath details. Kain, Raphael, Michael, Elizabeth, and Kassandra sat close together sharing fine champagne and words. Li, James, Carrie, and Rebecca were resting soundly in the makeshift infirmary alongside many others while Julie and Nancy had drifted off to their rooms for slumber.

"What's the schedule now?" Raphael inquired, taking a long sip from his glass.

Kain was silent for a moment, pondering as he swirled the alcohol in his own glass. "Tomorrow will be the celebrations. Those will carry on for the next few days I'm sure. But day after tomorrow, I want to get us out of here. We'll leave most of soldiers here, of course, so that they can enjoy what they've earned. But I want to get back to Arcainia as soon as possible." He gestured towards Kassandra with a large grin on his face. "And I'm sure you and your crew would like to get back home yourselves."

"It would be nice, Sir Viccon." she giggled softly.

"I know just how you feel, my dear. I'm feeling pretty homesick myself." he chuckled, sighing heavily as he did so. He did miss his home very much, his friends and the good times to be had. He did a quick calculation in his head and grunted. They had only been away from Arcainia for a little over a month and a half, but to him it felt like so much longer. He had never felt that way after a quest, that lingering homesick longing, ever after quests where he had been gone three or four months at a time. Perhaps it was the way this particular one had struck so close to his heart that made him long for the comfort of home. Or perhaps he had never before fought as he had this quest.

Feeling his heart beginning to sink, he quickly dismissed the issue and diverted his attention to the cheerful prince. "I'll need a full report on the state of Kuberica as soon as you can get it. The amount of damage, status of repair, the amount of aid Arcainia should send, that sort of thing."

"Not a problem." Michael assured him, putting an arm around his bride and drawing her close to his body. "It may take a few weeks, but I'll get it to you."

Kain gave a small half grin but said nothing as he took a long sip from his glass and narrowed his eyes slightly. There was a long silence among the small group, which Raphael finally interrupted by replying "What do you suppose happened to Noknor?"

Kain raised his eyebrows, sipped down the last few drops from his glass, and said "He ran away like the coward that he is. He tucked his tail between his legs and has run off to lick his wounds in some safe haven. Goddess only knows where he would have such a place. But he'll turn up again, trust me on that one. Probably sooner than later he'll be back to settle old scores. And when he does rear that ugly face of his, I'll be ready for him and I'll kick his sorry ass all over again, finish it once and for all."

"And I'll be there to help you." a soft female voice startled them. They turned to see Nancy enter with the stiffness of a sleepwalker.

"What are you doing here, pup?" Kain asked with a bit of a concerned frown. "Why aren't you in bed? You look beat."

"I couldn't sleep." Nancy mumbled behind a hearty yawn. She shuffled her way to her brother and gave him a weak embrace. However, there was no weakness in her serious face when she locked her eyes onto his. "I mean it, Kain. When Noknor does come back, I'm going to fight. I made a promise, and I do intend to keep it, no matter what I have to do."

Kain chuckled affectionately. "You needn't worry one bit, my love. When the time comes, you won't even have to ask me."

EPILOGUE: SIX MONTHS LATER

"Man and woman before me, and all children and elders gathered in the presence of our Divine Mother take heed of this that I say." the priestess, a middle-aged woman garbed in a simple white gown and wearing a beautiful golden headdress in the shape of long cow's horns with a brightly glimmering solar disc set in-between them, smiled brightly and called out as she stood before James and Li within the beautiful confines of the Auset Shine in Arcainia City. There was not a cloud in the deep blue sky overhead to cover the radiant sun as it shone its warm rays down upon the wedding party and their many guests. Birds chirped and sung sweet songs as a soft, cool breeze filtered through the courtyard, whistling gently as it caressed them. Except for a few muffled whispers and gentle sobs, there was silence as the hushed crowd listened to the High Priestess recite from her large prayer book with pages made of paper-thin silver.

"We are granted but one heart by our beloved Mother, and there is no gift that can surpass its value. No material thing can match it, not gold, silver, or jewels. It is life and not even death can cause its glowing flame to flicker. To be wed by the heart is for two to become one for all eternity, and this deed may not be undone for all time. The hearts of this man and this woman will forever belong to one another through all time. In truth they have already performed this coupling countless times before and so shall they continue to couple their hearts countless times more. Through all lives shall they live, they shall belong, in their hearts, to one another and no other. No other union brings such joy and blessings as the union of the hearts for their hearts have found each other in this life and are whole.

"I hold before you, those gathered to bear witness, James Elaxander Raptor and Li Hua who shall unite their two hearts unto one in the presence of our Heavenly Mother and become one child in her eyes."

The priestess gently placed her book down upon the altar and picked two beautiful red roses from two separate white vases in front of her. She held them over her head for blessings, calling out "Here two rose blossoms, the hearts of the man and the woman before you."

She handed the flowers over to the couple. They held their respective blossoms against their chests lovingly, daring to glance to each other out of the corner of their eyes like shy schoolchildren in the bloom of love. The priestess smiled and nodded before continuing the marriage rites.

"Know that these rose blossoms open their petals in full beauty only to the golden light and not for the darkness, and so will your hearts be in the golden light of your love. Take these blossoms and reflect upon your love and consider the seriousness of the pledge you will take which will lead you to new adventures before you could only dream of. Consider, this man and this woman, the wonderful gift our Mother has bestowed upon you in each other and the pledge you will make to Her."

There was a moment of silence broken only by the fluttering of the wind, the sweet songs of birds, and the muffled sobs of joy whispering in the audience. It was a time for the man and the woman to reflect upon their feelings for each other and cast away any doubts that they were meant to be together. If indeed there happened to be lingering doubts it was also the time to speak them. For James and Li there were no lingering doubts, no nagging voices in the back of their heads, no fears for the future or regrets of the past. They had only each other in their hearts with a love as fresh and new as the day it sprang forth.

The priestess bowed her head slightly to signal the coming end of the silence and turned her body to speak directly to Li. The look of the bride's radiant face brought a huge smile to her face. In her time since being blessed as a priestess of Auset, she had preformed probably hundreds of wedding ceremonies. She was always infinitely happy for the couple, but rarely did she find herself caught up in the wave of emotions flooding around her. However, there was something about this bride that sent the priestess's own heart a flutter, something in her eyes and in her smile that seemed to reach out and grasp one's very soul in a warm, tranquil light. Suddenly the priestess felt as if she were the one standing the bride's place.

The priestess stumbled upon her own cue but it was noticeable to no one but herself. She cleared her throat and spoke fondly the question "Knowing now the seriousness of this pledge, Li Hua wouldst thou wish to wed thy heart to this man?"

The beautiful Chinese blossom was absolutely stunning in her flowing pure white wedding dress of satin and lace. Her long dark hair was fixed into many daintily hanging curls and braids while a wreath of colorful flowers crowned her head. James had given her the choice of either a traditional Chinese wedding or a traditional Auset wedding, but it had hardly been a choice at all. She knew James really did want to be married in his homeland, and Li could hardly blame him. It really was a beautiful, albeit different ceremony, and besides with James being a Knight of Auset she knew he would never take well the fact of not being married in the Shrine. So she had agreed to it. Of course it had taken some coaxing to get her parents to make the trip and they had at first given her more than a little grief over the matter. But now that she stood with her husband before the altar of Auset, she really did feel she had made the right choice. It was so beautiful and peaceful.

But then, it really didn't matter where they were. All that mattered was that she was with her husband on the happiest day of her entire life.

She felt a tear of joy slip down her rosy cheek as she replied with a squeaky voice "I wouldst make my pledge to wed my heart to the heart of this man in never-ending love."

The priestess bowed her head slightly in recognition to Li's words, grinning at the extra words she had added to the end of the pledge. She turned to James and asked him "Knowing now the seriousness of this pledge, James Elaxander Raptor wouldst thou wed they heart to this woman?"

James took a very deep breath and held it in for several seconds before exhaling in a very shaky manner and clearing his throat. He felt his collar suddenly bind tightly around his throat and choke him off, but managed to croak out a nervous "I . . . I wouldst make my puh-pledge to wed my heart to the heart of Li . . . ah, this woman."

The priestess suppressed a giggle as an affectionate rumbled swept through the audience. She raised her hands over her head and said "Wouldst thou turn to your heart and repeat these words together."

At this, the priestess began reading from her book, pausing after every few words so that Li and James could recite along together and they stared longingly at each other.

"I swear that my heart, the very essence of my creation, shall belong only to you forever. I swear that I shall love no other as I love you and I that I shall hold no other as I hold you. Through all adventures good and bad, through calamities great and small, through sickness and strength, through times of prosperity and poverty, I shall love no other but you and I will nurture our love so that it may grow mighty as the oak and beautiful as the rose. May Auset bless you and me, and may Auset bless our love."

After they had finished the prayer, Li turned to her right and handed the rose over to Nancy Viccon, her Handmaiden. James turned to his left and handed his own blossom over to Kain Viccon, his Scribe.

"Wouldst the Messenger bring the Heart Rings?" the priestess asked.

James's young nephew stumbled forward after a coaxing push from his mother and raised a silken pillow to them. James reached down with a very shaky hand and snatched up one of the silver bands while Li did the same. James could barely slip the ring around Li's long, thin finger he was so nervous. He finally managed, however, saying as he did so "My love to thee forever."

"My love to thee forever." Li replied as she slipped her ring onto his finger. She sighed merrily as James reached down and gently grasped her hands in his. All of a sudden, she noticed that he wasn't shaking as much anymore and when she gazed deep into his dark eyes she saw that they held a calm, tender look to them.

While Li and James continued to hold hands and stare fondly into each other's eyes, the priestess slowly raised her hands up into the sky and called out "Oh, our dear sweet Mother! Please unite these children of Yours into one holy union. Please take them up into Your arms and guide them well down the golden path of light. Auset, please lay Your loving wings of protection around them and shield them from all harm and evil. Please be with them always and guide them in their life now and forever more. Oh, Heavenly Mother! Blessed be!"

"Blessed be!" the crowded repeated in a boisterous bellow of joy.

"As our Mother and Father show their love, so should you to complete this holy union." the priestess said softly, smiling as bright as the sun shining down. "Bestow a kiss and seal the bond you now forever share."

With hearts gushing love for each other, James tightened his grip on his Beauty's hands and gazed upon her gorgeous visage for a moment longer before drawing her closer to his body. They closed their eyes, their trembling lips touching softly before they wrapped their arms around each other for a passionate embrace. At the kiss, everyone erupted in joyous applause. Li felt her eyes grow moist and felt a lone tear run down her cheek like a rabbit racing to his doe. She never wanted to pull away from her James's lips, never wanted to leave his arms as the sky bellowed the cheers of friends and family.

* * *

Later that evening, people began collecting at the largest banquet hall in Arcainia Castle for the grand reception. The massive room was set up perfectly and decorated beautifully. There were many tables lined up in neat rows with enough comfortable chairs to seat just about all of Arcainia. There was a large wide-open area for dancing just in front of a high platform where the marvelous band played sweet, harmonious music. Off to the side there were several long tables piled with all kinds of wonderful foods and tasty drinks. There were roasted meats, glazed hams, a large variety of baked fowl, and steaming cooked vegetables to send out wafts of great smells into the air. The dessert table with its many cakes, pies, and sweetened breads made everyone's mouth water. Next to this was a circular table that held a terrific wedding cake. It was an enormous creation with nine separate stories each decorated with freshly picked edible flowers of many different colors and pure white icing. On the topmost level proudly stood two porcelain figures, a bride and a groom painted to expert detail to look like the real newlyweds, under a flowery wooden arch. Beside this table stood several more which, over the course of the evening, would become loaded down with gifts for the happy couple. On one of these tables sat a miniature wishing well made of light weight stone and painted in vibrant colors where people would toss in donations as well as happy wishes for the couple.

At the onset of the reception, Li and James stood at the main entrance to greet guests as they walked in. Each person gave the couple their fondest wishes, saying what a handsome groom he was and what a stunning bride she made. While James held his pleasant smile all the while, inside he was filled with a longing hopefulness that the one missing family member, in fact the one person he most wanted there, would stroll in to surprise him. Mara had sent word to him that she wasn't going to be able to make the event. She had expressed her deepest regrets that she had to be detained on business for the Ladys of the Elements and wished she would be able to make it for her beloved twin brother. James had totally understood, of course. After all, her being made Jestura was not something to be taken lightly. Still, he just couldn't help but be disappointed. So he put a smile on his face, held close to his sweet bride, and greeted his guests with his most pleasant demeanor while wishing for his sister to show.

Just as the bride and groom were about to abandon their greeting post to head for their seats at the main table, four large Chinese men stepped into the room and stood proudly before the couple. Three were very well built and fairly young looking, with long black hair and dressed entirely in Chinese garments made of the finest silk. The fourth man was slightly smaller than the others, but it was clear that he was the leader of the group. He was much older than the others, seeming to be ancient in comparison, with a long mustache and beard and long fingernails. There was a regal air about him, as if he were the emperor of China himself. They could have passed for mortal Chinese, except for their eyes, which were completely white and glowed softly with a pale light. Li gasped sharply in surprise and threw herself down to her knees, pulling her husband down with her. Several people took notice with great curiosity, but it was only Kain, Nancy, and Li's family that followed their lead.

The old man chuckled in a deep, rolling voice as he reached down to Li. She placed her hand in his like a small girl gripping the hand of her father and slowly rose as he picked her up to her feet. The man then gestured for James to rise as well before replying in a stout, booming tone of voice "My dear child, today is not the day you honor the Council of Dragons. Today is the day which we honor you."

The man lowered himself down to his knees before the couple and after a moment the other three men followed silently in suite and pressed their faces to the floor. At that very moment, her family was filled with a mixture of rapture and shock. However, Li's father by far was more proud of her than anyone else there, even Kain. When the four strange men had picked themselves up and walked into the hall to join the rest of the guests, he rushed to his daughter and threw his arms around her as he exploded his emotions over her. Li, quite flabbergasted herself, couldn't help ignore her father's gushing as she watched the Chinese dragons move about the hall to find themselves a seat in the company of the foreign mortals still whispering their gossip.

The reception was certainly a blast and everyone had a terrific time sharing the wonderful food and lively conversation, and dancing to beautiful music. Li and James led the first dance of the evening, holding each other close all the while. Afterwards Li suggested that they play something with a bit of a kick and everyone had a grand time dancing about wildly. When not on the dance floor, Li moved around the tables with Nancy and James's elder sister introducing herself and mingling pleasantly.

James chatted in a group with Kain, his father, his two brothers, and several of his friends as they all drank their beer. As they watched the three women shuffle about the tables, everyone was in agreement that James was pretty lucky to have found a girl like her. James consented readily and chatted briefly with the group before he excused himself to ask his wife for another dance.

It was such a perfect evening that nobody wanted it to draw to a close. However, all things must come to an end and before too long everyone was saying their good-byes and giving parting fond wishes to the happy couple.

* * *

Late in the wee hours of that morning, James and Kain stood in the Viccon living room chatting mildly over a beer while the women changed. While James had spent the past six months recovering from the wounds he had received from Garrison and reentering the life he had left out of, he and Kain had spent a lot of time together and rediscovered the friendship they had held so long ago.

"Thanks for hooking us up with your guest room." James told his best friend as he slowly sipped from his brass goblet. "I do not feel like going anywhere tonight."

Kain chuckled softly. "Don't worry about it. With as much as Li's used it, it's become more her room anyway. I'm just glad the bed was big enough." James raised a sly eyebrow of which Kain took notice and laughed loudly. He considered using the fuel to rib his friend, but instead chose to ask "So where are you two headed from here?"

"Well, we finally decided on Hurst. My folks booked us at the Karnak." he answered mildly. Kain's eyes widened and a low whistle escaped his lips. The Karnak was one of the finest hotel-casinos in Hurst. James grinned softly and chuckled "Yeah, I know. Hell of a wedding present. That was all Li needed, let me tell you. She jumped at the chance."

"I can imagine." Kain murmured, bringing his goblet to his lips and guzzling the last few drops down his throat. "I took her to Hurst not too long ago. We didn't stay at the Karnak of course, but she had a wonderful time. Ever since she's been bugging me to take her back. How long are you going to be there?"

"A week. Just long enough to lose all our wedding money." James chuckled mildly.

Suddenly female arms threw themselves around his neck and lips pressed tightly against his flesh. He jumped slightly and grinned while Li giggled playfully. She gave him another peck, on the lips this time, and asked "Are you ready to hit the silk sheets, airen?"

"If you are, Beauty." James answered, reaching his hands around behind him to gently touch his fingers to her waist.

"Hang on a second." Kain told them as he reached into his shirt. He pulled out Li's Dragon Heart talisman. He tossed it to her and said "Here, catch."

"How did you get this?" James asked, snapping his hand up quickly to catch it in air before it could reach Li's waiting grasp. "I thought Li was wearing it during the wedding?"

"I had him hold it for me at the reception." Li explained. "It was getting a little too heavy to dance with."

"Ah." James muttered, turning it over in his hands. "Hey, you ever figure out this inscription? Amor Vincit Omnia?"

Kain shrugged and shook his head mildy.

Li frowned slightly and took it out of her husband's hands. She glanced at it then at Kain and replied "Julie knows. You mean she didn't tell you?" Kain shook his head slowly. "Oh. She told me. She said it's a very old language that hasn't been used for thousands of years. She was really surprised to see it, and even more so on a Chinese artifact. You know, she's a real sweetheart. I think she's great and Nancy's seemed to have taken to her pretty well."

"Lovely." Kain chuckled and crossed his arms. "Well? Are you going to tell us what it means?"

"Yes, Li-Li." James told her as he moved behind her to wrap his arms around her waist. He gave her a strong squeeze and a kiss on her neck. "Be a dear and tell us what Amor Vincit Omnia means."

"Why, Love Conquers All, of course." Li replied with a large smile and a cocked brow as she turned her head and slowly brought her lips to rest onto those of her beloved husband.

Get Published, Inc!
Thorofare, NJ 08086
21 September 2009
BA2009264